MOTH

THE MOTH SAGA

BOOKS 4 - 6

DANIEL ARENSON

Copyright © 2014 by Daniel Arenson

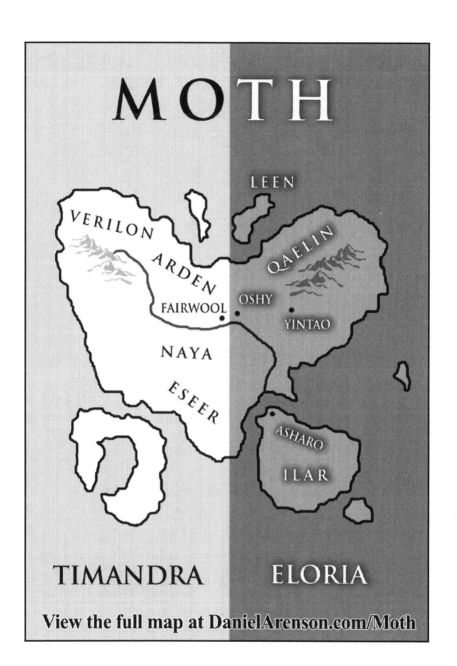

MOTH

LEEN

VERILON

ARDEN

QAELIN

FAIRWOOL

OSHY

YINTAO

NAYA

ESEER

ASHARO

ILAR

TIMANDRA

ELORIA

View the full map at DanielArenson.com/Moth

BOOK FOUR:

DAUGHTER OF MOTH

CHAPTER ONE
AN UNPLEASANT ENCOUNTER

The creaky, horse-drawn cart trundled across the bridge, taking Madori away from her homeland and old life.

Here it is, she thought and took a shaky breath. *The border.*

The Red River flowed beneath Reedford Bridge, beads of light gleaming upon its muddy waters. The cart clattered over the last few bricks, rolling off the bridge and onto the western riverbank. Madori looked around her, expecting more of a change—a different landscape, a different climate, at least a different shade of sky or scent to the air. Yet the grass still rustled on the roadsides, green and lush as ever. Elms, birches, and maples still grew upon the plains, and geese still honked above. A wooden sign rising from a patch of crabgrass, a crumbly old fortress upon a distant hill, and a twinge to her heart were the only signs that they had left Arden behind, entering this kingdom of magic and danger named Mageria.

Magic and danger? Madori thought, raising her eyebrows. She had heard tales of dark sorcerers, brooding castles swarming with bats, and creatures of both nightmares and fairy tales. Sorcerers? She saw only two distant farmers toiling in a turnip field. Brooding castles? The fort upon the hill—a mere crumbly old tower—looked liable to collapse under a gust of wind. Wondrous creatures? Madori didn't see anything wondrous about the cattle that stared from the roadside, lazily chewing their cud and flicking their tails. When Madori twisted in her seat to look behind her, gazing across the Red River to the eastern plains, she couldn't even distinguish between the two kingdoms—this new realm of magic and her old homeland.

And yet . . . and yet this *was* a new world. She knew this. She felt it in her bones, even if she couldn't see it. It wasn't in sorcerers or castles or creatures—it was in the chill that filled her belly, the tremble that seized her fingers, and the tightness in her throat.

I'm leaving my home forever, she thought as the cart trundled onward. *I will find magic here. I will find a new life. And I don't intend to return.*

Sitting beside her in the cart, her father patted her hand. "Excited, Billygoat?"

Madori rolled her eyes. She hated when he called her that. Her name was Madori Billy Greenmoat—"Billy" after Bailey Berin, the great heroine of the war whose statue stood outside the library back home. "Billygoat" was just the sort of groan-worthy pun her father would come up with.

"No." She stared forward over the head of their horse, an old piebald named Hayseed. "I don't get excited about things. And *please* stop calling me that."

Her father smiled and Madori groaned. It was a smile that practically patted her condescendingly on the head.

A sigh ran through her. She knew that her father was something of a legend in both halves of Moth, this world split between endless day and eternal night. He was Sir Torin Greenmoat, the famous war hero, the man who had fought in—and eventually ended—the war between day and night. The man who had made day and night cycle again, then broke the Cabera Clock, once more freezing Moth between light and darkness. The world saw him as a great warrior and peacemaker. But to Madori, he was simply her dull, boring father with his little quips and infuriating smiles.

She looked at him. Torin didn't even look like a hero. At thirty-eight years of age, the first wrinkles were tugging at the corners of his eyes, and hints of white were invading his temples and beard. He wasn't particularly tall, handsome, or muscular. He wore a simple woolen tunic and cloak, and he drove a humble cart pulled by Hayseed, an old horse no more impressive. Despite being knighted years ago, he wore no jewels, and soil hid under his fingernails. He didn't seem a warrior, a hero, a knight—simply a gardener, which was how Madori had always known him.

She knew the tales of Torin fighting in the great War of Day and Night, but that had all happened before her birth. Madori was sixteen now, the war was long gone, and to her, Torin Greenmoat was no hero but the most annoying man in both halves of the broken world.

"Are you sure?" Torin said, still smiling his little smile. "You look a little nervous. You're traveling into a new kingdom. You're going to try and gain admission to Teel University, the most prestigious school in the sunlit half of Moth. You're leaving everything you've ever known behind. You—"

Madori groaned. "Father! For pity's sake. Are you trying to get me to kill you? You're worse than Mother."

His eyes widened. "What? Never!"

"Mother scolds me nonstop, but you just smile and hint. That's a lot worse."

Torin grunted. "If your mother were here, she'd have spent the trip berating you about your clothes, your haircut, and your Qaelish lessons. You know that. Be thankful I'm the one taking you on this journey."

Madori had to admit he was probably right. Father was perhaps more embarrassing than britches split down the backside, but Mother was a terror. Koyee of Qaelin was as much a legend as Torin, and *she* actually acted like it.

While Torin was a Timandrian—a man of sunlight, his hair dark, his skin tanned—Koyee was an Elorian, a woman of the night. Her hair was long and white, her skin pale, her lavender eyes as large as chicken eggs. Koyee stood only five feet tall, but Madori thought her more terrifying than any warrior.

"Why do you wear this rubbish?" Koyee would say, tugging at Madori's clothes. "Why don't you wear proper Elorian dresses? And your hair! I've never seen a young woman with nonsensical hair like that. And your Qaelish—stars above, you've been neglecting your lessons. This turn you will read your Qaelish poetry books until you memorize them."

"I'm not Elorian!" Madori would say. "My hair is black. My skin is tanned bronze. I don't want to dress or talk or look like an Elorian, all right, Mother? Now will you—"

That's about as far as Madori would ever get. A slap usually silenced her, followed by screams, tears, and finally long hours in her bedroom, forced to study the language of the night.

Sitting on the cart, far away from her distant village near the darkness, Madori shuddered. She looked down at her clothes, which she had sewn herself. She wore a violet tunic over purple leggings, and leather boots heavy with many buckles rose to her knees—clothes strange in both day *and* night. Her hair, she knew, drew even more perplexed stares. She cut it herself, shearing it so short she could barely grab the strands between her fingers. She left only two long strands on top, both sprouting just above her forehead; they fell down to her chin, framing her face.

"I already look strange because of my mixed blood," Madori would often tell her mother. "I might as well have strange clothes and a strange haircut."

The argument never worked, but Madori thought it apt. Even if she wore proper Timandrian clothes—a skirt and blouse—or proper Elorian clothes—a slim, silken *qipao* dress and embroidered sash—she'd look out of place. She had inherited some Timandrian traits from her father. Her hair was black, not white like the hair of Elorians, and her skin was tanned, not pale like a child of darkness. But nobody would mistake her for a full-blooded Timandrian. Her Elorian blood—the blood of darkness—was clear to all. She was slim and short, barely standing five feet tall—normal perhaps in the darkness, but diminutive in the daylight. Most obvious were her eyes—they shone a gleaming lavender, large as owl eyes in her small, round face. A tattoo of a duskmoth—one wing black, the other white—adorned her wrist, a symbol of her two halves, of a soul torn between day and night.

A mixed-child. A child of both daylight and darkness. Perhaps the only one in the world.

And so I will seek a new home, Madori thought, throat tight. *A place where I'm accepted.*

The taunts rang through her memory, cutting her like icy daggers.

Mongrel!

Freak!

Creature!

As old Hayseed pulled the cart along, leaving their homeland behind, the pain still lingered inside Madori. She lowered her head and clenched her fists in her lap. Fairwool-by-Night, her old village, lay in the daylight near the border of darkness. Grown near the shadows, its people feared the night. Fairwool's children had spent years shoving Madori into the mud, spitting onto her, and mocking her mixed blood. Madori never told her parents—a father of sunlight and a mother of darkness—about how the other children treated her. She knew it would break their hearts.

And so now I'm leaving that home, she thought, and her eyes stung—those damn eyes that were twice the size of anyone else's here in daylight. Fairwool-by-Night was a backwater, a forgotten village full of ignorant fools; the entire kingdom of Arden was a land of fools.

But Mageria...

Madori looked down the road, and a tingling smile tugged at her lips. Ahead, the plains led to misty hills and a hidden world of wonder. Here was a new kingdom—only another kingdom of daylight, it was true, but a land of magic nonetheless. People here were educated, unlike at home, and they would accept Madori. At Teel University she wouldn't be simply a mixed-breed from a humble village. At Teel she would learn the secrets of magic. She would become a mage. She would grow strong.

She noticed that Torin was watching her, his eyes soft. He patted her knee. "Whatever happens at the trials, my daughter, I'm proud of you. Whether they accept you to the university this year, or whether we have to return for new trials next year, I love you. More than anything. To me you are magic."

She blew out her breath and rolled her eyes. "Oh, Father, you are such a horrible poet."

And yet tears filled her eyes, and she leaned against him and hugged him close. He kissed her head, lips pressing against the stubbly top.

"Even if your hair is too short," he said.

She managed to grin and tugged the two long, black strands that framed her face. "This part is long. It's good enough."

Torin groaned. "It looks like a damn walrus mustache is growing from your head."

For the first time since leaving her village long turns ago, Madori laughed. "Excellent. That's what I'll tell Mother next time she harasses me—that I simply have a head-mustache."

She was still laughing, and even Torin smiled, when hooves and horns sounded ahead.

Madori looked up and her laughter died upon her lips. She reached into her boot where she hid her dagger.

"Trouble," she muttered.

A convoy of armored riders—a dozen in all—was heading down the road toward them. Since leaving home, Madori had seen many travelers along this pebbly path—farmers, pilgrims, peddlers, and soldiers on patrol. But she had never seen anyone like the riders ahead. Each man wore priceless plate armor, the steel bright and gleaming in the sunlight. Their horses too wore armor—and these were no old nags like Hayseed but fine coursers, each more costly than anything and everything Madori's family owned. As the convoy drew closer, Madori tilted her head and squinted. She was well versed in heraldry—one of the few fields of study she enjoyed—but she didn't recognize the sigils on these riders' shields and banners. The symbol showed a golden disk hiding most of a silver circle—the sun eclipsing the moon.

Hayseed nickered and reared, raising the cart and pushing Madori and Torin back in their seats.

"Easy, girl, easy . . ." Madori said. Despite her calm words, she clutched the hilt of her dagger. These riders ahead were no good; she could smell it on them.

Raising dust and scattering pebbles, the convoy reached them, its formation not parting to allow the cart through. Torin had to tug the reins, pulling Hayseed to a halt. The riders ahead halted too, staring through eyeholes in their helmets.

Torin raised a hand in a friendly gesture, though Madori saw the tension in his jaw, heard the the nervousness in his voice.

"Hello there, fellow travelers!" he said. "Lovely day for a ride."

They stared down at him. A few riders gripped the hilts of their swords, and wondrous swords those were—the scabbards filigreed with silver motifs, the hilts wrapped in black leather, the pommels bearing gemstones.

The lead horse, a magnificent beast of snowy white fur, snorted and pawed the earth. Slowly, his gauntlets creaking, the horse's rider pulled off his helmet. The man had a cold, hard face, one that could have been handsome were it not so aloof. Wavy blond hair crowned his head, the temples streaked with white. Chin raised, the rider gazed down with icy blue eyes. Disgust filled those eyes like coins filled a rich man's coffers.

"Torin Greenmoat." The rider sneered. "So the rat has left his gutter."

Sitting in the cart, Torin glared up at the rider. "Hello again, cousin. I see the snake has left his lair."

The snowy horse sidestepped, and its rider clenched his fist around the hilt of his sword. "Yes, technically we are cousins." The man's voice was smooth and cold as ice around a frozen corpse. "Your mother's sister had the sense to marry into a proper, blue-blooded family, sense you clearly lack. But you will address me as all in Mageria do—as Lord Serin."

Madori had spent the trip here thinking her father the dullest, most insufferable man on Moth, but right now, she thought Torin Greenmoat a true hero. She leaped to her feet in the cart, drew her dagger, and pointed it at the riders.

"Get out of our way!" she said. "Ride your pretty little horses through the mud and let us pass, or by the stars above, we'll soon see how blue your blood truly is."

"Madori!" Torin hissed, pulling her back down into her seat. "Be silent."

The riders ahead snickered. Lord Serin glared at Madori like one would glare at dung upon a new boot. He raised a handkerchief to his nose as if Madori's very scent offended him.

"Learn to control your mongrel of a daughter," the lord said. "It's bad enough you bedded an nightcrawler, begetting a deformed half-breed, but you can't even keep the beast muzzled."

Madori stared, mouth hanging over. She could barely breathe.

Nightcrawler. It was a foul word, a dirty word for Elorians, the people of the night—the name of a lowly worm. She winced, remembering the names children in Fairwool-by-Night would call her. *Half-breed! Mongrel! Creature!*

All those taunts—years of them—pounded through Madori now, and somehow Serin's words were even worse. This was Mageria, the land of her dreams, not some backwater village. These were noblemen in fine armor, not peasant children.

Her eyes watered and Madori screamed. She leaped from the cart, ran across the road, and waved her dagger at Lord Serin.

"Draw your sword and face me!" she shouted. "I'm not scared of you. I have no muzzle and I can bite. I—"

"Madori!"

A hand gripped her wrist and tugged her back. Torin was pulling her away from the lords and onto the muddy roadside. Madori struggled and kicked, but she couldn't free herself from her father's grip. The riders roared with laughter.

"She's a wild animal, cousin!" Lord Serin said. He spat toward Madori; the glob landed on her boot. "She doesn't belong in Mageria. Mongrels belong in cages."

With that, the armored lord spurred his horse. The animal cantered forward, hooves splashing mud onto Torin and Madori. The other riders followed, spraying more mud.

"Send your nightcrawler wife back into the night!" Serin shouted as the convoy made its way around the cart, heading east down the road. "The Radian Order rises in the sunlight. The creatures of darkness will cower before us."

With that, the riders turned around a bend, vanishing behind a copse of elms.

Madori stood on the roadside, mud covering her clothes up to her chest. She clutched her dagger, fuming, and spun toward her father.

"I could have slain them all!" Her fists trembled. "Let's go after them. We'll leap up from behind. We'll—"

"We'll ignore them and keep traveling to our destination," Torin said calmly.

Madori raised her hands in frustration. "You'll just give up? I thought you're a war hero! I thought you fought in battles. How could you just . . . just . . . ignore them?"

She expected her father to scold her, but Torin sighed and lowered his head. Madori was surprised to glimpse a tear in his eye.

"Father . . ." she whispered, her anger leaving her.

He pulled her into an embrace, and she let her dagger fall into the mud.

"Yes, my daughter, I fought in battles. I still fight them every night in my dreams. And I don't want this life for you." He placed a finger under her chin, raised her face toward his, and stared into her eyes. "I want you to follow your dream of becoming a mage—not a warrior like I was. We'll keep traveling to Teel University and forget about those men. You will achieve greatness on your terms, not letting others drag you into the mud."

She gestured down at their filthy clothes. "We're already in the mud." She laughed softly and hugged her father. "All right, Papa. We keep going."

They climbed back onto the cart, and Hayseed resumed walking, taking them down the road. Madori had spent the past few turns dreaming about Mageria, this kingdom of magic and enlightenment, the home of the great University. She spent the rest of the turn in silence, staring ahead, a cold pit in her stomach.

Mongrel.

Beast.

A creature for a cage.

She lowered her head, clutched her hands together, and missed home.

CHAPTER TWO
THE TOWERS OF TEEL

After traveling by cart for almost a month, Madori saw the splendor of Teel University ahead. She gasped and tears stung her eyes.

"It's beautiful, Father," she whispered, clutching the hem of her shirt. "It's so beautiful."

He nodded thoughtfully, bottom lip thrust out. "The gardens aren't bad."

She punched his arm. "I don't care about the gardens!" She had to wipe tears from her eyes. "I've never seen anything like this."

When Madori had been a child, her mother would read her fairy tales of castles, their white spires touching the sky, their banners bright. Madori had always thought the stories just that—stories. Yet here before her was a fairy tale come to life.

She didn't know where to look first; her eyes wanted to drink it all in at once. She forced herself to move her eyes from the bottom up, admiring every bit in turn. Down the road, past green fields and a pond, sprawled a town of a hundred-odd buildings, their roofs tiled red, their walls built of timber foundations and white clay. Beyond the town, dwarfing even the tallest of its roofs, rose ivy-coated walls topped with merlons and turrets. Behind the walls rose four great towers, taller than any temple or castle Madori had ever seen; they seemed to scrape the sky itself. Between the towers rose a great, round building ringed with columns. A dome topped the building, looking large enough to easily contain all of Fairwool-by-Night with room to spare.

"Teel University," Madori whispered, her fists trembling around folds of her shirt.

A place of knowledge. A place of acceptance. Perhaps back in her village she was a mere creature to scorn. Perhaps ruffians along the road mocked her mixed blood. But here, finally, was the place Madori had always dreamed of, a center of enlightenment.

Torin pointed. "The dome is the Library of Teel. I've seen it illustrated in books. They say it's the largest library in the world." He pointed at the towers next. "Each of the four towers contains its own faculties of magic."

Others were traveling the road around them, heading toward the university. Madori saw thoroughbreds with braided manes pulling fine carriages, and behind their glass windows—real glass, a material as expensive as gold!—Madori saw youths dressed in finery, jewels adorning them. Parents spoke animatedly, and they too wore costly, embroidered fabrics.

"Ah, when I was a lad, I studied in Agrotis Tower," said one man, riding by upon a destrier. A samite cloak hung across his shoulders, and he patted his ample belly with a pudgy hand heavy with rings. "Of course, back in those days, I weighed a few stones less. Climbing all those stairs would be harder now."

The man's son, a scrawny youth of about sixteen years, nodded silently and nervously coiled his fingers together. Golden chains hung around his neck, and his sleeves alone—puffy things inlaid with rubies and amethysts—probably cost more than Madori's house back home.

She suddenly felt very plain, what with her humble woolen leggings and shirt—garments she had sewn herself—and muddy boots heavy with buckles. She owned no jewelry, and her prized possession was her dagger with the antler hilt, hardly the weapon of nobility. Her father looked just as humble, clad in a simple tunic and breeches. Madori had known that only noble children could attend Teel University, and officially she *was* highborn; her father had been knighted after the war. But riding here upon her cart, she realized that—despite the technicality of her highborn blood—she was as far removed from true nobility as lizards were from dragons.

Twisting her fingers in her lap, she looked at her father.

"They're probably just as nervous as you are," he said.

Madori bit her lip. "Their clothes are nicer than mine."

"Everyone's clothes are nicer than yours, Billygoat. That's what happens when you don't listen to your mother."

She snorted. "Mother wants me to dress in Elorian silk. Then I'd really stick out like a frog in a fruit bowl." She sighed. "Papa, when you went to the war years ago, were you ever scared? I mean . . . suddenly just so scared you didn't think you could do it?"

His eyes softened and he patted her shoulder. "All the time."

She looked around at the other youths with their rich clothes and jewels, then up at the university towers. "How did you go on? How didn't you run home?"

He mussed the cropped hair on the top of her head. "You're not going to war, little one."

"I know." She gulped and nodded. "But I'm still afraid."

He looked ahead at the rising walls of the university, seeming lost in thought. Finally he spoke softly. "I'll teach you a little trick I used back in the war—when I was afraid, when I was in danger. I told myself: To survive, you only have to breathe the next breath. That's it. Just the next breath." He took a deep breath, then slowly exhaled. "And then another breath. And another. I tried not to think too far ahead—just on taking that next breath, and every time that air flowed down my lungs, I realized that I'm still alive. I'm still going. And I could go a little longer and I'd survive that too. Some people say that you achieve great things step by step. But sometimes it's not even about moving—it's about living a little longer and realizing that you're still around, that you'll be all right."

She nodded and took a deep breath. "I like that, Papa." She leaned over in her seat and kissed his cheek. "Thank you."

Hayseed walked onward, pulling the cart into the town of Teelshire. The road was cobbled here, lined with houses that rose two or three stories tall, their roofs tiled, their windows filled with glass. Madori saw shops selling fabrics, pottery, sculptures, and books. An inn pumped out smoke from four chimneys, the sign above its door displaying a wolf in a dress and the words, "The Dancing Wolf." Everywhere she looked, she saw the other applicants—highborn youths with darting eyes. And among them . . .

Madori gasped. "A mage," she whispered. She tugged her father's sleeve. "Look. A real mage."

The man walked ahead, clad in a black cloak and hood. His eyes gleamed from the shadows. With a flourish of fluttering robes, he stepped into a shop with no sign, vanishing into the shadows.

Torin grumbled. "I've seen mages like him in the war—the black robed ones. Nasty folk. Your mother still has a scar along her arm from their foul magic." He winced. "Madori, are you sure you want to do this?"

She nodded vehemently. "Yes! Not all mages wear the black robes. Not all practice the art of war. I will practice the magic of healing." She thought back to that horrible year—the year her mother's belly had swelled, the year her little brother or sister had died in the womb, leaving her still an only child. She nodded. "I will do this. I will pass the trials. I will gain admission. And I will become a healer."

Because healers were respected wherever they went, she knew. Healers were not mongrels or monsters. Healers were beloved.

Past shops, around a pond, and along a road lined with cottages, they reached the walls of the university. An archway loomed here, its bronze doors open, tall enough that a cherry tree could have stood within it. Guards flanked the entrance, clad in burnished breastplates, red plumes sprouting from their helmets. A potbellied, mustached man stood in checkered livery, ringing a bell. His hand was coned around his mouth.

"All applicants to Teel University!" he cried out, bell clanging. "All applicants step through these gates! Parents shall wait in the town. All applicants—step through!"

Torin watched the portly crier. "His mustache looks a bit like that thing that's growing off your head."

Madori nervously tugged the two long, black strands that framed her face. "You sound like Mother. Now go—I saw a tavern farther back. Wait for me there. Swap war stories with the other fathers."

She made to hop off the cart, but he held her shoulder.

"Wait, Billygoat." He tapped his cheek.

She rolled her eyes, but she dutifully gave him a kiss. After climbing off the cart, she gave dear old Hayseed a kiss too, then gulped and began walking toward the gates.

"Good luck!" Torin cried behind her.

Madori dared not even look back at him. If she looked back and saw him waving, saw dear old Hayseed, saw all those memories of home, she thought she wouldn't dare keep going.

Breath by breath, she thought. *Like Father taught me.* She inhaled shakily and walked forward. *Just survive the next breath.*

Chin raised and legs trembling, she walked through the gates, entering Teel University.

* * * * *

Torin watched his daughter vanish into the university, then stood for a long moment, staring at the gates. Finally, with a deep sigh, he turned and headed back into the town of Teelshire.

"Good luck, Billygoat," he said softly, walking along the cobbled street.

A part of him, however, didn't wish her luck. That part, perhaps petty, wished that Madori failed at the trials. If she gained admission to the university, Torin would travel the road home alone. His daughter would remain here among these walls for four years—a journey of many turns away from Fairwool-by-Night.

I'd miss you, Torin thought. *Koyee would miss you too.*

Madori often clashed with her mother—the two would argue over everything from Madori's clothes and hairstyle, to her disdain of Qaelish lessons, to the tattoo on her wrist—but Torin knew that the two women deeply loved each other.

Women? Torin frowned. Since when had Madori become a woman? It was only recently that Torin was changing her swaddling clothes, teaching her how to walk, and delighting whenever she learned to speak a new word. And now—in a blink of an eye—she was a woman?

He sighed.

You became a woman somewhere between Fairwool and Teelshire, he thought. He was both proud and terrified of how fast she had grown up. Maybe he was scared to let her walk alone in the world. And

22

maybe he simply missed the child she had been, a child who had depended on him.

He didn't know how long the trials would last, but he saw many other parents ambling about the town, finding bookshops, teashops, and mostly alehouses to wait in. They were typical nobles, he thought, men and women adorned in embroidered fabrics, sporting bright jewels for all to see. Torin was the son of a knight, and after returning home from the war—a hero known across Moth—he had received his own knighthood. Yet he sought no castles, no riches, simply the humble life of a gardener. He knew that his simple peasant's garb, the dirt beneath his fingernails, and his humble demeanor dreadfully embarrassed Madori whenever they visited the courts of Arden—and even here in Mageria. Torin smiled grimly.

Good. It's a father's job to embarrass his children.

The houses and shops rose three stories tall around him, their windows displaying wares from across Mageria—rich woolen fabrics to rival even those from his village of weavers, statues and paintings of landscapes, armor and weapons, and all manner of books and scrolls. The shops were doing good business this turn; Torin guessed that the Turn of Trials was their busiest of the year, a time when the wealthiest parents across the world came to wait nervously . . . and spend.

Finally Torin passed by The Dancing Wolf tavern again. He decided that more than he cared to shop, he'd like to drown his worries in a big mug of ale. Worrying for Madori always gnawed on him—he hadn't stopped worrying about her since her birth—but now a new concern had risen. The encounter with Lord Serin still weighed heavily upon him. His cousin's warning echoed in Torin's mind.

The Radian Order rises in the sunlight. The creatures of darkness will cower before us.

Torin grimaced. He had heard similar rhetoric years ago. Last time, such hate-mongering had led to a war across the world. Torin had feigned indifference around Madori, not wanting to worry the girl, but now his belly twisted. The memories of that war years ago—the fire in the night, the blood on his sword, the countless dead around him—still haunted his dreams, and now those memories flared even here in this peaceful, sunlit town.

Shaking his head grimly, he stepped into the tavern.

A large, warm room awaited him. His usual haunt back home—a cozy little tavern called The Shadowed Firkin—was a place of scarred oak tables, a scratched floor, and commoners boasting about the size of their squashes and the longevity of their sheep. But here Torin found a tavern that looked almost as luxurious as a nobleman's hall. Tapestries hung on the walls, depicting scenes of hunters and hounds under a sky full of birds. Actual tablecloths covered the tables, revealing cherry-wood legs engraved in the shapes of horses. Armchairs basked in the heat of two roaring fireplaces, and sunlight fell through stained-glass windows. Casks of ale and wine rose along one wall, and a bar stood gleaming with polished brass taps. The tavern was still half-empty, but every moment the bell above the door rang as more parents shuffled in.

Nodding at a few other fathers—their cheeks were already red with ale—Torin made his way to the bar. He sat on a stool, placed a few coins on the counter, and ordered a dark brew.

He raised the drink in the air, silently making the same toast he always did—a toast to old friends. To Bailey. To Hem. To lost souls, old memories.

"It's been seventeen years, friends," he said, his voice too low for anyone to hear. "I still think about you every turn."

He drank for them, thinking of home, missing that old tavern near the dusk, missing his old friends.

Snippets of conversation, rising from the armchairs by the fireplace behind him, reached Torin's ears, interrupting his thoughts.

"Now the Radians!" one man was saying. "There are some folks with sense to them, I say. Proud. Get things done. They're doing some good work in Timandra."

A second voice answered. "I've been saying it for a while, I have. Can't trust the nightfolk. Damn 'lorians moving into the sunlight now—I saw some myself, right here in Teelshire! You let in a few, soon they'll swarm. Let the Radians deal with them."

Torin twisted in his seat, glancing toward the hearth. Two noblemen sat there, holding tankards of ale, their cheeks ruddy and their bellies wide. They noticed his glance and raised their tankards.

"Oi, friend!" said one of the pair, his yellow mustache frothy. "You agree with us, don't you? You're a man of Arden; I can tell from the look of you. Right on the border with the night, you lot are." He nodded. "The Radians will protect you. They'll protect us all from this infestation of filthy Elorians."

Torin winced. *Filthy Elorians . . .* His wife was Elorian. His daughter was half-Elorian. He had fought and killed to save Elorians from the cruelty of daylight.

The ale tasted too bitter in his mouth. He turned away from the men and faced the bar again. His heart sank.

Did I make a mistake? he wondered, throat tightening. *Should I have truly brought Madori here into the wide world—a world that is hostile toward her?* Part of him wanted to race outside, barge into the university, grab his daughter, and drag her home to safety. Madori would shout, claiming she was old enough to seek her own fortune. Even Koyee would insist that they could not shelter Madori forever. But how could Torin let his little girl go alone into this world—a world full of hatred and ignorance, a world that would hate her simply for her blood?

Torin stared at the suds in his mug. Before Madori's birth, he and Koyee had fixed the Cabera Clock. For a year, the world had spun around its axis, night and day cycling. For a year, the world had seen Timandrians and Elorians as one. With peace restored, Torin and Koyee had broken the Cabera Clock again; Koyee still wore a small Cabera gear around her neck. The world was frozen again between endless day and night, and now—only a generation later—hatred was returning.

Should we have never broken the clock? Torin wondered. *Should we have never restored Moth to the way it was, the way its people wanted it?*

A stool creaked as a cloaked, hooded man sat down beside Torin. After ordering his own mug of ale, the stranger spoke in a low voice.

"You're right to ignore those fools." He turned his head toward Torin, though his face remained hidden in the shadows of his hood. "You can't fix stupidity, only hope to avoid it for a while."

The stranger's voice seemed familiar, as did his slender, short frame. Torin leaned closer, squinting, trying to see into the hood's shadows.

"Bit warm in here for a hood and cloak," Torin said.

The man received his mug of ale, took a sip, then leaned closer to Torin, letting some light fill his hood. "Warm but safe."

Torin's eyes widened. He nearly choked on his drink. "Cam?"

His friend—Camlin, King of Arden—smiled thinly and pulled his hood further down, letting new shadows hide him. "Hullo, Torin old boy. I thought I saw you in the crowd outside. You stick out like a black sheep with those ridiculous clothes from home."

The weight instantly lifted from Torin's shoulders. The world was dangerous, his daughter was leaving home, and hatred lurked only several paces behind him—but his friend was here, and things suddenly seemed a little brighter.

"*I* stick out?" Torin said. "Look at your clothes." He pointed at Cam's shabby old cloak.

The slender man sipped his ale. "That's different. I'm in disguise." He dropped his voice to a whisper. "I can't just walk around without this cloak and hood. People would mob me. I'm the King of Arden after all."

"King consort," Torin corrected him. "Queen Linee is the real monarch."

Cam groaned. "Will we ever have a single conversation without you reminding me of that fact?"

Torin grinned. "Depends. Will your head ever shrink back to its previous size?" He grabbed his friend's shoulder and squeezed it. "It's good to see you, old friend. When's the last time we met? It's been... Merciful Idar, a year now. Not since last summer when Madori and I visited the capital. What are you doing here in Mageria?"

Cam glanced around the tavern, but it seemed like all the other patrons were busy speaking among themselves, bragging of their

children's prowess and making wagers on who'd gain admission to
Teel. The diminutive king turned back toward Torin.

"Tam's here—trying out for the university."

Torin's eyes widened. "Your son? The Prince of Ard—"

"Shush!" Cam glanced around, eyes dark. "He's here in disguise
too. I begged the boy to stay in Arden. We have fine schools there as
well, but the lad wanted to study magic. In fact, I blame you." He
gave Torin a stern look and jabbed his chest. "It's your daughter who
put that nonsense into his head. Turns out last summer, when Madori
and Tam were taking all those walks in the garden, they weren't
having a secret romance as we feared. Oh no. It was much worse
than that. Madori was telling my boy all about how she wants to be a
mage someday, and well . . . Tam hasn't stopped talking about magic
since." He gulped down ale and sighed. "It can't have been easy for
Tam, growing up in the palace, only several moments younger than
his twin. Imagine it, Torin! Robbed of a birthright by a moment in
time. The twins are identical—Idar, I can barely tell them apart!—yet
one is heir, the other not. I suppose I can't blame Tam for wanting to
find his own way, to find his own power. But I'll miss him. This isn't
his home. Honestly, I don't know if I wish him to succeed or fail and
return to Arden."

Torin nodded glumly. "I feel the same way. Children. They ruin
your life, don't they?"

Cam groaned. "You're getting rid of yours soon! I still have one
at home." He drained his ale and ordered another drink. When the
serving girl had left, he spoke in a lower voice. "Torin, there's another
reason I came here. I knew you'd accompany Madori here, and I
wanted to speak with you."

Torin raised an eyebrow. "How did you know it wouldn't be
Koyee taking Madori here?"

The king snorted. "I saw Madori and Koyee interact enough
times; the two would kill each other on the road. No. I knew it would
be you here. Torin, there's trouble. Trouble back home. Trouble here.
Trouble all over the sunlit half of Moth."

Torin blew out his breath. "Tell me about it. We ran into some
trouble on the road here. Radians." He grimaced; the word tasted

foul in his mouth. "I crossed paths with Lord Serin, my cousin. He's one of them."

Cam barked a mirthless laugh. "*One* of them? Torin, my boy, he's their *leader*. His fort rises right on the border with Arden, and his disciples are spreading through my kingdom, spewing their bile. They opened a chapter right in Kingswall—in the capital, Torin!—just a short walk from the palace." Cam placed down his mug as if the ale had turned into mud. "The words they speak . . . by Idar, they remind me of you-know-who."

Torin nodded. "I was thinking the same thing. I thought we got rid of that rubbish in the war."

Cam sighed. "Pluck one weed, another rises. If I've learned anything from sitting on the throne, it's this: Fighting ignorance is like fighting weeds—an eternal battle." He clasped Torin's arm. "My friend, I came here to warn you. Koyee is in danger. Madori is in danger, maybe even within the walls of Teel. You're in danger; the Radians see you too as an enemy. By the Abyss, we're all in danger from these fanatics."

A chill ran down Torin's spine. "Idar's Beard, how serious are these Radians? Will they turn to violence?"

"They already have." Cam winced. "Last month in Kingswall. A convoy of Elorian merchants entered the city, selling silk and silverware. The local Radian chapter hung them dead from trees and burned their wares, accusing them of stealing work from honest Timandrians. I found the Radians who did it; those bastards rot in my dungeon now. But more keep crawling across the kingdom. Torin, this is serious. And I need you to listen carefully." Cam leaned closer, staring at Torin. "Send Koyee into the night for now. Madori too, if you can talk sense into her. But you, Torin—I need you with me in the capital."

Torin laughed mirthlessly. "The capital? Cam, you know I don't belong in Kingswall."

"I know. But neither do these Radians. Many in Kingswall respect you, the hero of the war, Sir Torin Greenmoat. I need you to stand at my side, not a gardener but a great lord. I need you to preach peace and acceptance and counter Serin's rhetoric."

Torin had thought his spirits couldn't sink any lower. He stared glumly into his drink. "We've had peace for seventeen years, Cam. But now . . . this feels like the old days."

Suddenly he missed Bailey so much it stabbed his chest. If his old friend were here, she'd know what to do. She'd shout, pound the bar, and probably rush out to find and kill Serin right away. She had led their little group in the last war. If violence flared again, how would Torin fight it—older, his dearest friend gone, his own daughter in peril?

"Will you come with me, Torin?" Cam said, not breaking his stare. "I need you—not in your gardens by the dusk but in the heart of our kingdom. I can't face this alone."

Torin closed his eyes. He hadn't seen Koyee in almost a month, and he missed her so badly he hurt. How could he send her into the darkness while he stayed in the light? Again Serin's words echoed in his mind: *The creatures of darkness will cower before us.*

Torin opened his eyes and nodded. "Of course, Cam. Of course."

CHAPTER THREE
SON OF SHADOW

They rode through the sunlit forest, three people of darkness upon three black panthers.

Jitomi tugged the hood lower over his head, his eyes darting. Mottles of light fell between the trees, stinging whenever they hit his skin. His cloak was heavy, his hood was wide, and the forest canopy was thick, but still the light hurt. It baked his back and stung his eyes—large Elorian eyes the size of chicken eggs, eyes made for the shadows of endless night.

Not for this place, he thought. *Not the eternal daylight of Timandra.*

He grimaced, stroked the panther he rode on, and looked at his companions. His sister, Nitomi, wore tight-fitting black silk—the outfit of the dojai, assassins and spies trained in the night. Over them she wore a cotton cloak and hood, a garment purchased in the daylight. Two straps crisscrossed her chest, and many tantō daggers hung upon them. More blades hung from her hips, and throwing stars were clasped to her legs. A diminutive woman—halfway into her thirties but still small as a child—she looked at him, her large blue eyes gleaming, and grinned.

"Are you excited, little brother? I bet you are. I bet you're so excited you can't even talk so much, because the excitement is squishing all your words in your throat, but I don't have that problem! I'm so excited for you too, so much I can hop!" She hopped upon her panther. "Soon you'll be a real mage with real magic! Unless you want to turn back. We can turn back if you like, go back into darkness, and you can become a dojai like me, an assassin of shadows. We don't have magic, it's true, but—"

"We keep going," Jitomi said, interrupting her. He had been living with Nitomi for all his sixteen years; the only way to converse with her, he knew, was to interrupt a lot. His sister was twice his age—she had even fought in the great War of Day and Night alongside the heroes Koyee and Torin—but still had the heart of a child. "We don't turn back."

And yet a part of him did want to turn back. A part of him feared this land of daylight. He had been only a babe when the Timandrians had invaded his homeland of Eloria. The sunlit demons had marched into the shadows with blades, with torches, and with dark magic. Jitomi had grown up seeing the scars of that magic upon the warriors of Ilar, his island homeland in the darkness.

His nine sisters—Nitomi the eldest among them—were either dojai assassins or steel-clad warriors in Ilar's army. Yet what use were blades against magic? In the war, so many Ilari soldiers—brave, strong men all in steel—had fallen to the sunlit mages. His father had hoped that Jitomi—the family's youngest child and only boy—would become a great warrior, an heir to their fortress. But Jitomi had disappointed his father, had spat upon the family tradition, had left their castle in the darkness and journeyed here into the light . . . to find Teel University. To find the secrets of power.

"Qato blind," said the third rider, voice plaintive.

Jitomi turned to look at the man—if a man he was. His cousin, Qato, seemed more like one of the mythical giants of ancient days. While Nitomi was small—shorter than five feet—Qato stood seven feet tall, wide and stony as a cliff face. His panther, the largest of the beasts found in Ilar's wilderness, grunted under the weight. Normally bare-chested, even in the cold of night, here in daylight Qato wore a thick robe and hood, hiding himself from the sun. A massive katana, large as a pike, hung across his back. His eyes were narrowed to slits in the daylight, even this mottled daylight of the forest.

Jitomi rode his panther closer to his cousin. He patted Qato's knee. "We're almost there. Then you and Nitomi can return home. Soon you'll be back in the darkness."

Of course, home lay a two moons' ride away, but Qato needed all the encouragement he could get.

As for me, Jitomi thought with a sigh, *I won't be returning home for a while, not if I'm admitted to Teel.* He looked up at the sky, wincing in a beam of light that fell between the branches. *The university studies are four years long . . . four years in this strange light of endless day and heat and life everywhere.*

As much as the light seemed strange, the life that filled Timandra was even stranger. Eloria was a land of rock, water, and starlight, but here—here the entire landscape was made of life. Blades of grass grew under the panthers' feet, tiny creatures that survived even when stepped upon. Trees grew from the soil, giant creatures with rustling green hair. Birds and small furry animals crawled upon the trees like parasites, scuttling, crying, squawking. Jitomi had been in Timandra for two moons now, and while he was starting to get used to the sunlight—he could tolerate it with his cloak and hood— seeing life everywhere still seemed so strange. He had learned that not all these creatures were animals; many of them were called "plants," and they had no thoughts, no feelings, no sense of pain— much like the mushrooms back in Eloria but far taller and grander. Eloria had no plants, and still Jitomi struggled to distinguish between them and the strange animals of this place. To him it was all a surreal dream, an endless menagerie—life beneath, around, and above him.

He passed his fingers along his neck, up his cheek, and over his brow. A dragon tattoo coiled there, rising from collarbone to forehead. Jitomi could not see the tattoo, but he could imagine that he felt the inked scales.

Protect me here, Tianlong, black dragon of Ilar, he thought. *Lend me some of your strength.*

"Qato homesick," moaned the giant dojai.

"Me too, cousin," said Jitomi with a sigh.

Little Nitomi bounced in her saddle. "Not me! Not at all. I was so bored back in Eloria. It's so boring in the darkness what with all those boring shadows and boring stars and boring . . . well, that's all there is in Eloria, isn't it? Shadows and stars. That's why it's so boring! I love the daylight. It's an adventure! I love adventures. I once went on an adventure with Koyee, have I told you? We went to a distant island of secrets, and we saw a monster—a real monster with four arms!—and there were giant weaveworms who boiled their babies, and—"

"Qato knows!" moaned the giant.

Jitomi nodded. "Yes, sister, you've told us that story ten times this turn already."

"I can't help it!" The little woman was still hopping. "It's the best story I have, and—"

"Sister, look." Jitomi pointed between the trees and down a hillside. "I think we're finally here."

They rode a little farther, and the last trees parted. Grassy hills rolled in full sunlight toward a valley and farmlands. Past flowery meadows lay a town of many houses, a columned temple, and a walled complex containing towers and domes.

"Teel University," Jitomi whispered.

The panthers bristled and growled; creatures of darkness, they still feared open daylight. Jitomi dismounted and stroked his beast.

"Qato, will you stay here with the panthers?" he asked his cousin. "They're strong and noble animals, but they still fear the daylight. Let them remain in the cover of the forest."

The giant nodded. "Qato stay."

Jitomi smiled thinly. In truth, he worried more about Qato than the panthers; he had never seen his cousin so miserable.

Nitomi bounced off her mount. "I'm not staying! I'm going right with you. I bet we'll find another adventure down there. Do you think they have weaveworms? Do they have weaveworms in the daylight? Did I tell you about the time I traveled to the island with Koyee, and we saw weaveworms, and we saw a *real* monster with many arms, and—"

Jitomi placed a finger against her lips. "I think we better not speak of weaveworms and monsters here. The locals might think we're strange."

She nodded knowingly and clamped her palms over her mouth. She spoke in a muffled voice. "Okay!"

Leaving Qato and the panthers, the siblings began to walk downhill, their hoods pulled over their heads, their cloaks shielding their skin from the light. Jitomi sighed. Even without his sister prattling on about giant worms, the siblings seemed strange enough in this land. Jitomi had seen many Timandrians over the past two moons of travel: they were a tall, wide people, their skin bronzed, their hair dark, their eyes small. Jitomi was an Elorian, born and bred in darkness; his skin was milky white, his hair silvery and smooth, his eyes large and gleaming, his ears wide, his body thin.

I'm as strange to Timandrians as trees, grass, and sunlight are to me, he thought. He had to crush an instinct to turn back, to race home to Eloria. He had come this far, seeking the secrets of magic; those secrets lay in the valley below. He would be strong. He would not turn back. If he ever returned to Eloria, it would be as a mage.

They walked down the sunny hillside, found a pebbly path, and took it through the meadow. Many flowers—Jitomi wished he knew their names—swayed on either side, and small animals—furry creatures with long ears—raced away from his feet. When they finally reached the town and Jitomi stepped onto its cobbled streets, he lost his breath.

Towns in Ilar, his island of the night, were places of stone and fire, their black pagodas rising into the starry sky, their braziers crackling, their banners streaming in the moonlight like birds seeking flight. They were places of silence, of dark dignity, of a solemn beauty like crystal caves or underwater ruins. But here, in Teelshire, he found a town that spun his head—a place of endless color, sunlight, and life. Flowers bloomed in gardens. People wore not the dark silk of his homeland but colorful tunics and robes of cotton, wool, and fur. Stained-glass windows glittered upon the houses, and red tiles shone in the sunlight.

"It's beautiful," Nitomi whispered at his side, for once not launching into an endless stream of words.

He nodded. They stepped deeper into the town, heading toward the walls of the university.

As they walked, Jitomi's sense of wonder soured. At first it was a little boy who saw them, gasped, and fled. Past another street corner and a shop selling honeyed cakes, it was two women who pointed, muttered, and spun away on their heels. In a courtyard with a marble statue rising from a fountain, three men spat, and one shouted, "Nightcrawlers go home!" before storming off into a tavern.

"We're not very popular here," Jitomi said to his sister. He couldn't help but admire the ingenuity of the slur—nightcrawler, the name of a worm and, supposedly, the children of night.

The little woman was bouncing about, gaping at the many shops, taverns, statues, and gardens. "So what? Let them stare. Let them mumble. Jitomi, we are the children of a great lord! I'm a dojai and you're almost a mage already. They've just never seen an Elorian before. I bet they've never seen weaveworms either. Do you think we might still find weaveworms here? Maybe in the mountains up there, or—"

"Sister, hush. Let's go quickly. I want to reach the university and get off these streets."

A few men were glaring at them from a roadside ale-house. One held a knife. Another wore a strange brooch upon his lapel—it looked like a sun eclipsing a moon. The men spoke in low murmurs, and Jitomi caught something about how "Serin will send the creatures back into the night." He walked on, moving to another street.

The siblings hurried onward, and even Nitomi fell silent for once. Jitomi was too young to remember the great War of Day and Night, but his older siblings had told him many tales of those days. The fleets of daylight had sailed against Ilar, the great southern empire of the night. Those ships had smashed against the walls of Asharo, and many Timandrians—sailors and soldiers—ended up in chains, whipped, enslaved to their Ilari masters.

Yet now we're the foreigners, he thought. *Now we're nothing but creatures in a strange land.* He took a deep breath. *The war is over but hatred remains.*

They were near the walls of Teel University, walking across a courtyard, when they saw the demonstration.

A couple dozen Timandrians stood outside the university gates, raising banners with the same eclipse sigil. An effigy of an Elorian hung from a lamp post between them, formed of straw and wood—a twisted creature, its eyes cruel, its fingers clawed, its fangs red. The Timandrians chanted together in their tongue, which Jitomi had been studying for the past few years. He understood these words and they chilled him.

"Radian rises!" the people cried. "Radian rises! Elorians go home!"

One of the demonstrators, a young woman with long golden hair, rose to stand on a box. Cheeks flushed, she shouted, "Hear me! I am Lari Serin, a Radian warrior. Teel University is tarnished with the filth of nightcrawlers. Send all Elorian students home! Keep all magic in Mageria! Send the creatures back into the darkness."

Jitomi froze in his tracks, staring. So there were other Elorian students at Teel? That both comforted and worried him. He had hoped to fade into the shadows here; if other Elorians had come to study magic, and if tensions were rising, would he find himself caught in a racial war?

"Radian rises!" shouted Lari—the young, golden-haired woman. She saw Jitomi and his sister, pointed at them, and her voice rose even louder. "More creatures of the night walk among us. Nightcrawlers will burn!"

With that, Lari brought a candle to the hanging effigy. The Elorian of wood and straw caught flame. The demonstrators cheered, cut the burning effigy down, and stomped upon it. Their banners rose higher, and their voices cried out for Radian. Whether Radian was a god, movement, or leader, Jitomi didn't know, but whatever the case, the word meant danger.

Until now, Jitomi had been fighting the temptation to turn back, to run home to the night. Strangely, now he found himself clenching his fists, squaring his jaw, and marching forward with renewed determination. Nitomi walked at his side, silent for once, her eyes darting.

Leaving the protestors behind, they finally reached the university gates. Towers flanked a stone archway, its keystone engraved with two crossing scrolls, sigil of Teel. Guards in particolored livery stood at the open doors, their helmets plumed. When Jitomi peered inside, he saw a cobbled cloister, a towering elm tree, and columned halls. Many other applicants already stood within; some were fellow Elorians, hooded and cloaked.

Teel University... center of learning, wisdom, and magic.

Jitomi turned toward his sister. She stared at him, her large eyes damp, her lips quivering.

"It's time to say goodbye," Jitomi said softly and held her hands.

She nodded and sniffled. "I'll miss you, baby brother. I'll miss you so much. It won't be the same at home without you. Please do well here. Please become a very powerful mage very quickly, then come back to Ilar. I'll think about you every turn. I promise." She unclasped one of her many daggers from the strap across her chest.

She handed it to him. The tantō was curved, the hilt wrapped in silk, and the sigil of Ilar—a red flame—was engraved onto the blade. "Take this. It's good steel and it will protect you here. It's the only gift I have to give."

He took the dagger and slid it into one of his cloak's deep pockets. He was about to turn and leave when Nitomi leaped, wrapped all four limbs around him, and hugged him tightly.

"Goodbye, brother," she whispered.

"Goodbye, sister."

Tears filled his own eyes. He turned to step through the archway, leaving her there—wishing he had more to say, wishing he had more time with her. He felt stiff, awkward, afraid. He dared not look back.

If I pass these trials, I won't leave this place for four years.

He entered a cobbled cloister surrounded by columned galleries. Towers soared at all sides, and a great dome—large as a palace—rose ahead. Blinking furiously, struggling to keep his eyes dry, he stared at the elm tree. Its leaves rustled against the blue sky, and Jitomi thought of the stars of his homeland.

CHAPTER FOUR
FRIEND AND FOE

Head spinning, Madori took a deep breath and stared around at the fabled Teel University.

She stood in a sprawling cloister surrounded by porticoes. The place seemed large enough for an army to muster in. Many other youths walked around her, all highborn. All were better dressed, better bred, and quite a bit taller than her. Born to an Elorian mother, Madori stood barely five feet tall; women of the night rarely stood taller. Full-blooded Timandrians, children of eternal daylight grown on hearty sunlit fare, dwarfed her. As she moved among the crowd, Madori saw them stare at her, mutter, even point.

"An Elorian?" one boy whispered, gaping her way.

His friend shook his head. "Hair's black, skin's tanned. Half-breed, I reckon. I heard of those."

Madori sneered. She was about to march over to the two boys and clobber them—how dared they talk of her as of some animal!—but her father appeared in her mind. She could hear his damn voice again.

You will achieve greatness on your terms, not letting others drag you into the mud.

Madori grumbled. Father invented stupid puns, told jokes only he'd laugh at, and was overall a huge embarrassment, but he was also the wisest person Madori knew. Fists clenched, she walked away from the two slack-jawed boys, heading deeper into the cloister.

"Country bumpkins, they are," she muttered under her breath. "They'll never pass the trials."

She kept moving, worming her way through the crowd. She thought she caught glimpses of a wooden stage ahead. Used to being the shortest person around, Madori knew she'd have to step close if she wanted to see any speaker who might appear.

As she walked, she passed by some of the strangest youths she'd ever seen. Most applicants seemed to be local boys and girls, Magerians in cotton robes, their eyes bright and their hair golden. But many foreigners crowded the courtyard too. Some applicants seemed to be from Arden, Madori's homeland; they wore leggings, tunics, and tall leather boots. Others hailed from all over the daylight realms: jungle dwellers clad in tiger-pelts, their hair flaming red; northern Verilish youths, hulking and wide, wearing bear furs; southern desert children, their skin deep bronze, their tunics white; and even some dwellers of the distant savanna island of Sania, their clothes formed of many beads, elephants embroidered onto their cloaks.

Diverse as they were, all of them were Timandrians, Madori realized with a sigh. All were children of Timandra, the sunlit half of this broken world men called Moth. The day never ended here; these children had never known darkness. She, Madori, would always be a stranger among them—a girl born to a mother of darkness, an Elorian from across the dusk.

Her eyes stung. *Will I be an outcast here too?*

She was nearing the stage when she saw another group of applicants; these ones huddled close together, clad in robes and hoods. Madori tilted her head, squinted, and stepped closer.

Her heart burst into a gallop.

"Elorians," she whispered, a tremble seizing her.

Madori had seen many Elorians before. Her village was near the border with the night, and her mother often took her into the darkness. Madori had spent many hours admiring the stars and moon, feasting upon mushrooms and glowing lanternfish, and playing with Elorian children under the dark skies. Yet aside from her mother, she had never seen other Elorians in the sunlit half of Moth.

They were a slender folk, their skin milky white, their hair long and smooth and the color of starlight. Their ears were large, thrusting out, meant for hearing every creak in the deep darkness. Their robes were made of silk, embroidered with dragon motifs. Their most distinguishing feature, however, was their eyes. Those orbs were twice the size of Timandrian eyes, oval and gleaming blue and lavender. Madori herself—though tanned of skin and dark of hair— had those eyes.

Eyes for seeing in the dark.

She took a deep breath, sudden hope lifting inside her. Here in the sunlight, she was a curiosity, a girl for others to gape at. She was no more Elorian than Timandrian, but perhaps among the children of the night she could find some acceptance. After all, they too were curiosities here; Madori saw how the others stared and pointed at them. If Madori and these Elorians did not share the full bond of race, they shared the bond of alienation.

One of the Elorians noticed her. He raised his eyes and stared her way. His large, gleaming eyes were deep blue. A tattoo of a dragon crawled up his neck and cheek, finally coiling over the eyebrow. Strands of hair fell across his forehead, milky-white, and a silver ring studded his nose. He didn't speak, didn't step toward her, merely stared, his gaze penetrating. Slowly, the others in his group turned to follow his gaze, and Madori saw the confusion in their eyes. Like everyone, they too were trying to decide what she was—a girl with Timandrian hair and skin, her eyes large as an Elorian's.

She took a step toward them, needing that comfort, that acceptance, that security of a group. But before she reached them, she paused.

No.

A voice spoke in her head again, but this time it seemed to be her own voice, not her father's—a voice from deep within her.

This is not the path to acceptance.

She was in Timandra now, about to apply for admission in a university full of Timandrians. She had to make a choice how to live here, which side of hers to embrace. If she chose to mingle with Timandrians, perhaps she could still find some acceptance in the sunlight. If she chose to live as an Elorian, she would forever be an outcast here—just one more outsider, a misfit among misfits.

She caressed her own tattoo—a small duskmoth upon her wrist, its one wing white, the other black. Duskmoths were creatures shaped like the world, torn between day and night. They were creatures like her, forever halved. Madori tore her gaze away from that strange, tattooed Elorian boy and his comrades. Leaving them, she walked toward the wooden stage.

Several men and women stood upon this stage, clad in flowing robes. *Mages*, Madori knew—each from a different school. One mage, a stern looking man with cold eyes, wore the black robes of offensive magic—dark spells used in warfare. Several other mages wore white, green, and red robes, though Madori did not know what those colors signified; her father had met only the dark mages in the war. She wondered which of these professors could teach her healing; it was the skill she had come here for, the skill she refused to leave without.

One mage, an elderly woman clad in blue robes, stepped toward a podium on the stage. She was a frail little thing, barely larger than Madori, her hair white and her skin deeply lined. The woman raised her arms, and when she spoke, her voice boomed out, loud as a crashing oak. Applicants started and gaped as the thundering words pounded out of this dainty woman's mouth. Already they saw magic at work.

"Welcome, applicants, to the Teel Trials!" The mage gazed across the crowd. "I am Headmistress Egeria. You've traveled here from many lands to prove your mettle. I see applicants from across Mythimna. I see boys and girls from our homeland of Mageria." Cheers rose from the crowd at this; most here were local Magerians. "And I see applicants from the pine forests of Verilon, from the plains of Arden, from the cold arctic isle of Orida, from the jungles of Naya . . ." As the headmistress named every sunlit nation, its applications cheered. The old woman continued. "I see students from the swamps of Daenor, from the desert of Eseer, from the savannah of Sania." She cleared her throat and fixed the round glasses that perched atop her nose. "And, for the very first time in Teel University history, I am proud to see that Elorians—children from the dark half of Moth—have chosen to cross into the sunlight to join our quest for knowledge."

At those last words, the crowd fell silent. Madori cringed. The headmistress had spoken with good intentions, but looking around, Madori saw that the applicants weren't as pleased with the prospect. Some students glanced at one another; others gaped openly at the group of Elorians who stood clustered not far from Madori, hidden inside their silken robes.

One applicant, a golden-haired girl who stood not far from Madori, snickered. "What's next, letting pigs apply?" she said—too softly for the professors on the stage to hear, but loud enough for Madori to turn red.

A few of the girl's friends stifled laughs.

"Truly, Lari, you think Elorians are pigs?" said a boy, addressing the girl. He grinned. "Pigs smell better."

Lari tossed back her golden tresses. "Rotten pig carcasses smell better than Elorians. My father says they're lower than maggots."

Again the friends laughed.

The headmistress was speaking again, but Madori was paying no attention. She glared at the group of snickering youths. There were several of them—Magerians by the looks of them, all tall, golden of hair, and blue of eyes. They wore fine clothing of rich, embroidered cotton, and golden jewelry adorned their wrists and necks. They all wore the Radian sigil upon their lapels—a sun eclipsing the moon.

Madori ground her teeth. "Radians," she muttered.

The lead girl—Lari—seemed to hear her. She turned toward Madori, tilted her head, and narrowed her eyes.

"And what have we here?" she asked.

Madori clenched her fists. Lari was everything Madori was not. She had perfect clothes, perfect hair, a perfectly beautiful face—the kind to make boys trip over their own tongues. She was taller than Madori, obviously better bred, and about a thousand times wealthier. If Madori were a plucky little mutt, here was a prize racehorse.

"Somebody who'll punch your perfect little teeth out of your perfect little mouth," Madori said, raising a fist. "So I suggest you shut that mouth if you don't want this fist shattering it."

Lari laughed—a beautiful, trilling sound like rain upon leaves. "Oh my. Oh dear. This isn't an Elorian, my friends. This is . . ." She gasped and covered her mouth, feigning surprise. "A *mongrel*."

Her friends grimaced. A few made gagging noises.

Madori leaped forward. She barely stood taller than Lari's shoulders, but she didn't care. "A mongrel who'll bash your—"

"*Applicants!*"

The voice boomed across the crowd, louder than thunder. Madori froze, her fist inches away from Lari's face. She spun to see Headmistress Egeria glaring from the stage. The elderly woman was pointing at Madori. Around the headmistress, the professors stared at Madori, eyes boring into her.

"Is there a problem, applicants?" the headmistress said.

Madori forced herself to lower her fists, though she still fumed. Grinding her teeth, she stared back at Egeria and shook her head.

At her side, Lari pouted, a picture of innocence. The girl leaned closer to Madori and whispered, "Oh sweetness, such temper . . . truly you mongrels are rabid beasts. Someday we Radians will put you all down."

The headmistress was still staring at them; so were thousands of curious applicants. Madori forced herself to take several steps away from Lari and her friends.

We'll settle this later, Lari, she thought, her cheeks hot. *You might be a perfect little lady, but I'm a farm girl, grown up wrestling boys in the fields, and I can bash you and your friends to bits.*

After clearing her throat, the headmistress continued speaking to the crowd.

"As I was saying: Teel University accepts only the very brightest, the very strongest, the very wisest of all youths to learn the secrets of magic. Every year, we can admit only two hundred students to our school. Over two thousand of you have gathered here this turn." The headmistress raised her chin. "Most you will soon return home."

Grumbles rose across the crowd. Madori looked from side to side, judging the others' reactions. Some students seemed confident; Lari and her friends stood smiling, hands on their hips, sure of their victory. Other students looked worried; one boy wrung his hands, while another actually whimpered.

Ninety percent will go home, Madori thought. *But I won't. I lived my life an outcast, a misfit, a creature to be scorned or pitied.* She squared her jaw. *I will pass these trials, and I will become a mage. I will become powerful.*

"To weed out the chaff," Headmistress Egeria boomed out, "you shall partake in three trials. A Trial of Wisdom. A Trial of Wit. And finally a Trial of Will. Only those who pass all three trials shall attend Teel University. Your names will be called out one by one. When you hear your name, you will enter Ostrinia Tower." The headmistress pointed at an archway beyond the stage; it led into the base of a brick tower that scratched the clouds. "There your trials will begin."

With that, the headmistress stepped back. A young mage stepped forth to replace her, unrolling a scroll that dangled down to his feet. He began to read out names one by one. As each name was called, an applicant walked toward the tower.

Madori chewed her lip. She hadn't registered her name anywhere. How would they know to call her? She looked around, seeking somebody—perhaps a professor or other university member—to talk to. She cursed herself; how could she have missed signing up! As she scanned the crowd, she saw the Elorian boy—the one with the dragon tattoo and pierced nose—staring at her again.

Madori froze and narrowed her eyes, staring back, but the boy wouldn't look away. His eyes seemed to stare deep into her, his face expressionless, and something about him unnerved Madori. She had seen many Elorians before—after all, her mother was Elorian, and Madori spent many turns in Oshy, a village of the night—but never one like this, one so . . . the only word she could think of was *intense*.

She took a step closer toward him, intending to insist he explained his stare or she'd stab his eyes. Before she could take a second step, however, a hand reached out and tugged her sleeve.

"Billygoat?"

She spun around, for an instant sure that her woolhead of a father had stepped into the university grounds, the only parent here to utterly humiliate his child. But it wasn't her father who stood there, holding her sleeve. Madori's eyes widened.

"Tam?" She rubbed her eyes. "Prince Tamlin Solira?"

It was him. The Prince of Arden himself, her best—her only—friend in the world, stood before her.

Madori's father had spent the war fighting alongside the king and queen—his dearest friends. Madori spent half her summers in the darkness of Eloria, the other half in Kingswall, the capital city of Arden, spending time with the king, queen, and twin princes. The adults spent most of their time in dreadfully dull conversations, telling old war stories and discussing politics; so did Prince Omry, Tam's twin and heir to Arden. Meanwhile, Madori and Tam—bored senseless with the court—would sneak out into the gardens to chase butterflies, explore secret paths, and pretend to be adventurers.

Of course, they were older now, almost adults themselves. Tam was seventeen, a year older than her, and quite a bit taller. Brown, curly hair fell across his brow, and his smile was bright. Madori had always known him to dress in the finery of a prince, but here he wore simple woolen garments, clothes no finer—though perhaps more traditional—than her own.

"Hush!" His voice dropped to a whisper, and he winked. "Don't say my name here. At least not my full name. I'm sort of, well . . . undercover."

Madori grumbled. "And don't you call me Billygoat. You know I hate that stupid name. I am Madori Billy Greenmoat." She glared at him for a moment, then felt her eyes sting. She pulled him into an embrace. "What are you doing here, Tam?"

He grinned and mussed her hair. "Same thing you are. Trying out for Teel. Remember how we'd talk about becoming mages someday?"

She tilted her head. "I also remember talking about slaying dragons, forming a juggling troupe, and training elephants to play oversized musical instruments." She punched his chest. "For pity's sake! Why would you come here? I need to gain some power. You're already powerful. You're a damn prince and—"

"Billygoat, hush!" When she punched his chest again, he grimaced. "All right, all right—*Madori*." He rubbed his chest, wincing. "Look, my father is worried about you. There's been talk of . . . enemies. And, well, I couldn't let you come here alone. So here I am." He gave a little bow. "Your protector."

She rolled her eyes and snorted. "Last time we met, I was the one protecting you from the evil bumblebees."

"Those little buggers were nasty, and there's worse than bumblebees here." He leaned in close, whispering. "There's this fellow, a lord, his name is—"

"Serin!" The voice boomed across the crowd of applicants, interrupting Tam. "Lari Serin!"

Madori craned her neck, peering around Tam. The professor on the stage was still summoning applicants; Madori had blocked out most of the names, but this one sent shivers down her spine.

Lari—the girl who had called her a mongrel.

Serin—the name of the cruel lord on the road, her father's cousin.

The two names, in tandem, felt like mixing poison with flame. *She's a Serin.* Madori almost gagged. *She's a relative.*

Her chin raised, the sunlight gleaming upon her golden hair, Lari Serin strutted through the crowd, spreading smiles every which way. Other applicants clapped as she passed by; some even bowed. Obviously the girl was noble among nobles. Madori's belly soured and she gritted her teeth.

Lari caught her eyes, and the girl's grin widened. While walking toward Ostrinia Tower, she made a point of passing by Madori.

"Good luck at the trials, mongrel," she said and patted Madori's cheek. "Maybe they'll teach you to sit like a good little dog."

Madori growled, slapped Lari's hand aside, and leaped forward, intending to give the young lady two black eyes and a bloody nose. But Tam—damn the boy—grabbed her and held her back.

"Madori, no!" he said, dragging her away from Lari. "Let her go."

Lari laughed. "Keep her on a leash, boy! She's a wild one."

With a wink, Lari left them, heading across the cloister and into the tower.

Madori struggled and kicked in Tam's grasp. "Let go of me."

He refused and Madori cursed her small size; she didn't have the physical strength to free herself from his grasp, another reason why she had to learn magic, to gain power.

"Madori, listen to me," he hissed into her ear. "Do you know who that is?"

"A pretty little cockroach I'm about to stomp on."

"A pretty little cockroach who's the daughter of a very big, powerful cockroach. Her father is Lord Tirus Serin, the wealthiest man in Mageria—possibly in all eight sunlit kingdoms of Timandra." Tam sounded grim. "Not a person you want on your bad side."

Madori grumbled. "I think it might be a little too late for that."

Her fists were still clenched, but inside she trembled. The encounter on the road returned to her, and her eyes burned. She had fled the ignorance of villagers; now she found the same hatred even among the lords and ladies of sunlight.

Did I make a mistake leaving home? she thought, blinking away sudden tears. *Is there any home for me here—a girl of mixed blood, my Elorian eyes forever marking me a foreigner?*

Tam released his grip and she turned toward him, still held in his arms. She looked into his brown eyes and saw the same fear in them.

"What kind of place have we come to?" she whispered.

Before her friend could answer, the professor's voice boomed across the cloister again.

"Madori Greenmoat!"

She started. She wasn't sure how her name had ended up on the list—was magic at work here?—but she pulled away from Tam's arms.

"Good luck, Billygoat." A smile broke through the fear on Tam's face like sunlight through rain.

She nodded. "You too."

Leaving him, she walked through the crowd, heading toward the tower. As other applicants had walked this walk, their friends had clapped, cheered, patted them on the shoulders. As Madori walked, silence fell across the cloister, and thousands of eyes stared at her. She felt like a freak on show. She raised her chin high and squared her shoulders, forcing herself to walk with pride.

My parents are war heroes, she thought. *I am strong, wise, and determined. I am not a creature. I will pass these trials.*

She reached the tower. Jaw clenched, she stepped through its doorway and into the shadows.

Daniel Arenson

CHAPTER FIVE
TRIAL OF WISDOM

Madori stepped into a round chamber, probably the oddest applicant Teel University had ever seen.

My clothes are strange and my hair is stranger, she thought. *My mixed blood is a curiosity.* She raised her chin and stared at the professors who sat ahead. *But I will pass this trial.*

They sat at a table upon a dais—three professors in robes, all staring at her. She could barely see them in the shadows; they seemed like hulking vultures looming above prey. A beam of light fell from a window, illuminating a circle on the floor. Madori stepped into the light, blinked, and stared up at the professors, feeling like a prisoner at a trial.

One professor, a little old man with a bald head and white mustache, cleared his throat.

"Hello. I am Elixior Fen, Professor of Basic Magical Principles." He thumbed through a booklet. "You are . . . Madori Billy Greenmoat, yes?" His voice was scratchy and high-pitched. "From Fairwool-by-Night, in the kingdom of Arden. Daughter of . . ." He adjusted his half-moon glasses, peering into the book. "Daughter of Sir Torin Greenmoat, son of Sir Teramin Greenmoat. Oh my." He raised his eyes in surprise and peered down at her. "Your father is something of a legend in these parts—I wager, in all parts of Moth."

Madori raised her chin, pride in her father swelling in her. But another professor spoke, quickly crushing her rising spirits.

"Torin Greenmoat is a fool, not a true noble. I remember him from the war. I do believe we fought in the same battle once; of course, he was fighting for the wrong side. He is an insult to the purity of highborn blood."

Madori turned to look at this new speaker. Seeing him, her innards crumpled like old parchment.

48

This professor not only loomed like a vulture but looked like one too. His neck was long and scraggly, his nose was hooked like a beak, and his eyes were dark and glittering. His scalp was bald, and strands of oily, dark hair hung from his head in a ring like putrid feathers. He wore the black robes of warfare, the cloth dusty and tattered, and upon them gleamed a brooch of gold and silver—the Radian sigil.

A dark magician, Madori thought, anger bubbling inside her. *The kind father fought in the war. And a Radian to boot.*

"My father," she said, chin raised, "killed mages like you in the war."

The hooked-nosed Radian leaped to his feet, sneering. His fists clenched upon the tabletop.

"I would watch my tongue if I were you, *mongrel.* Your father spat upon the pure blood of Timandra, mixing it with Elorian filth." He snorted. "We see the result before us—an impudent, feral little—"

"Professor Atratus!" said Professor Fen, slamming his book shut. His white mustache bristled, and lines creased his bald head. The little old man seemed barely larger than Madori, but he spoke with authority. "Please, Atratus. We've not invited Madori here to discuss her parentage. Whatever happened between you and Sir Greenmoat during the war ended many years ago. We're here to judge young Madori, not any supposed crimes her father may or may not have committed." The diminutive professor cleared his throat and pushed his spectacles up his nose. "Now then, Professor Atratus, would you reoccupy your seat so we may begin?"

Never removing his withering stare from Madori, Atratus sat back down. His fists remained balled, and his lip curled.

The third professor, who had remained silent so far, finally cleared her throat. Clad in blue robes, she was younger than her companions—not much older than Madori's parents—with a head of bushy brown hair and olive-toned skin. A milky film covered her eyes; those eyes stared blankly over Madori's head.

She's blind, Madori realized.

"My name is Elina Maleen, Professor of Magical History," the woman said. "I will quiz you first, followed by my two colleagues. We desire for only the most learned youths to attend our university. Our questions will determine whether you are proficiently educated." The blind professor smoothed her robes. "You must answer *all three* questions correctly to pass to the next trial."

Madori gulped. Proficiently educated? She had grown up in a village, surrounded by farms. She had never gone to any school. All she knew was what she had read about in the village library. There were hundreds of books in that library, all donated by Queen Linee of Arden; Madori had mostly just read the books of epic tales and ancient deeds of valor. How would those help her at a school for magic? She wanted to object to this entire test. She wanted to tell Professor Maleen that she had come here to *become* educated. But before words could leave her mouth, the young, bushy-haired professor spoke again.

"Now, child, please tell me: What is the ratio of a circle's circumference to its diameter?"

Madori blinked.

What? she wanted to blurt out. How did that have anything to do with magic? Circumference? Daiameter? Only masons and shipwrights knew such things; she was from a village of shepherds and farmers!

She opened her mouth to object, to demand another question, but Professor Maleen leaned forward expectantly, and for a moment Madori lost her breath.

I don't know, she thought. Cold sweat trickled down her back. *I came here ill-prepared. I'll be among the ninety percent of applicants going home this turn.*

She froze. *Wait!* spoke a voice inside her. Percentages—she knew about those. She had just *thought* about them! Where had she learned about percentages?

She racked her mind, thinking back to Fairwool Library. When she closed her eyes, she imagined herself walking through that library again, passing by shelves of many books. In her memory, she reached out to one particular book, a dusty old tome with blue leather binding. She had loved its illustrations of stars, moons, and many graphs and geometric shapes.

A book of mathematics. Yes. She had read this book!

She opened her eyes, took a deep breath, and blurted out from memory, "It's a number that cannot be expressed in words or digits. It's roughly . . ." She mumbled under her breath for a moment, struggling to remember. "About twenty-two divided by seven. Three and a little bit." She nodded, hoping that was close enough. "Old Master Loranor, a mathematician from Eseer, referred to it as The Cosmic Number."

She took a deep breath, staring at the professor, and her heart pounded. For a long moment Professor Maleen was silent, and Madori barely dared to breathe.

Finally Maleen nodded. "Very good! Very good, child. You are correct."

Madori breathed out a sigh of relief. She managed a shaky grin and even gave a little curtsy.

Before she could catch her breath, however, Professor Fen rose to his feet. He was so short he actually dropped in height once sliding off his chair. He straightened his half-moon glasses, stroked his mustache, and passed a hand across his large, bald head.

"Now then . . ." he said, thumbing through his little book. "A question, a question . . . ah! Here we go. A very good question indeed, this one is." He smiled at Madori. "Listen carefully, child. Many years ago, both halves of Mythimna experienced both day and night, an alternating dance. Why is one half of Mythimna now always in daylight, the other always dark?"

Madori blinked. "Well, that's easy! It's because . . ."

She trailed off, frowning. Why *was* one half Mythimna—this world men called Moth—always in sunlight, the other always dark? She had always assumed that was simply the way of the world, that there wasn't any particular *reason* to it. This was like asking why the sky was blue, why mountains were taller than valleys, or why trees grew upward instead of down. She tilted her head.

"Well, it's . . ." she began, tapping her chin.

"Yes?" Professor Fen asked.

She chewed her lip, thinking back to the stories of the war. Her parents had told her this story! They had told her the story a thousand times, but Madori had always blocked it out, upset about her mother's latest lecture or her father's latest bad pun. Yet now she clawed at the memory. Her parents had been to Cabera Mountain, the heart of the broken world. They had fixed Moth. They had made day and night cycle again, only to freeze the world once more, what with Elorians blinded in the sunlight and Timandrians stumbling around in the dark. How had her parents done it? How had they made Moth turn again, then stop—

Turning!

"Because Moth no longer turns!" Madori blurted out, remembering. She nodded vigorously. "My parents told me that. Moth—well, Mythima is the world's real name—is round. A big sphere that floats in the sky, circling round and round the sun. And, well, Moth once used to turn around its axis—many years ago— letting day and night cycle." She did a little pirouette, mimicking the world. "But the world stopped spinning around itself." She stood still, facing the professors again. "So one side now always faces the sun, the other faces the darkness. Were the world to spin again . . ." She gave another spin. ". . . day and night would cycle again."

Professor Fen smiled and slammed his book shut. "Correct! Very good, young Lady Greenmoat."

I did it! Joy spread through Madori. She had answered another question correctly! She grinned and rocked on her heels. "Thank you, Professor."

Professor Atratus, clad in his flowing black robes, rose to his feet. His glare shot daggers at Madori.

"Do not be so quick to grin, girl." He sneered, upper lip twitching. "It is my turn to ask you a question." Fists upon the tabletop, he leaned forward like a bird of prey about to tear into her flesh. "My colleagues asked you simple questions of basic mathematics and cosmology, the answers to which any half-wit child would know. But I ask you a question of . . . zoology." He leaned even further forward, bones creaking. "List three examples of how the Elorian race—that subhuman species of darkness—is inferior to the purity of Timandrian blood."

The other two professors tsked their tongues.

"Professor Atratus," Fen ventured, his mustache twitching, "perhaps a different ques—"

"She will answer that question," Atratus said firmly, straightening and squaring his shoulders. He stared down his beaked nose at her. "Answer me, Madori." He made her name—an Elorian name—sound like an insult. "Speak—or are you ignorant?"

Rage flared in Madori. She sneered right back up at him.

"Very well," she said. "I will list why Elorians are, as you say, inferior. First of all, Elorians are less talented at warfare. They have a lower penchant for violence, leaving them inferior at killing, looting, and conquering." The professors sucked in their breath at this, but Madori plowed on. "Secondly, Elorians are less proud of their heritage. They do not claim to be superior to others. Their humbleness, their lack of hubris, is probably why they remain in darkness rather than invade other lands." She spoke louder. "Thirdly, Elorians are inferior to you, Professor Atratus, because they lack your marvelous buzzard's beak of a nose which you thrust proudly in all directions."

She stood panting, her heart thumping so loudly she thought it could crack her ribs.

For a long moment, only silent shock filled the chamber.

Professor Atratus began to tremble. His face turned red. With a sudden jerk, he pounded the tabletop and screamed.

"Impudent little maggot! Your words are folly, but they show to all the answer to my question. Your insolence, your lack of respect, and your crass effrontery to science prove you are inferior! Your very presence here shows the baseness of your Elorian blood, of—"

"So I answered the question correctly," Madori said, smiling thinly. "You just admitted it."

Atratus sputtered, for a moment lost for words.

Professor Fen cleared his throat and stroked his mustache. "Oh my, Professor Atratus, I do believe she is right. You did just confess that she answered correctly. Did you hear it too, Professor Maleen?"

The blind woman nodded, a thin smile on her lips. "Yes indeed, Professor Fen. I do believe young Madori has answered all our questions correctly."

Professor Atratus looked ready to burst. He pounded the table again, cracking it. "This is rubbish! This subhuman mongrel is not fit for a fine academic institution such as this. She—"

"She has passed this trial," Professor Fen said firmly, his mustache drooping with his frown. "Or do you wish me to summon Headmistress Egeria to judge?"

Professor Atratus froze in mid-sentence, his mouth hanging open like some wall-mounted fish. The other two professors merely looked at him, blinking, eyebrows raised. Atratus sputtered, unable to speak, spraying saliva. He pointed a shaky finger at Madori, his cheeks red, then spun around. Robes fluttering, he stormed out of the chamber.

Madori exhaled a shaky breath of relief. "I passed the trial," she whispered.

The two remaining professors nodded, smiling warmly.

"You have passed the Trial of Wisdom," said Professor Fen, his mustache rising with his smile. "Step through that back door, child. It will take you to a new place where you will partake in the second trial—a Trial of Wit."

Madori suddenly couldn't stop trembling.

I passed. I passed the first trial.

Tears budded in her eyes.

"Thank you," she whispered, curtsied, and ran through the backdoor.

CHAPTER SIX
TRIAL OF WIT

When Madori stepped through the back door, she expected to find another chamber or cloister. Instead she found herself in another world.

Blackness spread all around her; she felt as if she floated in the night sky. She stood on a stone bridge that spread over the chasm. A door stood before her—not encased in a wall but simply standing on its own. When Madori leaned sideways, she could peer around it. Many more doors rose along the bridge like battlements along a castle wall.

A contraption of ropes, wooden circles, and metallic rings hung upon the door. The jumble was connected to the doorknob, blocking Madori from twisting it. She jangled the hodgepodge, listening to the metallic rings clink and the wooden circles knock together.

"A riddle," she said. "An elaborate knot."

So, she realized, the Trial of Wit involved opening door by door—each one posing a riddle. At a summer festival once in Kingswall, Madori had seen a trained parrot that could solve elaborate puzzles, opening doors to get a treat. It seemed that now she would have to play parrot.

She stuck out her tongue as she often did when deep in concentration. She spent a moment trying to fit the wooden balls through the metal rings, twist the ropes, and undo the construction. She managed to free one ball, only for the ropes to tangle through a metal ring, blocking the process.

She sank an inch.

Madori blinked, stared down, and saw that the bridge had become less substantial beneath her. The stone suddenly looked like thick smoke; it swallowed the soles of her boots. She raised one foot after another, then let each sink back into the bridge. It felt like standing in mud.

Shaking her head, she returned her attention to the puzzle on the doorknob. After a few juicy curses, she managed to remove two metal rings, which she tossed aside.

Her boots sank another inch. Madori grimaced and looked down. The bridge beneath her seemed like thin smoke now; she could see the chasm below.

"So there's a time limit," she muttered.

She returned to the riddle. She freed another metal ring. Her boots sank deeper; she was now down past her ankles. Two wooden balls came free; she tossed them into the chasm.

She sank down to her knees. Her feet dangled over the pit.

With a curse, she tugged open a knot, freeing the last metal ring. The contraption fell off the doorknob.

The bridge vanished beneath her.

Madori grabbed the doorknob, clinging as she dangled over the pit. She twisted and tugged, and the door swung open.

Heart thumping, she climbed through the doorway. The next segment of the bridge was still solid stone. She stood upon it, knees shaking.

If I had failed to solve the riddle, would I have fallen to my death? She cringed.

A new door stood before her. Already the bridge beneath her feet, solid stone when she had first stepped onto it, began to fade. Biting her lip, Madori looked for a doorknob but found none, only a little hole in the door where a doorknob should be. Instead, many bits of metal—hooked, curved, circular, and spiky—lay scattered at her feet. She knelt, lifted the pieces before they could sink into the vanishing stone, and jangled them in her palm.

"It's the doorknob," she whispered.

She narrowed her eyes. Yes, she saw a doorknob here—a few round pieces that could snap into its shell, a few narrow shards that could fit into the door.

Her boot heels sank, the bridge dissolving beneath her. She cursed, spat, and got to work. Some pieces refused to connect; others snapped into place, only to block another piece from entering its proper slot. Her fingers were shaking and her boots had sunken past her ankles when finally she had assembled the doorknob. She snapped it into the door an instant before the bridge vanished beneath her. Once more she dangled. She swung the door open and climbed onto the next level.

A third door faced her; many more waited behind it. Madori twisted her lips, sucked in a deep breath, and got back to work.

One door had no knob at all but a panel of sliding, metal squares that had to snap into place for the door to open. Another door was engraved with a great wooden labyrinth; she had to slide a key through the maze as the bridge faded beneath her, bringing it to the keyhole fast enough to unlock the door. Another door lay in pieces, a great wooden jigsaw on the floor; an invisible field blocked Madori's passage farther along the bridge, and she could only step through after assembling the broken door and opening it. Every level the riddles became harder. Every level more sweat covered her, and she began to think her tooth marks would forever dent her bottom lip.

Briefly, she wondered where the other applicants were now. Were they too locked in great, black chasms, moving along their own bridges? If they fell, where would they end up? Would they magically appear outside the university, or would they fall forever into black death? But she had no time to consider this carefully, only solve puzzle by puzzle, opening door by door, moving ever closer toward the end of the bridge. Soon she could see it ahead—the end of the chasm. A brick wall loomed there, a golden door waiting within it.

Finally, weak and shuddering, Madori crossed the bridge, reached the great wall, and stood before the golden door.

She grabbed the knob and twisted it.

It was locked.

She looked down at the last segment of bridge, seeking jigsaw puzzles, hidden buttons, something—she found nothing. She returned her eyes to the door, looking for a knob, a lock, a maze, some puzzle to solve.

"Nothing," she whispered.

Musical symbols on the door glowed, then vanished.

Madori tilted her head.

"Do it again!" she said.

Again little musical notes glowed upon the golden door—different ones this time—vanishing as soon as she stopped speaking.

"Is there a password?" she said. Her voice made other notes glow, but the door would not open.

The bridge began to fade beneath her. She sank down to her ankles and winced.

A password . . . no. Not a word. Notes denoted a song. Music. But what music?

"What do I sing?" she said. Notes glowed and vanished.

Madori tugged the two strands of hair that framed her face. Music, music . . . she thought back to the lessons her mother had given her; she could still read notes. But what song could she possibly sing here to open this door? All she knew were old Qaelish tunes.

Her boots sank another inch.

She grimaced and began to sing softly, an old song villagers would sing back in Oshy across the dusk. A few notes glowed again, soon fading, and Madori tilted her head.

Wait! she thought. Some of the notes were glowing gold, but others shone a bright blue.

She sang the tune again. Again—some notes glowed gold, others blue.

"I have to sing the blue notes?" she asked the door.

A few golden notes glowed, their light softer. The blue notes were brighter, larger; it seemed those were the ones to sing.

Her boots sank down to the ankles.

"Damn it!" she shouted. Golden notes glowed.

She cursed and began to sing the practice scales her mother had taught her, rising from a deep baritone to a high soprano. A gold note. Another. Another. A blue note! Gold. Gold. Blue again. She tried to memorize each note, but how could she possibly read this music like this? She had trouble enough reading the sheets her mother would give her.

Think, Madori. Concentrate. Save the blue notes in your mind. Ignore the gold ones. Write them down inside your thoughts.

She took a deep breath, blocking out everything, and sang the scale again. She ignored the golden notes. They didn't exist. They were nothing. She forced herself to see only blue, to write down the score in her mind. After singing a few more scales, she had it.

"It's the song 'Darkness Falls,'" she whispered.

She knew that tune. She knew it! Her mother had taught her to sing this song.

The bridge faded to mere mud. She sank down to her knees.

Wincing, Madori sang her song.

It was a sad tune, an old tune of darkness covering the land of Eloria, of hope fading, of a distant ray of light shining to guide lost souls home. As Madori sang, the blue notes glowed upon the door, one after the other, no golden notes between them. In Madori's mind, she was a child again, back home, singing with her mother.

She sang the last note—a sad, soft sound.

All the blue notes began to glow together, the song 'Darkness Falls' etched in light.

The last door swung open.

The bridge vanished beneath Madori.

She leaped through the doorway and into shadows and light.

CHAPTER SEVEN
TRIAL OF WILL

Her legs still trembling and her mind foggy with exhaustion, Madori stepped into a towering hall, ready to face her final and greatest challenge.

"The Trial of Will," she whispered.

After the bridge, she had expected something fantastical—a dragon to tame, an ogre to slay, maybe a gauntlet full of spinning blades and swinging pendulums to knock her into rivers of lava. But she simply saw a columned hall—roughly the size of a large barn—full of other applicants.

An elderly professor stood at a podium across the hall. He wore red robes, and his white beard flowed down to his feet. His nose was so long and curved, it drooped past his upper lip.

"Welcome, Madori Greenmoat!" the elder called out. "The last applicant to emerge from the Trial of Wit. I am Professor Yovan. Welcome, Madori, to the Trial of Will."

Madori blinked, rubbed her eyes, and took a closer look, sure that dragons and ogres would still leap out at her. The chamber was simple but well built—the columns carved of solid limestone, the ceiling vaulted and painted deep blue. Many tables stood in neat rows, and upon each lay a strange device; it looked like a wishbone carved of iron. Two chairs stood at each table.

"Billygoat!" The voice rose from the crowd of other applicants. "I mean—Madori! Thank Idar."

Tam wormed his way through the crowd, coming to stand beside her. He grabbed her hands and smiled shakily.

"Tam, what's going on here?" she said.

He brushed back a strand of her hair which fell across her left eye. "I thought you wouldn't make it this far. You're the last one through."

She bristled. "Of course I made it!" She looked around her at the other applicants. "Idar's bottom, those last two trials weeded out quite a few."

From two thousand applicants, she doubted that more than four hundred remained. They stood clustered between the columns, talking amongst themselves, laughing nervously and discussing their ordeals. Most were Magerians, but there were some foreigners too, even a few Elorians. The latter stood in the shadows far from the windows—their natural habitat—and spoke amongst themselves in low voices. Madori saw that the strange boy with the dragon tattoo stood among them. Again he was staring at her, his eyes intense, boring into her as if peeling back the layers of her soul.

A chill running down her spine, Madori tore her eyes away from him. But as she kept scanning the crowd, her heart sank deeper. She cursed to see that Lari Serin—looking as pretty, prim, and proper as always—had made her way to this last trial. She stood among several other youths with Radian brooches, basking in sunbeams that fell through a window, laughing as if these trials were no more challenging than a garden stroll. When Lari noticed Madori, her eyes widened. She smiled and waved, her face oozing honeyed poison. It was the face a sweet-talking traitor gives his master before thrusting the blade.

Bearded Professor Yovan cleared his throat—a squeaking sound—and raised his arms, letting his sleeves roll down to his shoulders. He spoke again.

"I shall now divide you into pairs! As I call each name, step forth and sit down upon the glowing chair."

Madori narrowed her eyes and tilted her head, seeing no glowing seats. The other applicants all turned to face the professor, their conversation dying. The old man unrolled a scroll, leaned toward it, and called out the first name:

"Tam Shepherd!"

Tam—going by his father's old commoner's name, rather than his secret royal styling—gave Madori a little smile and pat on the shoulder.

"Good luck, Billygoat," he whispered and stepped toward the professor.

A seat began to glow, and Tam approached it and sat at the small table. When the professor read another name, the seat across from Tam glowed too, and another applicant approached to fill it.

Professor Yovan kept reading names from the scroll, and slowly tables were filled—two applicants at each. Upon every tabletop lay the iron wishbone.

"Madori Greenmoat!"

She stepped forward dutifully, made her way toward the next glowing seat, and sat down. The table was small, just large enough for two chairs. She stared at the item on the tabletop, finally getting a good look at it. The metal wishbone was as large as a lyre, its surface craggy; she couldn't guess its purpose. The seat across from her was still empty.

"Lari Serin!"

The seat across from Madori glowed.

Oh wormy sheep hooves.

Madori had not thought this turn could have gotten any worse. When Lari approached, a small smile on her lips, Madori's heart sank down to her hips. Lord Serin and her father were cousins; Madori felt ill to think that she and Lari shared blood.

Her hair a perfect fountain of golden locks, Lari neatly swept her skirt under her legs and sat down, knees pressed together, her back straight. She smiled sweetly at Madori.

"Hello, mongrel," she said, voice pleasant.

Madori leaped to her feet, clenching her fists. "I don't know how you made it this far, but you're failing this trial. You—"

A sharp clearing of the throat interrupted her. Professor Yovan came shuffling forward, nearly tripping over his beard.

"Is there a problem, Madori Greenmoat and Lari Serin?" he said, brow furrowing.

Lari blinked innocently, a sweet smile on her lips. "Not at all, Professor. I was simply telling Madori what a pleasure it was to meet one with such . . . famous parents." She gave Madori a little wink. "I see she's inherited much from them."

The professor seemed to miss the implied scorn. He tossed his white beard across his shoulder. "Very well then. But please, girls, you can be friends later. Now the trial is about to begin." He hopped back toward his podium and raised his hands. "Applicants! The Trial of Will begins. Please, every pair grab your iron wishbone, each applicant holding one side."

Madori lifted the wishbone, holding one side. The iron was rough and cold in her palm. Lari grabbed the other side, then suddenly yanked the wishbone toward her, tugging Madori forward in her seat, forcing her to lean across the table. Madori found herself only inches away from Lari; the two's noses nearly touched.

"You're going home soon, half-breed," Lari said, all the sweetness gone from her voice. There was nothing but malice in her eyes now.

Madori sneered, clutching the wishbone. "Tell me, my lady, when you inform your father you've failed the trials, will you cry?"

"Next time I see my father," Lari said, "I'll tell him how I made a little mongrel child burst into tears. I think he'll enjoy that story."

Professor Yovan was still speaking from the podium. "Four hundred of you are holding onto two hundred wishbones. You may not rise from your seat. You may not kick, punch, bite, or do anything but sit neatly, holding the iron. Whoever drops his or her wishbone first shall return home. Whoever remains holding the wishbone . . . will become a student at Teel University."

Madori blinked. Was that it? That was all she had to do? Hold onto the wishbone? She tilted her head. That seemed too easy. Were there no puzzles here, no questions, no challenges at all?

"Get ready to scream, little one." Lari smiled wickedly. She leaned forward in her seat, her fist tight around her side of the wishbone. "I'll enjoy hearing it."

"I bet you'll scream when you fail," Madori said. "I bet—"

She bit down on her words, frowning. The wishbone was tingling in her hand—a strange, tickling heat like a thousand tiny jabs.

Lari gave a mocking pout. "What's wrong, mongrel? Does your widdle hand huwt?"

Her hand *did* hurt. The tingling intensified, becoming a prickly heat. Madori ached to drop the wishbone but only gritted her teeth and tightened her grip. When she looked around the chamber, she saw other applicants wince, curse, and one girl even yelped.

"My hand feels fine," Madori said, returning her eyes to Lari. "You look a little pale, though."

Madori was lying; her hand did not feel fine, not at all. It was as far from fine as wine from poison. The pain intensified, almost intolerable, and Madori took deep, ragged breaths. She tightened her grip. The iron began to crackle, and little sparks like lightning raced across it.

At the table beside Madori, a boy yelped and dropped his half of the wishbone. His opponent whooped in triumph, the wishbone glowing in his hand. He raised the metal instrument like a trophy. At another table, a girl burst into the tears and dropped her wishbone; her opponent laughed, her admittance to Teel won.

Madori returned her eyes to Lari and glared. Lari stared back, a single bead of sweat upon her brow, the only sign of any pain she might be feeling. Madori's hand was trembling now around the wishbone. The pain blazed, racing up her arm to her shoulder. Her very teeth buzzed and shook in her jaw. Years ago, Madori had read a book about the charred victim of a lightning strike; she imagined that this felt similar. Her hair crackled, her hackles rose, and goosebumps appeared upon her arm. Her very clothes seemed to burn.

All across the hall, applicants were crying out and releasing their grips. One by one, failed applicants trudged dejectedly out of the room while victors stepped toward Professor Yovan, rubbing their sore hands.

"You look like a dying rat," Lari said, sneering now. More sweat beaded on her brow. "Will you squeal before the end?"

Madori's entire arm shook as she clutched the wishbone. She whispered through a clenched jaw, the pain nearly blinding her. "I won't let go. I—"

The pain burst out, doubling in intensity. She gasped and nearly dropped the wishbone. She saw the same look of surprise on Lari's face; the girl's eyes widened, showing white all around the irises, and she emitted a little cry. Across the hall, dozens of applicants screamed or whimpered, dropping wishbones.

Madori gritted her teeth, tears in her eyes, and held on. Lari sneered like a wild animal, clinging to her end.

"I won't let go," Madori hissed, barely able to speak, barely able to remain conscious. "I'll hold on even if my hand falls off. I—"

The pain flared again, growing even stronger, so strong Madori thought her skull could crack and her jaw could spill her teeth. Lari screamed but clung on. Lightning crackled along the wishbone and raced up Madori's arm, raising smoke. Sweat and tears mingled in her eyes. Through the veil, she saw the last few applicants drop their wishbones.

Only Madori and Lari were now still competing.

"Give up, mongrel!" Lari shouted, tears streaming down her cheeks, her face a rabid mask.

The wishbone emitted a whistle like steam from a kettle. Welts rose along Madori's arm.

"You can do it, Lari!" Madori shouted. "Hold on longer! I love seeing you suffer."

The other youths all gathered around them, forming a ring around their table. They were pounding fists into palms, cheering, chanting.

"Lari, Lari!" most cried out.

"Let the mongrel burn!" somebody shouted.

"Hold on, Lari!" another youth cried. "Hold on and watch her burn!"

Madori was weeping, trembling, screaming, but she held on. The iron wishbone burned red, trembling in her grip. The pain was a crashing sea.

A single voice cried out from the crowd—Tam's voice.

"Madori! Madori!"

A few other voices joined his, and now some in the crowd were chanting for her. Madori could now see only smudges, but she thought she saw the Elorians cheering for her.

Her hand slipped.

She nearly dropped the wishbone.

It was too much. Too much pain. Too much agony. It was lightning, it was fire, but it was also the pain of her mixed blood, of her childhood, of endless taunts, endless doubt. It the pain of a girl torn between day and night, and she wept.

I have to let go.

Before her, Lari was snarling, teeth bared, face red.

She won't let go. I have to. I have to.

She ground her teeth.

No.

She screamed and tightened her grip.

No. I will hold on. No matter how much it hurts. Because I know pain. I was born into pain. What is more agony? Pain has always been my companion.

Lari was shaking, her hair standing on her head.

"Enough!" Professor Yovan shouted. "Girls, enough! Let go!"

But Madori would not. Lari would not. They clung on and the wishbone burst into fire . . . then shattered in their grip.

Madori fell back, her chair flipping over. She slammed down onto her back. She clutched half the wishbone in her smoking, seared hand. It still crackled in her palm, driving fire through her. She would not release it.

She blinked.

Did I win?

She raised her head.

She saw Lari still holding her own half of the wishbone. The girl struggled to her feet, then came leaping down onto Madori.

"Feel this pain drive into your heart," Lari hissed, shoving her half of the wishbone against Madori's chest.

Pain exploded like thunder.

Madori screamed.

The agony drove through her chest, coiling around her ribs, wrapping her heart in fire, and she kicked and thrashed and—

The pain vanished.

I'm dead. She trembled. *I died. The pain is gone and I float now in the afterlife.*

"Madori!" The voice seemed to echo from miles away, from a different world. "Madori, can you hear me?"

She opened her eyes. Through a veil of mist, she saw a wrinkled, bearded face gaze down upon her.

Is this Idar, god of the sun?

She pushed herself onto her elbows.

"Madori!" A wrinkled hand touched her cheek. "Child, can you speak?"

It was Professor Yovan, she realized. When Madori sat up, her legs shaking, she saw the greybeard holding Lari back with one hand. Both wishbone halves lay on the floor, the heat and lightning gone.

"What happened?" Madori whispered. "Did I drop it?"

Professor Yovan wiped tears from his eyes. "In the name of sanity! I've never seen anything like this. I had to cast a spell. I had to stop the magic. You two would have died, my children. Oh dear . . ."

Madori rose to her feet, trembling. Sweat soaked her clothes, and her hand was blackened and swollen. When she looked around her, she saw the other applicants gazing in shocked silence. Tam stood among them, eyes wide and mouth wide open.

When Madori looked over to Lari, she found something new in the girl's eyes—not scorn, not pain, but unadulterated hatred, a rage as pure as the pain of the iron wishbone. Welts ran up Lari's arm, and her hair stood in a tangled mess, but she never removed her glare from Madori.

Professor Yovan, shaking his head in wonder, raised the broken wishbone halves and placed them back onto the table. He wiped his brow.

"For the first time in Teel University history," he said, his voice shaking, "we have a Trial of Will tie. Both Lari Serin and Madori Greenmoat shall attend Teel!"

The crowd erupted into cheers.

Madori swayed, nearly collapsing, but managed to grin.

"I passed," she whispered and rubbed tears from her eyes. "I'm a student of Teel."

Professor Yovan, still pale and trembling, opened the doors to the hall. It was like opening a floodgate. Hundreds of concerned parents spilled into the room, calling out for their children. Mothers embraced proud young students. Fathers patted sons on their shoulders. A few flunked applicants still lingered in the hall; their parents scolded, embraced, or awkwardly tried to comfort their embarrassed offspring.

When she saw her father, Madori gave him a shaky smile. Torin's eyes widened and his face paled. He rushed toward her.

"I passed," she whispered. "I passed, Papa. I'm a student of Teel."

Torin grabbed her wrist and examined her burnt hand. Ignoring her words, he spun toward Professor Yovan.

"What is the meaning of this?" the gardener said, voice harsh. "What kind of institution are you running here? I sent my daughter to trials; you return her to me with a burnt hand?"

Madori winced, feeling her cheeks flush. Several other students were snickering.

"Father, please!" she whispered. "You're embarrassing me."

Torin seemed not to hear her. He grabbed the professor's shoulders, demanding answers. Old Yovan mumbled something about how he'd never seen anything like this, and how their wishbone must have been faulty, and how he would send Madori straight to the infirmary and deliver a honey roasted ham to Torin's tavern of choice.

A tall figure moved through the crowd. A smooth, genteel voice interrupted the conversation.

"Ah, and so the humble gardener, the man who slew so many of his own countrymen, cannot bear to see a scratch mar the flesh of his little mongrel."

Madori growled, hackles rising. She looked up to see the man from the road.

"Lord Tirus Serin," she muttered.

He turned toward her, raising both chin and eyebrows, and stared down his nose at her. He had replaced his armor with a rich, cotton doublet and a jeweled belt. A samite cloak framed him, the fabric shimmering with golden thread and gemstones. A Radian amulet hung around his neck, a golden sun eclipsing a silver moon. His golden hair shone almost as bright, scented of rose oil.

"We meet again, little one," the lord said, and something new filled his eyes, something not only scornful but hungry, lustful. "I hear you've been accepted into Teel." He reached out, grabbed her wounded hand, and squeezed so powerfully she winced. "Allow me to congratulate you. I'm sure my daughter will give you the proper attention."

Madori tugged her hand free, glaring at the man. "I'm sure we'll be inseparable."

Lari walked up toward them, slung her arm around her father, and gave Madori a smile full of sweetness, innocence, and the promise of vengeance. "I'm sure we will be, dear cousin . . . I'm sure we will be."

CHAPTER EIGHT
MISFITS

Torin sat in The Dancing Wolf tavern, staring at his daughter over his gift of a roast ham.

He forced himself to swallow the bite he had just taken. Professor Yovan's gift—as if any gift could undo the welts on Madori's hand—tasted like ash.

My daughter is wounded, Torin thought. *Radians rise across the sunlight. My king wants me to leave my home and fight them. And I'm supposed to feel good about a honeyed ham.*

If Madori shared any of his concerns, she was displaying none of them. The young woman—by Idar, she had been only a baby last time Torin had checked—was digging into the meat, trying to speak while chewing lustfully.

"And would you believe Tam's here?" she said, stuffing another bite into her mouth. "The boy somehow passed his trials but—" She paused to swallow. "—but if you ask me, he had to cheat or something, because he's a bigger woolhead than you. Oh, and—" She gulped down cider and wiped her mouth. "—and I saw magic! Real magic. Lots of it. Magical bridges and doors and glowing seats. I'm going learn to make our chair at home glow." She grinned and bit off a chunk of ham so large a wolf would choke on it. She spoke as she chewed. "Would you like a glowing chair for home? I wonder if it'll work on animals too. Or even people. I could make our rabbits glow."

Torin said nothing, only sighed.

I have to break my daughter's heart, he realized. *I have to place her in danger or shatter her soul.*

He took a deep breath. He could no longer listen to her words; every one stabbed him.

"Madori," he said softly.

". . . and did you see how long Professor Yovan's beard is? Idar! Down to his feet! I wish I could grow a beard. Maybe I can grow a magical one. Why don't you grow your beard too? I—"

"Madori," he said again, "I can't let you stay here. You have to go into Eloria with your mother."

". . . and they asked me about mathematics, and—" She paused and tilted her head. Very slowly, she placed down her fork. She spoke even slower. "I . . . what?"

Torin figured the best approach was to blurt it all out at once. "It's too dangerous. Radians are rising across the land. There's a Radian professor here at Teel—one Atratus—and Lord Serin holds sway; apparently he built a good chunk of the university. It's too dangerous for you here. It's too dangerous for you anywhere in Timandra right now. I'm moving to Kingswall to help Cam deal with this threat. You will go to Eloria with your mother."

Madori leaped to her feet, letting her chair crash backwards. Across the tavern, patrons froze over their meals and stared.

"Like the Abyss I am!" she shouted. "Are you crazy, Father? Are you absolutely mad? Go home—now? After all this?"

He reached out to her. "Madori, please. Hush. Sit. Listen."

"I will not!" Tears budded in her eyes. "You always do this to me, Father! You always let me . . . let me build up my hopes, and then you destroy them. It's like when you told me we'd go visit the desert, and you changed your mind at the last minute, and we went on a damn fishing trip instead." The tears were now streaming down her cheeks. "I can't believe you. I can't! I wish Mother had taken me here instead. I'm going to Teel and you can't stop me."

She turned and ran, making a beeline for the door.

Torin cursed. He slammed coins onto the tabletop and made to run after her. He stumbled over a chair, cursed again, and steadied himself in time to see Madori bolt outside. When Torin finally made it to the door and stepped onto the street, she was gone.

"Madori!" he cried out, seeking her.

People on the street—shoppers, villagers, students and their families—turned to stare at him.

"Madori!" he shouted again, but she didn't answer. He couldn't see her anywhere.

Well, that went splendidly, he thought.

He began to trudge down the street, peering into shop windows, seeking the damn girl. Why did she have to make things so difficult?

"You used to be easy to be around," he muttered.

What had happened? Madori used to be his best friend—the girl he'd rock on his knee, tickle, laugh with, spend so many wonderful hours fishing, playing, and reading with. And now? Now Madori always found some other reason to think him the most horrible troll this side of darkness. He only wanted to protect her. How could she not see that?

He kept walking down the streets of Teelshire, seeking her. Where would the damn girl go? Would she have run into the university grounds? Perhaps into another tavern, or maybe she hid in an alleyway somewhere?

He groaned. Of course. *She went where she always goes when she's angry at me,* he thought. *To read.*

While Torin found comfort in gardening and Koyee in music, Madori's escape was reading. She spent many hours in Fairwool Library, delving into hundreds of books. Torin enjoyed reading books on botany on occasion, and Koyee enjoyed old tales of Qaelish lore, but Madori consumed books of adventure so quickly she had to order more from Queen Linee every year.

Torin spun around and walked toward the town's bookshop— an old little building whose sign bore the words, "The Bookworm's Banquet." He stepped inside, entering a dusty, crowded chamber chock-full of books. The leather-bound volumes stood upon shelves, rested on tables, and rose in tilting towers. Beams of light fell through stained-glass windows, gleaming with dust.

Madori sat between two bookshelves, her knees pulled to her chest, her head lowered.

Joints creaking, Torin sat down beside her. She would not budge.

He took a deep breath and spoke softly. "You know, I lost my parents when I was only a child."

She said nothing. She wouldn't raise her head.

He kept speaking. "I remember my father's last words to me. As he lay dying, he spoke not of himself, not of fearing death. He spoke of me. He was afraid, he said, that he wouldn't be here to look after me. When I had you, I finally understood his words." He smiled wistfully. "When you're a parent, you never stop worrying for your child. Being a parent is to always worry. Even when you're afraid for yourself, it's because you're afraid of abandoning your child."

Finally she raised her head. She looked at him, her eyes rimmed with red, tears spiking her lashes.

"Well, maybe you have to finally let me grow up." She wiped her eyes. "I'm sixteen, Father. Mother was my age when she sailed off to war. I think I can handle a university."

Torin sighed. *If it were only handling a university,* he thought. *But war again threatens to engulf Moth.*

"If I let you stay here," he said slowly, "you must promise me you won't pick fights with Serin's daughter."

"I never pick fights."

Torin snorted. "I've seen you beat up Kay Chandler's boy a dozen times back home."

She bristled. "He keeps touching the library books with greasy fingers!"

"And if I let you stay," he continued, "you must promise you'll stay near Tam at all times. At *all times.* He'll look after you, and I will talk to him, making it clear that if *anything* dangerous happens, he's to take you to Kingswall at once."

"Father!" She rolled her eyes. "I'm not a damn child."

"You are. You always will be. To me at least." He glared at her. "Promise me, Madori Billy Greenmoat. You make a promise now, or I swear *I* will enroll at Teel University myself so I can watch over you."

"Father!"

He pointed at her sternly. "Promise me. If you think your mother is the evil parent, you haven't seen me in action. Promise or you will."

She groaned so loudly she blew back both strands of her hair. "Fine! I promise. I promise I'll stay away from that pretty little toad. I promise I'll stay near Tam. I promise I'll hide away in the corner and barely squeak so that no trouble can find me."

"And . . ."

She rolled her eyes. "And I promise that if any trouble does find me, Tam and I will join you at Kingswall. Fine? Now will you please stop latching onto me? I swear someday you're going to sprout an umbilical cord and try to lasso me with it."

He wrapped an arm around her and pulled her close. She objected at first but gradually relaxed in his embrace.

"I don't need a lasso," he said. "I just need to hug you."

She leaned her head against his shoulder. She spoke softly, a tear on her cheek. "I love you, Papa."

He kissed the top of her head. "I love you too, Billygoat. No matter what happens, I always will, and your mother and I are always somewhere out there for you—even if we're half a world away."

She nodded and her voice was choked. "I know."

He closed his eyes.

And so I leave her in a viper's nest. And so I will always worry. Perhaps that's the price of letting your children fly. He sighed. *Cam will call me a fool, but haven't we always been foolish?*

He rose to his feet. "Now come on, let's go buy you some school uniforms. You can't walk into class dressed like a purple scarecrow."

They left the bookshop together, his arm around her.

* * * * *

Madori stood under the tree, gazing at the road that wound south through grassy valleys, heading toward misty plains. She waved, watching the cart roll into the distance.

"Goodbye, Father," she whispered. "Goodbye, Hayseed. I'll miss you."

She thought she could see Torin twisting in his seat to face the town, waving at her too. But with every wave he grew smaller, and soon the cart, horse, and rider were but a speck upon the horizon, and then they faded into the mist.

Madori blinked, her eyes damp. She had always thought her father infuriating, but now she missed him already, and her throat tightened. She longed to race down the road, to hug him one last time, to pat Hayseed, to beg them to stay, maybe even to go home with them.

She rubbed her eyes. *But I won't do that. I'll stay. I'll become a mage.* She nodded. *I'll be strong and I'll be amazing.*

She turned away, facing the town again and the university that loomed above it. A gust of wind blew, whipping back her two strands of hair and fluttering her robes. She looked down at her new garments. Instead of her old leggings and shirt—items she had sewn herself—she now wore flowing green robes. It was a color she detested—she detested all colors other than black and purple—but all first years were required to wear the green. At least she kept her boots; the leather creaked as she walked, and the many buckles jingled. Her pack hung upon one shoulder, full of the scrolls and books her father had bought her along with her new robes. She wasn't sure how Torin had been able to afford all this; a gardener, he had never been a rich man, and parchment cost a small fortune. She suspected that Tam's father—King Camlin himself, come in disguise to see off his son—had footed Madori's bill.

When she had crossed the town and stood at the gates of Teel University again, she paused and took a deep breath. Only last turn, she had stepped through these gates for the trials, but somehow now this seemed an even greater boundary to cross.

"Once I step through now," she whispered, "my old life is gone. Father. Mother. Hayseed. Home. Once I enter these gates now . . . this will be my new home for four years."

She stood for a moment, hesitating, fingers trembling, resisting the temptation to run after her father. Finally, with a deep breath, she took three great paces forward and entered the Teel cloister.

The first time she had entered this cobbled courtyard, she had seen thousands of applicants. Now only two hundred stood here, the lucky new class. Four columned walkways rose around them, enclosing the cloister within a square, and the four Towers of Teel rose at each corner. An elm tree rustled in the center of the cloister, and clouds drifted across the blue sky above.

As always, Lari stood with her group of cronies, all wearing their Radian pins. A jeweled tiara topped Lari's head, and golden embroidery adorned her green robes. While Madori's robes were secondhand, shabby, and shapeless, Lari's robes were obviously custom-tailored, fitting snugly and sporting golden hems. The young noblewoman was busy telling a story while her friends laughed, and Madori caught snippets about how "the mongrel burst into tears . . ." and how "her gardener father had to save her." Ignoring the group, Madori looked at the other students, her new classmates. A couple dozen Elorians stood under the elm, seeking the shadows, their hoods pulled over their heads; unlike Madori, who had inherited Timandrian skin that could tan, these pure-blooded Elorians had pale skin they dared not expose to sunlight. Finally, between the Radians and Elorians, sprawled a mass of unorganized students. Most were local Magerians, but many were from other sunlit kingdoms, their eyes more hesitant, their hands clasped together nervously.

Madori wasn't sure where to stand. Certainly not near Lari and her friends, but neither did she crave Elorian companionship; if she aligned herself with the Elorians, she would forever be an outsider here. If she embraced her Timandrian blood, perhaps she could still find a larger group of allies—obviously not among the Radians, but perhaps among the largest group, those Timandrians still unaligned.

She saw Tam stand in the middle group, and Madori felt some relief. The brown-eyed prince, now wearing green robes, was a welcome sight, a little bit of her old life, of comfort. She walked forward and stood beside him.

"Hullo, Billygoat," he said.

She raised her fist. "Don't make me punch you."

He rolled his eyes. "Fine! Greetings be upon you, Lady Madori Billy Greenmoat the First." He bit his lip. "Better?"

"No. But you got lucky. Punching your thick skull would probably cripple my hand, and one of my hands is already injured."

Tam grimaced. "Save your fists for you-know-who." He glanced aside. "I have a feeling you might need them."

Madori followed his gaze and saw that Lari and her friends were tossing a doll back and forth. The doll was a crude, ugly representation of an Elorian—its fingers ending with claws, its mouth sprouting fangs, its large eyes red. When the effigy fell into the mud, Lari made a point of stomping onto it. The young noblewoman raised her eyes, saw Madori, and gave her a little wink.

"You're next," she mouthed silently.

Madori was about to rush forward and attack the weasel. Before she could take a step, however, Headmistress Egeria emerged from the southeastern tower and marched toward the new students, her robes swaying. The elderly woman's hair was collected into a neat bun, and the sigil of Teel—two silver scrolls—hung around her neck.

"Students of Teel!" the headmistress announced. "Welcome. Welcome to the university."

The students all turned toward the woman. Lari gave Madori another wink before kicking the doll behind the elm tree. When everyone faced her, the headmistress continued speaking.

"Two hundred of you have passed the trials. Now you stand here before me in your uniforms, your books in your packs. You may think the hard part is behind you, that your education is now guaranteed. *But!*" The headmistress pointed to the sky, her sleeve rolling down to reveal a knobby arm. "You are mistaken. You are not yet safe. Many of you—perhaps most of you—will still return home. It is not uncommon for only half our students to successfully complete their first year. Many more flunk during their second, third, and fourth years." Egeria narrowed her eyes, staring from one student to another. "If more than fifty of you become true mages, I would be very surprised. *Now!*" She cleared her throat. "You will spend your first year in groups of four. Your quartet will be your most basic, important unit of university life. You will sleep four students to a room. You will sit four students to a table. Every quartet will have a name, a symbol, a leader, and a sense of pride. Perhaps more than any other decision you will make at the university—or in life!—will be who to choose for your quartet. No time is better than now to decide. And so, students—please, arrange yourselves to groups of four!"

Madori cringed. Choose three other students—others who'd be her constant companions for years?

She glanced around her. "Idar's bottom, I don't even want to spend four years with you, Tam, let alone any of these strangers."

He grabbed her arm and tugged her close. "Too bad, because you're stuck with me . . . and two others, if we can find them." He looked around him. "Say, Billygoat, you know anyone else here?"

She nodded. "I know Lari. Fancy inviting her to join us?"

"Oh, certainly! I'd also like to stick my head into a crocodile's mouth."

Near the elm tree, Lari had found three friends—twin girls and a tall golden-haired boy, all sporting the Radian brooches. A second quartet of Radians joined together beside them. Slowly other quartets were forming—four Ardish students here, four Verilish ones there, four Elorians in the shadows, and others.

Grouped by nations, Madori thought, her heart sinking. *But who'd join a half-breed like me?*

A voice spoke beside her, soft and dangerous as flames about to spread.

"Madori?"

She recognized that accent—it was the accent of Ilar, an Elorian nation south of her own moonlit homeland of Qaelin. She spun around to see the Elorian boy with the nose ring and intense eyes. His dragon tattoo stretched up his neck and coiled over his eye; it seemed to stare at her too. His white hair fell across his brow, and his hood and cloak were pulled tightly around him.

She turned away from him. "I don't join Elorians."

His voice was soft but still carried a hint of danger. "You are Elorian."

She spun back toward him, glaring. "I'm mixed. You know that." She tugged her two strands of hair. "You see my black hair, don't you? Go join your fellow Elorians, the pure ones."

He glanced toward where other Elorians were forming quartets, then looked back at her. He shook his head. "No. I did not travel into sunlight to stay in shadows. In this school, who you know matters. That is how you survive. I cannot stay in darkness." He looked at Tam. "He is Timandrian. He is with you. I will be too. I will learn your ways, Madori the half-Timandrian." He bowed his head toward her. "I am Jitomi of Ilar."

Tam raised his eyebrows and thrust out his bottom lip. "Might as well," he said to Madori. "It's not like we've got too many options left."

Madori grumbled. The young prince was right. Most other students had already formed quartets; many seemed to have known one another from before the trials.

She cursed and jabbed a finger against Jitomi's chest. "Fine! But you remember something, Jitomi the Ilari. I am half Qaelish. I have nothing to do with your island of Ilar, even if both our empires lie in the darkness. And I won't speak to you about anything Elorian—not the old foods of the night, not the starlight, not anything. We'll be quartet-members, but we will not be friends."

He nodded and spoke with his thick accent. "I join you, Madori, because you are of sunlight, not because you are of darkness too."

She sighed. "Lovely trio of misfits we've got here so far. But we need one more."

She looked around her, biting her lip. Only a handful of students were still unsorted. One among them caught Madori's eye. She squinted and tilted her head.

A tall Daenorian girl was walking around the courtyard, looking from side to side, trying to join different groups only for them to snicker and move away. She was the only Daenorian here and seemed to stick out just as badly as Madori. The girl wore a necklace of animal teeth, and beneath her green robes, she wore armor molded to look like crocodile hide. Under her arm, she held a steel helmet shaped like a crocodile's head, complete with a toothy visor. A sword hung at her side, its pommel shaped as another one of the reptiles. The girl had dark skin and smooth, black hair that hung down to her chin. Her lips were full, her eyes bright and eager, and Madori thought her very pretty—certainly pretty enough that Madori herself felt plain, scrawny, and homely as a true billy goat.

And yet, despite the Daenorian girl's beauty and bright smile, every other student she approached quickly moved aside, laughed, scoffed, or even cursed the girl.

"They're real crocodile teeth," the Daenorian said, showing her necklace to a group of Ardish girls with blue eyes and golden hair. "If you let me join you, I'll give you some teeth."

The girls grimaced and turned away.

Never losing the brightness in her eyes, the tall Daenorian turned toward another group, this one of local Magerian boys. "Do you like my sword?" she asked. "My father said it has magical powers. Do you think magical swords exist?"

The boys only rolled their eyes and turned away from her.

"Foreign freak," one muttered.

Madori sighed. She looked at Tam. "You did say you'd like to stick your head into a crocodile's mouth. I think I found the next best thing."

Her heavy boots clanking, Madori walked across the courtyard toward the Daenorian.

"Oi! Crocodile girl!"

The Daenorian spun toward her, and her eyes widened in delight. Her mouth opened into a bright smile. "Oh, aren't you tiny and cute! Do you like toffy? I have some toffy somewhere in my pocket, though it's a bit squished. You can have some if you let me join you."

The girl reached into her pocket, fished around, and produced something flat, dusty, and covered in lint. She held it out toward Madori.

Madori struggled not to cringe. "There's no need for that. I'm Madori. Who are you?"

The girl's grin widened. "I'm Neekeya! I'm from South Daenor. Remember that. *South* Daenor. Not the north part where people live in castles, wear ribbons, and pretend they're all proper and fancy. I'm from the swamps. We're real warriors there. My father says I'm the best warrior in the kingdom, and he gave me this sword, and it has magical powers. Do you believe in magical swords?"

Madori bit her lip. "I suppose so. Would you like to join our quartet?"

Neekeya gasped and tears budded in her eyes. She leaned down and pulled Madori into an embrace. She stood quite a bit taller than Madori, and her embrace was warm, and though the girl was odd—

her armor strange, her accent heavy—there was kindness and comfort and goodness to her.

"Thank you!" Neekeya breathed. "I'd love to. You're very kind. Would you like a crocodile tooth?"

Madori shook her head. "No thank you."

The four stood together: A girl torn between night and day, her eyes too large, her hair cropped short except for two long strands; a prince in disguise, a son of privilege masquerading as a commoner; a son of darkness, tattooed and pierced, in a land of light; and a swamp dweller of strange armor, eager eyes, and a smile that it seemed no darkness could crush.

"The headmistress said every quartet needs a name, a symbol, and leader," Madori said. "So what are they?"

Tam grinned. "That's obvious. You're our leader, little one. And our symbol is a duskmoth, like the one inked onto your wrist; after all, we're of both daylight and darkness here. As for our name? We will be known as Madori's Motley."

"No, Tam," Madori said.

But Neekeya grinned and hopped excitedly. "Madori's Motley! I like it. I like toffy too. Do you want some toffy, Tam?" She offered him a piece.

Jitomi too nodded. "Madori's Motley. I accept this name."

Madori only sighed. She had come here seeking acceptance in Timandrian society; now she found herself among a group of outcasts and misfits.

I suppose, she thought, *this is where I belong.*

With all the students in groups of four, Headmistress Egeria spun on her heel and led them toward a tower. Quartet by quartet, the students of Teel followed, beginning their life at the university.

CHAPTER NINE
CASTLE AND SCROLL

She stood by the grave of her father, staring up at the fortress that bore his name.

Salai Castle rose upon the hill, a pagoda three tiers high, its roofs tiled blue. A bronze dragon statue stood upon the top roof, the full moon haloing its roaring head. The stars gleamed above, and the darkness of Eloria spread to the east, blanketing the hills, valleys, and river. In the west, the dusk glowed like a palisade of lanterns, the borderland dividing day and night. The orange light gleamed against the black bricks of the castle, and its windows forever gazed upon the gloaming, eyes to guard the lands of darkness.

"You died defending this border, Father." Koyee looked down at the grave. "Now a great castle bearing your name guards this land. Eloria will never fall again."

She closed her eyes, the memories like ice in her veins. It had been many years since her father had died, and Koyee herself was a parent now, but the pain never left her. She still felt very young, very alone, very afraid.

"I miss you, Father," she whispered.

She opened her eyes.

But no, I am no longer a youth, she thought. *I am thirty-six years old, and I have a child of my own, and I will forever defend this home so many died for.*

She raised her chin, clutched the hilt of her katana—the blade her father had once wielded—and climbed the twisting path up the hill. The wind billowed her silken black cloak, making its embroidered blue dragons dance. Her hair streamed across her eyes, a white curtain, and she tucked it behind her ears. Her shirt of scales chinked, the armor she always wore here, the armor she would not remove even so long after the war.

Once you've seen war, you're always a soldier.

She reached the gates of Salai Castle. Two dragon statues flanked its gates, large as mules, roaring silently. Embers crackled within their mouths. The doors stood closed before Koyee, forged of bronze that reflected the dusk behind her. When she craned her head back, the castle seemed to soar forever, reaching the stars. Once this had been a simple steeple, a place called the Nighttower. Once she had stood here alone, gazing into the light of Timandra. For ten years, workers had labored here, turning a tower into a great castle. Koyee placed her hands against the doors. She paused for a moment, savoring the cold feel of them, letting that iciness flow along her arms. Then, with a nod, she shoved the doors with all her strength. They swung open upon oiled hinges.

She stepped into a tiled hall, columns holding its ceiling. Braziers shaped as fish, wolves, and birds stood in rows, their embers casting orange light. A table of polished granite stood in the center of the room, its surface engraved with a map of Mythimna, showing two continents like the wings of a moth—one continent painted white, the other black. Eternal day and endless night.

Three hundred men and women stood in the hall, clad in scale armor, silvery helmets upon their heads. As Koyee entered, they drew their katanas as one and raised the blades in salute. Their large Elorian eyes gleamed blue and lavender as they stared at her.

Koyee raised her own katana—the sword Sheytusung, a blade of legend, the blade she had fought with in the great war many years ago.

"Under this moon, we dedicate Salai Castle!" she announced, her voice echoing in the hall. "A fortress rises. Eloria will never more fall. We are the night!"

Three hundred voices called out together. "We are the night!"

Here were the greatest soldiers in Qaelin, this empire of the night. Koyee had chosen every one herself, the brightest stars of the darkness. They stood strong, brave, clad in steel, and they would defend their homeland.

Koyee lifted a goblet from the table. She raised it high. "Nearly twenty years ago, an enemy sailed down the river and rode upon the plains, and only a single tower stood here, its only guardian fallen. We have forged peace since then. And I pray to Xen Qae, our wise master in the stars, that this peace lasts ten thousand years. But if ever the fire burns again, if ever the light falls upon Eloria . . . we will be ready. Drink, children of darkness. May wine warm your bellies. The night is eternal; so is our strength. Our watch begins."

They drank. The wine poured down Koyee's throat, warming her belly.

Wine fermented from grapes grown across our border, she thought. *A drink of sunlight for soldiers of the night.*

They feasted then, the meats, mushrooms, and fish filling the chamber with their savory aroma. Soldiers talked and laughed as they ate, and one began to sing a song. A fireplace crackled at the back. Koyee ate little, spoke less, and did not sing, for too many worries lay upon her.

I built this castle to defend the darkness, she thought, *and yet I sent my daughter into the very heart of sunlight.*

Koyee had traveled across the sunlit lands of Timandra, and she had seen the looks people gave her and Madori—two women with eyes as large as chicken eggs, one an Elorian with pale skin and white hair, the other with dark hair and tanned skin, marking her mixed blood. The sunlit lands shunned them, yet what could Koyee have done?

"I'm shunned in Eloria too!" Madori had shouted at her, eyes damp. "I'm just as monstrous in the night—a girl with black hair and tanned skin—as I am in Timandra. So at least let me be monstrous at the university where I can learn magic."

Koyee had tried to embrace the girl, to tell Madori, "You are blessed, pure, and beautiful."

But Madori would not listen. She would shout, stamp her feet, and bring tears to Koyee's eyes. And finally Madori had left. And now she was gone. And even now, sitting here in this fortress across the border, Koyee missed her daughter and wished she could embrace her one more time.

"Wherever you are, Madori," she whispered as soldiers laughed and sang around her, "I love you, and I pray that you're safe."

After the meal ended, Koyee climbed the castle's coiling staircase. Still holding her goblet of wine, she stepped out onto the roof, climbed the tiled slope, and stood beneath the bronze dragon and the moon above. A soft smile touched her lips. She thought back to her youth, an urchin living barefoot and wild on the streets of Pahmey. She had often climbed roofs then.

"I was not much older than Madori," she whispered, "when I sat upon some shop's roof in that distant city, watching the floating lanterns and fireworks during the Moon of Xen Qae." She sighed. "May you have a better youth than mine, Madori. May you never know fear, hunger, and cold like I did."

She gazed downhill. South of the castle nestled the village of Oshy, its clay huts embracing the Inaro River, its boats swaying at the docks. When Koyee turned her head westward, she saw the dusk. The scar stretched across the land, gleaming orange, yellow, and gold. From up here, Koyee could just glimpse the green forests beyond— Timandra, the land of daylight.

You're there, Madori, she thought. *Somewhere in that light. Be safe.*

She whispered into the wind, speaking to her invisible friend, the shoulder spirit Eelani. "I built this castle and brought these soldiers here, praying their watch is silent, praying this castle forever remains only a thing of beauty, never of warfare." She gestured down at the river where boats were sailing in and out of dusk. "Look at them, Eelani. Merchants. They deliver our silk, mushrooms, and fireworks into the lands of daylight. They return with wine, fruits, vegetables, the fare we cannot grow in the darkness. Perhaps that is how we will prevent war. Trade. Merchants will defend us more than any fortress or wall. Where ships of trade sail, ships of war are less likely to fire their cannons."

She felt warmth caress her cheek, a hint of her invisible friend upon her shoulder. *If you truly believed these words,* a voice seemed to speak inside her, *you would be sailing upon one of those ships, not standing here above an army.*

Koyee raised her sword in one hand, her goblet of wine in another. "This will be Eloria—lifting the bounties of trade and peace in one hand, a sword in the other. Thus perhaps we will survive."

She left the castle.

She walked along the river, heading toward the light.

Rocky, lifeless hills rolled before her, but soon moss grew upon them, slippery under her boots. As she approached the light, thin grass rustled, then bushes, and finally trees. The sun emerged above the horizon, and Koyee pulled her hood over her head. She walked into the light. Trees grew taller with every step, their leaves dark and thin at first, then lush and sweetly-scented.

The shadows vanished behind her, and she emerged into the eternal daylight of Timandra.

The village of Fairwool-by-Night awaited her. Thirty-odd cottages rose around a pebbly square, their roofs made of straw, their walls formed of wattle-and-daub. An ancient maple tree grew from the square, and a stone library rose behind it, the place Madori would spend so many hours lost in. Past the buildings swayed fields of wheat and rye, and beyond them rolled green pastures dotted with sheep.

"Fairwool-by-Night," she said into the warm breeze. "My second home."

As Madori was torn between day and night, perhaps Koyee was too, spending half her time in the darkness, haunted by dreams of the war, and half her time here in daylight, being a wife, being a mother, seeking solace in the sun.

She walked into the village and approached her home. A garden bloomed outside the cottage, its sunflowers rising nearly as tall as the thatch roof, its peonies filling Koyee's nostrils with their sweet scent. She allowed herself a soft smile. This home would feel empty without Madori, but soon Torin would return to her. And in a few years, Madori would too, and perhaps someday—even if it's many years down the line—Koyee herself would feel at home here, would forget the memories, would find the peace she sought.

A scroll stuck out from Koyee's new mailbox, a little hollowed-out log perched upon a post. Soon after her accession to the throne, Queen Linee had founded the Sern Postal Company—two cogs that sailed along the Sern River every month, delivering mail between the capital and the riverside settlements. Koyee walked across the clover and pulled the parchment free. It was probably another letter from Linee; the queen enjoyed sending her letters full of poems, drawings, and tales from the capital. Holding the scroll and still smiling, Koyee stepped toward her front door.

She gasped.

The scroll fell from her hand.

Shock, then fear, then finally rage filled her.

With red paint—no, it was blood, its scent coppery— somebody had drawn a symbol onto the door. It looked like the sun eclipsing the moon. Below it appeared the words: "Elorian pigs go home."

A pig's head, a paintbrush still stuck inside it, lay upon the doorstep.

A slow whisper—more of a hiss—fled Koyee's lips. "Who did this?"

She spun around, her fist crushing the scroll. She stared across the village, seeking somebody who might be laughing, pointing, hiding. She saw nobody.

"Who did this?" she shouted.

Birds fled the old maple tree and a dog barked. Nobody answered. The villagers were all working in the fields, shepherding their sheep, or hiding in their homes.

The scroll crinkled in her fist, and she stared at it. The seal was blank; this letter had not come from Queen Linee. Fingers trembling, Koyee unrolled the scroll and instantly recognized her husband's handwriting; he had written in Qaelish, the language of the night which few in daylight could read. She read and reread the letter.

"Koyee, my love,

Billygoat has passed the Teel Trials and enrolled at the university. She is well but the world is not. A new movement—the Radians—are preaching hatred across the lands of sunlight. Sailith has died and they are its reincarnation. Tam Shepherd has enrolled at Teel too, and he'll look after Billygoat. She is safe. I've met Cam here and am returning with him to Kingswall; he needs my help fighting this new threat. Koyee, be careful. Stay in Oshy until this blows over. Stay in your new fortress, surround yourself with soldiers, and be safe. I'll come for you when I can.

I miss you and love you always.

Your husband,

Torin"

Koyee closed her eyes, the old war pounding back into her. Cruel leaders preaching hatred. Soldiers pouring into the night with torches, lanterns, swords, and arrows. Blood and death across the night.

Her daughter was halfway across the world. Her husband was traveling into danger.

"And you leave me here?" she whispered.

She turned back toward her door, stared at the symbol drawn in blood, and again she saw the blood of the war—it washed over her in a wave of memory.

She grabbed a rag. She dipped it in water. She began to clean the door, her eyes dry but her heart trembling.

CHAPTER TEN
THE PEWTER DRAGON

Madori sat at a table with her quartet, ready to learn magic.

Many other tables filled the room, each seating four students. Scrolls, vials full of bubbling potions, monkey skulls, and mummified reptile claws crowded the tabletops, the shelves lining the walls, and the great desk at the back of the room. Before that desk stood little Professor Fen, bald of head, white of mustache—one of the professors who had quizzed Madori at the trials. He rolled up his flowing sleeves and cleared his throat.

"Class!" he said. "Welcome to Basic Magical Principles. This turn I shall teach you, well . . . basic magical principles."

Madori opened her notebook and dipped her quill in ink. It was an ancient notebook, probably even older than Fen—the parchment pages had been used several times, scratched clean of ink after every use. When she squinted, she could still glimpse bits of the old layers of writing and even a few dirty drawings. Her father had bought her several notebooks before leaving, and even the used ones had cost a full silver coin each—a small fortune.

When she glanced aside, she saw that Jitomi had unrolled a parchment of rich Elorian vellum, its edges tasseled; Madori's mother would hang similar scrolls in their home, each illustrated with birds, dragons, and Qaelish runes. Neekeya, still wearing her necklace of crocodile teeth, had a notebook that looked even shabbier than Madori's; the pages were tattered, burnt at the edges, and already covered with Daenorian letters, leaving only the margins available. Only Tam had a shiny new notebook, its cover blue leather engraved with landscape scenes, its parchment pages fresh.

"You can share my notebook if you like," the undercover prince said to Neekeya, moving the book closer to her.

The swamp dweller smiled. "It's all right. My notebook is magical. Like my sword." She patted the pages. "You see the writing that's already here? I just need to tap my quill against the letters, and they'll reorganize themselves into whatever words I like."

Tam seemed unconvinced and Madori sighed. Neekeya had spent the past turn claiming that everything she owned was imbued with ancient magic: that her sword glowed around goblins, her necklace of crocodile teeth could bite dragons, her shoes could walk on lava, and even her meals—dried frog legs—gave her magical health and longevity. So far, Madori hadn't seen anything magical about the girl.

Beside them, Lari and her quartet sat at another table.

"Look at those creatures," Lari said to her friends, pointing at Madori's Motley. The girl snorted. "Their books must be made from rat hides."

Lari's friends laughed—the twin girls and the tall, golden-haired boy. The four had named themselves Sunlit Purity, and all four wore Radian brooches pinned to their pricey green robes. Madori's robes were shabby and second-hand, the hems worn and the elbows patched, but the Sunlit Purity quartet wore fitted robes of lush, embroidered cotton with golden hems, tailored to look as fine as gowns.

"Rat hide?" Madori asked, waving her notebook at Lari. "Do you recognize a relative?"

A few students snickered. Lari's face reddened, but before a fight could break out, Professor Fen raised his voice again.

"Students! Please. Pay attention. You can chat with your friends after class. Right now listen to your old professor."

Giving Madori a sneer, her eyes promising retaliation, Lari turned toward the professor.

"Is your book really made out of rats?" Neekeya whispered to Madori.

Madori shushed her. "Of course not. Now let's listen."

Professor Fen, barely taller than Madori's own humble height, paced before his desk.

"The Basic Principles of Magic!" he announced. "Three simple principles form the basis of every spell you will ever cast. The chasm of puzzles you walked through. The magic of mending broken bones . . . or shattering them. Magic to see to the stars and under the ocean.

All come from a remarkably simple foundation woven in incredibly complex ways. Once you learn the foundation, you will have the building blocks to create structures to dazzle the world. The principles are . . ." He paused dramatically, then raised three fingers. He tapped each in turn. "Choosing, Claiming, and Changing."

Students wrote furiously into their notebooks. When Madori glanced aside, she saw Neekeya tapping the existing words in her "magical notebook," then grunting as they refused to change shape. With a groan, the swamp girl scribbled her notes into a margin.

Professor Fen continued speaking. "These are the three steps to any magic. First you *choose* your material. Then you must *claim* your material. Finally, you will *change* your material. Choose, claim, change." He coughed into his sleeve. "Allow me to demonstrate. Say I wish to lift this vial off my table." He pointed as a glass vessel full of bubbling purple liquid. "How would I apply the three steps? Anyone?"

Lari's hand shot up. The young noblewoman smiled prettily, the proper and prim student.

"Yes, young Lady Serin," said Professor Fen.

Lari spoke as if reciting. "First you would choose your material—the air around the vial. Then you would claim the material—seizing control of the air. Finally you would change the material—changing the air pressure to levitate the vial." She shot a smug glance at Madori, then back at the professor. "My father taught me. I've been lifting objects at home since I was a toddler."

Professor Fen slapped his hands together. "Very nice, Lari! And very correct. Would you like to demonstrate for the class?"

"I'd love to." She looked again at Madori and spoke with just the hint of scorn. "Obviously, not all students are as knowledgeable."

Lari rose to her feet, smoothed her fine robes, and strutted toward the head of the class. She held her hands out toward the vial.

"First I choose the air as my material," Lari said. "The air will compress around the vial, eventually lifting it. Now I must claim that air. That is the hard part . . . hard for some, at least." Another look at Madori. "But I've been practicing claiming materials for many years. I will imagine the air—its little particles, the different gases floating within it, and claim control of it."

"The only gas here is the hot air leaving her mouth," Madori muttered to Tam.

Lari continued as if she hadn't heard. "I've now claimed the air and can change it." She raised her hand slowly. Two feet away, the vial began to levitate. "I am not magicking the vial itself; I am manipulating the air beneath and around it." She lowered her hand and the vial descended back onto the table. "Choose, claim, change."

She gave a little curtsy, then returned to her seat.

"Fantastic!" said Professor Fen, clapping enthusiastically. Several other students clapped too. "It's wonderful to see such a bright student. I'd have also accepted changing the glass itself to become lighter than air, but that would have been far less elegant, and would often cause the glass to shatter. Well done, Lady Serin."

Lari beamed and shot Madori a triumphant look.

Madori raised two fingers, knuckles facing Lari, a gesture so rude her mother—were she here to see—would have beaten Madori with a belt. Lari—raised in a palace where the rudest gesture was probably lifting the wrong dessert spoon—blanched and looked away, lips scrunching together.

"Don't goad her," Tam said.

Madori grumbled. "Just me being at Teel goads her. I might as well have some fun with it."

"Now!" said Professor Fen from across the room. "You will each find an assortment of items on your table. Choose one and levitate it. I will be moving between the desks to guide you."

Across the classroom, students began to mumble, squint, and thrust out their tongues, concentrating at lifting items off the tables. Conchs, animal skulls, chalices, and bubbling vials rattled across tables. Only Lari was successfully levitating an item: her Radian pin.

Madori stared at a pewter dragon statuette that stood on her table. She sucked in her breath, trying to claim the air. How did one claim air? When she glanced aside, she saw that Neekeya was staring at a wooden toy knight, her tongue thrust out in concentration; the figure was rattling. Jitomi was having some success levitating a Venus flytrap, but the pot kept falling back down after rising only an inch. Tam seemed as lost as Madori; the mouse skull he was staring at simply stared back.

Madori returned her eyes to the dragon statuette. It stood still upon the table, clutching a crystal.

Go on, Madori thought, *rise!*

"Having trouble, mongrel?" Lari came to stand beside her. She leaned against Madori's desk and smiled. "You don't seem to be doing too well."

"Get back to your desk, dear cousin, or I'm going to slam this dragon against your pretty face."

Lari pouted. "Oh, *tsk tsk*, such a temper on the little half-breed. Must be your savage nightcrawler blood." She crossed her arms. "Go on, let's see your magic."

Madori growled and returned her eyes to the figurine. She sucked in air through her nose, trying to detect its texture, the icy coolness, the smells of the bubbling potions.

Feel the air, she told herself. *Claim it. Make it yours.*

She let the air flow through her, moving down her throat to her lungs, then spreading throughout the rest of her, tingling her toes and fingertips. With every breath, she let that air flow through every part of her, tingling the hair on her head and wrapping around her bones.

Now change that air. Wrap it around the dragon and lift.

Upon the tabletop, the figurine began to rise.

Madori gasped.

"You're doing it, Madori!" Neekeya said.

Focus. Focus!

Madori tried to ignore everyone else, to direct all her attention toward the figurine. She raised it another inch, then another, until it hovered at eye level. A smile stretched across her lips.

With a *whoosh*, the dragon figurine shot forward and slammed into Madori's face.

She cried out and blood spurted from her nose.

The statuette clattered to the floor.

"Stupid mongrel," Lari said, smiling crookedly. "You didn't think it was you lifting it, did you?" She clucked her tongue. "Looks like the one with a face full of dragon is you."

Madori leaped to her feet and lunged toward Lari, fists swinging. Arms wrapped around her, tugging her back.

"No, Billygoat!" Tam said, pinning her arms to her sides. "You're only giving her what she wants."

Lari's eyes widened and she laughed. "Billygoat? Does the mongrel have a nickname?" She sighed. "She does smell like a goat."

Professor Fen rushed toward them, mustache bristling. "What is the meaning of this?" His eyes widened to see Madori's bashed nose. "What happened here?"

Suddenly Lari's face changed from cruel to distressed, and tears budded in her eyes. Her voice rose an octave, taking on a childlike quality. "Oh, Professor Fen! I was just trying to help her. She accidentally magicked the figurine onto her face, and when I went to check on her, she suddenly attacked me."

"I did not!" Madori shouted. "I— I mean— She hit me and—"

Lari covered her eyes. "Oh, Professor Fen! She frightens me. Can you punish her?"

"But—" Madori began.

"Enough!" Professor Fen's bald head flushed red. "Madori, go to the infirmary. Get your nose taken care of. Then report to the stables and spend the rest of the turn helping the horse master. You may return to your classes next turn—*if* you've learned how to behave."

As Madori stormed out of the class, her eyes burning, she heard Lari's voice rise behind her.

"I say, some girls simply can't curb their temper . . ."

When she was outside the room, Madori allowed her tears to flow. They streamed down her cheeks and dampened her robes, mingling with her blood. She heard the other students laughing inside the classroom, and Madori imagined them all mocking her. She leaned against the corridor's wall, her tears streaming, her chest shaking.

I never imagined it like this, she thought. *I miss you, Father and Mother. I miss you so much. I miss home.*

A lump filled her throat. She didn't want to go to the infirmary. She wanted to run outside the university, to hitch a ride with a peddler, to travel all the way home to Fairwool-by-Night. Why had she ever fought with her mother? Now Madori only wanted her mother to hug her, to smooth her hair, to tell her it would be all right.

"I'm sorry, Mama," she whispered, voice hoarse. "I miss you. I love you."

She walked outside, her sleeve held to her bleeding nose, and stood in the courtyard. Rainclouds were gathering and a drizzle fell. The columns and towers of Teel rose around her, marvels of architecture, and the domed library rose behind them, the world's greatest center of knowledge. Beauty and wonder surrounded Madori, but as rain and tears fell, she only wanted to return to her village.

"I can leave," she whispered. "I can sell my books and uniform in the town, and I'll have money for food, and I can travel home."

She let memories of Fairwool-by-Night fill her: her cottage with the garden of sunflowers and peonies, her horse Hayseed, her old bed and books, her rag dolls, her parents.

But even standing here, she knew that something was missing from that image.

There were no friends waiting for her at home. There was no future, no *dream*, not for her. Her parents had fought in the war; they had achieved greatness, and they had found peace in a quiet village and with each other. But she, Madori—what great things had she done?

She took a slow breath. Her father's words returned to her.

To survive, you only have to breathe the next breath. Breath by breath.

She took another trembling breath.

She was still here. She was still surviving, still at Teel.

"When you went to war, Mother and Father, you suffered too. And you could have gone back home, but you kept fighting." She laughed weakly. "You fought armies. I can handle Lari."

She nodded and wiped the blood off her face. A smile trembling on her lips, she decided to skip the infirmary. She headed straight to the stables, and when she stepped into their shadows, her smile widened.

For several hours, she tended to the horses—and she hugged them, and she whispered her fears to them, and they were her friends.

And I have human friends here too, she whispered. *I have Tam and Neekeya and Jitomi. My motley crew.*

When she left the stables, she felt better than she had in turns. She would stay, she vowed, no matter what. She would not let Lari drive her away.

"I swear to you, stars of Eloria," she whispered to the cloudy sky, imagining those stars hiding beyond rain, cloud, and light. "I will become a mage."

CHAPTER ELEVEN
SUNLIGHT AND MOTLEY

The bells of Teel University, high in the northeastern tower, rang the
end of the turn. Madori's parents claimed that thousands of years
ago, the world would turn, that night would follow day in an endless
dance. The bells of Teel—like the hourglass her parents kept at
home—tracked the old days and nights. With Moth frozen, Timandra
now basked in endless daylight, and Eloria hid in eternal shadow, but
still the bells rang, forcing the old cycle upon the university. Madori
supposed she was the only student here used to such a routine; each
turn was the same twenty-four hours her parents used back home.

Rubbing her sore shoulders—she had worked her arms down
to the bone in the stables—she stepped into the eastern arcade, the
dormitory for first year students. For a moment she stood in
shadows, staring ahead. Here was the long, covered walkway that
formed one of the cloister's four facades. A colonnade of many
columns rose to Madori's left, affording a view of the cobbled
courtyard and General Woodworth, the old elm tree. A long
succession of archways rose above her, engraved with ancient runes.
A brick wall, lined with doorways, rose to her right. First year
students were moving back and forth, stepping in and out of
chambers. Sounds of laughter, gossip, and even crying wafted down
the arcade.

Madori bit her lip. *My new home.*

With a deep breath, she took a step forward, emerging from
shadows.

At once, all the sounds of conversation and laughter died.
Everyone turned to stare at Madori.

She raised her chin, squared her shoulders, and walked down
the arcade.

Let them stare, she thought. *People have been staring at me all my life.*

She kept walking as eyes followed her. She was a half-breed. She was a freak on show for them. But she would walk with pride, as she always had—the girl with crazy hair, with the bronze skin of a Timandrian and the large, lavender eyes of an Elorian, with the famous parents adored or vilified across the world, with the fire inside her to learn magic—a fire none could tame. She walked by them all as they stared—Timandrians who whispered and gasped, Elorians who stood in shadowy corners. They were day and night, and she—she was the dusk.

Halfway down the gallery, she passed by Sunlit Purity, Lari's quartet. The four were leaning against the wall, the door to their chamber ajar. They had hung a Radian banner upon the door, and as Madori walked by, they shot her dirty glances. Derin, the tall blond boy, muttered something about mongrels under his breath. The twins—Fae and Kae—snickered.

"You stink of horse," Lari said as Madori walked by her.

Madori paused and turned to give Lari a cold stare. "I had a doll that looked like you at home—all golden tresses and freckled cheeks." Madori smiled thinly. "I ripped off her head and used it as a ball. Do you think your head would roll too?"

As Lari paled and covered her mouth, Madori gave her a wink and walked on.

Farther down the colonnade, Madori reached an open door and saw her friends inside the chamber. She stepped in and closed the door behind her.

"I'm telling you!" Neekeya was saying, standing with her hands on her hips. Her sword and helmet, shaped like crocodiles, hung on the wall behind her. "My pillow is magical! I brought it especially from home, and it always gives you good dreams."

Jitomi was sitting on a bed, painting a dragon onto a vellum scroll; it looked like the dragon tattoo that coiled up his neck. "I have never heard of such magic." The Elorian's eyes gleamed in the shadows of his hood.

Rummaging through his backpack, Tam groaned. "That's because no such magic exists. Her mother probably only told her that to get her to go to sleep."

Neekeya stomped her feet. "My mother is a great warrior! She wrestled crocodiles every day before breakfast. She wrestled a *magic* crocodile once, and—"

"Oh Idar's beard, here we go again!" Tam said, raising his hands in indignation.

Standing at the door, Madori cleared her throat. The others turned toward her, noticing her for the first time. Neekeya reacted first. She raced forward, her necklace of crocodile teeth jangling, and pulled her into a crushing embrace. Madori—almost a foot shorter—nearly suffocated in the swamp girl's arms.

"Air!" Madori gasped.

Neekeya only squeezed her tighter. "I'm glad you're here! I was worried. So much blood . . ." She stepped back, holding Madori at arm's length, and narrowed her eyes. "Are you all right?"

Madori nodded. "Bit peckish."

"I have some frog legs. And toffy!" The Daenorian reached into her pockets and produced both items of food. "Would you like some?"

"I was hoping maybe for some Ardish fare. Or maybe Qaelish food. Bread?"

Ignoring the request, Neekeya touched Madori's cheek. "Madori, you listen to me. I'm a warrior. A real warrior. I used to wrestle crocodiles with my parents. If Lari attacks you again, you step back and let me fight her." She snarled, revealing very white, very sharp-looking teeth. "I'll wrestle her good! I'm not scared of her. She and her friends . . . they think they're so mighty, what with their beautiful golden hair and blue eyes, proud Magerians in their homeland. They don't like us outsiders, do they?" Suddenly tears filled Neekeya's eyes. "But we're just as good as they are. We passed the same trials."

Suddenly Madori felt guilt pound through her. She had spent the past few turns focusing on her own misfortune—pitying herself, the girl torn between day and night. For the first time, Madori realized that Teel University was probably just as difficult for Neekeya. The swamp dweller—with her dark brown skin, heavy accent, and foreign ways—probably felt just as alienated here, just as threatened by the Radians.

Madori patted the taller girl's arm. "Thank you, Neekeya. You're right. We all passed the same trials. Every one in this room is just as smart, strong, and worthy as the Radians. We're all outsiders here, all far from home. And we'll face Lari and her gang together."

When she left Neekeya's embrace, Madori took a closer look at the chamber. It was small, no larger than her old bedchamber back at Fairwool-by-Night. Four beds took up most of the floor space, each carved of pine and topped with a mattress and woolen blankets. A large desk held scrolls, books, ink pots, and quills. A vellum scroll bearing an Elorian prayer hung upon a wall—presumably Jitomi had hung it up. A golden crocodile statuette, its emeralds eyes gleaming, stood upon the window sill—a Daenorian artifact, no doubt belonging to Neekeya. Meanwhile Tam was busy hanging up a painting from home; it showed the towers of Arden's royal palace.

Madori had no charms to add to this room, no mementos from her own home, nothing to make this chamber a new home. There was the dagger she kept in her boot, the one with the antler hilt, but she decided to keep this weapon hidden; she might yet need it, roaming a university rife with Radians. She reached into her pocket and fished out a copper coin, change from the meal she'd shared with her father at The Dancing Wolf tavern. It was a coin from Arden, showing Queen Linee—Tam's mother—on one side, and a raven— the sigil of Arden—on the other.

This is my memento, she thought. *A meal with my father, a last memory of my old life.* She placed the coin upon the shelf beside Neekeya's crocodile figurine.

Three of the beds already seemed claimed; her friends' packs, cloaks, and other belongings lay upon them. Madori made her way to the fourth bed, which lay under the window, and sat down. The straw mattress crinkled but seemed comfortable enough. Tam's bed lay to her one side, Jitomi's to the other.

Again, she thought, *I'm between night and day.*

She was about to kick off her boots and change into her sleepwear when chants rose from outside.

Madori froze. Her fingers tingled and her pulse increased.

The chants echoed outside in the corridor, dispersed and unorganized, and Madori could not recognize the words. But soon

the voices, one by one, solidified into a single mantra. Madori sneered
and leaped to her feet.

"Radian rises!" the voices chanted. "Radian rises!"

Boots stomped and the voices echoed across the hall. The floor
shook beneath Madori. Above the chant rose a high, pretty voice—
Lari's voice.

"Fellow students, do you wish to preserve the purity of
sunlight? Do you wish to cast out the filth staining our fine
university? Join the Teel Radian Society! Join us, receive your pin, and
help banish the darkness."

Madori raced toward the door.

"Billygoat, wait!" Tam cried and tried to grab her. She slipped
out from his grasp, yanked the door open, and raced outside.

Lari was marching up and down the columned gallery, chin
raised. Her cronies marched around her. Many students had stepped
out of their chambers; some gaped in silence, but others were
marching with Lari and her group, chanting the cry.

"Radian rises! Radian rises!"

Lari raised her fist. "Join the Teel Radian Society! We will bring
purity to magic. We will drive out the dark-skinned heathens, the
nightcrawlers of darkness, and the mongrels of impure blood. Radian
is purity! Radian is light!"

While Lari spoke, her friends were handing out Radian pins
and papyrus pamphlets. One scroll fell and fluttered toward Madori's
feet. On it appeared a drawing of an Elorian—the fingers clawed, the
eyes cruel—feasting upon a Timandrian baby, ripping out its entrails
with fangs. Below the drawing appeared the words: "Cast out
nightcrawlers, mongrels, and heathens. Radian rises!"

Lari pinned one of the pamphlets to the wall. "Join us!" she
cried. "Join me, Lari Serin, at the Teel Radian Society."

Madori had heard enough. With a growl, she made to leap
forward, intending to throttle Lari. She felt ready to kill the girl, then
flee into the wilderness.

Hands grabbed her.

"Madori, please!" Tam said, tugging her back. She thrashed in
his grip, but Jitomi and Neekeya soon joined him. The three grabbed

her arms and legs, holding her back. They stood in the doorway of their chamber.

Hearing the commotion, Lari turned toward them. A bright, toothy grin split her face.

"Look, friends!" she called out to the hall. "A swamp dweller, her skin like coal, a heathen and barbarian. A nightcrawler boy, a demon of darkness. A Timandrian boy, a traitor to his own blood. And finally, a feral little mongrel dog." She laughed. "The Radian Society will clean our university from their filth."

Madori screamed and tried to leap forward again, but her friends tugged her back into their room and slammed the door shut.

"Let me go!" Madori cried. "I'll knock her teeth in. I'll rip out her throat. Neekeya, you're with me, right? We'll attack her together."

"And if you do," Tam said sternly, "you'll only give her words credence." The prince released Madori and walked over to block the door. He glared at her. "If you hit her, you know what she'll do. She'll act the victim, cry fake tears, and trumpet the news across Moth that you're a menace. And all of Moth would hear that news. You don't know the power her father has."

"She doesn't know the power my fist has," Madori said, but she hated to admit it—though she fumed, kicked, and growled, she knew Tam was speaking truth.

If I attack Lari now, I turn her into a martyr.

"So what do we do?" Neekeya said, her voice hesitant. She let go of Madori and looked at the others, one by one. "Do we let her keep demonizing us?"

The chants still rose outside. More voices were joining them. Madori's heart sank to realize that, when she had stormed outside screaming, she had probably just made herself look like the wild animal Lari was painting her to be.

Jitomi spoke for the first time. The Elorian boy walked toward their table and slapped the pile of books. "What we do is study. The other students might call us barbarians. We will prove them wrong. We will prove that we can be smarter than them. We'll become more powerful than them. They want to banish us from their university? We'll beat them at their own game."

Madori heaved a sigh and leaned against the wall. "How? I can't even levitate a simple figurine."

"But I can," Jitomi said. "I know a little bit of magic. Neekeya does too. We'll work together. We'll learn to perform magic as well as Lari can—*better* than she can." He gestured at the door. "So let them chant. While they're outside parading like thugs, we'll open our books and study."

Demonstrating his point, Jitomi opened one codex and sat down to read.

Madori's body ached. She hadn't slept in over a turn, and she had spent hours working in the stables. She longed for a good half-turn of slumber, but Jitomi was right.

Next class, I won't let Lari humiliate me again, she vowed. She grabbed a book too. She sat beside Jitomi, opened the tome, and began to study.

CHAPTER TWELVE
CHAINS OF SMOKE

Her eyelids drooping, Madori began the next turn in a new class: Offensive Magic.

While Professor Fen taught Basic Magical Principles in a dusty chamber full of scrolls, vials, and sundry artifacts, this class took place in towering lecture hall with tiers of cold stone seats. There were no windows here; the light came from braziers that crackled upon the polished black walls. This looked less like a classroom, Madori thought, and more like the temple of a dark god.

She sat at the back of the hall with her quartet. The stage below was still empty, and students in the lower tiers rustled, leafed through books, and mumbled spells. Stifling a yawn, Madori tried to remember what she had studied last turn in her room, but the knowledge kept fleeing her mind.

"Who teaches this class?" she asked Tam.

Sitting beside her, the prince shrugged. "I don't know. Offensive Magic? Must be somebody angry."

Madori shuddered to remember her parents' war stories. They had fought the dark mages of Mageria during the great War of Day and Night. Mother still bore the scar along her arm, a coiling line like a serpent.

I saw Magerian magic tear flesh off bones, Koyee had told her, *flip ribs inside out, and crack skulls. I fought against siege towers topped with archers, cavalries of knights in armor, and great carracks firing cannons, but none frightened me like Mageria's black magic.*

Madori gulped.

"And now I learn this magic," she whispered to herself.

At her left side, Neekeya was whispering to Jitomi, "I have a ring of Offensive Magic. If I punch anyone while wearing the ring, it'll double my strength."

Jitomi tapped his chin. "Maybe the ring is just sharp."

Neekeya shook her head wildly, her black chin-length hair swaying. "No! It's magic. My father gave it to me, and he knows magic. I—"

"Hush!" Madori elbowed them. "Class is starting."

A door creaked open below and a shadow stirred. The students all fell silent, straightened in their seats, and stared down. A tall, balding man entered the room, wrapped in black robes.

Madori's heart seemed to sink down to her pelvis.

"Professor Atratus," she muttered.

The beak-nosed, hunched-over figure trudged across the stage toward the podium. The bald crest of his head shone, and what hair he did have—a ring around his back and sides like the feathers around a vulture's neck—shone with oil. He indeed reminded Madori of some great scavenger bird, here to sniff out rotten flesh. His black robes were so shabby they almost looked like a suit of feathers. The man's Radian pin shone in the light of the braziers, and Madori winced to remember their altercation at the trials.

He wasn't happy to see me pass the Trial of Wisdom, she thought. *And he won't be happy to see me here.*

"Class!" he barked when he reached his podium. He opened a few books and shuffled through them, then raised his eyes toward the tiers of seats. He cleared his throat—a horrible, gagging sound like a dying animal—and spoke in a voice that echoed through the hall. "You have come to study Offensive Magic. If any of you cannot tolerate pain, blood, or the gruesome damage our art can inflict upon the human body, I suggest you leave my university, return to your mother, and tell her you are a squeamish babe undeserving of true power."

A few scattered, nervous laughs rose from the crowd. Madori's heart sank even further; she swore she could feel it beating down in her foot.

Professor Atratus scanned the rows of seats, passing his eyes over each student in turn. "I see that this year, we have some students of excellent parentage." He let his eyes pause over Lari. "Indeed, the children of the purest pedigree are among us this turn." His gaze moved further along the seats, finally settling on Madori; that gaze changed into a withering glare. "And I see some among us are of . . . less distinguished heritage."

Madori clenched her fists in her lap. She wanted to leap down and challenge the professor, but Tam placed a hand on her thigh, holding her in place.

With a twitching sneer, Atratus tore his stare away from Madori and returned to his books and scrolls.

He spent the next hour rattling off magical theories, barking out fancy words like "material bindings" and "particle trajectory" and "physiological claims." Throughout the class, Madori could barely keep up; her wrist ached from scribbling down notes she didn't even understand. Lari, however, seemed the model student. Sitting at the head of the class, she kept raising her hand, answering every question properly, then turning toward the back tiers to give her fellow students smug smiles.

Throughout the class, as Madori kept furiously writing, Neekeya kept raising her hand. The tall Daenorian girl was practically bouncing in her seat, begging Atratus to answer his questions. Yet the balding professor wouldn't spare her a glance. His attention lay fully upon the Magerian students.

We in the back tier are the outcasts, Madori thought, glancing at her sides. Along with her quartet sat other foreigners, all ignored.

And no quartet is stranger than mine, she thought with a sigh, wondering how she'd ever pass this class. She could already see herself returning to Fairwool-by-Night a failure, flunked out of the university. Her mother would be furious, Madori thought. At first Koyee had not wanted to let her daughter—her only child—leave. Once Madori had insisted, shouting and kicking the walls, Koyee had agreed—on one condition.

"If you leave to the university," Koyee had said, jabbing Madori's chest, "you return to me a model mage. You will not loaf around at Teel like you do at home, sleeping entire turns, collecting stray animals, and wasting your time. If you go there, you will graduate at the top of your class, or by the stars of Eloria, do not return home at all."

As Atratus kept rattling out his lesson, Madori rubbed her sore wrist and heaved yet another sigh.

"Madori Greenmoat!"

The voice boomed across the hall and Madori started. Realizing she'd been lost in thought, she stared down at Professor Atratus.

"I asked you a question, girl," the professor said, brows pushed low over his beady eyes.

"I . . ." Madori's throat felt dry. "I'm sorry, Professor. May you repeat the question?"

Students muttered among themselves. Lari snickered.

Face turning red, Atratus grabbed a ruler and slapped his desk with a crack. "You will pay attention in class, girl, or this ruler will strike more than this desk. Do you understand?"

Madori ground her teeth and swallowed down her rage. She forced herself to nod silently.

With a disgusted grunt, Atratus left his podium and paced across the stage, tapping his ruler against his left palm.

"A volunteer!" he called out. "Step down. I normally wait a month before allowing magic in my classroom, but I believe that this year, with such bright minds, we may begin early. A volunteer! Raise your hand." Several hands rose in the class—none from the back tiers. Atratus didn't even turn to look. Still pacing, he cried out, "Lari! Lari Serin, step down please, darling child."

Lari rose to her feet, chin raised, a smug smile upon her face. She gave her fellow students a few nods, then strutted down the aisle and stepped onto the stage.

"I'm here, Professor Atratus," she said, voice sweet.

The stooped, balding man nodded and turned back toward the tiers of seats. He pointed his ruler at Madori.

"You! Greenmoat. Step down onto this stage. Since you've been daydreaming, you obviously know all about Offensive Magic already. Down!"

Madori glanced aside uneasily. Her friends winced, and Tam reached over to grab and squeeze her hand.

"You don't have to go down there," he whispered. "Just mumble an apology. You'll look a fool but it'll blow over."

Neekeya was struggling for breath. "Don't go," she whispered.

Madori stared down at the stage. Pretty and prim, Lari stared up from below, giving Madori her sweet little smile. And Madori felt it: the old rage rising inside her, the anger that always got her into trouble.

I once used this anger against you, Mother and Father, she thought. *I'm so sorry. I miss you so much now.*

She inhaled sharply through her nostrils and rose to her feet. She balled up her fists and walked down the aisle, moving between the rows of seats. As she passed by, hundreds of eyes followed her. Not a breath stirred. Her innards trembling, Madori stepped onto the stage.

You are the daughter of Torin Greenmoat, the great hero of the war, the man who united day and night, she told herself. *You are the daughter of Koyee of Qaelin, the great soldier who led armies, who slew the tyrant Ferius the Cruel.* She took a deep breath and squared her shoulders. *You don't have to be afraid of a bitter professor and a pampered girl.*

"Lari," said Professor Atratus, "I do believe it's time for a little demonstration of Offensive Magic. My fellow professors tell me you've been demonstrating levitation, transformations, and bindings to your classmates. Will you now demonstrate some . . . real magic?"

Lari nodded and stared at Madori, her eyes full of cruel delight. She spoke to Atratus, but she never removed her eyes from Madori. "Gladly."

"Excellent!" said the stooped professor. "Of course, to demonstrate hurting another human, we need a human to hurt." He looked at Madori. "But I think in this case, a mongrel will suffice."

Madori sucked in breath with a hiss. How could he speak like that? She wanted to march out of the lecture hall, to find the headmistress, to demand she discipline this professor for his bile. Yet she simply stood frozen. What could Headmistress Egeria do, after all? Take the word of a village girl? Like it or not, Professor Atratus had power here at Teel, and he had power across Timandra; as a member of the Radians, proudly displaying their pin, he served Lari's father, perhaps the most powerful man in all of Moth.

Madori growled. *So I'll play your game, Atratus. And I'll defeat you at it.*

Swinging his ruler, Atratus nodded toward Lari. "Now, Lady Serin, please explain the principles of magically attacking a foe."

Chin raised, Lari recited as from a book. "The Three Principles of Magic still apply: choose, claim, change. Advanced mages often choose human flesh or bone as their material. Once claimed, they can change this material—bending or shattering bones, tearing flesh, twisting the body into death. However, in the heat of battle, war mages often choose a faster, simpler approach. They choose particles of matter floating in the air. The air is full of matter—gasses, dust, dirt, smoke, even invisible metal." Lari smiled wickedly. "A mage can form a storm in the air, striking her opponent with a might greater than any mace or hammer. Advanced mages can even animate the particles into astral, striking beasts with minds of their own."

Madori bared her teeth and raised her fists. All of Professor Atratus's words—and all the words she had read in her books last turn—cluttered inside her head. She had learned something about forming a shield of air; she could swear it. She mumbled to herself, trying to claim the air around her, to weave it into a dense, soupy force field. Sweat beaded on her brow. Nothing seemed to happen.

"Excellent, Lady Serin!" the professor said. "Now demonstrate."

Lari nodded, smiling primly. "Gladly."

The girl's face changed. Her smile turned into a snarl, and her eyes blazed with hatred. Her hands rose, collecting the air into a dark ball of smoke. With a growl, Lari tossed her missile.

The projectile hurtled across the stage toward Madori.

Shield yourself! cried a voice inside her. *Block it with air!*

But she could not.

The smoky ball, large as a melon, crashed into her chest.

Madori cried out in pain and slammed down onto her backside.

The ball shattered, breaking up into smoky serpents. The tendrils wrapped around Madori's chest, squeezing, constricting. She couldn't breathe, and tears budded in her eyes. She tried to grab the tentacles and rip them off, but her fingers passed through them. Her ribs tightened; she felt like they might snap.

"Madori!" somebody shouted somewhere above; she thought it was Tam.

Lying on the stage, she saw nothing but the smoke, and then through the unholy fog, she saw Lari's face—cruel, smiling, her hands raised like claws. As the girl curled her fingers inwards, the smoky tendrils tightened further around Madori, and she screamed.

Why wasn't Professor Atratus stopping this? Tears streamed down Madori's face. She wanted to die.

He'll let me die, she realized. *Lari is going to kill me and I'll die here upon the stage as they laugh.*

She gritted her teeth.

No.

She thought of the scars along her mother's arm. Her mother had fought this magic before and triumphed.

I am the daughter of a great heroine, a woman who fought the forces of daylight and defeated them. I can defeat Lari.

Through the fog of pain, the words from her books returned to her.

She chose her material.

She claimed the smoky tendrils that constricted her.

She screamed, lashing her hands, tugging the serpents off like a woman tearing off chains.

The tendrils left her body, and Madori sucked in air. She leaped to her feet, lashing the tentacles of smoke forward like whips.

The magic crashed into Lari, wrapped around her, and knocked her down onto the stage.

Madori rose to her feet, snarling. She tried to cling to the magic, to tighten the smoke around Lari, to crush the girl and snap her ribs. But the magic vanished from her grasp like dreams from wakefulness. The smoke dissipated.

Lari lay on her back, moaning. Silence filled the lecture hall. When Madori looked at the rows of seats, she saw her quartet companions on their feet; Tam stood halfway down the stairs, mouth opening and closing silently, as if he had been rushing down to protect her.

An angry wheeze sounded behind her. Madori spun around and gasped.

She had seen Professor Atratus mad before, but not like this. His face flushed red, and sweat beaded on his bald head. His nostrils opened and closed as he breathed raggedly, and his fingers curled like talons.

Madori took a step back. The man's rabid glare seemed almost as powerful as Lari's magic.

"I did not allow you to do magic, mongrel," he hissed, each word labored.

Madori found her rage. She met his gaze. "I had to defend myself."

With a howl, Professor Atratus raised his hands. The smoke, which had dispersed, coalesced into dark ropes. The bonds wrapped around Madori's ankles, pinning her feet to the ground. More smoky ropes wrapped around her wrists, pinning her left arm to her side and tugging her right arm toward Atratus. She struggled and tried to break these magical bindings, to claim them too, but she could sense this magic was stronger than Lari's. She could not free herself.

Sneering, Atratus took a step closer toward her. His lips curled back to show his yellow teeth. "You will not perform magic in my class without my permission, mongrel. You will be punished now. Three lashes of my ruler upon your hand."

She tried to pull back, but she might as well have broken through iron chains. His ruler whistled through the air and cracked against her outstretched palm.

Madori bit down on a yelp.

He struck her again, and two weals rose against her palm. Her hand was still sore from holding the iron wishbone, and this punishment was like tossing oil onto dying embers. Tears budded in her eyes.

He swung his ruler a third time, and Madori nearly passed out from the pain, but she would not scream. When he released his magic, and the magical chains left her, she placed her wounded hand under her armpit. It tingled and burned, reminding her of the pain of holding the iron wishbone.

"Now return to your seat, half-breed," Atratus said. "Be thankful I only struck you three times. Next offense it will be thirty. To your seat! And after your classes this turn, you will report to the kitchens, where you will spend half a turn scrubbing pots and dishes. Understood?"

Madori nodded silently, not trusting herself to speak; she felt that if she tried to answer, she would either shout or cry. Holding her throbbing hand under her armpit, she climbed the stairs and returned to her seat. She could feel everyone's eyes upon her, especially Lari's.

CHAPTER THIRTEEN
A WHISPER FROM HOME

Her palm was still throbbing, three welts upon it, as Madori made her way down the corridor to her next class.

The rest of her quartet walked around her, forming a protective ring. Tam especially was fuming, his face red, his fists clenched at his sides.

"My father will hear of this," he said, barking out the words, as they moved down the columned corridor. "Who does that Atratus think he is? My parents donate to this university. Hundreds of books in the library are their gifts." He growled. "I'll get this Atratus sacked, I will, and I don't care what it takes."

"Tam, please," Madori whispered. "Lower your voice. It's all right."

Many other students were walking to and fro around them, not just first-years but older students too, clad in the lavender, gray, and orange robes denoting their seniority. The last thing Madori needed was for anyone to hear Tam's threats and report to Atratus; that would goad the old dog to new heights of fervor.

Neekeya too fumed. Her eyes were wide with rage, her teeth bared. "My father might not have donated to Teel, but he's a mighty lord and warrior, and his magic is far more powerful than Atratus's. He gave me a magical quill that can write curses to hurt anyone. I'm going to write a curse to knock Atratus's damn hands off!" She took the quill from her pocket and her expression became woeful. "I only need to learn how to use it. I think I might have broken it."

Madori doubted the "magical artifacts" Neekeya had received from her father—the quill, the ring, the sword, and dozens of others—had any magic at all. But at least Madori now knew: *I have magic within me.* Her hand still throbbed, and the humiliation still burned through her, but a hesitant smile tingled upon her lips.

I used magic. I defeated Lari.

As they walked down the hall, Madori raised her chin, letting that pride swell her chest. She knew she would face Lari again, and Madori vowed to study hard, to become stronger and stronger.

I came to Teel to learn healing, Madori thought, *but you, Lari, you will force me to become a warrior too. And you will rue your choice to make me an enemy.*

It took a while, but after exploring several corridors and chambers and making a few wrong turns, Madori's Motley finally found their next classroom—a sterile little chamber high up in Ostirina, the northwestern of Teel's four towers.

As Madori stepped inside with her friends, she breathed in deeply and her smile widened. It was finally time for the class she had awaited—Magical Healing.

A dozen other students were already here, seated at pale stone tables. Madori was relieved to see that Sunlit Purity was not attending this class. Of course Lari and her friends would have no use for healing magic; they seemed to care only for destruction. Madori sat down with her quartet at the last free table, opened her book, and caught a glimpse of her wounded hand. The welts were ugly and red and still hurt. Between them spread the faded scars from the iron wishbone.

"Students! Students, settle down."

The high, wavering voice drifted from the doorway. An instant later, Professor Yovan stepped into the chamber—the same professor who had supervised the battle with the wishbones, sending Torin a roast ham to atone for Madori's ruined hand. The elderly man's long, white beard rolled down to his feet, and his tufted eyebrows thrust out like the brims of hats. He seemed well into his eighties—even older than the bald, mustached Professor Fen, the teacher of Basic Principles. The greybeard reminded Madori of old Mayor Kerof, her great-grandfather, who had rocked her on his knee when she had been a girl. Dear old Grand Grand, as Madori called Kerof, had passed several years ago; old Professor Yovan, with his flowing beard and long, thin fingers, gave her the same sense of elder wisdom and grandfatherly love.

The students, already rather settled, turned their eyes toward the aged professor. Yovan made his way to his desk, slapped a hand against it, and announced, "Healing! Yes. Healing. Healing, healing healing . . . *Magical* healing, to be exact." He stroked his beard. "Magical Healing is about using magic to, well . . . heal." He cleared his throat. "And that is what I shall teach you!"

The students stared at him silently.

Seeming uncomfortable with the attention, Professor Yovan fumbled with the books, scrolls, and potions on his desk. "Who can tell me," he said, "how to heal the body using magic?"

It was nice, Madori thought, not to have Lari around to thrust up her hand at once. Hesitantly, glancing at her friends for encouragement, Madori raised her hand.

"Ah, yes!" said Professor Yovan. "You, little boy. What is your name?"

A few students giggled across the class.

Madori placed down her hand. "My name is Madori Greenmoat. And I'm a girl. Remember me from the Trial of Will?" She freed her two strands of long hair from behind her ears, letting them frame her face. With the rest of her hair cropped short and her body scrawny, she was often mistaken for a boy. "And . . . I'm not sure, but I'm guessing it has to do with the Three Basic Principles. Choosing your material—choosing the wound. Claiming your material—gaining control of the broken bone, injured flesh, or diseased tissue. And finally, changing the material—mending the wound."

Professor Yovan clapped his hands together, his face brightening. "Precisely, little boy!"

"Girl," she said.

He nodded emphatically. "You are most correct. However, reality of course is more complex. Any brute can magically shatter flesh. But to heal, ah! That requires the most innate, pure understanding of the body's structures. To injure is as easy as shattering a statue. To heal . . . that is to sculpt." He winked. "I use that metaphor every year. Rather proud of it."

The professor unrolled scrolls of human anatomy and launched into a lecture, describing the basic humors and energies that flowed throughout all living things. Madori found that, unlike with Professor Atratus, she could actually understand most of these words. Here was real magic, she thought—a force for goodness. Here was why she had come to Teel.

"Now," said Professor Yovan after an hour of speaking, "you will of course not be able to heal wounds for many months, maybe not for years. The effects of a mistake with such magic can be disastrous. When attempting to mend a bone, you could accidentally shatter every bone in the body. When attempting to withdraw poison from a wound, you could accidentally send the poison into the patient's heart. Many of you, throughout your studies at Teel, will learn to *harm*. Only the brightest among you will learn to *heal*. And so I demand from you, students: Do not attempt healing magic until your fourth year!"

But Madori was already summoning that power inside her—the power that had let her claim the smoky tendrils, let her change them to attack Lari.

"Madori, what are you doing?" Jitomi whispered at her side. He nudged her with his elbow. "You're not allowed to use magic."

But she ignored him. She closed her eyes and her lips whispered. Her nostrils flared as she claimed her material—not the welts upon her palm but the uninjured skin around them. Warmth filled her and tingled across her body as she changed her material— allowing her skin to push forward, erasing the wounds, pulling the injured flesh deep into her.

Gasps sounded around her.

Madori opened her eyes and stared at her hand.

The welts from Atratus's ruler were gone, leaving only pale scars.

Professor Yovan rushed over, eyes so wide Madori saw the white all around his irises.

"Little boy!" he said. "I told you! You may not practice healing magic. You— Oh my." He took her palm in his and examined the scars. "How old are these scars?"

"About ten seconds," she replied. "Professor Atratus struck me with his ruler only this morning. And I'm a girl."

Neekeya twisted in her seat, her necklace of crocodile teeth chinking. "It's true! Madori has magic—real magic!" She rummaged through her pocket and pulled out a lock of hair tied with a ribbon. "I have a magical lock of Healing Hair, and I tried to use it on Madori, but I think it only works on us Daenorians."

Professor Yovan clucked his tongue and patted Madori's hand. "Little boy—I mean, girl—you must obey me next time, and you must not heal without my permission—not even your own wounds. But . . ." His eyes watered and suddenly he was embracing her. "It's a delight to see such a naturally gifted healer. For sixty years I've been teaching here at Teel, and I've never seen a first year student heal a wound—let alone on her first day! You are a wonder."

Madori lowered her eyes.

"Thank you," she whispered. She could not speak any louder, and suddenly tears filled her eyes. For the first time in many turns, they were not tears of pain but of joy. Somebody appreciated her. Somebody thought she was a wonder. Perhaps Teel University was not the nightmare it had seemed but a place where she could learn, grow, become the woman she dreamed of being. Neekeya saw her tears and pulled Madori into an embrace, and Tam patted her healed hand.

After Magical Healing came Basic Principles again, followed by Magical History, then finally Magic and Sound—a class Madori had eagerly signed up for, teaching students to produce magical music. When the Teel Bells finally rang the end of the turn, Madori rubbed her shoulders, eager to return to her chamber for a solid sleep. Yet she sighed to remember Professor Atratus's punishment.

"I still have to report to the kitchens," she said to her friends. "Got to scrub some pots."

Tam sighed. "At least eat dinner with us first." He cringed. "We have to eat in the dining hall with hundreds of other students. Idar's beard, I'm not looking forward to that. Madori's Motley will stick out like monkeys at a banquet."

She smiled wanly. "I'm almost glad for my punishment. I think I prefer laboring in the kitchens than sitting in the dining hall. It's like polishing the armor instead of fighting in the battle." She bit her lip.

117

"I'll grab some food to eat while I work, and I'll meet you back at our chamber."

Leaving her companions, she made her way south of the library and cloister, down a path, and toward the dining hall. The building rose from a grassy sward, its walls columned, stairs leading up to its gates; it seemed a building as fine as the library or towers, topped with statues of birds and beasts. Students were gathering in a courtyard, lining up to enter and eat. Madori spotted Lari standing at their lead, holding a Radian flag; others of her order gathered around her.

Feeling relief that she had an excuse to skip dinner—her punishment was probably kinder than the meal—Madori skirted the building, leaving the main gates and heading toward a back door. No students stood in this little corner, and only a few geese ambled between the birches.

A sudden memory flashed through Madori: her mother standing in the window of their cottage at home, calling Madori home for dinner. Madori would be playing outside with Fairwool-by-Night's animals—a few stray dogs, geese like the ones here, maybe a duckling or two—covered in mud, her elbows scraped. Animals had always been her only friends. At first Madori would ignore her mother, but then the smell of the woman's cooking would waft on the wind, filling her nostrils: stewed chanterelle mushrooms, fried lanternfish, and spicy matsutake mushroom cakes—Elorian food, the food Madori loved.

I miss you so much, Mother, she thought, heading toward the kitchens. *I wish I could be eating with you now at home.*

She opened the back door and stepped into the kitchens. She found a hallway lined with several doorways. Through one doorway she saw a chamber full of cooking fires, and the scents of meats, stews, breads, and pies filled her nostrils. Her mouth watered. Cooks dressed in white tended to the meals—mixing stews that bubbled in cauldrons, turning spits of roasting pigs, and pulling bread rolls from ovens. Reluctantly, Madori kept walking until she reached the dish washing room and stepped inside.

Three walls here were built of bricks. Instead of a fourth wall rose many shelves like oversized window shutters, each shelf topped high with dirty dishes. Between the shelves, Madori could peer into the dining hall where a thousand students were eating. Every moment another student, belly full, stepped forward to place a dirty plate and cutlery upon a shelf. A stone aqueduct ran through the chamber, flowing with water; it was about the size of a horse's trough. Several students stood around the canal, scrubbing dishes. All seemed dejected, and all bore welts upon their palms—other victims of Atratus's wrath.

"Another prisoner!" announced one of the workers, a tall boy with a thick Verilish accent. Madori had seen Verilish traders before—burly men from the northern pine forests, thick of beards, clad in fur pelts, warriors who prided themselves on strength. She guessed that for a son of Verilon, scrubbing dishes like a woman was the ultimate insult.

Madori nodded. "Let's get this over with. I'm tired and want to go back to my chamber."

Another washer—this one a petite girl with black hair—laughed. She spoke with the accent of Eseer, a desert kingdom far in the south. "There are hundreds of plates still to wash, and hundreds of students are still eating. We'll be lucky to leave before next turn."

Sighing, Madori turned to look at the shelves of plates. Indeed, students kept walking by, adding more dishes to the piles; it looks like many hours of work. When she returned her eyes to the aqueduct, she realized that all the scrubbers—punished students—were foreigners. It seemed Atratus was loath to punish his fellow Magerians.

Madori bit her lip and got to work.

She dunked dish after dish into the flowing water, scrubbing it with a rag and soap. But soon the shelves threatened to collapse; at first only the fastest eaters had left their plates to clean, but now hundreds of plates were rising in a sticky, dirty mess.

"If we break one, Atratus will know," said the tall boy. "He's got magical eyes all over the place. My brother broke a dish here last year; Atratus nearly tore off his hand, he beat him so hard with his ruler."

Madori winced, scanning the chamber for magical eyes, imagining eyeballs moving in the walls themselves. She saw nothing but she wouldn't put such magic past Atratus; she winced to remember how his smoky ropes had bound her. She scrubbed faster, rushing back and forth between the shelves and the water. Before long, with hundreds of students placing down their dishes, Madori no longer bothered scrubbing one at a time. She rushed back and forth, towers of dishes in her arms, placing the clean ones upon trays for another student to whisk outside.

"Got to go faster!" said the boy. "Shelves running out of space."

Madori glanced at the shelves to see a pile of plates tilt. She rushed forward and caught three plates just as they fell. Wincing, she ran with them to the aqueduct, then back again. When she hurried to the water with yet another pile of plates, she slipped in a puddle, wobbled for a second, thought she could steady the structure . . . then saw one plate fall toward the ground.

The Eseerian girl leaped forward and caught it before it could shatter.

"Be more careful!" the girl whispered, face pale and eyes wide. "He'll know. By the great god Amaran, he'll know. He is a demon."

Heart lashing, Madori kept working. Her eyes stung, and soap bubbles filled the air, and she kept moving faster and faster, and she knew she couldn't keep up. They were only several dish washers, and the mountain of plates kept growing.

She forced herself to sing as she scrubbed, her voice low, her lips tight, her eyes burning. She sang "Darkness Falls," the song from her trials, a song of home—a song to remember a better place, a place of peace, of love. It was a song her mother used to sing her—a mother Madori had always fought with, a mother Madori could not wait to hug and kiss again.

I'm so sorry, Mother. I'm so sorry I always yelled at you for making me wash dishes at home. She laughed through her tears. *What I wouldn't give to be washing dishes at home now!*

She turned back toward the shelves, intending to grab another batch, when she saw two pretty blue eyes staring from the dining hall beyond.

"Lari," she hissed.

Past the stacks of plates, Madori couldn't see more than her enemy's eyes, but those eyes were smiling.

With a clatter, mountains of plates—a hundred or more—tilted on the shelves. Madori glimpsed Lari's hands shoving them forward, and she heard a cold laugh, before the plates all came crashing down.

Madori winced and leaped back, knowing that Atratus would know, that he'd lash her in a fury.

She waited for the crash of a hundred breaking plates but heard no sound. She realized she had closed her eyes, and she peeked . . . and gasped.

The plates were hovering in midair.

"Leave this place, Lari Serin!" rose a voice from behind Madori. "Leave or these plates will drive into your face."

With the plates hovering off the shelf, Madori now had a full view of Lari, who stood with her friends in the dining hall. The girl sneered but spun on her heel and marched off.

Madori too spun around—toward the back of the kitchen. Jitomi stood at the doorway, holding his hands forward, sweat on his brow. He managed to give Madori a tight smile.

"I think," he said, "I finally figure out levitation."

If she weren't worried about the plates crashing down, she'd have leaped toward the Elorian boy and kissed him.

Two more students stepped into the room—Tam and Neekeya—both grinning.

"We came to help!" said Neekeya. She looked around at all the dishes and winced. "I wish I had my magical dish scrubber here. My parents had one back at home. It would wash all the dishes itself, floating in the air; you just had to very lightly hold the handle to guide it."

Tam rolled his eyes and stepped around the Daenorian girl. "Well, we don't have magical scrubbers, but we have a bunch of hands and about a million dishes to wash." He reached toward the floating ones which Jitomi still kept magically suspended. "Now let's help the little billy goat."

Madori had expected to spend at least half a turn here, nearly going mad, but with her quartet's help, they were able to finish scrubbing everything within a couple hours. When their work was finally done, Madori didn't even want to return to her chamber; she wanted to plop down right here in the kitchens and sleep for turns on end. After staying up studying last half-turn, she was wearier than she'd ever been. Her friends had to practically drag her out of the kitchens, across the cloister, and toward the first years' dormitory.

The arcade—a colonnade on one side, a wall of doors on the other—was empty. The bedroom doors were all closed. Madori shuffled her feet, barely able to keep her eyes open, walking among her quartet. When they reached their door, she yawned and stepped inside, ready to collapse.

Instead she froze and stared.

At her side, Neekeya yelped and dropped the books she held. "What—" the swamp girl muttered. "What happened—?"

"Lari happened," Madori said.

Their books all lay torn on the floor, the pages scattered like autumn leaves. Their mementos from home—figurines, dolls, paintings—lay smashed. Somebody had drawn a large Radian symbol upon the wall in blood, and more blood stained Madori's bed; the coppery smell invaded her nostrils. The smell of rotten meat wafted too, and Madori nearly gagged.

A note lay upon her pillow. Moving carefully between the broken books and figurines, she approached her bed and lifted the note. Upon it appeared in neat handwriting the words: "Radian rises. Mongrels will be butchered like pigs."

Neekeya came to stand beside her. She grimaced and covered her mouth. "It stinks." She doubled over as if about to gag, then gasped and scampered backwards. Eyes wide, she yelped and pointed under the bed.

Madori lowered her gaze. When she knelt, she saw it too. She reached under the bed and pulled it out: a severed pig's head.

Tam made a queasy sound and turned green, and even Jitomi looked ill.

Madori placed down the head, turned around, and walked outside into the hallway.

"Madori, where are you going?" Tam said, hurrying after her. "The bells have rung. We're not allowed outside our chambers."

She kept walking, not turning to look back. "Stay behind. Stay safe and lock the door."

Neekeya raced up beside her, eyes wide. "You're not going to confront Lari, are you? Because if you are, I'm going with you. I'll fight at your side."

"No." Madori shook her head. "I will not fight Lari. That's what she wants. That's what she's waiting for—to lure us into a battle, maybe a trap. I'm going straight to Headmistress Egeria and putting an end to this." She turned around to face her friends; the hallway was empty around them, all the other students asleep in their chambers. "Go back. Clean up. Do not go outside into the hall; it's dangerous."

She left them there, heading between two columns into the courtyard.

Clouds hid the never-sinking sun of Timandra, and a drizzle fell. Madori's two strands of long, black hair stuck to her cheeks, while the cropped hair on her back and sides caught the raindrops like cobwebs catching dew. She made her way under the elm tree, across the grass, and toward the southeastern tower—the home of the headmistress. She found herself facing a brick archway, its keystone engraved with two scrolls, the sigil of Teel University. When she tried the towering oak doors, she found them unlocked; they slid open on oiled hinges.

I will find the headmistress, and I will tell her everything, Madori thought, stepping inside. She felt too hollow for emotion; no fear or rage filled her, unless these emotions lurked too deep for her to feel. She was hurt too badly, she had suffered too much; all she felt now was detached determination. *I will talk about my famous parents if I must, or I will talk about my friendship with King Camlin and Queen Linee. Lari isn't the only student here with lofty connections.* She walked down a hall, her clothes dripping, and tightened her lips. *I will end this.*

She rounded a corner, intending to stomp up the tower staircase, and found herself face-to-face with Professor Atratus.

Madori froze.

At once she raised her hands, sucking in breath, prepared to defend herself. Her heart leaped into a gallop.

He stared at her, looming like a vulture over prey, a foot taller than her. His eyes blazed and his nostrils flared, the hairs inside twitching. He bared his teeth.

"What," he spoke in a strained voice, "are you doing outside of your chamber after hours, mongrel?"

She refused to back down. She was half his size, a third his age, and as lowly as a worm compared to his power, but she faced him sternly.

"Move aside, Professor Atratus," she said. "I'm here to speak to the headmistress."

He raised his fist; it trembled, his knuckles white with strain. "Students are not to roam the university after hours. I thought that my punishments might have set on your the right path, but I see that you mongrels are truly rabid beasts."

His hand lashed out and struck her cheek. Before she could leap back, he slapped her again, a blow to the second cheek, rattling her jaw. She stood still, too shocked to react. She wanted to attack him. She wanted to cry, to scream, to run, to shout for the headmistress, but she could only stand frozen, and she cursed herself for her paralysis.

Atratus spat out spittle as he spoke, shaking with rage. "Since you obviously hate your chamber so much, you will sleep this half-turn outside in the rain." He grabbed her wrist and began tugging her down the hall. They burst outside into the cloister, the rain pattering against them. "You will remain standing outside until next turn, and if I ever catch you wandering again, I will show you no more mercy."

She tried to free herself from his grasp, but he was too strong. He dragged her across the cloister, down a gallery, past the library and dining hall, and finally toward a craggy wall. They stepped through an archway, emerging into a grove of elms and birches outside the university grounds. It was a cold, wet place in the shadows of the mountains, overrun with brush, a place forbidden to students. Atratus finally stopped walking behind a twisting oak with a trunk like a face. There he released her wrist.

She tried to run, to barrel past him. She knew that if she could only reach the headmistress, she'd have a sympathetic ear. But her legs would not budge. When she looked down, she found her feet sunken in the mud down to her ankles. Smoky tendrils wrapped around her legs, keeping her pinned in place.

"Atratus!" she began to scream when more smoke invaded her mouth, muffling her words.

"Spend a few hours outside the university," he said. "And think very carefully if you want to return. If I were you, when the spell is broken, I would wander deep into the forest, and I would live like the feral beast that you are. I cannot officially banish you, mongrel, not yet. But know this." He pointed a shaky finger at her. "If you do return, you will suffer. I will make you suffer greatly."

He glared at her and lightning flashed, sparking against his hunched form and hooked nose, gleaming in his eyes like white fire. He spat and turned to leave. He vanished back into the university, leaving her outside in the rain.

She could not move. She could not scream. She could only breathe through her nostrils, and lightning crashed again, hitting a nearby tree. Throughout the storm, she could hear the sounds of her friends calling for her, but she knew they wouldn't find her, not out there.

It was hours before the spell broke, freeing her legs and releasing the smoke in her mouth. She fell to her knees in the mud and took a ragged breath. She tilted over, lay on her back, and gazed up at the sky. The last clouds were dispersing, and a single beam of light fell upon her. A rainbow glimmered for just a few heartbeats before fading away.

Tears streamed down Madori's cheeks.

What do I do? Do I flee Teel? Do I try to make my way home?

She raised her head and looked at the university walls. The bells were ringing; a new turn of classes was beginning.

"I can't return," she whispered to herself, trembling in the mud, weary and weak and so afraid. "Lari would attack me, or Atratus would, and . . ." She covered her eyes. "I can't do this, Father. I can't, Mother. I'm not strong like you two are."

She closed her eyes.

She couldn't do this.

A faint hint of a caress, like a falling feather, tingled her hand.

Madori opened her eyes, and there she saw it, resting on her hand—a duskmoth.

She had seen duskmoths back home at Fairwool-by-Night; they were denizens of the borderlands, of the twilit strip that separated day from night. The animal was shaped like Mythimna, this world they called Moth, one wing white and the other black. A creature like the one tattooed onto her wrist. A creature like her, torn between day and night.

"What are you doing here?" she whispered. "So far from home . . ."

It twitched its feathery antennae. Perhaps, she thought, it was asking her the same question. Or perhaps it had come to comfort her, to remind her she wasn't alone. It seemed to meet her eyes, and she gently caressed its downy body.

It took flight, rising in spirals, and she watched as it ascended into the blue sky, and tears streamed down her cheeks. Lying in the mud, she reached up to it.

"Goodbye, friend. Be brave up there."

Trembling, her cheeks wet, she forced herself to take a deep breath.

Another.

Again.

Her father's words filled her, as warm and comforting as mulled wine: *To survive, you only have to breathe the next breath.*

"But how can I?" she whispered. "How can I even breathe when their magic can suffocate me?"

She saw her parents again in her mind. Her father's face was humble and kind, his eyes warm—one eye green, the other black, eyes torn between day and night like she was. She saw her mother too. Koyee's face was paler and sterner, but her eyes were just as loving, large Elorian eyes like Madori herself had. In her mind, they both embraced her, enveloping her with love.

"You fought a great war," she whispered to them. "Perhaps I don't face fleets of warships, armies of knights, or great battles like you did. But I'm fighting my own war here, a personal war, and one I'll need all your strength and wisdom for." She knuckled her eyes. "I promise you, my parents, I will fight. I will win."

She rose to her feet. Her knees shook but she took another deep breath, steeling herself.

"I'm like a duskmoth," she said. "I'm torn between day and night, and I'm far from home. But I will fly."

She walked back to the university, wet, muddy, afraid, and more determined than ever.

CHAPTER FOURTEEN
BLOOD AT HORNSFORD BRIDGE

They rode across the wilderness, two men in a horse-drawn cart, and beheld the might and terror of the Radian menace.

"By Idar's flea-bitten bottom," Torin cursed and tugged the reins, halting Hayseed. The nag snorted and pawed the earth.

Sitting beside him, Cam smiled bitterly. "I told you it was big."

Torin grimaced. "The Palace of Kingswall is big. The fortress my wife is building is big. This?" He gestured ahead. "This isn't a big fortress, my friend. This is more like a city."

Hayseed sidestepped and nickered, and the cart swayed. The slender king clutched his seat and nodded. "Aye, a city of nothing but soldiers bred for hatred."

Sunmotte Citadel rose upon a hill, surrounded by a circular moat, farmlands, and valleys. Behind the water soared the castle wall, topped with battlements, archers, and Radian banners. Towers rose at regular intervals along the wall, each a palace unto itself. Behind the battlements peered the tops of more towers and keeps—a complex so large Torin thought it could rival all of Kingswall. As if the soaring battlements didn't sufficiently unnerve him, he saw many troops mustering in the fields outside the citadel—ten thousand or more soldiers stood there, armed with spears and swords.

Hayseed whinnied. Torin stepped out of the cart and stroked the old nag, seeking to comfort himself as much as her.

"Serin isn't playing games here, my friend," he said to Cam. "This isn't just the fortress of a lord. This isn't just an army to guard his home. He's preparing for war."

The king nodded grimly. He too stepped out of the cart, shook his legs, and pointed northeast. "And our homeland lies just a couple miles away."

Torin followed his friend's gaze. Across grassy fields flowed the Red River, the rushing border between this kingdom of Mageria and their homeland of Arden. The ancient Hornsford Bridge spanned the water, half-a-mile long, built of ancient bricks. A fortified gatehouse rose at each side. The Magerian gatehouse was large as a castle, its two towers displaying the banners of Radianism—a sun eclipsing the moon—alongside the banners of Mageria—a buffalo upon a red field. Across the bridge, the Ardish gatehouse was smaller—a single, humble tower—its battlements displaying Arden's sigil, a black raven upon a golden field. Beyond the gatehouse rolled Arden's countryside, bereft of its own citadel or army. An empty land. A vulnerable land.

"Camlin, old boy," Torin said, "we're facing an armored knight with a bread knife."

Cam sighed. "A bread knife? I'd settle for a bread knife." He gestured toward the lonely guard tower on the Ardish side of the bridge. "That's more like a wooden spoon. Maybe even a napkin."

Torin grunted. "We move forces here. As soon as we reach Kingswall, we muster men. We send them west."

"What men?" Cam rubbed his temples. "Torin, my dear, it seems half the lords in my kingdom are loyal to Serin; they're raising his banners and receiving quite a bit of his gold. And those lords who *are* loyal to my throne? They wax poetic of an end to war, of peace on earth, of never more lifting arms and watching Moth bleed."

Torin grumbled. "Moth will bleed whether they want it or not. And they won't be there to staunch the wound." He narrowed his eyes. "Let's go home, Cam, but I'm not crossing that bridge. Not if you pay me with my own fortress. We ride south. We'll cross the river at Reedford; that's where Madori and I crossed over."

Cam raised an eyebrow. "Reedford? But my dear lad, Reedford is boring." He gestured ahead and grinned. "Here we get to inspect Serin's forces up close." He tugged at his rough, woolen cloak and scratched his stubbly cheeks. "We're no King Camlin and Sir Greenmoat here. We're simply two weary travelers seeking a way home." He climbed back into the cart. "Come on, Tor old boy, it'll be an adventure. Like in the old days."

Torin grumbled. "The old days weren't an adventure; they were a bloody nightmare." He rubbed his stiff neck. "And we were younger."

Yet he too climbed into the cart, and they began to move again.

The bridge still lay a couple miles away, and Hayseed was a slow old horse. Cam had wanted to buy two quick, sure-footed coursers at Teelshire; he had sold his own old horse at the town, as the beast had been too weary for a quick ride back. But Torin had refused. How could he sell Hayseed, his daughter's old friend? Madori was gone for years; the least Torin could do was keep her favorite horse—even if it meant the journey home would take twice as long.

He sighed. The journey home? No. He was perhaps returning to Arden, his kingdom, but not to his home. Not to Fairwool-by-Night, and not to his wife.

"The first time I traveled to Kingswall," he said softly, "I went there with Bailey to stop a war. Now we travel there to raise an army."

Cam nodded as the cart bumped down the pebbly road. "The two actions are not contradictory. We raise an army to stop a war. An army along your borders can bring peace more readily than the hearts of men. Hearts cannot be trusted; steel can be."

Torin raised an eyebrow. "Look at you, King Camlin. You almost sound like a military leader. Where is the young boy who fought for peace?"

"He grew up." Cam grunted and scratched his chin. "Idealism was fine when we were youths, just kids in a war the adults led. But we're the adults now. Idar's Warts, Torin. I actually have gray hairs now, do you believe it? I pluck them out, but they just grow back, and perhaps they bring me some wisdom. Let Tam and Madori be the new preachers for peace. Let us adults prepare for war."

Torin scratched his temple; he had been finding a few white hairs there himself. "I envy Koyee. She's always had white hair. Doesn't have to worry about plucking a thing."

Cam barked out a laugh. "The woman never ages anyway. You and I . . . we're halfway through our thirties already, and we're starting to show it." He reached over to pat Torin's hint of a paunch. "But that wife of yours; she still looks like a youth. People might think she's your daughter."

"I already have one daughter, and she causes enough trouble herself." He lowered his head, sudden pain overtaking him. "Damn it, Cam. Don't talk about our age. Not because I'm scared of growing old. But because—Idar damn it—I wish they could have grown old with us." He let out a sigh that sounded dangerously close to a sob. "That old loaf of bread and that braided madwoman. They should have been here with us now."

Cam nodded sadly, but suddenly a smile spread across his face. "Hem would probably be even larger at our age; he wouldn't fit on this cart, that's for sure."

Torin smiled to remember the old baker's boy. "He could *pull* the cart, that one. And Bailey, well . . . I bet you she'd insist that she's a true warrior and could run the whole way. Scratch that; she'd charge toward Sunmotte Citadel and take on Serin's army single-handed."

"You don't think she'd have mellowed with age?" Cam raised his eyebrows. "We've mellowed."

Torin shook his head. "She'd be as crazy as always. I miss her. I miss them both. It's funny, isn't it? They say time heals all wounds. What a contemptible lie."

As they drew closer to the bridge in the northeast, they were also drawing closer to the massive fort in the northwest. Serin's army stood only a mile away now, the sun glinting on thousands of spears. Every soldier, it seemed, wore a full suit of plate armor; back in Arden, only knights wore the expensive armor, while common soldiers wore the less efficient—but cheaper—chain mail or leather armor. The Radians not only had many horses but chariots too, their wheels scythed. Smaller than Torin's cart and much swifter, several of the vehicles raced around the field, their riders shooting at targets with bows. Behind these drilling forces, the walls of the fortress loomed taller than palaces, brimming with many troops.

Torin and Cam fell silent. The air felt too hot, too thick; Torin could barely breathe it. He cursed Cam for convincing him to take this route.

"They'll stop us," he whispered. The soldiers were still distant, but Torin couldn't speak any louder. "They'll send riders to the road. They'll think us spies."

"We *are* spies," Cam said. "Sort of. But no, they won't stop us. That bridge there—costs an entire silver coin to cross. How do you think Serin pays for all that fine armor, those chariots, those high walls?" He patted his purse. "Bridge tolls."

"Bridge trolls?"

Cam groaned. "You're either losing your hearing or developing a penchant for bad jokes. Both are worse signs of aging than white hairs or paunches."

Perhaps the Shepherd King was right; no soldiers appeared to stop their passage down the pebbly road toward the bridge, and if the armies saw them, they gave no sign of it. Before long the cart turned eastward, leaving Sunmotte Citadel behind. They trundled toward the river. An arched gateway led onto the bridge, framed by two guard towers, each large enough that, removed and placed upon a hill, it could have proudly housed a lord. Several soldiers stood upon the towers, holding crossbows, while several more stood beneath the archway.

Torin tugged his hood low over his head. Cam did the same. Hunched forward, clad in old wool, they hopefully looked like nothing more than two weary, common travelers. The guards at the gate stood sternly, clad in black plate armor, their faces hidden behind their visors. Their breastplates bore two sigils—the buffalo of Mageria on one side, Radian's eclipse on the other.

"Halt!" said one, voice echoing and metallic inside his helm, and held out his hand. "Stop for inspection."

Torin tugged the reins, and old Hayseed slowed to a halt, snorting. Several soldiers marched forward, their plate armor so well-fitting and well-oiled it barely made a sound. Moving with the urgency of starving men seeking food, they began to inspect the cart—lifting blankets, rummaging through packs, and sniffing at jugs of water.

"We're only two simple travelers returning home," Torin said, affecting a lowborn accent. "A friend of ours—we took him to a see a healer in Teelshire. Aye, they got real healers there, not like back home—*magical* healers, they got at Teelshire." He shook his head and tsked. "Still, all in vain. Our friend died on the road before we could even reach Teelshire; all we could do when we got there is bury him.

He was a dear friend, but I told him, I did, if he kept drinking spirits every morning and night, he'd soon come down with—"

"Silence," spat out a soldier. "We have no patience for peasant tales. Why didn't we see you cross from Arden? I never forget a face."

Torin sighed inwardly. A couple decades ago, in the war, he'd have charged at these soldiers with sword and shield, his friends at his side. He wasn't sure if that meant he was wiser or less brave; perhaps a bit of both.

"We crossed down south at Reedford," Torin said. "They got a nice inn there, they do. The smoothest ale you could taste. Do you like ale, friend? We got three casks in the back; feel free to take the small one for your troubles."

One of the soldiers stepped toward Torin and lifted his visor, revealing a hard, frowning face. The man's eyes narrowed. "Look at me," he demanded.

Torin gave the soldier a quick glance from under his hood. He held out a silver coin. "Here we are, our bridge toll, and that's real Arish silver, it is. Bite it if you like." Torin reached for his riding crop. "Now we hate to take up your time, so we'll just—"

Before Torin could tap his horse, the soldier grabbed Torin's wrist, stopping the crop.

"Wait a moment." The soldier leaned in, and his eyes widened. "I know you. One green eye, one black! We met in battle in the war. Torin Greenmoat, you are! Lord Serin said you might be passing here. He commanded us to bring you to him. You'll have to come with us."

The other soldiers—there were four of them—heard and stepped closer. Cam winced but Torin forced himself to laugh.

"Aye, I get that all the time. I always curse my eyes. Everywhere I go it's Terin Greenboat, Terin Greenboat—whoever that is. It makes a man weary. I—" He jerked his hand free and swung his crop. "Hayseed, go!"

As the horse burst into a gallop, tugging the cart onto the bridge, Torin grabbed the katana he kept hidden behind his feet—the same sword he would wield in the war. He drew the blade with a single, fluid movement and swung it across the cart's side. It clanged into a soldier's helmet, knocking the man back. Cam drew and swung his own hidden blade, knocking back another man, while a third soldier leaped away from Hayseed's hooves.

For two or three heartbeats, they raced unopposed upon the bridge.

Then that old sound Torin remembered and hated filled the air. Whistling arrows.

He ducked and pulled Cam down too. Arrows whistled above them, and one slammed into the cart inches away from Torin. Hayseed whinnied and kept running, her fear driving her.

"Now this is more like the old days!" Cam shouted, then winced and ducked lower as an arrow grazed his head, slicing a lock of hair.

The cart bounced madly. The river flowed at their sides, and the distant bank seemed miles away. When the cart hit a crack in the bridge, it bolted into the air, and Torin winced when they slammed back down. A cask of ale fell from the cart, and Torin spun around to see it roll and shatter, spilling its contents. Several soldiers were running across the bridge, slow in their armor; one slipped in the ale and crashed down.

For an instant hope leaped in Torin; they would make it across the bridge! But when he heard the hooves beating and the horns blowing, his heart sank down to his belly. He watched, grimacing, as a dozen Radian riders galloped onto the bridge, pointing lances.

"Hayseed, go, girl!" Cam was shouting.

Torin, meanwhile, climbed from his seat into the back of the cart. An arrow whistled, and he winced as it slammed into another cask of ale. He shoved, sending the cask tumbling down. A rider tried to dodge the rolling barrel but was too slow; his horse slammed into the obstacle and fell. Torin ducked, hiding behind more supplies as arrows flew. He shoved again, knocking down bundles of firewood; a horse entangled in the rolling logs and crashed down.

When Torin glanced back eastward, he saw that they had only crossed half the bridge. The remaining riders were gaining on them. Visors hid the Radians' faces, and their lances rose, ready to thrust.

Torin raised his sword, prepared to fight as best he could. But rather than charge from behind, the horses raced around the cart and came to block its passage. Hayseed whinnied and bucked, and the cart halted so suddenly it almost tilted over.

A ring of riders surrounded the cart, lances pointed inward like the teeth of a lamprey. The sunlight blazed against the Radian emblems upon the soldiers' breastplates and shields.

"Torin Greenmoat," said one rider, the tallest among them. He raised his visor, revealing the stony brow, haughty blue eyes, and strong jaw of Lord Serin. "Hello again. And . . . I do believe this is Camlin of Arden, the Shepherd King."

Sword raised, Torin nodded at the lord. "Hello again, cousin." He turned to glance at Cam and spoke in Qaelish, a language of the night they both had learned in the war. "The rider to my left—the shorter one?"

Cam nodded and spoke in Qaelish too. "After you."

Torin didn't waste another instant. He leaped from the cart, katana swinging, and lunged toward the knight. Cam leaped behind them. The horse bucked. The knight's lance thrust, and Torin's katana knocked it aside. Cam lashed his own blade, driving the horse back.

The two friends raced around the rider, free from the encircling enemy, and ran toward the bridge's ledge.

"Stop them!" rose a voice behind.

A crossbow thrummed and the quarrel whizzed by Torin's ear. He ran with Cam, arms pumping.

They reached the bridge's ledge and kicked off. Torin's heart hammered and his legs still ran in the air. They plunged down toward the rushing water, crossbow quarrels flying above them.

"Yes, definitely like the old days!" Cam shouted at his side.

With a a great splash of icy water, they crashed into the river.

They sank, kicking and swimming underwater. Torin's eyes stung and he kicked off his boots, propelling himself eastward—at least he hoped it was eastward. Arrows pierced the water around him, and one grazed his calf. Blood rose like dancing red demons.

Yes, I don't miss the old days, he thought as they swam, arrows filling the water like raindrops cutting through mist.

CHAPTER FIFTEEN
SEEKING MAGIC

She walked through the library of Teel like a woman walking through a temple.

"Here is my temple," she whispered. "Here is my solitude, my peace, the wisdom I seek."

She took a deep breath and smiled. She stepped forward slowly, head tilted back, her fingers tingling at her sides.

Madori had spent many hours of her childhood in the library of Fairwool-by-Night, a hall cluttered with creaky shelves, dusty books, and piles of scrolls. That had been a place like a womb, warm, comfortable, worn in, the book spines smoothed by many fingers, the air rich with the scent of papyrus and parchment. But here . . . here in the great Teel Library she found a different world. This was no womb; it was a palace. Porphyry columns rose several stories tall, their capitols shaped as Mageria's buffaloes, the beasts supporting a vaulted ceiling painted with scenes of sunbursts, pink clouds, and birds of all kinds. Marble statues stood every few feet, depicting the ancient gods of Riyona, their nude bodies paragons of beauty. Oil paintings of landscapes and ancient battles—the canvases as large as sails—covered the walls. Giltwood tables and upholstered chairs, themselves masterpieces, supported silver counter-square boards with jeweled pieces.

But more than any painting or statue, the books filled Madori's heart with warmth like mulled wine.

Thousands of books stood upon the shelves—*tens* of thousands, maybe millions. Some books were great works of art, their spines jeweled, their leather covers engraved with landscapes. Some books had jeweled covers of silver and gold, others covers of olive wood engraved with animals. Other books were mere bundles of parchment tied together with string. Some were great codices, three feet tall; other books were so small Madori could have hid them in her pocket.

She walked around in wonder, her smile growing, her head tilted back to take it all in.

"Books," she whispered. Portals to other worlds. Keepers of secrets. Chests of wisdom. Madori had seen the stars of the night, the white towers of Kingswall, and the pagodas of Qaelin, but to her books were the greatest wonders in Moth. They were more than objects; they were magic. Simple pages, that was all—pages with ink—and yet each contained a life, an entire world, a wisdom from beyond the ages.

As she walked here between the shelves, suddenly her troubles outside—Lari's aggression, Atratus's hatred, her troubles with this or that spell—seemed trivial. Here she felt safe, a star floating in a sky of light.

She pulled down a great, heavy book as long as her arm; inside she found ancient drawings of healing herbs. She spent a while reading an ancient codex with a red leather cover—a bestiary detailing all the animals of the world, from the humble shrew to the mighty elephant. For an hour, she read stories of adventure, the old heroes of Riyona battling sea serpents, cyclops, and dragons. She read a small book of ancient poetry—words two thousand years old—and shed tears for a pair of lovers whose song echoed through the ages.

The others have a home, Madori thought. Neekeya had the swamps of Daenor, Tam was from a great city of white towers, and Jitomi was from an island in the night. Madori caressed a pile of books on the table before her. *This is my home—anywhere among books. My home is the world of words.*

When she finally stepped outside the library and stood under the sky, she inhaled deeply and smiled. A new strength filled her, a tranquility like the sea after a storm. Whenever troubled, she knew she could return to this place, to her anchor.

"Madori!" The voice rose ahead, and Neekeya came racing toward her, panting. "Madori, where have you been? I've been looking all over for you. Professor Yovan said we have a test tomorrow, and you're the only one who understands healing magic." She grabbed Madori's hand and tugged her. "Come on! Back to our chamber. Tam cut his finger *on purpose* and tried to heal himself, but he can't, and Jitomi is laughing so hard I think he'll die. Quickly!"

Madori allowed herself to be dragged away. She looked back once, saw the library dome gleaming in the sunlight, and smiled silently.

* * * * *

The bells had rung, the turn was over, and most students and professors slept in their chambers, but Neekeya would not leave the workshop, not until she found a hint of magic.

"What about this one?" she said, placing her pewter mug upon the table. "It's a magical mug. My father said that you can drink and drink from it forever, and it'll never be empty. I tried it, and it doesn't work for me, but I think we just need to remove a little hex clinging to it, and—"

"Neekeya, please," said Professor Rushavel, his brow creased with weariness. His orange mutton chops, normally bristly like the cheeks of an orangutan, drooped like empty wine skins. "The turn is over. Return to your chamber to sleep, child. You must be weary."

Neekeya shook her head vehemently, her hair swaying and her necklace of crocodile teeth chinking. "I'm not! I'm wide awake! What about this one?" She took out a smooth river stone and placed it on the table. "This one is definitely magic. My father says if you add it to a pot of boiling water, the water will magically turn into soup. It sort of works for me, but I have to always add potatoes and carrots and leeks, so I think if you can just test it maybe, you know, with a spell to detect magic, we can—" She blinked and nudged the old man. "Professor Rushavel, wake up!"

The professor's eyes had closed, and he almost slipped off his seat. He woke with a snort and blinked a few times. His red, bulbous nose twitched as he sucked in air. "Yes, yes." He cleared his throat. "Perhaps next turn, child. Perhaps?"

Neekeya groaned so loudly it blew back a lock of her hair. She looked around her at the workshop. So many magical artifacts! They covered the shelves, the tables, even many of the chairs: figurines of animals that moved at the corner of your eye; horns that played any tune you just thought of; seashells that sounded like the sea, complete with seagull cries and the songs of sailors; model ships in bottles whose sails billowed and oars stroked; and a thousand others. Professor Rushavel himself had made many of these items. How could it be that none of Neekeya's own artifacts—and she had brought dozens from Daenor—wouldn't work?

"But my father told me these artifacts are magic," Neekeya said. "You have to help me fix them. I— Professor Rushavel?" She nudged him again. "Professor!"

But the old man was sound asleep, his cheek resting against his fist. His mutton chops rose and fell with every breath. When Neekeya nudged him, he only slumped down onto the table, his lips fluttering as he snored.

She sighed.

After a few more attempts, she gave up on waking the old man, wishing she had brought her magical snuffbox from Daenor, the one that could rouse a man from any sleep of weariness or wounds. She stuffed her artifacts—the mug, the stone, the ring of power, and two dozen others—back into her pack. With a sigh, she left the workshop.

She wandered across the university grounds, moving down columned galleries, along grassy courtyards, and through gardens full of statues and fountains. The halls and towers of the university rose all around, their bricks golden in the sunlight, their steeples so high Neekeya felt dizzy to look upon them. The library loomed to her right, a great dome rising into the sky. The first autumn leaves were scuttling along the grass and porticoes of Teel. With the hour so late, most of Teel University was deserted, the professors and students sound asleep. Only birds, squirrels, and an occasional lizard kept Neekeya company as she walked through the sunlit grounds, for which she was thankful. Animals were her friends, better than most humans here at Teel.

She sighed. "I'm like an animal myself to most of them," she whispered, and tears stung her eyes. Nobody outside her quartet ever spoke to her. Whenever Neekeya moved through a busy crowd—at the dining hall, in the cloister, or even the library—students moved aside, pointing, whispering, even laughing.

Neekeya paused by a pool of clear water in a garden. She knelt beside a statue of a winged cat, gazing into the pool.

"Who am I?" she whispered, looking at her reflection. "Who am I to them?"

She saw the same girl she had always been, a girl she had been proud to be. Her skin rich brown, her eyes large and black, her lips prone to smile, her smooth hair just long enough to fall past her chin. She looked at her crocodile tooth necklace, at the scale armor she always wore beneath her school robes, and at her magical bracelets of bronzed coffee beans.

"You are the most beautiful, talented, magical girl in the world," her father would tell her, muss her hair, and kiss her cheek. "You make me proud, and you are a great warrior."

He was a great warrior too, a lord of Daenor, a man who commanded a great stone pyramid rising from the swamps, wisely ruling over many people. He loved her dearly, and once Neekeya had loved herself too, but now tears streamed down her cheeks.

The memories of home—of her last turn there—pounded through her. She had walked through the swamps, leaping from stone to stone, a feral thing, hunting frogs with her long, silver-tipped spear. She had spent hours in the wilderness, needing to hunt, to run, to sweat, to drain herself of her nervousness, of her fear of leaving home. It had been a turn of fear.

"But I will face my fear," she had whispered that turn in the swamps. "I will learn magic—real magic."

The swamp waters gurgled around her, the frogs trilled, and the mangroves swayed in the breeze. All her life, her father had spoken to her of magic, gifting her his many artifacts, telling her tales of magical shields to block the fists of giants, cricket choirs that could sing so beautifully grown men would weep, and islands that floated through the sky.

"I'm going to study magic too," she told her father that turn. "At the great school they call Teel. I'm seventeen now, Father, and I must go. I must become not only a warrior but a sorceress."

They stood in their great hall, the mossy stone pyramid that rose from the swamplands, so tall only the bravest bird could reach its peak. From the throne room, Neekeya could stare out the windows at an endless land, green and lush and fluttering with birds, that rolled into the misty horizons. When she returned her eyes to her father, she saw a kindly man, his head bald, his eyes warm. Necklaces of gilded cocoa beads hung across his bare chest, and a sword hung from his side, its silver hilt shaped as a crocodile's claw.

"My daughter," he said to her, eyes dampening. "The outside world is cruel and dangerous. I fought in the War of Day and Night years ago. I saw not only the horrors of the night but the horrors of the day. We are Daenorians. We are outcasts even among the sunlit kingdoms. They mock our ways. They call us the backwater of Timandra." He rose from his wooden throne, stepped toward her, and held her hands. "Please, child, stay with me here. Daenor is lush, warm, a place of family, of friendship, of righteousness. Do not step out into the cold, cruel world where greed and hatred fill the hearts of nations."

She squeezed his hands. "But I would learn of these things! How can I fight for righteousness without knowing of cruelty? How can I be a just ruler some day, a lady of this pyramid, if I haven't seen injustice? How can I surround myself with your gifts, your artifacts of magic, when I don't have the power to use them?"

He could say no more; his voice choked. The tall warrior, stronger than any man in Daenor, pulled her into his gentle embrace and kissed her head.

"Goodbye, my daughter. Goodbye. I will miss you."

Neekeya sniffed, her tears falling. That had been many turns ago, and here she knelt in Teel University, this land that was so strange to her. This land where people wore cotton robes, not beads and iron and leather. This land where people whispered cruel secrets, taunted one another, mocked anyone who was different. Neekeya had never feared the swamplands' crocodiles or warriors who drank and cursed too much; she had always been able to fight them, but how could she fight in a place like this? She could survive in the wilderness, but how could she survive within the walls of Teel?

"I miss home," she whispered to her reflection in the pool, and her lips shook. "I miss you, Father."

Laughter rolled behind her.

A voice rose in exaggerated falsetto. "I miss you, Father."

Neekeya leaped to her feet, spun around, and saw them there. She growled.

Sunlit Purity—Lari's quartet.

"Well, look at what we have here," Lari said, hands on her hips. "The swamp monster."

Neekeya balled her hands into fists. The four were everything she was not—full-blooded Magerians, their hair blond, their skin pale, their eyes blue, their clothes woven of meticulous cotton, their accents perfect and highborn. Neekeya was the daughter of a great lord, but to them she was a barbarian, uncouth and no better than an animal.

She began to walk away from the pool, but they moved forward, blocking her passage. Lari stood before her, smiling crookedly. The twins—Fae and and Kae—blocked her left side, while tall Derin stood to her right.

"Get out of my way," Neekeya said.

Lari laughed. "Or what? Will you curse us with one of your 'magical amulets?'" She spoke those last two words in a mockery of a toddler's voice. "Will you hex us with a dead rat, attack us with an enchanted stick, or maybe kick us with a magical boot?" Lari's smile turned into a sneer. "You have no magic, Neekeya. You never did. You never will. You are nothing but a swamp monster and you need to go home."

Neekeya tried to shove Lari aside, but the girl stepped back, laughing, and slapped Neekeya's cheek.

"Oh, she's going to cry!" said one of the twins and laughed.

Lari too laughed. "Awful! I'm going to have to scrub my hand now. It already smells like the swamp."

Neekeya growled and tried to shove past them again, but they blocked her way. She tossed a punch but Lari dodged the blow, and one of the twins sneaked behind Neekeya and shoved her forward.

"I'm warning you, Lari," Neekeya said, raising her fists. "I used to wrestle crocodiles in my spare time, and if you don't step back now, I won't just slap you. I'm going to bash your skull against the cobblestones."

They only laughed harder.

"Crocodiles!" said Derin, his chest shaking with laughter. "I can just imagine her wrestling those creatures in a pit of mud."

"Just like in the story I drew," Lari said. She reached into her pack and pulled out a scroll. She unrolled it and held out the parchment.

Neekeya froze and her heart seemed to freeze too. Her eyes stung. Upon the scroll appeared a drawing of her—a cruel cartoon, displaying her not as a lord's daughter but as a savage barely better than an animal. Words appeared below the text: "The Story of Neekeya, the Half-Crocodile Swamp Monster." Below the title appeared a story; Neekeya only read enough to realize it portrayed her as a beast whose father was a crocodile.

Neekeya shouted hoarsely, tears in her eyes, and tried to snatch the parchment, but Lari pulled the scroll back.

"Calm down, savage!" Lari said. "We copied this scroll fifty times. It's all over the university already. Every first year quartet has a copy."

Neekeya didn't know if to weep or scream, and for a moment, she only froze.

Father was right, she thought. *Father warned me. I should have stayed home. I can't survive here. I can't face such cruelty.*

She closed her eyes. She wanted to run—across the gardens, outside the walls, all the way home to Daenor far on the western edge of the world. She was a joke here, nothing but a joke.

"Lari!" rose a voice from across the gardens. "Lari Serin! I heard you say you like magic?"

Neekeya's eyes snapped open and she gasped.

Tam stood under the stone archway that led into the gardens. Autumn leaves clung to his brown hair and green robes. He smiled, eyes bright, and thrust his hands forward.

With a chorus of shrieks, a dozen bats filled Lari's hair.

The young Magerian screamed.

"Get them off!" she cried. "Derin! Twins!"

But Tam pointed again, and suddenly bats were clinging to the others' hair too. They all shouted and ran, fleeing the gardens, tugging the bats off one by one.

Tam watched them leave and sadly shook his head. "They're only bats. I think they're cute." He pointed up at an oak. "They live in that tree. I only had to choose them as my material and move them a few feet downward."

Neekeya wanted to run to her friend, to thank him, to embrace him, but she only stood, still frozen like a damn fool. And her damn tears still flowed.

I'm acting like a baby, she thought. *I'm a warrior. I'm the daughter of a lord. I—*

She covered her eyes, her body shook, and her tears kept flowing.

Warm arms enveloped her, for for an instant Neekeya struggled, afraid, sure that it was Lari returned to torment her. But when fingers stroked her hair, she opened her eyes and saw that it was Tam who held her.

"It's all right," he said softly. "They're gone."

Her tears wet his shoulder, and her body pressed against him. "I can't do this, Tam. I don't belong here."

"None of us do." He touched her cheek, taking one of her tears onto his finger. "Not Jitomi, not Madori, not me. We're all outcasts at Teel but we have to stick together."

She looked away. "Jitomi? He has other Elorians here. Madori? She's half-Elorian herself; she often speaks to Jitomi of their home, a home they remember together. And you, Tam?" She looked at him. "You fit in here. You look like everyone else and you talk like everyone and—"

"And I'm not like everyone," he said, stiffening. "I'm from Arden. I'm the *Prince* of Arden. Maybe that's not a land of swamps and pyramids and crocodiles, and maybe like Mageria it's a fragment of the old Riyonan Empire, but it's still a different country . . . a country I miss." His voice softened and he sighed. "I'm sorry. You're right. Maybe I don't know how you feel. But I'm here for you. We all are."

She nodded. Her voice was choked; she could barely speak louder than a whisper. "I know." She smiled tremulously and held his hand. "Thank you, Tam. Our quartet means everything to me." She trembled and smiled through her tears. "Well, our quartet and those cute little bats."

He laughed softly, and she touched his cheek, and she didn't know how it happened, but somehow he was kissing her. Their laughter died, and as he held her close, it felt like she was melting into his kiss. His one hand stroked her hair, and the other held the small of her back. They kissed for what seemed like ages, desperate for each other, scared of letting go, wanting to forever stay like this in these gardens, together, one, whole, no longer afraid but warm and full of tingling joy. She had never kissed a boy before but it felt right, it felt natural, it felt like the best thing in the world.

They walked back to their chamber in silence, sneaking glances at each other, then lowering their eyes—a little afraid, a little embarrassed, a little joyous.

CHAPTER SIXTEEN
THE HOUNDS OF SUNMOTTE

Lord Tirus Serin—The Light of Radian, Duke of Sunmotte Citadel, Warden of Hornsford Bridge, and Lord Protector of Mageria—stood upon the bridge and watched the two Ardishmen breach for air.

At his side, Lord Imril—a wiry baron with a gaunt face and beaked nose—raised his crossbow, aiming it at Torin's head.

"Got him," he said, a hint of hunger and delight twisting his thin lips. He pulled the trigger.

Serin nudged the crossbow aside, and the quarrel skimmed over Torin's head, vanishing harmlessly into the water. Sir Imril turned toward him, and for an instant irritation filled the man's pale blue eyes. The show of defiance vanished quickly, however, replaced by the servility Serin demanded from all in his order.

"My lord?" Imril said.

"Let them be," Serin replied calmly. He waved down his other crossbowmen's weapons. "Let them swim."

His men lowered their crossbows as one, moving in perfect unison. Down in the water, Torin and Cam were still swimming to the Ardish riverbank, unaware that Serin had just spared their lives—for a while at least.

"But, my lord," said Imril and cleared his throat. The ratty nobleman was high ranking enough to speak while the others dared not. "The Shepherd King is a friend of the darkness. Sir Greenmoat is wed to one of the nightcrawlers. Why spare the lives of these scum?"

Serin turned slowly to stare at the shorter, gaunter man. Lord Imril's pencil mustache quivered just the slightest; to challenge Lord Serin himself, the Light of Radian, was an offense most men would be tortured for.

"You disagree with your lord?" Serin said softly, letting a hint of a smile tingle his lips. "Perhaps you think the Light of Radian is fallible?"

"No, my lord!" said Imril, that mustache twitching. He slammed his fist against his chest in salute. "I worship the Light of Radian. I only—"

"Tell me, Lord Imril." Serin placed a hand on the baron's shoulder. "Do you think I do not know who those two vermin are?"

"I only—" Sweat trickled down Imril's face.

"And tell me, Lord Imril, do you know the punishment for challenging the Lord of Light?"

Imril's throat bobbed as he gulped, and a glob of sweat ran down his cheek. "I— Yes, my lord."

"Describe it to me," Serin said, smiling, his voice pleasant. He leaned closer, his grip tightening on the man's shoulder. "In loving detail."

Lord Imril blinked and paled. He spoke hoarsely. "You whip them. You disembowel them. Then you tie them to four horses and send each running in another direction."

Serin nodded, his smile breaking into grin. "Excellent! And quite accurate." He laughed. "But of course, you are my loyal baron. You are far too high ranking for such lowly punishment. You feel free to speak your mind to me. I understand. I will show you mercy."

Imril laughed nervously and blinked sweat out of his eyes. "Thank you, my lord. I—"

He sputtered as Serin's dagger drove into his eye.

"This is my mercy," Serin said, twisting the blade inside the man's skull. "I give you a painless death. Your wife and children will enjoy the same mercy."

He pulled the blade free. Imril gave a last gasp, then collapsed upon the bridge.

"Remove his armor!" Serin barked at his soldiers. "Take his sword too. Then kick the body into the water; let the fish eat."

Upon the eastern bank, Greenmoat and the king were now climbing onto the Ardish bank, safely back in their homeland, that pathetic kingdom of magicless imbeciles.

Go back to your capital, Serin thought, watching them with a thin smile. *Tell your generals what you saw here. Tell them of the armies in my fields, of my mighty fortress, of the wrath that surely will descend upon you.* He licked his lips. *Tell them . . . and be afraid.*

The soldiers were unstrapping Imril's armor. Leaving them to their task, Serin mounted his horse and rode back west to the Magerian bank.

The world rose and fell as he galloped, and Serin smiled, still savoring the sweetness of the kill. It was not a good turn without at least one good kill. Ahead rose his fortress, large as a mountain, a city for an army, this army that would soon bring the light and truth of Radianism to the world.

He rode through the field, his banner raised high. Soldiers stood at attention at his sides, creating a path between them. Serin rode through this sea of steel. Men pounded their fists against their chests, chanting for their cause.

"Radian rises! Radian rises!"

When he reached his fortress, his guards pulled down the drawbridge, then saluted as Serin rode past them and through the gates. Past the walls, a vast courtyard awaited him, full of more soldiers. In great pits dug into the earth, collared slaves toiled, their backs lashed, their ankles chained. They were raising siege machines—catapults to hurl boulders, trebuchets to fire flaming barrels, and battering rams to swing on chains. In one pit, deeper than the rest, men stirred mixtures in great pots, creating the secret, flammable powder stolen from the night. The Elorians were weak, maggoty creatures, but they had invented cannons of fire, and Serin licked his lips hungrily to imagine turning their own weapon upon them.

"Greenmoat, you fool," he whispered as he rode between the pits. "Do you think I care a wit or jot for Arden, that cesspool you call a kingdom? Arden will be a wasteland when I'm done with it. Your only worth to me is the land to your east. You are a road to the night, nothing more, Greenmoat." He clenched his fist. "Your bones will pave that road."

Past the slave pits, he reached a second layer of walls, these ones even taller. A dozen towers rose along them like teeth from a stone jaw, topped with archers. The banners of Radianism draped the walls, displaying the triumph of the sun over the moon, the triumph of Timandrian blood—pure and hot and red—over the Elorian vermin, the subhuman creatures who spawned in the shadows. He rode through more gates here, across another courtyard, and toward his keep—the center of his domain. The building rose taller than any palace in Timandra, even taller than the palace of Serin's king in the south. Its towers scraped the sky, blades of stone. The King of Mageria perhaps wore the crown, but he—Lord Tirus Serin—ruled from the kingdom's greatest castle, commanding the greatest armies in all Mageria, perhaps all the world.

He dismounted his horse outside the gates of his hall, letting his stable boys lead the beast away. Servants bowed and guards stood at attention as he walked forth. He walked under an archway and entered his throne room—a vast hall lined with red columns, their gilded capitals shaped as sunbursts. A mosaic spread across the floor, depicting a battle of thousands, the soldiers of sunlight slaying the demons of the night. The mosaic was designed so that, as Serin walked toward his throne, his boots spared the Timandrian soldiers but stomped upon the faces of the twisted Elorians. He climbed the stairs onto his dais and sat down upon the throne, his banners hanging around him, framing him with their might. His soldiers stood across the hall, spears in hands, armor bright.

Serin clutched the armrests, leaned forward, and barked, "Bring them in!"

He had been waiting for this moment all turn, and he sucked in breath with delight and hunger as his guards stepped forward, dragging the chained prisoners.

Truly, these Elorians were pathetic beings, he thought, his nostrils flaring as he smelled their blood.

"Look at them!" Serin said, pointing at the chained wretches. "They are worms. They are subhuman."

The Elorians could barely stand; the guards had to hold them upright. Whips had torn into their flesh, and bruises surrounded their freakish, oversized eyes. They reminded Serin of naked moles. He had caught these creatures—seven in total—traveling into Mageria to peddle their silk.

"We will cleanse Timandra of their filth!" Serin cried, rising to his feet. "The lands of sunlight will be purified of shadows. We will allow no creatures of darkness to crawl upon our land."

The Elorians tried to beg in their language. One fell to his knees, bowing. Serin sneered.

Pathetic, he thought. *Groveling insects.*

Across the hall, the guards laughed. One soldier lashed a whip, knocking the bowing Elorian down, incurring more laughter.

Serin too laughed. "Bring in the dogs!" he shouted, voice echoing across the hall. "They are hungry. Let my pets feed!"

Growls sounded followed by mad barks. Guards stepped forth, leading chained dogs larger than men, creatures twisted and augmented with dark magic. The beasts howled, smelling the blood, hungry for meat. At a nod from Serin, the guards released the animals.

The Elorians yowled in fear. Some tried to escape only for the dogs to tear them down. Blood splattered the mosaic.

"Fantastic," Serin whispered, leaning forward in his seat, his eyes wide. "I wish you were here to see this, Lari."

As the dogs fed and guards cheered, Serin imagined bringing the mongrel—that little wretch Madori—here for a show. His pets would enjoy her young, supple, sweet flesh.

"Soon, Madori," Serin whispered. "Soon it will be your blood spilling across my hall."

The dogs fed and Serin grinned, inhaled deeply, and licked his lips.

CHAPTER SEVENTEEN
AUTUMN MOON

They sat in their chamber, sheets hanging over the windows, cloaking them in shadows.

"Are you ready?" Madori whispered.

The others nodded, huddling with her. They had pushed their beds back against the wall and sat upon the rug. Madori had prepared the scrolls, drawing Qaelish runes upon them—prayers to Xen Qae, father of her nation. The parchments now hung upon the walls. Jitomi had constructed the lanterns, stretching paper over thin wooden frames. They now floated, candles glowing within, tethered to the bedposts. Here in their little bedchamber, in the heart of a sunlit university, they had created a bit of home, an enclave of the night.

"It's beautiful," Neekeya whispered. She reached over and clutched Tam's hand. "Isn't it, Tam?"

He nodded. "It makes me want to visit Eloria."

"We *are* visiting Eloria now," Neekeya said and smiled.

Madori looked at the pair, and a strange chill filled her. She had seen the two hold hands, share hidden glances, and whisper many times these past few turns. The prince and the swamp dweller were growing close, and looking at them now, holding hands and smiling at each other, Madori felt something cold inside her. Was it jealousy? Did she herself want to hold hands with Tam, her childhood friend? Or did she feel outcast again—the half-Elorian, not good enough for the two children of sunlight?

Jitomi spoke at her side, interrupting her thoughts. "We're ready, Madori."

She turned toward him. He stared at her, his blue eyes solemn—large, luminous eyes, eyes like hers, eyes for seeing in the darkness of the night. Jitomi was from Ilar, a nation in the south of Eloria, far from Qaelin, the great empire of darkness where Madori's mother had been born. Their cultures were different—their two nations had fought many wars in the darkness—and yet here in the daylight, he was the closest thing she had to a kinsman, to somebody who understood the importance of darkness, the loneliness here deep in sunlit lands.

She nodded. "I've never done this magic before, but . . . I'll try." She took a deep breath and looked at her friends, one by one. "It's the Autumn Equinox. On this turn thousands of years ago, the great teacher Xen Qae arrived on the shore of the Elorian mainland, and there he met his wife, a young fisherman's daughter named Madori. I am named after her. Together they founded the Qaelish nation whose children spread across the night. This turn all Qaelish people celebrate their love."

She smiled softly, remembering the stories her mother would tell her of Xen Qae, the wise philosopher with the long beard, and his wife, a beautiful woman with hair like spilling streams of moonlight. As Madori sat here in the shadows, she felt almost like a full Elorian, a true daughter of darkness. When she spoke again, she found that even her voice changed, speaking with just a hint of a Qaelish accent—the accent her mother spoke with.

"On the Autumn Equinox, we pray to the moon, for we believe that its light blessed our great father and mother that turn. It is a time for moonlight."

At her side, Jitomi spoke softly. "I am from Ilar, an island nation south of the Elorian mainland, but we too celebrate the Autumn Equinox. We do not know the teachings of Xen Qae, but for thousands of years our people have danced under this moonlight. We call this autumn moon the *Domai Jatey*, the Half Light, a milestone between the turn of the seasons. It is blessed, a light of peace when our warriors may rest and pray."

Madori took a deep breath and closed her eyes. "Let us pray to the moon."

She looked at the soft light from the floating lanterns. It glowed a pale silver through the paper frames. A smile touched her lips as she chose the light, as she claimed it, and she changed it. She pulled wisps like glowing silk from the lanterns, weaving them together in the center of the room, a ball of twine woven from strands of candlelight. The others gasped but Madori only smiled silently, pulling the light more tightly together, raising the glowing ball to let it float above them. It pulsed softly under the ceiling, the size of an orange, a makeshift moon.

"It's beautiful," Neekeya whispered. "I've seen the moon from the daylight before. It's just a wisp from here like dust in a sunbeam. Is this how the moon looks in the night?"

Madori shook her head. "The true moon in the night is many times brighter, many times more beautiful. But this is the limit of my magic. Perhaps no magic can capture the true moonlight."

A low humming rose, and at first Madori thought it was the moonlight emitting the sound. Then she realized it was Jitomi singing, his voice low, a hum that soon morphed into words. Madori's eyes watered for she knew that tune. It was the song "The Journey Home," a song her mother used to sing, a song known across the lands of night.

Her tears fell and she clasped Jitomi's hand, and she joined her voice to his. She had never sung with anyone but her mother, and at first her cheeks burned with embarrassment, but then she closed her eyes and let the music claim her. In her mind, she was back in Oshy, the village in the night, the place where she had spent so many summers in her childhood. She was singing there again under the true moon. "The Journey Home" had always been the song of her childhood, but now she understood its true meaning. It was a song of being in distant lands, of dreaming of the moonlight, of taking a long path back into darkness.

My journey home will be long, she thought as she sang. *It will be years before I see the night again. And perhaps the night is not my true home, for I am half of daylight. And perhaps I have no true home. But here, now, holding Jitmoi's hand and singing our old songs, let the darkness be like a home to me. Let me sing to the moon and dream of the night.*

Their song ended, and she leaned against Jitomi, and he placed an arm around her and kissed her cheek.

Neekeya was blowing her nose into a handkerchief. "That does it, you two. That does it! When we graduate as mages, I'm visiting Eloria with you."

Madori laughed. "Only if you take me to visit Daenor too."

"Of course." Neekeya grinned. "But I'm not singing any Daenorian songs. My singing would make your ears fall off."

Madori wiped her tears away, the joke easing her mood of almost holy yearning. She smiled, hopped toward her drawer, and began pulling out Elorian foods she had taken from home and saved for this holiday: jars of chanterelle, matsutake, and milkcap mushrooms; salted bat wings; crunchy dried lanternfish; and sweet candies made from the honey of firebees, glowing little creatures that flew on the northern Qaelish coast. Soon the companions were laughing as they ate.

I miss my home in Fairwool-by-Night, Madori thought, listening to the others laugh about how Professor Yovan had stepped on his beard last turn. *And I miss my home in Oshy. My journey is still long, but maybe . . . maybe despite all the pain and fear, this is a home to me too, and this is my new family.*

Again her eyes dampened. Jitomi saw and gave her shoulder a squeeze, a small smile on his lips. She smiled back and reached for a handful of chanterelles.

"Eat," she said, handing him one. "A little taste of home."

* * * * *

They walked through the forest, hand in hand, an undercover prince and a swamp dweller, strangers in a strange land.

"Are you sure you want to do this?" Tam asked softly.

Neekeya turned to look at him. The forest canopy rustled above, casting mottles of light upon his sun-bronzed face and brown hair. His eyes gleamed in the light like amber. His face was kind, his voice soft. Neekeya couldn't help herself. She leaned toward him and kissed his lips.

"I'm sure," she whispered. "I have to do this. I have to let go. I have to become a new person."

She hefted her pack across her shoulders. Its contents jingled, a hundred artifacts her father had given her, claiming them to be magic—little figurines, rings, coins, seashells, and sundry other items. Neekeya had been collecting them since her childhood, sure that she owned a treasure, a magical horde worth more than a palace.

Now—a grown woman, a mage in training—she understood.

They're trinkets. Her eyes stung. *They're worth less than a single silver coin.*

"I've been a fool." Her eyes stung. "I believed my father's stories. I wanted to believe them. I wanted to think I'm powerful, magical, an owner of great artifacts." She wiped her eyes. "They were foolish stories told to a foolish girl. We'll find a place here, a peaceful place under a tree. We'll bury them." She nodded. "I've come to Teel to learn magic—and I will. Real magic. To do that, I must let go of the past."

He stroked her hair and kissed her cheek.

They kept walking, moving between elms, birches, and oaks. Neekeya wanted to walk farther; she could still see Teel's towers behind her. She needed a secret place, a place Lari and the other students would never reach. Chickadees and robins sang in the trees, crickets chirped, and pollen floated. The autumn air was cool, the leaves red and orange and golden. It was a beautiful forest, a forest for her secrets.

"This looks a lot like the wilderness of Arden," Tam said, looking around. "My brother and I used to spend many turns hunting in the woods. Just the two of us, a couple bows, and a couple hounds. We'd drive our mother crazy. She'd insist on sending guards, horses, knights in armor, a whole cavalcade to hunt with us, but where's the fun in that? So Omry and I would sneak out alone to a place like this, spend a turn or two away from the palace, and just be boys. Not princes. Not rulers. Just two regular people." He inhaled deeply, watching a cardinal flit from branch to branch. "We'd come home covered in scratches and bruises, our faces muddy, our hair a mess, our boots all torn up. Most times we wouldn't even catch any game. Mother would be furious, railing about how we ruined our priceless outfits, but Father always laughed. He was a commoner once, did you know?"

Neekeya smiled and slipped her hand into his. "I would go hunting too—just me alone. I'd hop from log to boulder in the jungle, a spear in my hand, hunting frogs. I'd collect whole baskets of them, bring them back home to our pyramid, and we'd feast on fried frog legs." She looked around her. "Daenor looks nothing like this.

155

The trees there are thrice as high, and you can barely see the ground; it's mostly water. The birds there are larger and very colorful, and great crocodiles roam around everywhere." She touched her tooth necklace. "Each one of these teeth is from a beast I battled. We'd eat them too, you know."

He wrinkled his nose. "Crocodile meat? Frog legs? I'd rather eat chicken and deer."

She shrugged. "One's as good as the other." She mussed his hair. "You speak so fondly of your home. Why did you come here? To Teel University? You're a prince! A prince of a mighty kingdom. I know that all students at Teel are highborn, their parents wealthy enough to pay the tuition, but princes? That's unique even here."

He blew out his breath thoughtfully. "I told you that in the forest, my twin brother and I were only two boys. But whenever we returned to our palace, we were different." He kicked a pine cone. "Omry is ten minutes older than I am—that's it, only a moment, the length of a song or two. That means he's the heir to Arden. He was ten minutes earlier than me . . . and now worth ten times more." Tam passed a hand through his hair. "I love my twin dearly, more than anything. I always will. But I had to find my own path, my own power. I couldn't watch us grow older together, him a great heir, myself always worth less. When Madori told me she'd try out for Teel, I knew that was my path too. To become a mage. To find my own strength. To feel . . ." He looked at Neekeya, brow furrowed. ". . . to finally feel equal to my twin."

Neekeya grinned. "Oh, you silly boy!" She tugged him toward her and kissed him again—this kiss longer and deeper—and when it ended, she tapped his nose. "I'm trying to keep walking here, and you keep making me kiss you." She squeezed him closer to her. "Your brother might become a king, Tam, but you'll be a great mage." She looked around her and smiled. "I think this is a good place."

A rivulet gurgled between alders, full of smooth, parti-colored stones and orange fish. Twisting roots, fallen logs, and carpets of autumn leaves covered the forest floor. A hole in the canopy let in a ray of light, gleaming with pollen. Boulders rose ahead, moss nearly hiding the ancient runes of old Riyonans, a people who had faded from the world many years ago. It was a secret place, Neekeya thought, a beautiful place. A place for hiding her childhood.

She knelt by an oak and began to dig. Tam helped her, and they worked in silence. When the hole was a couple feet deep, Neekeya upended her pack. Her trinkets spilled into the hole—pewter figurines, seashells, rare coins, spoons, scrolls, and more.

Her eyes stung. "Thank you, Papa," she whispered. "Thank you for letting a little girl believe in something secret, something magical. I love you. But now I seek true magic. Now I leave my childhood here for safekeeping."

She wiped her eyes and began to shove soil onto the items.

"Neekeya . . ." Tam spoke softly. "Neekeya, wait."

She shook her head. "No. I have to do this. This is right. I—"

"Neekeya, look! The seashell. It's glowing."

She tilted her head and squinted down into the hole. Indeed, the little shell—no larger than a coin—was glowing a soft blue. When she lifted it, the glow faded.

"A trick of sunlight," she said, yet when she placed the shell back down in the hole, it glowed again.

Tam scrunched his lips, reached into the hole, and rummaged in the soil. He smiled and pulled out a truffle. "Well, I do think you have something here, Neekeya." He held the seashell in one hand, the truffle in the other. When he brought them near, the shell glowed brighter. When he separated them, the glow faded. "A magical artifact."

Neekeya gasped and snatched the shell from him. She tested it again and fresh tears budded in her eyes. "It's true! My father was speaking truth. It's magic. It's a real artifact. It's . . . not very useful, is it?" She laughed through her tears. "It's a truffle finder. Hardly a great artifact."

Tam grinned. "It's very important. It means your father was right, that you spent your childhood surrounded by magic. Or at least, that one of these items is magic. That means there's hope for the other items too." He lifted a few of the figurines and examined them. "Professor Rushavel never found anything magical about them, but this might just be swamp magic, a different sort." He looked at

Neekeya and his face grew solemn. "I think you should keep these things."

She nodded. "We'll never lack for truffles again."

He rolled his eyes. "You'll never lack for *wonder* again. You'll never see your childhood as a lie." He began to place the items back in her pack. "Take these back, Neekeya. Keep them. They're important."

As they walked back through the forest, Neekeya grinned. "You know, some of these items might be *really* important, like . . . a magical shoelace un-knotter."

He nodded. "Or a magical nose hair plucker."

She grimaced. "Maybe something more pleasant—a magical cup that removes the skin off your milk."

"That's some powerful magic there. Maybe even some magical, wooden, Lari-biting teeth? A pair that would chase her around, biting her bottom?"

Neekeya laughed. "Now that would be a mightier artifact than even those Rushavel makes." She sighed and leaned against him as they walked. They stepped back into the university, carrying with them a little magic.

CHAPTER EIGHTEEN
WINTER SNOW

The bells rang and the seasons turned, and the first snow of winter fell upon Teel University, coating the gardens, walls, and roofs with white blankets. When Madori walked outside, the first to rise, she smiled for beneath her feet she saw a field of stars, a memory of the glistening sky of the night.

She smiled not only for the snow but because she was heading toward her favorite class, Magical History. As much as Madori enjoyed fostering her growing powers, she enjoyed learning about the wizards of old: how the wise mage Sheltan traveled to the distant isle of Orida and tamed the cyclops; how the Ten Rogue Mages holed up in the mountains for a hundred years before the Crystal Alliance hunted them down; and even tales of the war against Eloria where mages shattered the walls of Yintao but perished against the Eternal Palace.

It helped that Elina Maleen taught the class, the youngest professor at Teel; Madori had dearly loved the woman since Maleen had first quizzed her at the trials. The rest of Madori's Motley found Magical History to be a bore; Neekeya was taking Artifacts this morning while Tam and Jitomi were both at Magical Transformations. As much as she loved her friends, Madori savored this time away from them. It was a time to dream.

This turn we will learn the story of the ancient Elorian mages, she thought. She had been waiting for months for this lesson, for once the night had been full of magic now lost. Madori hoped that some turn she could return to Eloria with the lost art and teach magic again to the children of the night.

She walked to the back of the university, past the library and Agrotis Tower. She climbed a cobbled path, moving up a hillside dotted with snowy trees, their branches encased in ice. Cardinals and chickadees flitted between the birdhouses Professor Yovan had hung here, and a rabbit darted ahead, leaving prints in the snow. The old stone building rose between several maple trees, frost upon its bricks. Once a mill, the little building had become a classroom three hundred years ago when Teel expanded outside the cloister, its original complex. Now this was Madori's favorite classroom. Her smile widening, she opened the door and stepped inside . . . and her smile faded.

The other students were already in their seats—thankfully none of them Radians, but all of them Timandrians. But it was not Professor Maleen who stood at the podium as always, her wild brown hair falling in a great mane, her blind eyes staring up in wonder as if at living scenes of history. Instead, hunched over a book and wrapped in black robes, it was Professor Atratus.

The vulture-like man spun toward the door and hissed at Madori. She was so shocked she took a step back into the snow.

Atratus sneered and checked his pocket watch. "Late as usual. A lack of punctuality is typical of mongrels." He snorted. "Shocked to see me, half-breed? Your precious Maleen has taken ill, and you'll find I am less tolerant of tardiness. You will report to my office after class for three strikes from my ruler. Take your seat now lest I increase the count to thirty!"

Madori winced and rubbed her palm, already feeling the punishment; it seemed that a turn couldn't go by without him striking her. Ignoring the many eyes following her, she rushed to her seat and sat down.

Professor Atratus leaned over his podium, eyes blazing, and slammed his book shut with a shower of dust. "It says here," he said, a snarl twisting his voice, "that I am to teach you about ancient Elorian magic." He barked a laugh. "Elorians know only cheap tricks to fool their own feeble-minded kind. This class I will teach you something far more valuable about Elorians." He licked his lips. "I will teach you the history of their race and prove to you its inferiority."

Madori's heart sank. She wished she had fled the classroom the instant she had seen him. She wanted to bolt up now, to race to the door, but fear kept her frozen in her seat.

"Mongrel!" Atratus barked, pointing at her. "Stand. Come. To me, dog."

She could not move. She simply stared, mouth hanging open.

"Ten lashes from my ruler!" he shouted. "Stand! To me!"

Reluctantly, Madori rose to her feet. Before she could take a step, his magic shot out like grapples. The smoky ropes wrapped around her, tugging her toward him. More magic slammed against her mouth, stifling her scream. Across the classroom, students gasped, and one boy leaped to his feet, but glares from Atratus silenced them.

Madori struggled in the magic, trying to rip it off, to claim and change the bonds, but his magic was too strong. He pulled back his arms, moving her like a marionette, until he placed her beside him. She stood facing the class, trussed up like an animal awaiting slaughter. The students stared with wide eyes, faces pale.

"Behold!" said Professor Atratus. "Behold the menace of Eloria. Behold the wretched product of the nightcrawlers' invasion of our lands. Before you you see the corruption of our blood, the mingling of poison with purity. A mongrel! A creature of sunlight tainted with the blackness of night."

Madori tried to free herself, to scream, to talk back to him, even if it earned her a thousand lashes. But only a muffled whimper passed through the smoky gag.

He tapped her head with his ruler. Tap. Tap. Tap. Every blow rang through her skull.

"Observe the smaller cranium," he said to the class. "It is barely larger than a dog's skull—the result of the Elorian infestation." He smacked her chest. "Behold the frail frame. This specimen stands barely five feet tall, weighing less than a child. The Elorian blood weakens her." He placed his fingers around her left eye, tugging and stretching as if he'd let her eyeball pop out. "Observe the freakish orbs. Imagine how much space they take up in the skull, leaving less room for the brain. Those, my friends, are eyes for seeing in the dark—for sneaking up, scuttling, and snatching Timandrian children for their feasts of human flesh."

One student, a young girl of only fifteen years, raised her hand. "But Professor Atratus! This one is only half-Elorian. Does her Timandrian half not make her worthy?"

Atratus sighed and shook his head. "Sadly, my dear child, the presence of her Timandrian blood only increases her obscenity. A pure-blooded Elorian is like a maggot, a foul creature that crawls in the muck. But a mongrel . . ." His voice trembled with rage. "A mongrel is like a maggot found inside the body of a beloved pet— more foul by far, for it has ruined something pure." He stared at Madori and covered his mouth as if about to gag. "She sickens me."

Another student raised his hand. "Professor Atratus, how can we protect ourselves from the Elorian menace?"

The professor nodded. "A good question, my boy." He tapped the pin he wore upon his lapel, showing a sun eclipsing a moon. "The Radian Order will protect us. Lari Serin leads the Teel Radian Society; I urge you all to join, receive your pins, swear allegiance to Lord Serin, and learn how to protect yourself from nightcrawlers and mongrels."

A third student, this one a skinny boy with pale cheeks, spoke next. His voice shook, but he managed to stare steadily at Atratus. "Professor, the headmistress has said that Radians are dangerous. She says . . ." He gulped. "She says that Elorians are welcome in the lands of sunlight, that—"

Professor Atratus shouted so loudly the boy started and fell back into his seat.

"Headmistress Egeria is a fool!" Spittle flew from the professor's mouth. His fists shook. "And you are a fool to believe her! Who is the headmistress? A frail old woman, coughing and trembling, her one foot in the grave. Tell me, boy, do you have any siblings?" He trudged forward, grabbed the student's collar, and twisted it. "Do you?"

The boy—his face wet with Atratus's flying saliva—nodded silently.

Atratus growled like a rabid animal. "Do you want Elorians to snatch them from their beds, to cut them open in their solstice festivals, to feed upon their organs? Or perhaps you want Elorians breeding with your siblings, producing foul, mixed-blood offspring that are lower than animals?"

The boy, pale and trembling, shook his head.

Now, Madori thought, straining. *Now, while his back is turned toward me.*

Atratus was busy chastising the boy, railing against all the evils Elorians could perform to his parents, siblings, and countrymen. With the man deep in his tirade, Madori sucked in air through her nose, focusing all her effort on claiming the magical bonds he'd placed around her. She forced herself to clear her mind from anything else—to ignore Atratus's words, to ignore her humiliation, to ignore the eyes of the other students.

Choose your material.

Claim it.

Change it.

She tried but could not, and her eyes burned. All she had learned here at Teel, all her months of practice and studying, could not save her from his shackles.

Choose. Claim. Change.

Yet she could not; his magic was too strong.

"—and the Elorians will bring their disease, the Night Plague, into our wells, our farms, our very beds!" Atratus's words were piercing Madori's consciousness, rising and fading from her awareness. "I have jars of the Night Plague in my office, and I have seen its evil, and . . ."

Madori inhaled slowly through her nostrils, letting the breath fill her throat and her lungs, letting it flow to every part of her.

Breath by breath.

Her eyes stung. It was her father's voice speaking in her mind. She saw his kind face again, his wise eyes, his proud smile.

Breath by breath, Billygoat. That's all you must do to survive.

She exhaled slowly, inhaled again, savored the calming energy, and this too was like magic, a magic that cleared her mind. Breath by breath. Healing. Soothing.

Choose.

Claim.

And she had it.

His magic snapped into place in her awareness. She understood every single particle that comprised his ropes, saw the links between them, saw the logic that bound the magic like countless rings in chain mail.

Change.

She tore the links free.

The smoke fled her mouth and she gasped.

The tendrils tore free from her wrists and arms.

"He lies!" Madori shouted, tears in her eyes. "He lies to you! He's nothing but a liar. Elorians are not monsters, but Professor Atratus might be. Reject the Radians! Don't listen to their poiso—"

She could not finish her sentence.

His magic slammed against her with the might of war hammers.

Vaguely, Madori was aware of herself flying through the air. Her back slammed against the wall with a thud, knocking the breath out of her. She slumped down, pain clutching her chest, squeezing her lungs. She could not breathe.

Something was constricting her. Not the black smoke this time. She winced and tears ran down her cheeks, and the skin on her arms tightened, and she realized what material Atratus had chosen this time—not particles in the air but her own flesh. He was squeezing her like an orange.

With a jerk, he raised his hands. She rose into the air, her very skin tugging her body upward. She gasped, sputtered, struggling for breath.

"You will pay for your insolence, mongrel," he sneered, holding her suspended in the air. "You have hereby failed Magical History. I banish you from this class, and at the end of this turn, you will report to my office for thirty lashes, then go work in the kitchens for two straight turns."

He tugged the door open from a distance, then swung his arms. She flew outside like a discarded bit of cloth and landed in the snow. The door slammed shut, sealing her outside, bruised and struggling for breath.

* * * * *

"You have to go to Headmistress Egeria." Tam stood before her, staring at Madori sternly. "He can't do this to you!"

Sitting on her bed, Madori looked down at her throbbing palm. Professor Atratus had forbade her to heal the welts from his latest lashing, vowing to inspect the wounds every turn. Scrubbing pots for half-a-turn hadn't helped her hand feel any better.

"What could Egeria do?" Madori said softly. "She has no important family, no wealth, no influence . . . only a title. Lord Serin is the most powerful man in Mageria, possibly in all Timandra, and Professor Atratus is his pet."

Neekeya sat at Madori's side, wringing her hands. "But there's got to be something Egeria can do! Madori, please. Let's all go speak to her together."

Jitomi nodded. "We all go." His pale cheeks flushed, and the dragon tattoo twitched on his neck as he clenched his jaw. "We will demand she do something about this Atratus."

Madori lowered her head, her two strands of hair drooping. "No. I will go alone. Students are forbidden from entering her tower, and if Atratus catches us—if *any* professor catches us—I will not have you punished for my sake."

Her friends glanced at one another. Before they could argue, and before Madori could lose her courage, she rose to her feet and left the chamber, closing the door behind her.

The sun was bright and the hour was late; Atratus would be sleeping in his chamber, and if he caught her outside after hours, well, he had already punished so much there wasn't much more Madori feared.

She thanked both Idar, the god of her father, and Xen Qae, the wise philosopher her mother worshiped, when she reached Cosmia Tower without encountering any professor. When she creaked open the door and stepped inside—the place where Atratus had once caught her—she breathed in relief. This hall too was empty.

She climbed the spiraling stairs, looking out every window she passed, seeing more and more of the land as she ascended: the university grounds, with their columned halls and domes and gardens; the town of Teelshire beyond, its roofs tiled, its streets cobbled; and the fields and plains of Mageria. The road she had taken here snaked across the land, and a lump filled Madori's throat to remember the journey with her father. She had groaned at Torin's jokes, called him the dullest man in Moth, and couldn't wait to reach this university. Now she wanted nothing more than to see her father again, run toward him, hug him tightly, and never let go.

If you were here, Father, you wouldn't let any of this happen. You'd fight them all—like you fought the monk Ferius and his armies. I'm so sorry, Father. She stared at the road and the mist beyond. *I'm so sorry I never told you how much I truly love you.*

She knuckled her eyes dry. A few more steps, and she reached a door and knocked.

As if reacting to her touch, the door unlocked and slowly swung open.

The tower's top chamber was large and round, its brick walls covered with shelves. There were as many artifacts here as in Professor Rushavel's workshop. Madori saw animal statuettes with blinking crystal eyes; counter-square boards whose pieces—soldiers, horses, and elephants—moved as if locked in true battle; model ships whose sails billowed with air and whose oars stroked; toy soldiers with ticking hearts; books whose voices filled her head when she read their spines; little pewter dragons who blasted out sparks of true fire; and many more. An oak desk rose in the room's center, its top hidden under piles of codices, hourglasses, and scrolls. Behind the desk, in a great armchair that nearly swallowed her, sat the headmistress.

Madori expected Egeria to rail, to punish her, to shout that Madori was insolent for bursting in here uninvited and after hours. But the little old woman, barely larger than a child, simply smiled kindly, her face creasing into a map of wrinkles.

"Hello, my dear," the headmistress said.

Madori flinched, for an instant—a single heartbeat—sure that the headmistress was hurtling insults at her, was reaching for a ruler to strike her like Atratus. When the kind tone sank in, Madori realized that this kindness hurt her more than a ruler or insults could. Tears filled her eyes and streamed down her cheeks, but it was a good kind of pain, the pain of a scab peeling off.

"Child!" said Egeria, eyes softening.

The headmistress rose to her feet, rushed toward Madori, and embraced her. Madori was used to being the smallest person at Teel, but the headmistress was just the same size, her arms so warm.

"I'm sorry," Madori whispered. "I'm sorry I came here after hours, and I'm so sorry for everything. I had to see you. I had to tell you. I . . ."

She took a deep breath, and she told her.

She spoke of Lari and her quartet vandalizing her room, threatening her, attacking her. She spoke of Atratus binding her in front of the class, striking her palm almost every turn, and sending her to scrub pots after classes so that she could not study. She spoke of all her fear and pain, the nightmare that had been the past few months.

"I'm frightened," she finally said. "I'm frightened of the Radians and I don't know what to do."

She stared expectantly at the headmistress, waiting for soothing words, a promise of protection, some wise advice or at least another embrace.

Instead, the headmistress lowered her head and spoke in a soft voice. "I'm frightened too."

Madori gasped. "But . . . you're a great mage! You're powerful. You're—"

". . . the daughter of a shoemaker," the old woman said. "An old woman. A teacher who loves her students. That is all." She stepped toward the window and stared at the university grounds. "And I love Teel more than anything. For a thousand years the headmasters and mistresses have watched over our school from this tower. We defended Teel even through the great wars with Arden and the kingdoms of Eloria. We were a beacon of knowledge and light, and now . . . now I fear that a great light rises, a light to blind, to burn us all, a light that will sear Mythimna. The light of Radian." Her voice dropped. "They do more in Teel than write pamphlets, chant slogans, and spread hatred. Madori, I have sad news to share with you. Professor Maleen has died."

Madori gasped and covered her mouth. Her eyes stung anew. "Died?"

Egeria placed her hand upon a book of herbalism. "Poisoned. The Night Plague—a disease some claim comes from Eloria, a disease Professor Atratus has been studying. I myself have fallen ill with it; for ten turns I writhed in pain before finding the magic within me to vanquish the illness."

A growl fled Madori's throat, and she clenched her fists. "Atratus! He poisoned you! He— He murdered Maleen!" She clutched the headmistress's hands. "How can you let him still teach here? Can't you dismiss him or . . . or fight him? Or do *something?*"

Egeria seemed to age and wither before Madori's eyes. "I could do all these things, and then his master would come to avenge his wounded pet. You have met his master." Egeria's voice twisted in disgust. "You have met Lord Tirus Serin."

Madori nodded. "Lari's father."

She thought back to her encounter on the road. How she wished she could return to that turn! She would have stabbed the snake in the throat had she known the full extent of his evil.

The headmistress looked at a parchment map that hung upon the wall. She tapped a drawing of a northern fort. "In Sunmotte Citadel he musters an army, and many more of his forces spread across our kingdom. His pets bark in all centers of power: Professor Atratus here at Teel and other, even crueler men in our great cities. His servants whisper in the ears of our king, guiding all his actions. And his arm reaches beyond Mageria. In all kingdoms of the daylight his men work. Already Radian chapters rise in Arden to our east, Verilon to our north, and Naya to our south."

Madori spoke in a small voice. "So what do we do?"

The headmistress turned toward her and held her hands. "We must be brave. We must fight them at every turn. You will stay at Teel, Madori, and you will learn magic. I am old and I am fading; you and your friends must pick up this fight. We need mages like you— not warriors but healers."

Madori glanced down at her hand; welts still rose upon it. "Atratus said I'm not to heal my wounds anymore."

The headmistress winced, her eyes pained. She stepped around her desk, opened a drawer, and rummaged for a moment. When she returned to Madori, the headmistress held a ring in her hand; it was shaped as a dragon biting its tail, its eyes gleaming gemstones. When she placed it on Madori's finger, the pain of Atratus's lashes faded.

"A ring of healing," Madori whispered. "Neekeya will be delighted."

Egeria shook her head. "No, not a ring of healing, for Atratus would see your wounds healed and find other ways to punish you. It is a ring to soothe pain."

Madori caressed the silver dragon.

But it does not stop the pain inside me, she wanted to tell the headmistress. *It does not stop the pain of my mixed blood, my memories, the hatred of others and my humiliation.*

She spoke softly. "I don't want you to fade, headmistress. I don't want you to stop fighting, to tell me that I must fight without you. I'm only a child. My friends are only children." She blinked a little too much. "I've always depended on my parents, and on you, to guide my way. How can I face this enemy? I'm not wise. I'm not brave. I'm not strong."

Egeria smiled—a smile of kindness, warmth, and sadness all at the same time, a smile that lit her eyes and creased her face. "The greatest heroes are rarely unusually wise, brave, or strong. They are ordinary people who stand up and do what's right."

When Madori left the tower, she kept running her fingers over and over the dragon ring. When she returned to her chamber, her friends were already asleep, but even when Madori climbed into her bed, sleep would not find her. She lay awake, staring at the ceiling, caressing her ring.

CHAPTER NINETEEN
POISON AND STEEL

Torin stood on the city walls, staring down at the sprawling Ardish army.

"Thousands of our finest men and women," he said, the wind in his hair. "The might of Arden."

They mustered in the western fields outside the walls of Kingswall, the ancient capital of the kingdom. Thousands of horses stood in formations, bedecked in armor. Riders sat upon the beasts, all in steel, holding the banners of their kingdom: a black raven upon a golden field. Behind the horses stood the ground troops: pikemen clad in chain mail, their pole weapons hooked and glinting in the sun; swordsmen clad in breastplates, their shields and helms displaying the Ardish raven; and finally archers in leather armor, one-handed swords hanging from their belts, their longbows as tall as men. Finally, behind the warriors, gathered the support troops: engineers, cooks, washer-women, blacksmiths, arrowsmiths, fletchers, cobblers, jugglers and singers, and many other tradesmen.

"I don't know if it's enough," said Cam. "And it pains me to move these men away from the capital. But Hornsford Bridge is where Serin musters, and that is the border we must defend."

Torin looked at his friend. To him, Cam would always be the shepherd's boy from Fairwool-by-Night, his oldest and dearest friend—a scrawny boy with a ready smile, bright eyes, and an easy laugh. Yet now on the walls, Torin saw a leader burdened with worry. Cam had married Queen Linee of House Solira, and he'd been sitting upon the throne for seventeen years now, and those years of concern had left their mark upon him. The first hints of wrinkles spread out from Cam's eyes, and the first gray hairs had invaded his temples.

Torin placed a hand on his friend's shoulder. "Are you sure you should ride out with them?"

The wind billowed Cam's hair and cloak. Looking down at the army, he nodded. "Yes. I will ride out with them. Linee will stay here upon the throne, and you'll be here with her. Serin hungers for our kingdom; I don't doubt that. Mageria has been aching for revenge since our two kingdoms fought a few decades ago. They conquered this city once; it was King Ceranor who drove the mages out. They've never forgotten that humiliation, and Serin will want his revenge, even if he was only a babe during that war." Cam wrapped his fingers around the hilt of his sword. "I will ride to Hornsford. I will stare him in the eyes, and I will not let him cross that bridge."

Torin stood on the city walls for a long time, watching as Cam joined the forces, watching as the thousands rode and marched into the distance, their armor bright and their banners high.

When he closed his eyes, Torin saw the war years ago. In his memories, he sailed south along the Inaro River with Koyee, two youths in a little boat, witnessing the horror of Mageria's magic: villages burned to the ground; skeletons of children sprouting two skulls; the charred remains of men and women, their ribs flipped inside out; gruesome hills of bones and the scent of death; and everywhere the buffalo of Mageria painted with blood. He and Koyee had fled the mages in the night city of Sinyong, and Koyee's arm still bore the scars of dark magic.

The last raven banners were now flying over the horizon, and the sunlight glinted against the last troops' armor; it reminded Torin of the strip of dusk back home. He took out the scroll he kept in his pocket, unrolled it, and read Koyee's letter for the tenth time since he received it last turn. It was written in Qaelish, the delicate characters written from top to bottom in neat columns:

Dear Torin,

I miss you and Billygoat and think about you every turn. I've been alone many times in my life, but now the loneliness fills me like icy water invading a cave.

I am frightened. You wrote to me of a menace, of a great light to sear all in its way, of a sun eclipsing the moon. This menace has stretched its fingers across all Timandra; it has reached even our village of Fairwool-by-Night, and its sigils are drawn upon doors and raised as flags in our fields.

I've been spending more time in Oshy across the dusk, and I cannot speak to you of our defenses lest this letter falls into the wrong hands. But I will say this: If we must fight, we are ready. We stand strong.

I've written to Billygoat, but I've not heard back, and I worry our letters our being intercepted on the roads of Mageria. I'm so afraid for her but I know she's strong. I love you and her and pray to see you again soon.

Your ever-loving wife,

Koyee

Torin rolled up the letter. He missed his wife, he missed his daughter, and he missed home. He wore the armor of a lord now—a breastplate sporting a raven sigil, greaves and vambraces, and a helmet—and a rich cloak hung across his shoulders. Here in Kingswall he was a knight, a hero, a warden of the throne. Yet all he wanted to do was wear his old clothes again, return to his village, and be a gardener and husband and father.

He climbed off the wall, mounted his new horse—not Hayseed but a swift courser from the queen's stables—and rode through his capital city. He looked around him at the city: the narrow brick homes, their roofs tiled red; the workshops of potters, smiths, tanners, gem-cutters, barbers, and other tradesmen, their signs swinging in the wind; towering barracks, most of their soldiers gone to war; and finally the palace, a white castle rising upon a green hill.

As he looked at the gardens and towers, he remembered coming here with Bailey years ago, and the pain of missing her stabbed him.

"Twenty years ago, you and I first came to this palace, Bailey," he whispered, his eyes stinging. "We fought against this kingdom, but now I must defend it. Now I'm here, fighting for Arden lest evil once more corrupts the lands of light. I wish you were here, Bailey, still fighting with me."

Almost two decades, he thought, *and I still miss her so badly it hurts. Time heals all wounds; never was a greater lie spoken.*

He let the stable boys take his horse, and he spent a long time walking through the gardens, thinking of those old days and old friends.

As flowers bloomed and spring's leaves rustled outside the window, Madori sat in the classroom, prepared for her final exam.

The exam paper sat upside down on her table—printed on real papyrus, a rarity here in the north. All around the classroom, other students sat before their own exams, waiting to flip them over. Madori nibbled her lip, trying to bring to memory all she had learned about Magical Principles—not only the three basic axioms but the hundreds of theorems structured atop them. When she glanced to the head of the class, she cursed the sight of Professor Atratus there. The stooped, hook-nosed man was pacing, staring at a draining hourglass, and waiting to announce the exam's beginning.

The vulture will unnerve me through the exam, Madori thought. *He's going to do something to ruin this for me, I know it.*

"Good luck, mongrel," rose a sweet voice to her side.

Madori glanced to her left, and her belly tightened further. As if it weren't enough that Atratus was overseeing this exam, his favorite student—Lari Serin—was sitting here beside Madori. The girl smiled sweetly, her golden locks tied in blue ribbons. She sat straight, her hands in her lap, her quills and inkpot organized like soldiers upon her desk.

Wishing she had been assigned a different seat, Madori forced herself to stare down at her desk, trying to banish Atratus and Lari from her thoughts. She stared at her silver ring which the headmistress had given her, a dragon chewing its tail.

Bring me luck, Shenlai, she thought; it was the name she had given the ring, the name of the legendary Qaelish dragon her mother had once ridden in battle.

Finally Atratus flipped over the hourglass.

"Begin!" he barked.

Hundreds of papers rustled as the students flipped them over and began their exam.

Madori took a deep breath and quickly scanned the exam. She breathed a shaky breath of relief. Despite spending most of her time scrubbing dishes rather than studying, she knew this material. Professor Fen had prepared the exam, covering all those topics

Madori had mastered: application of the three principles to different states of matter, weaving Herafon's Law into the Fourth Principle, claiming multiple materials simultaneously, and other topics Madori had been practicing in lieu of sleep.

I already failed Magical History thanks to Atratus, she thought. *But I can pass this class.*

She began to write furiously, answering question by question. Thanks to Shenlai, the ring that dulled feeling in her hand, her wrist didn't even hurt.

". . . through application of Sheritel's Fifth Principle, we can prove that the links between particles grow denser in direct proportion to the length of the claiming . . ." She wiped her brow and kept scribbling. ". . . thus, as steam does not rise from water heating under a claim, we demonstrate Karn's Law that changing states of matter requires a new cycle of principles . . . " She blew out her breath, blasting back her two strands of hair. " . . .stacking multiple materials in a forked chain allows us to skip from one to another, stacking claims simultaneously . . ."

Soon her arm itself was aching from so much writing, and she wished she had a magical dragon armlet too.

The hourglass spilled its sand.

An hour went by. Two hours. Three.

A few students finished their exams and placed them on Atratus's desk. Madori shook her arm and got back to writing, putting down the final words.

Perfect, she thought with a satisfied breath. *This is one class I don't have to worry about fai—*

Something hard hit her leg under the table, interrupting her thoughts.

She grunted.

The blow struck her again, and when she looked down, she saw a pulsing funnel of air—magic flowing from Lari's direction.

Madori growled and snapped her head toward Lari.

The young Magerian gave her a wink, then gasped and raised her hand. "Professor Atratus! Madori is looking at me! She's cheating!"

Madori leaped to her feet, knocking over her inkpot. "I was not!" She spun toward Lari, growling. "You're a liar. You're a filthy liar!"

She couldn't stop herself; rage flooded over Madori, blinding her. She leaped at Lari, knocking her off her seat. The cousins crashed onto the floor.

"The mongrel is rabid!" Lari screamed.

Madori grabbed the girl's hair, tugging and tearing those perfect golden locks. "I *am* rabid, and I'm going to destroy you, Lari. I'm done with your—"

Her words turned into a scream as fingers grabbed and twisted her ear.

Professor Atratus dragged her to her feet; Madori thought he could rip her ear straight off. When she struggled against him, he grabbed her wrist and twisted her arm behind her back.

"Professor Atratus, she's crazy!" Lari said, lying on her back in a puddle of ink. "I only tried to be a good student, and she just attacked me, and . . . and . . ." She covered her eyes, giving a rather convincing show of weeping.

Madori struggled to release herself as Atratus dragged her to the head of the class.

"Professor, she wasn't cheating!" Neekeya shouted, leaping to her feet at the back of the class.

Tam too leaped up. "Professor Atratus, Lari is lying, she—"

"Silence!" the professor boomed. "Whoever says the next word fails this class." He glared at the students. "Everyone, back into your seats. I will not tolerate impudence." He gave Madori's arm a painful twist, nearly dislocating it; she yelped. "And I will not tolerate filthy mongrel scum copying their answers from pure-blooded Magerians. The half-breed will be punished for this."

Her friends still stood at their desks, cheeks flushed and eyes wide. Jitomi had his hands raised as if prepared to cast a spell against the professor.

Standing by Atratus's desk, Madori looked at them and spoke softly. "It's all right. Sit down, friends. Don't fail your test because of me."

Reluctantly, glancing at one another, they sat down. She had told her friends about her magical ring; they knew Atratus's punishment wouldn't hurt her. Dozens of other students filled the classroom, staring at Madori. A few—foreigners from Arden—stared with pity. Many of the Magerian students, Radian pins upon their lapels, stared with smug delight.

"Hold out your hand, mongrel," Atratus said, raising his ruler.

Madori gulped and stretched out her palm. His ruler would raise more welts, but she knew the ring would protect her from pain.

"Lari, sweetness," said the professor. "Please, step to the front of the class. You've suffered the bane of this mongrel; I feel it most fair that you administer the punishment."

Smoothing her robes, Lari nodded. "Gladly." She stepped toward the front of the class, chin raised, and took the ruler from Atratus. She turned toward Madori and a cruel smile spread across her face. "I will make you pay for what you've done, mongrel."

Madori's heart sank. Her ring would protect her from pain, but not this humiliation. To have Lari strike her? She pulled her hand back.

"No," Madori said with a snarl. "You are no professor here, Lari. You are nothing but a rich, pampered little—"

Lari swung the ruler. It sliced the air with a whistle and slammed against Madori's cheek. Blood splattered.

Madori gasped. Pain bolted through her, so powerful she nearly collapsed, and she raised her hand to her cheek. Her heart seemed to stop and she couldn't breathe.

Before Madori could react, Lari swung the ruler a second time, lashing it like a whip, striking Madori's other cheek.

Madori stood, shocked, in too much pain to react. She could barely see. She could just make out Lari standing before her, smiling in delight, raising her ruler for a third strike.

Madori blinked.

Thoughts raced through her mind as Lari licked her lips hungrily, preparing to strike again.

I have to stop this now. I have to end this. Even if I fail this class. Even if I'm tossed out of Teel. She growled and raised her fists, prepared to attack. *This ends now—*

The classroom door burst open.

Professor Yovan raced into the room, stepping on his long white beard and nearly crashing to the floor. He panted, his hair in disarray, his cheeks flushed.

"The king is dead!" he cried out, arms raised, tears on his cheeks. "The king of Mageria is dead!"

Everyone turned toward the elderly wizard. Lari froze with her ruler in the air, Madori with her fists raised. Her friends had run halfway across the classroom to join the fray; they too stood frozen as if somebody had cast a spell, turning everyone to stone.

Professor Yovan panted, his lips trembling. "They say he was poisoned; his sons too. Lord Serin has ridden to the capital. Until a new king can be chosen, Serin sits upon Mageria's throne." A sob fled Yovan's lips, but he managed to square his shoulders and raise his chin. "May Idar bless the king's soul! May Idar bless our new Lord Protector!"

Madori stared at the old man, and her horror was too great, too horrible, too impossible to exist, to feel, to shake her. Everything seemed like a dream. She felt numb, surprisingly calm, as if her terror had risen so high it formed a circle with calmness like her ring, a dragon biting its tail.

Yet no other king will be chosen, she realized as the blood dripped down her cheeks. *And even Idar cannot save us now.*

She turned to look at Lari, and Madori saw something new in the girl's eyes—no longer hatred, anger, or even mockery. Looking into those blue eyes, Madori saw victory.

CHAPTER TWENTY
SUNS AND SERPENTS

They huddled in their chamber, the door bolted shut with magic, a chair propped up under the knob for extra protection. More magic shielded the window, gluing the shutters shut, but still the chants pounded into the room, and the walls shook.

"Radian rises! Radian rises! Hail Lord Serin!"

Jitomi stood guarding the window, hands raised as if prepared to cast magic. In the shadows of the room, he had doffed the thick cloak and hood he normally wore, revealing a lean body clad in black silk and leather. The dragon tattoo that ran up his neck and face seemed almost a living thing.

"They are growing in numbers," the Elorian said grimly. His large, oval eyes gleamed a dangerous blue. "Hundreds now march outside, chanting for this tyrant."

Guarding the door, Tam sighed. "If only Serin *were* a tyrant, we could hope to rebel against him. But it seems he's more of a beloved leader, at least judging by the reception he's getting here at Teel."

While Jitomi stood ready to cast magic, the young prince had opted for his dagger. Weapons were allowed at Teel only for ceremonial reasons—family heirlooms, religious blades, or magical artifacts—to be kept sheathed at all times. Yet this was no normal turn, and Tam's blade gleamed. The prince's eyes were dark, his lips tight, his muscles stiff.

Neekeya too stood with a drawn blade. Her sword was long and thick, its silver hilt shaped like a reptilian claw. The swamp dweller—normally bright-eyed, ready to smile, a naive girl lost in a foreign land—became a fierce tigress here, a beast ready to pounce. Her lip peeled back, revealing her teeth, and her eyes blazed.

"I say we fight them!" she said. "I'm a warrior. I'm not afraid. We'll slay Atratus and take Lari hostage and not release her until Serin steps off the throne."

Tam raised an eyebrow. "That's not a bad idea."

They all turned to look at Madori—Neekeya growling, Tam somber, Jitomi staring silently.

Madori sat upon her bed, caressing the copper coin that was her last memento from her father.

Simple change from our meal in the tavern, she thought, looking at the coin. *I was so scared then, but now I miss that turn. Things were so much simpler then.*

Her cheeks still stung from Lari's assault. Madori had healed the wounds with her magic, but the scars remained, pale and prickling. As her mother bore the scars of nightwolf claws upon her face, Madori's countenance now too was marred, perhaps forever, mementos from a different sort of beast.

"Well, Madori?" Tam said. "What do you think? What do we do?"

She raised her eyes back toward her friends, and a lump filled her throat.

"Why do you ask me?" she said, not without anger, and closed her fist around the coin. "What makes you think I know what to do? Why listen to my words?"

Neekeya tilted her head, her crocodile tooth necklace chinking. "Because . . . we're Madori's Motley. This is our quartet and you're our leader."

Sudden rage filled Madori, and she leaped from her bed. The chants still rose outside, and the walls shook as hundreds of feet pounded down the hall outside their door.

"Your leader?" Madori's voice rose so loudly she was almost shouting. "I never asked to be your leader. I don't want to lead anyone. Who am I to choose for you?" She looked at them one by one. "Neekeya, your father is a mighty lord, ruler of a pyramid. Tam, you're a prince for Idar's sake. Jitomi, you're the son of a noble warrior of Ilar, heir to a great pagoda overlooking the moonlit sea. Me?" She gestured at herself. "I'm the daughter of a gardener. I'm a half-breed. I'm from a backwater village. I'm . . . I'm . . ."

Her words failed her, and her eyes stung.

"You are the strongest, wisest student in this school," Jitomi said, finishing her sentence. Leaving the window, he stepped toward her and held her hand. His grip was warm and firm, his eyes soft. "I will follow your guidance. If you ask me, I will fight for you."

Fight? Madori walked to the window and peered through the crack between two shutters. A hundred students or more were marching outside, trampling grass and raising torches.

"Radian rises!" they chanted over and over.

Lari led the march, shouting out her hatred. "The Light of Radian now rules Mageria! Our light will purify our kingdom, driving out the mongrels, the nightcrawlers, the swamp barbarians, and all the cockroaches that infest our fatherland." The crowd roared their approval and Lari cried out louder. "Undesirables will burn in our fire!"

Madori turned away, facing her friends again.

Neekeya was shaking with rage. "That spoiled daughter of a snake! I'm going to wring her neck. Who does she think she is to speak like that?"

Madori sighed. "She knows exactly who she is. Mageria's new princess."

"And I'm Arden's prince," Tam said. "We can go to Arden—all of us. We'll sneak out of the school. We'll take refuge in Kingswall at least until this blows over." He sighed and his shoulders stooped. "Maybe this is a fight we cannot win. Maybe all we can do now is flee."

Again they looked at her for guidance. Again they awaited her words.

And I? I just wish my parents were here. They're war heroes. They would know. She lowered her head. *But perhaps that is my greatest lesson at Teel University—that I must become my own woman now, no longer a girl in the shadow of heroes but a heroine myself.*

She spoke carefully. "We cannot flee. Serin's fortress guards Hornsford Bridge, the nearest crossing into Arden. Magerian castles watch all major roads and smaller crossings; with the king dead, those castles now belong to Serin too. If we flee this university, Lari will have her father hunt us. Nor can we fight Lari here; she's too powerful, and too many follow her."

Neekeya wrung her hands. "If we can't flee or fight, what do we do? Just cower?"

Madori thought back to Headmistress Egeria's words in her tower. *We must be brave. We must fight them at every turn. You will stay at Teel, Madori, and you will learn magic . . . you and your friends must pick up this fight.*

"We *survive*," Madori said. "Lari might march outside, and Atratus might be spewing his bile in his classrooms, but Headmistress Egeria still leads this university. This is still an oasis of reason, even with a few mad dogs within our walls. The Radian Society of Teel wants us to either fight or flee; one way they can crush us, the other be rid of us." Madori squeezed her coin. "So I say we do exactly what they hate, exactly what they're railing about outside our window. We stay. We study. We show them that we will not be intimidated, we will not be drawn into a war, and we will not run." She nodded, gaining confidence with every word. "The year's classes are ending. Next year we will take all our classes together, and none of those Atratus teaches. Madori's Quartet will remain together always. We will take turns watching even as we sleep. We are in danger, but we will withstand this."

Figurines shook on the shelves, and a picture frame fell, as the boots stomped in the hallway and the cries pealed.

"Radian rises! Hail Lord Serin!"

* * * * *

A strange silence blanketed Teel University next turn. As Madori's Motley walked along a columned gallery, heading toward their next exam, they heard none of the usual laughter, conversation, and songs that filled the university. The chants from last turn had died too. The ash of torches swirled upon the floor, the only remnant of the Radians' rally. The quartet passed by only one other student, a jittery girl who rushed down the corridor, her head lowered. Even the birds seemed subdued; only a single crow cawed as it circled above.

The quartet was near the northwestern Ostirina Tower, about to enter and climb to their classroom, when they heard the horns blare.

"The Horns of Teel," Madori whispered, a chill gripping her. "The headmistress calls."

She shuddered. Madori had spent many hours reading history books in Teel's library; according to them, the Horns of Teel blew only in the most dire circumstances, calling all students into the cloister to hear the headmaster or mistress speak.

The horns blared again—a high, ethereal sound like the cry of some unearthly being. Madori had never seen the fabled dragons of Eloria—it was said that only one still lived—but she had always imagined their cry sounding like this.

Students began to emerge from classrooms like ants from a disturbed hive. Eyes darted and hands were wrung. Madori's Quartet was caught in the stream as hundreds of students headed toward the cloister.

When the horns finally fell silent, every student at Teel stood in the courtyard, first to fourth years. An eerie silence covered the university. Then, with the shuffle of robes, the crowd parted to let Headmistress Egeria walk toward the stage at the back, the place where she had first addressed Madori and her fellow applicants many months ago. For the first time since Madori had met her, the old headmistress walked with a cane, stooped over, and it seemed that she had aged many years since the last turn. Egeria had always seemed old but also vigorous and vivacious; now she reminded Madori of how her great-grandpapa had looked in his final days.

"Headmistress," Madori whispered as the elderly woman hobbled by her.

Egeria raised her head to look at Madori. Tears filled the headmistress's eyes. She whispered, her voice so low Madori barely heard.

"You must look after them, Madori. You must look after the others." The headmistress glanced behind her and paled. Furtively, she placed a folded piece of paper in Madori's hand.

Glancing behind her again, the headmistress kept moving toward the stage. When Madori too looked behind, she saw Professor Atratus standing between the columns of the eastern gallery, his arms crossed, his eyes blazing as he stared at the headmistress. He seemed like a master watching an errant pup.

The headmistress reached the stage. Leaning on her cane, she hobbled up the stairs and turned toward the crowd. Even standing at a distance, Madori saw that fresh tears filled Egeria's eyes. Murmurs of conversation swept across the crowd.

The headmistress raised a trembling hand, and the crowd fell silent. Egeria spoke for them all to hear, her voice soft at first but gaining strength with every word.

"Dearest students, you have heard many stories, rumors, and whispers over the past turn. The tidings from the south have been confirmed. The old king of Mageria is dead. The cause of death reported is . . ." Egeria glanced to the shadows where Atratus was watching her. She swallowed and a tremble filled her voice. ". . . the Night Plague, a disease spread from Eloria. Lord Tirus Serin, Warden of Sunmotte, has been crowned our new king."

A new murmur swept across the crowd. Several cheers rose, along with chants for the Radians. Madori forced herself to keep staring ahead, her jaw tight, refusing to look at Lari who stood across the field; she had a feeling that Lari was staring right at her.

The headmistress gestured to two fourth year students. Both stepped onto the stage, carrying a chest between them. Both sported Radian pins upon their lapels. The students opened the chest and tilted it forward, revealing hundreds of pins.

Egeria kept speaking, her voice trembling. "Henceforth, on orders from our new king, all Timandrian students at Teel University shall wear Radian pins, showing the sun eclipsing the moon." Her voice cracked. "All Elorian and half-Elorian students will wear a different pin, this one shaped as a snake. You will now step forth, one by one as your names are called, to receive your pins."

Madori glanced aside at Jitomi. He met her gaze, his eyes dark.

Professor Atratus stepped onto the stage next, unrolled a scroll, and spent the next hour barking out names. Students approached, one by one, to receive their pins. The Timandrians accepted their Radian pins with pride, some adding a chant for Lord Serin and Radianism. Whenever an Elorian student stepped onto the stage, Atratus sneered and held out the serpent pin in disgust.

Finally Madori's name was called. She trembled with rage when she stepped onto the stage and faced Atratus.

"A serpent for a worm," Atratus said, glee in his eyes, his lips curled back in a mockery of a grin. He slapped the brooch against her chest. "All will now know that Elorians and mongrels are beasts that crawl in the dust."

When all the students had received their pins, Egeria addressed the crowd again. She stood upon the stage and let her cane drop; it clattered onto the stage. Madori thought the old woman would fall, but Egeria spoke in a loud voice, tears streaming down her cheeks.

"Students of Teel University! Be strong. I promise you—no Elorians will be hurt on my watch. You are safe, my students, regardless of what pin you wear. Be strong and know that I protect you."

Madori's Motley spent the rest of the half-turn in their chamber, guarding the door and windows. All classes and exams had been postponed; instead, the Teel Radian Society rallied in the cloister. The sound echoed across the university, shaking the chamber walls. Standing at the window, Madori heard Professor Atratus shout of sunlit domination, heard Lari—head of the Radian Society and now Princess of Mageria—demand to drive out the undesirables. After every slogan, the crowds cheered and the walls shook anew.

"Perhaps Tam was right," Jitomi said. The Elorian stood guarding the door, his snake pin fastened to his cloak. "We can still flee. While they rally."

Madori bit her lip.

Perhaps they're right, she thought. *Perhaps we should leave.*

She tried to imagine returning home—to her parents, to old Hayseed, to her old bed, to her books and dolls and the silver flute her mother always tried to force her to play. Back in Fairwool-by-Night, she was nothing but a lonely girl, a misfit, powerless and aimless. Here at Teel she had found a purpose, but what hope did this place now have for her?

"I understand, Jitomi," she said softly. She lowered her head, her throat tight. "When the bells next chime, and everyone is sleeping, you should leave." She had to blink rapidly. "This place is no longer safe for you. But I must stay."

Tam stepped toward her and clutched her arms. "Billygoat, your life is at risk here. Leave Teel too. I'll go with you. I'll shelter you and Jitomi in Kingswall—all other Elorian students here too, if they'll join us."

"And I'll go with you." Neekeya nodded emphatically, placing a hand on Madori's shoulder. "This place is too dangerous. We all leave together."

Madori laughed mirthlessly. "You are both Timandrians. You wear the Radian pins upon your lapels. Jitomi and I wear the serpent pins; we're in danger, but you're safe."

It was Tam's turn to laugh. He tugged off his Radian pin, tossed it onto the ground, and stomped on it. "What Radian pin?"

Neekeya tossed down her own pin and shattered it beneath her foot. "I don't see any Radian pins."

"Atratus won't be happy." Madori bit her lip. "Those pins might be the only thing that keeps you safe now."

"Then I'd rather be in danger," Tam said. Holding her, he stared into Madori's eyes. "Billygoat, we've been friends all our lives. I'm not going to toss you to the wolves. If you and Jitomi have to leave this university, Neekeya and I are going with you, and we'll keep you safe on the road."

He pulled her into his arms, and Neekeya joined the embrace. Madori—almost a foot shorter than them—disappeared into their warmth, and she could not curb her tears, for despite the pain and fear she felt beloved, and she felt safe.

And yet . . . Egeria's old words returned to her.

You will stay at Teel, Madori, and you will learn magic.

Her eyes stung.

She thought back to the war stories her parents had told her. Torin and Koyee, the great heroes of the war, had many chances to return home. They had kept going—traveling into the heart of darkness, the flames of war, determined to fight for what was right, willing even to die for truth.

I am Madori Billy Greenmoat, she thought. *Billy after Bailey, the great heroine who fought with my parents.* Bailey had died in that war, fighting against the evil sweeping across Moth. She had given her life and saved this world. *How can I, the daughter of heroes, flee an enemy?*

"No," she whispered, still wrapped in the embrace. "No, my friends. I will not flee. When you escape danger rather than face it, it will forever hunt you. Here within the walls of Teel will I make my stand. Evil rises; I will face it. Like my parents did. Like Bailey did. I will become a mage."

Her friends stepped away, looking at her strangely, as if she had changed before them like a creature in Transformations class. And perhaps she had changed.

Hardship changes us. It turns us into heroes or cowards. When disaster strikes, we metamorphose into the person who's been sleeping inside us.

She was about to say more when the door shook madly.

The Motley spun toward the door. Madori sucked in breath and raised her hands, already readying herself for magic. The door rattled again and chips of wood flew.

"Death to Elorians!" rose cries outside. "Drag out the nightcrawlers and show them Timandrian pride."

Tam and Neekeya raced forward and pressed themselves against the door. It shook again and more wooden fragments flew. A hinge came loose.

"Drag them out and make them pay for their sins!" somebody cried outside.

Madori was already whispering under her breath, repeating the theorems she had learned in her classes. She quickly claimed the floor, rattling the tiles to send the hinge into the air. She switched to claiming the air, shoving the hinge back against the door, then switched again, claiming the hinge and bolting it back into the door and wall. At her side, Jitomi was busy casting magic too. A funnel of air left his hands, drove toward the door between Tam and Neekeya, and flattened against it, providing extra weight.

The door held. The window shutters smashed open behind them.

Madori spun around at once, claimed the flying shards of shutters, and tossed them back at the window. A student outside—a fourth year—cried out in pain, the wooden chips driving into his face.

"The snakes are attacking!" he cried.

"Jitomi!" Madori cried. She was already tossing a cone of air at the window, sealing the entrance with an opaque, swirling blob. Jitomi added his own shield. The air in the room thinned, most of it shoving against the window and door, leaving Madori lightheaded.

Behind her the door shook again; a crack tore open across it. Hands reached inside. Tam and Neekeya were still pushing their weight against the door when magic coalesced outside, forming a smoky battering ram, and drove forward.

The door shattered into countless pieces. Wooden shards flew. Tam and Neekeya fell and sprawled against the floor.

The empty doorway revealed a columned arcade swarming with Radian students, all proudly displaying their pins. Some were raising Radian banners.

Lari stood among them, hands on her hips. She pointed into the chamber and screamed, "Grab the nightcrawlers! Punish the creatures who poisoned our old king!"

Not waiting another breath, Madori thrust both her arms forward, palms facing outward. Collecting particles of dust and wooden chips, she wove a ball and tossed it forward. The missile flew toward Lari, but the princess was too swift. She swept her arm, diverting the projectile with a blast of air.

Radians spilled into the room, eyes blazing, teeth bared, feral animals on the hunt.

"Call them back or you'll pay for this, Lari!" Madori shouted. "Your father's arse might be warming the throne, but Egeria still rules Teel."

Lari smirked. "Such a mouth on those creatures. I will enjoy smashing that mouth."

Violence filled the room with shouts, thuds, and splatters of blood. Neekeya swung her sword, keeping the blade sheathed, slamming the wooden scabbard against an assailant's head. Tam thrust his dagger in one hand, a chair in the other. Jitomi was muttering spells and Madori made an attempt to claim a Radian's boots and tug him onto the floor.

A student—Derin, the tall boy from Lari's quartet—leaped toward her. Madori jumped back but was too slow; Derin's fist slammed into her cheek, knocking her down. She blinked, seeing stars, and kicked wildly. Her foot hit Derin's shin and he fell, muttering curses. Three other Radians replaced him, leaping onto Madori, and she screamed and punched one's face. Her ring cut through his cheek and he fell back.

Elorian curses filled the air, and Madori kicked off another student to see Radians mobbing Jitomi. The Elorian boy was swinging his fists, shouting battle cries in Ilari, the tongue of his southern empire.

But the Radians were too many; a dozen filled the room and a hundred others filled the arcade outside. Boots pressed down on Madori, pinning her to the floor. Fists slammed into Neekeya and Tam, knocking them down. Hands grabbed Jitomi, tugging him outside.

"Jitomi!" Madori cried out, and another fist drove into her head, and for a moment she saw only shadows and lights, heard only ringing.

She thought that she would die here. Blood filled her mouth and dripped into her eyes. She had no time for magic; it was all she could do to keep breathing. She had to keep breathing. Breath by breath, like her father had taught her. Yet Torin had meant that breathing was easy, a rhythm always with her, an anchor to cling too. Right now breathing felt like the most difficult thing in the world, and boots drove into her stomach, and she doubled over.

No. I won't die here.

Lying on the floor, blows raining onto her, she balled her hands into fists.

Her parents had fought in the great Battle of Pahmey. They had sailed down the Inaro and slain mages in the port of Sinyong. They had faced the demon Ferius in Yintao, the greatest battle in the history of Moth, and finally slew him upon the Mountain of Time.

I am the daughter of heroes. I will not die in a school scuffle.

She pushed herself to her feet, and her magic blasted out of her.

Air slammed into her assailants. Furniture flew, crashing against them. Radians thudded against the walls, banged their heads, then slumped down, unconscious.

Neekeya lay on the floor, a gash bleeding on her forehead. Tam lay above her, shielding her with his body. Both were still breathing. Madori stood in the center of the room, feeling as if she held the air, the walls, the entire university in her arms. She had claimed objects before; now Madori felt as if she had claimed the world, held everything around her in her awareness.

Silent, her palms held outward as if carrying the weight of the air, she walked outside.

She stood in the cloister's eastern arcade—a portico of columns ahead of her, arches above her, the wall of chamber doors behind her. A mob of Radians had pinned Jitomi to one column. The Elorian was unconscious, his chin slumped to his chest, but the other students were holding him up. Fists and kicks thumped against the boy's thin frame. Blood ran down Jitomi's chin.

Madori thrust her arms out, palms facing toward the mob of Radians. Air blasted them, knocking them down. Standing a dozen feet away from him, Madori stretched out one finger, supporting Jitomi with a funnel of air. She gently lowered him to the ground.

A gurgling gasp sounded behind her.

Her strands of hair rising like seaweed in the water, crackling with energy, Madori turned around to see Lari.

The new Princess of Mageria stared, her own hair wild, her fingers curled up at her sides.

Madori smiled crookedly and took a step toward her.

With a strangled yelp, Lari spun on her heel and fled.

Madori wanted to chase the girl, to hurt her, maybe even to kill her, but her friends needed her. With the Radians all unconscious or fled, Madori released her magic, letting go of the awareness that connected her with all materials around her. She raced toward Jitomi and knelt above him.

Cuts covered him and blood dripped from his mouth. He was still breathing but that breath was shallow. Madori closed her eyes, trying to summon more magic, to heal his wounds, but she was too weary. Her body shook, and she found herself slumped next to him.

Footsteps thudded down the hall.

With a flutter of robes, Professor Fen burst into the hallway. The bald, mustached man gasped and sputtered.

"What— What—"

More feet shuffled, and old Professor Yovan raced from between two columns, nearly tripping over his beard. Madori tried to explain. She tried to tell them it wasn't her fault, but only slurred words left her mouth, barely words at all, merely sounds.

She tilted and Fen caught her head before it could slam against the floor. The last thing she saw was his concerned face, and then his eyes became blue oceans that she drowned in.

CHAPTER TWENTY-ONE
CAGED

Madori stood above his bed, her head lowered.

"I'm sorry, Jitomi." She tasted tears on her lips. "I'm so sorry."

He slept in the infirmary bed, breathing softly. Several other beds were occupied: some with other Elorian students, pulled from their rooms and beaten in the cloister, and other beds with Radians, many of whom Madori's magic had battered. Only by miracle had nobody died that turn.

But you came close to dying, Jitomi, she thought.

He seemed so peaceful, sleeping there. The dragon tattoo seemed to be sleeping too, its tail coiling along his neck, its head resting above his eye. Madori stroked the boy's hair. It was soft, smooth, and white as purest silk, the same hair her mother had, that all Elorians had. She leaned down and kissed his forehead.

"I'm sorry, Jitomi." Her tears splashed against him, and on a whim, not even realizing what she was doing, she kissed his lips.

He stirred and moaned. Madori pulled back, shocked at herself, raising her fingers to her mouth. She had kissed him! He was lying here sleeping, and . . . and . . .

She had never kissed a boy. One time back at her village, not long before leaving to Teel University, the brewer's boy had kissed her cheek and almost her mouth, a quick peck which had made her cheeks flush. But this—this had felt real, a kiss of compassion and excitement.

His eyes opened and he blinked a few times, struggling to bring her into focus.

"Madori," he whispered. "Why? Why are you sorry?"

She lowered her head and clasped his hand. "I'm sorry for Timandra, for the pain you experienced here. I'm half Timandrian. This is half my home. And . . . you came here, to our lands, seeking knowledge and magic. And this happened."

He smiled. "If you kiss me again, I will think it worth it."

She felt her cheeks flush and cursed herself. But she kissed him again. And it felt just as right.

Yet suddenly her eyes were damp, and a lump filled her throat, and she thought of the song she had sung—"The Journey Home." For a long time, Madori had thought that song meaningless to her, thought that her home lay hidden, a place she still had to find. But perhaps her home had always lain behind her old village, beyond the dusk, in the shadows of Eloria. Perhaps she had had to travel into sunlight to realize her home lay in moonlight.

"Someday, when we're mages, we'll return home," she whispered. "Our home lies in shadows . . . to the darkness we return."

She sat on his bed, then lay down beside him, placing her head against his shoulder. She laid her hand on his chest, and he stroked her hair—the stubble on the back and sides and the long, silky strands that framed her face.

"Do you remember just lying on a hill, watching the moon?" he said. "Did you ever imagine faces on it, dream of mountains and valleys?"

She nodded, smiling to herself, remembering her summers in Oshy. "Always. And do you remember the stars? I had a book of constellations, and I'd try to see them all in the sky. I used to imagine that the stars were distant worlds, millions of them, so far away I could never reach them. I imagined that I had a ship that could sail through the sky, and I visited every world, meeting dragons and clockwork soldiers and wise elders with long white beards."

"In Ilar we believe that the stars are great, distant flames, each borne by a great warrior." Jitomi smiled wryly. "In Ilar, most of our tales are of warriors, assassins, swordsmen, spies. Imagine me there—a thin boy who prefers to read books over swinging blades. My father thought me weak—no better than a girl, he said. You can imagine why I wanted to explore the lands of sunlight."

Madori thought back to her own kingdom of the night, the great land named Qaelin, a sprawling empire of crystal towers, pagodas as large as all of Teel University, and a little village by a starlit river. She nestled against Jitomi. "So when we graduate, come with me to Qaelin. Forget about Ilar if your people don't respect you. Forget about this land of sunlight. We'll both go to Qaelin, two mages. We can live by the river, imagine faces on the moon, and seek the constellations."

Robes fluttered and Professor Yovan shuffled toward them, clucking his tongue.

"Now now, little boy," said the professor, pointing at Madori. "You must let young Master Jitomi get his rest." The old man tossed his beard across his shoulder and rolled up his sleeves. "I've healed most of his wounds, but he's still weak, and he still needs more healing." He touched the scars on her cheeks, the ones Lari had given her. "Did you heal these wounds yourself, little one?"

Madori nodded. "I did."

The old healer beamed. "Excellent work! Since the first lesson I taught you, I knew you were a great healer, little boy."

"Girl," she said.

He snorted, fluttering his lips. "Same difference. Now get off that bed and let me do my magic."

Professor Yovan was rolling his sleeves back down, and Jitomi had fallen back asleep, when the Horns of Teel blew again.

* * * * *

When Madori stepped back into the cloister, answering the bells' call, she found the place transformed into a nightmare.

General Woodworth, the great elm tree, had been cut down. Where it had grown now rose an iron statue, twenty feet tall, depicting Lord Serin clad in armor. The tyrant was facing east toward the distant lands of night, his fist against his heart, his second hand holding his sword. From the galleries—four rows of columns that surrounded the courtyard, leading toward the dormitories—hung great banners of Radianism, depicting the sun eclipsing the Elorian moon. The old wooden stage was draped with more banners, and a podium rose upon it, displaying the sigil in gold and silver. Worst of all, soldiers surrounded the expanse, clad in black steel, holding pikes and shields.

For a moment Madori thought she had entered the wrong place. This seemed less like a university and more like a military camp.

When all the students stood in rows, the horns fell silent and Professor Atratus stepped onto the pulpit. He no longer wore his ratty old robes, the ones with the fraying hems. His new robes were darker than the night, hemmed in gold. Lari rose to stand at his side, wearing a golden tiara and holding a scepter, its head shaped as the eclipse of Radianism.

Across the cloister, everyone stared—other professors, Timandrian students with Radian brooches, and Elorian students with their snake pins. After a long moment, Atratus spoke, his voice so loud—magically amplified—that Madori started.

"Students of Teel. Fellow professors. I have some news that may upset—or delight—you. Headmistress Egeria has been accused of a terrible crime." Atratus sneered. "We all witnessed it at this very place only last turn. She stood upon this stage, vowing to defend Elorians—our enemy, the enemy of every pure-blooded Timandrian. Treason!" He pounded his fist into his palm, and students jeered across the cloister. "For her treachery, the illustrious Lord Serin, God of Sunlight, has sent forth his troops to protect us. Egeria has been sent to the capital in chains to stand trial for her crime." Some students gasped at this; others cheered. Grinning like a wolf over its prey, Atratus continued. "My great lord has named me, his humble servant, new Headmaster of Teel."

Madori could barely remain standing. Her head spun and Tam had to grab her lest she fell.

It's over, she realized. *My dream to become a mage, my hope of surviving here—gone.*

A drum beat and the sound of hooves rose from behind. Madori spun around to see two burly black horses—each twice the size of Hayseed—pull a wagon into the courtyard. The driver seemed almost as beefy as the horses, his frayed robe stretching tightly across his board shoulders, his hood revealing only a stubbly chin and thin lips. Upon the wagon rose an iron cage roughly the size of the Motley's bedchamber.

Atratus spoke again, restrained glee twisting his voice. "All subhuman undesirables, those wearing the serpent pin of shame, are henceforth banished from Teel University. You will step onto this wagon, which will transport you to the border of Mageria. There you may go where you will, so long as you never more set foot upon the lands of glorious Radianism."

The cloister burst into chaos.

Students gasped. Some cheered. At once the soldiers stepped forth, marching among the rows of students, shouting out the names of Elorians.

"Shen Quelon!"

"Heetan Doromi!"

"Danong Fan!"

A few of the Elorian students glanced around nervously, then followed the soldiers toward the wagon. Other Elorians were too slow to budge; the soldiers grabbed their arms, manhandling them toward the cage. The names kept ringing across the university.

"Keshuan Hatan!"

"Maen Hao!"

"Jitomi Hashido!"

Standing beside Madori, the tattooed Elorian boy glanced at her.

"Don't go," Madori whispered to him.

Jitomi touched her cheek. Fear filled his large blue eyes—but courage too. "It will be all right. I—"

Soldiers grabbed him, tugging him away from her. Madori shouted. She tried to tug him back. She leaped onto one soldier, only for the brute to shove her down. She landed hard on the cobblestones.

"Jitomi!" she shouted, a soldier's boot on her chest, pinning her down.

Jitomi looked at her, a sad smile on his lips, as the soldiers tugged him toward the wagon. Already they were shoving Elorians into the cage. One girl moved too slowly; a soldier backhanded her, spraying blood, and shoved her into the cage, slamming her against the bars. Jitomi climbed in solemnly, refusing to be shoved, holding his head high. He stood tall, staring at Madori between the bars, his face expressionless.

Finally twenty-five Elorians filled the cage, pressing against one another—the entire Elorian population of Teel. Madori still lay on the cobblestones, the soldier pinning her down, his boot nearly cracking her ribs.

It was Atratus himself who called her name, shouting it out like a curse. "Madori Greenmoat!"

The soldier lifted his foot off her chest and leaned down to grab her.

With a snarl, Madori hurtled a ball of air against him. With a clank of armor, the man fell.

"No!" Madori shouted.

Several more soldiers advanced toward her. She hissed and chose their armor, claimed the metal, and heated it. The metal turned red hot, and the soldiers screamed, pawing at the straps, trying to tear off the plates.

"I will not leave!" Madori shouted. She chose the air beneath her and shoved herself several feet above ground. She hovered, gazing at the crowd. "I am the daughter of Torin Greenmoat, a hero of Timandra, a warrior of sunlight. This sunlight flows through my veins. I will stay at Teel. I will become a great mage." She stared at Atratus across the crowd. "You cannot deny my Timandrian blood. I stay."

Atratus grinned—a horrible grin that seemed to split his face in two, stretching from ear to ear, revealing all his crooked teeth. He thrust out his palm, driving a ball of smoke and dust her way. The projectile took the form of a snake, hissing, fanged, its eyes blazing white. Madori tried to block the attack, but the snake tore through her defenses and wrapped around her.

She crashed down, writhing, the smoky serpent crushing her. Its fangs drove into her leg, and she cried out in pain.

"Chain her!" Atratus shouted, voice rising like steam, his amusement and hatred coiling together. "Chain her and toss her in with the others."

The soldiers tugged her to her feet. A fist drove into her cheek, and she saw nothing but darkness. Her chin tilted forward, and the magical serpent still wrapped around her torso, hissing, licking her with an icy tongue. She tried to struggle. She screamed, kicked, blasted out magic. But she was only one girl; she could not resist them all.

Chains clamped around her wrists, binding her arms behind her back. More chains hobbled her ankles. The guards dragged her toward the wagon.

"Look at me, Timandra!" Madori shouted as the guards lifted her. "Look at me and behold your shame! I curse you in the name of darkness."

Smirking, the soldiers shoved her into the cage. She thudded against the other Elorians, and the cage door swung shut. The lock was bolted, sealing her within. Blood dripped down her forehead, and she tugged at the door and bars, but they wouldn't budge. The cage was so crowded she had no room to sit; the Elorians pressed against one another like matches in a box.

The driver cracked his whip, and the horses began to move, tugging the wagon out of the cloister. The Radian students began to cheer, tossing mud and refuse onto the wagon. An egg flew through the bars and cracked against Madori's face. A rotten potato followed, spilling its liquid onto her. Every student they passed shouted in mockery, and one tossed a stone; it slammed into Madori's shoulder.

"Goodbye nightcrawlers!" the students chanted. "Radian rises!"

As the wagon trundled across the courtyard, Madori—covered in trash and blood—stared between the bars, and all her rage drained away. Chained, beaten, broken, she could only stare in stunned silence. Her eyes fell upon Tam and Neekeya; her friends were standing among the crowd of Timandrians, hugging each other, their faces pale and their eyes wide. Neekeya was weeping and Tam was shouting something toward Madori, but she couldn't make out his words.

She raised her eyes. Upon the stage, rising from the crowd, stood Lari Serin. The princess pouted mockingly at Madori, drew a fake tear down her cheek, and waved.

The wagon passed under the archway, and the doors of Teel University slammed shut behind Madori, forever sealing its secrets, knowledge, and magic.

CHAPTER TWENTY-TWO
GLASS AND STRAW

Cam stood in the rocky field, military tents surrounding him, and stared dubiously at the contraption.

"Are you sure this will work?" he asked, hearing the doubt in his voice. "It looks a little . . . wilted."

The camp bustled around him: troops marching between tents, smoke rising from a hundred cooking fires, swordsmen drilling in the dust, archers shooting at straw targets, and squires polishing the armor of knights. They had been camped here at Hornsford for several turns now, guarding the bridge from Mageria. Even from here, a couple miles away, Cam could see the tip of Sunmotte Citadel upon the western horizon.

You muster there, Serin, he thought, grimacing. *Twenty thousand of your troops drill for war. Soon you will try to cross Hornsford Bridge . . . and I'll be waiting.*

He returned his eyes to the contraption that swayed in the fields before him. The two dojai—assassins and spies from the darkness of Eloria—called it a hot air balloon. To Cam it looked more like a giant, half-inflated sack of wine.

He turned toward the two dojai who stood beside him. One was small, no larger than a child, clad in tight black silk. Many daggers hung on belts across her chest, throwing stars were strapped to her legs, and her large Elorian eyes gleamed in the sunlight. The second stood seven feet tall, his chest broad as a barrel, his long white hair flowing in the wind. His eyes, though also large, were narrowed to mere slits, mimicking the line of his mouth. A massive katana, large as a spear, hung across his back.

"Oh, you silly king!" said Nitomi, the smaller of the pair. "Of course it's looking a little wilted. It's not inflated yet! Once inflated it'll be the size of ten elephants! If you skinned them, that is, and sewed their skin together into a balloon." She tapped her chin. "Do you think it would float though? You know, because elephant skin is really thick and wrinkly, and besides, I like elephants and wouldn't want to skin them. Do you have elephants in this army of yours? I want to ride one! I rode a panther here—you know, we have lots of those in Eloria—but an elephant! With the trunk and all. Do you think their trunks can hold a sword? I can try to train one, maybe a whole army of swordsman elephants—I mean, swordselephant elephants. I mean—"

Beside her, the giant dojai groaned and covered his ears. "Qato hurts."

Nitomi looked at her companion, then slapped her palm over her mouth. She spoke between her fingers. "I've gone and done it again, speaking too much. My mother always told me: Nitomi, your mouth will fall right off. I've never seen a mouth fall off before, but once I think I saw a lizard's tail fall off, and—"

"Nitomi!" Cam said, interrupting her. The only way to have a conversation with the little dojai was to interrupt a lot. "Focus. The hot air balloon. Are you sure you know how to fly it?"

Her face brightened. "Of course I do! I've seen loads of hot air balloons! I—"

"*Seen?*" Cam asked, grimacing.

She nodded, grinning, and hopped around. "Oh yes, I've seen many paintings of them!"

Cam groaned. "Paintings?"

Nitomi nodded again. "Oh, they're so beautiful. I used to look at them all the time as a little girl. I can't wait to be in one myself! Hey, Cam, do you know how to fly hot air balloons?"

He gripped his head. "Nitomi! Idar's beard! You're the dojai here. You're the Elorian. You're the one who brought the hot air balloon here all the way from Eloria. How would I know how to fly it?"

She placed her hands on her hips, raised her chin, and glared at him. "Well, you're a king. You should really know these *spying* things, Camlin, especially since you intend to use this *spy* balloon to *spy* on the enemy. I mean, who do you think I am?"

"A spy!" he shouted. "Isn't that what dojai are? Spies and assassins?"

She looked down at her black silks, many daggers, throwing stars, and grapple, then back up at him. Her eyes widened. "A *spy*! That's what I am! Oh my, I did wonder why you brought me here. You know, I always thought dojai were just sort of sneaky and quick, but spying! That explains a lot." She turned toward Qato. "We're spies, Qato!"

The giant Elorian groaned. "Qato knows."

During the conversation, the hot air balloon had continued to inflate. The fire burned inside the basket, filling the balloon with more and more hot air. Soon the basket began to float, ropes tethering it to the ground.

Quick as a gazelle, Nitomi bounded into the basket and grinned. Qato followed, silent and grim; the basket dipped several inches, brushing the ground.

"Come on, silly!" Nitomi said, gesturing for Cam. "Step inside. We can't do all the spying for you."

Cam groaned. "That's the whole idea of me hiring spies."

Nitomi nodded vigorously. "And see? We brought you a hot air balloon. We've earned our keep. And I'm not flying without you! My mother always told me: Nitomi, if you ever meet a king, you can't fly off in a hot air balloon without him! Well, at least, I think she said that. She might have been talking about how I'm full of hot air, and how I'm not supposed to talk so much around a king, but I reckon I've already done a lot of that around you, so it's too late, and now you have to fly with me."

Cam couldn't argue with that logic. Sighing and rolling his eyes, he stepped into the basket and untethered the ropes.

The hot air balloon began to rise.

Cam leaned over the edge of the basket. Every foot ascended revealed more of their camp. The tents stretched out in rows. Between them, troops were drilling, sharpening swords, cooking meals, standing guard, and all awaiting the bloodshed. The balloon rose higher, revealing the edges of the camp: horses in corrals, palisades of sharpened logs, women washing clothes and pots in the river, engineers arguing over the construction of trebuchets, and dozens of supply wagons traveling along the road through the plains of Arden, bringing in supplies. Beyond the men rolled the vastness of the world: fields of swaying grass, hills speckled with boulders, copses of elms and birches, and the Red River flowing across the land.

The warriors of Arden, the bravest and strongest of their realm, are only ants from up here, Cam thought, the realization spinning his mind. *That's all we are, insects bustling across the world. Viewed from far enough above, the wars of men are no more significant than those of ants.*

"We're flying!" Nitomi's eyes widened. "Everything looks like toys from up here, as if I can just reach down and pick them up."

The little dojai leaned over the basket, reaching into the air, then yelped as she tilted over. Cam had to grab the seat of her pants and tug her back into the basket.

Qato groaned and clutched his belly. "Qato queasy."

Nitomi bustled about the basket, tugging ropes and pulleys. Vents opened in the balloon, releasing streams of hot air, propelling the vessel westward toward the riverbank. Cam himself felt queasy as the basket tilted, the balloon dragging it through the air, and he clutched the rim. Qato turned green.

Only Nitomi remained high-spirited. "It's like flying on a dragon!" She grinned. "Did you know that Koyee and Torin flew on a dragon once? Really, I saw it! Do you think they have hidden dragons in Timandra? Do you think we'll see one? Do you think they have elephants here?" She hopped about, rocking the basket. "Maybe it'll let us ride it—the dragon, that is, if they have one—though I hope it's not scared of this balloon, because when I was a little one, I saw a floating lantern once, and I thought it was a ghost, and then—"

"Nitomi!" Cam grabbed her. "We're sinking. Fly this thing!"

She gulped and nodded, tugging more ropes and twisting knobs. Vents closed and more heat blasted upward. The balloon began to ascend again, then veered westward. They left the riverbank behind, floated above the Red River, and were soon flying over the plains of Mageria. Hornsford Bridge seemed smaller than a toy from up here, its towers no larger than wooden counter-squares pieces. Further west, however, Sunmotte Citadel still seemed forbidding, even from this high above. Its mote, double walls, and guard towers shielded its inner core of many towers and banners. It seemed to Cam almost as large as Kingswall.

But Kingswall is a city of tradesmen, artists, thinkers, families, he thought. *This citadel houses nothing but soldiers dedicated to destruction.*

Myriads of those soldiers stood outside the citadel, drilling in the fields: swordsmen clad in black armor, riders upon horses, and mages in black robes. Lines and lines of the troops stretched across the fields, Radian banners rising among them. Most of the troops remained still, maintaining their orderly rows. Only a handful bustled about, pointing up at the balloon.

"Nitomi, take us a little higher," Cam said.

She nodded, tugging more ropes to seal the vents, then twisting knobs to release more heat. The balloon ascended higher, hovering over the army below. A few Magerian archers tugged back bowstrings, and arrows flew into the air. Cam winced and caught his breath, but they were high enough; the arrows reached their zenith below the basket and fell back downward.

Cam leaned over the basket, frowning. "Only a handful of archers are firing. Only a few soldiers are moving—mostly the ones on the perimeters." He tilted his head. "Something is wrong here. Nitomi, take us a little further west—over those lines of troops."

She nodded and the balloon moved across the sky. They hovered over the lines of horses and swordsmen. And yet the troops below stood frozen.

Nitomi opened a cylindrical case which hung from her belt and pulled out a long instrument. It looked like a leather scroll, but glass lenses sealed each of its ends. The little dojai brought one lens to her eye, leaned over the basket, and stared down. She gasped.

"Oh dear! They . . . Cam, they're just frozen. Frozen like freezing ice frozen by freezing spells!" She gulped, straightened, and handed him her instrument. "Look."

Cam frowned at the cylinder. "What is this tool?"

"A scope!" Nitomi grinned. "We build them in the Dojai School in the mountains. Nobody else in all of Moth knows about them, only us spies. Well, I guess you know about them now too. But don't tell anyone!" She growled and raised her fist. "It's supposed to be a secret, but I've gone and talked too much again, and now you know too, so you *have* to *promise* to be quiet, because if you tell anyone about scopes, I'd probably have to kill you—the Dojai School demands it!—but I don't really want to kill you, because I like you, almost as much as I like elephants, so—"

He patted her shoulder; the little woman seemed so agitated her eyes were dampening and her cheeks flushing. "I won't tell," he said. "I'll just look and return the scope to you."

Gently, he took the scope from her hands, placed the lens against his eye, and looked downward. His breath caught. He lowered the scope, raised it to his eye again, and shook his head in amazement. This piece of Elorian ingenuity amazed him as much as the hot air balloon. Staring through the scope, the soldiers below seemed several times larger, so large he could make out the Radian sigils upon their breastplates.

He frowned. "Something's wrong."

Nitomi nodded. "I'd say a massive army mustering right on our border is something wrong. Almost as wrong as skinning elephants. I—"

"Not that." Cam stared through the scope again, looking at the rows of swordsmen, horses, and archers. "They're . . . dummies. Straw dummies. Thousands of them."

Nitomi tilted her head, grabbed the scope from him, and stared down. She gasped and covered her mouth. "Evil magic! Somebody turned them all to straw!"

Cam's heart sank, and a tremble seized his legs. "No magic," he whispered. "A ruse."

He tightened his jaw and balled his fists. He thought of his wife, beautiful Queen Linee; of his best friend, Torin; of hundreds of thousands of people back in Kingswall.

He turned to the two dojai. They were staring at him silently— Qato somber as ever, Nitomi gasping.

"Take us back to our camp," Cam said, forcing the words past stiff lips. "Kingswall is in danger . . . and a month's ride away. We head back at once."

CHAPTER TWENTY-THREE
INTO THE WOODS

The wagon trundled down the road, jostling the Elorians inside their cage. With every bump, Madori slammed against the bars, and her fellow outcasts swayed and pushed her harder against the iron. They were only a few miles away from Teel University now, but bruises already covered her body. The gloomy sky and clammy rain did little to alleviate her discomfort.

"Damn shackles!" For the hundredth time, she chose and claimed the shackles that bound her wrists and ankles. Try as she may, she couldn't change the metal, only rattle it, nor could she snap the iron—it was too hard. "I can't break them."

Jitomi stood with his arms wrapped around her, providing only partial protection from the iron bars and the elbows of their fellow students. Still, she was thankful for his embrace.

"We're too weary for magic now." He kissed her cheek and tucked one of her strands behind her ear. "And it's hard to change something as intricate as a lock when the wagon keeps bouncing. When we stop, we'll try again."

She sighed and leaned her head against his shoulder, only for the wagon to bounce again and toss them against the bars. She winced. She imagined that under her robes, her body was striped like a zebra. Shivering with cold, weary, and aching all over, healing magic was beyond her grasp too. She made a halfhearted attempt—the latest in many—to claim and bend the cage bars, only to slump in weariness again.

"If only we had stayed at Teel another year, we'd be powerful enough to break out of this place," Madori said. She sighed. "I didn't think our first year at Teel would end like—"

"Silence, nightcrawler!" shouted the wiry, one-eyed soldier Madori had secretly nicknamed Patchy. Walking beside the wagon, the brute lashed his club between the bars. Madori tilted back just fast enough to avoid the blow. "You talk again, I open this cage and bash in your teeth."

On the other side of the cage, the second guard—this one a beefy, older man with white stubble—burst out laughing. "We'll soon do some bashing. Lord Serin said we reach the forest first. There we—"

"You too shut your mouth!" snapped Patchy. "I'll bash your teeth in too."

The larger guard fell silent. The two kept trudging through the mud, the rain pattering against their helmets and armor. Ahead upon the wagon, the third of their captors—the dour coach rider—leaned forward in his seat. Madori had still not heard that one speak nor seen his face. From the cage, the driver seemed like a gargoyle, hunched over and stony, the rain streaming off his cloak.

We'll soon do some bashing . . .

Madori looked at Jitomi. She saw the same concern in his eyes.

He leaned against her, pretending to kiss her ear, and whispered in Qaelish, the language of her Elorian homeland. A child of Ilar, his accent was thick but his words confident. "Conserve your magic. You might need it yet."

She stroked his head and nestled against him, pretending to nuzzle his cheek. "Where are they taking us, Jitomi?"

He held her close, stroking the stubbly hair on the back of her head. "I don't know but I doubt they'll just set us free." He let his hood droop, curtaining their faces, hiding them from the guards. When he spoke, his lips brushed against hers. "Whatever happens, I'll look after you."

She nodded, her eyelids brushing his cheeks. "And I'll look after you. I'm a better mage than you are."

He sighed. "With me battered and bruised, there are lumps of coal that are better mages than me right now."

She stifled a laugh, glancing back at the guards. "I've seen you in Magical Healing. There were always lumps of coal better at magic than you, at least in that class."

"Well, Madori, you are the best healer Teel has had in—" He bit down on his words and glanced out the bars; Patchy was walking near again, grumbling under his breath about nightcrawlers and their stench.

Madori too feel silent, deciding to conserve her breath along with her magic. She stood still, holding Jitomi, wishing the cage left her room to sit down or even stretch. The other outcasts pressed against them, silent and dour, rain dripping off their robes and white hair.

The hours stretched on and the guards gave them no rest. Thunder rolled in the distance and lightning flashed, illuminating a distant fort upon a hill. Madori was nodding off—even as she still stood on her sore feet—when she saw the marching army.

She stiffened. Jitomi inhaled sharply and held her closer. Around them, the other students narrowed their eyes.

Countless Radian troops were marching toward them along the road, each man clad in steel and armed with a sword, dagger, and spear. When lightning flashed again, the Radian eclipses shone upon breastplates, shields, and helmets. The wagon was moving north while these troops marched south, moving in two lines, mud staining their boots.

"Elorian prisoners!" one soldier cried out, his eyes widening to see the cage. "Damn nightcrawlers."

Another soldier guffawed and slammed his blade against the bars. "Hang these bastards. Death to Eloria!"

The wagon kept trundling south, and the soldiers passed them by, one line of troops on each side, as if the wagon were rolling down some great, steel throat. Some soldiers stared with wide eyes, others sneered, and some guffawed. One man began to sing a song, its words lovingly detailing the plunder of Eloria and the slaughter of "nightcrawlers." Soon all the troops were singing as they walked by. One man tossed a rock into the cage, hitting Jitomi in the shoulder. Another soldier dropped his pants and wriggled his backside at the cage.

"Kind of looks like Lari," Madori remarked to Jitomi.

"Enjoy your bars, scum!" one troop said and spat onto Madori. "Once we invade the night, we won't just cage you. We'll drive our swords into your bellies." He waved his sword as if to demonstrate.

It seemed an hour that the troops kept walking by, two by two; there must have been thousands. Finally the last stragglers passed them by, leaving the wagon to trundle alone along the cold, empty road.

"They're all riled up and look ready for war." Jitomi whispered. "Where do you imagine they're going?"

Madori chewed her lip. "Not to attack Arden; an army that size would have to cross at Hornsford, and they're moving the wrong way. Might be a battle on the southern border with Naya. Or maybe Serin just wants to bolster his troops in the capital, and—"

"Silence!" Patchy's club swung through the bars again, hitting Madori on the arm. "One more word and teeth spill."

She fell silent but her mind still worked feverishly. With Serin on the throne and his troops moving across the land, war was near. She had heard enough of her parents' war stories to smell it in the air. She thanked Xen Qae, Idar, and the constellations of Eloria that at least Mageria shared no border with the night. If Serin had access to Eloria, she had a feeling all those troops would be streaming into the shadows right now, plundering and butchering and burning.

Arden still separates Serin from the night, she thought, feeling some relief. *King Camlin and Queen Linee defend that land. Serin cannot cross.* She took a shuddering breath. *Eloria is safe.*

Trying not to remember the stories her parents had told her of the last invasion of Eloria, she leaned her head against Jitomi's shoulder. He held her close and stroked her hair, running his hand again and again between the stubbly back and the long, silky strands that drooped from over her brow.

They must have been traveling for at least a turn now, maybe two. Madori's belly ached with hunger, and her eyelids drooped with weariness. At some point she nodded off, pinned between the bars and Jitomi, sleeping fitfully even as the wagon bounced and her feet ached beneath her. When she opened her eyes again, the rain had stopped, though thick clouds still covered the sky; it seemed almost as dark as Eloria, and she was thankful for her oversized eyes. Jitomi was still awake, his own large eyes gleaming as they moved back and forth, scanning the landscape.

While she had slept, they had entered a forest. Oaks twisted around them, their trunks forming the shapes of beasts and cruel faces in her imagination. Pines coiled, sending branches like lecherous fingers to slap against the bars. With the canopy shielding the overcast sky, the light dimmed further. The leaves turned dark gray, the shadows dark like demons lurking between the trunks. Madori was reminded of the dusk, that twilit strip that lay many miles away, a land neither day or night. When lightning flashed, the trees—white, looming, twisted—seemed like goblins about to strike, their faces long and cruel.

Finally the wagon rolled to a halt.

The prisoners—Madori had come to think of them as prisoners rather than outcasts—jostled against one another. After moving for so long, even in stillness Madori's head spun and her legs swayed. Patchy—she still did not know his true name—spat into the dirt, unlocked the cage, and tugged its door open.

"Everybody out!" He banged his club against the bars. "Out, vermin! Out or I'll burn the lot of you."

Madori stood closest to the door. She had spent the ride wanting nothing more than to leave the cage. Looking around at the dark forest, she suddenly preferred staying behind the bars. Yet when Patchy raised his club again, she winced and began to climb out. Her ankles were still hobbled, her wrists chained behind her back, and she could only move slowly. Once past the cage door, she slipped off the wagon's edge, tilted over, and thumped facedown into the mud. The foul paste filled her mouth, and Patchy stood above her, his boot inches from her face.

"Up, maggot." He grabbed her by the collar and yanked her to her feet. Madori growled, spat out mud, and lunged toward him, intending to knock him down. He stepped back and Madori, weak and dizzy, fell back into the mud.

It was Jitomi who helped her rise, as gentle as Patchy was rough. The other Elorians emerged from the cage too. They stood together on the roadside, twenty-five banished students.

"Where are we?" Madori said. "You can't just leave us here. We're in the middle of nowhere. We'd never find our way home from here."

The trees creaked and a rider emerged onto the road, still cloaked in shadows. A voice rose, smooth and cruel as a blade.

"My darling Madori, that is exactly the idea."

The horse stepped closer, revealing the rider—a tall man in armor, his hair golden, his eyes cold and blue. The hard, handsome face twisted into a smile.

Madori sucked in her breath and took a step back.

"Lord Serin," she whispered.

CHAPTER TWENTY-FOUR
THE BATTLE OF MUDWATER

Torin walked through the palace gardens with his queen, missing his home so badly even the aromatic flowers, the bright birds, and his queen's company could not soothe his soul.

"I've never seen you so troubled." Linee's brow furrowed in concern, and she placed a hand upon his arm. "Torin, smile for me."

He looked at Linee—his queen and his very old friend. Her golden hair was raised in an elaborate construction of braids and curls, and her gown shone with jewels. Idar's sigil, a half-sun, gleamed upon her breast. Torin took her hands in his and squeezed them, thinking back to that turn—twenty years ago—when he had first come to these gardens and met his queen. Linee had been only twenty then, a silly young woman, flighty and careless as a butterfly. The years had filled her eyes with wisdom but had not dulled her beauty; her skin was still unlined, her hair untouched by white, the only sign of her age a lingering sadness that hung about her like a shadow over a summer garden.

"Queen Linee Solira," he said softly, her hands in his. "Few will know what we've been through, how we fought, how we suffered, what we saw all those years ago. We've lived in peace since then. We cannot let this peace burn."

"We will not!" she said. "Cam guards the bridge; it will not fall. Our walls here are strong; they will stand."

Torin watched a bumblebee fly from flower to flower. "Lord Serin sits upon Mageria's throne, and he will not sit idly, content to rule one land. He does not muster his forces for defense but for war. Eloria is the prize he craves . . . and we stand in his way."

Linee nodded. "And we will remain standing. We've sent word to the night; troops will arrive from Qaelin, swelling our numbers. Already our smiths work turn by turn, forging new swords and armor. Already our commanders train new men to fight upon our walls and in our fields." She touched Torin's arm. "We've faced enemies before and defeated them. Last war, we were not afraid."

He smiled thinly. "Last war we were young. Youths are too naive for fear, perhaps. But now we're older, and now, yes Linee, I'm afraid."

She smiled too, head lowered. "I lied. I was afraid last time too." She looked back up at him, and her eyes sparkled with tears. She pulled him into an embrace and laid her head upon his shoulder. "I'm glad you're here. I know how hard it is for you, being away from Koyee and Madori. Thank you."

He was still holding her when the alarm bells clanged across the city.

Linee gasped and stared at him with wide eyes. Torin grimaced and clenched his fists. The bells pealed across the gardens, not the high bells of festivals but the deep, harsh bells of war.

It's too soon, Torin thought. *Serin's forces are still at Hornsford. We're not ready.*

He tore apart from Linee. He ran.

He could barely remember leaving the palace gardens. Within what seemed like heartbeats, he was donning armor and riding his horse out the palace gates. A horseman met him there, riding up from the city streets, his face dripping sweat. Torin recognized the youth: Prince Omry, the heir to Arden, a seventeen-year-old boy several minutes older than his twin, Prince Tam.

"Sir Greenmoat!" said the prince, his brown hair matted across his brow.

Torin halted his horse. The bells still clanged across the city. "What's the news, Omry?"

"An enemy in the south!" Omry panted. "They're emerging from the forest across the river. They march onto Mudwater Bridge."

Torin cursed and spurred his horse. The beast burst into a gallop, and Omry rode at his side. They raced down the cobbled streets of Kingswall, passing between tall buildings of white bricks and red roof tiles, leaving the palace behind. Steeples, domed temples, and squat workshops all blurred as he galloped, and Torin's heart seemed to beat with the same intensity as his horse's hooves. Other soldiers were bustling around him, heading to the southwestern wall. City folk—merchants in dyed cotton, tradesmen in leather and wool, and commoners in homespun—rushed into their homes, climbed onto roofs to peer south, or prayed in the streets.

Finally Torin reached Tigers' Gate, one of Kingswall's seven gates. Two towers framed its archway, guarding the southwestern wall. A thousand years old, Tigers' Gate had long been a passageway for Nayan merchants. The fur-clad, fiery-haired rainforest dwellers often entered this gate, bringing the bounty of their realm: tiger pelts, ivory jewels, caged birds, cocoa and coffee beans, exotic fruits, aromatic sandalwood, and spices not found north of the Sern River. For a thousand years, Tigers' Gate had been the valve connecting Arden with Naya.

The bells still clanging, Torin dismounted his horse and entered the gatehouse. He climbed the spiraling staircase, finally emerging onto the top of the western tower. Standing between the battlements, he stared south and felt himself pale.

A cobbled road ran out the gate, traveling across the plains to the Sern River, the border with Naya. The Sern was a mile wide, gushing and uncrossable, aside from a ford a mile southwest of the city. Here, where the river thinned, the road connected with Mudwater Bridge. The bridge was narrow, half the size of the great Hornsford in the north—a passageway for merchants, its bricks mossy, its foundations overrun with reeds. A single tower guarded the northern, Ardish side of the bridge; the southern side disappeared into the Nayan forest. Mudwater was usually empty, only seeing traffic every seven turns when Nayan merchants emerged from their forest, pushing carts full of supplies.

This turn, standing atop the tower, Torin beheld a host of hundreds emerging from the forest, bearing Radian banners.

"Magerians," he whispered, staring at their black steel plates, their longswords, and the dark robes of their mages. "Serin's men."

Omry emerged onto the tower battlements too, stared at the host, and drew the symbol of Idar—a semicircle—upon his chest. "Idar save us."

The forest rustled behind the enemy troops; it seemed to Torin that thousands of soldiers still hid among the trees. The chants rose, ringing across the land.

"Radian rises! Radian rises!"

Torin clutched the battlements, understanding at once. Of course. He gritted his teeth, and his heart banged against his ribs.

We were fooled. Of course Serin let us escape at Hornsford Bridge. Of course he let Cam and I come here with the news.

"Serin never intended to attack at Hornsford," he muttered. "The bastard drove through Naya, hidden in the rainforest, like a clot crawling hidden through a vein. And now he strikes at our heart."

Below in the courtyard, Ardish riders were gathering before the gate, their horses armored. Spears glinted and shields displayed the raven of Arden upon gold fields. Behind them, along the streets of Kingswall, footmen were gathering, clad in chain mail and bearing longswords.

"It's not enough," Omry said, echoing Torin's thoughts. "With most of our troops in the west, this city is a ripe fruit for the picking."

Torin grunted. "Yet we will fight the enemy nonetheless."

The two men raced down the tower, ran into the courtyard, and mounted their horses, joining two hundred other riders. Several hundred infantrymen stood behind them, swords drawn. A squire blew a horn, and the doors of Tigers' Gate creaked open, revealing the countryside, the river, and the distant bridge. Already the enemy banners—the buffalo of Mageria and the eclipse of Radianism—were crossing toward the northern bank.

At the head of the city forces, Torin raised his katana—the sword Eloria had gifted him almost two decades ago, the sword he had fought the last war with, the sword he would finally wield again. "Men of Arden!" he shouted. "War! War is upon us. Fight with me, with Torin Greenmoat. Fight for Arden!"

With a sound like thunder, the riders of Arden burst out of the gates and galloped across the plains of their kingdom.

"Sons of Arden!" cried Prince Omry, rising at Torin's side. "Raise the raven banners and send the enemy to the Abyss!"

The land rose and fell around Torin—a river to his left, the plains to his right. They streamed forward, two hundred horses, tearing up grass and dirt, as behind them surged hundreds of footmen. Ahead, blood rose in a mist from the center of the bridge; the Mudwater's defenders, a mere fifty Ardishmen, were clashing swords with the enemy and falling fast. Before Torin could even reach the bridge, the last defender fell.

Banners raised high, the riders of Mageria streamed across the bridge, heading onto the Ardish riverbank. Horsemen rode at their lead, all in steel, a vanguard of two hundred riders. Behind rode robed figures upon midnight stallions, their faces hidden inside their robes. Finally, behind these dark mages, marched the infantry of Mageria, emerging from the trees in two rows like serpents of many steel segments. Leading this host rode its captain, a figure taller than any Torin had ever seen. The man—if a man he was—rode upon a horse the size of an elephant, and four arms sprouted from his torso, each holding a blade. Upon his black breastplate, burning like red fire, appeared the eclipse of Radianism, shining with horrible light.

"Here rides Lord Gehena!" said Prince Omry, riding at Torin's side. "Books speak of him, a man magically enhanced, mixed with the blood of ancient giants."

The dark captain raised his head, and he seemed to stare across the plains directly at Torin. Two hundred yards still separated the hosts, and a black helmet like a barrel hid the giant's face, but Torin saw red eyes gleaming within, staring into him, searing like two embers pressed against his flesh.

He swallowed down the fear that choked him, tore his eyes away from the horrible half-man, and shouted to his troops. "For Arden! For our home! Send the enemy back and know no fear!"

Hoisting the raven standards, outnumbered many times, the forces of Arden galloped to meet their enemy.

The armies crashed on the northern riverbank with a shower of blood and shattered steel.

Spears flew Torin's way. One slammed into his horse, snapping against the animal's armor. Another shattered against Torin's shield, showering wooden shards. Torin's head spun. His heart leaped into his throat. His pulse thrummed in his ears. His hand shook around the hilt of his katana, and he was there again, back in the night, a youth fighting the hosts of sunlight, Koyee at his side.

He gritted his teeth.

Breathe.

He sucked in air.

Survive breath by breath.

He leaned forward in the saddle, driving into the enemy.

A rider charged toward him, swinging a sword. Torin blocked the blow with his shield, swung his own blade, and shattered the joints of armor at the man's elbow. The arm bent with a sickening *snap*, and Torin thrust his sword again, denting the steel. Blood seeped. A second rider attacked from his left, and Torin swung his shield, driving the wooden disk into the enemy's helmet. His fellow riders fought around him, thrusting lances and slashing swords.

"Omry, get back to the city!" Torin shouted. "Organize a defense on the walls."

The young prince shook his head, sweat dripping down his face. "I fight with you, Torin! I—"

Horses screamed.

The air thinned, streaming away from Torin, leaving him gasping.

He stared ahead, saw them, and felt the blood drain from his face.

Mages.

A dozen rode from the bridge, the soldiers of Mageria parting to let them through. The mages' hands were raised, collecting the air into swirling balls thick with dust, smoke, and pieces of shattered steel. As one, the mages tossed forward their missiles.

Torin tried to dodge the projectile hurtling his way. He tugged his horse left, only to crash into another animal. His horse reared, wind shrieked, and pain and darkness flowed over Torin.

Blood splashed. Armor cracked.

He fell.

He saw nothing.

Pain drove through him, and he realized he had fallen onto his back. Still he couldn't see. The smoke clung to him, covering his visor, tearing at his armor like a demon. He grunted, blinded, unable to breathe. He pulled off his helmet and tossed it aside, and the darkness cleared, revealing a shadowy beast that wrapped around the fallen helmet, crushing it into a steel ball. More smoke clung to Torin's armor, scratching, tearing, denting. Torin screamed as he tugged off the steel plates and tossed them aside, freeing himself from the translucent creature. His armor had shielded him from the magical attack, but Torin's heart sank to see that his horse had been less fortunate; the smoky tendrils were crushing the lifeless animal.

Torin barely had time to catch his breath. Through the smoke they came marching—the ground troops of Mageria, moving in columns, two by two, covered in steel, their swords held before them, their shields guarding their flanks. Their boots moved in unison, reminding Torin of a great, mechanical centipede.

He lifted his fallen katana. Fellow Ardishmen came to stand at his sides.

"We will send them into the river," Torin said. "Soldiers of Arden, you will defend your border. Turn the river red with their blood!"

His fellow Ardishmen pointed their swords forward, shouted, and ran with Torin to meet the enemy.

The forces crashed together with spraying blood and clanging steel.

Thousands of blades swung.

It seemed to Torin that they fought for hours upon the riverbank. Men fell every moment, both those of Arden and the enemy, and the river turned red. Everywhere the enemy surged: swordsmen, riders, mages tearing off armor and shattering flesh. Swords cut into men. Magic tugged bones out of living bodies. Soldiers lay in the grass, clutching wounds, screaming, weeping, calling for their mothers.

Torin limped along the bloodied grass, an arrow in his leg, and raised his head to behold a horror from the underworld.

The captain of the Magerian hosts, the creature Gehena, had joined the fight, no longer content to command the battle from the sidelines. His four arms swung, each wielding a blade the size of a plow. Men flew like scattered toys. The captain's horse, a towering black beast, drove down hooves larger than human heads, crushing bodies beneath them. Arrows, broken blades, and spears pierced the dark captain's torso, but the creature seemed unaffected. Still his red eyes blazed within his black helm, and still his blades swung, cutting down the men of Arden.

"The bridge is fallen!" Prince Omry shouted, clutching Torin's arm. The young man's armor was cracked, and blood coated him. "We must flee!"

Torin nodded grimly. Hundreds of Magerians now covered the Ardish riverbank, flowing into the plains. More kept emerging from the forest.

The bridge is lost.

A squire brought him a riderless horse. Torin climbed into the saddle and raised his banner.

"Men of Arden!" he shouted hoarsely. "Back to the city! To Kingswall!"

They rallied around him.

They fled across the plains.

And they died.

With the bridge abandoned to the enemy, the full wrath of Mageria flowed across the river, a great shadow spilling forth. Arrows flew into the fleeing men. Magic tore through them. The laughter of Gehena echoed in their ears, high-pitched, the shriek of demons. Every step it seemed that another man fell.

Bloodied, limping, their armor shattered, the last defenders of Kingswall entered their city.

The gates slammed shut behind them, sealing out the enemy.

When Torin climbed the tower again, he clutched the battlements, shaking, barely able to breathe.

The enemy covered the land in a carpet of black steel. A hundred thousand troops or more hid the plains, chanting, waving the Radian banners. Dark mages rode upon dark mounts. Siege towers rolled forth, topped with steel, as tall as the city walls. Catapults and trebuchets rolled into formation, their boulders ready to fire. A great wheeled cannon rolled among them, forged as an iron buffalo; Torin had seen these weapons in Eloria but never in the lands of sunlight. And still more enemies flowed across the bridge, a never-ending stream like gushing oil.

"Death," Prince Omry whispered, standing at Torin's side upon the gatehouse.

Torin closed his eyes for only a moment.

I love you, Koyee. I love you, Madori. I miss you and love you both so much. I wish I could tell you that one last time.

He forced himself to take a deep, shuddering breath.

Again.

Again.

He opened his eyes, looked at Prince Omry, and held the young man's arm.

"Death," he agreed. "But first war. We die here, but not without a fight. We go down firing our arrows, swinging our swords, and singing of our home."

The prince nodded, his eyes damp, and raised his sword upon the wall. Around them, a hundred archers emerged to nock arrows and tug back their bowstrings.

Ahead in the fields, the trebuchets and catapults swung. Boulders, arrows, and blasts of dark magic flew toward the city of Kingswall.

CHAPTER TWENTY-FIVE
GRAVES

Lord Serin stood among the trees, smiling thinly as he examined the
Elorian prisoners.

"Men!" he said. "Step forth. Hand them their shovels."

Five Radian soldiers emerged from the forest. Three held
loaded crossbows, pointing them at the outcast students. Two other
soldiers tossed down long leather bundles; they thumped against the
ground and unfolded, revealing many shovels.

"What are you doing here, Serin?" Madori spat out. Her ankles
and wrists still chained, she hobbled closer to him. "Go back to your
lair and leave us."

The tall lord burst into laughter. He looked over his shoulder
and spoke to the shadows. "You were right about her, my daughter!
She's a vicious little thing. I do admire the scars on her cheeks. Your
work, no doubt?"

"But of course." A sweet smile on her lips, Lari stepped out
from the forest, holding a crossbow. She aimed the weapon at
Madori. "And I will hurt her worse if she tries to escape."

Madori sneered and made to leap at Lari, but the girl placed her
finger against the trigger. The crossbow creaked and Madori froze,
glaring at the girl and her father.

"Very good," Lari said, still smiling sweetly. "You will stand
still. If you try to attack me, you will die. If you try to escape, you will
die. You and your nightcrawler friends will do as we command." Her
voice rose to a shout. "Dig!"

Madori growled, looking between daughter to father. "How
about you two go suck on rotten eggs?"

Lord Serin sighed and nodded toward his daughter. Lari
grinned, raised her crossbow, and fired.

An Elorian student—a studious boy named Shen—clutched his
chest, a quarrel in his heart. He gasped, gazed at Madori, then fell.

Other Elorians screamed. Madori began to rush toward the fallen boy. Jitomi hissed and stepped toward Lari, hands crackling with magic. Soldiers laughed.

"Freeze!" Serin barked. "Any one of you nightcrawler scum moves an inch, unless it's to dig, your death will follow. Lari, if anyone else causes trouble, fire again. Fire at random." Serin's lips peeled back in a horrible grin. "Now, nightcrawlers, you will behave. Lift the shovels and begin to dig. Dig a trench here on the roadside. Go!"

Glancing around nervously, some weeping, the Elorians lifted their shovels. They approached the roadside and began to dig. Only Madori stood still, chin raised.

"I can't dig with these chains on me," she said, glaring at Serin.

He snapped his fingers, and her chains shattered and fell to the ground.

Madori brought her arms forward. After being chained for so long, her muscles screamed in protest, and blood covered her wrists. She was free! She could lunge at Lari and Serin. She could fight. She could—

Lari fired her crossbow. The quarrel whizzed by Madori's head.

"Dig!" the girl shouted, already loading another quarrel. "Dig or the next one hits your twisted mongrel heart."

Grumbling, her belly knotting with fear, Madori grabbed a shovel and joined the others. They dug along the roadside. Whenever Madori glanced over her shoulder, the soldiers raised their crossbows, and Lari shook her head while smiling her sweet smile. Madori returned her eyes to her work. The ditch was soon a foot deep, several feet wide.

Madori took a deep breath, summoning her magic. She was hurt, weary, and famished, and she doubted she had enough magic to fight with. But she could muster a little trick she had learned in her classrooms, a way to speak to her classmates without the professors hearing. Though her head blazed with pain, she chose and claimed the air between her and Jitomi. She formed an invisible barrier to block sound waves, then spoke softly.

"Jitomi!"

Digging beside her, he glanced at her. She saw in his eyes that he recognized her magic; they had often communicated like this in Professor Atratus's class. He whispered, allowing his words to reach her ear but not cross the magical barrier toward the Radians.

"Madori, I don't like this. We're digging our own graves."

She wouldn't look at him as she spoke. "I think so too. We have to attack them. Do you have enough magic in you to thicken this barrier of air? To block their crossbow quarrels?"

He nodded, an almost imperceptible movement. "Yes. Joined with your magic, yes. We'll create the barrier, then bolt into the trees."

"No." Madori tossed a shovel of dirt across her shoulder. "If we run, they'll track us. They'll catch us. We fight them."

Jitomi glanced over his shoulder, then back at her. "There are ten of them. Too many."

"Only two are mages—Lari and her father. The other eight are dumb soldiers. There are twenty-five of us and—"

A whip cracked. A soldier shouted behind them. "Get back to shoveling! Faster!"

Madori grunted and shoveled faster. She risked a glance at Jitomi and spoke before her shield of air could deteriorate, letting her voice through to the enemy.

"Pass the word on," Madori said. "On my signal, we raise barriers of air. The magic will block the first round of crossbow quarrels. Before the enemy can load again, we bang them with shovels."

Jitomi nodded and turned toward the Elorian beside him, conveying the information. The ditch was two feet deep by the time Jitomi glanced back toward her. He spoke two words, each one cold and hard as a blade.

"We're ready."

Madori took a deep breath, tossed a shovelful of dirt over her head, and spun toward the soldiers on the road.

"Now!" she shouted.

She claimed the air. She thickened her barrier. At her side, her fellow Elorians spun with her, and the air thrummed and solidified, forming an opaque shield.

The Radians fired their crossbows.

The air rippled like a pond under hail, wobbling as the quarrels slammed into the force field. The bolts shattered. Shards of metal and wood flew. Several shards passed the barrier and hit Madori's body, cutting her skin but not sinking deeper. The shield of air vanished, and the Radians began to load more quarrels.

Madori and the Elorians charged at them, shovels swinging.

A flash of fear filled Lari's eyes, bringing a smile to Madori's lips; she couldn't wait to slam her shovel into that pretty face. Lord Serin, however, smiled too—a smile lush with cruelty, amusement, and a hint of admiration.

Forget about Lari, Madori told herself. She screamed and charged toward Serin. *I go after the big fish.*

She lunged toward the lord, shovel swinging, as he thrust his sword toward her.

* * * * *

The enemy covered the land, spreading into the horizon, a sea of steel surging forth.

Their catapults swung. Their trebuchets twanged. From the ranks of enemy troops, dozens of boulders hurtled through the air, bristly with metal spikes.

Torin stood upon the walls of his city, hundreds of soldiers stretching to his sides. Protector of Kingswall, he raised his sword and cried at the top of his lungs.

"Archers! Fire!"

Around him, a hundred archers loosed their arrows. Whistles filled the air. A hundred glinting shards flew upward, reached their zenith, then plunged down toward the enemy. Below upon the fields, shields rose. Arrows slammed into wood. Three men fell dead, maybe four. Jeers rose from the enemy troops.

With a rumbling like thunder, the enemy's boulders slammed into the city of Kingswall.

One stone crashed into the wall beneath Torin, cracking the stone. The battlements shook. Another boulder sailed over his head, and Torin looked over his shoulder to see a steeple snap, tilt, and slam down to drive into the street. Other boulders slammed into houses, crashing through tiled roofs.

"Trebuchets, fire!" Torin shouted.

The contraptions of wood, metal, and rope twanged upon the city ramparts. Flaming barrels flew from the battlements of Kingswall, spinning and shrieking, to crash into the enemy below. Magerian troops fell, fire blazing across them.

"Archers!" Torin shouted and more arrows sailed.

Fire crackled in the field. Smoke rose. With a blast of smoke and flame, the buffalo cannon fired. The world seemed to shake. The cannon ball, large as a boulder, slammed into a turret only paces away from Torin. The tower crumbled. Bricks rained and archers fell. Dust filled the air. The blast nearly knocked Torin off the wall.

Mules grunted in the fields, clad in steel, tugging forth siege towers of wood and metal. Enemy archers stood upon them, firing onto the walls. Arrows flew around Torin, and one slammed into his shield. Another grazed his helmet. He fired his bow, hitting an enemy archer upon a siege engine. A trebuchet swung at his side, slamming its boulder into another engine, scattering wood and enemy soldiers.

One wooden tower reached the wall, and a plank slammed down. Magerian swordsmen rushed onto the battlements. Torin ran toward them, sword swinging, and locked blades with an enemy soldier. With a kick and thrust of his shield, he sent the man tumbling off the wall. More Magerians surged from the siege engine, and Torin snarled as he fought, slaying men, sending them crashing down. His comrades fought at his sides.

"Burn the siege engine!" Torin shouted over his shoulder. Men stood there with torches, lighting the wooden trebuchet projectiles. "Bring fire!"

Men rushed forth, holding torches and pots of oil. Cauldrons tilted over the battlements. Bubbling oil crackled over a siege engine. Torches fell, landed upon the wood, and the wooden tower burst into flames like a pyre. Torin stepped back and shielded his eyes from the heat. Those Magerian troops still in the engine screamed, engulfed in fire.

The tower collapsed but Torin found no rest. The buffalo cannon fired a second time, and another turret crumbled and fell off the wall. More catapult boulders sailed overhead. In the city, roofs shattered and houses crumbled. A domed temple crashed down, scattering bricks. Smoke, dust, and fire covered the city.

Through the screams of battle, shrieks of arrows, and roars of fire rose a deep chant. The voices boomed across the battlefield. Torin's heart sank.

"The mages," he muttered.

He stared between two merlons and a chill gripped him. The enemy troops parted below like a splitting sea. Down the path rode a hundred black horses, and upon them sat a hundred mages clad in black robes and hoods. At their lead rode the captain of Mageria's forces, the towering Gehena, his four arms raised like serpents about to strike. Swordsmen and archers chanted at the mages' sides, raising their swords and bows, cheering on their champions.

Torin turned back toward his men.

"Archers!" he shouted. "Aim at the mages! Slay the mages!"

He fired his own bow. His arrow sailed toward the mages, burst into flame in mid-air, and disintegrated. A hundred other arrows followed his, only to suffer the same fate.

The mages halted outside the city gates. At their lead, Gehena raised his head, his red eyes crackling like flames, staring straight at Torin. His four hands collected smoke and fire, forging them, coiling them into the shape of a great champion. Behind the captain, the lesser mages added their own smoke to the creation. The creature took shape in the fields—a great buffalo, large as a ship, its horns formed of countless metal shards. The ghostly animal shrieked, an unearthly sound, and charged.

Arrows rained upon the creature, passing through its smoke. The astral horns, each like a battering ram, slammed into the city gates.

The walls shook.

The doors smashed.

The gates of Kingswall shattered.

The mages moved aside. Cheering for victory, the enemy troops surged into the city.

It is lost, Torin knew, looking down to see the enemy racing into the inner courtyard. *The city has fallen. The city will be our graveyard.*

The world became a dream—a nightmare of smoke, blood, wounds, steel, arrows, death. They fought in the streets. They fought in homes, upon roofs, in the ruins of shattered temples. More and more Ardishmen fell, and ever the Magerians stormed forth, filling the streets like poison seeping through arteries. Torin fought for a turn, maybe more, ever falling back as the enemy claimed street by street. With blood, fire, and shattering stones, the city of Kingswall crumbled.

CHAPTER TWENTY-SIX
FLIGHT

We're too slow.

Cam panted as he rode across the countryside, leading three thousand armored riders. His horse foamed at the mouth, the courser's eyes rolling, nostrils flaring, ears lying flat against its head. The other beasts were just as exhausted. Cam knew he was driving them too hard, yet how could he rest?

We're too damn slow.

His family was at Kingswall. Torin was at Kingswall. Hundreds of thousands of his people were at Kingswall.

The serpent heads there now. Serin.

Cam clenched his fist as he rode. He did not doubt Serin's actions now; the man had fooled them, drawn them to Hornsford with his army of straw, leaving Kingswall a fruit ripe for the picking. Cam had sent Nitomi and Qato ahead in their hot air balloon, entreating the dojai to rescue whoever they could. But Kingswall needed more than two Elorian spies; it needed an army. It needed Cam and his riders.

Idar damn it, too slow!

The landscape rose and fell around them, grassy hills to the north, the Sern River to the south. Miles behind, his ground troops were heading east too, but Cam would not wait. In his mind's eye, he could imagine the Magerian horde assaulting the city, toppling walls, storming the streets.

With three thousand riders, I can tear through the enemy, he thought, gazing upon his forces. Every man wore good steel and carried a blade and sword. *We can still save our city. We can—*

Chants rose ahead, interrupting his thoughts.

Cam stared toward the sound and his breath died.

"Idar help us," he whispered.

The enemy covered the landscape, twenty thousand troops or more bearing the Radian standards. Thousands among them rode upon horses. Scythed chariots rolled forth. Men beat drums and sang for victory, and horns—thousands of horns—shrieked like birds of prey.

Behind Cam, his men raised their own horns. The song rose in the wind, the song of Arden, a song for victory. Men aimed lances and took battle formations.

"We will slay them, my king!" cried a lord.

"For Arden!" cried a knight.

The two armies stormed across the countryside toward each other.

We're trapped, Cam thought, a shiver taking him. *Of course.* He howled in rage. *He planned this too.*

He leaned forward in his saddle and drew his sword, prepared for battle—but he knew this was not a battle he could win. This was not a battle on his terms.

He flushed me away from my walls. He trapped me between Hornsford and Kingswall. Now my city stands alone and I'm caught like a sheep between wolves.

The fear—for his family, his friends, his people—stormed through him like an icy torrent.

The enemy roared as they charged, covering the land, thousands of horses and chariots with spinning blades upon their wheels. Thousands of arrows flew. Cam swung his sword, and blood stained the fields of Arden.

* * * * *

Lari grinned and licked her lips as she fired her crossbow, aiming at the filthy mongrel. When her quarrel shattered against the shield of air, Lari stared for an instant, disbelief freezing her.

The mongrel shattered my quarrel.

Lari felt her smile vanish, replaced with a snarl. She screamed.

The damn mongrel thinks she can magic her way out of this.

Growling, Lari placed another quarrel in her crossbow and began to turn the crank, tugging the string back. Crossbows were such crude machines—too slow to load. Weapons for commoners. The Elorians were racing onto the road, swinging their shovels. Abandoning hope of loading the second quarrel fast enough, Lari cursed and tossed her crossbow at the nightcrawlers. The weapon slammed into an Elorian's forehead, cutting a deep groove, and Lari smiled and hissed through clenched teeth.

Good. First blood.

She raised her hands, prepared to fight the way a proper, highborn girl should fight—with magic, cruel and twisting and dark, a force to rip bones out of flesh. Madori would die slowly, Lari decided. A quick blast to the heart was too good for mongrels.

I will coil your bones, pull out your organs, and make you watch and beg me for death. She licked her lips and her nostrils flared, already smelling the mongrel blood.

She took a step toward Madori, gathering the magic in her hands, when the other maggot—the one called Jitomi—swung a shovel toward her head.

Lari sneered and swung her arms, tossing the ball of magic—the one intended for Madori—at the shovel instead. Inches away from her head, the shovel jerked backwards, tugging Jitomi two steps back.

Lightning flashed and slammed into a tree nearby. Lari grinned, raised her palms, and sucked the energy toward her, forming two glowing balls. She smiled crookedly at Jitomi, that piece of nightcrawler filth.

"Toss down your shovel and fight like a mage," she said. "Or are nightcrawlers so weak with magic, you fight like gravediggers?"

Around them, the others were battling—Elorian students dueling soldiers, shovels clanging against swords. Jitomi tugged back his hood and stared at her with blue, monstrous eyes the size of limes. His white hair fell across his brow, and his skin gleamed when lightning struck again. The dragon tattoo coiling across his face seemed to stare too. Never breaking his gaze, he tossed his shovel aside and raised his hands, collecting metallic particles from the air.

Lari leaned forward, tossing her balls of lightning.

He reacted at once, lobbing his projectiles toward her. The balls of lightning crashed and shattered. A thousand bright shards hovered in the air for an instant, then pattered down.

Sneering, Lari chose his boot. She claimed the leather. She tugged and he fell. Quickly she chose the air around a rock, levitated it above the Elorian, and tossed it down toward his face.

Jitomi rolled aside, and the rock thumped into the mud. A blast of that mud showered upward, flying toward Lari, blinding her and filling her mouth.

She held one hand forward, shoving a field of air, and wiped the mud off her face to see him crash backward.

"Better." She spat out mud, smiled, and wriggled her fingers, collecting strands of smoke. "Now we're having fun."

She tossed the smoky ropes at him, the same magic she had used on Madori back at Teel. The murky tentacles spun around him. Lari tugged her arm back, tightening the grip, and Jitomi gasped. She shoved her palm forward, blasting out power and knocking him onto his back. She chose a branch above, claimed the wood, and cracked it. The bough slammed down onto Jitomi, pinning him to the ground.

Lari grinned and chose his foot—not just his boot this time but the flesh within. He lay, blinking, struggling to rise, still wrapped in the magical ropes.

Her grin so wide it hurt her cheeks, Lari tugged his foot, and he screamed. She spun him in the mud, dragging him toward the ditch until he teetered on the edge.

He tried to resist. He summoned a ball of mud, air, and wooden chips; Lari dodged the projectile easily. She stepped forward, pouted mockingly, and placed her foot against Jitomi's neck, smearing the dragon tattoo with mud.

"You dug your own grave, worm," she said sweetly. "Now fall into it."

She kicked, shoving him into the ditch. He fell into the grave and lay, groggy and bleeding. Lari stood above and laughed. She lifted a shovel and began tossing mud into the ditch, covering the Elorian, burying him alive.

"Die in the mud like the worm that you are." She laughed. "Your mongrel friend will join you soon."

She tossed in another shovelful of mud, lightning flashed, and she saw them emerge from the forest across the ditch.

Two figures, a boy and girl, blades in their hands.

Lari sneered.

"Tam and Neekeya." She spat. "The two traitors. So you've come to die too."

The two stepped to the opposite edge of the ditch. Tam raised his eyebrows.

"Hullo, Lari!" he said. "It's always strange meeting a student outside of your school, isn't it?"

Neekeya nodded at his side. "It is! And you know the best part?" She raised her sword with the crocodile-claw pommel. "At the university there are rules. But here . . ." The swamp dweller smiled toothily. "Here I do believe we can kill the girl."

The two lunged over the ditch, flying toward her.

Lari growled and tossed air their way.

Their own magic blasted forth, tearing through her defenses, and they landed before her. Lari leaped back, narrowly dodging Neekeya's blade. Tam swung his dagger and Lari screamed; the blade tore across her cheek, and her blood splattered.

"That," the boy said, "is for what you did to Madori's cheek."

Lari screamed and tossed dark tendrils toward him. Neekeya sliced the magic with her blade, then thrust the sword. The tip nicked Lari's other cheek, splashing more blood.

"And that," said Neekeya, "is for Madori's second cheek." She lunged forward, swinging her blade. "The next cut will be for me."

Lari screamed and stumbled backward. She had never cast so much magic before, and when she tried to claim Neekeya's sword, to heat the steel until the barbarian dropped it, she could not. The material slipped from her mind. She tossed a stone, but the projectile bounced uselessly off Neekeya's scale armor.

"You're nothing but a swamp monster!" Lari screamed. She turned toward Tam. "You're nothing but a pathetic traitor who mingles with scum!"

They thrust their blades toward her again, and Lari fled into the forest, screaming and cursing and clutching her wounded cheeks.

* * * * *

He stood in the tallest tower of Kingswall Palace, staring down upon a dying city.

The Magerian enemy covered the city slopes, clogging the streets with steel. Already the Radian banners rose upon the domes and steeples of Kingswall, capital of Arden. The city gates had fallen. The countryside still swarmed with the enemy, and ever more crossed Mudwater Bridge in the south. Only this palace still stood, a single island in the Radian sea.

Some banners, Torin saw, rose upon humble homes, willingly raised by city folk. Those people—his fellow Ardishmen—cheered along the streets and upon roofs, welcoming the enemy.

"Death to nightcrawlers!" they chanted. "Radian rises!"

More than the corpses at the walls, the enemy surging along the streets, or the dark magic coiling like smoke, the sight of these traitors disgusted Torin. In future tales, would bards sing of an Arden who fought nobly against Serin . . . or a kingdom that welcomed evil?

"Where are you, Cam?" Torin whispered, staring out the window at the ruin of his city. "Where are you, my king, my friend?"

Cam's army—myriads of archers, swordsmen, and riders— could have stopped this assault. But now the might of Arden languished in the west at Hornsford, useless as the capital shattered, as the ancient kingdom fell. When Torin lowered his gaze, he saw Magerian troops stream into the palace gardens, marching toward the gates. Soon they would storm through the throne room, climb the stairs, and finally emerge here into this tower. And it would end.

A hand touched his shoulder. A soft voice spoke.

"Torin. What do we do?"

He turned around. He saw them there and his eyes stung.

Queen Linee stood in the round chamber, her eyes wide with fear. She gripped a sword in her hands, but the blade shook. Beside her stood her son and heir, Prince Omry, his armor cracked and bloodied. He too held a blade, and a bandage covered his brow.

What do we do . . .

Torin looked down at his own blade, a katana of the night. Years ago, the Chanku Pack—great wolfriders of the Qaelish empire—had gifted him this blade. He had fought many men with this steel, yet now . . . now would the blade find another task?

What we do is fall on our swords, he thought. *What we do is die before they capture us. Because the fate they plan will be worse than death.*

He licked his lips, trying to speak those words. Somewhere below, men chanted, wood and stone crashed, and the tower shook.

"They're breaking in," said Prince Omry, eyes grim. "They will be here soon."

Torin nodded, for a moment choking, unable to breathe, unable to speak.

I will never see my wife and daughter again. I love you, Koyee and Madori. He looked around at the chamber—the tapestries on the walls, the jeweled raven statues, the lush rugs, the giltwood tables. It was a comfortable place, a good place to die.

He raised his blade. He spoke gently. "Let me do it. I will be quick. I—"

A cry sounded behind him.

Linee gasped and pointed.

Torin spun around to face the window and his eyes widened. He lost his breath.

Nitomi and Qato, the two dojai, hovered outside the window in a basket.

"Hurry!" Nitomi said, gesturing for them to enter the basket. "Hop on board! Did you know that there's a giant army of thousands of swordsmen and mages and riders and archers outside, and maybe they even have elephants, and they're all over the city, and they're breaking into this palace, and—"

"Yes, Nitomi, we know!" Torin said. He thrust his head out the window and gazed upward. Ropes connected the basket to a hot air balloon; Torin had not seen these vessels since the war in Eloria years ago. When he looked down, he saw Magerian soldiers streaming through the shattered palace gates; countless more spread across the city. A Magerian archer nocked an arrow and aimed up at the balloon; a bolt from Qato's crossbow sent the man sprawling.

Torin pulled his head back into the chamber. He held Linee's hands and guided her out the window and into the basket. The gondola dipped several inches under her weight. The queen stood still, her sword still in her hand, a tear streaming down her cheek as she gazed upon the fall of her city.

When Torin turned toward Prince Omry, the armored young man shook his head. He raised his sword. "I'm staying."

Torin clutched his arm. "No. Omry, you're flying away from here. You are the heir of Arden."

His eyes flashed. "Which is why I go down with this kingdom."

"Your kingdom does not fall this turn." Torin tugged the boy toward the window. "Your father still fights for this kingdom. Your mother will still lead Arden from safety. If you fall with this city—if the hosts of the enemy slay the heir of Arden—that would shatter the spirit of those who still fight. If you live this day, if you speak for Arden from a place of safety, you will bring hope to the hearts of all Ardishmen."

The prince hesitated, sword wavering. The sounds of boots stomped up the tower now; the chants of Magerians rose below.

"Go!" Torin shouted.

Reluctantly, the prince climbed out the window and into the basket. It dipped two full feet; it seemed barely able to stay afloat.

More arrows whistled from below. Two slammed into the basket. Qato leaned down and fired his crossbow, hitting one archer, then another.

"Hurry, Torin!" Nitomi cried, reaching toward him. "Into the basket! Now!"

Torin looked at the small dojai, then back at the chamber. The walls were shaking, and a framed picture fell and shattered. The cries of Magerians rose louder as they climbed the stairs.

The queen and prince must live to inspire hope, he thought. *But I am Lord Protector of this city. I cannot abandon a sinking ship.*

He turned back to the window. "Go, Nitomi! Fly."

Her eyes watered. "Torin, come on!"

Behind her, Linee and Omry cried out too. "Into the basket!"

Torin's eyes stung. "It won't support my weight." He shoved the gondola away from the tower wall. "Fly! I'll find another way."

Tears streamed down Linee's cheeks, and she cried out to him. "Torin, please!"

"Go!" He shoved the basket again and switched to speaking Ilari, a language of the night. "Nitomi, take them to safety. Take them to Oshy. I'll meet you there. Now go!"

Tears streamed down the small assassin's cheeks as she tugged ropes, letting the hot air balloon soar into the air. Linee was still shouting, reaching over the basket to him, as the vessel ascended and glided eastward, arrows sailing beneath it.

Torin stepped away from the chamber, raised his sword and shield, and faced the door just as it shattered open.

Four mages stepped into the room, clad in black robes, their faces hidden beneath their hoods. Their garments revealed only their fingertips—pale, clawed digits. They stepped aside and stood at attention, allowing a towering figure to enter the room—a man eight feet tall, clad in black, his arms spreading out like mandibles. Red eyes blazed from within his black iron helm. A voice like a hiss rose from that helmet, unearthly, deep, echoing, twisting with cruel mirth.

"Torin Greenmoat . . ."

His four blades burst into white flame, crackling, spewing smoke.

"Take him alive," spoke Gehena, field marshal of the Magerian forces. "Lord Serin will break him."

Torin screamed and charged, sword swinging.

The mages raised their hands.

The smoke blasted Torin's way, crashing against him. He swung his sword, cutting through the tendrils. Blackness covered the room, darker than the night. Pain drove through Torin, creaking his bones.

For Koyee. For Madori. For Moth.

He screamed and lashed his sword.

The katana clanged against Gehena and shattered into countless shards. The steel cut into Torin, and his blood spurted, and he fell.

Blackness enveloped him, almost soft, almost warm, cocooning him in deep slumber.

CHAPTER TWENTY-SEVEN
STEEL AND STONE

He stood before her—Lord Tirus Serin, the new King of Mageria, the Light of Radian—the man she must kill.

Screaming, Madori swung her shovel toward him.

His sword slammed into the handle, diverting the blow.

"Again we meet on the road, sweet Madori!" he said, smiling like a wolf at a sheep. "And again you lunge at me. Last time I spared your life. This time your grave is already dug and awaiting you."

The others fought around them—Elorian outcasts battling Radian soldiers. Madori would not spare the battle a glance; here before her stood her only target. She raised her shovel, prepared to strike again, but the wooden shaft caught flame in her hands. She yelped and tossed the shovel at Serin, but it clanged uselessly against his breastplate, then fell to the ground.

"Poor, innocent child." Serin took a step toward her. "Go on, attack me with magic. I see that you want to. I think I will toy with you a little before I—"

Madori screamed and tossed a ball of dark magic toward his face.

An inch away from hitting him, the projectile scattered and fell like ash.

"Good!" said Serin. "Good. You chose the particles in the air around us, formed a perfect missile, and tossed it within a heartbeat." He tsked and shook his head. "But you forgot to form new bonds between the materials, allowing me to easily disperse the projectile." He swung his sword, slicing skin off her arm. "Try again! Every time you fail, I will cut off another piece of you."

Madori yowled. Blood gushed from her arm. She had no time to heal the wound. Instead, she claimed his breastplate and began to heat the metal.

He sighed like a teacher at an erring pupil, shook his head, and transferred the heat from his breastplate into his sword. The blade turned red-hot, and he swung it again, nicking Madori's shoulder. She screamed, the wound sizzling.

"Not good enough!" Serin said. "Why heat armor without sealing the fire within?" He sighed. "Truly you mongrels are pathetic creatures. That is why you will die in our fire, and the true masters of magic—Magerians of pure blood—will rule both day and night. Try again!"

Madori trembled, her wounds dripping, barely able to focus, barely able to muster the strength to stand up. She needed help. She needed her friends. He was too strong. But the others were fighting their own enemies; Madori faced this man alone.

With a scream, she claimed his sword, trying to loosen the bonds within the blade, to bend the steel while it was hot. He responded by claiming the blade himself, curving it into a saber, and nicking her ear. She tried to claim the cobblestones beneath his feet, to tug them free and send him falling. He stepped aside, regained his footing, and stabbed her thigh.

Madori screamed, more blood spilling, and fell to her knees.

"My my." Serin shook his head sadly. "For a year you studied magic, yet you cannot even defeat an old man like me." He stepped closer to her, raised his hand, and blasted a cone of air at her chest. The blow knocked the breath out of her. She fell onto her back, gasping for air, her blood trickling.

He placed a boot upon her chest. His sword tore through her shirt, drawing a line across her chest, and more blood flowed.

"Foul mongrel blood," he said, pinning her down. He spat. "The pure blood of Timandra . . . mixed with poison of Eloria. It disgusts me. I will bleed you now, child—slowly, drop by drop, and you will stare upon me as your life trickles away, then join your subhuman friends in the grave you dug."

She tried to cast her magic; she was too weak. She tried to shove his boot off; he was too strong, crushing her, and she felt that her organs could burst, her ribs snap. Her eyes rolled back. She tried to cry for help, but only a whisper left her throat.

Breath by bre—

Yet his boot pressed deeper, and she couldn't even breathe.

Her eyes rolled back, and she thought she heard her friends calling to her: Tam, her oldest friend, a prince of Arden, a boy she had loved all her life; and Neekeya, her only female friend, a girl Madori loved more than life. How could they be here too? How could she fail, let them die here in the forest with her?

I'm sorry, my friends. I'm sorry, my parents. I love you all so much.

Tears streamed down her cheeks, mingling with the blood and mud.

Serin flipped his sword over, pointing the blade downward. He raised the sword slowly, prepared to drive it down like a tent peg.

No. How can I die here? I spent a year studying magic. How can I fail? She thought back to her professors: little Professor Fen, his mustache bristling as he taught Basic Principles; elderly Professor Yovan, a kindly graybeard who taught her the art of healing; wise Professor Maleen, poisoned by the Radians; and finally, the brightest light among them, Headmistress Egeria, the wisest woman Madori had known, a woman now imprisoned for her resistance.

They believed in me. They taught me to be strong. How can I let them down?

"And now," Serin said, digging his heel into her, "I gut you like a fish and watch your organs spill."

His face changed, turning cruel, delighted, red with bloodlust. He hissed, lips peeled back, and drove his sword downward.

With her last drops of strength, Madori chose and claimed the blade.

As the sword plunged down, she split the blade into two halves—down to the hilt. Each half curled outward like a great, steel jaw opening wide. The two shards slammed into the earth at Madori's sides, driving deep into the mud, missing her body.

She had no more power for magic. She grabbed a rock and hurled it, hitting his forehead.

Serin shouted and stumbled back, blood spurting and filling his eyes.

Dizzy and covered in blood, she tossed his broken sword aside and struggled to her feet. She stumbled a few steps toward a dead Radian soldier; she realized that most of the Radians were dead, and the Elorian outcasts were battling the last of them. Madori tugged the corpse's sword free and swung the blade at Lord Serin.

His sword gone, he tried to parry with his arms, relying on his armor for protection. Madori's blade slammed into his hand, severing a finger. She swung again, hitting the side of his helmet, denting the steel.

He emitted a sound like a butchered animal.

"We'll see who's gutted!" Madori said, stepping closer to him.

Around her, the other Elorians—bloodied, panting, and holding their own claimed swords—stepped forward with her, advancing toward the wounded Serin. Dead Radians lay upon the road around them.

"Father!" rose a voice from the forest behind—Lari's voice, sounding afraid and young. "Father, help!"

Madori lunged toward Serin, swinging her blade.

The mighty lord, the Light of Radian, the King of Mageria— spun on his heel and fled. He raced into the forest, clutching the stump of his finger, calling his daughter's name.

Madori tried to chase him. She wobbled and nearly fell. Arms caught her, and she found herself leaning against Tam.

"She's hurt!" the prince called over his shoulder. "Neekeya, bring bandages!"

Madori tried to free herself, to run into the forest. "We have to catch him, Tam," she whispered, blood in her mouth, blood in her eyes. "We have to kill him. We . . ."

The world spun. She was vaguely aware of her friends placing her down on the road, of Jitomi's warms hands upon her wounds, of Neekeya whispering prayers.

A raven circled above, cawing, the bird of Arden, of her home. Her eyes closed. She slept.

* * * * *

For a long time Tam stood in the rain, staring down at the grave, his fists clenched at his sides.

"I'm sorry," he said, voice hoarse, as the rain streamed down his face. "My friends, I'm sorry."

He lowered his head. Mud and stones covered the communal grave on the roadside, containing the bodies of Radian soldiers and five Elorian youths, outcast students fallen to Serin's cruelty. The rain pattered against the grave, and Tam wanted to kneel, to dig through the mud, to check again for life signs, to save them somehow. But he only stood, ashamed.

"You came into the lands of sunlight to learn our ways," he whispered. "You didn't distinguish between Magerians, Ardishmen, Daenorians, or any other children of sunlight; to you we were all foreigners. You came into sunlight trusting us . . . and now you lie dead. And now the forces of hatred march across this land."

Tam knew that he wasn't to blame. He knew that he'd done all he could to protect these Elorians. Yet still the guilt coursed through him—guilt for Timandra and the blood staining these lands of eternal daylight.

A hand touched his shoulder. He turned to see Neekeya gazing at him with soft eyes.

"We have to go." She caressed his wet hair. "Serin will be back with more men. We have to leave now."

He looked back at the road. The surviving Elorian students—twenty in all—were back inside the cage upon the wagon. Madori lay between them, her wounds bandaged, still unconscious. Jitomi sat with her, cradling her head in his lap. As the rain fell, the large Elorian eyes stared at him, blue and lavender, gleaming like lanterns.

"We'll take them to Arden," Tam said. "To the city of Kingswall, where they'll find rest and supplies. From there they can continue their journey to Eloria." He lowered his head. "My days at Teel University are over. I will not return there. In this time of bloodshed, I return to my homeland, to my city, to my family."

Neekeya clasped his hand. "And I go with you."

He tucked a loose strand of her hair behind her ear. "But your home lies in the west, Neekeya, in the swamps of Daenor."

She nodded. "And I will return there someday, but not yet. I will not leave you." She embraced him. "The Elorians need us; in the endless day, they are afraid, and they are weak, and they are alone. I will not abandon them any sooner than you would." She kissed him.

"And I will not leave you. We'll drive this cart east. We'll bring them to safety."

He held her for a moment longer, never wanting to break apart from her warmth, from her goodness. Cruelty raged across the land, war loomed, his best friend was wounded, and the bodies of five more friends lay underground—but there was some hope in the world, there was some goodness in the pain. There was Neekeya.

They donned cloaks and hoods, hiding their faces. They climbed onto the cart, replacing its fallen driver. The horses began to move. They would not stay on the road for long, only until Madori was well enough to walk; then they would travel through the forest, hidden until they could reach the border.

For now the wagon trundled, and the road stretched ahead between the trees, leading east into lands of water, light, and unknown shadows.

CHAPTER TWENTY-EIGHT
THE JOURNEY HOME

Madori was shivering by the campfire, the dark forest creaking around her, when she remembered the piece of paper.

Headmistress Egeria had slipped the little, folded paper to her turns ago; it felt like years. With all that had happened—the attack in the cloister, the long ride in the wagon, the battle on the road—Madori had forgotten. Perhaps she had wanted to forget. Perhaps the memory of the kindly old headmistress was too painful.

She reached into her pocket now, hand trembling, and felt the paper still there. Small. Folded several times.

A gust of wind blew. The trees swayed and sparks flew from the campfire. Her friends all shivered and huddled closer to the fire. Tam and Neekeya sat pressed together, sharing a cloak.

Madori sat apart from the others on an old log. Cold. Alone. Half her body in the light of the fire, half in darkness, torn even here.

Her eyes stung.

I miss you, Egeria. Teel is so far, and I'm so afraid.

She pulled the piece of paper out of her pocket. She stared at it but dared not unfold it. Were words written here? A farewell? A warning? Madori felt as if cold emanated from this paper. If she unfolded it, would she be releasing a beast she could not tame?

She lowered her head.

I never should have left home, she thought. *I should have stayed in Fairwool-by-Night. With my family. The people I love. I can't fight this darkness. I can't defeat this evil alone.*

She had come here for adventure, come to seek a new life, a new path. Come to grow up. Now, more than anything, Madori wished she could turn back time. Yet perhaps youth was something that could never be reclaimed, not its innocence, not its joy, not the warmth that was but a memory in the cold.

Hands numb, chest tight, she unfolded the paper.

Words were written here in Egeria's delicate script.

Dearest Madori,

I wanted to protect you for a while longer. I wanted to guide you. To teach you. To watch you grow up. I wanted to prepare you for the fire I knew would burn.

Yet perhaps we are never ready for fire. Perhaps we are always but children, afraid and crying out, when the flames burn us. Even the very old and very wise are still as children when tragedy strikes—scared, alone, seeking aid from parents we cannot find.

I will never see you again, Madori, and I don't know if you will ever find aid from another—from a parent, from a teacher, from a friend. I don't know if you will walk the burning paths alone.

But I know that you are strong.

And I know that you will walk them.

And I know that you will survive them.

Our time—the old guardians of Moth—has ended. We failed you. We vowed to bring peace to this torn world and we could not. Now—too soon, too soon!—this torch is yours to carry.

In the light of blazing hatred, carry the light of wisdom. Along the path of swords and arrows, carry hope.

Remember, child. Stars shine in the darkness. Life blooms from ash. The world is dark and cruel but full of goodness too, goodness that is worth fighting for. Fight for it. Always.

Your headmistress,

Egeria

Madori stared at the note a while longer, then folded it and placed it back into her pocket. She left the fallen log where she sat. She moved to nestle between Tam and Neekeya. They wrapped their arms around her, and they sat together, watching the campfire.

* * * * *

They walked up the hill, stood between two oaks, and gazed down at the dead heart of Arden.

Madori's eyes stung. She reached out and clasped Tam's hand.

"So it's true," she whispered. "Kingswall has fallen."

Tam drew his dagger, his face twisted, and he seemed ready to charge downhill, cross the fields, and attack the city walls himself. Instead he fell to his knees, lowered his head, and shook. Madori knelt beside him, pulled him close, and held him tightly. She gazed south with him, the pain like claws digging inside her.

Radian banners rose above the city of Kingswall, replacing the old raven banners. Magerian troops manned the walls, clad in black steel, and marched in the fields. The Magerian fleet sailed upon the Sern River, and more Radian banners rose upon Mudwater Bridge.

"The city's people live," Madori whispered to Tam, squeezing him, trembling with him. "Mageria conquered but did not destroy. Our families are alive."

He turned toward her, his eyes red. "My mother was in that city. My brother." His voice was hoarse. "Your father too."

She dug her fingers into him, baring her teeth. "Your mother is Queen, and your brother the heir of Arden. My father is a war hero. Serin will keep them alive. They're worthless to him dead. They're worth a fortune while they breathe."

The others walked uphill too and stood around them. Neekeya knelt on Tam's other side, stroked his hair, and whispered into his ear. Jitomi knelt by Madori and touched her arm, speaking of Torin being strong and wise, clever enough to escape. The other Elorians, outcast students from Teel, simply stood silently, hoods and robes protecting their skin from the Timandrian sun.

Madori wanted to say more. But her voice caught in her throat, and tears filled her eyes. For long turns, they had traveled through the wilderness, staying off the roads and rivers, hiding in forests and wild grasslands. All over Arden they had seen the remnants of battle: smoldering farms, ravaged towns, and castles now hoisting the enemy standards. For all these turns, Madori had told herself that Kingswall—fabled, ancient city of Ardish might—would withstand the Radian fire. Now she found it too overrun. Now her hope for

aid—from Queen Linee, from Price Omry, from her own father—
crashed like so many toppled forts.

"Come, friends," she said. "Further back. Behind the trees.
We're exposed here."

They stepped back and huddled in a copse between elms, oaks,
and pine trees. An ancient mosaic and three fallen columns peeked
from the grass, hints of a lost world, remnants of the ancient Riyonan
Empire which had ruled here a thousand years ago. Madori wondered
if her own kingdom would join the ghosts of Riyona. Tam sat on a
fallen column and placed his head in his hands; Neekeya sat beside
him, stroking his hair and whispering soft comforts to him. The
Elorians huddled together; they had hoped to find rest and aid here
on their way back home to the night.

Back home to the night, Madori thought, staring south. The wind
played with her hair, scented of old fire and blood. *We come from
darkness . . . to the night we return.*

She had thought to find sanctuary behind these sunlit walls, but
perhaps her home lay—had always lain—in the darkness.

"Now we must choose our paths," she said. "We fled the lands
of Mageria only to find the snake crawling upon Ardish soil too. This
land—the river, the city, these plains—is the road to the night. Lord
Serin will send his troops into the darkness." She turned to look at
the Elorians. "He will send them after your families . . . after my
mother. Now we must choose whether we hide or fight, whether we
dig hideouts or lift swords and make our stand."

* * * * *

For a long time, Teel's outcasts sat in the grove, whispering, praying,
huddling together as the world crumbled around them.

Tam paced between the trees, his boots stepping on pine
needles, rich brown soil, and the remnants of the ancient mosaic. The
head of a statue rose from the earth, a woman's haloed head. Tam
lowered his own head, the pain too great to bear.

*My father—trapped fighting a losing battle in the north. My mother and
brother—trapped in conquered Kingswall, perhaps dead. My kingdom—in ruins.*

He was a prince of Arden, the younger of the twins, never an heir, never one who mattered to the throne. He had fled this realm—to be with Madori, the only one who understood feeling torn, forgotten, afraid. And now . . . now as his kingdom burned, what path did he have? Did he travel with Madori into the darkness, abandoning his home to the buffaloes of Mageria?

The others were huddling together, the Elorians speaking in their language, Madori staring south in silence, the wind in her hair. Tam did not approach them. He needed to walk here, alone, to grieve, to pray. He wore only a tattered tunic and cloak, stubble covered his cheeks, and burrs filled his hair, yet he was still a prince of this land. He had to fight for it—to join his father in the northwestern battles, to sneak into the city, to find aid outside these borders, to lead rebels from the wilderness, to do something—anything—for his home. He had always relied on others for guidance—his parents, his professors, Madori's advice—and now he felt lost, trapped like in his recurring nightmare of racing through a labyrinth, desperate to escape but finding no exit.

Pine needles crunched behind him, and Tam turned to see Neekeya approaching him, her eyes soft, her crocodile helmet tucked under her arm.

Seeing her soothed him.   The breeze played with her black, chin-length hair, and the sunlight gleamed upon her dusky skin and scale armor. When she reached him, the tall swamp dweller took his hands in hers. Her grip was warm, the fingers long, the palms soft.

"I don't know what to do, Neekeya," he whispered. "Those we passed in the wilderness say my father still fights in the northwest, but none can say where. Even if I find him, he lies behind enemy lines. Do I seek him, Neekeya? And if I do, will you come with me?"

She touched his cheek, and her eyes dampened. "No. I return to Daenor, to the swamplands of my home. I will speak to my father; he's a great lord. I will tell him of the Radian menace. I will entreat him to send soldiers across the mountains, to strike at Mageria from the west. We will summon a great council of swamp lords in our pyramid. We are strong in Daenor. We will fight the tyrant."

He lowered his head. "I don't want you to leave me."

She took a shuddering breath and embraced him. Her tears fell. She cupped his cheek in her hand, and she kissed him—a deep kiss, warm and desperate and mingling with her tears. Her lips trembled against his, and their bodies pressed together—his clad in old cotton, hers in steel scales.

Finally their lips parted, and she stroked his hair. "Nor do I. Travel west with me, Tam. Travel into the swamps with me, then return to your land with an army behind you. Return here as a true prince, a true conqueror."

He wanted to laugh, but only a weak breath left his throat. "How would I be a prince among you? In Daenor I would be only an exile, a coward fled from his kingdom as the enemy marched across it. How princely would I seem then, returning here with the hosts of other men?"

She squeezed his hand. "Be my prince then! Wed me in the swamps. Be my husband, and you will not return as an exile but as a liberator. Let us forge an alliance between Daenor and Arden." She smiled through her tears. "When we return here, we will return together—husband and wife, strong, our houses joined, our armies roaring."

He looked into her large, earnest eyes. He stroked her cheek, trailing his fingers down to her chin. She was beautiful. She was strong. She was a woman Tam loved more than life.

"I don't want to wed you for power," he said. "Nor for armies. I will wed you for love. I love you, Neekeya."

She held him close and laid her head against his shoulder. "I love you too—always. Since I first saw you."

They stood together upon the old mosaic on the hill. The leaves glided around them, and in the south the enemy chanted and its horns blew for victory.

* * * * *

Madori walked alone, leaving the others in the grove. Upon the hill, she found the remnant of an old brick wall, only three feet tall, most of it long fallen or perhaps buried underground—a relic of Riyona, an empire lost to time. She climbed onto the wall fragment and stared at the four directions of the wind.

In the west her enemy mustered new power—the forces of Mageria and its corrupt ideology, the cruel Radian Order. When she turned to look north, she saw plains leading to dark forests; beyond them lay the realm of Verilon, a cold land of snow, ice, and pine trees, a realm she did not know, a realm she feared. In the south the capital of her home lay fallen, overrun with the tyrant's forces; even as she stood here, Madori heard the distant chanting of the enemy.

"Are you trapped within those walls, Father?" she whispered, eyes stinging. "Are you chained like I was chained, and are you thinking of me too? Or did you escape into shadows?"

Finally Madori turned to look east. The Sern River stretched across the land, the Ardish plains rolling to its north, the Nayan rainforest sprawling to its south. Mist and light covered the horizon, but beyond them, Madori knew—many leagues away—lay the shadows of Eloria, and that too was her home. There stretched her path, she knew—The Journey Home, like the old song, a journey into darkness.

She returned to the grove and saw the others standing, their packs slung across their shoulders, their eyes somber, staring at her.

Madori spoke softly. "I return to the darkness of night—the village of Oshy in the empire of Qaelin. That land is in danger now; the front line will move to the dusk. There I will make my stand. There I will fight with sword and magic against the tyrant—not in sunlight but in shadows." Her breath shook. "For many years, I thought that I could be a child of sunlight—like my friend Tam, like my fellow villagers, like my father." Her eyes stung. "For many years, I felt the pain of that sun and its people. I sought acceptance at Teel and still bear the scars—on my body, in my heart. Perhaps I've always been only a child of darkness; perhaps in the night will I find my home. My friends, join me there."

Jitomi came to stand by her side. He took her hand in his and squeezed it. The other Elorians, twenty in all, came to stand behind her, robed and hooded. Only Tam and Neekeya, the two Timandrians of their group, did not join her. They remained standing ahead under a pine tree, holding hands.

"We go to Daenor," Tam said softly. "Here our path forks. Here our quartet breaks."

He spoke some more—of forging an alliance with the western realm, of marrying Neekeya in her pyramid, of returning to Arden with a great host of men—but Madori heard little of it. As he spoke, she could only think of losing her friends.

She stepped toward them, her eyes damp, and embraced Neekeya—a crushing embrace, a cocoon of warmth she never wanted to be released from.

"Goodbye, Neekeya," she whispered and kissed the girl's cheek. "Goodbye, my sweet friend."

The swamp dweller smiled, tears in her eyes, and kissed Madori's forehead. "You're my dearest friend, Madori, now and always. We will meet again."

Her cheeks wet, Madori turned to look at Tam, and for a moment she hesitated. How could she part from him—her dearest and only friend for most of her life? The boy she had spent every summer with, had run through fields and gardens with, had daydreamed together with so many times? All her life, Tam had been the beacon of her soul. Now he was traveling away from her, an exiled prince, a man she might never see again.

He pulled her into his arms, and she laid her head against his chest, and she wept in his embrace. He kissed her tears away, and she never wanted to leave him, and when he finally walked downhill, Neekeya at his side, Madori stood for a long time, silent, a hole inside her. She stood there among the trees, watching her friends walk westward until they were only specks in the distance . . . and then were gone from her. Perhaps for years. Perhaps forever. And Madori knew that losing them was a wound greater than any her enemies had given her.

After a long time, she turned back toward the others. They stood silently, wrapped in their cloaks, their eyes—large Elorian eyes like hers—gleaming in the shadows of their hoods.

"It will be a long journey to the night," she said. "And danger crawls upon this land. We hoped to find safety behind brick walls; we will seek it in the shadows. Our road to darkness begins."

She began to walk, leading the way across the hills and valleys, for they dared not travel by road or boat behind enemy lines. Jitomi walked behind her, and the others trailed behind him in single file, slim figures in hoods and robes, outcasts, far from home.

They traveled as the moon waxed and waned, buying food in farms, hunting with magic, gathering mushrooms and berries. Every town they passed displayed the banners of Radianism, and every road they came across bore the soldiers of the enemy. They kept walking, hiding between trees, living off the gifts of the forest. Whenever they rested, Madori thought of those she loved—of her parents, of Tam and Neekeya, of Headmistress Egeria, and sometimes the pain was so cold inside her she couldn't breathe. Jitomi would hold her at those times, stroke her hair, and kiss her forehead, until she slept in his arms.

Autumn leaves rustled in the forests when Madori and her companions reached the dusk.

The village of Fairwool-by-Night lay to their south, Radian banners rising from the library roof. Madori stood between the trees, squeezing Jitomi's hand, staring upon her fallen home. A Magerian warship stood tethered at the docks, and enemy troops marched in the village square, clad in black armor. Madori's own home, the cottage where she'd been born and raised, stood enclosed in a new iron fence, its gardens burnt, its roof displaying an eclipse standard.

Eyes burning, Madori turned away. She stared east at the great, glowing line of dusk, the border between day and night.

"Into the darkness," she whispered, not trusting herself to speak any louder without weeping. "Quickly."

She walked between the trees, heading into that orange glow. The Elorians walked behind her, silent and grim. Only Jitomi walked at her side, holding her hand tight, and in his eyes Madori saw his compassion; he knew this was her home, and he knew her pain.

The sun dipped behind them as they walked, and shadows stretched across the forest, dark and tall like ghostly soldiers. With every step the light dimmed, turning a deep gold, then orange, then bronze. Their eyes glowed in the darkness, blue lanterns, eyes for seeing in the dark. The trees withered, thinning out, becoming stunted and weak. Soon the sun vanished beneath the horizon and they left the last trees behind. Only sparse grass and moss covered the hills here. Duskmoths rose to flutter around them, tiny dancers, their left wings white, their right wings black, creatures torn like the world. One landed on Madori's hand, and she remembered the duskmoth that had visited her at Teel University, and she wondered if this was the same one, a guardian, a soul that cared for her.

They walked on through the shadows, crested a hill, and there they saw it. The companions froze and stared.

"The night," Madori whispered. "Eloria."

The land of her mother rolled before them, cloaked in shadows. Lifeless black hills rolled into the distance, and the Inaro River snaked between them, a silver thread. The moon shone above, a silver crescent, and starlight fell upon Madori for the first time in a year.

"Eloria," Jitomi whispered. "Our home."

Your home, she thought, looking at him. *Your home,* she thought, looking at the other Elorians. *Yet what home is mine? Will I find any more of a home in darkness than I did in the sunlight?*

She kept walking.

They traveled across a valley and climbed a hill, and there above it loomed: Salai Castle, a pagoda with three tiers of blue, tiled roofs, the fortress named after Madori's grandfather. A golden dragon statue stood upon its topmost roof, and guards stood clad in scale armor at the gates, katanas at their sides. Their long white hair flowed in the wind, and their blue eyes gleamed. Below the hill nestled the village of Oshy, its lanterns bright as the stars, its junk boats floating in the river.

"We'll be safe here, friends," Madori said, turning toward her companions who stood upon the hill. "This is where we make our stand. In the darkness. War will come here too, and the cruelty of Serin will pour into these lands." She clenched her fists. "And we will fight it."

The castle doors creaked open. A gasp sounded. Madori spun around to see a slim figure emerge from within.

"Madori!"

Koyee rushed toward her, her white hair streaming, her lavender eyes filling with tears.

Madori's own tears fell, and suddenly she was trembling, and all the strength she thought she had—of a warrior, a leader, a mage—vanished like rain into a river, leaving her only a girl, so afraid, so hurt.

"Mother!"

She ran toward her mother, and they crashed together in an embrace. Their tears mingled.

"I'm home, Mother," Madori whispered. "I'm home."

* * * * *

They rode into the village in the chill of autumn, their horse's hooves scattering fallen leaves. Upon his mount, Lord Serin stared around in disgust and spat.

"A backwater," he said. "A sty. Barely worth the trouble."

His daughter sat beside him upon a white courser, a furred hood shielding her head from the wind. "Her home. A place that was dear to her." Lari sneered, turned her head around, and shouted toward their men. "Burn it! Burn it all down."

A hundred riders stormed down the hillside, clad in black steel, visors hiding their faces. Their banners rose high, streams of red against the gray sky like blood trailing along a corpse. Their torches crackled, raising columns of smoke.

"Slay them all!" Serin shouted. "Loot what you crave and burn the rest!"

The riders thundered between the cottages of Fairwool-by-Night, torching the thatch roofs. Children ran across the village square, crying for their mothers, as riders tore into them with blades. Villagers emerged from homes, the tavern, and the brick library, begging for life, praising Serin, chanting of Radian's might.

They begged and they died.

Serin sneered, riding his horse toward a young woman shielding a boy in her arms. He thrust his spear, skewering them both. At his side, Lari laughed as she trampled over a dead man, her courser's hooves snapping bones. Soldiers stormed into the library, tugged out books, piled them around the maple tree rising from the village square, and burned them all in a great pyre.

"Here's her house!" Lari said, pointing at a cottage. The word "Greenmoat" appeared upon the door. Lari laughed. "This little chamberpot of a cottage." She raced inside, then emerged holding a rag doll—perhaps a toy Madori had once played with. Lari spat. "The vermin are gone. The mongrel and her mother fled. Of course they did."

Serin handed her a torch. "Burn the house. This one is yours."

He watched, pride swelling within him, as his daughter set fire to the cottage, as the smoke and flames rose from the home of their enemies.

Blood stained Fairwool-by-Night, red as the fallen maple leaves. Bodies lay crushed and broken. Homes and fields burned. The autumn leaves fell upon nothing but death.

Serin withdrew his men to the hill. They gathered around the old stone watchtower, gazing down at the flaming ruins. A thin smile stretched across Serin's lips, and he wiped blood off his sword.

"The nightcrawlers will see this flame," he said. "The smoke will rise above the dusk, and the stench of death will carry on the eastward wind. The vermin are watching, my daughter. I do not doubt that the mongrel is among them."

He dismounted his horse and helped Lari dismount as well. They entered the watchtower, climbed its spiraling staircase, and emerged onto the battlements. A lone boy stood there, trembling, a youth barely old enough to shave. The lone survivor of Fairwool-by-Night, he made a clumsy attempt at some last honor, firing an arrow at Serin. The projectile missed the lord by two feet.

"Lari?" Serin said, raising an eyebrow.

She grinned, stepped toward the trembling boy, and slashed her sword across his belly. He fell, gasping, dying, his innards spilling.

Serin approached the eastern battlements and leaned forward between two merlons. Lari came to stand at his side, the cold wind billowing her hair and reddening her cheeks. Before them spread the dusk, the shadowy no man's land separating day from night. And there in the distance they saw it: the great shadow, the land of endless night. Eloria.

A castle rose in those shadows, perhaps a league away, a pagoda with three tiers of roofs. As his men emerged onto the tower top, raising a great Radian banner, Serin stared toward that pagoda, and he imagined that he was staring into her eyes.

"Hello, Madori," he whispered, stroking a merlon as if stroking Madori's head. "Do you see this fire? Do you smell this death? We will muster here, mongrel. We will raise an army like the world has never seen. We are coming for you." He licked his lips and caressed the stump of his finger—the finger she had removed. "Soon you will burn too."

Lari leaned against him, and Serin slung an arm around her. They stood watching the night, savoring the smell of victory.

BOOK FIVE:

SHADOWS OF MOTH

CHAPTER ONE
THE BUSKER AT DUSK

Little Maniko hobbled through the dusky forest, moving toward the searing light of the sunlit demons. He was seeking a gift for a child.

His every footstep shuffled. His gnarled fist clutched his cane. Black trees coiled around him, just as gnarled and knobby. They were small trees—they couldn't grow any larger here in the dusk, still far from the full daylight—but they towered over Maniko. He had always been small, under four feet at his tallest, and he had shrunk with age. His white beard trailed along the ground, longer than his body, thinner than he remembered. It seemed that beard grew thinner every turn, his back more stooped, his cane more wobbly.

"This might be my last trip into the dusk," he muttered, voice hoarse.

How old was he now? He did not remember. He had been old already when he first met Koyee—that scruffy urchin on the streets of Pahmey. And that had been a long time ago, he thought. A generation ago.

Little Maniko smiled, remembering. Ah, the lights of Pahmey! Lanterns floating toward the stars. Towers of glass rising to the moon. Dirty streets and shadowy corners, and him playing his lute for passersby, collecting his coins, feasting upon meals of stewed mushrooms and salted bat wings, and finally meeting Koyee, playing music with her, then fighting at her side as the sunlit demons swarmed through their streets. His same old lute still hung across his back. That city had fallen then, and now Maniko lived in a village by the dusk, a little place they called Oshy. And now he was old. And now his legs shook as he walked, and every season his eyes grew dimmer. Yet still he came here, walking into the dusk, seeking the gift, seeking a little hope in a world of darkness.

The trees grew taller as he walked, sprouting pale leaves, and moss soon covered the boulders. The light grew, casting orange beams between the trees. Pollen glimmered and the air grew warmer. The sun of Timandra was just over the horizon now; he was almost in the full daylight, in that land of his enemies, the land he had fought so many years ago. Duskmoths rose to fly around him, animals of the borderlands, this glowing strip between day and night. Their left wings were white, the right wings black, animals torn in two like this world the old books called Mythimna and most folk simply called Moth.

"Ah!" His eyes widened, and a smile curled his lips. He saw the bush ahead. The sun's rim rose behind it, a crown of gold. The plant almost seemed to burn in the light. Upon its coiling branches, like beads of blood, grew the duskberries.

Maniko hobbled forward with more vigor, his chin raised. His cane rapped against the hard earth, his lute swung across his back, and his beard whispered as it dragged along the ground.

"You've always loved duskberries, Koyee," he said, his smile widening. Or was it Madori? Sometimes Maniko stumbled, confusing the two, mother and daughter. Sometimes he thought Madori was the woman he had played music with in the dregs of Pahmey, his "partner in grime" as he called her. Other times he realized that Madori hadn't even been born then.

When you're old like me, he thought, *faces blur together, and all memories become like an oil painting under rain, smudges of color and light and beauty.* That was how Maniko knew his time was near, his life drawing to an end. All his life seemed to be unraveling behind him like the hem of his silken robe, all just strands of color fading into shadow.

"Best to just give both the berries," he muttered and barked a laugh. He reached the bush, squinting in the light of the sun, and began to pick the fruit into his basket.

The people of Oshy had told him to stop coming here, to stop collecting these berries. They said it was dangerous getting so close to Dayside. They said that the sunlit demons mustered here, preparing for war. Maniko snorted as he plucked the berries. He had fought hunger on the streets of Pahmey for decades. He had fought Timandrian soldiers in that city, and later in the southern empire of

Ilar, slaying many, even at his size. He was very old now, and he was no longer afraid.

"Let them come." He huffed, placed another berry into his basket, and patted the dagger that hung from his belt. To him it was as large as a sword. He had slain Timandrians with this blade before. If any attacked again, they would find that Little Maniko—though smaller than ever, stooped and wizened—still had a little fight in him. If he wanted to pick berries for Madori—or was it for Koyee?—he would travel into the very courts of sunlight and pluck them right off Lord Serin's plate.

He snorted again. "Lord Serin." A silly name. A silly man. They said the tyrant was mustering his forces right beyond these hills, prepared to invade the night—just like that fool Ferius had done in the last war. Koyee had slain Ferius, and if this new demon wanted to attack, they would slay him too.

Maniko drew his dagger and sliced the air. "That's right, Serin! If you step forth, you will taste Elorian steel." As he thrust and parried in the air, he could see it again—the old war, the enemies charging, and his blade flashing. "This old busker is also an old soldier. I still have some music in me. And I still have some fight too."

He smiled as he dreamed, remembering those old turns. He had been afraid then. But he had fought alongside greatness—with Koyee, with Emperor Jin of Qaelin, with Empress Hikari of Ilar, and with Tianlong, the last dragon of the night. He had risen from a humble busker on a street corner to a warrior. His breastplate had been only a frying pan strapped across his chest, and his sword had been only this humble knife, but he had fought with heroes. He had become more than a busker. Tears filled his eyes.

I became your friend, Koyee.

He sighed. Those turns were long gone. He sheathed his dagger, hefted his basket of berries, and prepared to shuffle back into the darkness. He had taken only one step away when the voice rose from the light.

"Look, Father! A little old nightcrawler who thinks he's a warrior."

Slowly, Maniko turned back toward the light.

A young Timandrian woman stood there, beams of light falling upon her golden hair, steel armor, and drawn sword. Her eyes were so small—half the size of Elorian eyes—and they glittered with cruelty. A tall Timandrian man stepped out from the light, joining the girl. His hair too was golden, and his eyes too were small blue shards. He wore priceless armor, the steel filigreed. An eclipse sigil adorned his breastplate, formed of many gemstones.

Maniko snarled. He knew that sigil—the sigil of the Radian Order, a new movement in the lands of sunlight. They said the Radians saw Elorians as lower than worms, pests to step on. Slowly, Maniko placed down his basket of berries. He drew his dagger. He pointed the blade forward with one hand, his cane with the other.

"Return to the daylight, Timandrians!" He knew his voice was high-pitched, wavering, weak, but he gave it all the gravity he could. "You step too close to Eloria. Leave now, sunlit demons, and never return."

The Timandrians looked at each other, then burst out laughing.

"Truly a worm, Lari!" said the man. "Barely larger than the worms in my garden back home. Is this the warrior they chose to guard their border? A decrepit dwarf?"

The Timandrian man raised his hand, and a blast of air slammed into Maniko. He cried out and fell down hard. His tailbone slammed against a rock, and he gasped in pain. Tears leaped into his eyes, and his dagger clattered to the ground.

The two Timandrians stepped closer and gazed down at him. The young woman—Lari, her name was—shook her head with mock sadness.

"Now he crawls through the dirt like a true worm." Eyes soft, she knelt and placed her hand against Maniko's cheek as if to stroke him. Then her expression changed, her lips peeling back in a snarl. Rather than caress him, her hand shoved his face into the dirt. "Eat the mud, vermin!" Her knee drove into his belly. "Eat the dirt like the nightcrawler that you are."

Maniko coughed as mud entered his mouth. He pawed for his fallen dagger but could not find it. Instead he swung his cane, rapping Lari's wrist.

The young woman hissed and straightened. Her knee left Maniko's belly, and he drew a ragged breath. He coughed out mud and pushed himself to his feet, legs shaking. His basket lay fallen, the berries spilled across the forest floor.

"Return now!" Maniko said. "Or—"

"Do you know who I am, nightcrawler?" said the tall man. He tapped the eclipse on his breastplate. "Do you know this sigil? We've met before."

Maniko's eyes had dimmed with age. He had trouble seeing and remembering faces. He spat. "You're a lout. Come here and I'll rap you too with my cane."

The tall man laughed. "Yes, I remember your spirit. You were spirited even back in the war, and you were ancient even then, if I recall correctly. I was only a young soldier, fighting my first battle. I assaulted the walls of Asharo, the capital of Ilar, and I slew many nightcrawlers. And I remember one among them—a little soldier who barely reached my belt. A frying pan formed his breastplate, and he bore a little dagger like a sword. I laughed at him then. And now, twenty years later . . . I see him again. It's funny. As I prepare to conquer the night, I find not the barbaric soldiers of Eloria opposing me here, but that same silly little creature."

And Maniko knew who this was, knew who this had to be. His eyes narrowed. "Lord Tirus Serin." He swung his blade through the air. "I do not remember you from the war; you were just another sunlit fool, one among many. A fool you are still."

Maniko looked around for his dagger, and his heart sank to see that Lari had lifted the blade from the muck. She held the dagger in one hand, her sword in the other. When Maniko took a step closer to the two, swinging his cane, Serin raised his palm again. This time no air blew to knock down Maniko. Instead, Maniko's cane cracked, then shattered into countless shards. Bits of the wood slammed into Maniko, cutting his skin.

These ones are no mere soldiers, he realized. *They are mages.*

Lord Serin drew his sword, a magnificent blade longer than Maniko's entire body. The steel glimmered red in the sun as if already bloodied.

"I forged this blade from the steel of slain nightcrawlers." Serin pointed the blade at Maniko's neck. "I slew over a hundred in the war. I collected bits from each—a shard of helmet here, a chip of a sword there—and had Mageria's greatest smith morph them into this blade. Sunsteel, I named it. A blade for cutting worms. You should be proud, little one! You will be the first nightcrawler to die upon it."

Maniko's dagger and cane were gone. But he still had what had always been his greatest weapon—the weapon that had served him for decades on the streets of Pahmey, that had helped him survive through grime and hunger, that had given strength to Koyee. With trembling fingers, he drew his lute from across his back. With stiff fingers, he began to play.

Gentle notes rose from the lute, taking form as he played, soon becoming that same old song he had first taught Koyee, the song called "Sailing Alone." And as he played, Maniko was there again, back home on the streets of Pahmey. The great public fireplace roared across the square, its iron grill shaped as dragons. The young women of the city's crest strolled toward the market, clad in fine silk dresses, their sashes embroidered. Peddlers rode upon bluefeather birds, hawking gemstones, ointments, charms, and sundry other items from many pouches. Past the tiled roofs of the city dregs, he could see them them there—the towers of the upper city, and above them all Minlao Palace, its dome shaped like the moon. Koyee stood with him again, a scrawny merchant in a tattered fur tunic, playing her bone flute. Two buskers in a world of dirt, hunger, fear, and darkness. Two warriors.

I played this song when we met, Koyee, he thought, eyes damp. *And I play it now in farewell to you.* It was an old song, a song of a girl who sailed alone into a new city. *And now I too sail alone . . . sail toward the great land beyond the stars.*

As the blade thrust into his belly, Maniko lost only a single note. Even as he fell, even as his blood spilled into the soil, he played on.

He lay on his back, his lifeblood draining away, the notes floating around him. He looked up. The two Timandrians stood above him, mere ghosts in the mist, and Maniko smiled as they faded away, as the lights of his old city washed over him, as the lanterns floated toward starlight.

"You are a natural, Koyee Mai!" he said. "Go and play your music. Make Little Maniko proud, and perhaps someday we will play together."

A girl with long silvery hair, bright lavender eyes, and a warm smile, she kissed his forehead. "Thank you, Little Maniko."

Koyee tried to give him the coin, but he brushed it away.

"This money is yours. Now go! Make beautiful music."

She left him that turn, and she left him now, a spirit of music and warm light. Little Maniko smiled, his notes weaker now, shaking like falling leaves in the wind.

Now go! Make beautiful music.

His tears flowed as she faded, as he sailed alone upon a shadowy river. One song ended, and then he heard it—the endless music of starlight, music welcoming him home.

Daniel Arenson

CHAPTER TWO
A LEGACY OF STEEL

"I'm joining the garrison." Madori stamped her feet. "I'm joining now and you can't stop me. I will wield a sword. I will fight. I already cut off one of Serin's fingers, and I'll cut the rest of him to shreds!"

She stood on the riverbank, panting with rage. The night was peaceful. The stars shone above, no clouds to hide them. Fishermen trawled up and down the Inaro in boats constructed of leather stretched over whale ribs, their lanterns bobbing, and every few moments a glowing fish emerged like a rising star, caught on the hook. The water sang softly, and wind chimes played among the clay village huts that rose behind her. Far beyond the huts, upon the hill, stood Salai Castle, its lanterns bright, and more music rose there: the song of soldiers chanting to the stars.

But one song is forever silenced, Madori thought, eyes burning. *Little Maniko will never more play his lute.*

Madori's mother stood beside her. Koyee had shed tears during the funeral, but now her large lavender eyes were dry. Clad in scale armor, her katana hanging from her belt, she stared at Madori sternly.

"No, Madori. You will travel east to Pahmey. I've sent word downriver, and Lord Xei Kuan will provide you with shelter in the Night Castle, and—"

"I will not be shipped away to safety while you stay and fight!" Madori's eyes burned, and her tears flowed down her cheeks, those cheeks scarred from Lari's assault at Teel. She pointed at those scars. "See these? My face is scarred like yours. We both fought battles. We both bear the marks. I fought Lari and Serin, and I will fight their army too. Give me a sword! I will fight here in Salai Castle." She gestured at the pagoda upon the hill. "I will wear armor and wield a sword, and I will slay the Radians if they dare invade. I will avenge Maniko."

264

Madori's body shook. She had grown up listening to Little Maniko's music. The little old man—Madori herself was short, and he had stood shorter than her shoulders—had once performed upon the streets of Pahmey. After the war, with so much of Eloria in ruin, he had settled here in Oshy. Madori had spent her summers here, and many of those summer hours had been idled away in the village square, listening to Maniko play his lute, pipe, and harp. He would play all the classic tunes of the night: "Sailing Alone," "Darkness Falls," "The Journey Home," "Call of the Clans," and many others.

Who will play the night's music now? Madori thought, gazing at the empty village square where Maniko used to sit. *Whose songs will now guide us through the darkness?*

She looked back at her mother. "Please," Madori whispered. "I'm seventeen already. You were younger when you sailed alone to Pahmey, when you fought with Maniko, when you saved the darkness. Let me fight too. I am the daughter of Koyee, the great heroine. How can I hide in safety when sunfire once more threatens the night?" She tugged at the two long, black strands of hair that framed her face. "True, I have dark hair and tanned skin. I'm half Timandrian. But my father too fought for the night. I don't know if Father is even alive or dead, and I'm so scared, and I have to fight. I have to."

Koyee's eyes softened, and she pulled Madori into an embrace. "My sweet daughter. Don't you see?" She touched Madori's scarred cheek, and pain filled her eyes. "I never wanted this for you. Yes, I was younger than you when I fought a war. And I was afraid then. I was hurt. I was alone in darkness, scarred, bleeding, so afraid . . . always so afraid. When I had you, Madori, I swore to the stars of the night, and to the memory of Xen Qae, and to any god who would listen . . . I swore that I would give you a better life. That you would never have to face war like I did. That you would never be alone, scared, bleeding in the dark. How can I let you fight now? How I can break my vow?"

"It is already broken," Madori said. "I already fought, and I was already afraid, and I already saw death. I watched Lord Serin and his men murder five of my friends on the road. I lay in the mud, bleeding as his sword drove into me. I saw the cruelty of sunlight. No, I did not fight a war like you did, but I'm ready to fight one. Bravely. At your side." She touched her mother's armor, fine scale armor forged by the master smiths of Qaelin, their empire of darkness. "Clad me in armor like the one you wear. Place a sword in my hand. And you will not see a frightened, bleeding girl but a proud woman of the night. I will make you proud, Mother. That is my own vow."

For you, Little Maniko. For you, my friends of Teel who fell on the road. For all children of darkness. Her tears no longer fell, and she raised her chin. *I was born split between day and night. I will find my honor as a pure warrior of shadow.*

A boat sailed by along the river, its lantern bobbing. Beads of light danced upon the gurgling water. The old fisherman, his beard long and white, reached over the hull. When a glowing lanternfish breached the surface, intrigued by the lamplight, the elder caught the animal in a net. Koyee and Madori stood in silence for a moment, watching the boat until it sailed by.

Finally Koyee spoke, her voice low and careful. "I will allow you to fight with me, daughter, but only if you train."

Madori's heart leaped. "Yes! I will train in the fortress. I will swing every sword you have, I will—"

"No." Koyee shook her head. "The soldiers in Salai Castle are hardened and grim, prepared for war. They don't need a pup scuttling between their feet. You will seek Old Master Lan Tao in the darkness. He trained your grandfather in swordplay. He will teach you to become a swordswoman, ready for battle, solemn and steady with the blade, not a rash youth. Only when he says you're prepared will I let you fight in this fort."

Madori wanted to shout again. Training? To be sent off into the darkness? The battle was near! Maniko had only been buried this turn, and—

And yet her rage faded as quickly as it had risen. To train with Old Master Lan Tao . . . the man who had taught Grandfather . . .

Madori had never met her mother's father, the wise warrior Salai, but she had heard many tales of his bravery. Salai had been the first Elorian soldier to face the attacking Timandrians in the Great War, perhaps the first Elorian to ever see a Timandrian. They said he had killed many of the sunlit demons before Ferius, the Lord of

Light, had murdered him. Grandfather Salai lay buried below the fortress that bore his name. In Madori's mind, Salai had always been old—even older than Little Maniko had been. She could barely imagine him as a young man, let alone that his teacher—who surely was even older!—could still live.

"He must be right old," she blurted out.

Koyee laughed softly. "Old Master Lan Tao is well into his eighties, but he's still quick of mind and blade. I myself only met him a year ago. I traveled into the Desolation, the craggy wastelands in the northern darkness. I found him in his cave, and I begged him to come to Salai Castle, to train my men. He refused. He said that after my father died, he swore to never train another soldier. He loved my father. He mourned his death. Now, Master Lan Tao claimed, he lives to meditate, to gaze upon the stars, and to breathe. Mostly to breathe, he said, though I'm still not sure of his meaning."

Madori bit his lip. "So why would he agree to train me?"

A gust of wind fluttered Koyee's long white hair and silken cloak. Koyee—the Girl in the Black Dress, the Heroine of Moth—solemnly met her daughter's gaze. They both had the same eyes, large and purple and deep as starlit skies. Wordlessly, Koyee unhooked her katana from her belt—the legendary Sheytusung. She held it out toward Madori.

Madori stared at the sword, hesitant. "You . . . want me to take it?"

Her mother stared at her, eyes unflinching. "Master smiths forged this blade in Pahmey under the light of its towers. My father fought with this sword in the great southern war against Ilar, then against the Timandrians in the dusk. I fought with this blade against the hordes of sunlight in Pahmey, in Yintao, and at Cabera Mountain. This blade has defended the night for two generations. Now it must pass to a third. Take this sword, Madori. Take it into the darkness, and learn how to wield it. I was never trained with the katana, but you will study with the master who first taught our family how to swing it. Master Lan Tao will not have forgotten Sheytusung." Koyee smiled thinly. "When he sees the granddaughter of Salai, bearing this sword of legend, he will train you."

267

Madori still hesitated. She had grown up hearing many tales of this blade, had grown up seeing this blade hanging upon their wall, a relic she was forbidden to touch. The sword that had killed so many Timandrians, that had defended Eloria, that had traveled with her grandfather to Ilar, that had been with her mother in her most desperate hours—on the streets of Pahmey, in the gauntlet of Yintao, in the carnage at Sinyong and Asharo, and finally at the great battle atop Cabera Mountain.

And now this sword comes to me. Madori took a deep, shaky breath. *Now a torch of starlight passes into my hand, my burden to bear. Now I shall become a protector of darkness.*

With a single, swift movement, she grabbed the katana and drew the blade. The folded steal gleamed, and she raised it above her head. It was light as silk and as deadly as dragon claws, and a chill ran through Madori.

She thought of Lari's mocking smile. She thought of Professor Atratus's sneer. She thought of Lord Serin's cruel eyes.

They're coming here, she thought. *The wrath and cruelty of sunlight prepares to wash over the night.* She looked up at her sword; it seemed to cleave the moon.

"With this blade, I will fight them. With this blade, I am Madori of the night."

* * * * *

Pain and memory.

It was all that remained.

A field of thorns had shredded the tapestry of Torin's life, and every thistle held a rent of cloth, scraps of memories over stabbing pain. Sounds. Smells. Reflections in shattered glass.

In the darkness, he was broken, scattered, clinging to those memories, reaching for them through the haze of his broken body.

He lay in a cart, he thought, the walls windowless, a box on wheels. He lay chained. He lay bruised, famished, cut, bleeding. For a long time—months, maybe years—he had languished in a dungeon. They were moving him now. He remembered them dragging him out of his prison cell, beating him, tossing him into this cart. How long had he lingered in these shadows? He didn't know. The cart jostled along a road, and every bump shot more pain through him. His head kept banging against the floor; he was too weak to raise it.

Like the scattered shards of broken bones, the memories spread around him, broken pieces.

In the darkness of the trundling cart, Torin saw the sky of Eloria again. The stars shone, a great field of constellations, a silvery path like a dragon's tail, a cratered moon, a wonder of endless depths. It was the first time he'd seen the night. He stood upon the hill with Bailey, with his dearest, his oldest friend.

"Bailey," he whispered in the cart, voice hoarse.

"Bailey," said a boy, his cheeks soft, a youth who had just joined the Village Guard.

Bailey stood beside him upon the hill, a year older, a couple inches taller, and a whole lot braver and stronger. She gave him a crooked smile, mussed his hair, and kissed his cheek.

"Scared, Winky?" she asked.

He nodded. "Yes, and you should be too. They live out there. Elorians."

Bailey only blew out her breath, fluttering her lips. "If you ask me, 'Lorians are just a myth." Then she laughed and grabbed his arm. "Come on, Babyface! Let's explore."

They ran. They ran through darkness. They ran through the fire in Pahmey. They ran through blood and death in Yintao. They ran through the fields of time, up a mountainside in the dusk, toward an ancient clock, and toward . . .

Pain.

Tears flowed down Torin's cheeks.

"Bailey!" he cried, holding her lifeless body, praying for her to wake up, to stay with him. "Please. Bailey. I love you. Don't leave me."

He stood under sunrise, and he placed flowers upon her grave. Darkness.

Trailing stars in a lifeless land of rock, water, and shadows.

And two more lights there in the darkness, as bright as the moon and stars. Two eyes, large, lavender, afraid. The woman peered from behind a boulder as he wheeled forth the bones of her father.

The woman stared from atop the city walls, firing her arrows at him. The woman lay naked in his arms, and he kissed her, made love to her. The woman walked toward him, clad in white, holding a lantern. His bride. His Koyee.

"Where are you, Koyee?" His lips cracked as he spoke. He tasted his blood. "He's coming. Serin. Into the night."

He groaned, the words scratching his throat. His many wounds throbbed. His belly clenched and his head pounded. More images floated before him, faces and smiles and bright eyes. A babe, newborn, lying in her mother's arms, wrapped in cotton. A daughter running through the fields of Fairwool-by-Night, gazing in wonder at the stars above Oshy, fishing with him in the river, growing into a wise, strong woman . . . then leaving. Vanishing in this war.

Where are you, Madori?

His family—broken like his body, scattered like these lanterns of memory.

The cart bounced, knocking his head against the floor, then rolled to a halt. Torin moaned and smelled his blood. He winced, anticipating more pain. The last few times they had stopped moving, they had hurt him. He felt too weak for more pain, for more screaming.

Curses and grumbles rose outside. A lock jostled. Rough hands tugged open the cart door.

Sunlight flooded the cart, blinding Torin. He moaned, wincing, able to see nothing but the searing light. It felt like fire burning him, driving into every cut on his body, raging inside his skull like flames inside an oven.

"Out!" rose the voice. "Out of the cart, traitor."

Eyes narrowed to slits, Torin saw them—Magerian soldiers. They had fought for Mageria long before Serin had taken power, and they still displayed a painted buffalo upon their chests—the ancient sigil of their kingdom. But now they also sported eclipse pins upon their cloaks—the symbol of Serin's Radian Order, the cruel ideology that had overtaken their land. The soldiers' eyes were cruel, their faces weathered and scarred. One man hefted a spear, thrust it into the cart, and goaded Torin. The spearhead nicked his thigh, drawing blood, and Torin shouted hoarsely.

"Into the sunlight, nightcrawler-lover." The soldier spat. "You're in Timandra now. Into the light."

Torin coughed and crawled out of the cart, chains dragging. He thumped down into grass, swayed for a moment on his feet, then fell to his knees, too weak to stand. He blinked feebly, eyes adjusting to the sunlight, and looked around him. The convoy had camped alongside a dirt road—a few wooden carts, a hundred soldiers, and three robed mages upon dark horses. Fields of wild grass sprawled toward faded blue mountains. A herd of buffalo roamed across a distant hill, and hawks glided overhead. Shattered columns rose on a second hill like broken ribs rising from a corpse—remnants of Old Riyona, the empire that had once ruled the lands north of the Sern.

We're heading down Riyonan Road, Torin thought, and a chill washed over him. *Toward Markfir, Capital of Mageria. Toward Serin's court.*

Torin knew what would happen once they reached the walls of Markfir. He had heard enough tales of Mageria's cruelty in its last war against Arden. Torin doubted he'd be lucky enough for a painless death. More likely they would torture him—cut open his belly, quarter him, and flay him before finally letting him die. They would hang his mutilated remains above the gates of the city, the traitor of sunlight, a lesson for all to see.

Torin winced.

But not before they hurt me some more.

Snorts rose from the head of the convoy. A massive dark horse, twice the usual size, moved off the road, a beast of black fur, oozing red eyes, and nostrils that leaked smoke and sparks of fire. Perhaps the creature had once been an ordinary stallion, augmented with magic, bloated into this terror of muscle and rank flesh. Flies bustled around it, and its stench wafted across the camp. Upon the beast rode a towering man, eight or nine feet tall, wrapped in a black cloak. Four arms sprouted from his torso, and each hand held a serrated blade. A helmet like an iron bucket encircled his head, and red eyes like embers blazed through the eye holes, staring at Torin, boring into him. Torin grimaced under the gaze; those eyes burned him like true embers pressed against his skin.

Lord Gehena, Torin thought, his teeth rattling and his jaw creaking. Serin's most prized soldier. The man who had crushed Arden. The man who would deliver the famous Torin Greenmoat to his capital.

The dark warrior dismounted and walked across the camp, heading toward Torin. Buckles jingled upon his boots, and each footfall crushed stones beneath it. Shadows writhed around the man—if a man he truly was—like smoky snakes. His cloak fluttered in the wind, its hem burnt and tattered. Tools hung from his belt: pliers, pincers, thumbscrews, hammers, and vials of acid.

Chains jangling, Torin struggled to rise to his feet. He stared at Gehena, forcing himself to meet the burning red gaze.

"My value to you lessens with every wound," Torin said. "If you want ransom, the queen will onl—"

Gehena raised one of his four hands. Bolts of magic blasted out of his black dagger, screeched through the air, and slammed into Torin.

He fell, writhing. The magic crawled into him, racing through his veins like parasites. Torin couldn't help it. He screamed. When the magic finally left him, he trembled.

One of Gehena's boots—twice the size of a normal man's foot—stepped onto Torin's chest. His ribs creaked, and Torin couldn't even scream, couldn't even breathe.

A hissing voice like astral smoke wafted out of Gehena's helmet. "I care not for ransom."

Another blast of magic slammed into Torin. The tiny shards of pain drove through him, exploring his innards, and finally tore out of his skin with a bloody mist.

"I've told you everything I know!" Torin shouted, almost blind with the pain. "I have no information to give you. I—"

Gehena laughed, a horrible sound like thunder rolling through a cave. Strands of magic tugged Torin to his feet, then into the air, squeezing him, crushing him. The magic levitated him to eye level with Gehena. The creature stared at him, those eyes all-consuming, burning with cold fire. Torin hovered two feet above the ground, his blood dripping into the grass.

"I don't care for information either," said Gehena. "You betrayed the sunlight. You fought for the night. I care only . . . for your pain."

That pain blasted out of Gehena in a holocaust of blinding fire.

Torin screamed.

The red light washed over him, and he saw no more.

CHAPTER THREE
THE LORDS OF LIGHT

Koyee knelt by her bed, her chest constricting, barely able to breathe. Her head spun and she had to force in air. She had fought many battles, yet now she felt faint, felt her world crashing down. Her home's walls, simple clay adorned with prayer scrolls, seemed to close in around her.

"We swore to protect her, Torin," Koyee whispered. "We swore to give her a better world. Swore she'd never fight like we did."

She trembled to remember that turn seventeen years ago when Madori had been born. Koyee had been so afraid then, holding the little bundle. Most mothers felt joy when holding their babes, but Koyee had felt fear, guilt, and crushing sadness. A child of both day and night. A torn child in a torn world.

"How could I have brought life into this world?" she had whispered to Torin.

He had comforted her, telling her that the world was healed now, that Ferius was dead, that peace had come. Yet now . . . now her dear husband was missing, perhaps dead in a new war that engulfed Timandra. And now her daughter, though returned to Eloria, would train to be a warrior.

"I wanted you to be a gardener, perhaps a healer," Koyee whispered, clutching her palms upon her bed. "Not this. Not a soldier."

Why had she given Madori the sword? She could have shouted, could have insisted Madori sailed to safety. She could have dragged Madori to safety herself. What kind of mother sent her child to train to become a killer?

Koyee sighed. She knew the answer.

"Because there is no safety anywhere in Moth," she whispered to herself. "Because only killers will survive now. Because the fire of sunlight is returning to our lands, and only with steel will Madori survive now. Only in the wilderness of Eloria, training to become a warrior, will Madori find some hope."

She silently added words she would not speak. *Please, spirit of Xen Qae, let her training in the darkness last for many moons. If the fire of war must blaze, let it burn and die before Madori can return.* Her breath trembled. *Do not let my sweet daughter turn into a killer. Do not let her take lives as I've taken lives.*

Koyee did not know how many men she had killed; she had slain too many to count, and each was a weight upon her soul, another scar inside her. Madori's cheeks perhaps were scarred now, but her heart was still pure.

Every time you take a life, you chip off another piece of your soul. Koyee lowered her head, eyes squeezed shut. *Please, Xen Qae, if you watch over me, keep my daughter's soul pure.*

A knock sounded on the door—so loud that Koyee started. An instant later, Madori stepped into the room.

Koyee rubbed her eyes. "Madori, by Xen Qae . . . I don't know why you even knock if you just barge in anyway."

Madori bristled. "I don't know why you even talk if it's just to scold me."

Koyee sighed. "What have you come for?"

"Well, nothing now." Madori's eyes reddened. "I had a gift for you, but I'm tossing it out." She turned to leave.

Koyee's heart twisted. She leaped forward and grabbed her daughter. "Madori, wait. Please."

The girl reeled toward her, eyes red. "What?"

"I don't want to fight. All we ever do is fight. Let's not part like this." Koyee guided her daughter into the room and they sat on the bed. "What have you brought me?"

Madori chewed her lip and clenched and unclenched her fists, seeming torn between her anger and forgiveness. Whenever they talked, it seemed like this—Madori forever torn between love and hatred, confusion and rage. Finally the girl relaxed, reached into her pocket, and pulled out a silver locket on a chain.

"For you," she said.

Koyee took the gift and smiled. "It's beautiful. Where did you get this?"

"Old Shinluan made it for me in the village. It's real silver. Look inside."

Koyee snapped the locket open. Inside she saw a delicate painting of Madori's face, perfectly lifelike.

The face inside the locket smiled and waved.

Koyee gasped and nearly dropped the locket. She spun toward her daughter, eyes wide. She saw that Madori was holding open an identical locket of her own, waving toward it.

"What . . ." Koyee began. She looked back into the locket Madori had given her, and she saw her daughter's face inside again. Only it was no painting, she realized. It was a reflection of the real Madori.

"The two lockets are linked," Madori explained. "Mine and yours. One peers out of the other. Look inside your locket again."

Koyee looked back at her locket in wonder. As Madori moved her own locket from side to side, the view changed.

"They are windows," Koyee whispered.

Madori nodded. "With our two lockets, we can always see each other. Each locket is a magical eye." She grinned. "I made them with magic. See, it's very simple! Each locket actually has a mirror inside. All I had to do was magically link the mirrors. Now your locket reflects whatever light goes into my locket, and vice versa. Essentially, when you look into your locket, you're just looking into my mirror—sort of. It's a bit more complex than that. It's an application of Feshavern's Fifth Principle as applied to artifacts and the bending of light. Professor Rushavel taught us this magic back at Teel University. I can explain more about how—"

"It's all right, daughter." Koyee smiled. "I think I prefer my magic with a tinge of mystery." She kissed Madori's cheek. "Thank you. I will worry less now that I can watch over you."

Madori nodded. "I'll keep my locket closed most of the time. I don't want you always watching! But whenever the moon hits its zenith, I'll open the locket and look inside, and I'll wave to you so you know I'm all right. Will you do the same?"

Koyee's eyes dampened, and she could barely speak without crying. "Of course." She embraced her daughter. "Of course. I love you, Madori. Be safe out there."

Madori nodded. "Ouch, Mother! You're crushing me. I'll be safe. Now let go and stop crying."

After her daughter left the room, Koyee slung the locket around her neck. It rested beside her other amulet—the little gear she had taken from Cabera Clock, the gear that kept the world locked between day and night. The two talismans—one of family, one of the world—rested side by side against her chest. She placed her hand over them and stared out the window at the night.

* * * * *

Tirus Serin, the Light of Radian, the Emperor of Mageria, stood upon the hill and watched his army muster at the border of night.

Once a village had nestled in the valley, a little backwater called Fairwool-by-Night, home to that mongrel Madori. Once the little beast's house had stood here, its roof woven of thatch, its gardens lush. Once an old maple tree had grown from the village square, shading the staircase of a columned library. Once five hundred souls had lived here on the border of darkness, the most eastern settlement in all Timandra.

The village was gone.

Where Madori's house had stood now rose a great marble statue, twenty feet tall, depicting him—Emperor Serin—gazing upon the darkness. Atop the ash of burnt houses stood iron cannons shaped as buffaloes; the filthy nightcrawlers had discovered the secrets of gunpowder, and now these Magerian guns would turn their own invention against them.

Beyond the cannons, where once fields had swayed, stood Serin's troops. Five thousand horsemen mustered here, each rider clad in steel and bearing lance, sword, and shield—a vanguard to charge through the gates of darkness and smash the walls of the Elorian cities. Thirty thousand soldiers stood beyond the horses: archers clad in boiled leather, their longbows taller than men, their arrows powerful enough to punch through armor; pikemen in chain mail, their pole-arms serrated and cruel; and many swordsmen in breastplates, their longswords wide, double-edged, and two-handed, blades to crash through the thin Elorian katanas. These men would swarm through the night cities, plundering, destroying, slaying every nightcrawler they found.

Finally, in the river, anchored dozen of warships. Shields hung across their hulls, each displaying the Radian eclipse. Their masts rose tall, and slaves manned their oars—mostly Ardishmen with whipped backs and collared necks. Upon the warships' decks stood Serin's finest warriors—his mages. Their robes were black, their faces hooded. Their magic would bring the nightcrawlers to their knees.

"All this is only a single fist," Serin said softly. "Very soon now, more troops will arrive from the capital. Very soon now, we will have a host to light every last corner of the night."

"I want her to watch," Lari said, voice strained. "I want Madori to see the night burn. To see her people scream in flame. To see her cities fall and shatter. I want my filthy cousin to watch every sword thrust into every heart, to see every babe ripped from its mother and crushed, to see every every throat slit." Lari clenched her fists, and the wind streamed her hair. "Madori will witness the anguish of the night before we drag her back into the day."

Serin looked at his daughter. Lari was a proud woman of the Magerian race, tall and strong and fair, her eyes blue, her hair golden—a paragon of purity. The nightcrawlers her scarred her cheeks on the road outside of Teel, but powder and rouge now hid the two pale lines. *How wonderful the Timandrian!* Serin thought, admiring her. *How superior we are to the sub-humans of the night!* Pride welling in him, Serin stroked Lari's cheek.

Serin's aunt had married Teramin Greenmoat, a weak knight with peasant roots—that had been bad enough. But then Torin Greenmoat, Teramin's son, had gone on to marry a nightcrawler, further polluting the family's blood. The ultimate insult was Madori, a half-nightcrawler in the family. Serin shuddered in disgust to imagine that he shared blood with that beast. As pure as Lari was, Madori was filthy, a stain upon his family, a stain he must efface.

"We will make Madori watch," he said. "She will see every death in Eloria before we take her to her father. And then she will see his death too." His hand, which caressed Lari's cheek, was missing one finger. Madori had taken that finger from him, and Serin's pulse quickened. "But Madori will not die. She will be the last nightcrawler in Mythimna, and we will keep her alive to a very old age. With magic, we can extend her age to hundreds of years." Serin sucked in breath, already imagining it. "She will travel the world in a cage, from town to town, a freak for the people of our empire to marvel at. The mongrel will become our pet, our circus animal. All will see her and scorn her."

Serin caressed the stump of his finger, and a thin smile stretched across his lips to remember Madori: her large lavender eyes; her strange black hair, cropped-short aside from two long strands that framed her face; and the fire in her heart, the fire that had driven her to attack him. It was almost a shame that she was half nightcrawler. With that much passion within her, Madori could have made a good warrior in his hosts, perhaps even a good mate to warm his bed; Serin had not been with a woman since his wife had died. Yet fire or not, Madori was a mongrel, tainted, filthy. When Serin met her again, he would break her.

"Look, Father!" Lari said, pointing west. "The boat arrives."

Serin clasped his hands together. "Splendid!"

It was a small vessel, its hull black, its sails displaying two crossed scrolls—emblem of Teel University. Several slaves sat chained to oars, propelling the boat onward. A stooped man stood at the prow, black cloak wrapped tightly around him. His nose was as curved as his back, his eyes were beady, and a ring of oily hair surrounded the bald crest of his head. He looked like some gangly vulture, and even his fingers, which clasped his cloak, looked like talons, complete with long sharp nails. As fair as Serin was, this man was foul. Serin was a warrior of nobility, of pride, of wide shoulders and a proud stance, a lion among lesser creatures; here before him emerged a scavenger.

A useful scavenger, Serin thought. *A tool, no different than my cannons and sword.*

"Professor Atratus!" Serin called out. "Welcome to the dusk."

The professor's small eyes stared across the mustering armies at the hilltop where Serin stood. The mage placed his fist against his chest.

"Radian rises!" he called out.

The boat navigated between the Magerian warships, a piranha moving between sharks. Two hooded mages stood upon the deck behind Atratus, holding whips of fire. Those whips cracked, slamming against the backs of rowing slaves. As the boat drew closer, Serin noticed that several Elorian skulls—the eye sockets freakishly large—hung upon the buffalo figurehead.

You are a twisted bastard, Serin thought, staring at Atratus. *A man after my own heart.*

The boat docked at the pier. Ardish merchant boats would once dock here, load the bounty of Timandra, and send the gifts of sunlight—fruits, grains, wines—into the night. Serin sneered. The Ardishmen had betrayed the sunlight, feeding the creatures of darkness. It was fitting, he thought, that from this very place—the docks that had once fed Eloria—the night's doom was kindled.

As Atratus stepped off the boat, the soldiers of Mageria formed a path between them and stood at attention, slamming the butts of their spears against the earth. Atratus did not spare the soldiers a glance. He walked between them, cloak wrapped tightly around him. A sneer found his lips, and his dark eyes glittered. When he finally climbed the hill and reached Serin, the stooped mage—the new Headmaster of Teel—knelt in the dirt.

"My Lord Serin!" A bubble of spit floated out of Atratus's mouth and popped against Serin's shin. If Atratus noticed, he gave no note of it. "I've come with the traitor, O Light of Radian. We hurt her. She is broken. But she still clings to life. We've kept her alive so that you may kill her yourself, dearest leader."

"*I* will kill her!" said Lari. The young woman tossed back her hair and smiled down at Atratus. "I suffered under her yoke at Teel for an entire year. The old crone nearly had me throwing up every time she summoned us to the courtyard." Lari drew her silvery sword. "I will gladly pierce her shriveled old heart, the traitor." She barked a laugh. "Letting nightcrawlers into Teel! Disgusting. She'll pay for her treachery."

Atratus rose to his feet and bowed his head toward Lari. "My Lady! Perhaps you would even care to demonstrate your magic on her? It would make your old professor quite proud. Besides, your

sword is too beautiful a weapon to bloody on the likes of the traitor."
He looked over his shoulder. "Here she comes."

Two younger mages were walking uphill, hands raised. Between
them floated a bruised old woman. Invisible chains held her aloft
between the robed men. Her white hair fell over her face, and
bloodied rags covered her body. She was barely larger than a child—a
dying, famished thing. When the younger mages reached the hilltop,
they saluted and released their magic.

The old woman fell to her knees, coughed, and raised her head.

She stared up at Serin, fire in her eyes.

She spat upon his boot.

Serin glanced at his daughter, then back at the old woman. He
backhanded her. It was perhaps crude—not an elegant attack like a
blast of magic—but it did the trick. Blood splattered and the old
woman fell to the ground.

"Headmistress Egeria," Serin said. "Or rather, *former*
headmistress. How lovely to see you. Are you impressed with the
armies I muster here? They will soon invade the darkness. They will
soon step upon the worms you sought to protect. They will soon
bring me Madori, the little vermin you harbored."

Though her eyes were bloodshot and puffed with bruises,
Egeria fixed Serin with a steady gaze. Blood filled her mouth, but she
spoke in a clear voice.

"Remember, Serin, what Madori's parents did to the last man
who invaded the night. Beware that Madori does not do the same to
you."

Serin sighed. "Ferius was a religious fanatic, a mere monk, a
fool who thought he could lead an army." He swept his arm across
the field. "Do you see these forces, Egeria? They are mine to
command. I am no village preacher who knows nothing of warfare. I
am a conqueror. I am . . . an exterminator. And the nightcrawlers will
perish under my heel. All but Madori, that is. Oh, that one will live a
very long time." He turned toward Lari. "What say we send the
mongrel a little gift—one of many to come?"

Lari nodded and a smile spread across her face, the smile a wolf
gives its prey before pouncing. "Gladly."

The princess stretched out both hands.

Egeria winced and struggled to raise her own arms, but magic bound her. Lari's blast of energy pounded against the old woman's chest, knocking her down. Lari grinned, stepped forward, and leaned over the former headmistress. Coiling strands of smoke materialized in the air. The astral tendrils snaked into Egeria's nostrils, ears, and mouth like serpents entering their burrows. Egeria thrashed on the ground, the serpents slithering under her skin, their forms visible like animals moving under sheets.

"I . . . I failed you, child." Tears streamed from Egeria's eyes. "I tried to teach you, Lari. I tried to teach you integrity, morals, goodness, I—"

With a scream, Lari balled her fists. The smoky serpents vanished from under Egeria's skin, digging deeper, crashing into her organs.

With a final gasp, Egeria went limp.

Lari looked up at her father, the rage gone from her face. Suddenly she seemed like a child again, desperate for her father's approval.

"Did I do it properly, Father?" She bit her lip. "I was hoping to drive the serpents into her heart right away. I didn't think they'd crawl under her skin."

"Keep practicing." Serin frowned at her. "I expect the best from you, Lari. Next time you kill, I want it quick. You will have to kill quickly on the battlefield. Do you understand?" He clenched his fist. "Do you remember what happened when you were a child, when you failed to play the proper notes on the harp?"

Lari blanched and her bottom lip trembled. Those bruises would linger for turns. To her father, the harp was almost as important as magic; whenever Lari had played a bum note, he would knock her onto the floor, would beat her with sticks, would leave her bruised, bleeding, and begging for another chance. Lari had grown into a woman, perhaps too old to beat, but Serin still expected perfection from her.

She nodded. "I will practice, Father. I promise. I will practice on as many nightcrawlers and traitors as it takes." She kissed his cheek. "I will make you proud."

Standing beside them, Headmaster Atratus cleared his throat—a horrid sound like a vulture gagging up a chunk of maggoty flesh. "And don't forget about your old professor. After all, I taught you much magic myself."

Lari smiled sweetly at the balding, stooped man. "Of course, Headmaster. I had to leave your university early to join the war effort, but I promise you—what I miss in classes I will perfect on the battlefield." She turned back toward the corpse. "And now . . . now I will bloody my sword. Now I prepare a gift for the mongrel. A little herald of what's to come."

Lari drew her sword and swung it down several times, finally severing Egeria's head.

They walked down to the river—an emperor in bright steel, a princess with a bloodied sword, and a mage in black robes. Myriads of soldiers stood at their sides, forming walls of steel, a force of sunlight about to swarm into darkness. The warships of the Magerian Empire rose in the water, masts like a forest. Serin barked a few orders, and soon a rowboat—an old landing craft the fleet could easily spare—was lowered into the water. Serin himself stuck the head onto a spear, then propped it onto the boat's prow, forming a lurid, dripping figurehead.

He took a scroll and quill from a servant, and standing on the river bank, he wrote in his fine, flowing script.

Dearest Madori!

Last we met, you took a finger from me. I now give you a head. Poor Egeria died knowing your fate. I wanted you to know it too. When we meet again—and it will be soon, my dearest Madori—I will take a finger from you. Then another finger. Then all your fingers and all your toes. But not your head. That will remain, so that you can see the crowds of Timandrians who gape at you, so you can hear their jeers, smell your own blood as they pelt you with stones. You and I will travel my empire together—you as a circus freak, I as your trainer. I'm afraid that dear old Egeria suffered a fate far kinder than what awaits you.

I am coming for you, and I will see you soon, sweet mongrel!

Your dear uncle,

Emperor Tirus Serin

He rolled up the scroll, nailed it onto the boat's hull, and sent the vessel floating eastward. He stood with his daughter, watching as the boat moved toward the dusk. Soon it entered the gloaming, and beads of light gleamed upon its wake like drops of liquid metal. Then the boat was gone into shadows, gone toward the village of Oshy. To Koyee. To Madori. To all the Elorians who would see his might and fear him.

"Perhaps they will fight as we march in," he said softly. "Perhaps they will beg. Perhaps they will flee. No matter what they do, the outcome will be the same. They will die."

Lari leaned against him. He slung his arm around her, and they stood together, watching the darkness. Behind them, the army stood ready to invade. Very soon now, the last troops would arrive from the capital. Very soon now, the darkness would burn.

CHAPTER FOUR
SWAMP AND STONE

Madori stood upon the hill, the wind whipping her cloak and two strands of black hair. She gazed down upon her home—the village of Oshy, the Inaro River, Salai castle, and beyond them the dusk. She had spent many of her childhood summers here. She had sought sanctuary here. When the invasion began, she would shed blood here.

"For now I say goodbye, Oshy." The whistling wind drowned her words and nearly tugged off her cloak. "I go into shadow."

For the first time in her life, she wore Qaelish clothes— garments she, half Timandrian, had once rejected. A *qipao* dress hugged her body, its indigo silk embroidered with golden fish. A silver sash encircled her waist, inlaid with pearls, and her silken black cloak sported dragon motifs. Across her back hung her greatest possession: Sheytusung, fabled katana of her father.

Now I travel into the Desolation, to find the master who trained my grandfather. She touched the silk-wrapped hilt. *I've learned to fight with magic. Now I will learn steel.*

She sighed. Once she had dreamed of being a healer, not a soldier. When her mother had miscarried years ago, leaving Madori an only child, she had vowed to learn to heal others, not slay them. At Teel University, she had made her greatest progress in Magical Healing class, not Offensive Magic. Yet now she—the girl who had wanted so badly to mend broken bodies and souls—would march into the darkness to become a killer. Perhaps her fate was to be torn—between day and night, between healing and hurting.

She turned to look northeast, away from the dusk and the village in its light. The full darkness of Eloria stretched there, empty, lifeless, nothing but black hills and plains beneath the stars. The wilderness. Madori was half Elorian, but the sight of so much darkness, such vast empty land, chilled her. She would not be sailing upon a river that reflected the stars, that glowed with lanternfish, that eventually led to cities of light. She would be traveling into the emptiness; she might as well have been walking across the surface of the moon.

She gulped.

"You're out there somewhere, Master Lan Tao," she whispered.

She unrolled her parchment scroll, revealing fields of stars. When Koyee had given her this starmap, Madori had only nodded, rolled her eyes, and insisted that she understood the directions. She had lied. She could barely understand the runes, arrows, and coiling lines that snaked between the illustrated constellations. Yet she had needed to quickly leave her home in the village, to leave her mother, to begin her quest. Every moment back in Oshy, she was tempted to defy her mother, to race into the dusk, to find Serin and challenge him to another duel. That would have meant her death, she knew. As much as she hated Serin, her training was not yet complete; a single year at Teel had not made her powerful enough to defeat her enemies. So she had stuffed the map into her belt. She had raced here to the hill, too anxious for teary partings. And now she stood out here in the wind, on the cusp of pure darkness, afraid, alone.

She took a deep breath. "I survived the searing light and cruelty of Timandra." She smiled crookedly. "I can survive the cold, empty darkness of Eloria."

She took a single step—the first of many, the beginning of a new journey.

A voice rose behind her, tugging her back like a rope.

"Madori."

She spun around to see Jitomi walking uphill toward her.

The young Ilari, once her fellow student at Teel, wore the raiment of his southern, island-empire. His black silk robes fluttered in the wind, embroidered with small red flames. Upon his belt hung a tanto dagger, a traditional weapon of Ilar. A red bandana encircled his brow. His nose ring gleamed in the moonlight, as did the smooth, white hair that hung across his brow. His dragon tattoo coiled up his neck and cheek, the scaled head resting above his eyebrow.

Madori nodded at him, a new lump forming in her throat. "Jitomi."

He stepped closer and stood before her. His blue eyes—large Elorian eyes like hers, twice the size of Timandrian ones—stared at her. "You are leaving without saying farewell?"

She looked away. "I don't like goodbyes." Her voice sounded too thin to her, too hoarse.

"I'm leaving Oshy too. I'm returning to Ilar, to speak to my father, to try and enlist help for the border." He stared south into the darkness as if already seeing his distant homeland. "This is not only the border with Qaelin but with all the night. I'll make my father understand; he holds sway in the court of Empress Hikari. When he speaks, she listens. Ilar will help us, Madori."

She turned back toward him. "I thought you came here to say goodbye, not to speak of armies and empresses."

Jitomi nodded. He held her hand, and he leaned forward, trying to kiss her. She pulled back and took a step away.

"Madori?" His voice was soft, hurt.

She shook her head and looked away. "Go, Jitomi." Her voice caught in her throat. She remembered that time in Teel, the time they had kissed in the infirmary, how she had lain in his arms. "Go to Ilar; that is your path. And my path leads into the wilderness. There's no need for farewells, no need for your kiss, no need for any of this." Her voice cracked. "We must tread different paths. Perhaps they will never cross again."

She hefted her pack across her back and began to walk away from him, heading into the darkness.

"Madori, wait." He stepped toward her, held her shoulder, and touched her hair. "Do you forget all we've been through? Do you forget the year we spent together at Teel, the long moons we spent together on the road?" His voice dropped to a whisper. "Those turns we slept in each other's arms, those secrets we whispered, those—"

"That's all over!" Her voice rose so loudly she was almost shouting. Tears burned in her eyes. "Don't you understand, Jitomi? We're not youths anymore. All those turns together have ended. It's war now. War like the one my parents fought, like we'll have to fight." She tasted a tear on her lips. "There will be no more embraces, no more kisses, no more sunlit turns of youth. We're in darkness now. We must walk our paths alone."

Pain filled his eyes. He touched her cheek, lifting her tear onto his fingers. His voice was barely a whisper. "Madori, I love you."

That only sent anger flaring through her, a rage fueled by her pain. "Well, I don't love you." She shook her head wildly. "What can love bring us now? Only heartbreak. Go, Jitomi. Go! Go to your homeland and I'll travel my own road. That is what's left for us." She laughed, though it sounded more like a sob. "I told you I hated goodbyes. I told you to leave. Now look." She gestured at her tears. "Now look what you've done to me. I hate you, Jitomi. I . . ."

Yet somehow she found herself embracing him. Somehow she found herself kissing him again, and it tasted of her tears.

She placed her hands against his chest and shoved him back. She turned away, eyes damp, and walked as fast as she could into the shadows. The stars spread above, and the icy wind cut through her, and she did not look back.

* * * * *

Tam Solira, Prince of Arden, and Neekeya, a daughter of Daenor, crested the rocky hill and beheld the swamplands sprawl below into the horizon.

"Daenor," Neekeya whispered. "Home."

The young woman stood bedecked in crocodile motifs—a helmet shaped as a crocodile head, a shirt of scales mimicking crocodile skin, and a necklace of crocodile teeth. Finally, a sword with a crocodile-claw pommel hung from her belt. Her tattered green cloak fluttered in the wind, as did those strands of her black, chin-length hair that escaped from her helmet. The rising sun gleamed upon her brown skin and lit her large, chocolate-colored eyes. She smiled wistfully, gazing with love upon her kingdom.

"I missed you, *Denetek*." She turned toward Tam, her eyes bright, and her smile widened to reveal her teeth. "Isn't it beautiful? We call our land *Denetek* in our tongue; Daenor is what the kingdoms of Old Riyona call it."

Tam looked back toward the view. Three years ago, he had visited the rainforest of Naya and thought that land harsh. Now, viewing the marshlands of Daenor, he understood what true harshness looked like. Daenor was not just lush and wet; it looked like a flooded apocalyptic nightmare. The water stretched for miles, covered in algae and lilies. Mangroves grew like spiders of wood and leaf, their roots twisting. Boulders jutted like islands from this green sea, looking as sharp and cruel as blades. Mist hung in the air, birds cried out discordantly, and distant pyramids rose upon the horizon, as grim as tombstones.

If ever the world fell to ruin, to flood, to decay, he thought, *it would look like Daenor.*

He suppressed a shudder and forced himself to nod. "It's lovely, Neekeya. It's very . . ." He thought for a moment. ". . . full of life."

Of course, "life" probably meant man-eating crocodiles, insects the size of his fist, and snakes that laid eggs inside human skulls, but he felt it safest not to vocalize those thoughts.

She held his hand and pointed across the marshlands. "Do you see that distant pyramid? That's my home. My father rules all these lands, as far as you can see. They'll be our lands one turn, Tam. We'll be married and rule together, a wise lord and lady of the swamps."

He looked at Neekeya—her ready smile, her bright eyes, the goodness that shone from her. Perhaps Daenor seemed forbidding to him, but Neekeya was beautiful and pure. He squeezed her palm. "But first we must stop the Radian menace. We must convince your father and the other lords of Daenor that Mageria must be fought. Or else these lands might fall as Arden fell."

A twinge twisted his heart to think of Arden, his homeland. The memories of its fall still hurt him—the enemy troops snaking across its roads, the Radian banners upon Kingswall's towers, and mostly the fear . . . the fear for his family, for his friends. He did not know if his family had survived. Would Serin keep the royal family alive, or was Tam the last survivor? He thoughts of them now—his wise father, King Camlin; his kind mother, Queen Linee; his twin brother, Prince Omry. Did they languish now in a Radian prison, did they lie dead in a field, or had they too fled to foreign lands? Even more than he wanted to free his homeland, Tam wanted to find his family again. With every breath, worry for them flared. It had been four months since he had parted from Madori outside the conquered city of Kingswall; he had heard nothing of his friends or family since.

Tam closed his eyes, the memories suddenly too strong to resist.

Catch me! little Madori cried, only a child, short and scrawny, her knees scraped. She laughed and ran through the sunlit gardens, and Tam ran in pursuit, a mere boy, laughing, his face tanned and freckled, his world full of joy. His twin, Prince Omry, was stuck in the stuffy court, heir to Arden, a serious boy groomed to rule. But Tam, a few minutes younger, laughed as he chased Madori outside. They splashed through the stream, collected frogs, and finally lay on their backs in the grass, watching the sky.

That one looks like a dragon, Madori said, pointing at a cloud. *I'm going to ride dragons some turn.*

Tam pointed out another cloud. *That one looks like a ship! We're going to find our own ship some turn, Billygoat, and sail far away from here, far away on adventure.*

So many summers they had lain like that in the gardens of Kingswall, dreaming, speaking softly of the distant lands they'd visit, of all the monsters they'd slay, the villages they'd save. Her—a girl torn between day and night. Him—a prince so jealous of his twin, his inheritance stolen by a few minutes of sleep in the womb.

They had finally gone on their adventure together, traveling to Teel to become mages . . . yet now Madori was so far from him. Now this adventure did not seem like much fun at all. It had been a journey of pain, of bloodshed, of fear and hunger. And now Madori was gone from him, traveling deep into the darkness on the other side of Moth.

I miss you, Billygoat, he thought. *And I must find aid here in Daenor. I must or all the night will burn.*

He turned back toward Neekeya. She stared at him, and her face hardened, and her eyes filled with determination.

"We will find aid," Neekeya said. "We've come here to prepare Daenor for war. We will protect our borders. Daenor will stand."

Hand in hand, they walked downhill, heading into the swamplands.

When they reached the water, Tam grimaced. The green, dank soup rose to his knees, thick with moss. Dragonflies flew around him, frogs trilled upon lily pads, herons waded between reeds, and he even saw a snake coil across the water. The mangroves rose around him, twisted like goblins. The air was hot and thick and filled his lungs like smoke. He wondered how he'd even walk a hundred yards here, let alone several leagues toward the pyramids. Neekeya, however, seemed to suffer no mobility problems. Despite her armor, she bounded from boulder to boulder, log to log, twisting root to twisting root. Her boots barely touched the water.

"Come on, Tam!" she said. "It's not a sea. You won't have to swim." She grinned. "Just hop your way over."

"I don't hop!" he said. "I'm not a frog."

She shrugged. "Well, you might not be, but you're wearing one as a hat."

He reached to his head and felt something slimy. When he pulled it free, the frog hopped away, and Tam grimaced.

They kept moving through the bog—Neekeya hopping from log to rock, Tam slogging through the knee-high water. He made a few attempts to leap like Neekeya, only to fall face-down into the muck, covering himself with mud, moss, and peat. The leafy mangrove branches hid the sky, and the song of the swamp filled his ears: squawking birds, chirping insects, trilling frogs, and gurgling water. An egret snatched a dragonfly. Snails perched upon a floating branch. Drops of water gleamed upon countless spiderwebs. Tall grass and reeds grew upon tussocks, rich with grasshoppers and toads.

"At least this land would be a nightmare to invade," Tam muttered as he waded forward, algae tangling around his legs. "I can't imagine Mageria's horses and chariots slogging through this."

Neekeya nodded. "I'd like to see them try. Our soldiers would rain arrows down upon them." She pointed up at the canopy, then waved. "Hello, boys!"

Tam looked up and lost his breath.

"Idar's shaggy old beard," he muttered.

Several Daenorians perched among the branches, clad in dark green cloaks and gray tunics. Brown and green paint covered their

faces, and leaves covered their helmets of boiled leather. They held
bows and blowguns, and daggers hung from their belts. With their
camouflage, Tam doubted he'd have noticed them were they not
waving back toward Neekeya. When he looked behind him, he saw
that many other Daenorians filled the trees he had already walked
under.

Neekeya gave Tam a solemn look. "Daenor is defended." She
nodded and gripped the hilt of her sword. "If Serin invades the
swamp, he will find his watery grave."

Tam stared east across the marshlands—east toward the distant
Teekat Mountains and beyond them Mageria.

Will Daenor remain a last island of freedom? he thought. *Will all the
world fall as Arden fell, and will the night burn, while we linger here in the mud?*
He did not speak these concerns. But he knew: *We cannot simply hide as
evil rises beyond the mountains. We must face that evil, and we must attack it, or
the Radian noose will choke us.*

They kept walking, heading east. The marshlands thickened.
The water soon rose to Tam's armpits, and the mangrove roots
twisted everywhere like a lattice. He was forced to hop forward with
Neekeya, jumping from root to log to mossy rock. After a few spills
and bruises, he got the hang of it. Soon, with the help of dangling
vines, he was able to move above the water almost at normal walking
speed. He marveled at how Neekeya, with her heavy armor, managed
the task; he wore only wool and felt clumsier than an elephant in
quicksand.

After hours of traveling, they reached mossy old ruins. Arches
of dark stone rose from the marsh, a hundred feet tall, like the ribs of
a fallen giant. No roof or walls rose among them, but Tam saw other
remnants half-submerged into bogs: the massive stone head of a
statue, large as a boat; an orphaned archway, its doors long-rotted
away; and sunken columns, their capitals shaped as crocodiles. At
first Tam wondered if Serin had already invaded and lay waste to
Daenor's cities, but he quickly realized that these ruins were
thousands of years old.

"Relics of the Ancients," Neekeya said. She nodded solemnly.
"They were great in magic, and many of their magical artifacts are still
hidden under the bogs. Now magic is lost to Daenor, but the

whispers of our forebears remain." She whispered a prayer in her language, clasping her necklace of teeth.

Tam thought back to the history books he would read in Arden. Like Mageria and Verilon, Arden had once been part of the Riyonan Empire; all three of those kingdoms, neighbors north of the Sern and east of the mountains, now spoke similar dialects and worshiped Idar, the god of sunlight. But Daenor, this swamp between the mountains and the western coast, had spent most of its history isolated from the rest of Timandra. Its people looked different, their skin darker, their frames taller, and they spoke a different tongue and worshiped older gods. It was said that even when Riyona herself had been young, Daenor had already been ancient.

They walked under the mossy arches, pushing back curtains of vines. They had just emerged from the ruins when Tam saw the men ahead. He froze and reached for his dagger.

Magerians, was his first thought.

A dozen men stood ahead, seeming as foreign to this swamp as Tam was. When he squinted, he saw that they bore the banners of Daenor—a black crocodile upon a green field—but they looked different from any Daenorian he'd ever seen. Their skin was a lighter brown, and their eyes were green. Their helmets were not shaped as crocodile jaws or their armor as crocodile skin; their helmets were simpler, their breastplates unadorned. Rather than green cloaks and necklaces of teeth, they wore gray cloaks clasped with silver brooches.

"North Daenorians." Neekeya froze, reached for her sword, and sneered at the men ahead. "What are you doing here in the swamps? I thought the south was too muddy for you fine, fancy folk of the northern plains." She spat and looked back at Tam. "They think they can bear a crocodile banner, maybe a little crocodile pin, and be as mighty as the beasts. They plow fields, live in castles, and look down upon their southern brothers and sisters."

One of the men stepped forward, his smile dripping disgust. He was tall and thin, perhaps forty years old, his black eyebrows plucked to perfect arches, his olive-toned skin scented of myrrh. Golden filigree shaped as herons bedecked his breastplate, and a diamond pendant hung from his neck, large as an acorn. A ruby-studded saber hung from his belt, and sapphires formed a decorative crocodile upon his shield. Here were pieces of artwork for display, not for battle.

"Look, friends." The man pointed at Neekeya. "One of the barbarians. The southerners are barely more civilized than beasts. It's no wonder the rest of Timandra sees our kingdom as a cesspool. The southerners are an embarrassment." His eyes flicked toward Tam. "And what's this now? A foreigner? You've strayed far from home, pup."

Neekeya drew her sword. "Out of our way, northerners. You speak to Neekeya, Daughter of Kee'an, a *latani* of *Denetek*. My family rules these lands you stand on. Return to your northern plains or I'll thrust this sword into your guts."

The tall, jeweled man did not lose his smile. "Land? Your family rules over a puddle. Do you not recognize me, Neekeya? We met once, many years ago, when you were just a little beast. I am Felsar, son of King Fehen, Prince of Daenor. Your lord."

Neekeya froze and sucked in air with a hiss. Then she seemed to recollect herself and spat. "Southern Daenor needs no fancy northern princes. For thousands of years, you minded your business in the plains, thinking yourself too good for us. You're more like Magerians than true Daenorians. You have no pride in our land; you only ape the Old Riyonans east of the mountains. *Denetek* needs no northern prince or king." She shoved her way past him. "Return north or drown in our mud, but whatever you do, spare me your prattle. Tam! Come with me. These louts are crocodile food."

She shoved past the men, elbowing them aside. They scoffed at her, and one spat at her feet, but Neekeya kept walking. Tam followed, moving between the North Daenorians. As he crept along a jutting mangrove root, he glanced more closely at the men, and his breath died. Upon their cloaks they wore small Radian pins. One of them, a mustached man with one eye, gave Tam a small nod and smaller smile.

"Tam, hurry up!" Neekeya shouted.

He looked away from the men and followed her, leaving the northerners behind and entering thick brush.

* * * * *

They must have been walking for a full turn, and they had barely halved the distance toward the pyramids. When Neekeya looked at Tam, she found him sweaty, wheezing, and ready to collapse. She sighed. In her eagerness, she had been driving him too fast. She had forgotten that he'd been raised in Kingswall, a city of cobbled streets and fancy carriages. While she hopped easily from rock to root, the journey through the marshlands had left Tam looking like a dying cat.

She paused upon a tussock of grass that rose from the water. She stretched out her arms and yawned.

"I'm so weary I can barely keep moving," she lied. Of course, she could have easily reached home on her own by now, and she could easily keep moving for another turn. But she didn't want to be dragging an exhausted, drowning boy out of the water, nor did she want to hurt his pride. "I need to rest and sleep."

He climbed onto the islet and stood beside her, breathing raggedly. Mud and moss covered him from head to toe. He managed to nod. "Very well. If you'd like to rest, I suppose we can."

She rolled her eyes. "Don't pretend you don't need a rest yourself." She mussed his muddy hair.

They lay on their backs in the grass. The frogs trilled around them, the water gurgled, and the leaves rustled above. Fireflies floated across them, and the hot, soupy air made their lids heavy. Neekeya had forgotten the richness of this place—the thick, lush scent of water and leaf, the languorous heat, the music of the life and water around her. She had gone to Teel University to learn magic, and now she realized that all of Daenor was magic; the very air here filled her with wonder.

Home. Would this home now be lost? She had seen the Radian pins upon the northerners—traitors to their own kingdom. Traveling here, she had seen Mageria's armies muster east of the Teekat Mountains, camps of many tents, archers, and swordsmen prepared for war. She had seen Arden fall under Serin's grip; would her own home now follow? Would this beautiful land burn in the Radian fire, its trees cut down, its waters dried, and the pyramid of her father crumbled to dust? As she lay here in this beauty beside the man she loved, a wave of fear rose within Neekeya, and she saw in her mind a great eclipse—a Radian sun not only hiding Eloria's moon but all lands of free folk.

Lying on his back, Tam reached out to hold her hand. He breathed deeply. "You know, lying here, Daenor isn't all that bad. I like the birds, and even the dragonflies are pretty. And the music of frogs and crickets is soothing. And—Idar's bottom!" He leaped to his feet and drew his sword. "Neekeya!"

She looked up, yawned, and stretched. "It's only a crocodile."

The reptile emerged from the water, placed its front claws upon the islet, and opened its jaws wide. Tam scrambled backwards, holding his blade before him.

"It's a bloody swamp dragon!" he sputtered.

Neekeya rose to her feet and approached the crocodile. "He's cute." She pointed back to the water. "Go, boy! Back into the water. No food for you here. Go!"

The reptile snapped its teeth, but after a few harsh words from Neekeya, it slunk back into the water and floated away in pursuit of less vocal meals.

"I'll never be able to sleep here," Tam said.

Neekeya shrugged. "There are worse animals that could visit. Take that python for example." She pointed across the marsh. A great snake coiled around branches, possibly even larger than the crocodile, deep in slumber.

Seeing the beast, Tam paled and fell to his knees. "I'm definitely not sleeping."

"Good." Neekeya nodded. "You can watch while I rest."

She pulled off her armor, lay back down, and closed her eyes. A moment later, she felt Tam lie down at her side. She peeked through narrowed eyelids to see him looking at her.

"I set up an alarm around the islet," he said. "I changed the grass and soil like Professor Fen taught us. The magic will trumpet if anything larger than a toad sneaks up on us. I suppose I should sleep a little." He yawned. "I've never been more tired in . . ."

He was asleep before he could complete his sentence. Neekeya looked at the muddy Ardish prince. As a child, she had been taught that the eastern royals beyond the mountains were cruel, that they looked down upon Daenor, seeing the swamp-people as little better than Elorians. But now Neekeya had met Elorians; she had met Madori and Jitomi and she loved them dearly, and she missed them. And now Neekeya had met Tam, and she loved him with more fire than a burning forest, more light than a blazing sun. She held him close, kissed his cheek, and nuzzled his neck. He placed his arm around her, and they slept entwined together.

When they woke, she built a fire and they ate a breakfast of grilled frog legs; she chewed hers lustfully while Tam only nibbled, looking queasy. They kept walking through the water, brush, and clouds of insects. After several more hours, they finally saw the pyramids ahead—the great realm of Eetek.

Thirteen pyramids grew from the swamps, thousands of years old, arranged into the shape of a great reptile. The pyramids seemed as alive as the swamps. Their lower bricks were green with thick moss. Higher up the pyramids, the moss faded, but many weeds, vines, and even trees grew between the craggy bricks. Birds fluttered above; their droppings stained the slanting walls. The pyramids were ancient and they showed their age. Those in the north, Neekeya knew, would mock the southern lords for letting nature invade their structures; they would call these pyramids neglected, infested with moss and leaves and wildlife. But to Neekeya and her family, these halls were not separate from nature but an extension of it, and the greenery upon the stone only enhanced their beauty.

She pointed at the largest pyramid, the one forming the reptile's eye. From this distance, she could just make out the gateway near the peak. Men in armor stood there upon a stone ledge. From here they seemed smaller than ants, but she could hear their horns. The silver trumpets were announcing a new turn, and the song brought tears to Neekeya's eyes. A song of home.

"We stand before Eetek Pyramid, the greatest in these swamps," she said, "and its song calls us home."

They walked through the marshlands, stepping over tussocks of grass and mangrove roots when they could, wading through mossy water when they could find no steppingstones. Other Daenorians traveled the marshlands around them. Men oared reed *sheh'an* boats,

holding baskets of fish and cages of birds. In the south, people
speared frogs and dived for mollusks. Reed huts grew upon grassy
hillocks, and other huts nestled among the branches of trees. Here
were the commoners of Daenor, clad in *seeken* homespun, a fabric
woven of lichen and leaves. Bracelets and necklaces of copper jangled
around their wrists, and beads filled their hair. They smiled at
Neekeya as she walked by, calling blessings toward her.

Finally she and Tam reached the great pyramid and stood at its
base. Chipped statues, shaped as men with crocodile heads, guarded a
staircase that climbed the pyramid's eastern flank. The pyramid rose
five hundred feet tall; Neekeya's father claimed it was the tallest
structure in the world. Priests stood upon a stone outcrop near the
crest, playing brass horns; the sound rained down, keening and deep
and metallic. At the pyramid's base stood several guards. They wore
scale armor, green cloaks, and crocodile helms with steel teeth, and
they held spears and bows.

"*Latani* Neekeya!" the guards said. "Welcome home, *Latani*!"

"What does *latani* mean?" Tam whispered.

"It is our word for 'lady,'" she said, feeling her cheeks heat up.

Tam's eyebrows rose so high they almost touched his hair.
"Lady! I didn't realize I was in the presence of a fine, pampered lady
of the court." He sketched a mocking bow. "My dearest Lady
Neekeya, would your ladyship care for some crumpets, perhaps—"

She nudged him with her elbow, scowling. "Be quiet! I'm no
fancy lady. I'm no North Daenorian or Ardishwoman. I'm a proud
swamp warrior. It's not my fault your language has no proper word;
your people don't even say the name of my kingdom properly. Just
think of me as a *latani*—a warrior lady, if you will." She grabbed his
hand. "Come with me and we'll see my father, and don't bow to me
again, not even in jest. The *Deneteki* bow to no one, not even to their
lords. We're proud. We're free. In the swamps, to bow is to be a
slave."

And we will never bow to Serin, she thought, lips tight. *Even if all the
world kneels before him, Daenor will stand tall, strong, unbent.*

They climbed the stairs up the pyramid, leaving the marshlands
below. Two guards framed every step, clad in their reptilian armor,
their spears decorated with bright feathers. Craggy limestone statues,

shaped as reptiles with hanging tongues, lined the staircase like bannisters, their backs furry with moss.

Tam was wheezing and even Neekeya felt lightheaded when they finally reached the top of the staircase. Above them still towered a good hundred feet of pyramid, and before them stretched a ledge of stone. Priests in green robes stood here, red feathers in their hair, blowing brass pipes. They lowered the instruments as Neekeya approached and called out blessings to her.

"Welcome home, *Latani* Neekeya!" Their old faces creased with their smiles. "May Cetela, God of Water and Leaf, forever bless you."

"May Cetela forever bless you too, my friends." Her eyes stung; it had been over a year since she had seen these dear old men. Abandoning decorum, she raced forward and embraced the priests one by one. "I'm so glad to see you again. I missed you. How is my father?"

Their smiles faded and shadows filled their eyes. Neekeya stepped back, frowning. A chill washed her.

"Many difficulties have tested us this past year, *Latani*," said Rekeena, the oldest of the priests, a wiry man with a bald, wrinkled head. "Many troubles have weighed upon your father's shoulders, though he still leads us wisely, and we still pray to Cetela. A great menace musters beyond our borders . . . and in our very kingdom. But it is not for us, priests of Cetela, to dabble in the affairs of men." He gestured toward the archway behind him. "Enter, child. We have seen you many miles away, and your father awaits you."

She glanced at Tam hesitantly, and she saw the same fear in his eyes. She thought back to the North Daenorians she had encountered on the journey. She had not spoken of it to Tam, but she had seen the Radian sigils upon their cloaks.

Radians . . . in our own land.

She swallowed, nodded at the priests again, and took Tam's hand in hers. They stepped forward together, under the archway, and into the shadows.

CHAPTER FIVE
THE DESOLATION

Madori walked through the darkness.

She walked alone.

She had thought the Elorian wilderness was empty. She had been wrong. The stars were a multitude, a sea of endless, distant life. They clustered above. They swept across the heavens like rivers of spilled milk. Madori had always thought the stars were white, but in the wild she realized that they were silver, blue, red, yellow, and countless other shades. They moved slowly or quickly, trailing above in an ancient dance. The constellations guided her: the leaping fish, the running wolf, the wise old philosopher, the glowing whale. Her parchment starmap was only a crude thing; the heavens above were a great tapestry whose secrets she would never fully understand. Headmistress Egeria had taught that some stars were distant worlds, that life flourished upon them too. As she walked, Madori wondered if any souls were traveling their own paths upon those worlds, looking toward Mythimna and also contemplating distant wanderers.

As a child, Madori would gaze up at the stars and imagine life on other worlds. She had imagined worlds of wonder and magic, of dragons and monsters, even one world where people could turn into dragons. She used to speak of building a great hot air balloon, of traveling with Tam up to the stars, of finding a place where day and night cycled, where she wouldn't feel so strange, so alone, where she could become a dragon—powerful, blasting out fire, a beast who could feel no pain.

The silly dreams of a child, she thought. Now those worlds in the sky seemed so distant, so out of reach, so cold.

Not only stars filled the wild. Other wonders filled the night. She had thought the wilderness black and jagged, but now she saw smooth lavender rocks in a dried-out riverbed, great indigo boulders shaped as men, and hillside crystals that reflected the stars. The bones of an ancient creature, as large as a dragon, rose from black dust, the ribs so large Madori could walk beneath them like she'd walk under the arches of Teel's cloister. Upon a cliff, Madori saw fossils of seashells and birds embedded into the stone, and even a fossilized tree—an actual tree, like in Timandra. Thousands of years ago, folk would say, the world had turned, and day and night would cycle around Mythimna. Here perhaps were the remnants of Old Eloria, the life that had flourished here and vanished when endless night had fallen.

She did not know for how long she walked. Koyee had given her an hourglass, but Madori did not bother using it; it would only tilt over as she walked. Time vanished here. When she was weary, she paused to sleep. Mostly she walked. She ate the foods she had taken from home: jars of matsutake mushrooms, salted bat wings, dry lanternfish, and even fruit imported from Timandra. She ate little; fear crushed her appetite.

Does the fire already burn in Oshy? she thought as she walked. *Does my father still live? Have Tam and Neekeya found safety? Has Jitomi found the road south?*

Her eyes stung. She hated people. She hated these bonds of family, fellowship, friendship, love. When you cared for people, perhaps you were always worried, always afraid. Even here in the wilderness, she was not a lone wolf. She was still a daughter, a friend, a soul torn away from those she loved.

"I will return to you." Madori drew her sword as she walked, and she raised the curving blade. Its weight and soft silk grip comforted her. "I will learn to use Sheytusung, and I will return. I will see you again, my parents, my friends, my Jitomi." She clenched her jaw. "But not before I drive this blade into Serin's heart."

She kept walking, navigating by the stars, seeking the Desolation, that wasteland of canyons, craters, and craggy boulders where lived Old Master Lan Tao. The wilderness spread on. A few scattered mushrooms grew from the soil, their innards glowing with coiling strands of light. As Madori kept walking, the few mushrooms became many, and soon she moved through a great field of lights like a second sky of stars. The mushrooms grew taller as she traveled— tall as her knees, then her shoulders, and finally taller than her head.

Their stems raced with dancers of light, and their great heads glowed, lanterns of blue, pink, and silver, lighting her way. She walked on, feeling small as a spirit, a mere moth in a forest of light.

She had begun her journey under a full moon. It was a sliver, a mocking dragon's smile, when Madori emerged from the mushroom forest and beheld a landscape of black, jagged hills.

"The Desolation," she whispered.

Boulders rose like the scattered teeth of giants. Valleys, craters, and peaks formed a jagged landscape like the ruins of an ancient city. Walking was slow here. She traveled along coiling paths, under overhanging stone, and between granite steeples that cut her hands if she touched them. Glowing eyes peered from inside caves, but when Madori approached for closer looks, the creatures within fled deeper into their lairs, and she dared not enter after them. Bats fluttered over her head, moving between hidden eyries. The towers and peaks of stone hid most of the sky, and hills became mountains, cruel and sharp and steep. She kept walking, knowing she was close now. They said the old master lived in a cave, and every time she saw glowing eyes, she wondered if it was him watching her.

"Old Master Lan Tao!" she shouted. Her voice echoed across the landscape. A boulder tilted. Pebbles raced under her feet. She winced, expecting an avalanche, and kept walking gingerly, navigating between fallen stones. She dared shout no more.

A tilted black mountain, shaped like a wilting sail, loomed ahead. She walked along a ragged path, pebbles creaking under her boots. She barely dared to breathe. A shelf of stone loomed above her, and boulders perched like dragon eggs at her side. She thought that if she sneezed, she'd set the whole structure tumbling. Below stretched a valley, perhaps a crater, strewn with many boulders. A stream flowed through it, reflecting the moonlight. The mountains, boulders, and canyons spread as far as Madori could see. For the first time in her life, she was thankful for her Elorian eyes, eyes that had branded her a foreigner in Timandra. Here they collected even the softest of lights, guiding her way.

"Where are you, Lan Tao?" she whispered. Her mother had only told her he lived in a cave. Madori saw dozens of caves here. If she shouted his name again, she was likely to send boulders tumbling.

If she began to enter each cave in search of him, she was likely to encounter some slumbering nightwolf or other beast.

Have I been a fool to come here? Have I traveled all this way to find only rock and water?

She was walking across a cracked valley, boulders rising around her like columns, when she heard the growl.

At once she paused and spun around. Her heart leaped into her mouth.

Yellow eyes gleamed above upon a mountainside, but the creature itself remained hidden in shadow. She saw only those eyes and long, sharp fangs.

Madori dared not move.

If you run, he'll see you as a prey. She forced herself to remain calm. *If he smells your fear, he'll pounce. Stand your ground, Madori.*

The growl rose again, loud and coarse as boulders rolling down a mountain. The creature padded forward, emerging into the moonlight. A nightwolf.

Madori sucked in her breath. She had heard of nightwolves before—her Uncle Okado and Aunt Suntai, fallen heroes of the night, had ridden them in the war—but Madori had never seen the beasts. She had always imagined them the size of Timandrian wolves, animals no larger than sheepdogs, but this creature could dwarf most horses. Its thick gray fur bristled. Its body was wide but graceful, made for leaping, and its claws were long, made for tearing flesh off bone. Madori remembered the scars that marred her mother's face; they had come from such claws.

She met the nightwolf's gaze. Its eyes were even larger than hers. Wise, deep eyes. This was no mindless hunter; this was a sentient being. And it was hungry. She saw the hunger in those eyes, in those bared fangs, in its lanky body. Yes, its fur was thick, but that pelt hung over a thinned frame. Its every movement spoke of hunger, the need for meat. Most nightwolves hunted in packs; if this one was alone, it must have been a wild beast, an animal too unpredictable, too proud to serve a master. It must have wandered the wilderness for many turns, far from the plains where its brethren claimed territory and hunted. It must not have eaten in as long, and Madori knew how she appeared to it.

Like a feast.

The animal took one more step forward. Madori stared upward. A good fifty feet separated the two, but Madori knew he could easily jump the length. Yes, she thought of the wolf as a *he* now, no longer an *it*; she saw his story in his eyes, and he became almost a companion to her, a fellow wandering, hungry, lonely creature.

Slowly, Madori chose the air between them.

The nightwolf snarled.

She claimed the air.

The wolf leaped.

She changed the air, forming a thick shield, pressing the material close together like bunching silk into a thick rug. The nightwolf slammed into the force field and yowled, shocked at the impact. But the beast was too powerful to stop completely—he weighed several times more than a man—and he tore through the air like a diver through water.

The nightwolf slammed into Madori.

She fell beneath him.

His weight nearly crushed her. A thick, soupy layer of air still lay between them, remnants of her shield. The wolf's teeth drove down, and Madori winced and funneled the air upward, knocking the wolf's head aside. His claws scratched along her arm, and she cried out in pain. Her blood spilled. He leaned in again to bite, and the pain of her wounds drove her magic away.

Focus. Think. Fight him!

She chose his fur. She claimed it. She changed it.

The fur rustled madly, crackling like Madori's hair when she dragged her feet across a rug. Several sparks flew across the wolf, little bolts of electricity. The animal yowled, and Madori kicked, pulled herself out from under him, and jumped to her feet. She snarled, nurtured the sparks upon the animal, and with a single *puff*, the fur burst into flame.

The nightwolf whimpered, turned tail, and ran a few steps. Then he fell to the ground and rolled, struggling to extinguish the fire. The smell of burning fur filled Madori's nostrils.

She doffed her cloak. She raced toward the animal, tossed the cloak over him, and patted out the flames. The nightwolf didn't attack, only lay and whimpered as she worked. Finally the fire was extinguished.

"There you go," Madori said. "Just singed a bit. Didn't burn the flesh."

The wolf lay before her. He rolled onto his belly, legs splayed out, a mark of surrender. When Madori patted his snout, he licked her with a tongue as large as her hand.

"Good boy." She rummaged through her pack, produced a dried lanternfish—her last one—and held it out. Still lying on his back, the wolf ate the paltry meal. "It's all I can give you, friend."

Her own belly grumbled. She had only a single jar of mushrooms left, barely enough food for another turn. Then she too would have to wander the wilderness, desperately seeking bats, fish, or moles. Perhaps she would turn into something like this wolf, a wandering, feral thing, slowly dying of starvation. She slumped beside the animal and stroked his fur.

"What are we doing here, boy?" She sighed. "We're both lost."

A voice rose from a hilltop behind her, an ancient voice like crumpling parchment.

"Why didn't you kill it?"

She spun around, drawing her sword in a single, fluid movement.

He stood on the mountainside upon an outcrop of stone. He was an old man—ancient—his face wrinkled, his beard long and white, his head bald. And yet he stood straight, his shoulders still squared, his eyes still sharp. He wore blue robes and a silver sash, and he kept his hands tucked within his wide sleeves. A katana hung at his side.

"He was hungry," Madori said, staring at the stranger.

The old man nodded. "An invader is hungry for your soil. A thief is hungry for your treasure. A murderer is hungry for your blood. Would you not deal death to them?"

She glared up at the elder. "That's different. Those are humans. Humans are cruel. Animals are kind."

He raised an eyebrow. "This kind animal almost ripped out your throat." The man hopped off the outcrop, and Madori winced, sure he would smash down into the valley, snapping every bone in his body. Yet the elder effortlessly glided down a good ten feet, landed neatly, and knelt to absorb the impact. He straightened and walked toward her. "A great nightwolf attacked you, and you did not draw your blade. You could have sliced out its throat before it reached you. Instead you fought with clumsy, crude magic like a Timandrian. Now you see a frail old man and draw your steel." He shook his head sadly. "A fool has come to see me."

She sneered. "I told you." She stepped closer to the old man, her blade drawn. "I don't like people. I like animals. Stand back or this blade will cut your throat." At her side, the wolf stood up and growled at the man.

He came to a halt a few feet away from her. His long white beard and flowing mustache fluttered in the wind. His gaze was haughty, she thought, and the hint of mockery twisted his lips.

"Kill it," he said. "Kill the nightwolf. It is hungry. So are you. You won the fight. Slay the beast and eat its flesh."

Madori pointed her katana at the man. "I'd rather kill you and feed you to him. He won't be hungry and I'll be rid of your prattling."

"And soon after you would die of hunger." He shook his head sadly. "You are foolish. You are rash and angry. Slay the animal. Prove yourself strong and I will train you. Otherwise turn and leave. I have no patience for fools."

Madori grumbled. "And I have no patience for cruel masters, Lan Tao. That is your name, is it not?" She spat at his feet. "I had a cruel master at Teel University. One was enough."

The old hermit smiled thinly. "Did that cruel sunlit master teach you to fight with magic? Perhaps he saved your life. If not for him, that wolf would now be digesting your flesh. Perhaps a cruel master is exactly what you need, for a great wolf of sunfire rises in the west. Yes, I have seen it, even from here—a great light mustering along the dusk. If you show the enemies any mercy, as you've shown your adversary here, they will cut through you and all those you love." He stepped closer, and his eyes narrowed. "Now kill the wolf."

She shook her head and sheathed her sword. "No. If I kill without reason, I'm no different from the sunlit demons. You cannot fight a monster by becoming one yourself. If you do, you've already lost. Salai of Oshy, my grandfather, was a noble man. He would scoff at your words." She turned to leave.

His voice rose behind her. "Did you know your grandfather, child?"

She froze. She looked over her shoulder back at Lan Tao. "I heard tales of his great deeds."

"Tales turn killers into heroes. Tales turn monsters into men of valor. Legendary men were rarely honorable; the poets of later generations ennobled them." Lan Tao nodded. "You bear his sword, Sheytusung. A sword I taught him to wield. A sword he slew many with. How many widows did your grandfather create, how many orphans? How many did your own mother slay with this blade? Most were not murderers, not criminals, not bloodthirsty beasts. They were boys and girls like you, caught in a war. They were souls like that wolf, simply hungry and lost, seeking a meal or a coin. And your grandfather killed them. He killed dozens of them. He did not let his morals get in the way. He did not pause to ponder the nature of life or death. He slew his enemy because that is all the world is, child. Enemies to slay. You kill or you are killed. That is all."

"The world is not black and white!" she insisted.

He nodded. "The world is infinite shades of gray. But not to a soldier. Not to a soldier who wants to survive. In war, a soldier must see the world in black and white, must destroy his or her enemy. We leave philosophy to the philosophers. We soldiers deal in steel."

With that, he drew his own steel. His katana arched down toward her. Madori parried. The two blades clanged together.

"You are slow," said Lan Tao. "I could have slain you a dozen times by the time you parried."

She summoned her magic. She chose his sword and began to heat the hilt. He replied by slamming the flat of his blade against her cheek, and she yowled in pain.

"Magic is slow." He slapped her again, a blow to her arm. "A blade is fast as lightning, sharper than a dragon's claws, and as elegant as a nighthawk across the moon."

Her wolf growled and leaped forward, placing himself between Madori and Lan Tao. The animal's fur bristled, and he bared his fangs at the old man, protecting Madori, shielding her with his body.

Madori stared over the wolf at Lan Tao. "I won't kill my nightwolf. He is mine now. I showed him mercy and I earned his loyalty. Now he defends me." She smiled crookedly. "You call my mercy weak, but it just saved me from another swipe of your blade. Perhaps I have a thing or two to teach you as well."

The old man stared at the nightwolf, then back at her. He nodded. "I will let you keep this companion, but I will not let you keep your pride. If you stay here, I will break you. I will shatter your impudent soul until, like the wolf you tamed, you are subservient. You will surrender your will to me . . . and I will forge your soul into a weapon harder than steel."

She placed her hand upon her nightwolf. "Teach me, Master Lan Tao." She sucked in breath and grinned savagely. "I could not defeat Serin with magic, but I cut off his finger with steel. Teach me how to cut out his heart."

CHAPTER SIX
THE STONES OF EETEK

Neekeya raced across the hall, tears in her eyes.

"Father!"

Kee'an, Lord of Eetek Pyramid, sat on an obsidian throne which rose upon a limestone dais. He was a tall man, powerfully built, his dark skin deeply lined. A string of gilded crocodile teeth and feathers hung around his neck, and nine gemstones—each as large as an egg—gleamed upon his silvery breastplate, symbolizing the Wise Mothers, founders of Daenor. His arms were bare and wide, and a headdress of golden claws topped his bald head. Two crocodiles lay guarding his throne, mouths open, their collars and leashes golden.

The lord rose to his sandaled feet, climbed down his dais, and stretched out his arms. "Daughter!"

For a moment she paused, staring into the hall, for the place had changed.

Gilded archways rose along the walls, affording views of the swamplands—miles of mist, mangroves, and mossy water leading to distant haze. Statues of men with crocodile heads—idols of Cetela, god of the marshes—stood in neat rows. Soldiers clad in feathers and iron stood holding spears and swords. The Hall of Eetek was as she had left it. She knew all its imperfections like the lines on her palms. The same scratches marred the floor, the same scars marked the guards, and the same patches of moss grew between the archways. Down to the last nick, the place was the same, and yet it could not have seemed more different to her.

Because I've changed, she thought. She looked down at herself. Her armor, the metal shaped as crocodile skin, was dented and chipped; the swords of Magerians had slammed against it. Her limbs were ropier; countless miles on the road had hardened them. But mostly her soul had changed, she thought. It too was leaner now, harder, stronger.

Over a year ago, I left this place a wide-eyed girl, a child who believed in magical rings, in heroes vanquishing villains, in adventure and wonder . . . a child who had never fought a battle rougher than a swamp-scuffle with the frog hunters' boys. She took a deep breath. *I return home a woman.*

Her father's smile faltered, and his eyes softened. "Neekeya?"

Her eyes dampened and something cracked inside her, a chip in the armor she had worn around her heart for so long. A hint of that old girl, innocent and full of wonder, leaked through, and Neekeya ran. Her boots thudded against the floor, and she crossed the distance in several bounds and leaped into her father's embrace. She held him tight as if she were a child again, not a warrior all in steel.

"Father." Her tears fell. "I'm home."

He kissed her forehead, held her at arm's length, and admired her. "These old eyes have missed you, Neekeya. Even in these dark times, you fill an old man's heart with joy."

"You are many years away from being old, Father." She smiled and wiped her eyes. Her father had fought many wars for many years, only taking a wife after returning from his final war, the great War Of Day and Night. The swamplord was sixty years old now, his body covered with many scars, and often Neekeya had caught a deep sadness in his eyes, haunting ghosts of those old battles. He hid that pain from her, she knew; whenever around her, even now, his eyes filled with warmth and his lips smiled. Neekeya had never understood those shadows she would see as a child, that memory in his eyes, those times he wandered the halls, seeming lost, alone, unable to find rest. Now, returned from her own war, her sword stained with blood, Neekeya understood something of old ghosts, and she understood something of the importance of family, of love, of joy in a dark world.

Kee'an raised his chin and looked over her shoulder. "And who is your companion?"

Neekeya turned to look at Tam too. She was about to announce him as the Prince of Arden, but she hesitated. Would Father only scoff? After their long journey through war and wilderness—six months had passed since leaving Teel—Tam looked nothing like a prince. His tunic and cloak were in tatters. Mud and moss covered him from head to toes, and stubble grew on his cheeks, thick with grime. Leaves still clung to him. Indeed, he looked like one of the mythical *heekeni*, monsters said to rise from the swamp and snatch misbehaving children.

"Father, this is . . ."

Tam stepped forth, leaving muddy footprints. He knelt before the Lord of Eetek. "My lord, I am Tamlin Solira, second son of Queen Linee and King Camlin of Arden. Our noble kingdom, an ally to Daenor, has fallen to the buffaloes of Mageria. I've come to you for sanctuary and for aid."

Neekeya looked at him, for a moment dazzled; for the first time perhaps, she saw the true prince in him. When she turned back toward her father, she felt a twinge in her heart. There it was—the old pain in Lord Kee'an's eyes, the old ghosts that lined his face.

"Tales have reached us in *Denetek* of the war in the east," Kee'an said. "Rise, Prince Tamlin. You will find sanctuary here, for Arden and Daenor have long been allies. Memories of my visit to Kingswall nearly twenty years ago still fill me with warmth; your parents welcomed me kindly, walked with me through their gardens, and we shared many laughs. I grieved to hear of Arden's fall, and I pray to Cetela that your parents find their own sanctuary in the wastelands of war." When the prince opened his mouth to say more, Lord Kee'an raised his hand to hush him. "You have many more stories to tell! That I know. But you are weary from the journey. First you and Neekeya will bathe, and we'll serve a feast for your return. Over a hot meal, you'll tell me all your tales."

Servants arrived to escort them out of the hall, down the pyramid's western flank, and to the public baths of Eetek. Columns surrounded the complex, each bearing a statue of another holy animal: not only reptiles but many birds, insects, and fish forged of bronze. Within the colonnades, wet tiles surrounded a pool of steaming water fed by a hot spring. Mangroves, ferns, and hemlocks grew between the columns, forming a green wall. Egrets flew overhead.

Tam blushed to see both men and women sharing the public bath, for the Ardish separated their baths by gender. But Neekeya only grabbed his hand and helped him undress. He entered the pool quickly, hiding his nakedness behind ferns and steam until he was submerged. Neekeya entered the water beside him; it was piping hot and luxurious, and the steam plumed around her. The water rose to their shoulders.

Neekeya waded closer to Tam and wrapped her arms around him. She pressed her nose to his. "We'll find aid here, Tam. I promise." She kissed his lips. "You'll see your family again, and we'll see Jitomi and Madori too. This war cannot last forever. I don't believe that the light of Radian will forever sear the world."

After they bathed, servants brought them new outfits to wear: soft *seeken* tunics, a grayish-green fabric woven from lichen and leaves; leather shoes inlaid with beads; and new suits of armor, polished and freshly forged. Undressed, Tam stood out in Daenor with his pale skin and shy, foreign ways. But soon he stood before Neekeya looking like a true warrior of Daenor; like her armor, his breastplate and helmet were forged to mimic a crocodile's skin and head, and a crocodile-claw sword hung from his belt. A green cloak hung across his shoulders. He could have easily been a prince of Daenor, and Neekeya felt her cheeks blush to think that, if her father approved their marriage, he *would* become a prince of the marshlands.

They met her father again in a courtyard west of the baths. The cobbled expanse lay within the jungle like a bald patch on a man's head. The marshes surrounded them—rustlings reeds, twisting mangroves, and ponds green with lily pads. Monitor lizards lounged in the water, occasionally emerging to sunbathe upon the cobblestones. Jabiru birds, as tall as men, wandered about on their long pink legs, pecking for food.

A table was set out, its legs carved as claws. Lord Kee'an sat at its head, and Tam and Neekeya sat across from him. Servants brought forth a feast of roasted meats, stewed vegetables, and steaming stews.

Neekeya drank from a clay mug of huckleberry juice, the blue liquid filling her with vigor. Bolstered, she stared at her father over the many steaming plates. "Father, I've not returned home only to bathe, to feast, and to see you again. I've come here with a warning. Tirus Serin has seized the throne of Mageria, as you must have heard. What you might not have heard is this: He musters many troops east of the mountains. For almost half a year, Tam and I traveled hidden across the wilderness of both Arden and Mageria, moving through the forests, surviving by hunting and gathering when we found no tavern or town. Whenever we stepped onto a road or visited an inn, we saw them—the Magerian troops. They no longer raise their old buffalo banners; they now hoist the Radian sigil, a golden sun hiding the moon. As they've attacked Arden, I fear they plan to attack Daenor."

Tam was struggling to crack open a crab leg. He gave up, placed down the claw, and turned toward Kee'an. "My lord, my kingdom has fallen to the enemy. I've heard no word from my parents or from my brother, Prince Omry." His eyes flinched with pain. "But should Arden rise again, and should her people throw off the yoke of tyranny, I would see Arden and Daenor aligned against the enemy. I ask that you help fight this enemy. So long as the eclipse banners rise, no kingdom of Moth is safe, not in daylight or darkness."

Neekeya swallowed a bite of spicy snake, the meat hot and springy. "Father, let us muster the warriors! Let the marshland clans gather, and let us march to glory. We will pass through the mountains, and we will cut through the enemy marshaling there, and we will march all the way to Markfir, capital of Mageria, and stick Serin's head on a pike." She rose to her feet, passion burning through her. "I will personally cut off his head. I have seen Serin upon the road. I battled his own daughter. He is a monster that cannot be tamed, only killed, and he hates Daenorians as much as he hates Elorians. He calls the nightfolk worms, and he calls us Daenorians barbarians. If we are barbarians, then let us show him our strength! He will not look down upon us as we crush the walls of his capital."

Her chest heaved, and lust for battle filled her. She had spent many turns on the road, hiding in forests, in farmlands, sometimes in barns when they could find them. She craved no more hiding; it was time to march to war, tall and proud and swinging steel.

Her father listened quietly, sipping from a mug and nibbling fried frog legs, stewed greens, and honeyed flamingo breast. He sighed and spoke in a low voice, and Neekeya heard the old weariness in him. "The Magerians have often looked down upon us Daernorians, it is true. All of Timandra has; even our northern brethren, Daenorians who live in the open plains, look upon us southerners with scorn, ashamed of their swamp-dwelling kin." He gripped his knife as if gripping a sword. "Yet if they march into our marshlands, the bogs will be their graves. We will fight them, Neekeya."

She placed her fists upon the tabletop and leaned toward him. "It's not enough to defend our borders. We must march into their lands. We must join the other pyramids. We must enlist the aid of the Northern Daenorians; they have horses, chariots, great siege engines of war. We must attack."

Before her father would reply, a smooth voice spoke between the trees. "Yet none will join you, lord and lady of the swamp. You are alone in this world."

Neekeya spun toward the voice. She growled.

A man emerged from the brush and stepped onto the courtyard. He wore fine silvery armor, and a jeweled crocodile appeared upon his shield. A saber hung from his belt, the hilt bright with gems. The man's light brown skin was perfumed; Neekeya would smell it even over the feast. She remembered the man she had encountered in the marshlands on her way here.

"Felsar," she said, not bothering to mask the disgust in her voice.

He nodded, a thin smile on his lips. "*Prince* Felsar. *Your* prince." He looked around him, lip curled in distaste. "I was told that the southern lords lived in palaces, finding some splendor even in the marshlands. I see only a decrepit pyramid—it should be torn down—and a courtyard of craggy bricks barely finer than a slaughterhouse floor." His gaze turned toward Lord Kee'an. "Ah, and here he is! The great Swamp Lord, Master of Mud." He turned toward Tam. "And the Hatchling of Arden, a baby raven who fled war in his homeland, forsaking his own kingdom to the buffaloes. A coward in the company of barbarians—what a feast this is!"

A glint caught Neekeya's eyes; the prince's Radian pin. She spat toward him. "You wear the Radian eclipse upon your cloak, proudly displaying your treachery." She drew her sword. "I will have your head for this."

The prince sneered and drew his saber. "I will teach you manners, girl."

She scoffed. "With that needle you call a sword? I clean my teeth with larger toothpicks." She swung her own blade—a wide, doubled-edged weapon. "Come closer, prince, and I'll show you how we treat traitors in the marsh—"

"Enough!" Lord Kee'an's cry rang across the courtyard. "Neekeya, sheathe your blade. Prince Felsar, I ask you the same. We are all *Deneteki* despite our differences. We will resolve these differences over a meal, not over spilled blood. Sit, Prince Felsar. Eat. Drink. And we will talk."

The prince glared at Neekeya, hatred simmering in his eyes. His lip trembled with hatred. Finally he nodded, sheathed his blade, and walked toward the table but did not sit. He lifted a skewer of grilled scorpions, sniffed, and tossed it aside. A monitor lizard scuttled toward the meal and crunched the scorpions between its powerful jaws.

"I will not eat this vermin you pass off as food," said the prince. "And I do not have many words to say to you, Master of Mud. I will speak simply so you may understand. You are an embarrassment. For centuries, we true Daenorians of the north had to suffer the swamps, the way a noble man would suffer the embarrassment of some twisted, parasitic twin growing from his torso. Yet we have found a way to join the true light of Timandra, to become an equal nation among the other kingdoms of sunlight. You say *Deneteki*? That is an old word, a word for barbarians, the word we used before we could read, write, forge metal, and live like proper men." Felsar's eyes flared. "Under the Radian banners, all are equal. All who serve Tirus Serin, the Lord of Light, will find grace in his court. I've come to these bogs to convey the order of my father, your king: Daenor will raise the Radian banners, and we will join Serin's empire in conquest of the night. A new order rises. All those who oppose it will perish. Daenor will not perish; we will join Radianism's great light."

"Join? You mean *serve* the light." Neekeya shook her head sadly. "You truly think Serin will see you as equal, Felsar? He loathes Daenorians. He sees us as lower than worms—even you, oh mighty northern prince. Do you truly think you can join him? No. You can at most serve him as a slave, a useful tool, a trained animal for him to sic upon his enemies. But I will never join Serin. I will fight him, and if you stand in my way, I will fight you too."

Neekeya bared her teeth, ready to fight. Even Tam now drew his sword and stepped forward, face red. Kee'an had to slam his fists upon the table, rattling the plates, to restore calm.

"Hear me!" said the Lord of Eetek. Suddenly he no longer seemed a weary old man. His old pride returned to him, and he stood tall, shoulders wide, back straight. "Hear me, Prince Felsar. You are young; you barely remember the last war. But I am old. Twenty years ago, I joined another so-called Lord of Light. I joined Ferius, ruler of the Sailith faith. I sailed with him into darkness with many ships. I fought the Elorians under the stars." His voice shook. "I fought that war hoping to forge an alliance with the rest of sunlight, to prove our worth to our fellow Timandrians. I killed Elorians for them. I spilled the blood of innocents, and their blood still stains my hand. And still the other children of sunlight mock our ways, see us as weak, as benighted, as uncivilized. Only a generation has passed, and already they ask us to spill Elorian blood again." Kee'an raised his chin and drew his sword, a mighty blade, five feet long and bright in the sun. "Never more will we join the forces of evil. We bowed before Ferius, killed for him, shattered our soul for him. Now we will stand against this new tyrant. Now we will redeem our honor. Leave this place, Prince Felsar! Return north and tell your father that we in the marshlands will not bend the knee."

The prince stepped closer to the old lord. Rage twisted his face. "You speak treason! You owe allegiance to my father, your king. The swamp is not its own kingdom, free to choose its wars."

"I am a free man," Kee'an replied simply. "And I choose the path of justice, not of service to evil."

"Treason!" The prince drew his sword, leaped forward, and swung the blade. Kee'an parried, and the two swords locked. The prince screamed, spraying spittle. "We will have your head for this!"

Neekeya and Tam snarled and stepped forth, blades drawn. The prince spun from side to side, glaring at each in turn.

"We do not bow before our enemies," Neekeya said. "We slay them. And you've made yourself our enemy."

The prince spat at her. "You cannot defeat Emperor Serin, fool. Thousands of Magerians muster to your east beyond the mountains. How can you hope to stop this swarm? Thousands of troops serve my own father; they marshal to your north, and when they hear of your treachery, they will crush you. In the south, the desert warriors of Eseer already raised the Radian banners; they too will march upon you. You are nothing but rebels to your own crown, and the noose tightens around you. The swamps will fall, and Daenor will serve the Radian Order, and—"

Kee'an swung his sword. The iron crossguard slammed into the prince's head, knocking him to the ground. The prince lay limp, moaning, blood trickling down his forehead.

The Lord of Eetek looked at Neekeya and Tam. His eyes were hard, his voice stern. "For twenty years, I have sought peace, yet now war is upon us again—not only with the enemy beyond our mountains, but with our own kin to our north. Felsar will remain with us in chains. And the marshlands will fight!"

Neekeya had spent the journey here praying to raise arms, to fight her enemies. Yet not like this. Not her father alone, a rebel to their own crown. A tremble seized her knees.

She looked at Tam and saw the same fear in him, but she saw strength too. He stared back at her, his sword drawn.

"We defeated Serin in battle before," Tam said softly. "We will defeat him again."

She nodded but little hope filled her. When they had faced Serin on the road outside of Teel, only ten troops had protected the emperor. Now myriads prepared to invade. Neekeya's breath shook in her chest, and her sword swayed in her grip. The trees rustled and the birds sang on, unaware that they soon might burn.

CHAPTER SEVEN
LOST SON

Jitomi stood at the prow of the *Do Tahan*—the *Salt Spirit*—staring across the dark sea toward the coast of his homeland.

"The Isle of Steel and Salt." His voice was so soft the wind nearly drowned it. "Land of the Eternal Flame. Blade of the Night. Ilar."

Ilar—the great island-empire in the night. Ilar—a land of warriors, fortresses, and flame. Ilar—perhaps the greatest military power in the world. Jitomi had not seen his home in over a year, and he dreaded his return.

Rain fell and wind shrieked. The sea was rough and the *Do Tahan*, a *geobukseon* ship, rose and dipped and swayed. Many rowers oared to the beat of a drum, their faces wet with rain and sweat, and their long white hair fluttered like banners. Two battened sails, their silk painted with Red Flame sigils, aided the rowers' efforts, pushing the ship toward the island. Ahead of Jitomi loomed the figurehead, an iron dragon that doubled as a cannon. It was shaped as Tianlong, the last dragon of the night and a symbol of Ilar.

Across the miles of black, salty waters stretched Yakana Peninsula, a tongue of black rock reaching into the sea. Clouds hid the moon, but many lanterns rose along the peninsula, their lights orange and red. Jitomi could make out the walls that lined the landscape, topped with parapets and turrets and banners. Beyond these battlements rose narrow houses, minarets housing archers, and pagodas with several tiers of red roofs. At the seaside edge of the peninsula, rising high above both the town behind and the water ahead, rose the ancestral home of his family: Hashido Castle. Seeing the black, jagged fortress perched like a demon above the water, Jitomi shuddered and swallowed down a lump. It was home, but it was also a place of dark memories.

"Good to be home, son?" said Captain Sho Hotan, an old man with a long white mustache, tufted eyebrows, and wise blue eyes. He came to stand beside Jitomi, the wind whipping his silken blue robes, and gazed toward the shore.

Jitomi sighed. "No. My father never wanted me to leave, to study magic. He called it the trade of an old, superstitious woman. After fathering several daughters, he hoped his only son would become a great warrior, a heir to his power. I thought to become a powerful mage—to prove to him that mages could be powerful—and yet now I return after only a year, a failure, a—"

He bit down on his words. Why was he telling all this to Sho Hotan, a man he barely knew? He felt like a fool, spilling his secrets to a stranger. Perhaps fear of seeing his father again made him foolish.

The wind whipped him, thick with rainwater and saltwater, and Jitomi tightened his black cloak around him. He missed his friends. He missed them so much his belly twisted and his chest ached. If Tam and Neekeya were here, he would feel braver. And if Madori were here . . .

His heart gave another twinge. He thought of the last time he had seen Madori, how she had scolded him, fled him into the darkness, shattered his soul with her talk of separate paths . . . but not without also kissing him. Not without giving him that memory of her warmth, the love and light he had still seen in her eyes.

If she came home with me, a half-Timandrian, I don't think my father would even scowl. His heart would crack and he'd fall down dead. And perhaps that would only make things easier.

He sighed. With the Radians mustering for war, he needed his father's help. The old lord held sway in Ilar's imperial court. He commanded many troops, and Empress Hikari heeded his counsel. Jitomi would need to convince the man that Magerians prepared to invade, that Ilar had to send troops into Qaelin to stop the attack. If Jitomi failed, the night would burn. Yet how could Jitomi speak sense to a man who loathed him, who thought him lower than the old women who washed his clothes?

As they navigated closer to the shore, Jitomi wanted to ask the captain to turn back. He wanted to dive into the water and swim away. He wanted to be anywhere but here, returning to this empire he had fled. He could try to find Madori, to walk whatever path she took, or he could even travel to find Tam and Neekeya, or perhaps he could still find his sister Nitomi in the wasteland of Arden, the last place he had heard from her.

No.

He forced himself to take deep breaths.

If I cannot enlist Ilar to fight this war, Madori will die in the Radian flames. Tam, Neekeya, my sister—all will perish in the inferno of war. I must do this. I need my father's help.

The *Do Tahan* navigated into the port, entering a calm harbor between two breakwaters. Many other military ships floated around them: triple-tiered *panokseons* with a deck for rowers, a deck for cannons, and a deck for soldiers; lumbering *geobukseons,* vessels similar to the *Do Tahan,* turtle ships with many oars and dragon figureheads that belched out smoke; towering *atakebunes,* floating fortresses covered in iron plates, pagodas upon their decks, their panther figureheads made for ramming into enemy ships. Civilian vessels navigated these waters too: the junk ships of Qaelish merchants, the small rowboats of fishermen, and cogs shipping everything from iron ore to silk. Their lanterns shone all around, and their sailors stared— eyes almost as large and bright—as the *Do Tahan* headed toward the pier.

Jitomi had been only a babe when the Timandrians, led by the monk Ferius, had attacked this empire, slaying many. Most of the enemies had attacked Asharo, the great capital city, which lay northeast from here, but some had landed upon Yakana Peninsula, and the wreckage of their ships still lay upon the rocks. If Serin attacked, igniting a second war between day and night, he wouldn't be a simple monk leading a rabble. Serin would be the greatest general in Timandra leading a trained army of killers. Would even these military ships, and the tall walls that rose ahead, be able to stop his light?

They docked at a pier. Jitomi walked along the plank and, for the first time in over a year, stepped onto the shore of his homeland.

Ilar. Land of my fathers. Land of—

He felt queasy. His legs swayed. He leaned over the pier and lost his lunch into the water.

He wiped his lips and sighed. *The proud warrior returns.*

Fishermen in silk robes moved about the boardwalk, pulling in nets of glowing lanternfish, angler fish that sprouted dangling bulbs of light, and octopi with glowing tentacles. Soldiers stood here too, beefy men in black and red armor. Their helmets were shaped as snarling faces complete with bristly fur mustaches, and many tassels hung from their breastplates. Katanas hung at their sides, and through holes in their visors, their blue and violet eyes stared at Jitomi. If they recognized him, the son of their lord, they gave no note of it.

Now I am a disgraced son, Jitomi thought with a sigh. Even the fishermen's children, scrawny little things who wore rags, had more honor here now.

A mountain rose beyond the boardwalk, its slopes jagged with boulders the size of horses. A narrow stone staircase stretched up between the boulders, the steps carved into the living rock. Two palisades of lanterns framed the stairway, their iron carved into the shape of demonic faces, red fire burning within their eyes and mouths. The passageway stretched upward, hundreds of steps long, leading toward the castle. Jitomi craned back his neck and stared at his old home.

"Hashido Castle," he said, the wind whipping his words away.

The pagoda loomed, five tiers tall. Its roofs were tiled crimson, their edges curling up like wet parchment. Upon the black walls, arrow slits revealed red fire that blazed within; the slits reminded Jitomi of blazing panther eyes. Upon the uppermost roof perched a dragon statue, life-sized and carved of iron, its jaws raised to the sky. From within those metal jaws rose a fountain of fire, shrieking and crackling, a living representation of the empire's Red Flame sigil. Hundreds of soldiers served in this fortress. A dozen warships patrolled its waters. Thirty thousand souls lived upon the peninsula it defended. In all of Ilar, perhaps only the Imperial Palace in Asharo was mightier. Here was the Blade of the Sea, the stronghold of the Hashido noble family, a family that had produced many warriors, dojai assassins, captains of warships, and . . .

"And me," Jitomi said. "A skinny failed wizard."

He raised his chin. He squared his shoulders. Perhaps he would seem weak here, but now he had a task, and he would complete it. He began to climb.

The stairs curved madly, tall and narrow, threatening to send the weak and infirm crashing down to the boulders below. Any invaders who attacked would have to climb these stairs in single file, heavy in their armor. When Jitomi glanced to his sides, he saw hidden pillboxes carved into the boulders. Soldiers lurked within, holding bows and arrows, ready to fire. Jitomi nodded at the arrowslits in the boulders, hoping the hidden men within recognized him as a son of this fortress. No words came in reply, but no arrows either. He kept climbing.

Not only living soldiers lined the mountainside. Skeletons lay between the boulders, still wearing rusted armor. The eye sockets were small, only half the normal size—Timandrian skulls. Here were the remains of the sunlit demons who had attacked Ilar years ago, who had fallen attempting to capture this fort. Jitomi's father had left the bones here, a warning to future invaders.

Some of these skeletons were mages trained at Teel University, Jitomi thought and winced. Every time his father climbed these stairs, he would think of Jitomi studying at Teel, and his rage would grow.

After climbing several hundred steps, Jitomi paused, winded. When he looked behind him, he could see all the port. The breakwaters stretched out like arms, holding the warships within their embrace. Lanterns bobbed as the vessels swayed. When Jitomi turned to look eastward, he could see the city sprawl across the peninsula: thousands of tall, narrow homes with curling red roofs; black temples to the Demon Gods; and many smithies to forge blades and armor.

Finally Jitomi reached the end of the staircase. The gates of Hashido Castle rose ahead, shaped as a great dragon's mouth complete with a fanged portcullis. Fire burned in two alcoves above the doors, the dragon's red eyes. Guards in lacquered black armor stood here, bristling with blades and spears and arrows.

"I have returned!" Jitomi said to them, struggling to keep his voice strong. "I am Jitomi Hashido, only son of Lord Okita. Open the gates for my homecoming, and may the Red Flame forever burn in your hearts."

One of the soldiers clattered forward. He was so heavy with steel, he reminded Jitomi of a great metallic beetle. No fewer than a ten katanas and spears hung from his belt and across his back, and a hundred red tassels decorated his armor. His black helmet was shaped as a scowling warrior, the mustache formed of white fur. His stare blazed through the visor's eyeholes.

"You are not welcome here, Jitomi, wayward son of Ilar." The man reached for the hilt of a katana. "You father has barred these gates for your return. Things are not as you left them, traveler of sunlight. Ilar has changed. So has this fortress."

"Then I will hear of these changes from my father," Jitomi said. "If he will cast me aside, let him do so, not you. Step aside, *guard*."

The man was of noble birth—only a noble son could defend a fortress of such might—and Jitomi knew that calling him "guard" was like calling a mighty mage a parlor magician.

The man sneered and began to draw a katana. "That I cannot do. I—"

Jitomi chose the sword. He heated the weapon, and the guard hissed and dropped the searing hilt.

"I will enter." Jitomi took a step forward, chose the air, and sent a gust of wind against the soldiers, knocking them sideways. Another gust of magic blew the great doors open with a clatter. "Try to stop me and your skeletons will litter the slope with the rest of them."

His heart thudded, and it was a struggle to keep his voice steady, but he forced himself to stare at the men, to keep advancing, to seem strong and proud. Strength and pride—those were the languages of Ilar, the only languages these men would understand.

"Sunlit sorcery!" they muttered . . . but they stepped aside.

Jitomi nodded at them. "I've learned the ways of our enemy, it is true. And I've come bearing warnings of that enemy's might."

Without sparing the men another glance, he stepped into the dragon's mouth, entering the shadows of Hashido Castle.

Along the hall, tapering columns rose in palisades like teeth. Arches stretched above like a metal palate. At the back of the hall, a hundred feet away, burned a great fireplace like a dragon's flaming gullet. Before the hearth rose a metal throne, shaped like a rising tongue; it loomed ten feet above the floor. A dark figure sat there, silhouetted by the raging fire.

Jitomi stepped closer, his boots thumping against the floor.

"Father!" His voice echoed through the hall. "I return with a warning. Enemies muster in the sunlight. We are in danger."

The lord did not reply, only sat still, perched upon that rising tongue of metal, only a shadow.

"Father!" Jitomi called again. "Will you not speak to me?"

Slowly, Lord Okita Hashido raised his head. Two blue eyes stared across the hall like forge fires. A gust of wind blew into the hall, and the lanterns that stood upon the columns—demon faces with flaming gullets—belched out heat and flames. The new light fell upon the lord, illuminating a burly frame, a white mustache, tufted eyebrows, and a black breastplate sporting the Red Flame sigil.

"And so, the boy who disgraced his father, who betrayed his proud empire, returns to grovel at the first sign of danger?"

Jitomi stiffened. He forced himself to take several deep breaths. "Father, this is no time for games of pride. The Timandrians are mustering for a new invasion of the night. Their armies gather on our borders. They—"

"On *our* borders?" Lord Hashido said. He rose to his feet, standing upon his dais. "Our borders are the sea, child. Or do you mean the dusk, the border of that wretched empire they call Qaelin? Dare you count the Qaelish, those weak rats, amongst our people?"

Rage filled Jitomi, overpowering his fear. "The enemy does not distinguish between Ilar, Qaelin, Leen, Montai, or any other nation of the night. To them we are all Elorians. Nightcrawlers, they call us— creatures to be stomped upon, and—"

"Nightcrawlers!" Hashido spat. "Worms. And who gave them that impression, boy? When they named us worms, did they see proud warriors of the Red Flame, killers clad in steel, swinging blades? Or did they see a weak, groveling, sniveling boy come begging to learn their parlor tricks?" He snorted. "Yes, you are like a worm that crawls in the dust. You have nine older sisters, each mightier than you. They are soldiers, dojai assassins, the captains of warships. And you!" Lord Hashido pointed, finger trembling with rage. "You, my only son, my heir . . . are weaker than them all. While your sisters, sharpen blades, you read from books. While your sisters slay their enemies, you come here as a weakling, begging me to fight your battles."

Jitomi closed his eyes for a moment, the pain driving through him. He had to steel himself with a deep breath before staring at his father again.

"No, Father, I am no warrior like my sisters. Yes, I traveled into sunlight to learn the magic of our enemies. And now those enemies threaten to burn us all. They—"

"Serin will not burn us," Hashido said. "He is not a fanatic like Ferius was, not a mindless brute. He is a sunlit demon, it is true, but his heart is a heart of flame and steel—a heart I admire. I know of his Radian Order, boy, and I do not fear it as you do. I am no coward. We will not fight against Serin but alongside him, warriors of darkness and light, and our empires will rise."

Jitomi blinked. He took several more steps forward until he stood right before the throne. Forgetting himself, he blurted out, "You're mad! You don't know the Radians. They hate all Elorians. They vow to kill us all, Qaelish and Ilari alike. An alliance? Empress Hikari would never agree to such a thing. She—"

"Do you mean this Empress Hikari?"

It was a new voice that had spoken—a crackling, cruel voice that spoke not in Ilari but in the tongue of Mageria. Catching his breath, Jitomi stared to the back of the hall. A figure stood there, cloaked in shadow; Jitomi had not seen the man until now.

The man stepped closer, clad in black robes. The firelight fell upon him, revealing a balding head ringed with oily black hair, a hooked nose, and beady eyes.

"Professor Atratus," Jitomi whispered.

The Radian held out his arm, and Jitomi nearly gagged. In his talon-like fingers, Atratus held a severed head. The hair was long and white, the eyes large and blue, and mouth still open in anguish. Jitomi had been to the capital city enough times to recognize it.

"You killed Empress Hikari." A tremble seized his knees.

Lord Hashido stepped off his dais and came to stand beside Atratus. The two men—a lord of Ilar and a Radian mage—stared together at Jitomi.

"Hikari was indeed a weak worm," Hashido said. "Much like you, my son. We travel to the capital! The Ilari and Radian empires will stand united. Together we will defeat the Qaelish rats and rule both day and night."

CHAPTER EIGHT
A BATTLE ON THE ROAD

The cart trundled on and Torin lay in the darkness, feeling his life slip away.

They had hurt him, but he could barely feel the pain anymore. He knew what awaited him at the end of this road—a public execution at Markfir, capital of Mageria. He looked forward to it. Death would be an end to pain. In death he would see them again.

"Mother and father," he whispered, lips bleeding. "Grandpapa Kerof. Hem." His eyes watered. "Bailey."

They had been waiting for him, he knew. They had waited for so long as he lingered here in the sunlight, in the darkness, growing older. Now he would join them. He did not know what the afterlife was like—even among Idarith priests, none could agree—but he knew they would be there. His only regret would be leaving the two women of his life behind.

Koyee. Madori. I'm sorry. I wanted to make this a better world for you. I failed.

The cart rolled on. He slid across the floor, chained, bruised, famished. He did not know how long they'd been traveling. He did not know how close they were to Markfir. He only knew that this was the last journey he would take. After so many travels—to the bright city of Pahmey, to the wonders of Yintao, to the terrifying beauty of Asharo, to the rainforests of Naya, to the gleaming towers of Kingswall—this was his last road. A road in darkness.

Shouts rose outside the cart and Torin winced. His captors often shouted, railing against Elorians, Ardishmen, and all other "undesirables." Whenever a man fell ill, a meal burned, or an item of clothing tore, they would take out their rage on him.

"Damn Ardishmen!" rose a cry outside.

Torin grimaced, anticipating their wrath.

A whistle sounded. A shard of metal and wood crashed through the cart wall. The arrow tilted and fell down by Torin's head.

"The bloody Ardish!" shouted another man outside. "The Ardish attack!"

Torin inhaled sharply. The Ardish.

Cam.

With strength he hadn't known remained in him, Torin shoved himself to his feet and stumbled toward the wall. He peered through the hole the arrow had left. Rye fields spread outside, and archers in black and gold—Arden's colors—were rising from among the stalks. Horses galloped and raven banners streamed. The Magerians—a couple hundred soldiers and mages—were already firing back, drawing swords, and casting magic.

Not all have died. Hope welled in Torin. *Arden still fights.*

His manacles clattering, he spun away from the cart wall. His head swayed and he nearly fainted. Stars floated before his eyes. Ignoring the pain—by Idar, every last inch of him was cut and bruised—he knelt and grabbed the fallen arrow. Its head was long, sharp iron made for punching through armor. As the ringing of swords and the whistles of arrows sounded outside, Torin twisted his wrists, grabbed the arrow's shaft between his teeth, and just managed to thrust the arrowhead into the padlock securing his chains.

"Slay the Ardish scum!" rose an inhuman shriek outside, a sound like shattering glass—Lord Gehena. The air howled—mages forming their projectiles.

Torin grunted. The arrow kept slipping, and he had to bend his wrists so far they almost snapped. Gripping the arrow's shaft between his teeth, he worked the head in the lock. His heart pounded. Sweat dripped into his eyes.

"Drag out the prisoner!" shrieked Gehena; it was a demonic voice that pounded through the cart walls, shrill as rusty nails on stone. "Drag out their favorite traitor so they can see him broken."

A gruff voice answered. "Yes, my lord."

Heavy footfalls moved toward the cart.

Dizzy and bleeding, Torin cursed and worked with more fervor.

Keys jangled in the cart door's lock. A heavy hand tugged the door open, revealing Hesh, one of the convoy's guards—a squat man in boiled leather studded with iron bolts. He had a gruff, unshaven face, a wide nose, and dry bloodstains on his gloves—Torin's blood. Behind him a battle raged; Torin could glimpse flying arrows and two men locking swords.

"Out you go, maggot." Hesh barked a laugh, spraying spittle. "Going to hurt you a little in front of your friends. Out!"

Torin curled up on the floor, moaning. He twisted the arrow in the lock one more time and heard a *clank*.

The stocky guard cursed. "Idar's hairy bottom! Come on, you roach." He stomped into the cart. "I'll drag you out by the ears if I have to." He leaned down to grab Torin. "Up or I—"

Torin thrust the arrow.

The iron head drove through Hesh's eye and deep into the skull.

Torin tugged the arrow back; it came free with a gush of blood and bits of eyeball.

Heart thudding, he kicked off the last chains binding him, drew Hesh's sword, and peeked outside. The battle was raging in the fields. Blood stained the rye stalks. Several Ardish horsemen were galloping around the Magerian convoy, firing arrows and thrusting lances. Other troops fought on the dirt road, swinging swords. Gehena stood with his back to Torin, brandishing four swords, one in each hand. His blades crashed into Ardish soldiers and sent them flying.

Cam's troops, Torin thought, and hope welled inside him. Last he had heard of his friend, Cam had been leading a host to Hornsford Bridge. Torin had assumed that force fallen. Were these the remnants of the king's army?

All his captors were busy fighting. While their backs were turned, Torin stumbled out of the cart. His bare feet hit the road, and for a moment he swayed, the sunlight blinding him. He took two steps and collapsed, nearly falling on the sword he held. With a bolt of pain, his face hit the dirt. Soil entered his mouth and stones jabbed his chest.

Breathe. Move.

He ground his teeth, struggling not to pass out. Clutching his sword in one hand, he crawled off the road and into the rye field. The golden stalks rose tall around him, swaying in the wind. The smell was intoxicating. The soft brown soil crumbled under him; several ants walked across it, holding seeds. The sky was blue and a cool breeze rustled.

It's beautiful, Torin thought, eyes dampening. *It's so beautiful.* He had forgotten the scent, the freshness, the beauty of the world outside the cart.

"Damn your hide to the Abyss!"

The voice shouted beside him. The stalks swayed. A boot slammed down near Torin and blood sprayed. With a thump, a corpse thudded down, cracking stalks. The head hit the ground beside Torin, staring at him with lifeless eyes. The man wore a black and gold cloak—a man of Arden. When Torin glanced upward, he saw a Magerian soldier tug his blade free. The man did not see him; he cursed and stepped away, already attacking another Ardishman.

Torin kept crawling.

Boots stomped around him, blood sprayed, and more bodies fell, but none of the living saw him. Torin kept moving. A horse galloped by, its hooves missing him by inches. A fallen helmet crashed down before him, and Torin placed it over his own head.

Soon Gehena's shriek tore across the field. "The traitor has escaped. Find him!"

Sword clutched in his hand, Torin kept crawling forward. The rye kept him hidden, but the field wouldn't shield him for long; the stalks creaked and bent as he moved. Boots thumped before him and a man leaned down. A cruel face leered.

"I foun—" the man began

Torin swung his sword, slamming the blade into the man's face. The Magerian crashed down with a shower of blood. Torin cursed, rose to a crouch, and ran while bent over. Another Magerian raced toward him. Torin swung his sword again, cut the man's hand, then slammed his blade into his neck.

"Find the traitor and drag him back to me!" The shout rose behind Torin, a typhoon. "Slay the scu—"

"For Arden!" rose a high voice—a familiar voice. "Slay the enemy!"

Hooves thundered by. Boots raced. The banner of Arden—a black raven upon a golden field—streamed above. And there Torin saw him, clad in armor, his cloak billowing in the wind.

"Cam," Torin whispered. He rose to his feet. "Cam!"

The king rode upon a white courser, a lance in his hand. His armor was dented and bloody, and a bandage covered his arm. Around him, his fellow riders looked scarcely better—their armor was cracked, their weapons were chipped, and their flesh bore both old and fresh wounds. Yet still the Ardishmen charged toward the Magerian convoy. Magic blasted forward. Smoky tendrils tore off a horse's legs, and the beast tumbled, spilling its rider. Swordsmen charged.

"Torin!" Cam shouted, then turned back toward the battle. His lance drove into a mage, piercing the robed man's chest. Swords, magic, lances, and arrows crashed all around in a storm.

Torin snarled and ran toward the fight. He was wounded, maybe dying. He was thin, feverish, famished, but still he ran. He would not cower as others fought. He would—

He swayed. The world spun. The ground seemed to shake.

Red eyes turned toward him, all consuming. Lord Gehena saw him, and the creature's malice drove into his heart.

Arrows slammed into the demon.

More Ardish forces swarmed across the field, several hundred strong. Torin could barely stand upright, but he forced himself to run with them. He swung his sword and slew another man. The Magerians fell, one by one, their blood splattering the field. Hooves trampled over mages, and spears drove into soldiers' chests.

Torin leaped over bodies and finally stood before Lord Gehena.

The giant towered above him; Torin's head did not even reach the creature's shoulders. A chill emanated from the mage's black robes, but his stare burned like fire. Arrows and lances pierced the dark mage, and black blood dripped from him. His blades swung.

Torin parried and thrust.

His sword drove through the black robes and into flesh.

With battle cries and bright steel, fellow Ardishmen thrust spears and swords, piercing the demon lord.

Even as blades cut into him, Gehena stared at Torin. Those red eyes narrowed with malicious mockery. A deep, unearthly voice spoke in Torin's mind, echoing within his skull, scuttling inside him like snakes.

We will meet again, Torin. And you will meet your daughter. Madori will be mine, and you will watch me break her.

Torin screamed and swung his sword.

The blade cut through empty cloth.

The black robes fell onto the road, no flesh within him. The iron helmet clattered down, empty and colder than winter's heart. Ardish soldiers cursed, kicked at the robes, and stabbed them. Some men laughed and chanted for victory, but Torin knew the dark mage would return.

He trembled. *He knew Madori's name.*

"Torin! By Idar, you look horrible." Cam raced toward him, grabbed Torin's arm, then looked over his shoulder. "Cade! Lale! Fetch a healer!"

Torin could no longer stay standing. He fell into his friend's arms, and he was only vaguely aware of Cam placing him on the road, holding a wineskin over his lips, and shouting for the healer to hurry. All colors blended together, then went dark.

CHAPTER NINE
YIN SHI

Madori spoke in a slow, strained voice. "Give me. Back. My sword."

The Desolation stretched around her. Pillars of stone tilted like the ribs of giants, a hundred feet tall. Boulders like the stone blades of giants rose from the earth. Cracks stretched across craters, full of tar, and the fossilized skulls of ancient reptiles gaped upon cliffs, embedded into the stone. The stars shone above but the moon was gone. Madori had been here almost a moon's cycle now, and still the old master withheld her blade.

That old master now stood before her, calm, his arms crossed and his hands tucked neatly into his sleeves. His long white mustache and beard fluttered in the wind.

"First you must learn how to breathe," he said. "Then I will return your sword to you."

Madori's rage exploded out of her. "I've been breathing for a moon now! Stars damn it, I've been breathing all my life. If I didn't know how to breathe, I'd be dead. I—"

"If you knew how to breathe properly, you would do so now instead of shouting," he replied calmly. "You are learning the breathing of Yin Shi, an ancient wisdom, not those snorts and huffs you call breathing. Now—again like we practiced."

Madori growled. It was intolerable! Only a turn after arriving here, the old man had snatched her blade away and hidden it somewhere in the Desolation. She had searched every cave and cranny but hadn't found it.

Huffing, she turned toward her gray nightwolf. She patted the beast's thick fur; she had cut off the charred bits and it was growing back nicely. "Come on, Grayhem, sniff. Use your nose and find the sword."

Grayhem only sniffed her fingers. She had given him that name a few turns ago, combining his color and the name of the statue inside The Shadowed Firkin tavern back home—Hem, the hero baker of the war. However, it didn't seem the nightwolf even understood the concept of names. He began to sniff at her pockets, seeking mushrooms.

"Go on. Grayhem! Sniff for the sword."

The towering canine, large as a horse, only snorted and slumped down.

Lan Tao stroked the animal and stared at Madori. "It is time, my student. Your Yin Shi lessons."

She gripped her head and shouted at the sky. "I came here to learn how to fight! You promised to teach me swordplay. How can I learn fighting without a sword?"

"That is the only way to learn," Lan Tao replied. "I've been teaching you swordplay from the moment you entered this place. With every breath, you learn to swing the blade. Now sit down. And we will breathe."

Grumbling, she sat down, crossed her legs, and closed her eyes. She heard pebbles creak as Lan Tao sat down before her.

"A deep breath," he said, voice calm. "In . . . slowly . . ."

She dutifully inhaled, letting the air fill her from the bottom of her lungs to the top.

"Good," he said. "Focus your awareness on the air in your lungs. Let it flow to your feet. Let it fill your fingers, your head, all your body. And . . . exhale."

She exhaled slowly, trying to focus all her awareness on the air leaving her lungs. Yet her mind kept racing. She thought back to Teel University and how the Elorians had died on the road. She thought of Jitomi, who had traveled alone into Ilar, and she wondered if he was safe. She thought of her father, who had gone missing in the battle,
and of Tam and Neekeya who were seeking aid in Daenor, and—

The air whistled and pain slapped against her arm. She opened her eyes to see Lan Tao holding his katana; he had slammed the flat side against her, as he had so many times.

"Ow!" She glared and rubbed the red mark.

"You are not focusing. I can practically hear your thoughts. Your mind is a storm, but the Yin Shi mind must be a clear pond.

Now—try again. Every time a thought comes into your mind, let it go. Let it be as a cloud in the sky, floating away. Let it be as a ripple on a pond. As every thought enters, gaze upon it curiously, like gazing at a passing light . . . then let it leave you. Keep returning your awareness to nothing but the air, nothing but the breath entering and leaving your body. No thinking. No remembering. Simply *being*."

"Can't I even think of swordplay?" she asked.

He raised his katana again. "You will do as you're told. Now again—we breathe."

She muttered but she closed her eyes. She breathed again. A slow breath in, letting it fill her slowly, letting the air flow to every part of her: her toes, her legs, her torso, her head, her fingertips. She held the breath, and at once those damn fears returned to her, anxiousness for her friends, for her family, for Serin's armies mustering. She had to stop them! She had to learn to fight. She—

Let your thoughts be a cloud. Watch them float away.

She tugged her awareness back toward her breath, exhaling slowly. She let those thoughts flow away with the air.

"Good . . ." said Master Lan Tao. "Very good. The Yin Shi mind lets all thoughts ripple away. The Yin Shi mind is a clear, still pond. And breathe in . . ."

She breathed in again, held the air, released it slowly.

"Remember, child, the mind of a Yin Shi warrior is pure, focused only on existing. Never on the past. Never on the future. Only in the present. Only on what you are feeling right now, where you stand or sit, where you breathe, where you exist." He inhaled deeply. "Feel the air. Feel the wind around you, the starlight above, the cold stone beneath you. Only sensing. Never thinking."

She kept breathing slowly, trying to do as he taught, to only *be*. She pretended that she were some mollusk in a shell, clinging to stone, unable to think, to remember, to plan, only to exist in the present moment. Yet her thoughts kept rising. Every breath or two, the damn fears returned to her. She saw the dead. She saw the enemy soldiers. She—

She breathed.

Let the thoughts flow away.

She breathed in. She breathed out. Only being. Never thinking. Never remembering. Slowly, breath by breath, her mind cleared.

They sat like that for hours most turns, simply breathing, never thinking.

His voice flowed across the night. "Become like a stone, like a river, like a beam of light, part of the world, always in the present, always here."

When finally their session was done, he allowed her to eat. They sat together, three souls—Madori, Master Lan Tao, and Grayhem—gathered around a fire. They ate from an iron pot, a simple meal of stewed mushrooms and wild *shabani*—furry black animals who lived in the burrows of the Desolation, the size of Timandra's hares. After so long in silence, Madori kept speaking between mouthfuls.

"When will I get to swing my sword? When will I learn how to parry and thrust?" She gulped down a piece of the fatty meat. "Will you teach me how to pierce armor?" She bit into a greasy mushroom. "I want to learn how to fire arrows too, so I can fight from the walls of Salai Castle. Do you know how to fire arrows, Master Lan Tao?"

He simply stared over his bowl, smiling thinly. "You are learning all these things already."

She licked the bottom of her bowl. "Nonsense." She snorted. "I only learned boring breathing so far. I want to learn how to *fight*, Master." She jumped to her feet and snarled across the campfire at him. She swung an imaginary sword. "To slice! To cut! To kill my enemies! To—"

He vaulted over the flames so quickly she barely saw him move. His palm connected with her cheek with a flare of white light. The pain blinded her.

"Why did you not see this blow?" he said. He slapped her again, harder this time. "Why don't you defend yourself?"

She gasped, the pain blazing. She gulped and raised her arms defensively, then felt pain on her ankle—his foot slamming into her leg. She fell.

He loomed above her, his face no longer calm but a cold, hard mask. The firelight painted him red, and he no longer seemed an old man but a demon. His sheathed sword flashed, and the scabbard hit her shoulder.

"Go on, fight! You wanted to learn violence?" He snorted. "You wanted to learn to defeat an enemy? I am your enemy! Defend yourself. Defeat me!"

She growled and leaped to her feet. When his hand lashed toward her again, she blocked the blow. She claimed the air like she had learned at Teel. She sucked in the smoke from the campfire, particles of ash and dust, forming a ball to hurtle against him, to—

His hand thrust again, slapping her face a third time. Her magic dispersed.

"You have no time for magic." Another slap. "You must defeat me *now*—within the space between heartbeats. Fight!"

She tried to block his blows. She howled, lunged toward him, and attacked. He blocked every fist, every kick, and his blows kept landing upon her. The pain throbbed. She knew that bruises would cover her. Ahead she saw all her enemies. He became Emperor Serin, Professor Atratus, Princess Lari, a million soldiers of Mageria. She had to stop him! Surely she could defeat him, but the pain was too strong, and he was too fast, and her fear flooded her. Another blow from him sent her sprawling to the ground.

He leaned above her. He grabbed her collar.

"Why do you not fight?"

"I am fighting!" she shouted, blood in her mouth. "You're too fast."

He laughed. "Fast? I'm an old man. I'm over eighty years old; you're not yet twenty. You're faster, stronger, lither. Why then do I defeat you?"

She growled and tried to rise, but he pinned her down. "I don't know!"

He shook her. "Because I am *aware*. That is why. In battle, I am only in the present. I sense every movement. Every tension in your muscles and in mind. Every flick of your eyes. Every twitch of your legs or arms. But you . . ." He shook his head in disgust. "Your mind is a storm. You think of the past and future." He snorted. "You think of your enemies—how they wronged you, how you crave revenge, how you hurt from their blows. A warrior of Yin Shi cares not for revenge, not for the past, not for the future, not for the faces of foes. A warrior of Yin Shi does not *think*, does not *feel*; only *senses*. A warrior of Yin Shi lives the air, the starlight, the dance. Ah, yes, it is a dance. It is the same as breathing, that is all—the breath of battle, the air coming and going."

She blinked up at him, tasting blood in her mouth. "How is breathing anything like this? Breathing is simple."

He nodded. "Laying one brick upon another is simple, yet that is how you build a palace. The turning of a gear is simple, yet attach enough gears together and you can build a great clock. To fight is to be aware. The way you are aware of your breathing, focusing all your consciousness on the air coming and going, thus you can be aware of a battle. The sluggard *thinks* while she fights. The coward *fears*, the brute *hates*. The wise Yin Shi warrior never thinks, never feels; she is simply *aware*. Do you understand?"

She nodded. "I do."

He grunted. "You lie. There is no understanding in Yin Shi; understanding is a thing of thoughts. There is only *awareness*. You will *know* this wisdom when you experience it, not when you claim to *understand* my words. Words are thoughts. Words are the invention of the mind. Yin Shi is not about the mind. You are not your mind, no more than you are your foot or hand. You are not your thoughts. You are your *soul*. Only when you become your soul, removing your thoughts from your essence, will you become Yin Shi."

She nodded slowly. She rose to her feet. She took a deep breath, and she felt the air around her. She let the starlight fill her eyes. She let her awareness spread through her.

"Good . . ." he said. "Let the awareness spread like roots. Let it flow through your body and into the stone beneath you, to the canyon walls, to the wind, to the sky above. Hold it all in your awareness. Be part of it. You are not Madori, a trapped mind in a skull. You are the world around you."

She nodded, took another deep breath, and let that awareness spread. She gasped. Suddenly she was no longer trapped in her body; he was right. She was one with the Desolation.

"It's like magic," she whispered.

With magic, she had to choose her material, then claim it, and finally change it. *Yin Shi is the same!* she realized. *Yin Shi is simply another application of the same principles!* She had to choose not just *one* material but the universe and herself in it—the air in her lungs, the landscape around her, all other souls . . . and claim them all, hold them all in awareness the way she held materials in her magic. But instead of *changing* them, she simply experienced them, become . . . aware.

She was one with the night.

Lan Tao's muscle twitched.

Madori raised her arm.

Before his palm could strike her, she blocked the blow. At once she saw the subtle tension in his leg, knew he would kick her. She hopped back, and his foot passed through air. She blocked another blow. She thrust her hand, and her fist drove into his chest.

Master Lan Tao fell.

Madori gasped.

"Master!"

At once she dropped her Yin Shi awareness. It felt like waking from a dream. She knelt above the fallen old man and touched his cheek.

"Master, I'm sorry! Are you all right?"

Lying on the ground, he smiled up at her. "Finally," he whispered. "Finally you learn."

She helped him stand, and suddenly she realized how frail he was; he weighed no more than she did, maybe even less. She supported him, and they climbed the craggy hill together. Grayhem walked at their side, eyes bright in the darkness. They entered their cave, and Madori helped the old man lie down upon his bed—a simple stone alcove in the wall.

Once Lan Tao was sleeping, Madori tiptoed toward the cave opening. Grayhem stood at her side, and she placed her hand in his fur. She stood for a long time, looking out into the night. She knew that Lan Tao did not like her thinking, remembering, planning, yet as she stood here, she imagined fighting Serin with her new skill, and she smiled.

CHAPTER TEN
THE RAVENS IN THE NORTH

Five hundred Ardish soldiers rode through the snowy forest, bearing the treasures of their raid: two hundred Radian swords and shields, three coffers of the enemy's gold, and one freed prisoner.

Torin swayed on his horse, still weak. Bandages covered his wounds, and as he rode, he nursed a wineskin. His head still spun, and his limbs were thinner than he'd ever seen them. He had been imprisoned for almost eight months, Cam had told him, most of them spent in a Kingswall dungeon. It had felt like eight decades.

But he was healing already. After several turns of riding in the open air, eating real food—bread cooked fresh over campfires, roasted venison, and wild berries—the pain had begun to fade, the haze to lift. He wore armor now, no longer rags. Arden's raven appeared upon his breastplate, and a new longsword hung at his side. He looked around him at the other riders, the survivors of Arden's army. They looked healthier than him, but they too were haggard. Stubble covered their faces, dents and scratches marred their armor, and their eyes were sunken and hollow.

"All right, old boy?" Cam rode his destrier closer to him.

Torin nodded and scratched his newly trimmed beard. "I feel like one of your shorn sheep. My beard and hair grew monstrously long in captivity. I must have lost half my weight when I finally trimmed them."

Cam smiled wanly. "You're looking stronger every turn."

"I'm ready to face Serin himself in battle." Torin gazed at his hazy reflection in his vambrace. "Even if I have a few more white hairs on my head. A prison cell will do that to you."

Snow began to fall around them, and icicles hung from the oaks, maples, and birches. Several coyotes stared from between the trees, eyes golden, then turned to flee. As the riders traveled northward, the land became colder. Torin had lived most of his life at

Arden's southern border along the Sern River, the great pipeline connecting Mageria, Naya, Arden, and Qaelin in the night. Here they were traveling across the northern hinterlands of Arden, a thickly forested land near the border of Verilon, the sprawling kingdom that ruled the sub-arctic realms of North Timandra. Frost covered the riders' armor, their breath plumed in clouds, and steam rose from the horses' backs. Here was a vast, cold, empty wilderness, a place to hide, to survive, as the Radian fire burned in the south.

"There it is," Cam finally said. He pointed north between the snowy trees. "Welcome, Torin old boy, to what remains of Free Arden. Welcome to our camp."

A palisade of sharpened logs stretched between the trees, forming a crude wall. Trophies hung from some logs—the helmets and cloven shields of the Radian empire, still coated with blood. Ardish troops patrolled the perimeter, clad in frosted steel, and upon makeshift, wooden towers stood archers in snow-coated cloaks. A dirt path led toward gates in the wall, and the convoy—led by King Camlin—rode into the camp.

Riding close behind his friend and king, Torin gazed around. After long moons of war and fear—parting from his family, seeing Kingswall fall, enduring torture and hunger—Torin finally felt a little ray of hope pierce the clouds.

Arden has not yet fallen.

Thousands of Ardish men and women moved about the camp, most of them soldiers in steel, swords at their waists. Tents and wooden huts stretched in neat rows. Deer cooked upon campfires, and fur pelts hung on ropes, freshly cured. In a dirt square, men were drilling with blades, polishing swords, and practicing their archery. Many here were wounded—some bandaged, others burnt, and a few missing their limbs—but most still seemed strong, ready to keep fighting. The raven banners rose proudly above the camp, thudding in the wind.

"We have fifteen thousand men and women here," Cam said to Torin. "Most are soldiers, the survivors of the war, but many are townsfolk and farmers who fled the Radian onslaught. Food is lean and the winter is harsh, but we're surviving. We're still fighting."

As they rode by, soldiers bowed and cried out, "King Camlin! King Camlin returns!"

Cam nodded to all those they passed. Behind the king, the soldiers who had ridden south upended sacks, spilling out their treasure—the armor, weapons, and gold of the Magerians they had slain on the road. Men cheered and rushed forward to collect the bounty.

"We'll use the armor and weapons for those who joined our camp," Cam said. "We must all become soldiers. Now come, we'll find something to eat—and some good company too."

Riding side by side, Cam and Torin made their way down the dirt road between the soldiers. They rounded a great oak, rode into a dirt square, and approached a campfire. Several people stood here, tending to roasting deer.

Torin's eyes widened. "Linee! Omry!"

The Queen and Prince of Arden ran toward him. Rather than a gown—her usual raiment—Linee now wore tan leggings and a vest of boiled leather. Her golden hair spilled from under a round helmet, and a sword hung from her belt. Prince Omry wore heavy steel armor—a breastplate, greaves, and wide pauldrons—and a double-handed sword hung across his back. When Torin dismounted his horse, the two crashed into him, wrapped their arms around him, and squeezed.

"Go easy on me!" Torin winced. "I'm still wounded."

Laughing and shedding tears, Linee jabbed his chest with her finger. "You're late."

He nodded. "I was delayed. Took a little detour with our Radian friends." He pulled Linee back into his embrace. "It's good to see you again."

A high-pitched voice rose from farther back. A small dark shape bounded forward. "Torin! Torin, you've come back! I was so worried about you. We searched all over with our hot air balloon, but they took you away, and it was horrible, and I had to take the others here, I had to!" Little Nitomi, the Elorian spy, jumped onto Torin, wrapped all four limbs around him, and clung. Tears filled her eyes. "Thank the Red Flame you're here. I've been watching over the others while you were away. Are you hurt? Do you want to eat some

342

mushrooms? We have mushrooms here! Not as good as the ones in Eloria, but I found some that I like, and I'm so happy you're here!"

Tall, pale Qato—never far from his cousin—stepped forward. The towering Elorian stared at Torin with a blank, stony expression. "Qato happy."

Soon the companions sat around the fire on logs, eating a meal of roasted deer, stewed mushrooms Nitomi had cooked, and oatmeal. They washed the food down with red wine and cold ale, bounty captured in a previous raid. As they ate and drank, Cam talked, bringing Torin up to speed.

"Serin's mustering on the eastern front now, Tor," he said, chewing on a strip of venison. "I didn't want to tell you on the road, not with you still recovering from your injuries. Serin plans to invade Qaelin. Maybe the invasion has begun already."

The food turned to ash in Torin's mouth. He turned toward Linee and spoke softly. "Any news of Koyee and Madori? Last Cam heard from them, both were in Oshy across the border. Has any news arrived while Cam and I were away?"

The queen lowered her head. "No news from the east for a month now. According to our last report, Madori had crossed Arden behind enemy lines, entered the darkness, and joined Koyee at Salai Castle. We know nothing more."

Torin's eyes stung. "That plucky little thing. All my months of captivity, I was so worried about the Billygoat. And there she is! She made it across the war and into the darkness."

But Cam's eyes remained dark. "Tor . . . there something else I didn't want to tell you on the road. Last we've heard, Serin had destroyed Fairwool-by-Night. He burned down the houses. He . . ." Cam's voice choked. "He slew everyone there, we think, and now he musters an army on the ruins. Koyee and Madori are right across the border. I pray to Idar that they fled to safety deeper in the night."

Torin lowered his head and his eyes burned. "After I saw what Serin did to Kingswall, I feared as much." His breath shook in his lungs. "Our home is gone."

A dead, empty space filled Torin, a cavity in his chest. Fairwool-by-Night. His home. Burned down. The Shadowed Firkin, the tavern where he had spent so many hours with his friends. His

home, the cottage where Mayor Kerof had raised him, where he had
grown up with Bailey, where he had married Koyee, where he had
raised Madori. The maple tree. The library. The fields of rye and the
gardens he had spent his life tending to. All gone. All his friends and
neighbors—fallen.

How can I go on? he thought. *How can I keep fighting when it feels like
I have nothing left to fight for?*

Nitomi looked up from her bowl of mushrooms. She spoke
softly, interrupting his thoughts. "And I pray for my brother, for little
Jitomi. He was with Madori at Teel, did you know? In her last letter
to us—it was a whole moon ago!—Koyee said that Jitomi was with
her in Oshy, but that he planned to leave, to return to Ilar, to my
father." Nitomi shuddered. "Oh, my father was always so mean to
him."

Torin rose to his feet, his appetite gone. "Serin is attacking
Qaelin through the dusk? So we cut off his supplies." He pounded
his fist into his palm, sudden rage washing over his grief. "Mageria is
in the west. Qaelin is in the east. We're here right in the middle,
sitting above his supply lines. We keep raiding the roads. We cut off
his eastern host from his western kingdom. He can't fight a war if
he's starved for food." He gripped his sword. "Why are we here? Let
us organize another raid, a larger raid. Surely Serin's wagons are
rolling east along the roads, his ships sailing east along the river. We'll
burn them."

Cam sighed, placed down his bowl, and stared at the campfire.
"Not so simple, old boy. There's a new Radian army mustering in
Kingswall. They're not just Magerians either; a whole lot of Nayans
have joined them, and even Ardishmen who've turned coat and now
raise the eclipse banners. They're calling themselves a united army of
the Radian Empire. And they're about to march north, to seek us in
the forests, and to try and stamp us out. They're fifty thousand
strong, we hear." Cam grimaced. "They have mages. Chariots.
Cannons, Torin! We have ten thousand weary, hungry soldiers and
five thousand refugees to protect. The enemy might already be
marching; they might be here by the full moon."

Nitomi nodded. "Qato and I saw them from our hot air
balloon. They have elephants too, Torin! Real elephants. I always

thought I'd love elephants, but these ones are wearing armor, and there are little towers on them—howdahs, they're called—and there are archers inside, and they're going to come here, and I really don't want to kill those elephants, and . . ." The dojai covered her eyes. Hulking Qato patted her shoulder, silently comforting her.

Torin felt queasy. He couldn't take another bite of his meal. "Serin might have rallied Nayans and even some Ardishmen, but not all in the sunlight flock to his banners. On the road, I heard Gehena and his soldiers speak." Torin grimaced to remember those long turns of pain in darkness, tortured and famished. He suppressed a shudder. "They spoke of battles along the Icenflow northwest from here. The kingdom of Verilon has refused to join this so-called Radian Empire. From snippets I've heard, it sounded like Serin has been sending troops across the Icenflow to raid Verilon's forests. Only one Magerian returned from each raid, speaking of Verilish warriors butchering his comrades and feeding them to the bears."

Cam blew out his breath, eyebrows raised. "Lovely folk, the Verilish." He chewed his lip. "Right now, I don't even know if I'm serious or sarcastic."

Torin clutched the hilt of his sword, seeking comfort from the heavy leather grip. "My father fought Verilon in a war many years ago—before I was even born. He spoke of horrible barbarians, great bearded warriors who rode on bears and wielded hammers that weighed more than a man. In his stories, the Verilish were like monsters. If they now fight Serin, we have powerful allies." He stared at Cam over the campfire. "We need not fight the Radians in this forest, humble wooden walls around us. Verilon lies only a three turn ride north. Let us join our forces to theirs. When Mageria's buffaloes open a northeastern front, they will meet an alliance of bears and ravens."

With creaking armor and creaking joints, Cam rose to his feet and paced around the campfire. "Will Verilon welcome us? The raven and bear have never been the best of friends."

"The enemy of my enemy is my friend, as the old cliche goes." Torin smiled wryly. "Serin has committed the bulk of his troops to the eastern front, to conquering the night. Many of his other troops are mustering in the west, besieging the marshlands of Daenor; many

Daenorians too fight against him. Serin thinks his army at Kingswall is enough to conquer the north." He sneered, surprised by the sudden rage that flowed through him. "We will make him bleed in the north."

Cam stepped closer to Torin, grabbed his arm, and whispered into his ear, "Tor, I've seen Orewood, the great Verilish city on the border. Massive towers. Huge walls coated in ice. Thousands of iron-clad warriors thrice my size. If we march there, there's a good chance Verilon will slay us and feed us to the bears."

Torin smiled grimly. "And if we stay here, the Radians will crush our camp. I'll take my chances with the bears. Massive towers? Huge walls? Burly warriors? Good. I'd like that on our side."

They turned toward the others—Queen Linee, Prince Omry, and the two dojai. Beyond them, many soldiers moved back and forth, preparing for battle.

Torin looked back at his friend. "What do you say, Cam? You and me. We'll ride ahead, just the two of us, like in the old turns. We'll knock on those great frozen walls and forge us a little alliance, then invite the rest of this lot over."

The king rubbed his shoulders. "The last time we rode out together, we ended up jumping into a river, arrows raining down onto us."

"Exactly." Torin smiled. "It's always fun. But if you insist, we'll bring a few guards this time."

As fresh snow fell upon the forest, Torin, Cam, and a handful of soldiers rode out of their camp, heading north through the wilderness toward the distant city of ice and snow.

CHAPTER ELEVEN
BLOOD IN THE DUSK

Ten thousand Elorians stood in the dusk, the orange light shining upon their scale armor, the silver moonstars on their shields, and their drawn katanas. Ten thousand pairs of blue, silver, and purple eyes gleamed, staring west, waiting. Ten thousand hearts beat with fear. The Host of Twilit Spirits, the Qaelish empire's western division, waited for battle.

Koyee sat at their lead upon a nightwolf, a shaggy black beast named Senduan. Her scale armor hugged her, and her long white hair hid within her helmet. She held a round shield in one hand, its surface engraved with a moon within a star, sigil of her empire. In her other hand, she held a new katana, a sword she had named *Tuanshey*—slayer of light.

"Once more, we stand ready for battle, Eelani," she whispered.

Her invisible friend rested upon her shoulder, a hint of warmth and a barely perceptible weight. Little hands seemed to caress Koyee's cheek.

"I know you're scared, Eelani," Koyee said. Her voice was so low she barely heard herself. "I am too."

She thought back to her first battle—a great dance of fire and steel upon the walls of Pahmey. That had been twenty-one years ago, and she had been only a youth, only a girl of sixteen—younger than her daughter was now. Back then she had been quicker, perhaps braver, a mere urchin with nothing to lose but a bone flute and a few copper coins. Now she was a wife, a mother, a leader, a protector of an empire. And the fear was greater than ever, the weight upon her shoulders nearly too much to bear.

Yet I will bear it nonetheless, she swore to herself and tightened her fist around the silk-wrapped hilt of her sword. *And I will fight with more courage than ever.*

She gently nudged Senduan. The shaggy nightwolf—he was large as a horse—stepped forward, parting from the ranks of troops. The gloaming spread around Koyee, the orange light falling upon pale grass, twisted trees, and brambles—the only flora that could survive in the shadows. Duskmoths flew around her, and one landed on the hilt of her sword. She turned to face her troops. The ten thousand stood in orderly lines, a machine of metal as fine as any clock. They were young men and women, many barely older than her daughter, all clad in the same scales, all holding the same swords. Boys. Girls. Their eyes frightened but determined, shining in the twilight.

"Soldiers of Eloria!" Koyee called to them. Her voice carried across the dusky forest. "I am Koyee, Daughter of Salai. You've heard tales of the battles I fought. Many of you were just babes when I slew Timandrians in the great War of Day and Night. Now the sun rises to burn us again. From the towers of Salai Castle, we have seen them muster, and now we have seen them enter the dusk. Twenty years ago, they took Eloria by surprise. This time we will cast them back into the light." She banged her sword against her shield. "We are the night!"

Ten thousand blades clanged against shields. Their voices rose as one. "We are the night!"

"Show no fear!" Koyee shouted. "Show no weakness to the enemy. Do not despair in the face of battle, not even in the face of death. We will shed the blood of Timandra! We will defend the darkness. For Eloria!"

"For Eloria!" they cried, swords rising like a forest of steel.

Though her words perhaps inspired courage, Koyee's innards trembled. Yes, she had seen the enemy from the rooftop of Salai Castle. She had seen a hundred thousand troops gather—swordsmen, pikemen, archers. She had seen five thousand horses bearing armored riders. She had seen scythed chariots, siege engines on great wheels, battering rams on chains, catapults and ballistae, and even cannons shaped as life-sized buffaloes. Worst of all, she had seen hundreds of mages in black robes. At the thought of them, the scars that snaked around her arm—given to her by a mage in Sinyong years ago—blazed with new pain.

This is a battle we cannot win, she knew. She had sent messengers to all corners of the night. She had begged for aid, for more troops, for anyone who could wield and sword. Yet here were all the swords Eloria could wield. For every ten living souls in Timandra, only one lived in Eloria; there were no more soldiers to spare.

She tightened her lips. *They outnumber us ten to one. So each among us will have to kill ten of them. And I will kill many more than that.*

The enemy's chants rose in the west, and Koyee turned back toward the light. Her heart pounded and her breath fluttered in her mouth. Her nightwolf growled beneath her, fangs bared.

"They're here."

She couldn't see them yet, but their sound rose slowly, louder with every heartbeat. Thousands of thumping boots. Stamping hooves. Chinking armor. War drums that beat a rhythm of slaughter. *Boom. Boom. Boom.* A blaring horn that sounded like a dying beast. Chants in many languages all united under the eclipse banner. More drums. *Boom. Boom.*

She heard their voices. At first they were too distant to hear clearly, but with every beat of the drum, with every thud of boots, those voices grew nearer, coalescing into a mantra.

"Radian rises! Radian rises!"

Koyee snarled upon her nightwolf and held her sword high. "We are the night!"

The soldiers of darkness howled behind her. Koyee breathed heavily through clenched teeth, her pulse thrumming in her ears. And then she saw them.

They emerged from the sunlight, marching between the trees, the hosts of the Radian Empire. Horses rode at their vanguard, clad in armor. Some horses bore riders armed with lances and swords. Other horses pulled scythed chariots, archers within them. They filled the dusk, more plentiful than the stars.

Lances rose, crested with bright steel, and the riders of sunlight charged.

Koyee shouted wordlessly, kneed her nightwolf, and raced toward them. Around her, hundreds of other nightwolves raced forward, their riders howling and pointing their swords.

With shattering steel and spraying blood, the hosts crashed together.

Koyee's nightwolf roared and snapped his teeth. A lance drove toward Koyee, and she swung her katana, slicing its shaft. A horse reared before her. She thrust her blade. She severed a knight's leg, cutting deep where his plates of armor met. Another horse galloped toward her, and Koyee's wolf leaped. They soared over the rider, then plunged down like a comet, fangs and blade driving into flesh.

Around her, the myriads fought in the dusk. Nightwolves tore off pieces of Timandrian armor and dug into the meat beneath. Horses trampled over Elorian swordsmen, and lances crashed through scale armor. Trees burned. Every heartbeat, more fell dead. The corpses covered the land, and severed limbs lay strewn like so many fallen branches.

"Hold them back!" Koyee shouted. "Elorians, defend the night!"

More nightwolves fell. Chariots raced between the trees, as agile as the wolves, crashing into the lines of Elorian infantry. Blades rose upon their wheels, mowing down men and women. Archers fired from within them. One of the projectiles hit Koyee's shield, and another sank into her nightwolf. The beast cried out in pain, blood spurting.

"Senduan!" Koyee cried. She leaned down, grabbed the arrow, and tugged it free from the nightwolf's flank. "Keep fighting, Senduan! We must hold them back. We—"

Fire sparked ahead.

The smell of gunpowder flared.

The Timandrian troops parted, and Koyee beheld a horror that froze her blood.

The cannon rolled forth on wooden wheels, twenty feet long, a beast of black iron shaped as a buffalo. Embers burned in its nostrils, and its mouth was open in a crackling roar. Timandrian soldiers stood around it, waving their longswords, chanting for victory.

Koyee sucked in air and tugged her wolf aside.

"Elorians, scatter!" she shouted hoarsely to the troops behind her. "Scatter to the trees!"

They began to move. They were too late. Racing away, Koyee returned her eyes to the cannon in time to see it fire.

Flames blazed out in an inferno like a collapsing sun. Koyee had an instant vision from years ago—Ferius crashing into the mechanical sun at Cabera, igniting a blast of heat and light. Smoke engulfed the dusk. The cannonball drove forward, so fast Koyee could barely see it, a projectile larger than her head. It slammed into the lines of Elorian troops, pulverizing those it hit. Blood, scales of armor, and bits of hair and flesh flew across the forest, pattering against the soil. Trees ignited. Fire blazed across corpses and fallen branches.

For a moment the forest seemed still and silent. Koyee could only hear the ringing in her ears. She could only see the death, the bodies broken into smudges.

Then, with renewed howls, the Timandrian swordsmen charged forth. The surviving Elorians, their armor red with the blood of their friends, swung their katanas and ran to meet them. The dusk exploded with the song of ringing steel.

Ahead, Timandrians poured new gunpowder into the muzzle, then loaded a new cannonball. Koyee sneered.

"To the cannon!" she shouted. "Elorians, to the cannon!"

She kneed her wolf, and the beast burst into a run. Senduan bounded from boulder to boulder, corpse to corpse, claws lashing, fangs digging into men. Whoever the nightwolf could not kill Koyee cut with her sword. The cannon rose ahead from smoke. One man lit a new fuse, and sparks filled the air.

Koyee sneered and raced onward.

Her wolf leaped through smoke. Her sword swung. The blade severed the lit fuse.

Men shouted around her. Swords swung and arrows flew. Koyee leaped off the saddle. She sailed through the air and landed atop the searing-hot cannon; her boots sizzled against the heated iron. She swung her sword in arcs, chopping men down. An arrow slammed into her vambrace. Another snapped against her armor, and a third scraped along her helmet.

Her eyes fell upon barrels of gunpowder below.

A wry smile twisted her lips.

She leaped into the air, swung her sword, and slew two more men before her feet hit the ground. She raced, rolled, and jumped up, stabbing another man—the one who had lit the fuse. He fell, and his torch thumped into the dirt.

"Slay the nightcrawler!" rose a shriek. "Kill her!"

"Hold them back, Senduan!" Koyee shouted to her wolf. The beast was tearing into men, teeth bloody. Two other nightwolves joined him, forming a circle around Koyee, holding the enemy back.

She lifted the guttering torch. Grinning savagely, Koyee sliced a barrel open. Its gunpowder spilled.

"Senduan, to me!"

The nightwolf ran toward her.

She leaped into the saddle.

She tossed her torch into the gunpowder.

The nightwolf raced along the cannon and vaulted off, and they soared forward like a cannonball.

For an instant, silence filled the world.

Then that world seemed to fall into the sun.

White, shrieking, all-consuming fire blazed. The dusk lit up, brighter than a sunlit desert. Flames howled. Smoke roared. Koyee and her wolf kept leaping through the inferno, and blasts of air hit her, slamming into her back with the strength of hammers. Her head rang. Her cloak burned.

They hit the ground, singed.

Koyee looked behind her in time to see three more explosions, one after another, rock the forest—three more barrels exploding.

She tumbled off her wolf, fell onto her stomach, and covered her ears. Chunks of iron, chips of wood, and drops of blood pattered down onto her. Her ears rang and smoke engulfed her. Soil fell like hail.

When she finally rose to her feet and looked around, she sucked in air between her teeth. A crater loomed in the dusk. The cannon was gone. A hundred Timandrian bodies, maybe more, lay in a ring around the crater. Of those who had stood closer to the cannon nothing remained.

Behind her, the Elorians roared with new vigor and raced forward. They slammed into the remaining Timandrians, cutting them down. Koyee climbed back onto her wolf and fought with them.

We slew hundreds, maybe a thousand, she thought. *Yet ninety-nine thousand remain.* Her eyes stung in the smoke. *We can bleed them, but this is a battle we cannot win. This is a battle we cannot survive.*

The Elorians fought but the enemy kept coming. Lines of swordsmen. Iron-clad towers on wheels, archers in their crests. Catapults that rained boulders into the Elorian ranks. Dark mages on dark horses, blasting out living serpents of magic that wrapped around Elorians and crushed their bones. The forces of sunlight covered the dusk, streaming forth like a rising sun, and Koyee shouted until she was hoarse and would not stop swinging her sword.

CHAPTER TWELVE
THE RED FLAME ARMADA

The Ilari Armada, Terror of the Night Sea, sailed across the black waters toward the coast of Qaelin.

"Father, you cannot do this!" Jitomi said. "Please. Listen to me! Listen to reason. You are sailing against the wrong enemy. The Qaelish are our allies. Your enemy lies in the sunlight."

Standing at the prow, Lord Okita Hashido turned to stare at his son. His eyes narrowed and his lip peeled back in a sneer. "Silence your sniveling, boy, lest I stripe your back and toss you to the sharks. Your words are treachery. Were you not my son, I'd have you flayed and burned. If you anger me further, that can still be your fate."

The fleet stretched across the dark sea. Hundreds of *geobukseon* ships sailed in formations; each was a hundred feet long, their battened sails wide, and their iron figureheads, shaped as dragons, could spew out smoke to conceal their position in battle. Among them towered the *panokseons,* great ships with three tiers of decks: the lower deck for rowers, the middle deck for cannons, and the upper deck for soldiers. Those soldiers wore heavy, lacquered armor, the metal black and red, and helmets shaped as snarling faces hid their heads.

Jitomi and his father, meanwhile, stood on an *atakebune*—a floating fortress—one of only three in their fleet. Named *Daroma Tai*—Terror of the Water—the massive ship was large as a castle, its deck four hundred feet long and lined with dozens of cannons. Oars emerged from holes in its iron-clad hull like centipede feet, propelling the vessel forward. An entire pagoda, three tiers tall, rose upon the deck. A thousand troops filled the *Daroma Tai*: swordsmen in heavy steel plates, armed with katanas and throwing stars; archers in black silken robes; and gunners in boiled leather. A massive dragon figurehead thrust off the prow, and from its mouth emerged a cannon like a tongue.

A true dragon—Tianlong, the last dragon in the night—flew above the ship, coiling and uncoiling like a great banner. His body was long and narrow and covered in black scales. Only two small arms grew from that body, barely larger than human arms and tipped with claws. In sharp contrast, Tianlong's jaws were massive enough to swallow men whole, and his teeth were long as katanas. The dragon's eyes blazed, and his fiery red beard, mustache, and long eyebrows fluttered in the wind.

"Magnificent beast," said Lord Hashido, staring up at the dragon. "Strong. Fearless in battle. A mighty warrior." He looked back at Jitomi. "The qualities I wanted in a son. Instead you stand here as weak as a woman, begging to return home with our tail between our legs."

"I would have you fight with strength and pride," Jitomi said, "but not against our Elorian brethren. I would have you fight against the Radian Empire. Against those who invade the night."

"Those who invade *Qaelin*!" Hashido laughed—a horrible, barking sound. "Those who attack our old enemy. The Magerians are strong, and the Radian Order that rules them is a movement of pride, honor, and nobility. Like the Ilari, the Radians respect the might of the sword, the cannon, the arrow. Together we will defeat the Qaelish Empire and carve her between us."

"And what then?" Jitomi shook his head incredulously. "Do you truly think that Lord Serin, the man who preached death to Elorians, will simply lean back and let an Elorian empire rule in the south? No. He would turn his wrath against Ilar too. He's simply using divide-and-conquer tactics, Father. I'm no general, but even I know this old trick. He's pitting Elorians against Elorians, and when we shatter one another, he'll be there to sweep the pieces away."

Hashido snorted. "It is true, Jitomi. You are no general. You are nothing but a weak boy who failed at every task he was given. I tried to teach you swordplay; you failed to wield the blade. I tried to enlist you into the Dojai Order like your sister; Nitomi is a prattle-mouthed, empty-headed fool, but even she became a dojai, a feat you refused to even attempt. Finally you went off to study magic like some illiterate village woman who believes in charms and spells, and even at that you failed. But I, Jitomi, *am* a general. And now I am an emperor. And I will soon be a conqueror. Look, worm! We can see the Qaelish coast. Our enemy awaits."

Jitomi stared ahead and his heart sank. He recognized this place. The Qaelish town of Xinsai sprawled along the coast, a strip of light. It was not a major city like Sinyong, the great Qaelish port further west upon the coast, a stronghold that connected the sea to the Inaro river. It was surely not a bastion of power like Pahmey or Yintao, the two great lights of Qaelin. Here was a simpler place, a town with only five pagodas, their roofs blue and topped with brass dragon statues. A couple hundred tall, narrows houses nestled between the pagodas. A few junk ships—Qaelish vessels with triangular, battened sails—floated in the water, humble fishermen upon them.

Why are we sailing to Xinsai? Jitomi wondered at first, belly curdling. It was only a small town. It was no threat. It was—

As the Red Fleet sailed closer, he understood.

A port bit into the town, surrounded by walls and turrets. Moonstar banners rose here, and archers guarded the battlements. Hundreds of Qaelish workers bustled upon planks and scaffolds, swung hammers, bent iron, and pounded leather. The skeletons of several junk ships were taking form in the water, not humble fishermen's vessels but mighty warships. As Jitomi watched, several men turned a wince, guiding down a cannon onto a deck. It was a shipyard, massive in size, serving the Qaelish navy.

"Here do the Qaelish worms build their so-called fleet," said Lord Hashido. "We will show them the might of a true armada."

Bile rose in Jitomi's throat. He grabbed his father's arm. "Father, these people are not soldiers. They are workers struggling to feed their families. You cannot—"

Hashido backhanded him. His gauntlet connected with Jitomi's cheek with a spray of blood.

"They will die in our fire, boy." The lord pulled down his visor; it was shaped like a snarling demon, forged of lacquered steel, its mustache made of panther fur. "If you do not silence your words, you will die with them." He turned toward the soldiers who stood behind him on the deck. "Warriors of Ilar! We sail to conquest!"

The soldiers on the deck, hundreds of demons in steel, raised their swords and roared for the Red Flame. Upon the pagoda that rose from the deck, a fortress of metal and clay, archers tugged back their bowstrings. All across the water, the other ships of Ilar—hundreds of them—sailed to war. The dragon figureheads of the *geobukseons* belched out smoke; cannons hid within their iron jaws. Upon the three-tiered *panokseon* ships, more cannons were lit, and warriors formed ranks around landing craft. Above the fleet, Tianlong the dragon soared, and his cry pealed across the sky.

"Father!" Jitomi said, clutching his cut cheek. "Do not destroy! If you must conquer, then conquer. Seize these ships for our fleet, and let the townsfolk live. They can serve us. They need not die."

But Lord Hashido seemed not to hear. He pointed his sword toward the coastal town, and he shouted, voice storming across the water, "Armada—fire!"

The cannons blazed.

"No!" Jitomi tried to grab his father, but the soldiers held him back. "Father, stop this!"

Smoke enveloped him as their own ship's cannons fired. He watched, eyes burning, as the cannonballs slammed into the town of Xinsai. Several projectiles slammed into junk ships, shattering their hulls. Others crashed into walls and turrets, cracking bricks, sending men falling. Another volley blasted out from the Ilari ships, and cannonballs now slammed into city homes, shattering clay walls. A pagoda crumbled, raining screaming men.

"Watch, boy," hissed a voice beside him. "Watch as nightcrawlers turn against nightcrawlers."

Jitomi spun around to see Professor Atratus, wrapped in his black robes, standing on the deck. As always, the Magerian wore his Radian pin. His eyes glittered, reflecting the firelight, as he stared at the destruction. His lips peeled back in a hungry grin. He turned to stare at Jitomi, glee in those beady eyes.

"Do you see?" said Atratus. "Do you see how pathetic your kind is? You turn against each other, unable to unite even as my lord invades your lands in the north." He cackled, spraying saliva. "Your folly will be your doom. You will watch this doom unfurl, boy. I am still your teacher. I now teach you the true wretchedness of your own kind."

Rage and fear pounded through Jitomi. He growled at Atratus, tempted to draw his katana and slay the man. Before he could act, whistles filled the sky. A rain of arrows lit the night, glinting red in the firelight.

The soldiers on the deck, Jitomi among them, raised their shields.

The arrows, fired from the town's battlements, rained down with a clatter. Most snapped against shields and armor. A few sank into the deck. One or two managed to punch through steel and draw blood. When the barrage subsided and Jitomi lowered his shield, the Magerian professor was gone.

Jitomi looked across the battle and winced. The Ilari fleet was dropping its anchors. Cannons blasted out again, slamming into the coastal town. Only three Qaelish warships guarded the shipyard, and they were now burning. Chanting for the Red Flame, Ilari warriors climbed into landing crafts and began oaring toward the blazing town.

"Drag the worms out of their holes!" Lord Hashido was shouting; he still stood at the prow, sword raised. "Slay the men and children and capture the women! Destroy every last home and ship!"

In the town, women and children were fleeing from their homes and running to the northern hills. Some Qaelish men stood upon the walls, firing cannons and arrows, but the Ilari firepower tore into them, scattering down bodies and bricks. Corpses burned upon the streets, houses crumbled, and the Qaelish ships sank. Firelight danced upon the bloody water. The first landing crafts reached the shore, and Ilari troops emerged from them to race into the town. Clad all in steel, their helmets demonic, they looked more like beasts than men. Their swords swung, cutting into Qaelish shipwrights, fishermen, and fleeing children.

"Tianlong!" Lord Hashido shouted. "Tianlong, to me! I will ride upon you and command the battle from above."

The black dragon coiled above, wreathed in smoke, but did not dip lower. The beast roared but was not yet fighting, and he did not heed his emperor's command.

"Tialong, beast of Ilar!" Lord Hashido shouted. "Bear me upon your back, and we will spill the blood of Qaelin."

But the dragon would not obey. He rose higher, streaming above the battle like a banner, and his roar pierced the night sky.

Cursing, Hashido turned away and marched toward a landing craft. He spat into the water. "If even the dragon is cowardly, I will lead this battle on the front line, swinging my sword with men." The new emperor huffed. "There is more honor to that." He placed one foot into the landing craft, which was already filling with more troops, and turned to look at his son. "Stay here upon this deck, son. Stay here and watch men do their work. You're as worthless to me as the reptile who flies above."

Men turned winches, lowering the landing craft into the water. Hashido stood at the prow, leading the boat toward the town. A hundred other vessels rowed around the emperor, bearing soldiers. Soon Hashido emerged onto the coast, raised his sword, and fought with his men. The lord's katana swung into a fisherman and emerged bloody. Qaelish bodies littered the coast and floated in the water.

Jitomi watched from the deck of the *Daroma Tai*, eyes damp.

"Glorious," whispered Professor Atratus. He came back to stand at Jitomi's side. He licked his small, sharp teeth. "Glorious."

I must end this, Jitomi thought. His hands clutched the balustrade. *I must stop this carnage.*

He turned and ran across the deck, which was now empty of soldiers. He reached a mast, grabbed the ropes, and began to climb. Wind whipped him and arrows sailed around him. A cannonball, fired from the town walls, sailed alongside him with a shriek. It crashed down onto the *Daroma Tai*'s deck, punching a hole. The ship tilted, and water gushed on board. Jitomi clung onto the mast, gritted his teeth, and kept climbing even as the ship listed.

"Tianlong!" he shouted, climbing higher. "Tianlong, hear me!"

More arrows sailed from the walls. One slammed into Jitomi's armor and shattered, driving pain into him. He grimaced and climbed higher. Below upon the deck, sailors were scuttling about, and more water gushed. The ship was beginning to sink. Jitomi kept climbing, moving as fast as he could. His armor was too heavy. Despite the arrows still flying his way, he tugged off the steel plates and sent them crashing down onto the deck.

"Tianlong!" he cried. "I am Jitomi! I am a companion to Madori, daughter of Koyee, your old rider. If you remember Koyee, hear me, Tianlong!"

The black dragon seemed to hear him, but he still coiled far above, looking down at the battle, seeming torn. Smoke and flames puffed out from his great jaws. Jitomi scuttled higher up the tilting mast until he reached the basket at its crest. An Ilari sailor stood there, pierced with arrows, dead eyes staring. Grimacing, Jitomi climbed into the basket with the corpse and waved his hands.

"Tianlong, last dragon of Eloria! Hear me. For Koyee, hear me!"

The dragon finally descended. His red beard fluttered as a great banner, and his scales reflected the firelight from the burning town. His eyes narrowed, staring down at Jitomi, and a deep rage burned in them.

"You dare speak of Koyee," the dragon rumbled. "I bore her upon my back, and we fought sunlit demons together. She is a daughter of Qaelin, this very empire we burn, and the most noble soul I ever met." He roared and blasted out smoke. "Now Elorians fight Elorians. Now you betray Koyee's honor."

Jitomi had to shout to be heard over the roaring battle below. Hundreds of ships sailed all around, firing their guns, and thousands of soldiers were streaming along the town's docks. The mast kept tilting; soon it would crash down into the sea.

"Then let us stop this, Tianlong!" Jitomi cried. "Let us stop my father. He leads this host, and Atratus, a mage from the sunlight, whispers into his ear. We must stop them."

He reached up and touched the dragon's scales. Tianlong dipped lower in the sky. Jitomi climbed onto the dragon, straddled his scaly neck, and grabbed his horns. Tianlong rose higher just before the mast finally cracked and crashed down onto the sinking deck. They soared above the battle. The wind shrieked around them, and the cannons still blazed and swords still rang upon the coast.

"Warriors of Ilar!" Jitomi shouted. "Stop this madness! These are not our enemies. Hear me! I ride upon Tianlong, the last dragon of Eloria, and I call to end this violence. Our fellow Elorians are not our enemies!"

Some soldiers looked up at him. A handful hesitated, swords wavering. But most still fought, moving along the streets like metal serpents through a labyrinth. They kicked open doors, dragged out families, and sliced their throats. Upon the water, ships were still firing their cannons, tearing down the city walls. The shipyard burned and crumbled, reduced to mere crackling flotsam.

Jitomi pointed down to a city square. His father stood there, leading a hundred soldiers in tasseled armor. Facing them stood a dozen Qaelish soldiers—probably the last to survive in this town—along with a score of townsfolk armed with knives and clubs. As Jitomi watched, his father sliced a woman's belly open and laughed.

The black dragon flew above the square, and Jitomi cried down, "Father, stop this! Men of Ilar, hear me. This is not the way. The Radians are not our allies; we only serve the sunlight when we battle fellow dwellers of darkness. Sheathe your swords and—"

His father unslung his bow off his back, tugged back an arrow, and fired at Jitomi.

The dragon banked, and the arrow scraped across his scales, showering sparks.

"Tianlong!" cried Lord Hashido, standing in the courtyard below. "Cast off the boy and obey me. Fight for honor! For Ilar! Slay the Qaelish for the glory of the Red Flame."

Jitomi clung to the dragon's horns. The wind whistled around him. He spoke softly into Tianlong's ear. "And if we reach the north, and if we face Koyee, would you let him kill her too?"

The dragon roared.

His cry shook the city below, louder than thunder, so loud Jitomi covered his ears and clung to the dragon with only his legs. Smoke blasted from the beast, and his beard crackled with fire. The dragon swooped and roared as arrows pounded into him.

"You are a fool, Hashido!" the dragon bellowed. His jaws opened wide.

"Tianlong, no!" Jitomi cried.

But the dragon would or could not hear. His great jaws closed around Lord Hashido. His teeth punched through armor. The dragon tossed back his head, lifting the new emperor of Ilar. Hashido's sword swung, and the katana chipped the dragon's scales, and Tianlong bit deeper. Armor cracked. Teeth drove into flesh and blood leaked through steel.

Jitomi winced. Terror thrummed through him, and suddenly he was a boy again, a simple child in his father's fortress, marveling at the powerful lord, knowing he could never be as strong. Did some love for his father remain, even now?

"Spare him," Jitomi said. "Spare him, Tianlong. He's my father."

The dragon looked over his shoulder at Jitomi. Some of the rage left his eyes. Hashido was still alive, moaning in the dragon's jaws, his blood seeping. With a grunt and puff of smoke, the dragon tossed the new emperor down. Hashido clanked against the cobblestones.

Jitomi dismounted the dragon and leaned over his father. The battle died down around them. Ilari soldiers crowded near, gasping and muttering. The Qaelish lay dead or had fled the courtyard.

"Father, can you hear?" Jitomi said. The emperor was moaning, blood seeping from his armor. Jitomi lifted the man's visor, revealing an ashen face. "Father, I'll find you a healer. But you must call off the troops. We must end this war."

The wounded man, eyes sunken, spat. The glob of saliva hit Jitomi's cheek.

"Leave me, traitor." Blood leaked from Lord Hashido's mouth. "You killed me. You killed your own father. Curse you! Curse you forever. Your hands are covered with your father's blood. The spirits of the underworld will forever haunt you."

The emperor's breath died. He slumped to the ground.

For a long moment, Jitomi held his father's lifeless body. His throat and eyes burned. Around him, fire and smoke engulfed the city. Finally Jitomi raised his head to gaze at the warriors who surrounded him, steel demons with dripping blades.

"Emperor Hashido is dead!" Jitomi said. His knees shook, but he forced himself to take a deep breath and rise to his feet. "I am his only son. I hereby take command of this army. Back to our ships! We leave this place. We end this battle."

The ring of demonic faces drew nearer, the visors reflecting the firelight. Armor creaked. Swords rose higher. One of the soldiers stepped closer, a towering man, his lacquered armor painted crimson, his helmet horned. He held a massive katana the size of a pike, and his eyes blazed within his helmet's eyeholes. Instead of tassels like most breastplates sported, this man's armor was decorated with gilded finger bones—trophies from his enemies.

Jitomi recognized him. When he spoke the man's name, it tasted like ash. "General Naroma."

The man raised his demonic visor, revealing a face just as cruel. Tattoos covered it, black and red, and his eyes burned under tufted eyebrows. His white mustache twitched as he sneered.

"You are nothing but a lost pup." The general spat. "You were a shame to your father, whom you slew. You will pay for your crime, boy, And I shall sit upon the throne." He raised his sword and shouted for the army to hear. "I am Naroma, new Emperor of Ilar!"

Laughing, Naroma swung his massive katana toward Jitomi.

Jitomi leaped back, dodged the blade, and stumbled over his father's body. He fell down hard on the cobblestones, arms raised before him.

The surrounding soldiers burst into laughter.

"Behold the Pup of Hashido!" said General Naroma. His face turned red as he laughed. "Cowering like a woman. Should I kill him slowly and hear him beg?"

Covered in his father's blood, Jitomi rose to his feet. The soldiers all stared. The dragon hovered above, watching silently. The general laughed and raised his sword again.

"I am no woman, General Naroma," Jitomi said slowly. "Though I've met women whose strength and wisdom I would be proud to possess—strength and wisdom you lack. Strength is not measured by the power of the arm but that of the heart." He chose the general's blade and claimed it. "And a man who relies on steel to display his might is a fool."

With a sharp breath, Jitomi changed the blade, heating the steel so that it melted, red and hot as if fresh from the cauldron.

The liquid metal spilled across Naroma's hand, and the general roared. His gauntlet cracked, leaking blood and skin.

With his other hand, the general drew another sword—a curved blade engraved with a panther motif. The katana swung toward Jitomi before he had time to muster his magic again.

Heart thudding, Jitomi parried.

The blades clanged and locked.

"Yes, I think you will die slowly, wizard," said the general. "You will die squealing. Begging. Scre—"

Jitomi chose the man's helmet and heated it.

The man roared.

The steel helmet melted, the horns dripping, the visor flowing in rivulets down Naroma's face. Still the man swung his sword, and the blade crashed against Jitomi's armor, cracking the steel but not cutting the skin beneath.

Jitomi swung his own katana.

The blade sliced through the man's dripping helmet, scattering droplets of blood and liquid metal.

The man crashed down.

Jitomi stood in the bloody courtyard of a burning town, and he wanted to collapse, to tremble, to weep for his father. But now he would have to be strong—to show the strength his father had never seen in him.

"Hear me!" He raised his sword. "I am Jitomi Hashido, son of the fallen emperor. I take command of Ilar. You will obey me, or you will die like Naroma died—squealing like a rat." Those words tasted foul, but they were words these soldiers, proud killers of Ilar, would understand. "I am a sorcerer, and I am a warrior, and I am your emperor. Return to your ships, men of Ilar! A new enemy awaits us. We will shed blood for the glory of our empire. We will not waste our arrows and blades on weak Qaelish worms. We will face the sunlit demons, and we will crush them!"

The soldiers stared at him for a moment in silence. Hundreds more streamed into the square and watched.

Then they roared their approval. Their blades rose in a forest. They chanted for him. "Emperor Jitomi! Emperor Jitomi! For the glory of the Red Flame!"

Jitomi stared at them, and his head spun. He had spoken propaganda, and his belly felt ill. He had spoken like Professor Atratus.

He clenched his jaw. *I spoke the words I had to. When swords are thrust toward me, I will thrust back my own blade. When poisonous words rally hordes against my people, I will spill poison too.*

Leading his soldiers, he marched out of the courtyard, down the streets, and back toward the port. The warriors climbed back into the ships, but Jitomi—his own ship sunken—rode upon Tianlong high above the fleet.

As the Red Flame Armada sailed away from the ravaged town, Jitomi flew over ship by ship, scanning their decks for Atratus, but the mage was gone.

* * * * *

A hundred thousand strong, the Radian army rolled out of the dusk and into the darkness of Eloria.

Siege towers of wood and iron moving on great wheels. Scythed chariots full of archers. Mages, hooded and shadowed. Knights on armored stallions. An endless sea of archers and swordsmen bearing torches and roaring for the death of darkness. Catapults swung, their boulders hurtling. Cannons fired, blasting out smoke. Ballistae shot their iron arrows. The projectiles lit the night sky and slammed into Salai Castle upon the hill.

Koyee stood in the village of Oshy, her armor splashed with blood.

The village was empty around her—a ghost town of clay huts, barren squares, and guttering lanterns. She had ordered the people of Oshy evacuated last turn; they now sailed toward Pahmey in the east, seeking sanctuary from the sunlit onslaught. Her sunlit home, a cottage in Fairwool-by-Night, had burned. Koyee now stood by her nightside house, a humble clay hut, and watched the castle upon the hill crumble.

Its roof tiles rained down. Its walls cracked and collapsed. The bronze dragon upon its crest crashed onto the hillside. The cannons and catapults kept firing. As every projectile hit the castle, the hosts of Timandra cheered.

"Koyee!" rose a voice behind her. "Koyee, we must flee. Now."

She stared at the castle, eyes damp.

"For so many years, I built this place," she whispered. "For my father. Now it falls like a house of cards."

A hand grabbed her arm. "Koyee, we must leave now."

She turned around to see Xenxua, a young soldier with large indigo eyes. He was barely older than Madori. He panted. Scales were missing from his armor, and blood leaked through the holes.

"The last boats are loading." He tugged her. "We have only moments. Quick, Koyee."

She stared at him. Such a young, frightened face. She could barely hear the battle behind her anymore. Her ears still rang from the cannon fire, and everything felt so numb. Perhaps this was but a dream. Just a nightmare.

"Koyee!"

She turned back toward the castle and the dusk beyond. She could barely see anything but the Timandrian army now. The enemies covered every last stretch of land, and they were climbing what remained of the castle walls like insects upon a dying animal. Thousands of the troops, bearing torches, came marching toward the abandoned village. Their faces burned red in the firelight, and their eyes stared at her, hungry for her blood.

How can I flee? How can I abandon my post?

She clutched the locket that hung around her neck. She tightened her lips.

For Madori. I am a mother now. I must live.

"Koyee, please!" Xenxua begged, trying to tug her back.

She nodded. "We flee."

They turned and ran. Arrows sailed over their heads, and one glanced off Koyee's helmet. They raced between the huts as the enemy roared and laughed behind them. At the docks, the last few junk boats were sailing away along the Inaro. In the east, she could just make out the junks' forms; they had extinguished their lanterns. A single boat remained, a few Elorian soldiers within it.

"Come, Xenxua," she said. "Into the boat. Enter first. I—"

An arrow whistled. It slammed into the back of Xenxua's helmet, punched through the steel, and emerged from the middle of his forehead.

Koyee gave herself only an instant of frozen horror, of guilt, of crushing grief. Then she jumped into the boat as more arrows whistled around her.

They grabbed oars. They rowed off the pier. The current caught them, tugging them east, leaving the village and fallen castle behind. When Koyee turned and looked back west, she saw dozens of ships emerge from the dusk—towering, wooden, bearing the eclipse sigils, lumbering beasts that swayed upon the water. The fleet of sunlight.

She turned away and clutched her locket so tightly it cut her palm.

CHAPTER THIRTEEN
LIGHT OF THE MARSHES

All the marshlands danced with light as Neekeya daughter of Kee'an, *Latani* of Daenor, rowed through the water to meet her groom.

She stood in a *sheh'an*, the small reed boat of her people, holding an oar. She rowed slowly, solemnly. Lily pads coated the water, their flowers blooming, a carpet of green and lavender that parted around the prow. All around Neekeya, glass jars of fireflies hung from the mangroves, lanterns to guide her way through the mist. Upon fallen logs, twisting roots, and mossy boulders they stood—her people, the children of South Daenor. They wore garments of *seeken*, and their jewels shone upon them—gold and silver for the wealthy, humble clay beads for the poor. The firefly light danced upon their dusky skin, and warmth filled their brown eyes.

"*Latani*," one woman whispered. She tossed a lily into the boat.

"Daughter of the marshes," whispered an old man, bowing his head. He tossed a flower of his own.

"Neekeya," said a little girl, her voice awed, and tossed her own flower.

Neekeya smiled to all those she rowed by. Soon her reed boat was overflowing with the purple blossoms, their scent intoxicating.

She no longer wore her armor of steel scales nor her helmet, and no sword hung from her side. She wore a *leeri*—the traditional marriage garment of her people, a silvery tunic woven of gossamer, its fabric strewn with wildflowers. Around her shoulders hung a green *seeken* cloak woven of lichen. She wore the marshlands upon her body, for all Daenorian brides were to be of the land, in harmony with all around them.

Frogs trilled, the water gurgled, and birds sang—the music of the swamps. The people around her raised wooden flutes to their lips, and they added their music, the notes frail and beautiful to her, a song of both sadness and joy. Tears stung Neekeya's eyes, for she had never loved her home more, even on the eve of this home falling to the fire.

Perhaps all the marshlands will burn and dry up, she thought as she rowed. *And perhaps the enemy will cover this land and my life will fall in the fire. But here, this turn, I am a bride, and I am a proud* latani *of my homeland. This turn I am joyous.*

Dragonflies and fireflies danced around her and haloed over her head, forming a crown of light. A statue rose ahead from the water—the god Cetela, a man with the head of a crocodile, vines dangling between his teeth and lilies blooming around his legs. She rowed around the statue, and there—upon a platform of stone between two columns—she saw him. Prince Tam Solira. The man she was marrying.

The people had mended his old clothes of Arden, filling the tatters and holes with gossamer and *seeken,* forming a patchwork that did not look old and worn but new, healed—a garment of both the plains of his homeland and the swamps of his new home. A garland of ivy crowned his head, and a beard was thickening upon his cheeks, and Neekeya no longer saw the boy she had known. She saw a man, a prince, a soul with whom to forever walk the dark paths ahead.

The stone platform rose from the water, carved into the shape of birds and reptiles, the old engravings mossy and wet. The columns that framed it rose taller than men, and their capitals supported baskets of sweet-scented flowers. All around hung the mist, dragonflies flew, and egrets waded through the water. Neekeya docked her *sheh'an* at the platform and rose to stand beside Tam. She smiled tremulously, her fingers tingled, and her eyes dampened.

Perhaps next turn the fire will fall, but this turn I am in love, and I am happy.

Her father stood upon the stone too—once a lord of a pyramid and now King of the Marshes, of the free Southern Daenor. He wore a cloak inlaid with gold and silver disks, and a breastplate covered his chest, nine jewels upon it—symbols of the Nine Mothers, founders of Daenor. Kee'an looked older than Neekeya had ever seen him, and deep lines marred his face, and on the eve of war, worries too great to bear hung upon his shoulders. Yet joy too filled his eyes, and he spoke in a deep, clear voice.

"In the words of our Old Scrolls, whose wisdom Cetela taught to the Nine Mothers: In times of death, let there be life. In times of peril, let there be hope. In times of sadness, let there be joy." He reached out and joined hands with Tam and Neekeya. "There is no light without darkness, no courage without fear, but one force needs no counterpart. Love. Love can exist without ever having heard of hatred. Love lights the hearts of both the innocent and broken. And this turn, surrounded by the life and light of our marshlands, we celebrate the love of Neekeya and Tam, children of sunlight."

Neekeya reached into her pouch, then handed Tam a gift: a gilded crocodile tooth amulet. She hung it around his neck and couldn't help but grin as it rested against his chest, a grin she suspected looked silly and far too wide but one she couldn't curb.

He handed her a gift too: a ring of braided silver and gold.

"I worked it myself with magic," he said. "You can't see it, but inside the silver strand is a hair from my head, and inside the golden strand is a hair from yours."

She gasped. "Did you go plucking hairs off my head while I slept?"

He looked a little guilty, then nodded. "It's a custom of Arden. I hope you like it."

She let him slip the ring onto her finger. "I will never remove it," she vowed.

Lord Kee'an spoke some more, reading from the Old Scrolls, and Tam and Neekeya spoke too, exchanging vows they had written. Finally Kee'an opened a golden box, and many fireflies flew from it, beads of light swirling and rising through the mist. And thus Neekeya was wed. She pulled Tam toward her, and she kissed him, a deep kiss of love and fear, and though joy filled her, she wondered how many more kisses they would share and how long before the Radian fire burned her.

* * * * *

Tam stood in the chamber, stared into the mirror, and did not know who he saw.

He had turned eighteen this year, had come of age by the customs of his people. Were he back in Arden, the kingdom would have celebrated. King Camlin and Queen Linee would have tossed a great banquet in the palace gardens, and all the lords and ladies of Arden would have attended, come to see the twin princes—Tam and Omry—become men. There would be flying doves, pies of all kind, blooming flowers, and wandering jesters and pipers. Corgis would scuttle underfoot, and children would laugh, and wine would flow.

And you'd be there, Madori, he thought. His eyes stung. *You and I would sneak away from the festivities, hide ourselves in cloaks, and go down to the docks.*

He smiled to remember those times Madori and he would wander among the fishermen and sailors, compete to see who could spit farther into the water, pay copper coins for oysters, and talk about the exotic lands the ships must have come from. They would talk of boarding one of those ships, sailing to the distant islands of Sania or Orida, even far into the night, and finding lands of adventure.

"Our real adventure came out quite differently, didn't it, Madori?" he whispered.

He looked around him at the room. The chamber was small and stood high in the pyramid of Eetek. A bed lay in the corner, topped with tasseled cushions, and murals covered the walls, depicting egrets, crocodiles, dragonflies, and a hundred kinds of trees. Through the window, Tam could see the true swamps of Daenor, a land of mist and water. But instead of exploring and seeking adventures, he was waiting for war, for the fire to descend upon this wet land and sear it dry.

He looked back into the mirror. And he was different too. Where was the Tam he had been, had dreamed to be? He saw no prince of Arden. He saw no adventurer. He saw no mage. Instead, he saw a lost man, far from home, far from his family and friends. He missed them. He did not know if they still lived, if his home still existed, and the pain constricted his throat.

The door to the chamber opened, and in the mirror, he saw Neekeya enter the room.

He spun around and lost his breath.

"Hello," she whispered, then lowered her eyes and smiled shyly. "I'm ready."

Some of his fear washed away. No, he was not alone. He had Neekeya. He had a wife. He stepped toward her, feeling the pain melt.

"You look beautiful," he said.

She smiled demurely. She stood clad in a chemise woven of gossamer; the garment revealed more than it hid. Her smooth black hair hung down to her chin, scented of flowers, and her ring encircled her finger. Tam placed a finger under her chin, and she raised her head. Her eyes were huge, dark pools, and her full lips parted. He kissed those full lips, and she kissed him back, a deep kiss, their bodies pressed together, their arms around each other.

She took him into her bed; here was the bed of her childhood, now the bed of her womanhood. They would not stop kissing, even as they undressed, and they lay together, moving together, sometimes laughing, sometimes solemn, something staring into each other's eyes, sometimes closing their eyes and surrendering to the heat. They were as different as day from night—his skin was pale, hers dusky as the shadows, a prince from a palace and a warrior from a marshland pyramid. And he knew that, no matter what the next turn might bring, he loved her fully, and with her he was complete.

They made love for what seemed like hours, then lay in each other's arms, gazing up at the mural of birds upon the ceiling. She nestled close, her arm and leg slung across him, and playfully bit his chin, then grinned up at him. He kissed her nose.

"My husband," she whispered.

"My wife," he whispered back. "My *latani.*"

He closed his eyes, and though she was warm against him, and the soft sunlight fell through the window and birds sang outside, he was afraid, and he was back on that road in Mageria, the Radians swinging their swords and his friends dying around him.

CHAPTER FOURTEEN
THE VIEW IN THE LOCKET

"Slowly tilt to the left." Old Master Lan Tao demonstrated, swaying his frail body. "Slowly . . . slowly . . . let your right foot rise until just your toes touch the earth. Focus your awareness on the movement, on how your muscles work, on your breath, on—"

"I can't focus when you talk so much!" Madori wobbled, nearly fell, and glared at the old teacher.

He sighed. "In battle, when arrows fly and swords swing, will you tell your enemy that you cannot focus while they try to kill you? You must be able to focus even as they attack; you should be able to handle words from an old man's mouth. Now—tilt! Slowly . . . to the left . . . be aware of every breath . . ."

She grumbled but she obeyed. As he had taught her, she cleared her mind of thought, focusing all her awareness on the movement of her body as she tilted to the left—the muscles stretching, the weight shifting, her strands of hair falling free from behind her ears, the feel of the ground beneath her bare feet, and the air entering and leaving her lungs. When they swayed to the right, she kept breathing deeply, letting every thought that entered her mind flow away.

For long moons now, she had been training with Master Lan Tao, and still he did not allowed her to swing her sword. Sometimes, he had her sit still all turn, focusing her awareness on each part of her body in turn—her toes for what seemed like hours, then finally her feet, then her legs, then her hips, gradually moving up to her head as the turn ended. Other turns, he had her focus her awareness on sounds she heard: the wind in the canyons of the Desolation, the creaks of rocks, the snorts of her nightwolf, the scuttling of animals and bats, and a thousand other sounds she had never imagined could exist in this wilderness. Other turns Lan Tao insisted that she simply breathed, monitoring her mind for thoughts: memories, planning, fears, or sometimes just random daydreams . . . allowing all thoughts to flow away, to disperse like clouds, letting her awareness return to her breath again and again, a rebirth every time she inhaled.

When they were finally done, Madori rubbed her shoulders. She asked the same question she asked every turn. "Master Lan Tao, when will you teach me how to fight?"

And he gave her the same answer he always did. "I already am, my student. With every breath."

"But I want to learn with the sword!" she countered as always.

He would only shake his head. "First you must learn to fight with your awareness, with your soul, with your body. Once you have mastered Yin Shi, then, child, you may lift your sword and let the blade be a part of you."

Madori sighed. She had been here for three moons now, and she had spent all that time training in Yin Shi. She couldn't wait much longer for battle. Whenever she gazed into her locket, she saw new Elorian forces mustering at the dusk. One time, Koyee had stood upon the roof of Salai Castle, held the locket up, and let Madori see the tips of distant enemy towers—siege engines prepared for war. Any turn now, Madori knew, the invasion of Eloria would begin.

"And I'll be stuck here," she muttered. "Without even a sword."

With their training done for the turn, Master Lan Tao prepared their usual dinner—a bland paste of mushed mushrooms sprinkled with dried eel flakes. As always, the old man sat perched on a hilltop, staring into the distance as he chewed slowly, mouthful after mouthful. Madori had stared at that landscape so many times—she had memorized every nook and cranny in the Desolation, and she could have drawn from memory the jagged boulders, snaking canyons, the cracks in the craters, and the scree upon the hillsides. This turn, instead of eating with her master, she simply grabbed her bowl of food, stomped toward the cave where she slept, and entered the shadows. Barely any moonlight filled this place, which suited Madori. She sat cross legged, took a spoonful of food, and grimaced at the taste. Forcing herself to swallow, she pulled her locket from her shirt.

"I miss you, Mother," she whispered. A lump filled her throat, and it was not from the stew. "I'm so worried. I'm so scared for you and Father and everyone else."

She peeked outside, waiting for the moon to reach its zenith, the time she and Koyee had agreed to open their lockets in tandem. Her bowl of stew was empty and her eyes were drooping when the time came. With a deep breath, she opened her locket, expecting to see her mother smile at her.

Madori gasped.

She dropped the locket.

Her eyes burned.

By the stars . . .

Trembling, she lifted the locket again and stared into it. She grimaced. Instead of Koyee's smiling face, she saw fire burning. Magerian troops marching. Enemy warships in the water. The land rose and fell, and the vision spun madly, sometimes vanishing, sometimes appearing at odd angles. It took a moment for Madori to understand; her mother was running, the locket bouncing and spinning upon her chest, sometimes clattering shut, sometimes knocked open.

"The invasion is here," Madori whispered. She gripped the locket. Her voice rose to a shout. "Mother! Mother!"

But the locket could convey no sound. Madori watched, clutching it so tightly it nearly snapped. Koyee's locket swayed madly, and for a moment Madori saw only steaks of color and light. When the image settled, she realized that Koyee had leaped into a boat and had begun to sail downriver. Arrows flew overhead. When the locket spun west, Madori caught a glimpse of Salai Castle. It crumbled before her eyes, its roofs collapsing, its walls cracking. Beyond the castle spread an army of thousands, its Radian banners held high.

"Mother!" Madori cried again.

The locket spun—Koyee turning back eastward. Several other Qaelish soldiers sat in the boat with Koyee, faces grim and bleeding, their armor cracked. One soldier was shouting something. Madori could read his lips: *Oar faster! Retreat!*

"Mother, can you hear me?" Madori shouted into the locket. "Mother, are you all right? Mother!"

A voice rose from the cave's entrance. "Calm yourself, Madori. Breathe. Like I taught you."

She spun toward the cave entrance, her eyes damp, her chest heaving. "Master Lan Tao! Timandra invades! Armies flow into the night and—"

"Let your thoughts leave you," he said. "Calm yourself. Breathe. In . . . slowly . . . feel the breath—"

"This is no time for a lesson!" Madori shouted. She shoved herself past him. "Where is my sword? War! I have no time for your Yin Shi breathing now. War is h—"

It was his turn to interrupt. "This is *precisely* the time for breathing. When the sky is falling, that is when we must remain most calm. Breathe. Slowly." He inhaled deeply as if to demonstrate. "Hold the breath . . . and release." When she opened her mouth to object, he silenced her with a glare. "Do it."

Her insides trembled, and her mind was a storm, but she forced herself to obey. She took a deep, slow breath, yet still her mind raged. Her mother was in danger! The enemy attacked! Perhaps her mother was dead already. She needed to look into the locket again, she—

"Focus all your awareness on your breath," said Lan Tao, voice soothing. "Let all your thoughts leave you."

She wanted to object. How could he force her to train now?

This is not training, she realized. *This is mastery of Yin Shi in a true storm.*

She let all thoughts flow away. She exhaled. She inhaled again. Her mind cleared, becoming like a still pond. After a few more breaths, she looked back into her locket.

It had fallen dark.

Madori looked back up at her master. "My mother is fleeing down the Inaro River. She will be heading to the great city of Pahmey where more soldiers await. I must join her, Master. I must fight at her side."

Suddenly Master Lan Tao seemed very old. He had always seemed old to her but vigorous too; now he truly showed his age, his wrinkles deep, his eyes sad.

"Your training is incomplete," he said, and she heard the pain in his voice.

"Perhaps we're never ready for a storm," Madori said. "But I've learned so much. I cannot linger here, safe while my mother flees and fights, while our people need me. Return my sword, Master. Please. I will wield that blade proudly—as my grandfather did, as my mother did. I will make you proud, Master, and I will not forget all that you taught me."

He lowered his head. For a moment his shoulders stooped. But then he straightened, raised his chin, and turned to walk down the hillside.

Madori bounded outside of the cave and ran after him. "Master Lan Tao! Will you let me leave? Will you return my sword?"

He kept walking, not turning back toward her. Madori ran behind him, panting. Grayhem raced up toward her and loped at her side.

The old master walked toward a crater full of still, silver water that reflected the moonlight. Kneeling, he reached into the water and pulled out Sheytusung, the blade of legend. The moonlight reflected against it. The Yin Shi master turned back toward Madori and held out the katana.

"It has been blessed with moonlight and with water," he said. "And now it truly passes to other hands, to a student of Yin Shi. It no longer shall be named Sheytusung, for that was its name in other hands, a name that means the light of the river, a name of brightness and swiftness. Now I name it *Min Tey*, the glow of the water, a name of calm and stillness."

Madori took the blade reverently, and it felt warm in her hand, and the light and water still clung to it.

I will make you proud, Grandfather, Mother, Master, she thought. She hung the sword across her back and climbed onto Grayhem. *I will remember all that I learned.*

She rode out of the Desolation, her sword upon her back and her locket hanging around her neck. She stared into the southern, dark emptiness, and she traveled by the starlight, heading to Pahmey, heading to war.

CHAPTER FIFTEEN
THE RAVEN AND THE BEAR

The limestone bear rose from the forest, craggy and frosted, a sentinel taller than any tree. Snow gathered around its feet, and eras of wind and hail had beaten its form. Perhaps once every strand of its fur had been lovingly carved, every fang and claw detailed, but now the statue looked like molten rock, barely more than abstract. Torin had to crane his neck all the way back to see its roaring face high above; the statue must have loomed three hundred feet tall.

"A statue of Gashdov," Torin said. His horse nickered beneath him, breath frosting. "The fabled Guardian Bear of Verilon, a god of the north. They say the true Gashdov isn't much smaller than this statue, a beast to dwarf all others."

Cam bit his lip, staring up from his own horse. "This marks the border between Arden and Verilon. The city of Orewood is near."

Behind Torin and Cam rode their retinue—five knights and thirty men-at-arms, all clad in steel plates, the ravens of Arden upon their shields. Their banners fluttered in the cold wind, and snow coated their woolen cloaks. Torin himself wore a woolen tunic under his armor, and a thick black cloak hung around his shoulders, yet he couldn't stop shivering, and his teeth chattered. Verilon seemed even colder than the darkness of Eloria, or perhaps he was simply older, thinner, still wounded and weary. Whatever the case, a cough kept rising in his throat, and he couldn't wait to finally sit by a roaring fire, a mug of mulled wine in his hands.

Torin sighed. *Last war, when I was half as old, I didn't care about the cold, and I didn't long for a hearth or wine.* He was turning forty this winter, and with every year, he cared less for swords and more for mugs, less for saddles and more for armchairs.

They kept riding north, leaving the bear statue behind. The forest had changed over the past few leagues. Few of the maples, birches, and oaks of Arden grew here. Here was a forest of towering pines like steeples. Wolves ran between the evergreens and hawks glided above, and several times the riders saw true bears; the beasts fed from icy streams, catching salmon in their jaws. The snow kept falling, and with every gust of wind, clumps of snow fell from the trees with *thumps*.

Torin kept looking around for Verilish soldiers, guardians of the border, but saw none. Here was a vast land, as large as Arden and Mageria combined, covered with ice and boulders and thick woods. Perhaps Verilon depended more on its harsh hinterlands for defense than any wall or guard along its borders.

They were weary, but they did not wish to set camp here in the wilderness of a foreign land. They rode on, breath frosting, lips blue, and the snow would not stop falling. They ate as they rode, and Torin found himself nodding off in the saddle, despite the pain in his limbs and the blisters growing on his thighs.

Dreams of half-wakefulness filled his mind. He was young again in these visions, traveling into the night for the first time, Bailey at his side. When wolves stared between the pines, eyes glowing, he saw Koyee's eyes—large and lavender, peering from behind a boulder near the village of Oshy, a turn almost two decades ago . . . the first time he had seen her. And he saw Madori's eyes, just as large and purple. Those eyes stared at him, blinking, confused, after she had first emerged from the womb. They stared at him with love, a girl still innocent about the horrors in the world. They stared at him with anger, a rebellious youth, as he took her to Teel University in the vipers' nest.

Will I see their eyes again? he wondered. A lump filled his throat. He missed his family so badly his chest ached and his belly felt full of snow.

And as always, he thought of those he had lost: of his dear friend Hem, that lumbering giant of a boy; of his parents, fallen to the plague; of Bailey, the dearest friend he'd ever had, the twin light of his heart. No matter how far he traveled from home, those he left behind still filled him with memories and pain.

They had ridden for several more hours when they saw the walls rise ahead.

"The city of Orewood," Torin said, and a chill ran through him. "Looks more like a mausoleum for giants."

The great wall stretched across the snowy forest, rising a hundred feet tall. Built of rugged, dark gray bricks, the wall reminded Torin of many tombstones cobbled together. Icicles hung from the battlements, and snow topped the merlons. As the Ardish convoy rode closer, Torin saw the banners of Verilon rising from guard towers; they displayed a brown bear upon a green field. Soldiers stood upon the walls. Their beards were brown and bushy, and they wore crude, iron breastplates over fur, and more pelts hung around their shoulders and peeked from under their helmets. Their bows were long and their spears longer, and their eyes were dark.

Torin and Cam rode closer, leading their convoy toward a gatehouse. Two round towers rose here, each large enough to be a fortress in its own right. Across a ravine rose a stone archway, its doors hidden behind a raised drawbridge. A dozen Verilish soldiers stood upon the gatehouse battlements, staring down with nocked arrows in their bows.

The Ardish company halted across the chasm. The snow rose a foot deep, hiding their horse's hooves. Their banners unfurled once in the wind, revealing the ravens of Arden, then wilted. Torin glanced at his companions, then rode several feet forward, bringing himself to the edge of the ravine. He hefted his raven shield, coned a gloved hand around his mouth, and cried up to the guards.

"Men of Verilon! I am Sir Torin Greenmoat of Arden. With me rides King Camlin, lord of our realm. Three knights and thirty men-at-arms are with us. We've ridden for many turns and seek your hospitality."

The guards upon the gatehouse battlements seemed to stare at one another; it was hard to see from so far below, especially with the snow in the wind.

"We've come as allies of Verilon!" Torin cried. "As war rages across Mythimna, and as the Radian Empire clashes against Verilon along the Icenflow, we offer our friendship. Will you let us enter and speak with your king?"

For long moments nothing happened. No voice from above answered. But no arrows fell either; Torin took that as a good sign.

Finally, after what seemed like an eternity, metal chains creaked, and the drawbridge began to descend. When it clanked down across the gorge, it revealed a rising portcullis and swinging, iron-banded doors.

Torin turned his head and looked at his companions. They stared back. Cam nodded and the companions rode onto the drawbridge, leaving the forest and entering the city of Orewood.

Torin entered first. He found himself in a cobbled courtyard surrounded by a hundred archers and swordsmen. More archers stood in towers ahead, pointing their arrows down at him. Beyond the courtyard he glimpsed many log houses, the stone domes of temples, and several distant fortresses.

A Verilish man wobbled forth, his cast iron breastplate barely able to contain his massive gut. His beard was almost as large, hanging down to his belt, and his cheeks were ruddy. He must have stood seven feet tall, and a war hammer—its head was large as a boot—hung across his back. Beneath his armor, he wore fur pelts, and he carried a pewter tankard overflowing with frothy ale.

"Men of Arden!" he boomed. "I am Hogash, Captain of the Southern Gates. We will welcome you into our halls, where you will feast upon bloody meat and drink frothy ale, but first you will disarm yourselves. No swords, no arrows, no blades. Leave all your weapons at the gates, and leave your horses; they will be tended to. And if you try to slip any weapons past us, we'll flay you alive and feed your living, writhing remains to the bears." He slapped his belly and burst out with laughter, as if he had just told the world's funniest joke.

Cam glanced at Torin, then back at his men and nodded. The Ardishmen dismounted and began to unhook their weapons and hand them over to the Verilish guards: longswords, daggers, bows, quivers of arrows, and lances. Cam watched the weapons and horses being escorted away, looking like a starving man who had just seen a dog snatch away his meal.

"When I was a shepherd, I never thought I'd miss having a sword," the king muttered to Torin. "Now I feel naked without one."

The corpulent captain turned and waddled toward a street, and the Ardish company followed. As they walked, Torin looked around, soaking in the sights of Orewood, capital of Verilon.

Log houses lined the streets, their sloping roofs coated with snow, and icicles hung from their eaves. Chimneys pumped out smoke, and through open window shutters, Torin glimpsed bear rugs and crackling hearths. The city folk wore fur and leather, and their cheeks were red. Men sported proud beards and women hid their hair under shawls. They were a heavyset people, wide of bodies and wide of faces, but their eyes seemed kind to Torin, their ways simple and old. The sounds of the city rose in a symphony: chickens clucking in backyards and pecking for seeds in the snow, cats mewling upon roofs, hammers ringing in smithies, men singing drunkenly in taverns over mugs of ale, and stocky housewives beating the dust out of rugs. Like its music, the city's aroma was intoxicating; Torin smelled rich stews cooking in homes, tangy sausages hanging in butcher shop windows, oiled iron and soft fur pelts, and finally the stench of gutters flowing with the contents of emptied chamber pots.

As they kept walking, heading deeper into the city, stone buildings began to rise among the log homes. Several buildings seemed to be temples, their roofs topped with bronzed domes, and statues of bears stood outside their gates. Others buildings were manors for the city's wealthy; several sported silver domes, and one's dome was even gilded. Finally, Torin saw several fortresses, and many soldiers stood outside them, massive men with barrel chests, bushy beards, and war hammers. Each warrior of Verilon seemed twice the size of an Ardish or Magerian soldier.

After walking for an hour or two, Torin saw the fabled Geroshahall—palace of Verilon.

"By Idar's swollen feet," he muttered.

Geroshahall was massive, easily five times the size of Arden's royal palace back at Kingswall. It was carved of the same rough, gray bricks as the rest of the city, and icicles hung from its turrets and battlements. Soldiers stood upon its encircling wall, and between them rose the bear banners. Beyond the wall rose a dozen wide, circular towers topped with gold, bronze, silver, and iron domes. While Arden's palace was elegant, pale, and delicate, here was a powerful, looming structure, more a fortress than a palace. While guards in Arden wore polished steel and golden cloaks, here the guards looked as scruffy as woodsmen, their cast iron breastplates as crude as peasants' frying pans, their furs coated with snow and mud, their beards untamed.

Arden's palace is a fine maiden, perfumed and fair, Torin reflected. *Verilon's palace is the gruff, burly enforcer who tosses drunkards out of the tavern.*

Hogash, Captain of the Southern Gates, spoke to the guards of Geroshahall. The surly men gave the Ardish companions stern looks, muttered under their breath, and hefted their hammers. Finally, cursing and spitting, they shoved open Geroshahall's iron-banded doors.

Hogash drank deeply from his stein, wiped suds off his mustache, and lumbered into the hall. Torin, Cam, and their retinue followed, entering the heart of Verilon.

They found themselves in a massive hall—the largest indoor structure Torin had ever seen. Six rows of columns, each as wide as a guard tower, supported a ceiling so distant it all but vanished into shadows. The floor was rough and pitted, and a dozen great fireplaces roared in the walls, filling the chamber with heat, light, and smoke.

Men and women feasted at pine trestle tables. Upon iron platters lay steaming venison, smoked sausages, and roasted geese. Ale flowed from tankards. Clad in fur and metal, the diners ate with only large knives for cutlery, carving up meat and stuffing it greedily into their mouths. Ale beaded upon beards, and grease dripped down iron breastplates. Belches, laughter, and crude songs wafted through the air like the meaty scents. Dogs scurried underfoot, feasting upon bones and scraps the diners tossed their way.

"By Idar," Cam whispered to Torin, his eyes wide with awe. "This is what we need back in Arden. Not fancy lords nibbling on crumpets with forks thinner than my pinky finger."

Torin grimaced. "Right now, Serin's troops are feasting in Arden's palace. I'd take all the dessert forks in the world over a hall full of Radians."

As they walked closer to the trestle tables, the diners noticed them and raised their tankards in welcome, spilling droplets of the amber ale. At the head of the table rose a chair larger than the others; Torin assumed that it served as Verilon's throne. The massive, wooden seat was carved into the shape of an upright bear complete with iron claws that sprouted from the armrests. A man sat here, looking much like a bear himself. His chest was wide as a wagon, and his belly seemed large enough to digest a entire roast pig. Ale and grease filled his beard, and his cheeks were flushed red. He stared at the Ardishmen from under bushy eyebrows. Above his furs, he wore a dark breastplate engraved with the emblem of a rearing bear. Upon his head perched a crown—not a crown of gold as southern kings wore but a heavy, iron construction shaped as bear claws thrusting upwards.

Hogash shouted out the introduction, "Here sits Ashmog, son of Fargosh, King of Verilon!"

The king belched, wiped suds off his mouth, and rose to his feet with the sound of clanking armor and creaking wood.

"Look at that one!" the king boomed, pointing a turkey leg at Cam. "I've eaten meals larger than him. And that one!" He thrust the turkey leg toward Torin. "His beard is shorter than the hairs on my backside."

The king roared with laughter, spraying out bits of half-chewed meat. The hall roared with him, and men banged tankards against the tabletop in approval.

Hogash gestured at the Ardish companions. "My king! Here before you stands Camlin, King of Arden. And with him thirty ravens of his flock."

King Ashmog snorted. "Former king perhaps. I hear the Radians' backsides are warming his throne now." The king lumbered around the table and across the hall, his feet pounding against the stone floor. Two war hammers hung across his back, their heads as large as loaves of bread. He came to stand before the Ardish company, towering above them; Torin's head barely reached the man's chin, while Cam stood shorter than his shoulders.

"Your Highness." Cam bowed his head. "I've come here to—"

Ashmog thrust out a massive hand—it looked more like a paw—and grabbed Cam's chin, forcing his head up. "Look me in the eyes! No man who bows can call himself a king." Ashmog snorted and spat sideways. "Is that why you lost your throne, runt? Did you bow as the Radians invaded rather than fight?" He raised his arms and roared for all the hall to hear. "But King Ashmog fights! Ashmog will lead the Motherland to victory!" Across the hall, his men roared and banged the tabletops. Ashmog spun in circles, arms raised, bellowing. "The Radian scum think they can cross the Icenflow, that they can invade our forests, that their magic makes them strong. But Verilon is stronger! We crushed their ships on the Icenflow, and we will drive them out of our forests." He spun back toward Cam, leaned down, and narrowed his eyes. "Here you see true might, little king, true warriors who will crush the enemy like a bear crushes a deer."

Cam's cheeks reddened. He stared up at the larger man. "We in Arden have been fighting this war every turn. I've led many raids against the Radian supply lines. I fought Serin's forces upon the open fields. I thrust my sword into Lord Gehena. I—"

"You," said Ashmog, "are now here, seeking sanctuary." He jabbed Cam's chest with his turkey leg. "If the Ardish were so mighty, your kingdom would still stand." He stuffed the turkey leg into his mouth and sucked up all the meat at once, leaving a clean bone. He spoke as he chewed. "Why are you here, ravens? Have you come to seek safety from the cold of winter and the Radian fire?"

"We've come to forge an alliance," said Cam. "Ten thousand Ardish troops camp along the border. South of them, at Kingswall, a Radian army of fifty thousand prepares to march north . . . and they will come here. They will lay siege to Orewood, and their machines of war will smash your walls and towers as they did at Kingswall. Let us aid you, King Ashmog. Let my army join yours, and together we will defend these walls."

Ashmog snorted and swallowed his meat. He grabbed a tankard of ale and drank deeply. "So I was right. You've come here for safety. You fear to face the Radians in the field, and you seek to shelter your forces behind my walls." He snorted. "You think that Serin, that lump of bear dung, poses a threat to me? Verilon is stronger than he can imagine. If Serin marches here, we don't need a few Ardish birds to help us. Our gates can withstand any catapult or battering ram."

Torin spoke for the first time. He stepped closer to the king and met the large man's gaze. "But can your gates withstand magic?

Have you ever faced mages in battle? I have." Torin shuddered at the
memories. "I saw mages spew out dark smoke, crumbling the walls of
Sinyong, a great port city in the night. I saw mages smash down the
walls of my own city in Arden. I saw their magic crush steel armor as
if it were tin, tug bones out of flesh, and melt stone." He clenched his
fists at his sides. "You not only face a great horde of soldiers. You
face mages, King Ashmog, and to defeat them, you need all the help
you can get. In this hour, all free folk of Moth must fight together
against the rising Radian Empire."

The king's brown eyes narrowed, becoming sly slits beneath his
bushy eyebrows. He leaned down, scrutinizing Torin. Slowly his
cheeks reddened and his teeth clenched. He spun around, staring at
Captain Hogash.

"Hogash! Who is this man? I've heard tales of men with
mismatches eyes, one green like Timandra, the other dark as the
night."

The Captain of the Gates raised his chin. "He identified himself
as Sir Torin Greenmoat. He—"

"Torin Greenmoat!" roared Ashmog. The king tossed back his
head and raised his hands, spilling ale from his tankard. His howl
seemed to shake the hall. "Torin Greenmoat, son of Teramin! Here is
the son of Fargosh's Bane!" The king slammed his fist against a table,
shattering it. Iron plates and pewter mugs crashed onto the floor. He
spun back toward Torin, face red, saliva spraying. "Your father was a
murderer, a coward, a sneaky beast who stabbed my own father in
the back."

Torin felt the blood drain from his cheeks. He cleared his
throat. "My father fought the previous king of Verilon. It's true. But
he never killed him. He took the war hammer onto his shield, and—"

Ashmog roared and tossed his tankard across the hall. "Our
last king lived to an old age and died with only daughters. He was my
uncle. He raised me as a son—after your father slew mine in the
forest. Or do your people not tell that tale?"

Torin gulped, remembering his old lessons of heraldry. Of
course! Ashmog was not the son of Verilon's previous king; his
father, Fargosh, had been only a prince, had fallen in the great war
many years ago.

"Perhaps our fathers met in battle," Torin said, "but Teramin Greenmoat would never stab a man in the back. He—"

Ashmog swept his hand across another table. Plates flew and slammed into Torin.

"How dare you enter my hall!" Ashmog bellowed. "You, the son of the cursed Demon Raven." He pointed a finger at Torin; it trembled with rage. "You, the spawn of Verilon's greatest enemy. I would sooner name Serin my heir than allow this worm into my hall. Hogash! Men of Verilon! Seize him! Grab Torin Greenmoat, and we will feed him to the great bear!"

Cam began to shout, as did the Ardish knights behind him. Torin spun from side to side, trying to hold back the soldiers rushing toward him.

"King Ashmog, listen to me!" Torin shouted. "We cannot fight each other anymore. We—"

Several Verilish guards jumped onto him, fists raining down. Chains clasped around Torin's wrists, a sack was thrust over his head, and for the second time since this war began, all the world went dark around him.

Daniel Arenson

CHAPTER SIXTEEN
BLOOD ON THE MOUNTAIN

Neekeya crouched behind the boulders, staring down the mountainside at the winding path. She waited. She kept her hand on her bow. Her heart thrashed and her jaw clenched, but she would not turn away.

The mountains of Teekat spread around her. Above soared their peaks, capped with snow, but all around Neekeya the limestone was gray, bare, and craggy. Boulders rose like great, scattered crocodile teeth, and mist floated between them. Far below in the west, when she turned her head, she could see the distant haze of Daenor's marshlands. But this turn she focused on the east, for Teekat Mountains—a great range that soared thousands of feet high—separated the marshes from the plains of Mageria. And this turn, from the east, the wrath of that cruel empire would overflow.

Other soldiers of Daenor spread across the mountain, hidden behind boulders and in nooks. They wore mottled cloaks of gray and white, blending into the mountains. Beneath those cloaks they wore scale armor, and under their hoods hid toothed, reptilian helmets. Gloved hands clutched bows and spears, and swords hung from belts. The mountain pass stretched between them—a rough trail that crawled up the slope, many miles long. The ancient men of the mountain had carved it ten thousand years ago; along with smashed pottery in caves and a few runes etched into the boulders, this path was all that remained of that ancient civilization.

And this turn blood will wash this path, Neekeya thought. *This turn it will become a red river.*

She looked to her left. A few feet lower on the slope, Tam crouched behind another boulder. He too wore a mottled gray cloak, looking much like a boulder himself, and he too held a bow. Only the raven drawn onto his shield separated him from the three thousand Daenorians who waited here.

388

"They will be tired after their climb," Neekeya whispered to him. "They will have climbed Teekat Mountains for miles before reaching this place. We are strong, well-rested, quick, and we know these mountains. The enemy will fall."

She wondered if she was trying to comfort him or herself. She thought it was more of the latter. Now she wished her father had come to this fight. The Lord of Eetek had wanted to accompany her and the troops, yet Neekeya had insisted he stay at their pyramid.

"Danger crawls from every direction," she had told him in his hall, standing under an archway in the pyramid, gazing down at the marshlands. "The North Daenorians will not forgive the capture of their prince; they will march against us. In the south, the kingdom of Eseer has raised the Radian banners; they sail against us and land upon our coast." She had hugged the tall Lord Kee'an. "Stay here, Father. Stay here and lead. I will return. I promise."

She had kissed him then—perhaps for the last time—and come here with Tam. Come to kill, perhaps to die. To war. And now she missed her father, and she wondered if she'd ever embrace the old warrior again.

Not even two years ago, she thought, *I was but an innocent who believed in magical rings and enchanted fairy tales.* She tightened her lips for fear of them trembling. *Now I will spill the blood of my enemies.*

She thought back to Teel University. She remembered how Lari Serin had tormented her, and Neekeya wondered if Lari was fighting in this war, and if their paths would cross again—perhaps even here upon this mountain.

Crouching behind his boulder, Tam looked up toward her. He opened his mouth to speak, then shut it and tensed.

Neekeya sucked in her breath. Across the mountains, the other Daenorian soldiers nocked arrows.

She could not see the enemy yet, but she heard their thunder. Thudding feet. Clanking armor. A drumbeat. Above all other noises, trumpeting rose—not the trumpets of brass instruments, she thought, but an organic sound, enraged.

Neekeya sneered. "The Radians."

She stared east down the coiling path. She could trace it for about a mile; further down, the trail vanished behind a stony crest.

The sounds rose from behind that peak of stone, echoing across the mountains. A chant began, deep and rumbling, a song about Emperor Serin burning the heathens. And still that trumpeting rose, shrill, sending chills down Neekeya's spine.

Be strong, Neekeya, she thought to herself, holding her nocked arrow steady. *Be strong and you will survive this turn.*

Across the Daenorian outposts, the hidden soldiers were silent. Not a scale of armor chinked. They were only three thousand—it was all the men the marshlands of Eetek could spare—and toward them marched the horde of an empire.

A gust of wind blew, scented of oil and metal, and billowed Neekeya's cloak. Stones tumbled below, and then she saw them.

Neekeya lost her breath.

Three massive beasts walked at the Radian vanguard. They were several times the size of horses, gray and wrinkled. Their ears were wide, and their noses were as long as pythons.

"Elephants," Neekeya whispered.

Their tusks were gilded, and when they tossed back their trunks and cried out, she recognized the trumpeting she had heard. Howdahs rose upon the elephants' backs—towers of wood and leather—and archers stood within, clad in tiger pelts. The soldiers sported braided red beards strewn with beads, and tattoos covered their bare chests.

Nayan warriors, Neekeya realized—dwellers of the rainforest south of Mageria. Now they bore the Radian banners, joined to Serin's cause.

Across the mountain, the Daenorians remained hidden, crouched behind boulders, arrows ready. Neekeya raised her hand, urging the soldiers to wait. She looked back toward the path.

The elephants came climbing higher. At first Neekeya had seen only three, but now many more emerged to climb up the path; she counted a full twenty. Behind them marched lines of Nayan footmen, spears across their backs. Tiger skins hung from them as cloaks, the heads still attached and serving as hoods. Live tigers walked among them too, chained and growling. Rather than fly the flags of Naya, these troops raised the Radian eclipse banners.

Neeeya held her hand raised, palm open. "Wait," she mouthed. "Wait."

The enemy kept marching up the path. Soon the elephants at the vanguard were only five hundred yards away. As more Nayan troops emerged from behind the lower peak, they revealed other soldiers. Magerians marched here too, wearing the black armor of their kingdom, but their breastplates no longer sported the buffalo—sigil of their old dynasty—but the eclipse of Lord Serin. While the Nayans walked in a mass, their red beards and hair wild, the Magerian troops marched in perfect precision, automatons of metal.

The Nayans are wildfire, Neekea thought, *and the Magerians are cold steel. But both raise the Radian banners, and both will die as one. Their blood will flow the same.*

She kept her hand raised.

Wait. Wait . . .

The enemy kept snaking up the path. Neekeya saw thousands of them. Soon the vanguard was only three hundred yards away, then two, then close enough that Neekeya could stare into the elephants' eyes.

She growled.

She formed her hand into a fist.

"Now!" she shouted.

She leaped to her feet and shoved the boulder she hid behind. Around her, dozens of other Daenorians did the same.

The boulders creaked.

The elephants trumpeted and men shouted below.

The boulders tilted over and rolled down the mountain pass.

Neekeya crouched and stared down, sneering as the boulders slammed into the enemy host.

Elephants tumbled, their legs shattered. Some boulders rolled between the great beasts to slam into the lines of infantry. Men fell, bones snapping. Some troops leaped aside, slamming into their brethren, sending men cascading down the mountainside.

"Arrows!" Neekeya shouted.

Heart pounding against her ribs, she loosed her arrow. The projectile sailed toward a howdah and slammed into a Nayan archer within. The man clutched his chest, crashed out of the howdah, and fell off the elephant. The beast, wounded and enraged, stepped on the man in its confusion, crushing him. More Daenorian arrows sailed downward and slammed into the enemy. The arrowheads were smeared with the venom of the marshlands' golden frogs; just a drop was enough to still a man's heart.

Dozens, maybe hundreds of bodies littered the mountain path.

The enemies shouted below. Nayan commanders barked orders from atop elephants, pointing spears at the Daenorians' locations. Magerians mustered alongside the path, drew swords, and began to march upwards, shields held before them.

"Fire!" Neekeya shouted, hoarse. "Shoot them down!"

She fired another arrow. Her fellow soldiers fired with her. Some of the projectiles slammed into the elephants, enraging the beasts. Other arrows slammed into enemy soldiers; some snapped against armor but many sank into flesh.

With battle cries, the Nayan troops fired their own arrows.

Neekeya crouched behind another boulder, this one deeply embedded into the mountainside. Arrows crashed against the stone and clattered around her. At her side, Tam fired an arrow, then crouched and raised his shield above his head.

"Slay them!" a man cried below, speaking in the language of Mageria. "Archers, fire!"

Whistles filled the air. Arrows sailed upwards, glinted in the sun, then came falling like comets. Neekeya grunted and raised her shield overhead. Three arrows punched through the wood, emerging only an inch away from her head. Another arrow scratched along her thigh, tearing her skin, and she grunted. Around her, hundreds of arrows peppered the landscape—clattering against stone, piercing shields, and some shedding blood. One Daenorian took an arrow to the neck; he gave a strangled cry and tumbled down the mountainside.

Neekeya stood up, her shield bristly with arrows, and raised her sword over her head. "Daenor—attack!"

Her army—thousands of swamp warriors, roaring through their crocodile helms—swept down the mountainside, swinging their swords.

The battle exploded with a clash of steel and showers of blood.

A rainforest warrior lunged toward Neekeya, and she raised her shield, blocking the swipe of his scimitar. She shoved against her shield, pushing the man down. He tripped on the rocky slope, crashed onto his back, and Neekeya swung down her sword. The blade cracked open his iron breastplate. She swung again, the breastplate shattered, and blood sprayed the man's red beard and braided hair.

Two more warriors leaped toward Neekeya. She swung her blade in a wide arc, parrying both men's scimitars. She thrust her shield in one direction, knocking one man down the mountain, and her sword in the other, piercing the second man's neck. Both soldiers tumbled down and knocked against their climbing brethren. Neekeya roared with fury, blood on her armor, fear and rage consuming her.

"Turn back, Radians!" she shouted, voice echoing across the battle. "Turn back or this mountain will be your graveyard."

Yet thousands were still climbing. An elephant's corpse lay before her, and she scuttled onto the dead animal to survey the battlefield below. She felt the blood drain from her cheeks.

"By Cetela," she whispered.

Most of the enemy host was still snaking up the mountainside. There were tens of thousands: Nayans in tiger pelts, Magerians in black armor, and further back marched Eseerians—desert warriors clad in white tunics, bearing sickle-shaped swords. The army was so massive it snaked down to the misty valleys.

This was not only a host to carve a path through the mountains. Neekeya grimaced. Here was a host to overwhelm all of Daenor and send the pyramids crumbling down.

Tigers raced up the mountainside, free of their leashes. Neekeya sneered. One of the animals pounced toward her, and she held out her shield. Its weight slammed her down. She tumbled off the dead elephant, the tiger clawing at her shield.

"Neekeya!"

A cloak fluttered. Metal flashed. Tam leaped forward, and his shield drove against the tiger, shoving the beast off. Neekeya rose to her feet and swung her sword in arcs, holding the animal back. Tam spared her only a glance before a Nayan warrior raced his way, thrusting a spear. The prince of Arden cried out, swung his sword, and parried.

"Crocodiles!" Neekeya shouted to the Daenorians who stood farther up the mountain. "Send out the beasts!"

Upon the mountains, Daenorians in gray robes pulled blankets off concealed cages. They unlocked the cage doors, and dozens of famished and furious crocodiles raced down the mountainside, jaws snapping. The reptiles, trained to avoid the soldiers of Daenor, ran toward the battle and drove through the enemy lines.

The battle raged on.

Neekeya fought with fury, sometimes slaying men with her sword, other times casting forward blasts of magic, using the powers she had learned at Teel. Always Tam fought at her side; his sword danced with hers, and his magic slammed into enemy armor, cracking the steel and breaking the bones within. All around them, the hosts fought: tigers, elephants, crocodiles, rainforest warriors, swamp dwellers, and knights in black steel. An hour into the battle, robed mages joined the fray; they rode upon black horses, and their blasts of magic tore across the mountain, sending boulders tumbling down to crush men.

"Do not let a single man pass!" Neekeya shouted as she fought. "Protect Daenor!"

Several scales were missing from her armor. Chips marred her sword. Blood seeped down her thigh, arm, and forehead. Yet still she fought, refusing to retreat.

At Teel I was only a weak girl, so afraid, a foreigner for the Radians to torment. She roared and swung her sword, cutting men down. *But now I am a warrior.*

"Neekeya!" Tam shouted. He grabbed her. Blood dripped down his face and covered his arm. "Neekeya, we can't hold them back."

"We must!" She slew another man. "Daenor, fight! Hold them back!"

Several Magerian troops came racing up toward her. She summoned particles from the air, wove them into three balls, and tossed the projectiles down the mountainside. The magic crashed against the soldiers' legs, sending them tumbling down. Desert warriors raced over the fallen, their white robes flowing, and swung scimitars toward her. Tam and Neekeya fought side by side, cutting the men down. Yet tens of thousands were still climbing, and the corpses of Daenorians littered the mountain.

"We've lost most of our men already!" Tam said. He spat out blood. "We can't win."

Neekeya trembled with fear and weakness. "Then I will die with my men! I will not run." Her eyes burned. "I cannot run."

A man rode up the mountainside toward them. Enemy troops moved aside, letting him pass. It was a mage, his robes black and flowing, his face hooded. He raised a pale, withered hand.

Neekeya growled and summoned her own magic, weaving a protective field of air. But the mage was too fast. A bolt of lightning shot from his fingers and slammed into her armor, and Neekeya screamed and fell.

The lightning raced across her, raising smoke. She screamed. Tears flowed from her eyes. She pawed at her armor, struggling to tear it off. Her hair crackled and she couldn't breathe. Wincing, she saw the mage dismount and walk toward her, grinning within his hood, driving more of the lightning into her. Scales on her armor sparked and cracked, and she wept.

"Tam!" she screamed, but he was writhing at her side, lightning crashing against him too. He too was screaming.

No. Not like this. I'm not done killing yet.

Though her body convulsed, wreathed in lightning, Neekeya manage to stand up. She stumbled forward and slammed herself against the mage.

The lightning passed from her to him, and he howled and fell backwards. He crashed down onto the mountainside, his cloak caught flame, and his magic died.

Trembling, tears streaming, Neekeya thrust her blade into him.

Tam struggled to his feet, coughing, his hair singed and his face sooty.

"Neekeya," he managed to say, voice hoarse and weak. "The mountain is lost. Look around you." He gestured at the dead Daenorians; perhaps only five hundred remained alive, facing tens of thousands of enemies. "We must fall back. We'll fight them in the marshlands, firing arrows down from the trees. That is the true domain of Daenor. That is where we'll make our last stand."

As men fought around her, Neekeya gazed across the battle. Her eyes burned with tears. The best of Daenor had come here—the noblest of her sons and daughters—and here they had fallen. Here forever their souls would reside and their glory would whisper in the wind. She knew Tam was right.

"The mountains are lost," she whispered. She raised her voice and shouted to her kinsmen. "The mountains are lost! Fall back, children of Daenor! Fall back to the marshlands!"

She slew a man who raced toward her. She screamed as an arrow grazed her cheek, and her blood dripped. She began to race up the mountain, shouting as she ran.

"Daenor, fall back! To the marshlands!"

She leaped over the bodies of her kinsmen. Their eyes stared at her, glassy, condemning. *How dare you leave us here, latani of Eetek? Do not leave us upon the stone! Return us to the marshes.*

Yet she had to leave them. She raced over the dead, rallying the living around her. Arrows flew. One slammed into a Daenorian at her side, slaying him—a mere youth, younger than herself. She kept running.

The last defenders of Daenor, only several hundred, fled down the western mountainside, bleeding, shouting, heading down into the swamplands. Behind them like a rising sun charged the Radian forces, beating drums and chanting for victory.

CHAPTER SEVENTEEN
SHATTERING

Madori rode through the darkness, the wind ruffling her hair and Grayhem's fur. She leaned forward upon the nightwolf, staring south into the shadows.

"Hurry, Grayhem," she pleaded. "We have to hurry."

The wolf panted but kept racing across the wilderness. The land was flat and rocky and black, the great emptiness north of the Inaro River and west of the Iron Road. The lights of the night sky shone above: the constellations, a crescent moon, the faded trail of light men called the White Dragon's Tail, and those moving stars Koyee claimed were distant worlds, sisters to Moth. But Madori kept waiting to see other lights—the lights of Pahmey, the great western city of Qaelin, a hub of life in the darkness of endless night.

She held up her locket and flicked it open as she rode. As before, it showed nothing. If Koyee still had her locket, it was closed.

"Stars damn it, Mother!" Madori cried into the wind. "Where are you?"

She had not seen a vision in the locket for hours, or maybe it had been full turns now. The last vision had shown Koyee sailing on a boat of refugees, heading toward the glass towers of Pahmey. Madori had never been to that city, but she had seen it painted upon many scrolls: a city of high walls bedecked with lamps, of glass towers that shone with inner lights, of domes like the moon, and of floating lanterns. If Serin's forces had truly driven into the night, would the Elorians meet them there in battle?

"Keep running, Grayhem," she said, stroking his fur as he raced across the land.

Her sword hung across her back—the blade renamed, no longer Sheytusung but Min Tey, the glow of the water, for her mind was now like a clear pond reflecting the moonlight. With the wisdom of Yin Shi, she knew she could keep her rage and fear under control, could keep her mind clear even while in danger. She hadn't completed her training in Yin Shi, as she hadn't completed her training of magic at Teel University, but she would take all knew of both skills, and she would use them in battle.

I will meet you again, Serin, she swore. *And this time I will not just cut off your finger but your head. You have not yet met Min Tey in battle.*

She rode on through the endless night.

She rode for many turns.

When they were too tired to continue, Grayhem and she slept under the stars. When they were hungry, they searched the moist earth for mushrooms and truffles, and when they raced over rocky plains, they dug for underground beetles, worms, and rodents, horrid little things that made Madori queasy but kept her alive. She drank melted snow. She rode on.

Through the cold and darkness, a song kept playing in her mind, and soon she was singing it as she rode, her voice soft. She sang "The Journey Home," one of the oldest songs of Eloria, the song her mother had taught her. Koyee had sailed alone upon the Inaro as a youth, and "Sailing Alone" had become an anthem to her, the song she had played on the streets and in the glittering burrows of the yezyani. But Madori, torn between day and night, always seeking a home, had another song to her heart, and in the darkness, seeking Pahmey, seeking a battle to fight, seeking a home, her voice rang with her song and filled the night.

Ten turns after leaving Master Lan Tao in the northern Desolation, Madori finally saw the lights of Pahmey ahead.

Upon a hilltop, she halted her nightwolf and gasped, staring at the distant city.

Pahmey rose upon the northern bank of the silver Inaro River. Black walls surrounded the city, topped with many lanterns. Beyond the walls, Madori saw thousands of homes built of opaque glass bricks, their roofs riled red, green, and gold, their edges curling upwards like scrolls. Many pagodas rose among the houses, dragon statues atop their roofs—temples to Xen Qae and to the constellations. At the city's crest, glass towers rose toward the sky, and they shone with inner lights of silver, lavender, and blue. The greatest tower among them—Minlao Palace—supported a silver dome shaped like the moon. Even higher up, hot air balloons hovered in the sky between floating lanterns.

It was a city of light, of beauty, of knowledge, an oasis in the dark wilderness.

It was a city under attack.

Myriads of Magerian troops surrounded the city. The enemy's warships floated in the river, eclipses painted upon their sails, showing the golden sun hiding the moon. Thousands of riders sat upon horses, and countless footmen stood behind them, their black armor reflecting the light of their torches. Barely visible, mere specks in the night, were the mages. Madori had never seen so many of them in one place, not even at Teel—a thousand mages or more rode upon black horses, the vanguard of the host. The Radian army surrounded Pahmey like a colony of ants surrounding a fallen morsel.

"Mother," Madori whispered, chest shaking. "Mother, where are you?"

She pulled the locket from under her shirt. When she flipped it open, a gasp fled her lips.

"Mother!" she cried.

Koyee's locket was open, and some hope filled Madori. Did that mean Koyee was still alive? The view in the locket showed the Radian host up close: lines of troops in dark steel, their torches crackling; mages upon horses, hidden in black robes; warships in the river, cannons on their decks; and beyond the soldiers and masts, the towering walls of Pahmey, and upon them Elorian archers in steel scales.

"Why . . . why are you among the Radians?" Madori whispered. How could Koyee's locket be showing her a view from *outside* the city?

The view in the locket spun madly. When the locket finally steadied, it revealed a familiar face.

Madori felt faint.

It was Serin.

The Emperor, Lord of the Radian Order, stared through the locket directly into Madori's eyes . . . and smiled.

With a cry, Madori slapped her locket shut.

She trembled. Her heart beat madly. Her head spun.

"Mother . . ."

Was Koyee dead? Had Serin killed her and claimed her locket?

"Mother!" she cried toward the distant city. Her tears burned.
She panted. She—

Breathe. Slowly. Focus.

It was Master Lan Tao speaking in her mind. Nostrils flaring,
Madori obeyed him. She slowly inhaled, filling her lungs from bottom
to top, letting the soothing air flow across every part of her, down to
her toes, along her arms, and inside her head. With every new breath,
she let the panic flow away. With every breath, she focused her
awareness on where she was: the feel of Grayhem's fur against her
thighs, the softness of her silk dress against her body, the chill of the
wind that streamed her two long strands of black hair. Slowly she
became fully aware of herself, in control again, grounded.

"I have to find you, Mother," she said into the wind. "I have to
fight at your side."

Distant shouts in Qaelish rose from the city walls. The banners
of Qaelin rose from the city's battlements—a silver moon within a
star upon a black field. Soldiers in scale armor cried out the words of
their empire: "We are the night!" And under this night sky, Madori—
born half of sunlight—felt a full child of darkness. Under this sky,
facing this battle, she was a child of Qaelin, of Eloria, and she would
fight for the darkness.

"We are the night!" they cried below, and their arrows flew
from the walls toward the enemy hosts. Bronze cannons shaped as
dragons fired from the battlements, and their cannonballs crashed
into the forces of sunlight.

The battle began.

Madori drew her sword, kneed her nightwolf, and leaned
forward over his back.

"Run, Grayhem! To war!"

He ran.

Madori raised her sword, charging down the hills toward the
enemy troops. She would die here, she knew; she was a lone woman
charging toward thousands. But she would not cower as her mother
needed her, as her city—and this turn Pahmey was her city, the
beacon of her heart—lay surrounded by light.

She had ridden only halfway toward the enemy when the walls of Pahmey began to shake.

Madori hissed, eyes wide.

The thousand mages surrounded the city like a noose, riding upon their black mares, and each bore a crackling red torch. Their free hands pointed toward Pahmey, and dark magic oozed from them, tendrils of black and silver coiling like serpents.

One glass tower, hundreds of feet tall and filled with blue light, cracked. The sound of shattering glass pounded against Madori's ears even as she rode. With a great shriek, the tower collapsed. Elorians—small as ants from here—tumbled from its windows. Shards of glass showered over surrounding roofs. Finally the tower vanished in a cloud of dust.

Madori could barely breathe.

"Serin!" she shouted. She doubted her voice could be heard; thousands of voices were now screaming from the city. "Serin, stop this!"

A second tower crashed down, its glass walls shattering. Screams rose from the city. Cracks raced along the walls. The mages kept casting their magic, and Madori rode as fast as Grayhem would carry her, but she could not help, could not avoid seeing the devastation.

One chunk of wall fell, its turrets and ramparts slamming into the ground. Behind it, houses collapsed and vanished into sinkholes. More towers crumbled. Dust rose in clouds, thick with glass fragments that flew like snow, a million lights reflecting the fires. More of the wall fell. Canyons were tearing open. Sinkholes greedily swallowed buildings like gluttons guzzling down food. Elorians began to flee the city, racing out the gates into the wilderness, only to encounter the enemies' swords.

Madori was only a mile away, charging toward the enemy troops, when a great *crack* tore across the land, louder than anything she had heard. She was forced to cover her ears, and even Grayhem yowled. A thousand buildings in Pahmey tilted inward, their walls crumbling. Dust blasted out. A massive sinkhole opened within Pahmey's center . . . and the ruins of the city vanished.

Mewling, Grayhem stopped running, stared down, and whimpered.

When the dust settled, all that remained of Pahmey was a ring of cracked walls, a few odd houses clinging to the rim, and a great hole in the center.

"They're all gone," Madori whispered. "Thousands of buildings. Countless people. A history of thousands of years. Gone."

Her tears flowed. She had never seen such devastation. She had heard stories of the last war, of how King Ceranor of Arden had attacked this city, how thousands of Elorians had died defending it. But this . . . this wasn't conquest. This was genocide. This was the effacement of a civilization.

Madori stared in horror. "Pahmey is gone."

For long moments, the land was eerily silent.

Then the Radian troops began to cheer.

Men waved banners and blew trumpets. Joyous songs erupted. Effigies of Elorians, constructed of wood and straw, were set aflame. White doves were released into the sky. Everywhere the troops cried out in joy, celebrating the destruction.

Only a few Elorians had survived along the sinkhole's rim—a couple thousand, that was all, a fraction of the city's lost civilization. The Radian soldiers mobbed them, chained them together, whipped them, kicked them, and howled with laughter as they bled.

Madori watched from the distance, still hidden in shadows, her wolf panting beneath her.

"What do I do?" She shuddered. "Stars of the night, what do I do?"

She looked into the locket again but saw nothing; its twin locket was closed. Was Koyee dead, one of the hundreds of thousands of fallen? Even Yin Shi could not calm Madori now, and her tears flowed.

"And so I will die with my mother." She raised her sword, and she roared into the darkness. "We are the night!"

A lone woman upon a lone wolf, she charged down toward the tens of thousands of Radian soldiers.

They turned toward her, amusement in their eyes, and Madori crashed against them, screaming and swinging her sword.

She fought in a mad fury. She fought with magic, blasting out bolts of power. She fought with Yin Shi, aware of every swing of a sword, and she cut men down, driving her katana through steel as easily as silk. Beneath her, Grayhem bit and clawed, driving through the enemy. Madori fought with tears in her eyes, a roar in her throat, a wild woman of darkness. Blood flew around her. Men toppled at her wolf's feet.

She was still screaming as blasts of magic knocked her off her wolf, as clubs slammed against her, as hands grabbed her, as chains wrapped around her ankles and wrists. Pain exploded across her. Fists drove into her face. Her wolf growled somewhere in the distance, and all she saw was a sea of Radian soldiers.

"Mother!" she cried hoarsely, blood in her mouth.

Hands yanked her to her feet. A canvas sack was thrust over her head. Blows drove into her stomach, and she doubled over, and a kick sent her sprawling. Her head hit something hard, and Madori wept for the loss of darkness.

Daniel Arenson

CHAPTER EIGHTEEN
THE BEAR OF VERILON

Torin stood in the arena, chained to the pole, as the crowd roared around him.

Many years ago, Torin had stood in the arena of Asharo, Capital of Ilar, in the darkness of Eloria. There he had seen Koyee fight Tianlong, the black dragon of the night. Despite its horrors, that had been a grand amphitheater carved of polished stone, a marvel of architecture. This place, in the sunlit kingdom of Verilon, was only a crude pit dug into the dirt. The hole was a good ten feet deep, perhaps a hundred feet wide, and around it rose a ring of wooden bleachers. Hundreds of Verilish men and women sat upon the crude wooden seats, roaring down at the pit. They drank from pewter steins, dribbling ale onto their beards and thick fur cloaks, but their true thirst this turn was for blood.

My blood, Torin thought.

In the arena's center, a wooden pole rose from the frozen earth. A chain ran from the pole to Torin's ankle, perhaps ten feet long. He stood barefoot on the cold soil, clad in nothing but a woolen tunic, armed with nothing but the humble dagger they had given him. Like this, chained and shivering with cold, thousands of men watching and roaring for his blood, Torin waited to die.

I survived the great War of Day and Night—the dark magic at Sinyong, the inferno at Yintao, the bloodshed in Naya. I survived the torture of Lord Gehena. I lived through fire, through darkness, through war and disease. He clutched his dagger. *And now I die like this, a fool for their amusement.*

He scanned the crowd above, finally locating Ashmog. The King of Verilon was chewing on a pig's trotter between gulps of ale.

404

Grease filled his bushy brown beard. Two young women sat on his lap, one on each knee, stroking the king's hair as he feasted.

"Ashmog!" Torin shouted up toward the king. "Ashmog, hear me! This is not the way. I've come here to aid you, not to fight for your pleasure."

The king gulped down a chunk of meat, looked from one of his women to the other, then burst out laughing. His two companions laughed with him, and soon the entire amphitheater was roaring.

"Oh, I don't expect you to fight much, murderer's son!" the king shouted down. He drank deeply, coating his mustache with foam. "You'll probably curl up and die begging for mercy." The king rose to his feet upon the bleacher, knocking his companions down. He pointed at Torin from above, his eyebrows pushed down, and his voice boomed. "My father fought nobly. He died with a bloody sword in his hand, slaying enemies, even as your father stabbed him in the back. But you . . . you will die squealing."

Torin grumbled. He refused to believe his father would ever stab a man in the back. His father had been a noble knight. Torin was about to shout back at the king, to defend Teramin Greenmoat's honor, when iron doors creaked open in the arena's wall.

Torin spun toward the exposed tunnel. A roar sounded from within. A great paw reached out from the tunnel, the claws as long as swords. All around the arena, the spectators upon the bleachers roared with new vigor.

By Idar . . .

The beast was too large to stand in the tunnel; it had to crawl out like a creature emerging from the womb. Its fangs were like spears, its eyes like smelters. When it rose to its feet, it towered like a great oak, twenty feet tall. Here stood the great bear Gashdov, a deity of the northern pine forests, symbol of Verilon—an ancient creature who fed upon the flesh of men.

Torin raised his dagger—a puny piece of metal.

The towering bear slammed its front paws against the ground. The arena shook. The crowd cheered. Roaring, Gashdov raced toward Torin, strings of saliva quivering between its teeth.

"*Shan dei!*" Torin cursed, switching to Qaelish in his fright. He ran behind the wooden pole. His chain clattered. An instant later, the bear's paw slammed down where Torin had stood, the claws digging into the frozen soil.

Torin's heart pounded and sweat washed him even in the cold. He clutched his dagger but knew he could not win this fight. He could barely even call this a fight; it was an execution.

I'll never see my wife and daughter again, he thought. He did not fear death, but how could he let Koyee become a widow, to let Madori live without a father?

The bear lolloped around the pole and faced Torin again. It rose to its hind feet, roared, and swiped its claws again.

Torin leaped back. The chain pulled tight, and he fell onto his back. The claws swiped over his head. Torin thrust up his dagger, and the blade cut into the bear's paw. The beast roared; the dagger was like a thorn's prick, enraging the bear but doing no harm.

The claws lashed again, each like a katana. One claw nicked Torin's shoulder. His blood splattered the icy floor. The crowd roared with a sound like a thunderstorm, and the arena shook.

"Eat his flesh!" Ashmog cried above. "Eat, Gashdov!"

The bear roared above Torin, mouth stretched wide. All Torin saw was the great gullet, the massive teeth, the swinging uvula.

Thrust your dagger! whispered a voice inside him. *Fight it! Stab it!*

Ignoring that voice, he tossed his dagger aside.

He forced himself to go limp.

I did not win the last war with violence, he thought. *I won by fixing the Cabera Clock. By healing something broken.*

"If you must feed," Torin whispered to the bear, "feed and enjoy your meal. But if you will suffer your hunger, I will provide you with more than a meal. I will offer you friendship." He stared at the roaring beast, and he recognized something in Gashdov's eyes— something lonely, something lost. "What is the greatest pain they caused you, friend? Hunger or loneliness?"

The great bear bellowed and Torin winced, waiting to be eaten. Surely Gashdov could not understand. It was a mindless animal, a vicious killer. But as the roar went on, those teeth did not rip into him, and Torin heard the loneliness in that cry, the pain. He stared up at the howling bear.

This is not merely an enraged animal, he thought. *Gashdov is an ancient deity of the forest, one who is no less a prisoner than I am.*

"I understand," Torin whispered. He reached up a hesitant hand and stroked the animal's brown fur. "I understand what they did to you. You're meant to roam the forests, to protect this ancient land, your domain, to watch over your people." Torin's eyes stung. "But they imprisoned you here, forced you to kill men for food. To entertain them."

The bear's roar now sounded like a plaintive cry of pain. His paws thumped down onto the soil, and Torin stroked the animal. The bear's head nuzzled him, as large as Torin's entire body.

"It's all right," Torin whispered. "I understand. I'm your friend."

The bear emitted soft, deep gurgles, sounds of old kindness almost crushed under hunger and imprisonment.

Across the arena, the roars of the crowd—like the roars of the bear—faded.

One hand upon the bear's head, Torin pointed up at King Ashmog.

"You imprisoned this animal!" he said. Blood dripped down Torin's arm but he barely noticed the pain. "You turned against your own protector, your own god. Even in Arden, we tell stories of the ancient Gashdov, a guardian of the forest, a noble deity of the northern hinterlands. And you turned him into this." Torin shook his head sadly. "Into a starving animal for a bear-baiting spectacle."

He stood in the arena, chest heaving, waiting for King Ashmog to call for archers, perhaps to call for a bow and shoot Torin himself. If he had to die, at least he'd die speaking truth. Truth is what he had always fought for, had always been willing to die for. Snow glided down, coating the arena, turning the bear white. Silence. No movement but for the falling snow.

Finally Ashmog spoke, and his voice was soft, awed, and in the silence it carried down from the bleachers, as clear as if shouted.

"He tamed Gashdov." Tears streamed down the beefy man's cheeks. "He tamed the beast!" The king rose to his feet, unslung his war hammer from across his back, and raised the weapon above his head. "He spoke to the bear, and the bear heard his words. Kava Or has risen!"

Torin blinked. Who had risen?

The bearded king trundled down the bleachers, shoving men aside, and entered the arena. He rushed toward Torin and the tamed bear. Torin half-expected the man to swing his hammer, and he winced. But King Ashmog knelt before Torin, holding out his hammer as an offering. Tears streamed down the king's ruddy cheeks, and his bottom lip trembled.

"Forgive me, Kava Or, He Who Talks to Bears." Ashmog's chest shook. "Forgive me, Old One, Spirit of the Forest. I did not know." He was weeping now. "You tamed Gashdov, Guardian of Verilon. You spoke to him. You are Kava Or, prophesied to rise in Verilon's greatest hour of peril, to return our god to sanity, to help us fight evil."

Along with relief for his spared life, anger rose in Torin. He stared at the kneeling, weeping king. "Saved him from sanity? Maybe if you hadn't imprisoned him, hadn't forced him to slay men for food, he would not have gone mad."

Ashmog prostrated himself. "Forgive us, Kava Or! The great god Gashdov went mad many generations ago, and we could not tame him, could not speak with him. But you spoke. And he listened." The king rose to his feet, eyes solemn. "I understand now. The prophesies spoke truth. An evil has arisen, and it storms forth from the south—the evil of the Radian Empire. Gashdov is restored to sanity. Kava Or has joined us." He turned toward the crowd. "Kava Or has risen!"

The crowd cheered and their voices soon rose in song, a prayer of the forest. In the arena, Gashdov moved closer to Torin, nuzzling him with his wet snout.

Stroking the animal, Torin looked at King Ashmog who stood beside him.

"Will you let the forces of Arden into your walls, Ashmog? Will you fight with us against the Radians?"

Ashmog tightened his lips and clutched Torin's shoulder. His eyes burned, and his lips peeled back in a sneer. "Kava Or, we will not just fight. We will crush the Radians as a hammer crushes stone."

CHAPTER NINETEEN
A MEMORY OF MUSIC

Emperor Tirus Serin sat on his horse, staring down at the smoldering sinkhole, and clenched his fists.

"Gone," he whispered, voice choked. "You're gone, Pahmey. As I had vowed to you."

Around him, the hosts of his empire cheered. Men beat drums, blew trumpets, and sang the songs of Radianism. A hundred thousand troops roared for victory. In the river, men cheered atop ships, and cannons blasted out in triumph. Even Lari, sitting at Serin's side upon her horse, raised her fist and howled with joy.

But Serin watched silently, his jaw tight, the memories pounding through him. Most of the others were too young to remember. But he, Tirus Serin, had been to Pahmey before. The memory gripped him like a fist of magic.

He had been a young man, not yet thirty, when the last war had flared across the night. Sir Tirus Serin—handsome, the firstborn of a proud lord, heir to Sunmotte, a favorite son of sunlight. He was a man of Mageria, but that war he fought alongside Arden, the kingdom of his betrothed. His bride—a fair but weak-willed woman named Ora—waited back in Kingswall, and Serin had come here to kill, to shed as much blood as he could before settling down with a wife.

"Slay them all!" Serin shouted, marching through the city gates. "Slay the nightcrawlers!"

They stepped over the corpses of Elorians and through the shattered gates, entering the city of Pahmey.

And there Serin saw her.

His sword bloody, his blood pumping, he lost his breath.

An Elorian woman stood ahead on the boulevard. She was not a soldier; she wore no armor, only a black silk dress. Blood and cuts covered her, and she held a katana. Her oversized purple eyes met his gaze, then moved to stare at the dozens of soldiers around him.

"I am Koyee of Eloria!" she called out to the advancing Timandrians. "I am a warrior of the night. I am a huntress of the moonlit plains. This is my city. This is my land. You cannot enter. Return to the day! This city is forbidden to you. You cannot enter. We are the night!"

Serin had always thought the Elorians weak, sniveling creatures, nefarious and pathetic.

Here he saw strength. Here he saw beauty.

At that moment, Serin loved his enemy.

His comrades jeered around him, mocking Koyee. His king— the proud Ceranor—led men forth to slay the girl. But Serin could not fight, barely move.

She's beautiful, he thought. She intoxicated him, more alluring than wine, than killing an enemy. She was the most beautiful woman he'd ever seen.

Then the battle flowed over the city. Swords rang. Arrows flew. Blood splattered the glass buildings of Pahmey. And she vanished.

And he killed.

Serin marched through the streets, slaying all in his path. He cut down Elorian soldiers. He cut down women, children, leaving a path of dead, slaying all those weak worms, seeking her—the only one who had stood up, had challenged him, had faced him with defiance. The single strong, noble, beautiful Elorian he had seen. Koyee.

"Where are you, Koyee?" he whispered, slicing through the fleeing enemy.

The city fell that turn. The banners of sunlight rose. The blood of Eloria washed the streets.

"Return to me," his betrothed pleaded in her letters. "Return to me, my sweet Tirus, so we may wed in the bright gardens of Kingswall or the proud halls of Markfir."

Ora sealed all her letters with a kiss, and Serin—a soldier in Occupied Pahmey—tossed the scrolls into the fire.

For months he lived in the Night Castle, a pagoda claimed from the defenders of Pahmey. For months he patrolled the streets of that city, keeping the Elorians in line, hunting down any who dared resist the conquerors of sunlight.

For months he sought her.

"Koyee," he whispered whenever he lay down to sleep in the Night Castle. "The Girl in the Black Dress."

He was not alone in seeking her, of course. The Sailith monks, led by the squat and cruel Ferius, searched every warren for Koyee— the girl who had wounded Ferius himself in the battle. None found her.

She must be dead, Serin thought as he lay in bed, as he patrolled the streets, as he dreamed of her. *Or perhaps she fled the city. She is gone.* His throat tightened. *And I must return to my betrothed in the sunlight, to a lesser woman.*

The desperation clawed at him. Serin was not a drinker, not a smoker, but that turn he needed to forget, to drown his worries in ale and the *hintan* spice the Elorians puffed in their dens. Clad in his armor, he walked along the cobbled streets. Houses of opaque glass bricks rose at his sides, their tiled roofs curling up at the edges. Many lanterns shone, their tin shaped as laughing faces, and eyes glowed inside bat houses of iron and silver. The towers of the city's crest rose above, glass beacons of light. Public fireplaces, their grills shaped as dragons, roared at every street corner. Few Elorians walked the streets these turns—a few men and women, clad in silken robes and embroidered sashes, hurried between houses on slippered feet, quickly vanishing into shadows. Most shops were closed. Most taverns had boarded up their doors, refusing to serve the enemy. All but one place.

"The Green Geode," Serin said, staring at the place. His soldiers had spoken of it in hushed tones. From the outside, it seemed a simple building, not even constructed of glass but simple dark stone. The Green Geode was a rock in a field of flowers. This neighborhood sprawled near the city's crest, a place for the wealthy, and the other buildings here were grand, their columns soaring, their lanterns bright, places of welcoming light and song. Through their wide glass windows, Serin could see Elorian dancers and actors entertaining the Timandrian troops. But Serin cared little for dances or plays; he sought only forgetfulness. He would find forgetfulness in what the Elorians called "pleasure dens"—places for lost souls.

He entered the Green Geode, this little nook in the shadows. Once inside, he understood the den's name. While the outside was crude rock, green light washed the inner chamber. Crystals hung from the ceiling. Lanterns blazed upon the walls. Several Timandrian soldiers sat at tables, drinking ale and wine, and some even smoked *hintan* from hookahs—the Elorian spice that softened the mind, that erased memories. The purple spice bubbled in glass vials, and green smoke wafted through the air.

Upon stages stood the yezyani—Elorian women trained in the arts of dance, song, music, and seduction. They wore scanty silks that revealed more than they hid, and jewels shone upon them, little glass vials that trapped the light of angler fish. Two of the yezyani swayed upon one stage, dancing seductively. Another performed with marionettes. The third, clad in an indigo *qipao* dress and a clay mask, played a flute.

Serin's eyes narrowed. He stared at the flutist.

His heart burst into a gallop.

Her mask hid her face, but Serin knew that proud stance, that flowing white hair, those lavender eyes that gleamed within her mask's eye holes.

"Koyee," he whispered.

She met his gaze, then looked away, playing on. Serin sat at a table, but he no longer craved to forget. He ordered no wine, no spice, merely sat and watched and listened.

Beautiful, he thought, mesmerized. *A beautiful song. A beautiful woman.*

"You are the only one who resisted me," he whispered, thinking back to his first turn in Pahmey, to marching through the gates and seeing her defiance, her sword, her flashing eyes.

He knew that he loved her—hopelessly, eternally.

When her song ended and she stepped off the stage, he approached her. She tried to leave the common room, to climb upstairs to her chamber, but he blocked her way. His bulky, armored form was twice the size of her slim, silk-clad body.

She stared up at him. Through the mask holes, her eyes narrowed.

"Move," she said, speaking in Ardish, her accent heavy.

For a moment, Serin did not know what to say. He simply stood, blocking her passage.

How do I speak to her? How do I tell her how I feel?

"Move!" she said again.

He reached out to touch her hair. "My dear, I would very much like a private song. Would you play for me in your chamber?" He hoped she understood his words. He pulled a silver coin from his pocket. "I will pay you. I—"

She recoiled from his touch, her eyes flashed, and she shoved him aside. She spoke through her mask, voice brusque, accent thick. "No. Go away."

Rage flared in Serin.

How dare she refuse him? He was Sir Tirus Serin, a great lord, heir to Sunmotte! His father commanded armies. His coffers overflowed with gold.

"Do you know who I am?" He grabbed her wrist, refusing to let her climb the stairs. "Do you even understand my words?" He tugged her closer to him. "I am Lord Tirus Serin! If I tell you to play for me, you will obey. You—"

She slapped him.

Her hand connected with his cheek so powerfully it stunned him. Before he could react, she kicked him swiftly in the chest, knocking him back. He tripped over a chair and fell down hard onto his backside. Mugs of ale tumbled off a table and spilled across him.

The hall erupted with laughter.

Timandrian soldiers brayed, cheered, and pounded the tabletops. Upon the stages, the other yezyani giggled. Koyee fled upstairs, cursing, and everywhere the laughter rose. Serin sat on the floor, drenched in ale. He had banged his tailbone; the pain was so great he couldn't stand. The great lord, the great soldier—dripping wet, humiliated.

"Beaten by a woman!" cried out one soldier and roared with laughter. "Smacked down by a little Elorian lass half his size!"

Serin's eyes stung with tears. He stared around the room, and there he saw him, sitting at the back—Torin Greenmoat, his cousin. The young soldier was not laughing like the others; Torin stared at Serin with something far worse than mirth. He stared with pity.

Rage exploded through Serin, and he rose to his feet, only to slip in the ale and crash back down onto the floor. More laughter rose.

"Let me help you," Torin said, approaching. He tried to help Serin up.

"Let go of me!" Serin screamed. He shoved Torin aside. He leaped back to his feet, grabbed a table for support, and all but raced through the room. He stumbled out into the street to the sound of laughter.

Serin stood in the darkness, ale dripping from his hair, and spun back toward the Green Geode. Through the door he heard the yezyani sing again.

I loved you, he thought. *I loved you, Koyee, and you . . . you did this to me.*

He clenched his fists. He tossed back his head. And he bellowed in rage.

With that, Serin spun around and marched down the street, marched through the city, marched outside the gates and into the open night. He boarded his family's ship. He said nothing as they set sail, only stood at the stern, staring at the lights of Pahmey grow smaller in the distance, then fade beyond the horizon.

He returned to the sunlight, and he married his betrothed, and he fathered Lari, and he watched his father die, and he inherited Sunmotte, and he claimed the throne of Mageria, and he founded an empire, but Serin never forgot her. Never forgot the humiliation he suffered in the night.

"And now you are fallen, Pahmey, city of shadows," he whispered, staring at the smoking sinkhole. "You hurt me, so I destroyed you. And I will destroy you all."

He looked around him. His soldiers—a massive army of a hundred thousand—were not mocking him, were not laughing, were not jeering. They were chanting his name. They were killing for him. Before him, the sinkhole gaped open like a dark soul—the magic

Serin himself had developed in the depths of his dungeons, a magic the mages of the last war had lacked, a final solution to the vermin of the night.

"And you will suffer more than all, Koyee," Serin whispered. He clutched her locket in his hand, its edges digging into his palm. "You will regret what you did to me."

"Radian rises!" the soldiers chanted. "Radian rises!"

Serin allowed himself a single, small smile.

CHAPTER TWENTY
BLOOD MARCH

Pain exploded across Madori's face.

"On your feet, mongrel!"

The voice was distant, muffled, echoing as in a dream. But the pain was real. It blazed across her cheek again, then drove into her back, and Madori cried out. Tears flooded her eyes.

"Get up, half-breed, or stay here and die in the cold."

Pain drove into her side again, and she gasped and opened her eyes.

I'm alive, she thought. *Stars, I'm alive.*

She coughed and tasted blood in her mouth. When she blinked, bringing the world into focus, she couldn't see the stars above, only dust and smoke. Magerian soldiers were staring down at her, Radian eclipses upon their breastplates. One of the men, his gruff face covered in stubble, raised his hand above her. Blood stained his fingers—her blood, she realized.

"If it were up to me, I'd leave you here in the dust." The man spat onto her; the glob hit her forehead and trickled down her face. "Emperor Serin wants you to live." The man's face split into a cruel grin. "Though he didn't say we couldn't shed some of your blood on the way."

He backhanded her again, and Madori yowled. Blood flew from her mouth, and she growled and leaped to her feet, ready to attack.

Chains clattered around her ankles and wrists, and she slammed back down onto the ground.

The Magerian soldiers roared with laughter. When Madori blinked, she saw that dozens of them stood around her. Ignoring the pain—every last inch of her hurt—she tried to summon her magic, to claim and heat their armor, to blast them with air, or to set their hair on fire. But she was too weary, too hurt.

Breathe, she thought. She inhaled slowly as Master Lan Tao had taught her. *Brea—*

"Up!" the gruff soldier shouted. He grabbed her by the ear and tugged, and Madori screamed in pain and scrambled to her feet, sure he would rip her ear straight off. "Now go. Walk! Move—the lot of you. Go, nightcrawlers!"

Madori blinked and turned around. She gasped. Before her gaped the great sinkhole that had swallowed Pahmey; only a few walls and homes surrounded the chasm in a ring. Those few Elorians who had fled the city stood outside the devastation.

Fresh tears filled Madori's eyes. She saw a thousand survivors, perhaps two thousand—no more. Blood covered many of them. They wore ragged burlap tunics; no more silk dresses, scale armor, or simple fur garments distinguished between Elorian nobles, soldiers, and commoners. All stood trembling, their bodies bruised and bleeding, their wrists and ankles bound with chains. The prisoners gazed at Madori with their gleaming Elorian eyes, large and blue and purple like lanterns in the night. A few were only children, weeping and unable to even cling to their parents, their limbs chained.

When Madori looked down at her body, she saw that she too had been dressed in burlap rags. Dust, mud, and blood covered what parts of her the ragged tunic did not. Manacles encircled her ankles and wrists, and chains ran between them, long enough to let her walk but not run or fight. She pawed for her locket, but it no longer hung around her neck. Grayhem, her dear nightwolf, was nowhere in sight.

She spun back toward the squat, scruffy Magerian who had struck her. He wore golden eclipses upon his pauldrons, she saw; this one was a commander. She spoke in a slow, steady voice simmering with rage.

"Let. Us. Go." She bared her teeth. "I don't know who you are, but if you don't release us, I will—"

He drove his fist into her belly.

She doubled over, coughing and spitting out blood. Her eyes burned. She could barely breathe.

"Chop off her head, Sir Gora!" shouted a soldier.

"Gouge our her eyes!" cried another.

Through her tears, Madori saw the gruff captain—Sir Gora—shake his head and spit. "This one's a mongrel. Only half nightcrawler, she is. Her hair ain't white and her skin ain't pale enough to be full-crawler. Serin said to keep mongrels alive." He shook blood off his fist. "She'll get to the emperor, one way or another." He pulled a whip off his belt and cracked it in the air. "Nightcrawlers—move!"

Around the chained prisoners, the Magerians soldiers mounted horses and cracked whips. Several of those whips landed across Elorian backs, shedding blood.

"Move!"

One by one, the Elorians began to shuffle forward; their chains only allowed them to take short, heavy steps. A few wept as they walked, their manacles clattering, their chests shaking. Others glanced around nervously. Some walked while staring with defiance, eyes hard, fists clenched. A few were were strong and healthy; they walked straight. Others were too old, too young, wounded, or weak; they limped and swayed as they hobbled forward.

Her mouth still bleeding, Madori walked with them. When she missed a step, Gora—he now rode upon a stallion beside her—cracked his whip. Stones cut into Madori's bare feet, her chains felt heavier than boulders, and her head spun so wildly she barely knew north from south. As the convoy of prisoners moved, the Magerians kept shouting and lashing their whips. They herded the prisoners into a long, snaking line, three or four Elorians wide.

"March!" Gora shouted from his horse. "Move, nightcrawlers! Stop and you die."

One Elorian, a little boy barely ten years old, swayed and collapsed.

"Move!" Gora shouted. "Up!"

The Radian's whip hit the boy's back. Blood splattered.

"Stop that!" Madori shouted. She lunged forward, trying to reach the fallen boy, but Radian soldiers grabbed her, tugged her back into the line, and shouted at her to keep walking.

"Let go!" She managed to tear free, even with her chains, and hurried toward the fallen boy. Gora was leaning across his saddle, beating the child, whip landing again and again. Madori screamed and placed herself between the boy and the whip. The lash struck across her chest, and she yowled.

"Back into the line!" Gora shouted.

"Let me help him," she said, blood dripping across her. She knelt and tried to raise the Elorian boy, to revive him.

Oh stars . . .

She lowered her head, weeping.

The boy was dead.

"Walk!" Gora shouted. He dismounted his horse, grabbed Madori under the arms, yanked her to her feet, and shoved her back into the line with the other prisoners.

She kept moving, her chest constricting with fear. Before her, the two thousand survivors stretched across the dark plains. They moved on, leaving the ruins of Pahmey behind.

Madori could barely walk. She had lost too much blood, was too hurt, and her chains were too heavy. Yet she forced herself to keep moving one foot after another, refusing to fall.

Breathe. Focus. Be a still pond.

The procession continued to move across the landscape. Madori counted several hundred Radian troops on horseback, their whips ready to strike any Elorian who fell.

At first the Elorians marched close together, some weeping, most silent. But the road stretched on. After walking for several hours, some began to fall. An old woman. A wounded soldier, his hand severed. A young girl. They fell to their knees, begging for rest, begging for mercy.

They found neither.

The Radian whips tore into flesh.

"Up! March!"

A few of the fallen rose and shuffled on. Other simply lay on the ground, too weak to continue. The whips kept cutting into them, and Radian lances drove into their backs. As the march continued, the prisoners moving deeper into the darkness, the fallen remained behind upon the barren land—broken bodies for the night to claim.

As Madori walked, she kept scanning the crowd of prisoners. She stood at the back of the line; the two thousand Elorians stretched ahead of her, heads lowered. Their long white hair flowed like banners, and blood and dust covered their bodies.

"Are you here, Mother?" Madori whispered. She kept rising onto her toes, even hopping in her chains, trying to find Koyee in the crowd. But she could barely distinguish between the Elorians ahead; bloodied and chained, they had become a single mass of broken souls.

And they kept falling.

Whenever one prisoner crashed down, the Radian whips landed, and spears thrust. Most of the fallen never rose again. Every few moments, Madori found herself stepping over another corpse. And with every corpse, her heart trembled, and she expected to see her mother lying dead beneath her. She saw so many dead faces: children, elders, wounded soldiers . . . but never Koyee.

"Are you still alive, Mother?" Madori whispered, trudging on. "Have you fallen in the battle of the dusk? Or in the ruin of Pahmey?" She trembled. "Or do you march here ahead, so close to me?"

"Silence!" Gora shouted. He rode his horse beside her, swung his whip, and lashed Madori across the shoulders. "Walk!"

She cried out in pain, and she kept walking, blood trickling down her back.

The moon rose and fell above. The stars moved. The Magerians changed their shifts; some retired to a wagon to sleep, and others emerged to ride the horses and goad the prisoners on. They had soon walked for a full turn—the length of a day and night back when the world had still spun—and the Magerians gave them no rest. The second turn of marching stretched on, and the whips and spears kept lashing, and the Elorians kept falling. Their captors laughed as they rode their horses, drank wine, and feasted upon meat and bread and grapes. Whenever an Elorian fell dead, they roared with laughter and trampled over the body, leaving it crushed behind. Whenever Madori looked over her shoulder, she could see the trail of the dead—hundreds stretching into the north.

They had left Pahmey with two thousand Elorian survivors. By the time the second turn of marching ended, only a thousand still lived.

The moon and stars kept moving across the sky. Based on what Madori knew of their dance, they must have been walking for three turns now. The Magerian shifts changed again, the sleepers emerging from their wagon with renewed cruelty. Madori swayed as she walked. Tears streamed down her face. Her knees ached and her lungs could barely suck in air. She kept trying to summon her magic, to break her chains, but could not; she was too weak, too wounded. Dying.

Breathe, she thought. *Like Master Lan Tao taught you.* Yet how could she breathe when her lungs blazed with fire?

"Hurry up, mongrel!" Gora called from his horse. He swung his spear, cracking the wooden shaft against her back. "You're slowing down."

The pain was too much.

Madori fell to her knees.

An instant later, her face hit the dirt.

I can't go on. It's over.

Gora dismounted his horse and knelt beside her. He grabbed her hair and tugged her head up.

"Stand!" he barked. "Serin insisted you live. Stand! Walk."

She tried. She pushed herself onto her elbows, but her arms wobbled, and she crashed back down.

Gora's boot drove into her belly. "Up!"

She wept. She could no longer move.

I will die here, she thought, staring at the dust around her. *I will die here under the stars of my home.*

"Up!"

She stared up, and she saw them there—the constellations of Eloria. The racing wolf. The leaping fish. The proud warrior. She remembered seeing these constellations in her book back in the daylight. Her mother would read the book to her, describing all the great beings in the sky. Madori remembered the taste of the tea her mother would brew, the softness of Koyee's silken dresses, the warmth of the hearth in their home, the comfort of her dolls.

I miss that home, she thought, *though it lies in ruins. And I miss you, Mother, though I don't even know if you live or lie dead. But I can't go on. I can't.*

With her last drop of strength, Madori raised her head, and a glint caught her eye.

She gasped.

Gora, cruel captain of the march, was wearing her locket around his neck.

He must have been hiding it under his shirt until now. In his fervor of kicking and shouting, the locket had emerged from under his collar and swung open. Inside Madori saw the view from the second locket.

This time, it did not show Emperor Serin.

Instead, it was Lari's face in the locket.

The young woman was dressed in splendor: she wore gilded armor, a samite cloak, and a jeweled tiara. Her golden hair flowed across her shoulders, rich and lustrous. Powder and rouge hid the scars Tam and Neekeya had given her cheeks outside of Teel, and fine cosmetics adorned her eyelids and lips. Through the locket, she stared into Madori's eyes and smiled—that old smile that dripped both honey and poison.

"Look," Lari mouthed silently.

The view in the locket moved.

Madori cried out.

"Mother!" Tears sprang into her eyes. "Mother!"

Koyee lay in the dirt, covered in dust and blood. She was barely recognizable. Koyee too wore a burlap tunic, and her captors had sheared off her hair, leaving her scalp nicked and dripping blood. Bruises covered her face. But Madori knew it was her mother, and she cried out to her.

Trembling, Koyee looked up into the locket. She saw Madori and tears filled her eyes. She reached out a trembling hand, crying out words Madori could not hear.

Gora grunted, snapped the locket shut, and tucked it back under his collar.

Even through the pain and weariness, even as she lay on the ground, perhaps dying, rage flared in Madori.

Lari and Serin are torturing my mother.

She roared.

I will save you, Mother. I'm coming. I promise.

Teeth clenched and limbs shaking, Madori pushed herself to her feet.

She rejoined the Elorian procession. Her chains rattling, she walked with the others, jaw clenched, eyes narrowed.

Step by step, she thought. *Walk. Ignore the pain. Pain is irrelevant.* She focused only on her breath, letting the pain flow away like her thoughts. *Even if your body blazes with agony, keep walking. Never stop.*

Her eyes leaked, and she clenched her fists. She stepped over a fallen body. She walked on.

"I'm coming for you, Mother," she whispered. "And I'm coming for you too, Lari and Serin . . . and somehow, with magic, with my chains, or only with my fingernails and teeth, I will kill you."

Another body crashed down before her. Chin raised, Madori stared ahead across the marching prisoners and laughing Radians.

The march continued into the endless, cold darkness of the night.

CHAPTER TWENTY-ONE
INTO DARKNESS

The Red Flame Armada sailed up the Inaro River, driving deep into the dark wilderness of Qaelin.

Jitomi, the new emperor of Ilar, flew above his fleet upon Tianlong's back. The dragon coiled beneath him, red beard fluttering and black scales chinking. Below, upon the silver river, the five hundred ships formed a great serpent of lights, their lanterns red and orange. Battened sails rose high, catching the wind. Many oars pounded the river, driving the ships upstream. Cannons, soldiers in steel, and pagodas bearing archers rose upon the decks. It was the greatest fleet in the world, a machine of war, a floating empire. Tens of thousands of troops stood upon these decks or within the hulls, waiting to kill. Thousands of cannons stood ready to fire into the enemy.

"This is," Jitomi whispered, "the hope of the night."

Tianlong grunted, his scales chinking. "Ilar has always been smaller than Qaelin, but its armies greater, its ships mightier. For too many generations, we tormented the northern coast, slaying our own brothers and sisters." The dragon bared his fangs. "But now the might of Ilar will crush Timandrians, even if we must sail into the very lands of sunlight." The dragon looked over his shoulder at Jitomi, and his red eyes narrowed. "You will lead us to glory, my emperor."

Jitomi took a shuddering breath. Emperor . . . No, he had never wished to be Ilar's Emperor. His head still spun to consider it. For many generations, the Hashido family had been powerful, wealthy, a protector of the coast. But to usurp Empress Hikari, to begin a new, imperial dynasty . . .

"I never wanted this, Tianlong," he said softly. "I never imagined my father would seize the throne. I never imagined he would die and I would inherit that throne. I'm not a leader." He

425

looked down at the hundreds of sailing ships. "They will know. They will find out that I'm not a warrior, not an emperor to fear. And fear has always been the glue holding Ilar together."

Coiling across the sky, Tianlong puffed smoke out from his nostrils. "Jitomi, I have protected Ilar for thousands of years, and I have seen many emperors rise and fall. I have seen a dozen dynasties claw their way up from the dirt, reach glory, and fade. One dynasty ends, another begins. This has always been the way of Ilar."

Jitomi nodded. "I know the history. But all those emperors were great warriors—like Hikari. Like my father. Like all the conquerors before them. What chance do I have?" He shook his head. "I defeated Lord Naroma, but how long until another lord rises to challenge me, to usurp my reign with armies and many ships?"

The dragon raised his eyebrows and thrust out his jaw. "Probably not very long." He looked back at Jitomi, and a hint of amusement filled his eyes. "Were you hoping I'd tell you that you're strong too, or that you can find inner strength and lead this nation for many years? No. That would be a lie." He laughed, spewing smoke. "Truth is, Jitomi, you won't last long upon this throne. You are gentle and kind—admirable qualities for a man, poor qualities for an Ilari emperor. If you were to seek my advice, I would tell you to flee into the wilderness, to hide, to never emerge back into the night, for you speak truth: the lords of other houses will rebel against you, and even within your own house you will face challengers, for your elder sisters will lust for the throne. They will see you for what you are: a mere boy. And they will crush you."

Jitomi tightened his hands around the saddle's horn. He stared forward along the Inaro River that snaked northward through the dark lands of Qaelin. "So I cannot keep this throne. But maybe I can lead this fleet for just long enough—long enough to find her." His throat felt too tight. "To find Madori. And long enough to fight Serin. Tianlong, will you help me? Will *you* be loyal to me, at least until we can win this war? I can't do this without you. The nobles will not fear or respect me, but they still respect you."

The black dragon licked his chops. His fangs gleamed. "I am loyal only to Ilar, little emperor. For thousands of years, I fought only for the Red Flame, not for any mortal man or woman." He snorted.

"Some emperors claimed to be immortal, to be deities of the night. They lie buried underground and I still fly." Fire kindled in his eyes. "I am the last dragon in all of Mythimna. Did you know that, Jitomi?"

Hail filled the wind, pattering against Jitomi's armor. He pulled down the visor of his helmet. The ice crashed against the steel. "I do." His voice barely carried over the wind. "Your two last siblings—Shenlai of Qaelin and Pirilin of Leen—fell in the War of Day and Night. The Timandrians slew them. I emerged into the world as Pirilin fell. I was born during that great last battle in Asharo."

Rage and pain twisted the dragon's voice. "The Timandrians slew them. I was there when Pirilin died. I saw the cruelty of sunlight. I fought with Hikari, a noble empress, against the hosts of the light." He tossed back his head and let out a roar. "And I mourn my siblings still. Now Timandra attacks again. Your father wanted to join the Timandrians, to lie down with demons. You, Jitomi, want to fight." The dragon's face split into a horrible, toothy grin. "So yes, I will help you for now. I will keep you alive even as the nobles may plot to slay you. And we will fight the sunlight together."

Jitomi closed his eyes. He thought back to his first battle. It had been on the road outside of Teel University in Mageria, his friends at his side. He had fought Lari herself then, and he had nearly died in the dirt. He had been only a boy, cast out from his father's court, alone, afraid.

He opened his eyes and looked back down at the fleet, the legendary mighty of Ilar. Upon hundreds of decks, men were beating drums. Thousands of oars rowed to the beat. Thousands of soldiers all in steel, their helmets shaped as snarling demon faces, prepared for war. Jitomi clutched the hilt of his own sword.

Now I return with an army.

The armada sailed on through the night, heading north toward the fires of war.

* * * * *

They stood outside the pyramid gates, hundreds of feet above the marshlands, watching the enemy close in like a noose.

"Daenor is fallen," Lord Kee'an whispered, eyes damp. "The swamps are lost."

Standing beside him, Neekeya snarled and clutched her sword. "Not as I still breathe. Not as I still wield steel."

They stood on a stone ledge outside the throne room. Behind them rose the archway that led into the pyramid's crest. Before them a staircase trailed down the pyramid's southern facade, leading to the swamp. A hundred soldiers of Eetek Pyramid stood upon this staircase, guarding the passage to the throne room, but Neekeya knew they were but ants facing a herd of buffaloes. Her eyes stung to gaze at the lands around her.

The swamps shook and wept as the Radian forces poured in.

From the east came those enemies Neekeya had failed to stop in the mountains. Nayan elephants waded through the marshlands, archers upon their backs, and many Nayan warriors, their beards and hair flaming red, walked behind them, leading leashed tigers. Magerians walked there too, their steel plates tinted black, and mages moved among them, their dark horses walking knee-deep through the water. The enemy covered the land like a swarm of insects, and as they moved, they destroyed—cutting down trees, burning the huts and gardens of farmers, crushing fruit groves.

When Neekeya turned to look south, she saw more enemies arrive. Here marched Eseerians, warriors of the southern desert realms. Thousands of years ago, Eseerians and Daenorians were said to have been one people, a tribe of mountain dwellers; still many of their words were the same, and even their gods shared kins of family. Yet the Daenorians had migrated north into the marshlands, the Eseerians south to the desert, and now these warriors, clad in white robes and bearing scimitars, advanced north to crush their cousins, and they too bore the Radian banners, sworn to Serin.

Neekeya stepped to the edge of the platform, climbed onto a statue of the god Cetela, and stared around the pyramid's crest toward the north. There too she saw an enemy, and these forces chilled her most of all. Fellow Daenorians swarmed from there, her northern kin who dwelled in the open plains, their skin lighter, their clothes, castles, and customs mimicking those found east of the mountains in the realms of fallen Riyona. For many years, the North

Daenorians had turned against the old ways of their southern kin, building castles instead of pyramids, donning wool instead of crocodile skin, dining upon fine pastries instead of frog legs and chestnut stews.

They forgot who they are, Neekeya thought, staring at the advancing soldiers. *They're ashamed of the crocodile banner, and so now they raise the Radian eclipse upon their flags, and they seek to crush us southerners.*

She climbed off the statue and rejoined those upon the ledge: her father, thirty soldiers in steel, and her husband.

"Nations from across Timandra have joined the Radian Order," she said. "Even our own kin from the north have betrayed us. But I will never join Serin." She drew her sword with a hiss. "We are perhaps the last free land in sunlight. And now is our last stand."

Tam's eyes lit with fire, and he drew his new sword, a reptilian sword of the marshes. "A last stand for freedom. I will die here if I must."

All across the horizons, the marshlands trembled. Trees collapsed. Villages burned. Birds fled across the sky, abandoning the crumbling land. And everywhere the enemy advanced, and their drums beat, and their horns blared, and their chants rose, praising Serin and the Radian Empire. Everywhere flew the Radian standards, a thousand suns hiding the moon.

The forces reached the smaller pyramids first, the twelve lesser halls of the marshes, sisters to Eetek Pyramid. The Radian hosts charged up the staircases along their flanks, firing arrows, thrusting spears. The pyramid guards fought back, tall men in crocodile armor, their swords wide, their arrows swift. Thousands of corpses slid down the pyramids' facades. Neekeya watched as her brothers in arms slew hundreds, perhaps thousands of enemies.

Yet the Radians kept swarming. One pyramid—the smallest one, the ancient Se'antak, Tail of the Crocodile—fell first. The Radians—these ones were Magerians, lords of the new empire—reached its crest and knocked down its statues. The eclipse banner rose there, replacing the old standards of Daenor. Another pyramid—the lofty Te'anta, the Hall of the Marsh Light—fell next, its last defenders slain. Nayan troops crushed the statues on its crest, dug out gems from stone, and raised their banners. One by one, the ancient halls of the swamps fell.

"Thus does Daenor fall," said Lord Kee'an, voice low. The old warrior held a shield in one hand, its rim bristly with crocodile teeth, and in the other he held a great curved sword. "But not without a fight. In many ages to come, people will speak of Daenor's Last Stand, of the blood that we spilled here. They will speak in whispers in the halls of an enduring Radian Empire, or they will sing of honor in free lands. Whether we are painted as vanquished foes or fallen heroes, we will be remembered for eternity."

A gust of wind blew, scented of fire. Smoke rose from a dozen villages across the land, and the groves of bobwoods burned. The last banners of Daenor fluttered above Neekeya, displaying a green crocodile upon a golden field. Below the staircase, the first of the enemy's elephants reached the pyramid of Eetek. The first warriors—Magerians in dark steel—began to climb the stairs.

Tam, seemingly by instinct, stepped closer to the staircase, shielding Neekeya with his body. She moved forward too, coming to stand again at his side.

"We will fight bravely together, Tam," she said.

When he looked at her, his eyes narrowed with pain. "I don't fear death, but I fear losing you, Neekeya."

She held both bow and arrow, and she could not hold his hand, but she moved closer to him, and their bodies touched. She stared into his eyes. "I married you, my love, only turns ago, and I found joy in life. If I must die, let it be here and now, weapons in my hands, the banner of my people rising above me, side by side with my husband. I will take this end over old age under the banners of a tyrant."

The clash of steel rang below. She looked back down the staircase and saw the last soldiers of South Daenor dueling the climbing enemies. All around the pyramid, more Radian troops arrived—oaring boats, wading through the water, or riding beasts. They began to swarm up the pyramid, climbing the stairs, climbing the sloping walls, rising like ants over a tasty morsel.

Neekeya, Tam, and the other soldiers upon the platform fired their bows. Their arrows, tipped with the poison of golden frogs, sent enemies crashing down the pyramid's flanks. But too many soldiers were climbing; new men replaced all those who fell, an endless supply. Neekeya kept firing, taking down man by man. As they fell, they crashed into the soldiers climbing below them. Corpses tumbled down into the marshes. The pyramid's defenders rolled down logs bristly with metal spikes, sending Radians crashing down. And still the enemy attacked, more emerging from the swamps every breath, swallowing the land, climbing higher and higher.

Soon the last Daenorians upon the staircase had fallen to the swords of the enemy. That enemy climbed all four of the pyramid's facades, ascending foot by foot.

For my home, Neekeya thought. *For my husband. For my father. For Madori and Jitomi and all lost friends.*

The enemy reached the top of the staircase. Neekeya screamed and swung her sword.

She fought in a fury, screaming, knocking men down. Tam, her father, and her fellow soldiers fought around her, their swords forming a ring of steel, cutting into the climbers. Magerians tumbled down the pyramid, slamming into their fellow soldiers. Blood poured like lava spilling down a volcano. And still the enemies climbed.

One Daenorian soldier, a beefy man with a bald head, fell at Neekeya's side, impaled by a spear. Another warrior, a woman with braided hair and fierce eyes, screamed and tumbled, her chest pierced with a crossbow bolt. Enemy arrows clattered around Neekeya. One slammed into her armor. Another arrow whistled and cut into Tam's shoulder, and his blood spurted. A third Daenorian fell. Several Magerians leaped onto the platform, and Neekeya howled and raced toward them, cut them down, and sent their corpses tumbling. More kept climbing.

"Fall back!" Kee'an shouted. He thrust a spear into a Radian soldier, piercing the man's neck. "Into the pyramid—fall back!"

Neekeya swung her sword, parried an enemy's attack, then drove her blade into the man's armpit and out of his throat. She tugged her sword back with a shower of blood, looked at her father, and nodded. Swords flashing, the last defenders of Eetek—no more than a score—raced off the platform, under an archway, and into the triangular throne room. Grunting, men slammed the pyramid doors shut.

Daniel Arenson

"Tam, help me!" Neekeya shouted. Together they lifted and dropped an oaken beam into the doors' brackets. Already Magerians were slamming at the doors from outside, and when Neekeya raced toward the archways lining the hall, she saw more Magerians climbing the craggy facades; they would reach these side entrances within moments and swarm the hall, and no doors had been built to block these passageways.

Kee'an turned toward his men and gave them a silent stare and nod. The soldiers nodded back, approached the great wooden throne of Eetek, and shoved the seat. Their muscles bulged and the throne scratched along the floor, revealing a trapdoor.

"Daughter," Kee'an said, turning toward her. "Now is the time to flee." Men opened the trap door, revealing a tunnel. "The passageway leads deep into the pyramids and below them the mines. The tunnels run deep and exit in the western hills. That is your path now."

Neekeya paused. The doors rattled and cracked. One Magerian soldier reached an archway on the eastern wall, and Neekeya fired an arrow, slaying him. She spun back toward her father.

"I vowed to fight until death!"

Kee'an's shoulders stooped, and his eyes seemed so sad to her, so old. "Will you have me die seeing my heiress perish?" He stepped toward her and clasped her arm. "Do not let my line die here, daughter. The line of Eetek must survive, if not in our halls or marshlands, then in exile. Flee with Tam! Seek his father, whom men say still fights in the north." Tears streamed from the old warrior's eyes. "*Live*, Neekeya. Live to bear a child, to carry on our line. Please."

Tam fired an arrow at another Magerian who reached the hall. He turned toward Neekeya and held her hand. "If your father commands it, I will see you to safety."

"I command it," said Kee'an. "Take my daughter to the halls of your parents, Tam—to King Camlin and Queen Linee, if they still live—or to whatever free land you can still find." His tears fell. "Let me die knowing that my line does not perish with my kingdom."

The door cracked and shattered. Magerians stormed into the hall, shouting and brandishing their swords.

432

Kee'an stared at Neekeya one last time.

"Go," he whispered. "I'll hold them off. Run, my daughter! I love you always."

With that, the old warrior howled. With his last few soldiers, a mere dozen men, he raced toward the shattered doors and the swarming enemies.

Neekeya stood, bloody sword raised, torn.

Tam grabbed her arm. "Come, Neekeya! Into the mines."

She stared at her father, tears in her eyes. He was roaring, swinging his sword, cutting down the enemy. His men fell around him. More Magerians entered through the archways, racing into the hall.

"Neekeya!" Tam shouted.

She wept.

Goodbye, Father. Goodbye.

She let Tam drag her into the tunnel. They plunged into darkness.

Fires blazed above, men laughed, and a single cry rang out: "Run, Neekeya! Run and live!"

She ran, tears in her eyes, into shadow.

CHAPTER TWENTY-TWO
IRON MINE NUMBER ONE

"Dig!" the overseer shouted. "Dig or more will die."

Overseer Nafar was a towering man, nearly seven feet tall and thin as a blade. A patch covered one of his eyes, and he was missing his left hand. Instead of a wooden hand or even a hook, a whip was attached onto the stump. Standing in the mine, he swung his arm and cracked the whip. The lash landed against an old Elorian woman, cutting the skin.

"Dig or die, nightcrawlers." The overseer licked his lips. "Faster!"

The old woman, back bleeding, swung her pickaxe with shaky hands. The sharp iron head barely chipped the canyon wall.

Koyee's limbs shook, and rage simmered inside her. Her fists trembled around the shaft of her own pickaxe. She wanted to charge at the guards, to climb the canyon walls, to attack and slay them.

There are hundreds of us! she thought, looking around the canyon. *All with sharp pickaxes. We can attack, we can—*

"Dig, worm!" Overseer Nafar marched toward Koyee, and his whip cracked against her shoulders. She yelped. "Dig or I'll kill another one as you watch."

Koyee spun around, back bleeding, and stared at the Timandrian. Nafar was a brutish thing, a giant of a man, missing a hand and eye but still strong, still deadly. Other Magerians stood around him, all in armor, all armed with whips and swords.

I can slay at least one or two, Koyee thought. *I can swing my pick into Nafar's face, even as I'm weak, even as—*

Nafar snorted. "Very well." He approached an old Elorian man with a long white beard. He held a dagger to the elder's throat. "Dig now or he dies. His blood will be upon you. Just like the last one."

Koyee narrowed her eyes. She could see the blood of the overseer's last victims on his arms.

Slowly, she turned back toward the canyon wall. She swung her pick. She chipped into the stone.

"Good," said the overseer. "Good. But this old man is useless anyway."

A gurgling scream tore through the air. Koyee spun around to see the overseer pull his knife free from the elder's throat, then kick the corpse aside.

"You said you—" Koyee began.

Nafar lashed his whip, hitting her cheek.

"Dig or I'll kill a hundred others! And not just old men. We got children here too. Back to work, nightcrawler."

"Please," whispered the young woman who worked beside Koyee. "Please, Koyee, my son is here. He's only ten. Please dig. Please don't cause trouble."

Her innards trembling and her teeth grinding, Koyee returned to digging. Blood dripped down her cheek to the corner of her mouth. She swung her pick against the canyon wall with all the strength she had.

Hundreds of other prisoners worked around her—Elorians captured in Oshy and other villages across Western Qaelin. Fishermen. Mushroom farmers. Captive soldiers. They were all the same now, all prisoners of the Radian Empire. Like her, they worked with chained ankles. Like her, their heads were shaved, the scalps nicked and encrusted with dry blood. Like her, they wore burlap rags. Like her, their shoulders were branded with the Radian eclipse. Koyee's brand still blazed every time she swung her arms, and she winced to remember the hot iron pressing against her only turns ago, forever marking her a slave to the Radian Empire.

Have we really been here for only a few turns? she thought. It felt like years.

She looked around the canyon at the poor souls, her fellow prisoners. Dust from their digging rose in clouds, hiding the stars and moon. Koyee had never seen such a wretched lot. Not only were they bald and branded and bruised, they were famished. At first, their Radian masters had fed them scraps—vegetable peels, thin broth, a few apple cores—and even these scraps had stopped coming two turns ago. Koyee had not eaten since. Her body, like the bodies of her fellow slaves, was fading away.

They do not truly care for iron ore, she thought, swinging her pickaxe into the stone again. *They want to torture us, to work and starve us to death, and to laugh as we dwindle down to bones.*

Indeed, a hundred Magerian troops stood atop the canyon, staring down at the Elorians who worked below as if watching a show. They drank from wine skins, ate salted meat and bread, and laughed as they watched the prisoners work.

"Faster!" shouted Overseer Nafar. The whip that sprouted from his arm swung, hitting a young boy. "Dig, nightcrawler." The whip swung again, splattering blood across the child's back.

Koyee raced forward, chains rattling. "Stop it! He's only a boy."

The one-eyed, one-handed Magerian laughed. "I told you to dig, nightcrawler. Now I will have to kill another one."

The whip flew again and again, slamming into the screaming child. Koyee screamed too. She couldn't resist the rage anymore. She leaped toward the overseer, but two other Magerians caught her arms and tugged her back. She watched, shouting, as Nafar beat the child, cutting the frail boy over and over.

"Please!" Koyee begged. "Stop!"

Nafar turned toward her, cheeks red, grinning. "Return to digging like a good nightcrawler, and I will stab the boy's heart." The overseer laughed. "Keep screaming like a pig, and I'll keep whipping. It can take him hours to die this way."

Too weak to fight, famished and wounded and feverish, Koyee still tried to lunge forward, to attack. But the Magerians held her back, and she only lowered her head and nodded. She returned to the canyon wall, and she dug again. She heard the child's last gasp, and she smelled the blood.

Be at peace now, she thought, tears in her eyes. *The rest of us will soon envy you, child.*

The prisoners kept swinging their pickaxes, digging out clumps of iron ore. Deeper in the canyon, great smelters sat upon fires, melting the rocks to extract the iron. Molten metal bubbled in cauldrons, and smiths forged fresh blades, helmets, and arrowheads.

436

With our blood and tears, Koyee thought, *we're building the weapons of our enemies.*

After what seemed like turns of digging, the overseer finally blew a horn, and the Elorians shuffled in their chains toward a chamber cut into the canyon wall. They entered the crude cave, a shelter for a few hours of rest.

Koyee huddled among the others. The cave was so small they all pressed together; they barely had room to lie down. Cold wind shrieked through the entrance, and the prisoners shivered. Yet cold as the wind was, Koyee felt hot; when she touched her forehead, it felt on fire, and her limbs would not stop trembling. Around her, she saw sweat bead upon brows. Prisoners coughed blood. She wondered what would kill them first: the whip, the cold, the hunger, or the fever.

She closed her eyes, remembering a time many years ago when she had been but a youth, no older than Madori was now. She had worked in the Hospice of Pahmey, wearing the uniform of the Sisterhood—a heavy leather cloak, thick gloves, and a mask with a beak full of herbs. That outfit had protected her from the diseases that Timandrians carried, illnesses they were immune to but which ravaged so many Elorians. Now she was exposed. Now, instead of a healing, she was dying.

Does my life end here? she wondered, coughing and huddling with the others in the darkness. *After all my battles, all my victories, all my pain and joy, do I—Koyee of Qaelin, the Girl in the Black Dress—fade away in darkness?*

"I miss you, Torin," she whispered and tasted her tears. "I miss you, Madori. Remember me as I was, a warrior in armor, a brave woman, her white hair streaming in the wind." She was almost grateful her family could not see her now, the creature she had become.

"Please, Madori," she whispered. "If you're alive, run from here. Run as far as you can. Run and hide."

The Elorians around her wept, prayed, and shivered, and Koyee closed her eyes, hugged her knees, and struggled to take breath by breath.

* * * * *

Pahmey's prisoners entered the mine with screams, the cracks of whips, and the smell of blood. Madori stared in silence.

Serrated steel fences surrounded the camp, tipped with blades, and many Magerian guards patrolled them, clad in dark steel and armed with longswords and crossbows. Large dogs barked between them, tugging at their chains, their fangs bared; they seemed desperate to rip into Elorian flesh. An archway broke these walls of steel, and above it hung a sign in both the languages of Mageria and Qaelin: "Labor Brings Light"

Gora, the squat captain who had led the march here, shouted, "Nightcrawlers, enter your new home! Move, worms!"

The survivors of Pahmey, coughing and trembling, hobbled under the archway and into the camp. Chains jangled between their ankles and wrists, and dust and blood caked their skin. Madori blinked, barely able to drag her feet forward. Every last inch of her was bruised, cut, or swelling. She coughed and tasted blood.

"The journey is over," she whispered. "Finally over."

She trembled as she walked. Even in the shrieking cold wind of Eloria's winter, her skin burned and sweat dripped down her brow. How long had she been marching? She did not know; it felt like many turns. She vaguely remembered many Elorians leaving Pahmey, two thousand or more. When she blinked, looking ahead at the others, she saw only several hundred. The rest still lay in the wilderness, a long road of death, fallen to the march. Their bones would perhaps forever mark the path of Eloria's fall.

And hundreds of thousands vanished into the sinkhole that was Pahmey, she thought, shuffling forward with the others. *And perhaps millions of nightcrawlers now lie dead across the rest of the night.*

She blinked and clenched her fists.

No! We are Elorians. Not nightcrawlers. I must never let them reduce me to a worm. I am Elorian, as pure as any other now. We are a proud people, even as we bleed, even as we shuffle through the dust. We will never be the creatures they want us to become.

Gora rode his horse beside her. "Be a good mongrel." He drank deeply from a wineskin. Crimson liquid dripped down his chin. "Your little pleasure walk is ending. Here you will find no mercy."

The prisoners filed into the camp. Madori, walking at the back, entered last. Here, at the end of her journey, every step was a battle of will, requiring all her strength. Every step blazed like a thousand whips. She forced herself to keep walking. If she fell, she would die. If she fell, she would never see her mother again. And so she forced herself to keep going, past the archway, into the camp.

She blinked, looking around at the swaying world. Several long black tents rose here, their walls painted with Radian eclipses. Magerian troops moved among them, armed with swords and crossbows. Iron braziers crackled, full of red flames; while Elorians could see by moonlight alone, these soldiers of Timandra needed the light of fire.

Farther back rose a fine tent of lush, black fabric rich with golden embroidery. Guards surrounded it, armed with pikes. This was no simple military tent but a place of wealth. Madori stared at it, her belly knotting.

Serin must be in there, she thought. *Maybe Lari too.*

She wanted to race across the camp, to challenge the pair, to slay them with magic or with tooth and nail. But she could barely even walk, and a hundred soldiers separated her from the emperor.

Not yet, Madori, she told herself. *First learn the lay of the land. First find Mother. First regain some strength. Then fight.*

She looked away from the tent. To her left gaped a shadowy canyon; with the braziers filling the camp with smoke, she hadn't seen it until now. This was no natural chasm, she realized, but an iron mine. Cauldrons belched out fumes below, full of molten metal. Pickaxes rested in a pile, and Madori shuddered to see bloodstains on the stones. She couldn't see any miners.

"Line up, nightcrawlers!" Gora rode his horse around the Elorian prisoners. "Line up for inspection. Gather here! Line up."

With whips and spears, Gora and his men herded the Elorians into a fenced courtyard. Torches crackled and blood stained the stony ground. A butcher's block rose ahead by a smoking brazier.

"Line up!"

With a few cracks of the whip, the Elorians entered the courtyard and lined up before the stone block. Madori swayed on her feet. She wanted to do something—to flee, to fight, to scream for her mother. Yet she could barely stay standing, and when once she swayed, Gora's whip bit her shoulder, lapping at her blood. It was all she could do not to fall. One Elorian, a young man who stood before her in line, did fall, dead before he hit the ground. Two Magerian soldiers guffawed and dragged the corpse away.

Stay alive, Madori. Just stay alive for now.

"One by one, to the block!" Gora shouted. "Go on, nightcrawlers, to the block! You first." He pointed at a pale Elorian man with sunken eyes. "To the block."

Madori winced. *That's a butcher's block.* Her eyes stung. *They marched us all the way here to behead us.*

The man made a half-hearted attempt to flee. Gora kicked, driving his steel-tipped boot into the small of the man's back. The Elorian gasped with pain, and Gora manhandled him forward. The man was too weak to resist, famished after long turns on the road, broken and bleeding. Chortling, Gora shoved the man's head down onto the block and drew a curved, ugly knife.

Madori grimaced. *Oh Idar . . . oh stars of Eloria . . .*

Licking his chops, Gora brought the blade down close to the Elorian's face.

Madori closed her eyes.

She heard the Elorian grunt, heard the prisoners gasp, heard Gora laugh. She peeked through narrowed eyelids, expecting to see a rolling head . . . but Gora had not beheaded his prisoner. Instead, he was using the blade to shear the man's hair. The brute chuckled as he worked, tugging the strands violently, cutting the scalp as often as the hair.

"We'll keep you scum alive for now," he said when the man was finally bald. His grin widening, Gora grabbed an iron poker from the brazier, hefted it lovingly, and brought a red-hot brand down onto the Elorian's shoulder.

The prisoner screamed. His flesh sizzled. When Gora finally pulled the brand back, an ugly Radian eclipse smoldered upon the Elorian's shoulder.

"Next prisoner!" Gora shouted.

Some Elorians tried to escape, others to fight. Blades quickly thrust into their throats, and Magerians dragged the corpses away. Most of the prisoners shuffled forward, too weak to resist, to suffer having their hair sheared and their shoulders branded.

I won't scream, Madori thought as Gora shaved her head, scraping his dulled blade against her scalp. Blood dripped down her forehead and neck. *I won't—*

When the brand pressed against her shoulder, she gritted her teeth, and she thought of the Desolation, of Master Lan Tao, of the dear eyes of Grayhem who was lost to her. Even as he held the brand against her for agonizing moments, laughing above her, she did not scream.

Magerians shoved her back toward the others. The prisoners huddled together, beaten, chained, famished, and now bald and branded.

They truly turned us into worms, Madori thought. *They preached that we're not human, so they made us less than human.*

Suddenly the Magerian soldiers, who had spent turns laughing and spitting and singing rude songs, stood at attention. They slammed their fists against their chests.

"Radian rises!" shouted Gora, standing stiff, chin raised. "Blessed be Emperor Serin!"

A trumpet blasted. Hooves thundered. With a flourish of golden banners, a pair of white horses entered the courtyard. Upon them sat two riders—two resplendent deities. Their armor was bright and worked with silver filigree. Cloaks of samite hung across their backs, fastened with golden pins. Strings of jewels hung around their necks and gleamed upon the pommels and scabbards of their swords. The two riders gazed down at the prisoners with haughty blue eyes, and smiles played upon their lips.

A beaten waif, only half-alive, Madori stared up at them and her innards burned.

Serin and Lari.

The emperor and his daughter stared at the hundreds of Elorian prisoners. Lari held an embroidered handkerchief to her nose.

"These ones stink even worse than the first batch," the princess said. "Disgusting creatures."

Madori glared up at the pair, fists clenched. Her father was Serin's cousin—the two men's mothers had been sisters—and Madori shared their blood, but she felt as different from these two as a dog from toads. They didn't recognize her. How could they? If Madori saw herself in a mirror, she doubted she would recognize herself. She no longer looked like a fiery mongrel with strange hair; she was now only a starving, bleeding imitation of a woman, just another branded prisoner, one among all the rest. Lari had perhaps recognized Madori when first staring into the locket, but as Madori now stood among the others, bald and beaten and caked with blood and dust, she blended in—just another nightcrawler.

Emperor Serin cleared his throat. He spoke in a deep voice, addressing the prisoners. "Welcome to your new home! Welcome to Iron Mine Number One, the first of many that will dot the night. Here you will aid the war effort. Here you will dig for iron, melt the metal, and forge new blades and arrowheads and spearheads. With the weapons you make, we will slay your brothers and sisters. With the weapons you bleed for, we will crush the rest of the night. For your service, you'll be allowed to live a few months longer. But be sure, dear nightcrawlers, you will not live forever. And you will be grateful for it."

Lari grinned at his side. "We will show the world what pathetic, sniveling creatures nightcrawlers are. You are nothing but worms. Stinking, disgusting worms. Look at you." She made a gagging sound. "You sicken me."

Lunge at her, Madori told herself. Her fists trembled. *Pull her off her horse. Wring her neck!*

Yet how could she? They wore armor and bore blades, and many soldiers stood around them. Madori was so weak she could barely stand, and chains hobbled her.

Now is not the time to fight, she thought. *I'm too weak to use magic, and I have no weapons. But in the mine they'll give me food, and they'll give me a pickaxe.* She gritted her teeth. *And first chance I get, I'll drive that pickaxe into Lari's head.*

"I will be returning now to the war!" Serin announced, voice ringing across the camp. "There are many more Elorian cities to destroy, many more nightcrawlers to kill or enslave. As you work, slaves, think of them. Think of their agony. And think of how you suffer. Radian is the true light of the world. You now feel its burn." He turned his horse back toward the camp gates. "As I conquer and kill, Princess Lari Serin will remain to command you. Obey her every order, or I promise you: she has new ways of hurting you that will make you miss the whip."

With that, the emperor spurred his horse and rode off, leaving Lari in the courtyard.

The young princess, her golden hair cascading in perfect locks, turned toward Gora.

"Toss these ones in with the others, soldier," she said. "Those worms have lazed about long enough. Let them all dig together. Let them dig for the iron that will slay their own miserable kind." She snorted. "And next ones that die, burn them outside the camp; my tent still stinks of the last nightcrawlers you burned."

Gora bowed his head. "Yes, Your Highness." He turned toward the Elorian prisoners. "All right, worms! Move! It's into the mine with you. Time to dig or die. Go!"

He cracked his whip, and the Elorians began to shuffle out of the courtyard. Their chains jangled, and their brands blazed against their shoulders, raw and red. Most of the prisoners were too weary to lift their heads. Madori herself struggled for every breath. How could she possibly dig in this state? She doubted she could even raise a quill, let alone a pickaxe.

"If you want us to dig," she blurted out, "let us eat and drink and rest first!" She knew she was being a fool, but she couldn't stop the stream of words. "We're almost dead. We've just walked for turns. If you want us to be good workers, give us a meal! Give us water. Give us a turn to sleep."

Gora growled and, as expected, his whip slammed against Madori's back. She fell to her knees, gasping for breath.

Hooves pounded as Lari rode her horse near. The princess laughed icily. "A feisty one we have here! Beat her to death, Gora. Make it last a while. I would like to—" Lari froze. Her eyes narrowed.

The princess inhaled sharply, dismounted, and knelt beside Madori. "By the sunlight . . ."

Madori stared into Lari's eyes, saying nothing.

Lari's face split into a huge, toothy grin. She looked like a child who had just been given the world's largest cake. "I know this one!" Lari laughed. "The mongrel! It's Madori the mongrel!" She turned toward Gora. "I changed my mind. This one will live. In fact, this one will not be a miner." Lari looked back at Madori, and her smile turned cruel, predatory. "She will be my personal servant. I'm in need of a handmaiden in this camp. Yes, this mongrel will suffer a special fate."

Madori cursed herself. To the song of whips and wails, the Elorians' slavery began.

CHAPTER TWENTY-THREE
UNDERGROUND

Neekeya ran through the tunnel, Tam at her side.

Father . . .

She panted. Her eyes stung.

Father, where are you?

The tunnel walls raced at her sides, painted with murals of crocodiles, cranes, and reed boats navigating marshlands. The torch she carried flickered, the only source of light. The floor sloped steeply, and the tunnel wound like a corkscrew, moving down the pyramid. They had been running for what seemed like ages; surely they were beneath ground level now, plunging deep into the earth, fleeing the threat above.

"We will live." Tam, who ran at her side, met her eyes. "I promise you."

Live? What use was there for life as a coward? She was fleeing battle. She had left her father to die. She had left her kingdom to burn and all her people to perish in the Radian fire. She wanted to shout these things at him, but she only nodded silently.

Yes, perhaps I must live now, a last promise to my father. The pain squeezed her chest. *To bring new life to a fallen dynasty. To live as beggars, exiles, wandering the world, alone, forgotten . . . carrying a secret light.*

"Find the swamp wench and the boy!" rose a shout above. "Slay them!"

Neekeya growled. She recognized that voice.

"Prince Felsar," she muttered.

Last she had seen him, the Prince of North Daenor, traitor to the kingdom, had been caged outside the pyramid, imprisoned for joining the Radian Order and threatening Eetek with destruction. Now destruction had fallen, and Neekeya felt sick at the thought of the traitor freed.

"You cannot escape me, Neekeya!" His voice rang above, and his laughter echoed. "I have seen you flee into the tunnels as a rat. Come face me, coward, and die salvaging some of your honor."

Neekeya drew her sword and made to spin around, to charge back up and face him. Tam grabbed her arm, holding her fast.

"No, Neekeya." He tugged her. "I promised your father I'd lead you to safety. Felsar will have many men with him. Now is not our time to fight him."

She trembled with rage, but she nodded and kept running further down the tunnel with Tam. She cursed herself for not slaying the prince when she'd last faced him.

The tunnel leveled off and widened into a great hall, large enough for a dragon to fly through. They had reached the great Eetek Mines, the source of her family's power and wealth. Many crystals gleamed upon the cavern walls, and carts full of mined gems gleamed upon tracks. Amethysts, topaz, emeralds, sapphires, and diamonds all shone here. The miners were gone—whether they had left to fight or seek safety elsewhere Neekeya did not know. Metal tracks plunged into shadows, leading to the deeper mines. A crevice split the floor, and peering down, Neekeya saw a rivulet of lava gurgling in a red river.

"The Mines of Eetek," she whispered. "A place of wealth, beauty, and magic." Even in the horror of war, she paused for a heartbeat, marveling at the beauty of the place.

Shouts rose behind her.

Tam and Neekeya spun around, swords raised.

Prince Felsar emerged from the tunnel into the mine. With him ran a hundred soldiers or more—Magerians in black steel. Felsar himself wore a black breastplate now; it sported the Radian sigil.

He pointed his sword at her—the long, thin sword of a Magerian. "There they are."

Neekeya sneered. "Felsar! You are a fool." She spat. "Do you really think you're one of them? You clad yourself in Magerian armor, but I still see your dusky skin. You wear the sigil of the eastern empire, but the blood of a Daenorian still pumps through your veins. You are a traitor."

The prince shook his head. "No, *Latani*. You fail to understand. Daenor can no longer stand alone, an outcast in the sunlight. The time has come to join the rest of Timandra, to be equals in a sunlit empire. That is what the Radian Order gives us—equality. All who serve Serin will find honor. And all who seek to fight my master will perish. And so will you and the prince pup." He turned toward the Magerians around him. "Slay them."

The Magerians raised crossbows. Quarrels whistled.

Neekeya and Tam dived and ducked behind a metal cart. The bolts slammed into it, and gemstones cascaded.

Boots thumped as the enemy ran forward. Growling, Neekeya shoved against the minecart she hid behind. It tilted over, spilling hundreds of gems across the floor. Three Magerians, racing forward with swinging swords, tripped and crashed down, clumsy in their armor. Others knelt and began to collect the gems.

Neekeya tugged the emptied cart back onto the track. She jumped inside and gestured to Tam.

"Well, come on! You wanted to save me, right?"

He nodded and leaped into the cart too. More crossbows thrummed. They ducked and the quarrels flew over their heads. Neekeya grabbed a lever and tugged, releasing the cart's brakes. With shrieks and a shower of sparks, the trolley began racing down the metal rails, heading deeper into the mine.

Wind whipped their hair. They gripped the sides of the cart, ducking as more quarrels flew overhead. The tracks plunged down into darkness, and craggy walls raced at their sides, their gemstones blurred into streaks. Only several scattered torches provided illumination.

"Idar's Beard!" Tam cursed. "Is this thing safe?"

Neekeya shook her head. "Not at this speed. But neither are Radians with crossbows."

As the minecart trundled down the track, she glanced behind her and cursed. Several other carts were racing in pursuit, the enemy within them. Prince Felsar sat in the lead trolley, and Magerians filled the carts behind him. All bore crossbows and swords. Another bolt fired and Neekeya ducked, dodging the projectile.

"Neekeya, watch out!" Tam shouted.

She winced to see a sharp turn in the tracks. Desperately, she grabbed the lever and tugged on the brakes. The cartwheels screamed. Sparks rose in a fountain. As the cart skidded along the turn, it tilted over, nearly spilling Tam and Neekeya. Below, she could see the darkness plunging down to the river of lava. She screamed and leaned the opposite way, and the cart's wheels slammed back down onto the track. They kept racing downward.

"Idar's Soggy Britches," Tam muttered.

An instant later, Neekeya saw Felsar's cart just barely make the turn; it too tilted and nearly tumbled down before righting itself. The cart behind Felsar, however, did not break in time. It began to make the turn, then veered off the rails and tumbled down. Men screamed inside before crashing down into the lava.

Neekeya's cart made another sharp turn, plunging into a dark, narrow tunnel that led deeper into the earth. Diamonds shone in the walls around her, and the ribs of ancient reptiles rose like archways above. The enemy carts pursued. Crossbow quarrels flew, and Neekeya ducked. The missiles whistled and slammed into the cart. One quarrel slammed into a wheel, and the cart leaped and nearly overturned. It crashed back down onto the tracks with shrieking sparks.

"Tam, grab the lever!" Neekeya shouted.

She sucked in air and rose above the edge of the cart. A quarrel whistled and she tilted, dodging it.

Focus. She inhaled deeply. *Summon the magic.*

She chose the tracks behind her. She claimed the metal. She changed the material, lifting the rails like the tusks of a rearing elephant.

The minecart behind her hit the shattered metal and flew into the air. Behind it, other carts bolted and tilted, slamming into one another. Felsar screamed, his cart tilting madly. Trollies crashed down into the lava below. Smoke and dust obscured the tunnels, blinding Neekeya.

Her cart kept racing downward.

No enemies pursued.

She breathed out a shaky breath of relief.

We're safe.

"By Inagon's moldy pits!" Tam shouted, laughing. "That was brilliant. Absolutely brilliant."

The tracks led them onward, soon leveling off. They slowed down in a towering, craggy hall the size of a palace. The track here stretched over a chasm, and the lava roiled and bubbled below. Only the thin, rickety track—humble rails cobbled together into a bridge—separated the cart from the inferno below.

The track finally ended at a stone platform that thrust out from the cavern wall. A staircase stretched ahead, leading upward into shadows. The minecart rolled to a stop at the platform. No other carts followed; they all must have fallen off the broken track.

Legs rubbery, Neekeya and Tam climbed out of the cart onto the stone ledge. The platform was only a few feet wide, trapped between the lava and the staircase.

Growls rose to her side.

Eyes narrowed, Neekeya turned toward the sound. A barred door was worked into the stone wall. Beyond lay a chamber full of furry black creatures the size of boars. Tipped with claws, their forepaws were massive; they formed half of each animal's mass. The creatures' tapered heads were eyeless, their noses were long and pink and whiskered, and sharp teeth filled their mouths.

"What are they?" Tam asked, eying them wearily.

"We call them minemoles," Neekeya answered, "though their true name in our tongue is *da'altin*. They are excellent diggers—they dug these mines—though they're also nasty, hungry creatures who thirst for human blood." She shuddered. "Several times, miners cut their fingers upon sharp stones. The minemoles smelled the blood like sharks and . . ." She shook her head wildly. "Never mind that." She pointed at the staircase. "Here the mine ends. These stairs will lead us into the western swamps, hopefully beyond the battle. From there we'll travel, hidden between the trees, to the sea."

Tam nodded and took her hands. "We'll find the sea. I promise you. We'll sail to safety. If my parents still live, we'll find them. We'll survive." He pulled her into his arms and kissed her forehead. "I'll look after you always. I'll love you always."

They stood holding each other for long moments, the chasm of lava to one side, the cellar of minemoles to the other, and the

449

staircase behind them. Finally Neekeya broke apart from the embrace. She placed one foot upon the staircase and reached out to him.

"We climb."

Before she could take another step, a voice rose from across the chasm.

"You cannot escape, Neekeya. It's over."

Prince Felsar came walking along the rails over the pit of lava. Behind him walked a dozen Magerian soldiers and three mages in black armor.

Neekeya hissed, crouched, and claimed the track. She tugged the metal, intending to shatter the rails again, to send the enemy plunging down into the lava. The rails began to bend. But the three Magerian mages—they seemed to hover above the track—seized control of the magic, pressing the rails back into place. They raised their hands, and blasts of magic shot across the chasm to slam into Neekeya and Tam.

The two fell, writhing in pain.

The pain ended as fast as it had begun. Neekeya lay gasping, electricity crackling across her. She struggled to her feet, and Tam rose beside her, coughing. Sweat dripped down their foreheads.

Neekeya took another step onto the staircase.

More magic blasted out, knocking her down. She screamed. Blood dipped from her mouth, and the minemoles shrieked in their enclosure, banging against the bars, begging to feed.

When the pain ended, Neekeya spun back toward the track that spanned the chasm. Felsar and the mages had crossed half the bridge now. Hoods hid the mages' faces, but Neekeya could see Felsar clearly. He was smiling.

"You cannot escape us," the prince said. "Even if you make it up the stairs—and perhaps I will let you climb them for sport—we will hunt you in the marshes. Perhaps I will keep you alive. Perhaps I will drag you to Emperor Serin in chains, so he may torture you himself. The *Latani* of Eetek and the Price of Arden . . . fine prizes." The prince licked his lips. "Fine prizes that would elevate me to glory in the court of my lord."

Tam coughed and hugged himself. Blood dripped from cuts the magic had left across him. The minemoles were shrieking, reaching their paws between the bars of their enclosure, consumed with bloodlust, desperate for their crimson drink.

Neekeya's limbs shook. Her head spun. Coughing and bleeding, she struggled back up to her feet. Tam grasped her arms. He stared at her, sweat dripping into his eyes.

"Climb, Neekeya." He stroked a strand of her hair; it was wet with blood and sweat. "Run."

She looked back at the tracks. The enemy was advancing, the lava gurgling below. If she stepped onto the stairs again, the mages would blast their magic, she knew. What could she do? She was trapped. She had failed. She—

"Run!" Tam shouted.

He spun toward the enclosure in the wall. Magic blasted out from his hand, shattering the metal bars. With a single swift movement, Tam swiped his hand across his blade, then lifted his bleeding palm.

The minemoles raced toward him, clawing over one another in a mad dash.

"Up the stairs, Neekeya!" the Prince of Arden shouted . . . and leaped onto the track.

"Tam!" she shouted.

He ran across the metal track over the chasm, heading toward the enemy. Neekeya cried out and tried to run after him, but the minemoles raced around her, each as large as a boar. They slammed into her, knocking her down, in their mad dash after Tam's dripping blood. The creatures scurried along the track like rats along a rope.

Upon the track, high above the lava, Tam swung his sword, parrying a bolt of magic. Shouting wordlessly, he slammed into Felsar.

"Tam!" Neekeya shouted, tears in her eyes.

An instant later, a dozen minemoles leaped onto Tam, Felsar, and the soldiers on the track. Magic blasted out. Men screamed. Blood showered. Fire exploded.

With creaks and snaps, the iron rails shattered.

Both men and minemoles fell.

Neekeya reached across the chasm, screaming, watching the rails plummet.

The lava showered up toward the ceiling and walls, greedy tongues licking chops of stone, satisfied after a hearty meal.

"Tam . . ."

Neekeya remained upon the stone ledge, reaching down toward the lava. Her body shook. Tears gushed from her eyes.

"My husband . . ."

The lava settled and gurgled peacefully, a red river. The bridge had vanished, leaving only a few shattered spikes of metal. All that remained of men and minemoles was the echo of a scream, perhaps only a memory. All that remained of Neekeya's life was a hollow, empty shell.

She wept. Her life was saved. Her husband was gone.

"Tam . . . please," she whispered. "Please, let this be a trick. Let this be some illusion of your magic. Tam . . ."

More Magerian soldiers emerged across the chasm from the opposite tunnel. They saw Neekeya, raised crossbows, and fired. Several quarrels clattered around her, and one drove into her thigh. She screamed.

I'm sorry, Tam. I'm sorry.

She turned and ran up the staircase, quarrels pattering around her feet. She climbed for hundreds of steps, moving higher and higher, her blood dripping, her tears falling. Finally she emerged back into the marshlands, turned around, and saw the Pyramid of Eetek a mile away. Radian banners rose from its crest, and Magerians blew horns in victory.

Covered in blood, dust, and mud, Neekeya stood in the marshes, the water up to her knees. She lowered her head and clutched the hilt of her sword.

CHAPTER TWENTY-FOUR
THE BLOOD OF ELORIA

Lari leaned back in her lush armchair, placed her feet upon her embroidered footstool, and sipped from her glass of wine.

"Well, well." She examined Madori. "The war hasn't been good to you, has it?"

The camp outside—Iron Mine Number One—was a nightmarish land of screams, blood, and death. Here in this tent was an oasis of comfort and splendor. The tent walls were woven of rich, crimson wool embroidered with golden thread. Golden bowls of fruit, jeweled jugs of wine, and ivory cutlery rested upon giltwood tables. Statues of rearing buffaloes—symbols of Old Mageria—held crackling embers in their mouths, and their ruby eyes gleamed.

And in the center of this splendor is me, Madori thought.

She looked into a tall mirror, its frame golden. She did not recognize the creature she had become. Cuts bled upon her naked scalp. Grime covered her body. That body was thinner than she'd ever known it, her ribs visible between the tatters of her rags, her joints knobby. The brand still blazed upon her shoulder, raw and red, and the stripes of Gora's whip marked her skin.

She looked back at Lari. As wretched as Madori was, Lari was resplendent. The princess wore a burgundy gown strewn with golden suns, and rubies hung around her neck. Her blond hair cascaded, scented with sweet oils, and even here in the camp, the princess kept her face finely painted—her eyelids powdered blue, her lips tinted red, her cheeks kissed with pink. On her fingers shone rings, each one worth more than Madori's old house and everything it had contained.

"What do you want from me?" Madori asked.

Lari sloshed the wine in her mouth, swallowed, and raised her eyebrow. "Why, I should think it clear, mongrel. I want you to suffer. I want you to stay alive to endure all the pain I can give you. I want you to remain the last living nightcrawler after all others have perished, and to remain by my side, to watch the destruction of the night with me." Lari leaned forward, her teeth stained red with wine. "And then, mongrel, I will return you to the sunlight, where I will parade you around as a freak, a creature for a menagerie. Men and women from across the empire will travel to see you, to pelt you with stones, to laugh at the deformed creature of darkness that I tamed. That is what I will turn you into."

The princess's cheeks flushed, and her grin stretched obscenely wide—so wide it almost seemed to split her face. Her eyes blazed with fire. With her garish makeup and hissing grin, she suddenly seemed less like a woman and more like some demonic jester.

She's insane, Madori realized. *She's not just cruel, not just hateful. She's utterly mad.*

"So why keep me here?" Madori said. "Why not toss me into the mine with the others?"

Lari plucked a grape from a bowl and chewed. "Too easy for you to kill yourself down there. I've seen one do it—slam the pickaxe right into his own head." She laughed—a trill shriek of a sound. "You will not leave my sight. You will not be a miner. You will be my servant; that is a better fate for you. Until the war is over and all the nightcrawlers are dead, you will prepare my meals, wash my clothes, empty my chamber pot, clean my dishes, and mostly watch with me. Yes, mostly you will stand with me above the canyon, watching as the nightcrawlers wither away, watching as they die." Lari rose from her chair, approached Madori, and held her arms. Her eyes blazed with the white light of a madwoman. "It will be glorious."

Madori stared into those two blue orbs of insanity. She shook her head. "I refuse. I will not serve you, Lari. You've gone mad with your power." Hesitantly, she touched Lari's shoulder. "You don't have to become this person. You don't have to let your father turn you into this. I can help you. I—"

Lari screamed and backhanded her. Madori clutched her blazing cheek.

"Be silent, mongrel, or I'll cut out your tongue." Lari grabbed a pitcher and tossed it at Madori. It slammed against her chest and spilled its wine. "I thought you might refuse. I knew you would. But I have ways of forcing you to obey."

"If you hurt me," Madori said softly, "I will endure it."

"May be." Lari laughed. "But I think, if I hurt another, you will find it harder to resist." She shouted toward the tent's entrance. "Gora! Bring her in!"

The tent flap opened. Gora and two other guards dragged in a bald, beaten Elorian.

Madori's eyes dampened.

Her heart seemed to fall still.

Mother.

"Mother!" she cried, leaped forward, and pulled Koyee into an embrace.

Tears streamed down Koyee's bruised face. "Madori! Oh, Madori!" Koyee trembled, caressing Madori's cheek again and again. "I'm so sorry. I'm so sorry, daughter."

Madori could not speak, only weep. Gone was the proud, noble mother she had known, a warrior of starlight. Koyee was now battered, bleeding, her head bald, her hands raw and blistered, her limbs stick-thin. Tears flowed down Madori's cheeks.

"It'll be all right, Mother," she finally whispered through shaking lips, holding Koyee close. "Help will come to us. We—"

"Pull them apart!" Lari shrieked. "Gora! Make the mother suffer. Let the mongrel watch."

With a few grunts and curses, the Magerians grabbed mother and daughter and tugged them apart. Madori wailed and reached out to Koyee, but the guards only laughed, their grips like iron.

With a grin, Gora struck Koyee, knocking her down.

"Damn you!" Madori howled. She struggled against the guards gripping her but couldn't free herself.

Gora chortled and raised his whip above Koyee. Coughing out blood, Koyee struggled to rise, but her arms wobbled, too weak to support her.

"Stop!" Madori cried. She turned toward Lari. "Stop. I'll do as you say. Just let her go."

Gora froze, his whip held in the air, and glanced at Lari. The emperor's daughter nodded. Disappointment clouded Gora's face, and he hawked and seemed ready to spit, then apparently remembered where he stood and swallowed. With a grunt, he grabbed Koyee and manhandled her out of the tent.

"Be strong, Mother!" Madori called after her. "I love you. I love you . . ."

The other guards shuffled out, leaving Madori alone again with Lari in the tent.

Lari cleared her throat, sat back down in her armchair, and placed her feet back upon the footstool. "Now, my dear mongrel, I thirst for wine. Pour me a new cup. Afterward you may fetch me my dinner from the kitchens, then wash my boots and gown; both are dirty from my ride last turn. Well . . . get to work. Or shall I call your nightcrawler mother back in?"

For the next few hours, Madori worked in silence—serving Lari, cleaning her plates, cleaning her clothes, grooming her horse, and obeying her every command. Her head would not stop spinning, and her limbs would not stop shaking, and she wondered how long she would remain alive, how long any of them would. Her chains rattled with every step.

Soon, she thought as she worked outside in the cold, polishing Lari's armor. *Soon, once I've regained my strength, I'll be able to cast magic again. Soon I'll be able to get my hands on a blade or pickaxe. And then, Lari . . . then the madness in your eyes will turn to fear.*

* * * * *

He rode across the night, leading a host of sunlight.

He was a conqueror. A lighter of darkness. An exterminator of vermin. He was Emperor Serin. He was a light to the world and a hammer to crush the worms that infested it. He was the god of Radianism, a deity among men.

"The darkness vanishes," he whispered, licking his lips. "The light rises."

Ahead of him, the great hive of nightcrawlers crumbled. Yintao, they had named it. The capital of their filthy, infested land. The magic tore into the hive, smashing walls, crumbling towers, and his hosts cheered. A hundred thousand Timandrians, children of pure sunlight, streamed into the ruins, slaying the weak, capturing the strong. Thousands of Elorians marched in chains, whipped, beaten, shivering in their nakedness and wretchedness.

"Make them suffer before they die," Serin commanded his generals. "Make the world see their baseness. Strip off their clothes. Shear off their hair. Brand their skin and let them serve us. Let them dig. Let them forge the weapons of their own destruction."

He laughed as he rode through the darkness, leading his hosts, carving the mines for the worms. He laughed as they labored, building him more swords, more spears, more arrows, more cannons, more tools for his glory. Pathetic beings—so eager to serve him, so eager to help him destroy their own kind.

This is why I rise, he thought. *And this is why they fall. This is why I am their master and they are my slaves.*

He rode through another town, another city, watching the towers crumble, watching the slaves emerge, watching all the darkness turn bright with his fire.

"Glorious," he whispered, sitting astride his horse, staring down the hill. Tears stung his eyes. "Beautiful."

Below him, his soldiers rolled out wagon after wagon from a crumbling city, each piled high with Elorian bodies. Serin watched, hand held to his heart, as the soldiers stacked up mountains of corpses and lit them in great pyres. The fire rose high to the sky, casting out sparks, scented of burning meat, of his glory. Serin watched these great lights in the night, and tears of joy and awe streamed down his cheeks.

"The night has ended," he whispered. "Radian has risen."

CHAPTER TWENTY-FIVE
THE WALLS OF OREWOOD

They stood upon the walls of Orewood, capital of Verilon, waiting for blood and fire.

The soldiers covered the battlements and filled the courtyards below. Ten thousand Ardishmen, banished from their homeland, waiting for vengeance. Twenty thousand Verilish warriors, meaty men with cast iron breastplates, thick fur cloaks, and beards just as thick and warm. Ravens and bears. Swords and hammers. Two forces united, ready to face the swarm.

"Bloody cold turn for a battle," Cam muttered. The short, slender king shivered, armor clanking. Snow covered his helmet, piled up upon his pauldrons, and clung to his stubbly cheeks. "We should have fled to the warm south."

Torin patted his friend's shoulder, scattering snow. "Soon we'll be warm enough. Battle heats a man's blood more than mulled wine or the love of a woman."

Cam sighed. "I'd take warm wine and a woman's love instead."

The snow suddenly seemed colder. The talk of women made Torin think of his wife, of Koyee missing. He lowered his head. "As would I."

Cam looked at him and his eyes softened. "I'm sorry, Tor. I pray every turn that we hear from her. Koyee is strong and brave, among the strongest people who live in Moth. If anyone can survive this, it's her."

Torin nodded. He stared off the rampart at the pine forest. The evergreens spread into the horizon, white with snow. A frozen stream snaked between them. The snow kept falling, and still the enemy did not appear, though Torin knew they were out there, moving closer, seeking them, seeking him.

"And the children are out there too somewhere," Torin said softly. "Madori and Tam. No word for months now." Torin clutched the merlon that rose before him. Suddenly it was a struggle to even breathe.

"I worry about them every turn, every breath." Cam's voice sounded choked. "It's a horrible thing, isn't it? Being a parent when your children are in danger. I often feel guilty, Tor." He stared at Torin with haunted eyes. "Guilty for bringing children into the world. We should have known. You and I, more than anyone. We fought in the last great war. We knew about the ugliness in the world, the cruelty in the hearts of men. And yet we brought children into this world, and now . . . now . . ." He lowered his head, overcome.

"There's not much hope," Torin said softly. "But I think that there's a little hope still. Let us cling to that sliver of hope now. It's still better than despair." He looked around him at the lines of soldiers upon the ramparts, then at the thousands of soldiers waiting in the courtyards within the city. "And that little hope lies here at the walls of Orewood."

Cam patted the icy merlon that rose before him. "Good, solid limestone." He sighed. "As if I know limestone from any other rock. Could be chalk for all I know." He looked back at Torin. "You know, I think back to the last round. To all those battles we fought. And I remember standing beside our friends, but all those old walls and battlefields merge together. I can no longer remember where it was Hem swallowed that apricot seed and nearly choked—was it Yintao? Pahmey? I can remember Bailey standing in some grand hall, trying to sing 'Old Riyonan Fields' and accidentally singing the rude lyrics Wela Brewer had invented for it." He laughed. "But I no longer remember if it was in the court of Qaelin's emperor, the halls of Ilar, or maybe just some knight's manor in the sunlight." He wiped his eyes. "I remember lots of bloodshed, horror, pain . . . but also good times. You know, I do think that old war—when we were just kids— was both the worst and greatest time in my life."

Torin nodded, head lowered. "Mine too. It's all memories of pain, but also memories of dear friends, the last memories of them we have." He caressed the hilt of his sword. "This war is turning out quite differently. And I begin to wonder if we'll ever have peace. I lie awake in bed, and I question why we fight for this world. It seems that whenever you slay one tyrant, another rises to take his place.

Whenever you win one war, a generation later a new fire rises to burn the world. Do we fight for everlasting peace, or do we only fight for those brief moments in the sun, a respite from violence before blood washes us again? Perhaps the hearts of men cannot tolerate peace for more than a few years. Perhaps violence is the way of man, and all hope for ending war is just a hope for temporary victory, not an enduring end to arms. Sometimes I think that if this is so, perhaps it's better to lay down our swords, to let the enemy slay us, for even should we slay this enemy another will knock on our door. And yet I keep fighting. Not because I believe I can hold off the tide forever. I fight for those brief moments in the sun. For seeing my daughter smile. For smelling flowers bloom in spring in my gardens, even as I know winter will come again. For a dream of peace, however brief. If we vanquish this enemy, our children will fight another, or their children will, and they too will keep fighting. There will always be ugliness in the world, but perhaps there will always be beauty too. It's for those flashes of beauty that we're willing to face the endless stream of terror."

Cam nodded sagely. "I was just going to say all that myself."

Torin laughed. "I know. I . . ."

His voice died.

Men across the wall stiffened.

A distant drumming rose in the forest, and the trees upon the horizon swayed.

Cam spoke in a soft voice, barely more than a whisper. "They're here."

Across the walls of Orewood, the Ardishmen raised their bows and raised their chins. They stared into the southern forests, solemn, proud, ready to fight any terror that might emerge. Their banners unfurled in a gust of snowy wind, revealing the black raven upon the golden field. At the sight of these banners, pride welled in Torin.

Let the enemy see that Arden still stands with honor and pride.

Further along the walls, the soldiers of Verilon reacted somewhat differently. Here were no noble, steely soldiers in plate armor, no proud eyes, no solemn stares. The Verilish host erupted into wild jeers. Burly men—most were twice the size of the typical Ardishman—bellowed and lifted their hammers and shields high.

Many held flagons of ale, and they drank between roars. Their fur cloaks billowed in the wind, and in lieu of drums, they pounded their hammers against their own iron breastplates, raising a ruckus that sent birds fleeing. Several men went even further; they turned their backs toward the forest, lowered their breeches, and gave the south a good view of their wriggling, hairy posteriors.

"They know how to enjoy war, I'll give them that," Cam muttered, watching the warriors of the bear.

The drums kept beating in the south, and the trees kept creaking, snow falling off their branches. The last birds fled the forest, and then Torin saw them, and he gripped his bow and cursed.

The Radians covered the forests, countless soldiers. This force seemed even larger than the army that had attacked Kingswall. Here was a great horde from many nations: Magerians in black steel, traitorous Ardishmen in pale armor, Nayans in tiger pelts, and even Eseerians from the distant south. Among them marched warriors Torin had never seen before—tall, broad men, as large as the Verilish, but golden haired and fair of skin. They were warriors of Orida, Torin realized, the island nation from the northern sea; they too now raised the Radian banners.

Catapults rolled forth among the enemy troops, followed by ballistae—great crossbows on wheels, large as cannons. True cannons emerged next from the forest, shaped as iron buffaloes. Wheeled battering rams swung on chains, and trebuchets swayed like pendulums as they rolled forth. But worse than all these tools of siege were the dark riders among them—robed and hooded mages.

One of these mages rode ahead of the army, twice the size of all others. Torin winced, pain shooting through him at the sight. Those red, burning eyes seemed to find him across the distance, to pierce him like spears. Four arms rose, holding four severed heads, trophies from the southern battlefields.

"Lord Gehena," Torin muttered. "He's back."

"Like a bad rash," Cam agreed.

Over the past few turns, Orewood's defenders had cleared out about a mile of forest, leaving a field of tree stumps beyond the canyon and walls. The enemy hosts paused before this cleared stretch of land, their backs to the forest; they stood just beyond the range of the defenders' arrows.

Only Gehena rode forth. His horse, several times the usual size, snorted and huffed, blasting smoke out of its nostrils. The dark lord's cloak gusted in the wind, revealing tattered, burnt hems. A stench of smoke and vinegar wafted from the mage toward the walls of Orewood.

Several soldiers beside Torin raised their arrows. Torin raised his hand, holding back the fire.

"Wait," he said.

Gehena kept riding forward until he had crossed half the distance between the forest and walls. His horse sidestepped, sneering. With a hiss that sounded halfway between water on fire and a laugh, Gehena tossed the four severed heads he held.

The grisly projectiles sailed through the air and across the walls. Torin grimaced as one landed right between him and Cam.

"By Idar," Cam said, blanching.

Torin stared down at the head and ground his teeth. It was the frozen head of Kay Wooler, his neighbor from Fairwool-by-Night, a mere girl of twenty. Her face was still twisted with fear.

A shriek rose from the field, morphing into words, high-pitched, demonic, a sound like a hailstorm.

"Here are the heads of your neighbors," cried Lord Gehena. "Here are the heads of those you abandoned, those you failed, those you let die. They are four among thousands." He looked over his shoulder. "Men of Radian! Show them your trophies!"

Across the field, thousands of Radian soldiers roared. They raised thousands of spears; each held a severed Ardish head.

Gehena laughed and turned back toward Orewood. "You tried to fight my lord, the mighty Serin. He repays treachery with death. Though as great as his might is his mercy. On his behalf, I give you one more chance to live. Surrender now. Open your gates and swear allegiance to my lord. Raise the Radian flag, fight with us against the night, and you shall live. Refuse me . . . and you will die." His laughter rose like steam. "You will all die in agony, and your heads will pelt the next city we crush."

"I say we fire those arrows now," Torin said.

Cam nodded. "Capital idea." The king raised his voice to a roar. "Archers of Arden! Fire!"

Hundreds of soldiers upon the wall raised their bows. Hundreds of arrows flew skyward, reached their zenith, and flew downward toward Gehena.

The mage pointed his four hands forward. The arrows disintegrated and fell as ash.

An instant later, the Radian soldiers blew horns and charged toward the walls of Orewood.

CHAPTER TWENTY-SIX
THE WAR ETERNAL

Koyee swung the pickaxe. Again. Again.

Pain flared across her. Again. Again.

The whips cracked. Again. Again.

The turns faded together into a long, unending nightmare. She rose. She worked in the mine, chained, with a thousand others. She suffered the shouts, the lash, the steel-tipped boots. She returned to the cave with the others, huddled together, praying, whispering.

Their captors did not feed them. While forced to clean the camp above the canyon, they scrounged around in the trash, picking out bones, peels, and whatever else remained from the Radians' meals. They drank melted snow when it fell; usually they thirsted. Their fat and muscles melted off, leaving them famished, rubbery, skin hanging off bones like white silk off hangers.

And they died.

Always they died.

A body collapsed. Again. Again.

The wheelbarrow rolled out a pile of corpses. Again. Again.

Sometimes it was hunger or thirst. Sometimes the lash of an over-eager overseer. Often it was disease; the Timandrian illnesses still ran through the mine, bringing chills, boils, fever, death.

And yet, through this pain, their labors bore fruit. Piles of arrowheads, spearheads, and swords rose in wagons, shipped off to war.

Thus we die, Koyee thought, swinging the pick. *Working to slay our own people.*

They worked. They suffered. They died. And sometimes . . . sometimes they fought.

One turn it was a young man, though he looked old now, who shouted in agony, tears in his eyes, and swung his pickaxe at a guard. The Magerian only laughed, dodged the blow, and knocked the

Elorian down. That turn, the Magerians enjoyed hanging the prisoner above the canyon, only to lower the rope instants before death, allow the man to recover, then tighten the noose again. It was hours before the man died as the other prisoners toiled below, hearing the gasps, knowing this would be their fate too should they rebel.

Yet another prisoner, a diminutive woman with large indigo eyes, shouted the next turn after watching her son collapse. She too attacked a guard, and her pickaxe hit the man's armor, denting the steel. The Magerians beat her to death, laughing as she bled.

How can we fight them? Koyee thought, chipping out the iron ore, one chunk after another. *We are weak, nearly starving, dying. They wear armor, and they carry shields and swords.* She lowered her head. *It's a fight we can't win.*

Yet as the turns went by, she realized: *We must fight nonetheless.*

The next time they entered the cave to sleep, she began whispering of her plans.

"Gather, friends." She gestured for them to approach. "Gather, hear me."

The prisoners lay across the cave like discarded rags, so weak they could barely raise their heads. The cave was small; the prisoners covered the floor, leaving no room to spare. They barely seemed human to Koyee, only ravaged things, half-alive. They reminded her of the plague victims she had seen in the Hospice of Pahmey, still drawing breath but only a mockery of true life. She could clearly see the bones and joints of her fellow prisoners; their skin hid nothing. Their eyes peered, huge and glazed, from bald, skull-like heads. She no longer knew man from woman, child from adult; all had become sickly, starving, dying things.

Now we truly look like the worms they always called us, Koyee thought.

"Come, friends, gather near."

They crawled toward her, the stronger dragging the weak. A few only raised their heads, blinking, uttering silent words. Koyee struggled onto her stick-thin legs. She stared around her, meeting gaze after gaze.

"We've been here for over a moon," she said. "If we do nothing, we will die here. So many of us have died already, and I no longer believe help will come to us. If we fight, our fate will be the same." She tried to make a fist, but she was too weak to close her fingers. "If only death awaits us, we can still choose how to die. And I say we die fighting. Together."

One of the prisoners, an Elorian youth named Baoshi, struggled to his feet too. He leaned over for a moment, coughed, and finally righted himself. He met Madori's gaze. Sweat dripped off his forehead, and the glaze of illness coated his eyes, but he managed to nod.

"I will fight with you, Koyee," he said. "I know of your tales. You are the great heroine of the first war. The Girl in the Black Dress. The Rider of Dragons. The Slayer of Ferius." He turned to look at the others. "She is a heroine. We must follow her. She will lead us to victory."

Another prisoner, a man named Chenduon, shook his head. "She will lead us to death." He coughed, holding his frail chest. "I do not want to die a hero. I want to live as long as I can. Maybe aid will arrive. Maybe Emperor Jin will send a great army to free us."

The younger Baoshi laughed bitterly. "You are delirious. There is no aid for us; the emperor might be dead, all his halls fallen." He shuddered. "I was in Pahmey. I saw the mages of sunlight sink the whole city into the pit. Now I envy those who fell. And I do not believe there is hope for aid. All of Eloria must have fallen, not only Qaelin but Ilar and Leen too. Perhaps we are the last Elorians alive."

A woman struggled to her feet—Shinquon, once a fisherman's wife. "If all Eloria is fallen, maybe the sunlit masters will show us mercy." A tear streamed into her sunken cheek. "They will no longer need weapons if their war is won. Maybe they will soon free us." She turned to glare at Koyee. "I too want to stay alive as long as possible. Every turn that we still live brings hope, if only a whisper of hope. If we fight, we know for certain that we die."

Young Baoshi spun toward the woman, then had to lean down for a moment, coughing. Finally he managed to speak again. "I'm willing to die fighting. But perhaps we will win." He looked at Koyee. "Right, Koyee? We have a chance to win, do we not? I believe."

Koyee sighed. She looked around her. Everyone was now watching from across the cave. She spoke softly. "Our hope to defeat our masters is as small as our hope for rescue. I believe that there is almost no hope at all. I will not lie to you; I would lead you to fight not because I think we can win, but because I prefer to die fighting, to die proud, to show them—with our last breath—that we are no worms, that we are proud Elorians, proud children of darkness. But if hope drives you, and if hope is what helps you swing a pick at a soldier, then cling to that hope. Foster it. Because even though hope is small, barely more than a speck, I do not believe that hope is ever dead. We were born in the night, and more than anyone, we know this: Even in the greatest darkness there is some light. Even beyond the greatest fear there is courage. Even in the greatest pain there is joy."

Their eyes gleamed with tears. Koyee had to close her own eyes; seeing them looking at her, finding hope in her, was suddenly too much. She was a woman now with a grown daughter, and she was a leader, a heroine and legend, so why did she so often still feel like a child? Even now, she often felt no older, no braver, than that youth who had sailed alone upon the Inaro River, an orphan girl more than twenty years ago. Back then, she had sought the aid of others—from leaders, from soldiers, from emperors. She had relied on so many others to teach her—on Little Maniko and his courage, Empress Hikari and her strength, and Shenlai the dragon for his wisdom. Always there had been somebody older, somebody wiser and stronger, somebody to guide her. Yet all those souls had died, and now she was the wise one, the one others approached for leadership. And the weight nearly crushed her.

Inside I still feel like a child . . . somebody who needs leadership in others. How can I now lead them, give them the strength and wisdom others gave me?

She looked at them. They nodded, one by one.

"When the moon is gone from the sky, and the Timandrians' eyes are weakest, we attack together," Koyee said. "We will raise our pickaxes. And we will swing them not at stone but at our oppressors. We will slay them or we will die as heroes, and any who survive this war will sing of our courage for eternity."

* * * * *

Jitomi stood on the prow of the *Tai Lar*—the *Waterfire*—the new flagship of his armada. Behind him sailed hundreds of ships, the might of his empire. Ahead, flowing down the dark waters of the Inaro, sailed the sunlit fleet.

"Now the true mettle of the night will be tested," Jitomi said. "Now the might of the Red Flame will be judged not by burning fellow Elorians . . . but by facing an empire of sunlight."

Lord Dorashi, Captain of the *Tai Lar*, stood beside him. A gruff man of fifty years, Dorashi wore crimson armor, the bulky plates tasseled and engraved with black dragon motifs. His face was leathery, his eyes hard and narrowed. A thick white mustache drooped over his thin mouth. His shoulders were broad, his helmet horned. His family ruled the distant, southern coast of Ilar, and they had long been aligned with the Hashido nobles, Jitomi's family from the northern peninsula.

"We will smash through them," Captain Dorashi said. "The Red Flame Armada has never been stronger, and Tianlong flies with us."

The leathery captain raised his eyes skyward. Jitomi followed his gaze. Clouds hid the moon and stars, and in the darkness, Tianlong was but a shadow, a coiling serpent of the night. The dragon's red beard fluttered like a banner, a hint of red like blood staining the clouds.

This battle I will fight upon the water, Jitomi thought. *With my people. One among them.*

He had removed his mage's robes, and now he wore the armor of an Ilari warrior—armor he had once refused to don. Now he bore a katana and shield. Now he led an empire, a nation. Now he fought for all the night.

The Radian fleet sailed closer, moving toward them across the mile-wide river. Hundreds of carracks sailed there, their white sails sporting the golden eclipse of the Radian Order. Cannons lined their hulls, the knowledge of their construction stolen from Eloria in the last war. Lanterns hung from their masts, casting light upon thousands of archers and swordsmen. This force had smashed the towns and cities along the river, moving south, crushing all in its path, devastating Qaelin, the mainland of Eloria.

They stop here, Jitomi thought.

He turned to look behind him. Hundreds of Ilari warriors stood upon the deck of the *Tai Lar:* swordsmen all in steel, gunners manning their cannons, and even riders astride growling black panthers. A pagoda rose from the deck, three tiers tall, and archers stood within it, bows ready. Behind the *Tai Lar* sailed many more ships, all ready for battle.

"Ilar!" Jitomi shouted. He drew his katana and raised the blade. "Sons of Ilar, hear me! I am Jitomi Hashido, Emperor of the Red Flame. An enemy of sunlight approaches. The Radian Empire which has deceived us, which has slain our brothers, sails to crush us. We will smash the enemy! For the Red Flame and for Eloria, we will triumph!"

They roared, thousands of voices. Thousands of swords rose. Thousands of horned, demonic helmets blazed in the light of torches. Above, the dragon Tianlong let out his cry.

Captain Dorashi raised a red banner. "Smoke!" he roared. "Light the dragons!"

Across the Ilari fleet, men lit the dragon figureheads of their ships. Black and yellow smoke rose from the iron jaws, scented of sulfur, obscuring their locations. Ilari warriors loved fighting in shadows and smoke, hidden, smashing through their blinded enemies.

Jitomi turned to face the north again. He could see only smoke now, not the enemy fleet. But he could hear the Radians. Their war drums boomed. Their horns blared. Their voices shouted out as one: "Radian rises! Radian rises!"

Jitomi squared his jaw. *For the darkness. And for Madori. For the woman I love.*

He stepped closer to the prow. He shouted at the top of his lungs. "Fire!"

Fire crackled. Black smoke blasted out. Ahead of Jitomi, the dragon figurehead of the *Tai Lar* blasted out fire. The ship shook. A cannonball shot through the smoke, cutting a path of clear sky. A ship emerged from the clouds ahead, and an instant later, the cannonball slammed into its hull.

A thousand other cannons blasted from both fleets.

Fire and sound washed over the world.

One cannonball slammed into the *Tai Lar*'s hull only feet away from Jitomi. The iron-clad ship shook madly. Jitomi nearly fell. For an instant he thought the hull had collapsed, but its iron flanks had withstood the blow. A dozen other cannons fired upon the deck. Men screamed. Fire blazed across the Radians' wooden ships.

"Archers!" Jitomi cried. "Fire!"

Flaming arrows flew through the night to slice through the enemy's canvas sails. The sails burst into flame, and firelight lit the darkness. Enemy arrows flew in response, and Jitomi raised his shield. Flaming projectiles slammed against him, shattering against his shield and armor and peppering the deck around him.

Cannons blasted again. The fleets kept sailing toward each other . . . then crashed together with blood and flame.

A Radian ship rammed into the *Tai Lar*, its figurehead denting the iron starboard. The *Tai Lar*'s own figurehead scraped across the enemy's weaker hull, scattering shards of wood. Planks drove down from ship to ship, and soldiers charged into battle.

Jitomi grimaced as two Radian swordsmen ran toward him, swinging longswords—blades heavier and longer than his katana. He chose and claimed one man's sword, then heated the hilt; the soldier screamed and dropped the weapon. The second soldier thrust his blade, and Jitomi blocked the blow with his shield, then swung his katana upwards. He drove the blade into the man's armpit where his armor was weak, and blood showered. Another swing of the katana and the man fell.

All around Jitomi upon the *Tai Lar*'s deck, soldiers of day and night battled. Men raced across the planks or swung upon ropes from deck to deck. All across the Inaro, ships burned, archers fired, cannons blasted, and men thrashed in the water. Tianlong roared above, dipping down to slam through enemy hulls, sending the ships into the water.

"Drive through them!" Captain Dorashi was howling, holding a bloody katana in each hand. "Smash the enemy!"

Arrows sailed overhead from the ship's pagoda. Men screamed and blood washed the deck.

Jitomi swung his blade again and again, parrying, killing. One arrow punched through his armor and entered his arm. He growled but kept fighting with blade and magic. All around him, the fire lit the night and the blood painted the river red.

* * * * *

The assault on Orewood began with cannon fire, swinging catapults, and shrieking ballistae.

"There will be no siege!" Lord Gehena's voice rose like a storm, inhumanly loud, high-pitched like shattering glass. "All who oppose Serin will die, and Orewood will be his trophy."

A boulder slammed into the rampart beside Torin, cracking the stone. A ballista's iron projectile, longer than a man, sailed overhead to smash a home beyond the walls. A cannonball drove into a guard tower, and the turret collapsed in a pile of bricks.

"Fire your arrows!" Torin shouted. "Men of Arden, take them down! Aim at the gunners! Aim at the catapults!"

He nocked an arrow and fired. Across the walls of Orewood, thousands of archers fired with him. Thousands of arrows flew from the walls, the guard towers, the roofs behind. A rain of steel, wood, and flame descended upon the enemy. Radian troops fell, pierced with arrows, only for their comrades to trample the corpses as they charged.

"Scale the walls!" Gehena screeched upon his horse. "Shatter the gates! Claim this city for the Light of Radian!"

The Radian hordes swept forth like the sea. Great ladders swung, snapping onto the walls with iron brackets. A battering ram swung on chains, slamming into the doors, chipping the wood. Trebuchets twanged in the field, tossing flaming barrels and spiked boulders over the walls and into the city. Log homes collapsed. Fires crackled. People shouted and fled deeper into the city, clogging the streets.

"Oil!" Torin shouted. "Burn them!"

Across the walls, oil bubbled within cauldrons. Torin helped tilt one pot over a murder hole carved into the rampart. The oil slid down the stone tunnel, fell through the open air, and sizzled over the troops below. The Magerians screamed, the oil trickling under their armor and searing their flesh.

And still the enemy kept coming.

Mages shot black, astral whips that rose hundreds of feet tall. The lashes grabbed onto the ramparts and tugged back, tearing down merlons and turrets. Bricks rained down into the field. Men rained with them. Cannonballs sailed overhead and crashed into homes beyond the wall. Fires spread across the city. Red smoke rose in clouds, hiding the sky.

It is a war we cannot win, Torin thought. *It is a war without end.*

He shouted hoarsely. He fired arrows. He spilled oil. When the enemy climbed the ladders, he swung his sword, and he fought them on the walls, and he slew men, and his blade ran red with blood. But through roaring fire, blasting cannons, and the screams of the dying, all seemed muffled, the whole world a haze.

It is the war eternal. It is the curse of Moth. Will we always bleed?

He knew they could not win this battle. Not with the magic tearing the walls apart, ripping down brick by brick. Not with the cannons firing, the rams swinging. The gates shattered below. A mile in the northwest, he heard distant screams, and he saw the city's western gates shatter, the enemy stream into the streets. To his right, a great section of wall crumble, and the enemy surged, climbing over the rubble into Orewood.

The dams collapsed.

The Radian forces swept into the city with chants, with galloping horses, and with myriads of swinging swords.

A war eternal, Torin thought, standing atop a pillar of stone, one of the few sections of wall still standing. *Blood without end.*

"Torin!" The voice seemed miles away, ages away, a voice from another world, from memory. Was it his wife calling to him? He had fought his wife once. In the city of Pahmey, she had fired an arrow at him. She—

"Torin, damn it! Come on!"

A hand grabbed his arm. He looked down. Cam was tugging him, shouting something. Torin could barely hear. His head rang. When he touched his forehead, his fingers came away bloody.

"I don't remember being hit," he whispered.

"Tor, come on, damn you!" Cam shouted.

Torin nodded. Cam tugging him, they raced down a stone staircase instants before it collapsed. Bricks and dust rained. They ran into a courtyard covered with bricks, cloven helms, and bodies. A few scattered Ardishmen stood with raised swords. Hundreds of Radians surrounded them.

"Does it end here?" Torin asked his friend.

Cam spat and raised his sword. "If it does, we go down together, old boy. Now let's kill a few of these bastards first."

The two men shouted and charged toward the enemy.

Across the city of Orewood, buildings collapsed, horses galloped, cannons fired, and blood flowed. A temple's columns cracked and fell, and the roof slammed down onto men. Fire blazed across wooden homes. Helmets rolled across the streets. Hammers swung, cleaving breastplates. Men fell and cannons rolled through the city, their wheels bristly with arrows. Bears charged at horses and lances thrust. Everywhere the fire burned. Smoke rose, black and red, hiding the crumbling city under a blanket of heat and ash.

CHAPTER TWENTY-SEVEN
DAGGER AND BONES

Madori knelt on the cold, rocky ground of the courtyard, polishing Lari's armor. She had been working for an hour with rags and oil, shining each piece at a time—pauldrons, breastplate, vambraces, greaves, gauntlets, and helmet. Each piece of steel was filigreed with golden buffaloes and Radian eclipses, symbols of Old Mageria and the new Radian Empire it had become. Each of these pieces was priceless, worth more than anything Madori had ever owned, probably worth more than all that had been in Fairwool-by-Night.

You destroyed that village, Lari, Madori thought as she worked, shining the rubies inlaid into the breastplate. Her eyes stung. *You crushed and burned it to the ground. And some turn I will avenge it. I don't know how, and I don't know when, but you will pay for your crimes.*

She lifted one of the Lari's gauntlets—the one that had struck Madori's own cheek only last turn, leaving an ugly gash. She began to polish it carefully, moving the oiled rag over each finger, cleaning off her own blood. Last time Madori had failed to polish the armor carefully enough, Lari had ordered her men to beat Madori unconscious. Luckily, in her weakened state, that had not taken more than a couple blows, but it was enough that Madori had never missed a spot since.

She had been here for two moons now—two moons of beatings, of hunger, of disease—and Madori was fading away. Every turn as she awoke, she was surprised to find herself still alive.

"Lari doesn't even need armor in this place," Madori mumbled as she worked. "We're so weak we couldn't crush a mouse beneath our heels."

A voice boomed out behind her. "Work silently, worm, or you'll taste the back of my hand."

She looked over her shoulder. One of Lari's guards stood there—a yellow-haired, rat-faced man named Derin. Madori scowled at him, prepared to talk back, but when he raised his hand, she swallowed her words and returned to the armor. Derin had beaten her often enough—it seemed every guard here had—that she had lost the appetite for defiance.

If I were still strong enough to cast magic, I would crush you like a bug, she thought. Often she had tried to use her magic here, to cast a shield of air around her, to protect herself from the blows. But her body was too weak, her mind too muzzy. Whenever she tried to use magic, her skull seemed to contract, and she saw stars. A few times she had managed to create a protective shield of air around her during the beating, but the effort had sucked up so much energy, she had spent hours afterward dizzy and gagging.

The tents of soldiers rose around her. Beyond them, scaffolding rose in the night; workers bustled there, constructing a fortress for the Magerians. To her east, Madori could make out a line of soldiers guarding the canyon. The sounds of the mining rose from the chasm—pickaxes against stone and whips against flesh. Several times, Madori had tried to creep toward that canyon, to gaze down into the shadows, to see if her mother still lived. But guards always caught her and tossed her back to Lari and her wrath. And so Madori remained above in the Magerian camp, the only Elorian here, serving the princess.

"Make way!" rose a voice. "Make way—nightcrawler corpses! Make way!"

Oiled rag in hand, Madori sucked in her breath. She spun toward the voice, and she saw him there. It was Peras this time, a wiry soldier with graying hair, who was shoving the wheelbarrow through the camp. Within lay a dozen starved Elorian corpses.

Forgetting the armor, Madori hobbled toward the wheelbarrow. The chains around her ankles jangled, and tears filled her eyes.

"Please, Peras," she said. "Let me see them."

Radian soldiers gathered around, chortling.

"Let her look!" said rat-faced Derin. "I like it when she looks."

Another soldier, a tall woman named Ferla, barked out a laugh. "Remember, Derin, if she finds her maggot mother before the new moon, you owe me a silver coin."

Derin spat. "Won't be till after the new moon. Her mother's a tough one."

"No one's tough in the mines, boy." Ferla snorted. "And you're going to owe me that silver coin."

Ignoring the soldiers, Madori rummaged through the wheelbarrow of bodies, seeking her, seeking Koyee. The dead were almost unrecognizable; fallen to starvation, disease, and their cruel masters' whips, even freshly killed they looked like old corpses, shrunken and shriveled. She found men, children, youths . . . all strangers.

Madori breathed out a shaky sigh of relief. "She's not here," she whispered.

A few Radians roared with laughter. Ferla muttered and spat, while Derin boasted of the coin she owed him.

You're strong, Mother, Madori thought, returning to the armor. *You'll survive this. We both will.*

She gave the armor a few last passes with the rag, then turned to her next task: preparing Lari's dinner. The princess often went out riding for hours in the darkness, claiming the camp stank of death. When she returned, weary and hungry from her ride, she demanded her meals waiting on her table.

Madori hobbled to the wide tent that served as the camp's kitchens until the fortress was completed. Wobbling on her chained, bony legs, she carried plate after plate into Lari's embroidered tent, setting out the feast upon the giltwood table. Lari was a slim young woman, not much heavier than Madori had been before arriving at this camp, and yet she could eat as much as the burliest soldier, her appetite knowing almost no bounds.

Perhaps cruelty sucks up a lot of energy, Madori thought, arranging the silver cutlery.

Soon the meal was set: a roast honeyed duck upon a bed of shallots and wild mushrooms; grainy bread rolls still steaming from the oven, topped with butter; a silver bowl of dried figs, persimmons, and apricots; and a wooden box full of sweet almond clusters dusted with sugar. It was all fine Timandrian fare, imported from the day, and intoxicating with its aroma. Madori's mouth watered and her head spun. She craved a bite, desired it more than anything. Her head spun and her body shook as the smell entered her nostrils.

Only a bite, she thought, reaching toward one of the figs. *Only a little . . .*

She stopped herself.

No.

The first few times Madori had set this table for the princess, she had stolen a few morsels. And each time, somehow Lari knew. Each time, Madori was punched in the gut, forced to gag. Each time, Koyee was dragged into the tent, punished for Madori's crime.

There is magic here, Madori knew, looking around at the tent. *Magic like my locket.* Some item in this tent—perhaps one of the chalices, perhaps one of the jewels sewn into the walls—had the magic of sight, allowing Lari to spy upon her from afar.

And so Madori placed her hands behind her back, desperate for the food but daring not take a single morsel. She was slowly starving, but she wouldn't risk more punishment for her mother.

Finally trill laughter sounded outside, and the tent flap opened. Lari stepped inside. She wore a fine riding gown trimmed with fur, the skirt cut down the sides to allow her to straddle her horse. Her cheeks were flushed pink, and sweat dampened her hair.

"Mongrel!" she said, kicking off her boots. "Come. Polish them."

Madori nodded and rushed forward. The boots splattered mud across the rug as Lari kicked them aside. Madori knelt, rag in hand, and got to work, polishing the leather again and again.

As Madori knelt, polishing away, Lari sat at her table and began to feast. The duck's crunchy skin cracked. Gravy dripped off the shallots as Lari tossed them into her mouth. Her throat bobbed as she drank the wine. Madori had always imagined princesses to only nibble their food, a few bites here and there of lettuce, but Lari guzzled down her meals; it was an obscene, unfathomable sight. Madori did not know where all that food went, for Lari remained slender. Perhaps some magic was involved, a way for Lari to feed like a pig and magically transport the food away from her belly.

Or perhaps she simply burns up the energy by tormenting me, Madori thought, her mouth still watering.

Finally Lari was done eating. She slapped her feet onto the tabletop, causing the plates to bounce. She tossed one of those silver plates at Madori. It crashed onto the rug, scattering the duck's bones and fat.

"Eat your meal," Lari said. "Eat it all up, then clean up this mess."

Madori wanted to refuse. She wanted to toss the plate back at Lari. But she needed this meal, as poor as it was. She leaped onto the morsels, stuffing the duck skin into her mouth and crunching the bones between her teeth, then licking the gravy off the plate.

"Truly you creatures are pigs," Lari said, watching the spectacle, disgust in her eyes.

Madori ignored her, picking out the last bits of fat and skin from the rug. She no longer cared for Lari's mockery; any dignity Madori had once possessed had vanished here long ago. These scraps would keep her alive a little longer, long enough to find the right moment.

Chewing on a bone, she glanced up and stared at the tabletop. A knife lay here, stained with the duck grease.

If I move fast enough, Madori thought, *maybe I can grab the knife. Maybe I can—*

Lari lifted the knife and tilted her head. "You'd like to thrust this into my heart, wouldn't you, little one?" Lari balanced the knife in her palm. "Perhaps one turn you will try to grab it. And when you do, this blade will enter flesh—your mother's flesh." Lari licked the knife. "And if by chance you do manage to stab me, mongrel— perhaps freeing yourself from your shackles and cutting me in my sleep—you better also stab every guard in this camp. If anything is to happen to me, they have their orders." Lari grinned hungrily. "They are to immediately torture your mother before your eyes, making it last for turns, until she dies. And only then will your torture begin. So keep staring at this knife, worm. Keep dreaming of ways to kill me. You are only planning your own nightmare."

Madori looked away.

Not yet. Not while Mother is imprisoned. I have to free her first.

She did not know how she'd reach the canyon where the miners worked. Guards patrolled it around the clock. All Madori could do was bide her time, grow stronger, keep eating whatever scraps were tossed her way, and wait for her wounds to heal. If she obeyed Lari for long enough, perhaps the beatings would stop. Her bruises would fade, and with the pain lessened, she would find her magic again.

With magic I can sneak past the guards into the mine, she thought. *With magic I can free my mother and everyone else.* Her eyes dampened. *I miss you, Mother. I miss you so much.*

Kneeling here before Lari, eating scraps like a dog, Madori thought back to her time back in Fairwool-by-Night, living with her parents. How she had clashed with her mother then! How often she had yelled at Koyee, rebelled, made her mother cry! Whenever Koyee would scold Madori for her hairstyle or clothes, Madori would shout, smash things, storm out of the house and not return for a turn or two, leaving Koyee in tears. She had hated her mother then, had thought Koyee the most ruthless tyrant in the world.

I'm so sorry. Madori's tears fell. *I love you so much, Mother. I'd give everything in the world to live with you in that old house again.*

Sniffing, she tried to remember that house which the Radians had burned; it still stood in her memory. She remembered her father working in the gardens, tending to sunflowers, tulips, and sweet summer peonies. She remembered her soft bed and quilt, and how she would lie there for hours, reading in the sunlight that always fell through her window. And she remembered good times with her mother from before her rebellious youth, back in childhood when the world had seemed so bright: walking with Koyee to the river to look at the fish, entering the night with Koyee to watch the stars, or simply listening to Koyee sing her old songs of Qaelin.

At the memory of warmth, music, and love, Madori's tears would not stop falling, and she vowed that if she ever saw Koyee again, that if the two ever escaped this place, she would never yell at her mother again.

I will always love you, Mother. Always, whether we die this turn or in many years.

Lari finally left her table and lifted a lantern. She stared down at Madori's tears with a smirk on her face. "Follow me, mongrel. I have a new task for you this turn."

The two left the tent and moved about the camp. The other tents rose at their sides, and soldiers moved among them. In the east, the workers were bustling across the scaffolding, and a great wooden lever—dozens of feet tall—was lowering a basket of bricks onto a half-completed wall. In the west lay the mine; Madori could not see into the canyon from here, but she heard the cracking whips and the screams of workers. As usual, she was the only Elorian up here outside of the canyon.

Lari led her toward the camp's serrated iron fence. Guards moved aside from the gates, and Lari walked outside into the open night, beckoning for Madori to follow.

Madori stood frozen, hesitant. *Why is she leading me out of the camp?* She swallowed. *Does she intend to kill me out there, to leave my body for the worms?*

"Follow!" Lari barked. "Here, mongrel."

Madori raised her chin. Whatever Lari planned out there could be no worse than the camp. Chains rattling, Madori hobbled through the gates and outside into the darkness. The only light here came from Lari's lantern; the moon was gone from the sky.

Her eyesight will be weak here, Madori thought. *She has small Timandrian eyes. I can fight her here.*

They walked for a stretch before reaching a wheelbarrow of Elorian corpses. A smoking pit gaped beyond it, and a stench hit Madori's nostrils like a blow.

"Come, stand on the edge," Lari said, inviting Madori forward. "Look into the abyss."

When Madori stepped forward and looked down into the pit, she had to cover her mouth. She felt her paltry meal rise back up.

"By Xen Qae," she whispered.

Hundreds of charred skeletons filled the chasm. They were Elorian skeletons, Madori saw; the skulls' eye sockets were twice the size of a Timandrian's. Shreds of burnt flesh still clung to the bones, and a foul smoke rose to sting Madori's eyes.

"Beautiful." Lari stared down into the mass grave with delight and awe in her eyes. "It's the most beautiful sight I've seen—the purification of the world, the light we bring to the darkness." She turned to regard Madori. "Some turn soon, your mother will burn in this pit too. That turn, I will spit upon her bones. But that won't be for a while longer. I have a task for you while you still live."

Madori stared at the emperor's daughter. "You're mad," she whispered. "Lari, how can you delight in death like this? How can you slay innocents?" She gestured down at the smoking bones. "These were women, children, not soldiers. They were—"

"They were nightcrawlers." Lari licked her teeth. "Have you truly not understood yet, mongrel? They are all my enemies. Their very presence in this world disgusts me."

"Why?" Madori whispered.

The princess caressed Madori's cheek. "Because they corrupt all that they touch. Everything they approach turns to rot. Like you, mongrel. Your blood is half Timandrian; your father is a man of sunlight, sharing my own blood. The nightcrawler whore tempted him, lured him into her bed, and they produced you. A monster. An abomination. You could have been pure, Madori. You could have been like me, a lady of sunlight. We are cousins, and we could have ruled the world together, two companions, two mistresses of light. Now you are ruined, a freak."

"I'd never be like you." Madori shoved Lari's hand away. "Never. My father is a pure Timandrian, and he's also pure of heart. But your heart is rotten. There was never impurity in the night nor in me. I realize that now. For many years, I too thought I was impure." Madori shook her head. "But I'm not. The true disease is not in my mixed blood but in your heart, Lari, and in the heart of your father. If you will kill me for these words, then kill me. There is no value left to my life. Not here."

Lari smiled thinly. "Madori, have you heard tales of the old empire of Riyona?" She gazed back into the pit and seemed to contemplate the bones. "The empire was mighty and ruled all lands north of the Sern River, all the way to the coast in the north, the mountains in the west, and the darkness in the east. All other lands in sunlight paid tribute to Riyona's glory. Do you know how the Riyonans built an empire?" Lari's lips peeled back in something halfway between grin and snarl. "With cruelty. With strength. They stamped out their enemies and they intimidated all others to obey. The Riyonan emperors had a practice. When an enemy was truly great—a warlord or rebel leader—the emperor would skin him alive, then create a book out of the skin. Human parchment. Upon the book, the emperor would write the names of those he had slain." Lari turned back toward Madori. "Some of those old books survive. I've seen them in Markfir, capital of a new empire—the Radian Empire. We are the new Riyona. But unlike that old empire, we will rule forever." She gestured at the fresh corpses in the wheelbarrow. "I will have you create me a new book, made from the skin of my enemies. Choose one body. Peel off its skin, and we will write the names of all those I kill upon the parchment."

Madori found herself strangely calm; perhaps after so much pain, so much terror, she was too hurt, too jaded for shock. She met and held Lari's gaze.

"Then hand me your dagger." Madori nodded toward the dagger that hung from Lari's belt. "I'll need a blade."

Something strangely subdued, almost calm but fully dangerous, filled Lari's eyes. Not breaking her stare, she drew her dagger and held it out, hilt first. Madori took the weapon. For a moment the two women stared at each other, saying nothing.

Finally Lari broke the silence. "You have a choice now. You can attack me. Maybe you'll even kill me. And then my soldiers have orders to torture your mother to death." Lari shrugged. "It might be worth it. Koyee is nearly dead anyway; I doubt she'd last more than another month here. And if you slay me with this dagger, well . . . that would be a great boon to the nightcrawlers, would it not? And a great act of vengeance for you; you might even get a chance to flee into the darkness after slaying me. There are no guards here to stop you." Lari tapped her chin. "But I wonder . . . I wonder if you'd be willing to flee, to abandon your mother here to death and torture. Let us see how honorable a mongrel is. So choose, Madori. Thrust this blade into a corpse and bring me its skin . . . or thrust this blade into me. Your choice."

Madori held the dagger before her. She looked to her right; skeletons smoldered in the pit and corpses lay in the wheelbarrow. She looked to her left; the camp fence rose in the distance, and screams sounded from beyond it.

What do I do? Madori thought. Her belly twisted. She raised the dagger an inch, desperate to attack Lari, to thrust the blade into her heart. The princess made no move to flee or fight.

It's a trap, Madori thought. It had to be. If she attacked, Lari would use magic to thwart the thrust. Perhaps magic was already shielding the princess with invisible armor. And yet . . . maybe if Madori thrust hard enough, fast enough, maybe she could kill Lari. Maybe she could have her vengeance, then run into the darkness, flee this place, be free.

And leave my mother behind.

A part of Madori screamed inside her: *Koyee is already dying! She might be dead already. How could you give up your vengeance and freedom for a dying woman?*

She looked east, across the chasm, to the open night. *Mother would want me to flee,* Madori thought. *She would tell me to kill Lari, to escape, to leave her . . . yet it's something I cannot do.*

"Have you chosen?" Lari asked.

Madori looked at the corpses in the wheelbarrow. A dead youth, younger than her, hung across the rim, glassy eyes staring at Madori, mouth still open in a silent scream. This was not something Madori could do either. She would not disgrace the dead.

"Choose!" Lari said.

She had only one choice left, Madori knew. The only choice she had ever had, perhaps. The only choice that could thwart Lari's plans and end this pain.

Madori placed the tip of the dagger against her own neck.

She closed her eyes, the steel against her skin.

She saw the swaying rye fields of Fairwool-by-Night, golden in the sunlight. She saw her mother smile, singing softly as she tucked Madori into bed. She saw her father wave from his gardens, saw herself run to him, jump into his arms, and kiss his cheek. She saw all her friends: Tam, the boy she had once thought she would marry; Neekeya, her dear, brave friend from distant lands; and Jitomi . . . the only boy she had ever kissed, ever loved as a woman loves a man.

Goodbye, she thought. *Goodbye, my family, my friends. Goodbye, Timandra. Goodbye, Eloria. Goodbye, this world we call Moth. I love you all.*

She took a deep breath, prepared to shove the blade.

"Madori."

The voice was distant, soft, carrying on the wind. *His* voice. The voice of Jitomi, the voice she had thought she'd never hear again.

"Madori!"

"I have to do this," she whispered to his memory. She saw him in her mind: a young man with white hair, his nose pierced, a dragon tattooed across his face. "I have to."

"Madori!" His voice was louder now, torn with pain, coming from above her, from the stars. Perhaps he had died before her, and she would join him now in those celestial halls.

"Madori, wait!"

A chinking sound rose above, and a roar pierced the world, louder than thunder. The dagger still clutched in her hands, Madori opened her eyes, looked up, and gasped.

A black dragon flew above, and Jitomi sat upon its back, calling her name.

"Jitomi!" she shouted back at him, tears in her eyes.

A choked sound ahead of her drew her attention. Madori looked back down to see Lari trembling, her skin pale. Her eyes widened with rage. Her hands balled into a fists.

With a roar, Lari leaped forward, slammed against Madori, and knocked her down. The two women tilted over the edge of the smoking pit . . . then fell, crashing down toward the shadows and skeletons.

CHAPTER TWENTY-EIGHT
UPRISING

Koyee swung her pickaxe again and again, chipping away at the wall. Around her, a thousand other slaves worked with her. All were silent this turn. None wept, wailed, or so much as groaned. Nervous eyes darted toward Koyee, then up at the sky. She followed their gaze.

The moon is gone, she thought. Only the stars shone above.

It was time.

Yet Koyee kept working, loathe to give the signal to attack. She kept chipping away, waiting for . . . for what? A shred of hope? A sliver of courage?

She looked behind her. Upon the chasm's eastern ledge, a hundred soldiers stood in steel, staring down into the mine. Beyond them lay a camp of tents, and somewhere up there Madori still lived, still needed her, needed a mother.

Once I swing this pickaxe at a soldier, I will never see my daughter again, Koyee thought.

She took a shaky breath, and her arms trembled. Guilt coursed through her along with her fear. Why had she always been so hard on the girl? Once Madori had grown up, had learned about her mixed blood, she had begun to rebel, to shout at her parents, at anyone who approached. Koyee had always responded with shouts of her own, even with a few slaps to Madori's cheeks, and now the guilt seemed too great to bear.

I should have hugged you then, Koyee thought, *not fought against you. I should have held you close, told you that I loved you, told you that your crazy hair, your crazy clothes, your crazy ways are fine, that I love you as you are. Instead I scolded you, and I drove you away from me.*

Koyee would have sold the treasure of an empire for another life with Madori, even just another moment—to hold her daughter, to tell her that she loved her always, that she was sorry.

I might never see her again, Koyee thought. *But if Madori must see me die, if she must see my body wheeled away, at least she will know I died fighting.* Koyee's eyes stung. *The way my father died when I was young.*

She took a deep breath, remembering that turn—so many years ago—when Torin had returned to her the bones of her father. Koyee squared her shoulders. She raised her chin. She turned toward the other miners, and she shouted as loud as she could: "Elorians! We are the night!"

Across the mine, the Radian overseers stared, confusion twisting their faces.

An instant later, a thousand miners swung pickaxes at their masters.

Koyee screamed as she swung her tool, now her weapon. Overseer Nafar ran toward her—towering, gaunt, and sneering. The Magerian raised the stump of his right arm, the one which ended with a whip instead of a hand. He swung that whip toward her. Koyee's pickaxe drove into his face before the lash could strike her. The overseer—the man who had whipped her so many times, had slain so many Elorians around her—crashed down, blood gushing from the ruin of his face. Koyee was so weak she nearly collapsed, but she swung again and again, slamming the pickaxe down until the overseer moved no more.

That is for all those times you beat me, she thought, panting, blood on her face.

"The nightcrawlers are attacking!" shouted Gora, the squat Magerian who had led Pahmey's survivors here, who had beaten Madori bloody too often to count. Koyee silenced the brute with a swing of her pickaxe just as he drew his sword. When Gora fell, blood gushing from his belly, she drove the pick into his neck, finishing the job.

That is for my daughter, she thought, drenched in his spurting blood.

She glanced around her, panting and dizzy. Across the mine, the Elorians were swinging their picks against their masters, but only three other Radians had fallen; many more remained. Dozens of Elorians already lay dead, pierced with Radian swords or simply fallen to exhaustion and disease, the attack taking out the last of their strength. Koyee watched, frozen for an instant, as the living Radians plowed through the herd of slaves, swinging their swords, cutting Elorians down. Most of the picks rebounded harmlessly off the Radians' armor.

"Aim for their faces!" Koyee shouted. "Don't attack the armor. Elorians, aim for—"

Whistles filled the air. Arrows descended from above the canyon. Koyee turned to see many Radian archers standing upon the rim, firing down. The arrows drove into the crowd of Elorians, and screams rose. Blood splattered. Elorians fell dead.

Koyee screamed and swung her pickaxe again. Two other Elorians fought at her side; the three picks took down another Radian soldier.

And so here I die, Koyee thought as more arrows fell from above. *Here, in darkness, fighting, a weapon in my hand.* It was not a bad way to die.

"Fight your way out!" Koyee shouted. She pointed at the craggy staircase the Radians had carved into the canyon wall, letting them move between the mine and tents above. "Up! To their camp! Overwhelm their tents and slay them all!"

She knew it was hopeless. Not with a hundred thousand slaves could she defeat men in armor, not with the slaves so famished and ill, already nearly dead, chains hobbling them. But if she could, she would die seeing Madori one more time. Her daughter would see her fighting as a free heroine, not dying as a slave.

"Eloria, we are the night!" Koyee cried, leading the way toward the stairs. Behind her, those Radians already in the canyon were butchering Elorians one by one. From above, arrows still fell. Soon a hundred slaves had died, but Koyee climbed onto the staircase, and she swung her pickaxe, knocking a Radian down. The other Elorians climbed behind her—bald, battered, weary, and free warriors.

"We are the night!" they cried together. "For Eloria! For Koyee!"

She kept climbing, knocking men down. Her ankles were hobbled, the chain only a foot long, just long enough to let her climb step by step. She had fought in battles before—upon the walls of Pahmey, in the canal of Sinyong, in the streets of Yintao, in the heart of Cabera Mountain—but here was her greatest battle, the last battle of her life. Here she was stronger and nobler than ever before.

She reached the edge of the staircase, emerged from the mine, and hobbled into the camp. Her ankles were still shackled. Her arms were so weak she could barely hold her pickaxe. Twenty Radians or more rode toward her upon their horses, all in steel, bearing lances, and Koyee raised her pickaxe, ready to fight and die.

Steel arrows flew through the night.

Battle cries rose.

Koyee winced and swung her pickaxe blindly.

The Radian riders crashed down, arrowheads bursting out from their chests. Their horses reared, whinnied, and scattered.

Koyee stared and gasped. Tears flooded her eyes.

"Hope," she whispered. She trembled. "Hope is here."

With battle cries and swinging katanas, a hundred Ilari soldiers rode into the camp upon black panthers, slaying the Radians and roaring for the night.

Koyee ran. Her chains clattered between her ankles. She fell and found that she could not rise. She crawled.

"Madori!" She climbed over a Radian corpse. At her side, an Ilari warrior astride a panther locked swords with a Radian rider. "Madori! Daughter!"

No answer came. Koyee tried to stand up. She fell again. Her head thumped against the earth, and her pickaxe fell from her hands.

* * * * *

They rolled among the smoking bones, the daughter of an emperor and a famished, dying woman torn between day and night. Above in the sky, the dragon howled and swooped. Magic shot out from Lari's hands, blasted skyward, and stretched across the pit's opening like a membrane. Tianlong the dragon crashed down against the black, quivering shield; Madori could see his fangs and claws scratch against it, unable to break through. Jitomi's muffled voice cried from beyond: "Madori, Madori!"

Lying with Madori among the bones in the mass grave, Lari laughed maniacally. "They cannot break through! Even the dragon of the nightcrawlers is too weak to resist my magic." She looked back at Madori. "It's just you and me now, mongrel. You tried to steal my plaything. You tried to kill yourself. But you are mine to torment, and you will be mine for many years." She grabbed Madori's wrist. "Return me my dagger so that I may cut off your fingers. You won't be able to try that trick again without any fingers."

Madori screamed and tried to hold onto the dagger. But she was too weak. She cried out as Lari twisted her wrist, and the dagger fell from her grip.

"You cannot win!" Madori shouted. "Ilar attacks. Eloria fights back. You will die this turn."

Lari laughed and drove her knee into Madori's belly. Madori coughed, unable to breathe. She gagged, losing the paltry meal she had eaten in the tent.

"I will live forever!" Lari shouted, laughing. Shreds of magic still clung to her fingers, and her hair crackled and rose like a fire. "No nightcrawler can harm me. I will turn you into a creature. Give me your hand! I will cut off finger by finger."

She grabbed Madori's wrist again. Lying on the pile of skeletons, Madori screamed, grabbed a bone, and tugged. The bone detached from the skeleton, and Madori swung it like a club. The femur connected with Lari's head with a *crack*.

"You cannot win," Madori repeated, her voice hoarser now, weaker. Every breath drained out precious energy. "I defeated you at the trials at Teel. I will defeat you now. Your kind will never win."

She swung the bone again. Lari's temple bled, but the princess managed to catch the bone. She shattered it in her palm as if it were a twig.

"We've already won, mongrel." Lari smiled and licked blood off her lips. "Your kind is all dead, all but a few scattered wretches. You will be the last nightcrawler alive."

She swiped her dagger.

The blade sliced Madori's finger, cutting through the joint.

Madori screamed.

Her blood gushed out, spraying Lari's face. Her finger fell, dangling from her hand by only a shred of skin. There was no pain, only horror, only so much blood.

"I love the taste of your blood." Lari greedily licked the blade. "Now for the next finger. Slower this time, so you can feel it."

The princess grabbed Madori's hand again and lowered her dagger.

Madori's eyes rolled back. She felt ready to faint. She felt the blade begin to cut her skin.

I'm sorry, Mother. I'm sorry. I failed you.

Koyee was smiling down at her, rocking Madori in her arms, singing a lullaby, a song of the night. They were back in Fairwool-by-Night, and Madori was very young and felt very safe. Sunlight fell through the windows and a robin sang outside. The music soothed her, the song "Sailing Alone," a song of fear, of longing, of passageways in the dark.

You survived, Mother, Madori thought. *You survived, Father. You fought great enemies and you defeated them.*

The blade cut deeper.

"Good . . . bleed for me, mongrel," Lari said.

Madori screamed in rage.

"I am Elorian!" Her voice roared, torn with pain. "I am a daughter of Eloria. We are the night!"

She formed a fist with her four remaining fingers. She drove that fist upward and slammed it against Lari's face.

Lari fell back, her nose crushed, her tooth knocked loose. The dagger fell from her grip and clattered between the bones. As the skulls watched, Madori lifted the dagger, stumbled toward Lari, and drove the blade downward.

The dagger crashed into Lari's chest, thrust between the ribs, and sank deep.

Lari screamed, gurgling on blood.

"You could have lived," Madori whispered. "You could have lived in peace, an empress, an ally." She twisted the blade. Lari twitched, kicking, gasping. "Now you die among the bones of those you murdered."

Madori pulled the dagger out. Lari gave one last twitch, one last gurgle, then lay still and silent.

The magic vanished above, revealing the sky again.

Madori fell.

She lay on her back atop the skeletons. Her head tilted sideways, and she saw the skulls looking at her, and it seemed to Madori that she could see their eyes again. They were watching her. Thanking her.

Arms wrapped around her, and blinking, Madori thought she could see Jitomi's face. He was kneeling above her, calling her name, but then he faded like the world, and she smiled.

CHAPTER TWENTY-NINE
THE DISTANT LIGHT

"Hush now, little Madori. You are home. You are home."

The little girl smiled softly, her nightmares easing. Whenever she dreamed of monsters under her bed or ghosts in her closet, her mother's soft words could soothe her. Mother was stroking her hair now, and Madori felt her fear flow away. The pain of fever dreams melted like the candles they used in the night.

She blinked softly, struggling to open her eyes. The bed was soft around her, warm and safe, womb-like, enveloping her. Mother looked down from above, her lavender eyes loving.

"Mama?" Madori whispered. "Are the monsters gone?"

"Yes, sweet child." Koyee wiped the sweat off Madori's forehead. "All gone. We defeated them."

Madori shivered. These dreams had been worse than monsters or ghosts. She had dreamed of cruel men in steel, and many bones, and starvation in darkness, and . . .

She frowned. She sat up in bed so quickly her head spun. The room swayed around her. And she remembered.

She was no longer a child but a woman. The iron mine. The chasm of bones. Lari. Jitomi.

"Mother!" Madori's eyes flooded with tears. "Mother, you're alive."

Koyee looked thin, almost skeletal, her cheeks sunken and her eyes huge. White stubble covered her head, all her long, silvery hair gone. But she wore a cloak of lush black silk, the cloth embroidered with red flames. She smiled warmly and color touched her cheeks.

"I'm alive, sweetling. We're both ali—"

Madori would not let her complete her sentence. She leaped up and wrapped her arms around Koyee, squeezing so hard, never wanting to let go. Hot tears flowed down her cheeks onto Koyee's cloak.

"I'm so sorry, Mother." Madori shook, barely able to breathe. "I'm so sorry for everything. For everything. For how I was. For fighting, rebelling, running off to Teel. Please forgive me."

Koyee laughed and her own tears fell. "Only if you forgive me for being a horrible, stern nightmare of a mother to you. My own mother died when I was so young, and I didn't know how to handle you." She held Madori tight. "I'm so glad we're both here."

Held in her mother's embrace, Madori looked around her. Where was "here?" She saw curving clay walls, iron beams, and a small round window. The room was still swaying. At first Madori had thought herself dizzy, but now she realized—she was on a ship.

Gingerly, she released her mother, stepped off the bed, and stood for a moment on bare feet. She was wearing a silken gown, and her wounds were bandaged. A thought struck her and she looked at her hand. Her finger, which Lari had cut off, was reattached and bound tightly. A smile tingled across her lips, and Madori tiptoed toward the porthole and peered outside.

A gasp fled her lips. Many other ships sailed outside, a great fleet—their sails battened, their decks lined with cannons, their figureheads shaped as dragons and panthers. Red flames were painted onto iron hulls.

"The Armada of Ilar," she whispered in awe. She spun back toward her mother. "Jitomi! I remember. He brought aid." She laughed. "Not all Eloria has fallen. There is hope."

A voice spoke softly behind her. "There is always hope."

She turned around, saw him standing at the door, and her eyes dampened anew. "Jitomi."

He smiled, though there was pain and sadness to that smile, and suddenly Madori hesitated. She had parted from Jitomi in anger at Oshy. Would he still be mad at her? Were things still broken between them? But then his smile widened, and his eyes softened, and he held out his arms. She raced toward him and they embraced. He kissed the stubbly top of her head.

"Silly little Billygoat," he said.

She gasped. "Nobody but my parents is allowed to call me that." A thought struck her, and she turned back toward Koyee. "What of Father? Have we any word of him?"

Koyee still sat upon the bed, her hands in her lap. Her eyes darkened. "Only rumors. They say that your father was captured in Kingswall, but that Cam freed him from his Radian captors. Men speak of a Free Arden in the northern forests, joined to Verilon. A northern front rages there. I believe that Torin still lives, that he still fights." She placed a hand against her chest. "Our hearts are joined, and I can feel his heart still beating with mine."

Madori breathed a sigh of relief. Father was fighting in the war, but he had not died, at least not that they knew of. She sniffed and turned back toward Jitomi. "What of Tam? And Neekeya?"

Jitomi lowered his head. "Of them we have no words, no whispers, no rumors. All we know is that, when we parted last year, they were heading to Daenor. We've heard talk of Daenor falling to the Radians, but not of our friends' fate."

Madori nodded silently, and fear for her friends gnawed on her. "I need to see the water and the sky." She wobbled toward the door, still so weak. When she passed by a mirror, she looked at herself, and she barely recognized the reflection. The girl she had been—with tanned skin, fierce eyes, and two long strands of black hair—was gone. Instead she saw a pale, thin woman, only black stubble on her head. Her purple eyes seemed even larger than usual in her gaunt face. She tightened her lips, looked away, and exited the chamber.

She found a staircase and climbed, holding onto the rail for support. The smell of oil, steel, and water filled her nostrils, and she breathed in deeply and climbed onto the deck.

"We're sailing on the Inaro," she whispered in awe. She would recognize this river anywhere; it was the river that ran south of Oshy, her home in the night, and that morphed into the Sern River upon which Fairwool-by-Night had stood. She did not recognize what part of the Inaro this was, only that here was the starlit water of her childhood.

The deck stretched hundreds of feet long, and many Elorian soldiers bustled across it. They were not the soldiers of Qaelin, her homeland; Qaelish soldiers wore steel scales and elegant, curving helmets. These soldiers wore heavy, lacquered plates painted red and black, tassels hanging from them. Their helmets were shaped as snarling demons complete with horns and fur mustaches. Many katanas hung across their backs, the grips wrapped with red silk. Here were the soldiers of Ilar, the southern empire Jitomi was from.

When she looked across the water, Madori saw many other Ilari ships, all bearing the Red Flame sigil. She gasped to see some Timandrian ships too—tall carracks built of wood, their sails woven of canvas. When she noticed that Ilari banners rose from them too, she tilted her head.

"We captured them in battle," Jitomi said, coming to stand beside her. He placed his hands against the balustrade and leaned forward, gazing at the rest of his fleet. "Many sailed against us further southeast. Many sank." He smiled thinly. "I took a few for my fleet."

She looked at him, eyes narrowed. "Your fleet?"

He smiled wanly. "For a while longer."

He spoke then of the past few moons—how he had traveled to Ilar, how his father had died, how he had become Emperor of Ilar. He spoke too of sailing north along the Inaro, of meeting the Radian fleet in the water, and of sailing onward until he reached the ruin of Pahmey.

"I had hoped to find you in the city," he said. "When we saw that Pahmey was gone, we captured a few Radian soldiers who were lingering around the ruins. We questioned them. When I learned of the mine, hope sprang in me, hope that you still lived." He took her hand in his. "And you are alive."

She leaned her head against his shoulder. "For a while longer."

He placed an arm around her and pulled her close. "Now we must choose, Madori. We must choose our path. We are a lone army in a sea of enemies. A lone beacon of hope in a land where all other hope is lost. Do we land our fleet upon the bank, then march across the darkness of Qaelin, seeking survivors?"

"Where is Serin?" she asked.

Jitomi looked out across the water. "Radians we captured spoke of him returning west into sunlight, back to his palace in Mageria."

"Then that is where we go." She walked along the bulwark, moving between soldiers, until she reached the prow of the ship. An iron figurehead, shaped as a dragon, thrust ahead. The western waters were dark and calm; their ship led the way. Darkness waited there in the distance, but beyond it, Madori knew, lay the light of day. Jitomi came to stand beside her, and they stood together, staring at the horizon as behind them sailed hundreds of Ilar's ships.

"We sail on," she whispered. "We sail through darkness and we sail into the light. We sail along the Inaro, and along the Sern River, until we reach Serin's backyard. We will do what no Elorian army has ever done: Invade the daylight."

Jitomi wrapped his arms around her and kissed her head, but Madori would not relax in his grip. She kept staring ahead into the shadows, and pain filled her.

I will never forget this pain, she thought, and her eyes stung, and her throat constricted. *I will never forget how the whips hurt me, how the hunger clawed at my belly, how I watched my people die. Forever, in darkness or in light, that nightmare will fill me. We will meet again, Serin. I promise you this. I vow this by the stars of my forebears. We will meet one more time, Serin . . . the last time. The time I kill you.*

The fleet sailed on through the darkness. Ahead, across many miles of shadow, the dusk blazed with light.

BOOK SIX:

LEGACY OF MOTH

Daniel Arenson

CHAPTER ONE
THE WHALE AND THE DIAMOND

Prince Eris Grimgard, second son of King Bormund of Orida, stood at the prow of his longship and watched the sun rise over the water.

"Home." His voice nearly vanished in the wind. "After three years of darkness . . . sunlight." He turned around to face his men. "We are home!"

The Oringard sat in the long, narrow ship—a hundred warriors. Each man held an oar, propelling *Orin's Blade* forward. The ship was shaped as an orca, sigil of their kingdom, and more orcas appeared upon their banners and round wooden shields. Each of the Oringard, legendary warriors descended from the first king himself, wore a horned helm, a fur cloak, and a wide blade at his hip. Each man also carried a gilded horn around his neck, amulets to bless them in battle, then drink mead from in the halls of victorious afterlife. As they oared the ship forward, the men cried out Eris's name, blessing him.

"For three years," Eris said, "you've followed me through darkness. You defeated the undead of the crystal forests in Leen, the beasts of the watery chasm off the Qaelish coast, the bloodthirsty wolves of darkness, and many more enemies. Now we return home with our prize." He raised his own horn, larger than the others, older, holier. "We return with the Meadenhorn! With glory!"

The Oringard roared for that glory, and Eris turned back toward the west. The sun had fully emerged from the water now. The light reflected against his armor, his blade, and the Meadenhorn in his hand. The wind billowed his cloak and filled his nostrils, and after three years of cold, finally warmth filled him. The wind smelled like salt, like water, like sunlight—like Timandra, the lit half of the world, the realm Eris had begun to think he'd never see again.

"So this is the sun."

The voice that spoke beside him was soft, hesitant, almost afraid. Eris turned to his right, gazed upon his wife, and felt all his warrior's strength, his pride and glory, his haunting nightmares of bloodshed and darkness, all fade into a haze like veiled sunlight in the rain.

Yes, I return with the lost artifact of Orida . . . and with a treasure even greater.

Eris took her soft, pale hand, so small in his, a lily in the paw of a bear. "Does it burn you, my love?"

She stood wrapped in a white silk cloak and hood. The sunlight fell upon her pale face and large indigo eyes—Elorian eyes, the size and shape of chicken eggs, far larger than his. She was a small woman, no taller than his shoulder, so thin she was almost frail. Strands of her white hair escaped her hood and billowed as banners. Around her neck, rather than a mead horn, she wore a diamond, the stone of her people. She was Yiun Yee, a princess of Leen, a daughter of darkness, and his wife.

"The sunlight burns me no more than moonlight can burn a diamond," she replied. "No more than starlight upon the crystals of our forests. No more than the light of your love, my Eris, within my breast. The sunlight is no brighter than that love, and it can no more burn me than you can." She smiled—the fragile, hesitant smile which had first drawn Eris to her like a siren's song. "I've always wanted to see the sun. How beautiful it is."

How beautiful you are, Eris thought, gazing at her pale cheeks, her gleaming eyes, her silken hair. *How brave you are. How noble. How precious to me.*

He had defeated the undead in the icelands, the wolves in darkness, the great beasts of the chasm, and she had fought at his side. She had left her palace of crystal and moonlight, had traveled with him through blood and fire and shadow, and now into daylight. Now into his home. Now into a world that, to her, was as strange as a land beyond the stars.

"You've left a great palace," he said, holding her hand. "You've left the fabled city of Taenori—the Light of the North—in your empire of Leen, abandoning your birthright for a chance to live at my side. And I vow to you, Yiun Yee: You will become a great princess of daylight, a great jewel of the Orinhall upon our sunlit island, more precious than diamonds."

The Oringard, these stout one hundred men who had fought at his side for three years, kept rowing. The longship emerged from the dusk, and now the sun shone fully. A chill still lingered in the air, and a drizzle fell, but to Orin this light seemed as bright and warm as summer in the southern deserts of Eseer. The last shadows of Eloria faded behind them, and the blue sea—by Orin, he had almost forgotten the color blue!—spread ahead toward the horizon. Beyond that horizon lay Orida, his island, and upon it the great city of Grenstad. The city had lost its heart, lost the Meadenhorn, lost what he—Prince Eris, Hero of Orida—would return to its breast.

"I care not for palaces or royal titles." Yiun Yee gazed at the blue sea, then turned to look at him, her eyes bright. "I care only for a life at your side. I care only for you, Eris, the light of my heart, the love of my soul."

Eris held her hand as they sailed onward. He was a man of sunlight—his beard and hair long and golden as sunbeams, his eyes blue as the sky and water, his frame tall and strong like the mighty oaks of Orida. Yiun Yee was like the moon—softer, paler, a thing of fragile beauty. A Prince of Orida and a Princess of Leen. A son of light and a daughter of darkness. The great War of Day and Night had ended twenty years ago, and Eris had found the treasure his father had lost in that war, and he found a wife among the old enemies, a marriage of peace, of an old wound finally healed.

They kept rowing through the open sea for long turns. Fifty men rowed as fifty slept, cycling again and again. They ate the food they had collected in the night—mushrooms, bat and snake meat, and lanternfish that glowed with inner lights. For the first time, they caught the fish of Timandra in their nets, and Eris dreamed of the great feast that awaited them at the Orinhall.

Soon we'll feast on succulent boar, wild deer from the forests, and fresh breads and pies from the ovens. Soon we'll drink mead from Orin's horn. He caressed the Meadenhorn, this reclaimed treasure, admiring the gold and jewels inlaid upon it.

Finally, after ten full turns of rowing through the light, they saw it ahead.

Tears filled the Oringard's eyes. The men cried out in joy. "Orida! The island of Orida!"

Eris raised the Meadenhorn, and it caught the sunlight. "The Sons of Orin return home!" He turned toward Yiun Yee. "And with us a treasure of the night. This will be your home too, Yiun Yee, my princess of darkness and light."

Orida was known by many names: Orca's Isle, Orin's Landing, The Meadenrock, and a hundred others. Eris stood at the prow, watching it grow nearer. It was a massive island, nearly as large as Leen in the night. Its shores were white, and great pine forests stretched across its hills and mountains. Above all other crests rose the great Berenhorn, the tallest mountain in Orida, named after Beren the Wise who had climbed its slopes and planted Orida's banner upon its crest.

As they rowed closer, the city of Grenstad appeared. A port of stone and wood spread across the coast, and many longships anchored here, shaped as orcas and lined with oars. Wooden halls rose on the hills beyond the shore, their roofs thatched. Above them all rose the mighty Orinhall. The great mead hall, home to Orida's king, stood in the shade of the Berenhorn, and it gazed upon the city below and the sea beyond. Its roof was thatched like the roofs of lesser halls, but gilt coated its wooden beams, and its banners rose high, displaying leaping orcas. True orcas, great killers of the sea, swam alongside the *Orin's Blade*, welcoming the heroes home.

They rowed into the port, docked at a pier, and for the first time in three years, Eris and his Oringard set foot upon their homeland. For the first time in all her twenty years, Yiun Yee, a princess of Leen, stepped onto sunlit land.

They walked through the city, heroes returning home. Men and women emerged from their houses, their hair long and golden. They wore fur and cotton, and silver rings were woven into the men's beards. They cheered for Eris, for he returned with the Meadenhorn, the kingdom's lost treasure, and they gazed in wonder at Yiun Yee, and she seemed to them as mystical as their reclaimed artifact. Yiun Yee in turn gazed upon the city with equal wonder, her Elorian eyes growing even larger than usual. She smiled at Eris.

"The city is smaller than Taenori." She spoke in his tongue, which he had taught her, her accent thick. "But it's just as fair. It is a wonder of sunlight." She wrapped her silk cloak tighter and pulled her hood low. "Though it will take me time to adjust to this great lantern in the sky."

They kept moving through the city and its crowds, and finally they made their way uphill toward the Orinhall. The great mead hall loomed above them, the crests of its giltwood beams carved as orcas. Guards in steel stood before its gates, their helmets horned, their cloaks black and white, their shields round and their swords wide. They raised the horns that hung around their necks on chains, and they trumpeted for the glory of Eris and the Oringard, and they opened the gates of the hall.

Eris stepped inside, a hero to enter legend, his wife at his side, his Oringard behind him . . . and found the hall changed.

All his pride, his joy, his glory seemed to crumble.

In some ways, the hall was the same. Oak columns still rose in two rows, engraved with sea monsters, orcas, and the faces of old gods. The wooden floor was still smoothed by the heels of many feet over many generations. Round wooden shields hung upon the walls, upon them the sigils of the great lords, and among them hung ancient swords of iron and bronze. Iron candelabra hung from the ceiling, and a fireplace roared at the back of the hall. Guards stood here, proud Sons of Orin, clad in fur and steel, their blond beards strewn with beads and golden rings.

The back of the hall, however, was not as Eris had left it. The old banner of Orida, an orca upon a white field, no longer hung here. Instead a great banner of gold and silver covered the wall, displaying a sunburst hiding the moon. Eris knew this sigil. He had seen the Radian ships sail in the darkness, raiding the coasts of both Leen and Qaelin. He had heard tales of Tirus Serin, a cruel Magerian lord, forging an empire in the sunlight, collecting other kings to serve him. But Eris had never imagined that this banner would hang here, that his own father—King Bormund Grimgard, a proud Son of Orin— would bend the knee to this southern sorcerer, would hoist Serin's banner in the Orinhall.

"Father!" Eris said, stepping forth.

As always, King Bormund sat upon his throne of giltwood, but he was not the man Eris had parted from three years ago. Bormund had once been a proud warrior, his shoulders wide, his chin always raised, his beard a deep gold, his eyes bright. Those wide shoulders stooped now. Silver strands invaded the gold of his beard. His eyes had darkened, and cunning now filled them, and beneath the cunning lurked fear like boulders hidden underwater. A horned helm still topped the king's head, and a gilded breastplate still shone upon his chest, but he seemed less a proud warrior now, more like an aging predator, grown too slow to hunt, devious and peering from the shadows of a den.

Eris's mother, Queen Tylgra, normally stood at the throne's right side. A new woman stood there now, a woman Eris did not know. She was fair and no older than Eris's thirty-five years. Her golden hair cascaded across her shoulders, and her eyes were blue and bright. She wore a green gown with a plunging neckline, and a golden chain hung around her neck, holding an amulet with the Radian sigil.

The woman stepped forth and raised her hand. A sunburst was tattooed onto her palm, hiding the moon. "Halt, Sons of Orin, and kneel before your king!" She spoke in Oridian with a thick Magerian accent. "You stand in the presence of Bormund Grimgard, son of Fengard, Slayer of Fen Shoo the Light of Leen, Defeater of Oshmog the White Bear of Verilon, King of all Orida." The woman turned to stare at Yiun Yee, and her eyes narrowed with hatred, and her lips peeled back. "You have brought evil into this hall, Sons of Orin. Kneel and beg for your lives, for you come here with a daughter of darkness."

Eris looked at his wife. Yiun Yee stared back with large, shocked eyes. Behind her, the Oringard—a hundred stalwart men— knelt before their king, but Eris would not bend the knee. He turned back toward his father and the strange woman and stepped closer toward them.

"I've returned, Father, to find a home less welcoming than before." He glanced at the tall Radian woman. "Who stands beside you where my mother once stood, and who cloaked your hall with the eclipse of a southern empire? You were once a proud king of Orida, not one to bend the knee to a foreign ruler."

King Bormund rose from his throne. His shoulders curled inwards, and his neck hung low as if barely supporting his head, but his eyes glittered with greed, and his lips twitched. He hobbled forth, reaching out thin fingers toward the Meadenhorn which hung around Eris's neck on a chain. The old king laughed, a sound like crackling ice.

"You've found it, my son! The Meadenhorn." Tears streamed from the king's eyes. "The great horn that Orin himself drank mead from two thousand years ago. The blessed artifact of our island, the horn lost in the darkness." He pawed at the heirloom. "Hand it to me, my son, so that we may drink mead from this holy vessel once more."

Eris took a step back, pulling the Meadenhorn out of the king's reach. The old man gasped.

Eris's heart pounded. "Father, I've been gone for three years from your hall. I fought for you. I slew men and beasts for you. Twenty-three of my Oringard lie dead under the dark waters of Eloria. I return here, and you offer me no welcome, only fingers greedy for your prize, like a starving dog reaching for a morsel. Who is this woman who stands where once my mother stood? Answer me!"

King Bormund stared from under his brows. His scraggly, graying hair—once thick and lustrous and golden—hung loosely around his weathered face. "A starving dog for a morsel? It seems to me that you here are the dog, a mere pup begging for approval from his master. Are you truly a warrior or a mere boy, desperate to impress his father?" Bormund snorted. His eyes narrowed shrewdly, and his lips twitched. "You call Serin a foreign ruler. That he was once, perhaps. Yet now Serin is more than some distant emperor. Now he is . . . a brother." The king stepped toward the Radian woman and wrapped his arm around her waist. "Here stands Iselda Serin, sister to Emperor Tirus Serin, and my new wife. Yes, my son. Your mother has fallen ill and died while you were away. You were not here by her side, even as she called to you. Iselda Serin is our new queen . . . and your new mother."

The news hit Eris more mightily than a war hammer. His mother, dead. His father, married to a Radian, the sister of the emperor whose tales of cruelty traveled across the night. Eris's grief exploded, and he tossed back his head and howled. His keen echoed across the hall.

Yiun Yee rushed toward him and placed a pale hand upon his arm. "I'm sorry, Eris," she whispered.

King Bormund stared at Yiun Yee, and loathing filled his eyes, and his lip curled up in disgust. "And who do you bring into my hall, son? A woman of Leen stands before me, a woman of the dark empire I fought twenty years ago, the empire that stole our Meadenhorn."

Eris took a deep breath, the grief shuddering in his chest. He had not expected giddy excitement from his father upon meeting Yiun Yee, but neither had he expected outright hostility. He held Yiun Yee's hand.

"Leen is the empire you invaded and sacked twenty years ago, Father," Eris said. "It is the empire where you dropped the Meadenhorn upon the coast, losing our heirloom in the heat of battle. You stand now before Yiun Yee, a princess of Leen, a brave woman who helped me scour the darkness, who helped me retrieve the Meadenhorn from the creatures who had guarded it. You've taken a foreign wife in my absence. As have I."

It was King Bormund's turn to roar. He cry echoed across the mead hall, a cry of fury and grief. "What dark times have come upon this hall, that a Prince of Orida should wed without his father's consent, and that he should take a daughter of darkness no less?" The king licked his lips and reached out his hands. "Hand me my Meadenhorn, and perhaps I will forgive your transgression. Hand me my prize."

But Iselda Serin stepped forth and raised her palm again, displaying the eclipse tattooed upon it. "There can be no forgiveness for marrying a nightcrawler." she said. "These creatures are utterly evil. My dearest Bormund, did you not send your eldest son to raid the nightcrawlers' coasts and slay them? And now you would allow your second born to bring one into your hall?" The new Queen of Orida shook her head. "The daughter of darkness must suffer the fate of all her kin, as commands my brother, the great Light of Radian, Emperor Tirus Serin. Like all other Elorians, she too must die. Slay her, King Bormund. Prove yourself a mighty king, worthy of sitting upon this throne and serving my brother." Her eyes narrowed. "Or would you show me your weakness, and would you have Emperor Serin hear of a nightcrawler in this court he has allowed you to keep?"

King Bormund's eyes flicked between her and Eris, and for a moment the old king seemed torn.

"Father . . ." Eris said. "What has happened to you? You were once a proud king! I remember. I left you here a proud king. Now your shoulders stoop, and your eyes turn to another for guidance, and you let this foreign sorceress command you, to order you to spill the blood of your own daughter-in-law." Eris drew his sword. "By my steel, I am sworn to protect my wife. You will not touch her. You will accept her as my wife, Father, or I will leave this place—with her and with the Meadenhorn."

The king's eyes lit with fury, and he snarled and leaped forward. "The Meadenhorn is mine! It is not yours to keep. Ever has it hung around the necks of Orida's kings, not the necks of second born sons, of lesser princes." Bormund drew his own sword, the pommel shaped as the sun. "You have disgraced my court! Your wife must leave."

"His wife must *die*," said Iselda, also stepping forward. She placed her hand on Bormund's shoulder. "Slay her here. Slay her before me." She leaned closer and whispered into the old king's ear. "Show your strength in your court, and you may show me your strength in your bed."

The king shook, his face red, and let out a hoarse, wordless cry. He lunged toward Yiun Yee, swinging his blade.

Eris roared and swung his own sword, parrying. The two blades clanged together.

"Father!" he cried.

Yiun Yee stepped back, eyes wide with fear. The old king lolloped toward her, blade swinging up and down, madness in his eyes. He seemed like a man possessed, and though old and frail, he shoved Eris aside with the strength of a great warrior. The king's sword swung downward like a comet, slashing through Yiun Yee's gown, tearing open the silk and her skin. The Elorian princess screamed and stumbled backwards, blood spilling.

Eris roared.

He leaped forward, blade arching.

"Yiun Yee!" he cried. "Father, no!"

The guards of the hall stepped forward, reaching for their swords, as did the Oringard, but Bormund waved them back. The old king leaped toward Eris, roaring in madness, swinging his blade. Eris held out his sword.

"Stand back, Father!"

Eris tried to parry, tried to stop this, but the old king was too given to his madness. Like a fish leaping mindlessly onto the hook, King Bormund drove onto his son's blade. Eris's sword crashed through the king's chest.

Blood showered.

King Bormund's sword clanged to the floor.

Yiun Yee screamed and stepped back, clutching her wounded chest.

Yet while her wound was skin-deep, King Bormund was hurt more gravely; Eris's sword emerged from the old man's back.

"My horn . . ." the king whispered, impaled upon the blade. "My treasure . . ."

The old man's fingers reached out, curling like talons, making a last attempt to grab the Meadenhorn from Eris's neck. Then blood filled the king's mouth, and he fell to the floor, his weight tugging the sword's hilt free from Eris's grip. King Bormund lay at his son's feet and rose no more.

Eris stood, shocked, silent, still. He stared down at his dead father—the father he himself had slain—then raised his eyes. Iselda stood before him. Clad in her lush gown, her jewels bright, she met his eyes and smiled—a hungry, predatory smile.

Before Eris could speak to the Radian sorceress, the doors to the hall slammed open behind him. Eris spun, his father's blood upon his hands, to see his older brother step into the Orinhall.

Prince Torumun was a tall man of noble bearing, his beard thick and golden, his arms wide. Eris had known his brother to be honorable, a brave warrior, yet now Eris saw grisly trophies hanging from Torumun's belt. Elorian skulls dangled there upon chains, the eye sockets twice the usual size—the trophies of enemies slain in battle, an old practice not seen in Orida for many years.

Prince Torumun stared at the scene: his father dead upon the floor, his brother's arms coated in blood, a wounded Elorian princess, and a smiling step-mother with cruelty in her eyes.

"Your younger brother has returned, Prince Torumun!" said Iselda. "He has returned with an Elorian to usurp the throne. He has slain your father. Will you not take up arms against him?" The Radian turned toward the soldiers lining the hall. "Guards of Orida, will you not strike down this traitorous brother?"

Across the hall, soldiers of Orida drew their swords and stepped forth. The Oringard—Eris's own men—drew blades and stepped around their prince, protecting Eris and Yiun Yee.

"Brother!" said Torumun, voice torn in pain. "What have you done? You've slain our father!" The heir of Orida tossed back his head and howled. "You've slain him!" Torumun drew his sword. "Murderer! Usurper! Guards of Orida, slay him, slay the traitor! For the Light of Radian, slay Prince Eris!"

The palace guards stepped forth, swinging blades. The Oringard, who had fought with Eris for three years and remained loyal even in this hall, parried and thrust back.

"Stop!" shouted Eris, and his voice echoed in the hall, so loud he knew even the city beyond could hear. His eyes burned. His breath shook in his chest. "Stop this madness! Too much blood has spilled here already." He pointed a bloody finger toward Iselda. "Evil has come into this hall. The cruelty of the Radian Order has driven this place to bloodshed, to madness, to hatred. Iselda Serin, I banish you from Orida. Leave this city, and leave this island, and never more return. Go now!"

The Radian Queen only smiled at him. She stepped between the soldiers toward Torumun. She placed an arm around the prince's shoulder.

"Prince Torumun is now King of Orida!" she announced. "He has slain many Elorians in battle while you, Prince Eris the Traitor, brought an Elorian into our holy hall. By the laws of Orida, it is

509

Torumun who now rules, and Torumun who is now my lover." She stroked the prince's cheek. "For long years, we longed to love in the open, my prince, my sweet Torumun. And now the throne is yours, and now my love is yours for all to see."

The queen pressed herself against Prince Torumun and kissed him deeply, once his step-mother and now his lover. When the kiss ended, she pointed at Eris.

"And now, my sweet Torumun, slay him. Slay your murderous brother and his wife. Slay them and we will mount their skulls in our hall, and the Meadenhorn will be yours, as I am yours."

Torumun nodded, sword raised, and stepped forth.

Eris knelt, grabbed his sword, and pulled it free from his father's corpse. With his other hand, he held Yiun Yee. She leaned against him, clutching the tatters of her gown and her dripping wound.

"Brother!" Eris said. "How can you desecrate this hall? Turn aside this witch who seduces you."

Torumun raced forward, sword swinging. "I will have your Elorian's skull for my trophy. You slew our father, and I will bring you to justice."

The two princes locked swords. The blades clanged. Across the hall, the Oringard fought against the soldiers of the palace, and more men streamed in from the city. Blood washed the hall. One of the Oringard fell, chest pierced. Another cried out and tumbled. Men rushed into the hall, firing crossbows, and more of the Oringard fell. One bolt slammed into Eris's thigh, and he cried out in pain.

He fell to the floor, landing by the corpse of his father. As men fought around him, Eris gazed at the dead king. Bormund's eyes seemed to accuse him. *You murdered me, son!*

"I didn't mean to," Eris whispered.

You slew your father. You are forever cursed.

Eris rose to his feet, grimacing. He pulled his wife into his arms, and he raced across the hall, moving between the combatants, and burst out onto the hill. The city flowed across the slopes, many halls of wood and thatch leading to the sea.

"Slay him!" Torumun cried behind him from the hall. "Slay him and his wife!"

Eris made his way downhill, and his Oringard fought around him, carving a way through soldiers, suffering the wounds of swords and arrows, until they reached the sea and entered their longship. A great host flowed down the hills toward them, a thousand men or more, firing arrows, crying out for their blood. Prince Torumun ran among them, and his voice rang across the city.

"You are cursed, Eris! You murdered our father, and I will hunt you down!"

And above that voice rose a cruel, high laughter—the laughter of Iselda Serin. The Radian Queen stood upon the pier, chin raised, smiling as the *Orca's Blade* sailed away.

Eris had returned here as a hero, a proud son bearing an ancient prize. He fled the island as an exile, covered in blood—his own blood, the blood of his wife, and the blood of the father he himself had slain. His ancient gift, the Meadenhorn, still hung around his neck upon its chain.

The surviving Oringard rowed, and Eris lay upon the deck. Yiun Yee lay at his side, and their blood mingled. They fled into the open sea, a dozen ships in pursuit, and the sounds grew hazy. Eris could no longer hear the waves, the shouts of his men, or the whistles of arrows. All he could hear was that distant, echoing laughter, and all he could see were his father's accusing dead eyes.

CHAPTER TWO
ASHES

Madori stood upon the ship's deck, the wind ruffling her short black hair, as the Ilari Armada emerged from the dusk into the ruin of her old home.

"Fairwool-by-Night," she whispered. "Our home is gone."

In the space of a blink, she saw a memory: Fairwool-by-Night as it had been in her childhood. Thirty cottages of clay and wood stood in a ring, their roofs thatched, their gardens blossoming with sunflowers, peonies, tulips, and other flowers her father grew. Old Maple rose between them, leaves shading the staircase that led to the village library. Fields of rye, wheat, and barley swayed in the wind, and beyond them sheep grazed in green pastures. Robins and blackbirds sang overhead, and wooden piers stretched into the river, shading the weedy homes of bass and sunfish. A place of lazy turns spent reading under the tree, racing through the fields in search of butterflies, and dreaming of distant adventures. Madori had grown up here lonely, a girl of mixed blood shunned by her peers, but in her long exile she had come to miss her old village, her dog-eared books, her warm quilt, her garden, her childhood, her home.

Now this home was gone.

She took a shaky breath, her memory vanishing. The fields had been trampled and cut down. The old maple tree was gone. The cottages and gardens had burned, and a great statue of Serin rose among them, gazing east toward the darkness. Only the library still stood, its columns sooty, but Radian banners now hung upon its walls. Serin's eastern garrison had mustered here before invading the night, and many soldiers still lingered. Radian archers stood in makeshift wooden forts and upon the Watchtower, the village's only stone fortification. Three warships swayed at the docks, lined with cannons, and more of the great buffalo guns lined the riverbanks.

Hundreds of soldiers moved about the ruins of the village, and at the sight of the Ilari flagship emerging from the shadows, they cried out and raised their bows.

Koyee walked across the deck of the *Tai Lar*, flagship of the Ilari Armada. Clad in Ilari armor, she was almost unrecognizable. Steel plates, tasseled and lacquered, enclosed her slender form. A helmet hid her face, the visor shaped as a snarling demon with furry eyebrows. Madori could see only her mother's eyes, large and lavender.

"This turn we fight side by side, daughter," Koyee said and drew her sword.

Madori swung down her own visor; she too wore Ilari armor, its black plates making her feel like a great steel beetle. She drew her own katana, the blade that had once been Sheytusung but renamed Min Tey. The blade had been stolen from her in the darkness; she had found it among Lari's belongings in the iron mine, and now once more Madori carried it to battle.

"Side by side," Madori whispered. "For our home that was."

Tianlong, last dragon of the night, streamed above, emerging from the dusk into the full daylight. Jitomi sat on his back, and the young emperor blew into a horn, a great wail for blood and conquest.

Behind the *Tai Lar*, other Ilari warships emerged into the daylight, the vanguard of the Armada, a great fleet of five hundred vessels. For the first time in the history of Mythimna, this world frozen between day and night, an army of darkness emerged into the sunlight.

With whistling arrows, the roar of a dragon, and blasting cannons, the invasion of Timandra began.

"We are the night!" Koyee cried, and a sea of swords rose across the decks, thousands of warriors roaring for battle.

"We are the night!" Madori cried among them, sword held high, for this turn, emerging into the sunlight, she too was an Elorian. She had been born of a sunlit father, but in this war she was a daughter of darkness.

Enemy arrows rained from above, slamming against the Elorians' armor as they dropped anchor and lowered planks toward the docks. Cannons blasted from the riverside, slamming into the ship's iron hull, and the Elorian cannons answered from their decks, tearing into the enemy's lines. Madori screamed as she ran with the hosts, racing across a plank and onto the riverbank. She swung her sword, tearing into the Radians who stood upon the ruins of her village. Her mother fought at her side, and Jitomi flew overhead, and everywhere was smoke, blood, arrows, and steel.

Perhaps a thousand Radian troops garrisoned here; the bulk of Serin's Eastern Division was still crawling across the night. The Elorian invaders outnumbered them a hundred to one. Ilari warriors raced through the camp upon panthers, swinging katanas at the enemy. Cannons tore down tents and huts and wooden walls. At first the Timandrians tried to fight back. A soldier raced toward Madori, and she swung her blade, parrying his every thrust, and finally drove her katana through his shoulder and into his chest. Koyee slew another man, and around them, a hundred more Timandrians fell dead.

The rest turned to flee, but the Ilari—warriors bred in the light of the Red Flame for war and conquest—showed them no mercy. The blood of Timandra spilled upon the trampled fields and burnt remnants of Fairwool-by-Night. When the battle ended, all that remained of the Radian force were the dead.

With the enemy slain and its ships seized, the Ilari troops cheered for victory, and even Tianlong roared with triumph above, but Madori found no joy inside her, only digging pain like a dagger buried deep within her chest beyond the reach of any healer. She moved among the ruins, boots slogging through blood, her eyes wide and damp.

"Fairwool," she whispered.

She walked over a corpse, around an Ilari panther and its rider, and through a puddle of blood. She knelt by a severed arm and a cloven shield.

"The Shadowed Firkin rose here," she whispered, caressing the earth. Only piles of ash marked the place where the tavern had once stood. When Madori closed her eyes, she could see the place again: the chimneys belching out smoke, light glinting on the stained-glass windows, and the bronze statue of Hem Baker sitting inside by the hearth. She could hear the laughter of patrons, the songs Tera Brewer would sing upon the tables, and the crackling of the fire. She could smell the cooking beef stew and fresh bread, taste the cold ale, feel the oiled wooden bar beneath her palms. Yet when she opened her eyes, it was gone; only ash and blood and death.

Madori rose to her feet and walked around a group of laughing Ilari soldiers. She felt dizzy and nearly fell but dragged her feet onward. She knelt by a blackened stump and placed her hand upon it.

"Old Maple rose here," she whispered. She could see the tree in her memory again. She had spent many hours of her childhood climbing its branches, pretending to be Bailey Berin, the great heroine of the war whose statue had once stood in its shade. She was Madori Billy Greenmoat, her middle name given to her in honor of Bailey, yet now the heroine's statue was gone, and the tree both women would climb had been cut down.

Madori left the stump. Her boots squelched through blood as she walked forward to where her old house had stood.

Her childhood home—the old cottage where she had been born and raised—was gone. Upon the blackened earth where it had stood now rose a stone statue, taller than the fallen Old Maple, of Emperor Serin.

Rage filled Madori like the fire of a thousand cannons.

She roared, grabbed a stone from the ground, and drove it against the statue. She cried out, tears in her eyes, and pounded the statue again and again, chipping Serin's leg.

"You killed my friends at Teel!" she shouted, thinking of the Elorian students he had slain on the road. She pounded the statue. "You destroyed Pahmey!" Tears streamed down her cheeks. "You ruined my home. I am coming for you, Serin. I will find you and I will destroy you."

She kept pounding the statue with her rock, chipping bit by bit, until the stone cracked in her hand, and Madori fell to her knees, panting, chest heaving.

She felt a hand on her shoulder, and she spun around to see Koyee staring down at her, eyes solemn.

"Try this," Koyee said, handing Madori a chain.

Ilari troops stepped forward with more chains, which they wrapped around the statue and attached to their panthers. The beasts tugged and Madori tugged with them, straining as she gripped the iron links. The statue tilted, then crashed down and shattered. The Ilari soldiers cheered, but Madori remained silent, staring at the fallen colossus. The head lay at her feet, larger than her entire body. She looked into the stone eyes.

We will meet soon, Serin. You wanted to light the darkness, but now this darkness rises against you. And I rise with it.

A howl sounded behind her.

She spun toward the east and narrowed her eyes.

The howl rose again—the cry of a wolf.

Madori tilted her head, and her heart burst into a gallop.

A great beast, large as a horse, emerged from the dusk and raced across the battlefield. A nightwolf, she realized, a great hunter of the Qaelish plains. As it drew nearer, racing between the troops, Madori saw that its fur was gray, its frame lean, its eyes large and blue.

"It can't be," she whispered.

Yet as the nightwolf raced toward her, she knew it was him. Tears flooded her eyes anew, but this time they were tears of joy.

"Grayhem!" she cried.

He ran toward her, and Madori raced over the dead toward him, and she leaped onto her nightwolf and embraced him. The great beast nearly knocked her down, licking her cheeks and nuzzling her. He whimpered in pain and happiness to see her.

"Where were you?" she whispered, nearly choking on her joy. "By Xen Qae, boy! I haven't seen you for moons, not since Pahmey."

The nightwolf almost seemed to try and speak. Sounds almost like words rose from his throat, and he licked her again and again, pressing against her. He was so frail—by the stars, she could feel his ribs—and he must have traveled for countless leagues in the darkness before finding her.

She walked toward a toppled Timandrian tent where Ilari troops were digging through the enemy's supplies. She found a string of sausages and fed them to Grayhem; he swallowed them one by one, barely pausing to chew, and Madori laughed and rubbed the tears from her eyes.

Not all is lost, she thought. *Not all was taken from me.*

"You found me, boy," she whispered and kissed Grayhem. "I missed you. I love you."

He was still thin and frail but the meal seemed to give him strength. Madori climbed onto the nightwolf and straddled his back.

The Ilari Armada—five hundred ships bearing the banners of the night—sailed along the river, away from the dusk and into the sunlight. To war. To Markfir, capital of the Radian Empire. To Tirus Serin. Jitomi rode upon his dragon, and Koyee and thousands of other soldiers sailed upon the ships, but she, Madori, remained upon the riverbank, riding her wolf, her dearest friend.

As they headed into the west, Madori kept staring forward, imagining the turn she would meet Serin again. She did not look back once to the ruin of her home.

CHAPTER THREE
THE FINCH AND THE RAT

A finch flew above, warbling, a lone beacon of song and beauty in the world. Hunkered down in ruins of broken stone and shattered wood, Torin gazed up at the bird, marveling at how life could still survive here, how a bird could still fly and sing when so much death had befallen the world.

At his side, Cam nocked an arrow and tugged back the bowstring, aiming at the bird. Then, with a sigh, he slowly released the bowstring's tension and returned the arrow to his quiver.

"Ah, to Inagon with it," Cam said. "Even if I hit, there's barely any meat on it. Looks like it's rat on the menu again, though the damn rats are as skinny as we are."

Cam, shepherd turned King of Arden, himself looked like a starving rat. He had always been slender, but now Cam looked downright cadaverous. His cheeks were sunken, his skin ashen, his hair limp. His eyes darted nervously and he licked his dry lips with an equally dry tongue. The king still wore his plate armor, but dents, cracks, and stains covered it.

Torin suspected that he himself looked no better. When he gazed down at his body, it seemed to drown inside his own armor. He had barely recovered from his captivity in the Radian dungeons— a nightmare of pain and darkness spanning eight months—when he had found himself here, fighting in the ruins of Orewood.

At least, this place had once been Orewood. The proud capital of Verilon, once among the largest cities in Moth, had crumbled. Half the city's log homes had burned down; they spread across the hills in charred remains like the sooty skeletons of oversized beetles. Most of the stone structures too had collapsed. Cannons had punched holes through walls. Towers had fallen, and their domes of bronze, tin, and silver lay upon cracked streets like the massive, discarded spinning tops of giants. Shards of walls, orphaned archways, and lone columns rose from ash and piles of bricks. The once-mighty city, bastion of the north, had become a graveyard.

It seemed to Torin that only the city smithies and foundries, great buildings of stone, still stood; neither side had dared destroy them. Orewood had been built around iron mines, giving the city its name. Its foundries produced half the iron and steel in Timandra. Most turns Torin wanted to smash those foundries to the ground and end this carnage in their name.

"We can't keep eating rats," Torin said softly. "Not while the enemy is feasting on salted pork, fresh bread, and ale. Every turn we grow weaker. We must advance. We must take the temple."

Cam's eyes darkened. "Tor, there must be hundreds of Radians between us and the temple. Their archers line the roofs. Their swordsmen patrol the street."

Torin gestured around him. A hundred Ardishmen huddled here in the shell of an old chandlery. One wall and the roof had collapsed. They crouched against the remaining walls, armed with bows and arrows. Across the road, several Ardish troops stood on the roof of an abandoned tannery. They were all thin. Ashen. Maybe dying. They had been fighting in Orewood for almost a month now; they had barely eaten since the battle had begun.

Torin looked below him. A trapdoor led to the chandlery's cellar, and a dozen eyes peered up from the shadows. Verilish children hid here, their parents slain in the war, and they too were hungry. They too were dying. The rats and beetles had sustained them at first, but now even those animals were going scarce.

"We must reach the temple," Torin repeated. "That's where the food is stored. That's where we'll survive."

They had smelled the food cooking in the temple before— roasted meats, breads, stews. When the wind was just right, and the smell wafted down to this hovel, it was almost intolerable. Some turns Torin could only sit against a wall between skirmishes and bloodshed, smelling that distant food, dreaming of biting into the feast.

Cam rose to his toes and peered through a hole in the wall. The temple lay down the street, only five blocks away. Normally it would be only a short walk. Now, with the enemy troops on the roofs, it seemed more distant than the southern deserts of Eseer.

"Do you think," Cam said, "that they might be in the northern quarters? Maybe . . . maybe even close to the temple?" He turned toward Torin, eyes desperate. "Do you remember the banner? We saw the Ardish banner fly from the north. It had risen beyond the temple. A pocket of Ardish survivors maybe." His fingers shook around his bow, and his voice dropped to a whisper. "Maybe Linee and Omry are there."

Torin lowered his head. "I don't know, my friend. There are pockets of survivors all over this city, both fighters of Verilon and Arden. They could be anywhere."

Cam stared out the window again, and this time his gaze did not go toward the distant temple. His eyes moved lower toward the bodies strewn across the street. Some were old, barely more than skeletons. Others were fresh, crows and rats picking at them. More than once Torin had wondered if the rats they had caught here in the chandlery—the rats they had eaten when no other food could be found—had contained the flesh of men in their little bellies.

"I want to tell you that they're still alive," Torin said softly. "I want to believe it myself. I want to tell you how Linee and Omry are strong and brave, and how if anyone can survive this slaughter, they can. But the truth is I don't know. I don't know if they live. I don't know if my own family has survived and fights somewhere in the darkness. I don't know if you and I will live come next turn. Some turns I don't know if I myself am alive or already dead, trapped in the eternal nightmare of Inagon, that cursed land of afterlife. But I do know that we must advance." He gripped Cam's arm. "We must take the temple, and we must retake this city, and if Linee and Omry are alive, we must find them. We must advance. We must fight."

Cam tightened his lips and nodded. "Like in the old turns, right, Tor, old boy?"

Torin felt a lump in his throat. In their first war, they had lost their dearest, oldest friends. They had left the bodies of Hem and Bailey buried in the killing fields. Four youths had left Fairwool-by-Night. Two had returned.

Will we be the last survivors now too? Torin thought. *Will Cam and I emerge to fight, maybe even survive, to find ourselves alone again, our families slaughtered?*

He lowered his head. *Perhaps,* he thought. But he would fight nonetheless.

Cam moved among the troops, giving the order in hushed tones. A hundred troops stared back grimly and nodded. Those who had bows nocked arrows. Others drew their swords. Even the children in the cellar, their parents slain in the war, grabbed knives, rocks, and sticks and emerged to stand among the soldiers. A warble sounded above, and Torin raised his eyes to see the finch again; it fluttered across the ashy sky and vanished among the distant ruins.

Fly far from here, friend, Torin thought. *Fly and find a life away from the wars of men, for everything around us turns to ruin and rot.*

Cam returned to him, sword drawn, and suddenly the short, slender king looked like a giant. His eyes burned with determination, and his sword shone in a beam of light that fled the clouds. Torin drew his own sword and hefted his shield. He met Cam's gaze. The king nodded.

"For Arden!" Cam shouted. He leaped over rubble, raced through a shattered doorway, and emerged into the street.

"Men of Arden, to the temple!" Torin shouted. "With me!"

The men roared. Torin ran, leaping over the ruins, and emerged onto the cobbled street. He ran alongside Cam, and a hundred soldiers ran behind him. Between the men, dressed in rags, ran the children from the cellar. A little girl clutched a rag doll, and a young boy ran with a knife, lips tightened and eyes flashing, ready to fight. One soldier raised the banner of Arden, a black raven upon a golden field. The finch had fled from the sky; the raven had emerged.

"For Arden!" Torin shouted hoarsely, running forward.

The cobbled street stretched before them, lined with ruin. Most of the houses alongside had burned or crumbled. Those that still stood looked ready to collapse, their walls full of holes. Radian troops stood behind their windows and on their roofs, and a great eclipse banner swung from a tilted statue. The temple rose in the distance, one of its domed towers fallen, its two remaining domes shining silver in the veiled sunlight.

For a moment, the Ardish force ran unopposed toward the temple.

Then, with whistles and the howls of men, a hundred Radian arrows flew toward them.

Torin kept running. One arrow slammed into his raised shield, and another glanced off his helmet. At his side, an arrow punched into an Ardishman and sent him tumbling. Grunts rose behind as more men fell. The running children screamed. As they ran, the surviving Ardishmen fired their own arrows at the roofs and windows. Most clattered harmlessly against stone and wood, but one arrow sank into a Radian archer. The man tumbled off a roof and slammed down onto the street.

"To the temple!" Cam shouted, running forward as more arrows rained.

The new volley slammed into them. Two arrows pierced Torin's shield. Another pierced his armor and nicked his chest, drawing blood. One arrow slammed into Cam's arm. Other Ardishmen fell, pierced by many shafts. An arrow sank into a girl's leg; her brother lifted her and kept running.

We're almost there, Torin thought. The world swayed around him. The temple rose and fell. There would be food there. Better shelter. A chance to find others. Hope.

They had run another block when, with battle cries, dozens of Radian troops burst out from side streets, swinging their swords.

Torin snarled and kept running. His fellow soldiers ran around him, brandishing their blades. With thuds and the ringing of metal, the two forces slammed together.

One man—a Magerian in dark armor—swung an axe. Torin blocked the blow on his shield, then swiped his sword low, slamming the blade into the man's leg. As the Magerian was forced to kneel, Torin swung his shield, knocking the axe aside, and thrust his sword into the man's neck. Another Magerian leaped at him, swinging a longsword in wide arcs. Torin parried, and the blades sparked together. The man fought in a fury, blade lashing again and again, until it slammed into Torin's breastplate and dented the steel. Torin grunted, his armor pressing into his skin, and slammed his sword down with all his strength. The blade cut deeply into the enemy's arm. Another thrust of Torin's sword knocked the man down.

All around him, the others fought. Cam was dueling two men at once. Even the children fought with rocks, knives, and sticks. More arrows rained from above, and men kept falling dead. One Radian soldier roared and raced toward them, and Torin winced. The man wore armor in the style of Arden; a raven was still visible upon the breastplate, chipped away and crudely painted over with an eclipse. He had the brown hair and dark eyes more common among Ardishmen than Magerians—a traitor to his kingdom joined to Serin's cause. A sword's thrust from Cam sent the man sprawling down. Torin drove down his own blade, piercing the traitor's chest, and he grieved for slaying a man of his home, grieved that a man of his home had fallen to evil.

In a lull, Torin looked around him. His head spun, and the world seemed hazy, slow, stuck in some transparent syrup. The dead lay everywhere, their eyes staring at him. The enemy. His comrades. Men and women, all the same in death.

The war eternal, Torin thought. *The blood of Moth. The blood that will forever wash us.*

More arrows rained. More men fell. Torin tightened his lips and kept running.

They raced through a hailstorm of more arrows, cut enemies down, and reached the temple. A stone staircase rose toward dark gates. The walls soared, peppered with holes, and one fallen tower lay across the street, its bricks strewn and its dome cracked. Two towers still rose, topped with silver domes. A Radian banner flew from one.

As Torin, Cam, and the other surviving Ardishmen raced up the stairs, three mages in black robes emerged from the gates.

Torin knelt, dropped his sword, and unslung his bow from across his shoulder. He fired an arrow and hit one mage. The man tumbled down the stairs. But the other two mages were already casting their magic. Smoky tendrils blasted downward, slamming into the climbing Ardishmen.

Torin dodged one astral strand and kept climbing. Other Ardishmen fell, the magic wrapping around them, crushing their armor and bones. One man screamed as the magic shattered his breastplate, cracked his chest, and tugged the ribs from his flesh. The magic raised another man in the air, crumpling him into a ball and dropping him back onto the stairs. Torin raced up the last steps when one of the remaining mages turned toward him.

Black magic slammed against Torin, a dozen shrieking snakes with white eyes that wrapped around him. He screamed as his armor dented, pushing inwards. He refused to fall. He raced forward, thrust his sword, and drove the blade into the mage's chest. Cam raced up at his side, and the king's sword swung into the second mage, sending him falling down the stairs.

The magic vanished. Torin fell to his knees, groaning as his dented armor cut into him. He tugged the straps free and pulled shards of metal from his skin. Cam grabbed him, and Torin slung his arm across his friend's shoulder. Perhaps fifty Ardishmen and twenty children had survived the dash from the chandlery, and they stumbled into the temple.

"Lale, Roen, guard the gates," Cam said to two archers. The men nodded, and the rest stepped deeper into the shadows. A handful of Magerians were scrambling up from makeshift beds and reaching for swords. The Ardishmen cut them down before they could swing a blade.

"There might be . . ." Torin gasped for breath. "Might be bandages here. Healing herbs. Food. Oh stars, there will be food. Let's look."

Cam glanced down at Torin's wounds. "You need to lie down."

"We need bandages. We need food. We'll rest later."

They stumbled through the temple between piles of bricks and shards of wood. Finally they found the kitchen and pantry, and Torin felt more pain than the bites of arrows or swords.

The kitchen was empty. The pantry shelves held only a single sack of flour, a single jar of preserves, and a few rats.

"More rats," Cam said. "Rats and raspberry jam. Lovely."

Torin fell to his knees.

There is no hope. We will die here. We will die in the ruins of Orewood and I'll never see you again, Madori. I'll never hold you again, Koyee.

Suddenly the pain was too great to bear—of his wounds, of his worry, of those he had lost. How many Ardishmen had died on the street to claim this temple? All for this. He lifted the jar of jam, closed his eyes, and lowered his head. A rat gazed up at him curiously, as if contemplating this miserable creature who looked even hungrier and more ragged than itself.

CHAPTER FOUR
THE LEPER OF KETEN

Breathing heavily, her armor smeared with mud and moss, Neekeya
stumbled out of the marshlands and onto the coast of her fallen
homeland.

The beach stretched ahead of her, sloping down toward the
blue water. A few palm trees and mangroves grew above the sand,
and the air smelled of salt. Neekeya had been traveling through the
marshes for twenty turns now, nearly a whole month, crossing the
fallen kingdom of Daenor. Here, at the edge of the world, she fell to
her knees and gazed at the sea.

When she had been a girl, Neekeya had come here once with
her father, and she had walked toward the water, gazed at the blue
horizon, and announced that here was the edge of the world. Her
father had laughed. Neekeya had grown up and studied the maps of
Mythimna, this world shaped as a great moth split between day and
night, and she knew that more of this world lay beyond the sea.
South from here lay the island of Sania, a land of vast savannahs,
roaming herds of elephants, and noble people related to her own
race.

"There will be aid there for me," she whispered. "There will be
hope."

She struggled to her feet, weak with hunger, and took several
steps along the sand toward the sea. Five distant ships sailed
northward on the horizon, and when Neekeya squinted, she could
see great scorpions painted on their sails. Here were Eseerian ships
from the southeastern desert—followers of the Radian Order. They
would be sailing north toward the pyramids of Eetek, pouring more
soldiers into Neekeya's homeland.

She turned in the sand and gazed at the marshlands. Mangroves
rose here, their roots nearly as tall as her, leading to shadows. Mist

floated between the branches, and herons waded through a delta. Neekeya clenched her fists and lowered her head.

"Daenor," she whispered. "My home. I will return. I will not forget you, *Denetek*." Tears stung her eyes. "And I will not forget you either, Tam."

The loss of her husband clawed inside her, nearly too great to bear. She had traveled into these marshlands with him, to wed him here, to rule this land alongside him. Now she stumbled out from the swamps, a widow, both her home and her husband fallen to the enemy.

"I cannot bring you back, Tam," she whispered. "But I can keep fighting. I will stay alive for you. For your memory. I will keep fighting the enemy so long as breath fills my lungs."

She caressed her wedding ring, which Tam had forged himself with magic—a strand of gold containing one of her hairs, a strand of silver containing one of his. She turned away and walked along the beach, and she did not look back to the marshes.

She walked southward for several hours, perhaps a full turn, until she saw the port ahead. Here lay the city of Keten, the Gates of the Sea. For centuries, Keten had connected Daenor to its neighbors, the desert realm of Eseer and the more distant, southern island of Sania. For centuries, the ships of those realms—their people sharing old bonds of kinship, language, and gods with Daenor—had found safe harbor here, bringing spices, wines, jewels, fabrics, and even pets from exotic lands. In her old chambers in the pyramid, Neekeya had owned jeweled rings, bottles of colored sand, scarves of silks inlaid with coins, richly illuminated books, and many other treasures brought into Daenor through this port. This turn she would welcome no treasure here from distant lands; she herself would sail away to find those lands of her childhood dreams.

She had fuzzy memories of the port from her childhood: the ringing of bells on ships, the smells of fish and oil, the creaking of ropes, the swaying of ships, the song of sailors and the caws of gulls. She remembered a place of warmth and wonder.

This turn she saw a nightmare.

Radian banners rose from the stone towers of Keten and draped across the columns of its temple. A great statue of Cetela had once stood here upon a breakwater, gazing at the sea, a man with the head of a crocodile. The head had been knocked off; it lay at the statue's feet like a bloated whale, its eyes shattered. The enemy ships filled the port—the long, narrow boats of Eseer, scorpions painted onto their sails. Radian soldiers from many lands stood on the walls and patrolled the piers. Neekeya saw Magerians in black plate steel, their hair golden and their eyes blue, their swords wide and long; Eseerians in white robes, desert warriors armed with scimitars fashioned as scorpion tails; and even Nayan warriors of the northern rainforest, tiger pelts hanging around their shoulders, their long red beards strewn with bones and beads. All these troops now hoisted the Radian banners. All served Lord Serin.

"But I will never serve you," Neekeya whispered. "Though you crushed my home, I still live, a *latani* of Eetek, a princess of the marshlands. And I will still fight you with every breath, Serin." She clutched the hilt of her sword. "Your people slew my husband. And I will avenge him. I will avenge Tam."

Standing in the sand outside the city, Neekeya could almost see Tam again. She imagined that he stood beside her, and her eyes dampened. She gazed upon his apparition: a young man of nineteen years, the same age as her, his hair brown, his skin tanned gold, his eyes bright and warm. A memory shot through her: Tam racing across the bridge toward Felsar in the underground, then crashing down into the lava, giving his life to save hers.

She tightened her lips and raised her chin. Dwelling on her pain would not bring him back, would not liberate her fallen homeland. The desert of Eseer had joined the Radian Order. So had the rainforest of Naya. But Sania, the southern savannah, still stood tall and free; she had seen none of its soldiers in the swamps, and none of its ships sailed here. In Sania she would find allies. She would find a hope to fight again.

"And to reach Sania, I need a ship," she said.

She could not wander into the port looking like she did, she knew. She still wore her crocodile armor—the breastplate shaped like crocodile skin, the helmet sharp with iron teeth—clearly denoting her a warrior of Daenor. Even should she doff her armor, her deep brown skin marked her a South Daenorian, an enemy to the Radian

Order. Yet perhaps, entering the city as a simple marshlands girl
come seeking a meal, the Radians would let her live. Serin sought to
slay all Elorians; with Daenorians, at least, he sought only
subjugation, not yet genocide.

For the first time in many turns, she removed her armor—the
armor she had worn at Teel University, in the wastelands of Arden,
and throughout the war in Daenor—the armor that had protected
her body and soul for years. Like her home and husband, it too
would leave her. She buried it in the sand and rolled a boulder atop it,
vowing to return. She could not bear to part from her sword. She
used the blade to cut down a thick bamboo stalk along the border of
the marshes. She split the stem down the middle, hid her sword
within it, then reattached the halved stem with vines. She hid the
protruding crossguard within a garland of leaves and vines. She
walked on, holding her makeshift *he'tak*—the holy staff of a Cetela
priestess, a ring upon a rod. *He'taki* were items of divinity and
healing; hers hid her sting within.

She walked along the sand toward the town, the mangroves to
her left, the sea whispering to her right. Finally she reached the
northern gates of Keten. The city walls rose above her, built of tan
bricks. Flowering weeds grew between the cracks, and an eclipse
banner hung from the battlements. Eseerians archers stood above,
arrows knocked in their bows. More of the desert warriors stood
guarding the gates, their scimitars—shaped as scorpion stingers—
drawn and gleaming.

"Turn back, swamp dweller!" said one of the guards, a tall man
with olive skin and dark eyes. "This city is forbidden to your kind."

Neekeya stepped closer. She spoke the language of Eseer; it
was similar to her own tongue, for the two peoples—of the southern
desert and the northern marshlands—shared a common ancestry.

"I'm a daughter of this city," she said, speaking in flawless
Eseerian. "My father was an Eseerian sailor; my mother is a child of
Daenor." She knew that, with her darker skin, she could not pass for
a pure Eseerian, but perhaps they would believe her to be mixed like
Madori. "I've heard that Eseer captured this city, and . . ." She
allowed tears to fill her eyes. "I've come seeking my father. Please, sir.
Allow me to enter the city, so that I may seek him. I've not seen him

in many years, not since he sailed back to the desert, leaving me in the marshlands with my Daenorian mother. Please let me find him. My mother is dead."

She let tears stream down her cheeks. It didn't take much effort; she simply had to think of her true father, the fallen Lord Kee'an, for her eyes to water. For extra effect she added a wobble to her lips and a heave to her breasts.

The guard's eyes softened. He spoke gently. "My father too left me as a child. He too was a sailor." He glanced around him, then back at Neekeya. "What's your name?"

"Asai," she said, using the name of an Eseerian lady who had visited Daenor years ago and had been Neekeya's friend for a summer.

"I am Jatef," the guard said. "My emperor perhaps hates Daenorians; you'll find that few of his soldiers do. If you don't find your father, seek me at the gates or the tavern by the docks, the one with two chimneys. I'll buy you a bottle of wine and shelter you for the night in a warm bed."

She nodded, wondering if he cared less for her safety and more for her company in said bed. "I will seek you," she lied. "Thank you, Jatef."

Leaving him at the gates, Neekeya—now Asai the bastard daughter—entered the city of Keten.

The lively streets and markets were gone. No more children ran upon the cobblestones, spinning metal hoops. No more peddlers shouted out their wares. No more sailors swayed between the taverns and pleasure houses, seeking games of dice, bottles of wine, or women to warm their beds. That old city of sound and sin had died; a military camp awaited Neekeya here. Soldiers of the enemy stood everywhere: Eseerian archers upon the roofs, Magerians in dark steel at every street corner, and Nayan warriors along the docks. Some Daenorians still lived here, but they were frightened, meek; she saw their eyes peering from within boarded windows, a people conquered.

And she saw the dead.

Cages hung from trees and walls, and within languished the bones of dead Daenorians. She knew they were her people; the skeletons still wore the armor of Daenor, and strings of crocodile teeth hung around their necks. Neekeya covered her mouth and nose; the stench spun her head.

I'm in danger here, she thought. Even without her armor, even with her sword hidden. Already she saw soldiers staring at her, eyes cruel.

"Off the streets, swamp rat!" shouted one man, a Magerian brute with sandy stubble on his cheeks. "We don't let you vermin scamper about anymore. Run home to your mama, or I'll stick my sword in your gut."

Neekeya nodded and shuffled along. Walking like this, her dusky Daenorian countenance revealed to all, would not get her past this block, let alone to the piers where she could hope to book passage on a ship. A plan began to formulate in her mind. She hurried down the road until she spotted a fabric shop, rolls of cotton and canvas and wool hanging in its windows. She stepped into the dusty brick house, finding herself surrounded by reels of fabric, cloaks on hangers, and many scarves. An elderly Daenorian woman sat here on a wooden chair, wrapped in a cloak and tasseled scarves.

"Priestess of Cetela," the woman whispered in awe, gazing at her bamboo *he'tak.*

Neekeya was no true priestess, but perhaps this turn Daenor needed blessings more than warriors or mages. She nodded at the fabric merchant.

"May Cetela bless you, Wise Mother." Neekeya reached into her pocket and produced an emerald ring, one of her last mementos from home. She had once thought this ring enchanted; these turns it was hard to believe in enchanted jewels. "I have no coin to give you, but would you accept this ring for a cloak and scarf?"

"I would not," said the merchant. "All coins and jewels have lost their meaning; all that matters now is our people, our memory of freedom. Take what cloak and scarf you need, and let them be gifts to you, as your blessing is a gift to me."

As Neekeya donned a heavy woolen cloak and a *seeken* scarf, guilt filled her, for she was only a priestess in disguise. As she left the shop, she secretly placed the ring onto the windowsill. Neekeya would need no ring in the open sea, but perhaps this woman would still find use for it—a bribe for a soldier or perhaps just a thing of beauty, a memory of kinship.

Wrapped in her white cloak and hood, a scarf hiding her face, Neekeya walked back onto the street. Only her eyes were now uncovered, and though she still held her bamboo staff, she doubted that the Radian invaders would know its significance to Daenor—or what she hid inside it. Cloaked and hidden in white, she hoped she looked like an Eseerian woman, perhaps a camp follower, the wife of a soldier, a healer, or peddler come to hawk charms to the soldiers.

She walked along the street, head bowed low. She passed by a temple to Cetela. The statues of the crocodile god had been smashed, and the banners of the enemy draped across the walls. She walked down a narrow, sloping street between brick houses and palm trees until she reached the port.

Several stone towers rose here, airy and pierced with narrow windows, weeds and flowers growing between their bricks. Two breakwaters stretched into the harbor, lined with columns, and a hundred vessels nestled within their embrace—fishermen's boats, merchant cogs, and the warships of the invaders.

Neekeya paused and closed her eyes, thinking back to the memory of the great mural in Eetek Pyramid, showing this southern port. She had spent much of her childhood standing before that mural, admiring the details of merchants bringing in cages of parrots, leashed tigers, exotic spices, and baskets of jewels from distant lands, and she had often wished she could step into the painting and sail off herself on adventures. The port she faced now was no place of magic, for enemy soldiers stood upon its boardwalk, and the ships of a cruel empire filled its cove.

She walked toward the boardwalk, trying to formulate a plan as she approached. Could she book passage on a ship, paying with her labor, scrubbing the deck and peeling potatoes? She doubted that many merchant ships would be sailing back and forth during the war, and what Radian warship would hire a Daenorian? Did she dare, then, to steal one of the Radians' rowboats, to try and make her way to Sania alone? That seemed just as impossible. Could such a small vessel, built for navigating between the boardwalk and the towering brigantines with their many sails, truly cross the open sea?

As a child, Neekeya had read stories of sailors abandoned at sea, building rafts, and finding their way home. If those castaways had survived on rafts, surely she could survive in an actual boat . . . couldn't she? Neekeya sighed. Perhaps not. Perhaps death awaited her in the sea. But death lay on the land too; maybe only on the water could she find a sliver of hope.

As she took another step closer, five Magerian soldiers on the boardwalk turned toward her. One drew his sword.

"Halt!" the man said. "The boardwalk is closed. Leave this place now or the fish will feed on your body."

Neekeya kept hobbling forward, wrapped in her cloak, hood, and scarf and leaning on her staff. She coughed. "Please, kind sirs! I was told to come here." She reached the soldiers on the boardwalk, coughed again, and stooped over. "I was told to leave the city."

The soldiers muttered. "Did you hear me, rat? The port is—"

Neekeya coughed wildly and spoke in a hoarse voice. "But the city guards! They said that Keten is closed to lepers. They said that before I infect anyone else, I'm to get on a boat, to—"

"Idar damn it!" one soldier shouted. The men stepped back, eyes wide, and covered their mouths and noses.

Neekeya took two more steps toward them, coughing violently. "Dear sirs, a boat. Is there a boat for me? I need to leave. I already made three men sick, and—"

The soldiers turned tail and fled across the boardwalk, cursing. Neekeya smiled behind her veil and walked onto a pier that stretched into the water. A rowboat was tethered here, a humble fishing vessel; a net, a bucket, and a fishing rod lay within it. Neekeya guessed that it had belonged to a Daenorian, a fisherman banished from the port, perhaps killed. She climbed inside, untied the rope off its peg, and grabbed the oars. She began to navigate away from the pier and across the cove.

Raised voices sounded behind her on the boardwalk. Neekeya turned her head to see the soldiers—those who had stopped her—exchanging heated words with a Magerian knight, his golden pauldrons denoting his nobility. One soldier pointed at Neekeya, and the knight cursed.

"Stop that boat!" shouted the knight and waved his sword.

Neekeya grimaced and rowed with more vigor.

Upon the walls and towers that surrounded the port, soldiers raised their bows. Neekeya ducked as arrows sailed down toward her. Most sank into the water. Two pierced the hull of the boat, and one scraped across Neekeya's arm. She kept rowing, her belly tight, navigating her boat between two towering brigantines. The massive vessels, each the size of a castle, shielded her from the barrage of arrows. A handful of sailors stood upon them, pointing down at her and shouting.

"Stop the boat!" rose the knight's voice. "I'll be damned if I let a filthy leper steal one of the empire's vessels."

When Neekeya looked over her shoulder, she saw several rowboats following her, soldiers within them. She rowed with all the strength in her arms, emerging from between the brigantines. She had nearly reached the edge of the cove. The breakwaters ended ahead of her, curving inward like embracing arms, leaving only a small exit to the open sea. An archer stood upon the tip of each breakwater.

Neekeya grabbed the fishing rod and swung it. The string sailed through the air and the hook grabbed one archer's bow, yanking it free. The second archer fired, and Neekeya ducked; the arrow sailed over her head and sank into the water. With a few more strokes of the oars, she cleared the breakwaters and shot into the open sea.

Men shouted behind her and more arrows flew, sinking into the water. The waves were rough here outside the cove, tossing her boat up and down.

"You fool!" shouted the knight from his boat, still within the port. "A rowboat can't survive in the open sea."

Neekeya ignored him and kept rowing, leaving the port behind, heading into the deep waters. The soldiers in the other boats cursed and turned back toward the boardwalk. She heard them muttering about how no damn leper was worth this much trouble. Then she heard nothing but the waves and the gulls above.

As the port grew distant behind her, a chill flooded Neekeya, and suddenly she felt trapped within this small vessel. She had felt no fear during the chase, only cold determination, but now the fear filled her. When she leaned over the boat, the water seemed endlessly deep, the waves endlessly powerful; she was a mere insect on a leaf, floating in an ocean.

She squared her shoulders.

"I will survive here," she whispered to herself. "I survived traveling for months across occupied Arden and the Magerian plains. I survived war in the marshlands. I will survive the sea, and I will make it to Sania. I have a net. I have a rod and hooks. I will *live*. I will see you again some turn, Tam, but not yet. Not yet."

She rowed on, leaving her homeland of Daenor . . . and heading into the endless blue.

CHAPTER FIVE
WINGLESS

Eris Grimgarg stood upon the tor, a rocky outcrop that rose from the gray sea like a bone from a wound, and he stared across the water toward his home.

Orida was but a faded line on the horizon, a shore forbidden to him. For three years in the darkness, Eris had dreamed of returning to his homeland, the island which his ancestor, the legendary King Orin, had conquered from the wraiths of the underworld. And now . . . here he stood. Upon a barren rock. A refugee and outcast, the blood of his own father on his hands.

Yiun Yee walked up to him and placed a hand on his shoulder. The wind streamed her white hair and silken gown, and her large Elorian eyes—made for seeing in the darkness of night—shone with love for him, a love that had given him the strength to search for the Meadenhorn in caverns and forests and dungeons, a love that gave him strength even here upon the tor, upon this rock far from any land or hope for glory.

"I am sorry, Yiun Yee," Eris said. The wind ruffled his beard and tossed strands of his blond hair across his face. "I wanted more for you. I wanted my father to embrace you, to call you a daughter. I wanted a feast in our honor, to sing old songs of glory, to drink mead from the horn we fought for." He caressed the horn which hung around his neck, passing his fingers over its golden filigree—the horn Orin himself had drunk from. "Instead, we stand here now, your chest cut by my father's sword, my hands stained with the blood of that father, a man I slew." Eris lowered his head. "I did not bring you out of darkness for this."

She touched her chest, where he could see the outline of bandages beneath her silken gown, and stood on her tiptoes. She kissed the corner of his mouth, and she spoke softly in his tongue, her accent thick. "Your father's blade nearly pierced my heart, but this heart will forever beat for you. I need no palaces, no feasts, no songs or tales of old lore, no golden mead from legendary horns. I would rather stand here on this desolate rock with the man that I love, free to love him."

The waves broke against the rocks below, splashing up to dampen her gown and spray salt against Eris's armor. His longship swayed madly below. Carved into the shape of an orca, it looked like a struggling whale about to drown. Somewhere in the open sea, his brother led a hundred other longships on the hunt, seeking him.

If they find us, Eris knew, *they will slay my Oringard, but they will not slay Yiun Yee and me, not at first. Not before they bring us home, before they display us to the city, then cut off our heads for all to see.* Eris gripped the hilt of his sword.

"The sorceress has taken over our land," he said, "spilling poison first in the ears of my father, then in the ears of my brother. Prince Torumun has fallen under the Radian curse." He turned away from the sea and faced his Oringard. Ninety men—the survivors of the slaughter in the mead hall—crowded upon the boulders and rocky slopes of the tor. "Torumun has fallen to madness. We, bearers of the Meadenhorn, must resist him. We must dethrone him."

One of the Oringard detached from the others and approached Eris. He was a stocky man, his yellow mustache curling upwards to connect to his sideburns. A horned helm topped his head, its gilt chipping and old, and a painted boar reared upon his shield. His face was leathery, his eyes small and blue and hard. He was Halgyr, Chief of the Oringard and greatest among its warriors.

"Torumun is king by right," said Halgyr. "He is your elder brother, Eris. He is a serpent that crawls among weeds. He is a coward who would hide behind others in a fight. But he is eldest son of your father. How will you claim the throne by right?"

Eris raised the Meadenhorn. "With this. The gods have led me to the Horn of Orin. I still bear our greatest treasure. I am second born but first in Orin's eyes. Back in our city of Grenstad, in our great mead hall, an evil lurks. Iselda, sister to Serin, a witch of Radian, cannot be tolerated within our realm. We must cleanse the Orinhall."

Halgyr glanced at Yiun Yee, then back at Eris. The gruff old warrior lowered his voice. "My lord, there are those in Orida who would speak similarly of you. As your father wed a Radian, and as your brother took the same Radian for his own bride, you have married a woman of Eloria. To many in Orida, the Elorians seem stranger than Radians, creatures of darkness."

Rage crackled inside of Eris. "Yet you and I know that's not true, that Leen—which our ships so often attacked—is home to noble, strong people. The Radians are not noble; they're cruel and cowardly. We've seen their ships slay women and children upon the coasts of Leen and Qaelin. We've heard tales of Serin's forces attacking lands of sunlight too, bringing all under his dominion. I cannot let Orida fall into the clutches of that empire. Two thousand years ago, it was Orida that first overthrew the yoke of the Riyonan Empire, who led to its collapse. Now it will be Orida that stands strong against the Radian Empire. My father joined the monk Ferius, shaming our island; I refuse to let Orida serve another foreign ruler." He looked at the Meadenhorn, and his voice softened. "For years, I thought that finding this horn would be my greatest glory, my life's quest. But now I know that this horn is a symbol, leading me to my true battle." He raised his eyes and looked at his Oringard, ninety stalwart men. "To free Orida."

They stared at him and raised their own horns. "Strength and freedom!" they cried, the old words of their isle.

"Strength and freedom!" Eris repeated, raising the Meadenhorn. "Torumun has forgotten both words, but we—true Sons of Orin—do not forget. Oringard! For three years, you traveled the darkness with me, and we now hold a treasure, a symbol of our old realm, of our strength and freedom. Will you fight with me again? Will you fight with me for the throne, and will you see me sit upon it?"

They raised their horns high, and they roared their approval.

"We will reclaim our land!" Eris shouted. "We will drive out Torumun and his sorceress, and we will cleanse the isle of the Radian curse. We will restore the true glory of Orin, our greatest hero, and we will drink mead in free halls."

As the Oringard chanted for war, Yiun Yee approached Eris, her brow furrowed with concern. She placed her small, pale hand against his wide sun-bronzed arm, a gentle lily growing by a lion.

"Eris, the Oringard are mighty; I do not doubt their strength or courage. Yet I've seen your brother command a thousand soldiers, and many more must fill his kingdom." As the wind billowed her hair and the waves splashed the hem of her gown, she looked upon the Oringard. "How can so few, brave though they might be, defeat so many?" She tightened her lips and turned to stare east. "Let us return to Leen, to my homeland, a dark twin to Orida. I will speak to my father. He will send his armies into the sunlight, for he fought in the war twenty years ago, and he remembers the ships of Orida raiding our coasts. They flew under the Sailith banners then, back when my father was only a soldier, when we had no true king. My father will not allow another banner of sunlit domination to threaten our home in the shadows."

Eris cupped his wife's cheek and kissed her lips. She was everything he was not—small while he was hulking, soft while he was rough, pale while his skin was bronzed, a woman of purity while his hands were stained with patricide.

"The people of Leen are noble and brave, no less than my Oringard," he said. "I've seen their archers clad in white steel, their arrows flying true. I've seen their glittering halls of crystal and glass, wonders of their empire's beauty and strength. But I cannot be seen returning to Orida with another's army. If the hosts of Leen help me reclaim my throne, forever will the children of Orin see me as a usurper, a foreign invader, a man no more noble than Torumun. No." Eris shook his head. "I cannot rededicate Orida with the hosts of Leen."

Gruff Halgyr raised his wide sword, its blade shaped as an orca about to strike. "One of the Oringard is worth a hundred of Torumun's men. We will recover our strength. We will return. We will cleanse the isle of the enemy."

Again Eris shook his head. "No, Halgyr, for Yiun Yee spoke truth. She sees us with the eyes of an outsider, and she judges us true—strong, noble, yet deeply outnumbered, unable to win this fight alone." A great wave crashed against the tor, spraying him with water and salt. He stepped higher upon the islet, rising to stand above his men. "We've all read the Saga of Orin. We've all sung its song. Two thousand years ago, demons and ghosts lived upon our island, and they drank the blood of the ancients, and they built their lairs from bones. It was Orin, a wandering warrior, who woke the giants of the icy north. Creatures of rock and ice and snow, they rose from the water, and they challenged him, yet Orin defeated their chief in battle. The giants followed him then, a first Oringard, and they cleansed the island of the creatures that infested it. He named that island Orida." Eris raised his horn. "I hold the very horn that Orin drank mead from in the first hall at Grenstad. Now a new evil infests our home, not ghosts or demons but a sorceress in crimson, a cruelty called Radian. So I will do as our forebear did. I, Eris Grimgard, will wake the giants of the north again. I will cleanse our island."

Most of the Oringard cheered and sang. All but Halgyr. The gruff captain frowned and tightened his cloak around him. He leaned close to Eris and spoke in a low voice. "The giants are but a myth, Eris. An old story, existing only in song and on parchment."

"A myth?" said Eris. "Once we thought Elorians a myth, yet I found a wife among them. Once we thought dragons a myth, yet my father fought the dragon Pirilin in the great War of Day and Night. If Elorians and dragons live in Mythimna, so do giants. Will you sail north with me, Halgyr? Will you fight at my side?"

The squat, leathery man raised his chin and puffed out his chest. "Always, my king. To the edge of the world and back." He raised his sword. "Drink mead, Oringard! Drink for Eris, true King of Orida!"

They stood upon a desolate rock in exile, but they opened a cask of mead from their longship, their last one. They poured the drink into their horns, and they drank and sang as if back in the Orinhall upon their homeland. Eris drank from the Meadenhorn, the artifact he had fought for, the artifact which would name him king.

Yiun Yee leaned against him, and he held her close. They stared into the north as the wind whipped their hair and the waves splashed against them.

* * * * *

He is a hero, Yiun Yee told herself, staring at her husband. She clutched the wound on her chest. *He was defending me, that was all. Defending my life.*

Eris stood at the prow of the longship, staring north, his sword raised. He looked almost like a statue, a noble Son of Orin, a legendary warrior from an epic poem. The wind streamed through his golden hair and ruffled his thick beard. His eyes shone blue—small Timandrian eyes but no less beautiful than large Elorian orbs. The sunlight gleamed upon his armor, his shield, and the horn that hung around his chest.

A hero, Yiun Yee thought, eyes stinging. Yet she could not stop seeing it—the blood on Eris's hands . . . the blood of his own father. Again and again, whenever she closed her eyes, Yiun Yee saw her husband stab King Bormund, tug the blade free, shout for war.

Pain flared on her chest, and she touched her bandage again. King Bormund had given her this wound. Eris had saved her life. Saved her! That was all. He was no killer. No murderer.

I fought by his side for two years in the darkness, she told herself. *I know him. He's noble and kind.* She lowered her head, and her eyes stung. *Yet here in the sunlight, do I see a different man?*

The Oringard chanted as they rowed, an old song of heroes battling sea serpents, dragons, and trolls, a hearty song sung with pride, with deep voices, with raised chins. Standing here in the sunlight of a foreign sea, Yiun Yee closed her eyes, and she tried to remember the songs of her homeland. She remembered soft tunes of haunting beauty played on harps and flutes. In her mind, she could still hear "The Light of the North," the great song of her people, a song sung for Taenori, the city of crystals and moonlight.

As a child, Yiun Yee had stood in the halls of Leen's palace, surrounded by crystal columns, marble tiles, and vaulted ceilings painted with stars, and she had listened to priests play the old songs of Eloria, and she had pretended to be Koyee of Qaelin. In the stories, Koyee was a musician and a great heroine, and Yiun Yee had tried to master the flute, to emulate her heroine, but she could never remember the right notes to play. She had tried to learn swordplay instead, to become a warrior like Koyee, but she could never master the blade either.

She had begun to see herself as one with no talents, an ordinary woman who could never become great like those she admired. Her father, the king, praised her beauty, and suitors from across Leen, Qaelin, and even distant Ilar had come to court her. She was Yiun Yee, Princess of Leen, her indigo eyes and fair countenance legendary, and yet she had turned down all those men. For Yiun Yee never forgot those old books, the stories of adventure and war, and she wanted to be like her heroines—like Koyee of Qaelin, like Suntai the Wolfrider, like Bailey Berin of the sunlit lands—not just a fair face but a woman of substance.

And so she had left.

With only her silk cloak and her diamond pendant, Yiun Yee had abandoned her palace, her father, her home, the very darkness of night. She had fallen in love with a man from the day, a sunlit demon, and for two years she had fought at his side. For two years she had thought herself a heroine like in the old tales. She could still not play the flute, still not swing a sword, but she had found love, and she had helped her love reclaim his treasure. She had traveled with her lover into the sunlight itself and to a foreign palace—one smaller than the one she had abandoned in the darkness—only to see him . . .

The image pierced her again. Her husband, strong and noble Eris, slaying his own father.

"Saving me," she whispered. "For me."

He turned toward her, perhaps hearing her words, and his face split into a smile—the confident, toothy smile that she loved, that even now could melt her heart.

"Will you sing with us, Yiun Yee?" he said.

She smiled too and shook her head. "I would scare the fish away from the sea, and we would have no more meals to catch."

Eris had spent the past few turns brooding, his eyes dark, and often Yiun Yee had seen him stare at his hands, contemplating the lines upon his palms, perhaps still seeing the old blood. But now Eris wrapped his arm around her, his chin raised and his smile bright, and pointed ahead across the water.

"Do you see them ahead? Icebergs. We're far north now. That means we're getting closer. Orida still lies in the west just beyond the horizon, but in a few turns, we'll have left that island far behind, heading to the great ice lands of the uncharted north."

She squinted, barely able to see it. Her eyes were still weak here in the daylight, the way Timandrian eyes were weak in the darkness. Yet as they oared closer, the icebergs came into view—towering islands larger than castles.

"Are they made of salt water or fresh water?" she asked, turning to eye their dwindling supplies of water, wine, and mead.

Eris opened his mouth and seemed about to reply when a deep cry rolled across the ocean.

The Oringard's song died. The warriors reached for their swords. Yiun Yee narrowed her eyes, staring around at the sea.

The sound rose again, a keen from the depths. It rippled the water, and to her left she saw something breach, a spine bristly with spikes. The cry rose a third time, and then the creature vanished.

She stared at her husband, then back to the water. A few of the men drew swords, but it seemed to Yiun Yee that the creature's cry had been mournful, more a dirge than a battle cry.

Then it leaped out of the water only feet away from their prow, and it bellowed so loudly it blew back their hair.

The serpent was as long as their ship, maybe longer, and covered with gleaming, turquoise scales. Its mouth opened wide, full of sharp teeth, and blue horns grew from its head, wrapped with seaweed. Barnacles grew upon its belly, and its eyes stared at Yiun Yee, the color of the sea. Many spikes, each as long as a katana, grew upon its back.

"A jormungand!" shouted Halgyr. The old warrior raised sword and shield. "Sea serpent!"

The creature bucked, and while most of it still lay underwater, Yiun Yee could see its tail far away; the creature was massive.

With battle cries, men of the Oringard raised their bows and fired. Arrows slammed into the serpent, shattering against its scales.

The creature howled. Its head swung and slammed into the longship.

Horns punched through the hull. The *Orin's Blade* tilted madly. The creature sank under the water, and for a moment silence fell.

The waves settled.

"What . . . what was that?" Yiun Yee whispered.

Eris stared around with narrowed eyes. The Oringard stood behind him across the ship, some with drawn swords, others with nocked arrows. The creature did not reemerge.

"Jormungand—a fabled serpent of the northern sea." Eris turned toward Halgyr and smiled wryly. "Another myth come to life for you. A live jo—"

Before he could complete his sentence, the beast burst out from the sea again, dripping seaweed and water and roaring with rage. It swam furiously, wrapping around the longship like an anaconda constricting its prey.

The *Orin's Blade* began to creak.

The Oringard rained down arrows, but they shattered uselessly against the creature's scales. Eris snarled, ran across the deck, and leaped overboard. He landed on the serpent, small as a mouse upon a python, and drove down his sword.

The blade crashed through scales and into the creature's flesh.

The serpent squealed. Its grip on the ship loosened, and it rose high from the water like a trained cobra from a basket. Eris clung to its back, lashing his blade, a dozen feet in the air.

"Eris!" Yiun Yee cried.

At the sound of her voice, the serpent flicked its head toward her. It met her gaze, and pain filled its eyes. Then it flailed its neck wildly, flinging Eris off its back.

The Prince of Orida sailed through the air and crashed into the ocean many feet away.

With battle cries, a dozen other warriors leaped from the ship onto the serpent, driving down their swords. The blades crashed through its scales.

The serpent howled, a cry of agony, rage, fear. The Oringard kept firing their arrows and lashing their blades. The creature loosened its grip on the boat and its body began to sink.

Tears filled Yiun Yee's eyes.

"Stop!" she cried. "Stop hurting it. It's leaving us! Let it swim away."

Yet the serpent would not swim, perhaps too weak. Its blood filled the water, and it laid its scaly head upon the ship's deck. Its eyes stared at Yiun Yee, large orbs like crystal balls, the lashes long and white and feathery. It whimpered and Yiun Yee approached it. She laid her hand upon its scales. They were cold and smooth like mother of pearl, and the animal seemed to calm as she stroked it.

"It's all right," Yiun Yee whispered, caressing its snout, "you're safe."

When she had been very young, a mere toddler, she had seen Pirilin the dragon in the court of Leen. The white dragon had fallen in the War of Day and Night, and this serpent reminded Yiun Yee of that legendary beast. All this serpent needed to look like a dragon were wings, and—

She gasped. When she looked at the creature's back, she saw two long scars.

"You had wings once," she whispered. She turned toward the Oringard who had paused their assault. "It had wings!"

A deep, rumbling voice drew her gaze back toward the serpent. It stared into her eyes, and it spoke in her language, the tongue of Leen, though its dialect was ancient like the oldest books in Leen's libraries.

"I was a brother to Pirilin," the creature said. "I flew above the dark mountains of Leen long before palaces rose there, long before Elorians had built cities and ports. The wild men of the mountains cut off my wings, leaving me to crawl in the dust. I found my way to the sea." Tears streamed from his eyes. "I've been swimming here for so many years, feeding on fish and seaweed, and I have forgotten my name."

Yiun Yee gasped. "But I remember. You are Imoogi, the Sky Serpent! Our books tell of a dragon who was lost. They say the men of the mountains slew you. That they built sails from your wings for their ships. But you lived." She wept. "I will bring you home, Imoogi. I will return you to Leen, and you will no longer crawl there in the dust like a snake. You will live in the palace of my father, wrapped around his throne, a being worshiped, adored, forever a symbol of our land."

"Imoogi . . ." said the dragon. "Yes. I remember my name. I remember. I—"

The dragon gasped.

Blood spurted from his mouth.

Eris rose upon the dragon's head, grunting as he drove his sword deep between Imoogi's horns.

Yiun Yee screamed.

Eris twisted the blade, tugged it free, and leaped back into the ship. With a last gasp, Imoogi's head slid off the deck and into the water. Blood spread across the ocean. Imoogi rose no more.

"Yiun Yee, are you all right?" Eris said, walking toward her. "Did it hurt you? Did—"

She screamed and shoved him.

"Why did you slay him?" Tears poured down her cheeks. "He was tamed. He could have lived." She shook with sobs. "He was a dragon of Leen."

Eris stared at her, eyes pained. He reached out to her. "Yiun Yee, my love! It was a jormungand, a cruel beast. It could have hurt you. It could have bitten right into you and—"

She shoved him again, slapped him, and spun around. She walked across the deck, stood at the stern, and hugged herself. As the Oringard kept rowing, the grief of Imoogi's death filled Yiun Yee, and along it a deep, cold fear.

Who is my husband? She lowered her head, and her hair streamed in the wind. *Who is the killer that I married?*

The longship sailed on, leaving the blood behind, heading into the cold, icy north.

CHAPTER SIX
LOVE AND SHADOW

Jitomi stood in the belly of the *Tai Lar*, flagship of the Ilari Armada, and stared out the porthole. The wilderness of Arden spread north of the riverbank, lit with the endless sunlight of this land. They had left the ruins of Oshy and Fairwool-by-Night behind, and they sailed on toward Kingswall, the great Radian stronghold of East Timandra.

Oshy and Fairwool . . . two homes to Madori. Two villages burned to the ground. Jitomi narrowed his eyes in sudden pain. His home, Hashido Castle upon the peninsula, still stood in the darkness, awaiting him. How must it feel to lose not one home but two, to have every part of your past effaced?

He turned around from the porthole and faced his cabin. The captain's quarters of the *Tai Lar*, a mighty *atakebune* ship, was a place of splendor. Scrolls hung from the walls, illuminated with colorful warriors, maidens, and dragons. Suits of gilded, decorative armor stood in silent vigil, tassels hanging from their breastplates, and katanas with jeweled scabbards hung above them. Porcelain plates and cups stood on a stone table, their surfaces painted with birds and fish. A large bed stood beyond the table, topped with pillows, silk blankets, and Madori.

She sat at the edge of the mattress, wearing indigo silk robes, silent. She stared at him with her large, lavender eyes. Her hair, shaved off in the Radian camp, had grown an inch; the black strands fell across her brow and the tops of her ears. She had small ears, Jitomi noticed. Timandrian ears, smaller than Elorian ones. He had never noticed this before.

He stepped toward her, sat on the bed beside her, and touched one of those small ears. "Your hair is growing out. It almost covers your ears."

She nodded and lowered her head. Still she was silent, and her hands bunched up together on her lap.

Jitomi felt the pain in his chest grow. "I'm sorry," he whispered, the words he had wanted to whisper since leaving the darkness. "I'm sorry about what happened to Oshy. To Fairwool-by-Night. I'm sorry about what happened in the iron mine. By the Red Flame . . ." Jitomi held her hand. "I cannot even imagine such pain, and I don't know how to comfort you. But know this: I'm always here for you, Madori. I will always look after you now. With an armada. With an army. With every beat of my heart, I vow to you, I will protect you."

Finally she met his gaze, and her eyes flashed, and some anger overshadowed her pain. "I've never needed anyone to protect me. I am a mage. I am a warrior of Yin Shi. I am the bearer of Min Tey, a sword of legend, and a great nightwolf awaits me upon the deck, a wild beast that I tamed. I'm no weak damsel needing a warrior to save me."

Jitomi laughed softly. "I'm not much of a warrior. I had never fought in a battle until this mess began. And I'm not much of a mage." He lifted his hands and tried to summon enough magic to levitate a pillow, but it quickly thumped back onto the bed. He sighed. "Madori, do you think that once the war is won, once we cleanse Timandra of the Radian Order, we could return to Teel? I'd go back there. I miss it sometimes."

She looked at him as if he'd just announced he's marrying a frog and moving into a swamp. "Miss it?" She groaned. "Jitomi, it was a miserable time. Don't you remember Atratus torturing us, Lari mocking us, how everyone treated us as vermin?"

"Radians did," Jitomi said. "And now we're sailing back into the sunlight with an army at our backs." He smiled wryly. "I bet old Atratus never expected that from us. But no, I don't miss that vulture or Lari. You rid the world of a monster when you thrust your dagger into Lari Serin, and I hope I get to do the same to Atratus. But I miss . . . well, I miss being a child." He sighed. "Look at me. I'm wearing silk embroidered with gold, and priceless armor hangs on my wall. Treasures covered my table, and every sheet on this bed probably costs more than most panthers."

Madori nodded. "Yes, I can see why that would be intolerable."

He rolled his eyes. "What I mean is: I miss not having all this responsibility, the treasures, the ships, the people who look to me for leadership, and the fear. I'm always afraid, Madori. That I make a wrong move. That we lose a battle. That I lead my men to death. That one of those men tries to overthrow me. Already I had to quell three revolts against my rule, and Tianlong says that my sisters will challenge this rule as soon as I return. Dealing with Atratus back then was a nightmare, but it seemed somehow simpler. And it wasn't all bad." He smiled thinly. "Do you remember the night you summoned a magical moon in your chamber, and Tam and Neekeya were with us? And do you remember those times we walked in the northern forest, the four of us, collecting berries and talking about our homelands?" He sighed. "But I suppose those turns are over for good. Too much has changed. Too much has burned."

"Perhaps we'll go back some turn." Madori stared ahead, face blank. "I swore to become a healer. It was a few years ago. My mother was pregnant, and she was so happy, telling me over and over about how I'll have a little brother or sister. Then one turn she wasn't pregnant anymore, and she spent many turns in her bed, weak and mourning. Her babe died, and I swore then—I swore that I would learn how to heal people, to make sure nobody ever got ill again, ever lost a babe, ever lost a family member to disease, ever lost a limb to rot or life to a roaming plague. My mother had been a Sister of Harmony once, tasked with guiding the terminally ill into the afterlife, but I didn't want to work in a hospice. I wanted to *heal* people, to bring the ill back to life. And on my journey, I became a soldier." She looked at him, eyes damp. "That's never what I wanted. So yes, Jitomi. Let's go kill Serin, and let's go back to Teel, and let's become what we wanted to become. Two mages. Not an emperor and a soldier. Just Madori and Jitomi."

His hand returned to stroking her hair, and he leaned closer and kissed her cheek. Her skin was soft, the tanned, golden hue of a Timandrian, dark by his milky-white skin. She turned her head toward him, gazing at him with those lavender eyes, and those were the eyes of her Elorian side, huge and endlessly deep. He kissed her lips.

She lowered her head, and her hair brushed against him. When she raised her eyes again, he kissed her a second time, and this was a deeper kiss, and now the walls around her broke. She kissed him back, and it felt like melting into each other. He held her in his arms, and she slung her legs across his lap. She felt so soft, so fragile, a little bird fallen from a nest, and her arms wrapped around him, and still they kissed.

"I love you, Madori," he said. "I have for a long time. I would make love to you if you'd allow it."

She smiled thinly. "I've traveled the world. I've fought battles. I've faced armies. But . . ." She lowered her eyes, suddenly shy. "I've never done *that*. But I want to." She bit her lip. "I want to try."

She stood up and doffed her cloak, remaining naked before him, and grabbed his own clothes and tugged at the silk. Soon they lay on the bed beneath the silken covers, holding each other close. He kissed her mouth, then trailed his lips down to kiss her neck, her small breasts, her flat belly, her soft thighs, then back to her mouth. He had slept with a woman before—his father had insisted, demanding it was time to become a man—but this felt different. Warmer. Softer. A thing not of cold mechanics but of heat and passion and love.

And I love you, Madori, he thought as he lay above her, as his body flowed into hers, as she gasped and closed her eyes beneath him. *I love you always. I will never let you go again.*

She nestled against him and kissed his chin. "Now don't think I'm going to marry you or anything now, Jitomi Hashido, or that I'll do this with you every turn. I just wanted to try it. Not that I'm disappointed. I . . ." She bit her lip and her cheeks flushed. "I'll be quiet. I don't know what to say. I feel awkward sometimes, and I'm a little shy, and—"

He kissed her lips, and she gratefully kissed him back.

They were putting their clothes back on when shouts rose from above the deck.

Jitomi froze, his shirt only halfway laced.

"Where's the boy?" rose a shrill cry above. "Where's the little pup. Bring him to me, so he may grovel for his life."

Jitomi felt queasy. "Oh by the Red Flame." He quickly laced up his shirt, grabbed his sword, and headed to the door.

"What's wrong?" Madori cried after him. She raced in pursuit, clad in only her silken robes, her feet bare.

"My sister," he said, heart sinking.

He began racing upstairs toward the deck. Madori ran after him.

"You mean Nitomi?" she said. "The little dojai, the one who talks a lot?"

"We are not so lucky." Jitomi's words tasted like ash. "I have several older sisters. Most . . . I don't talk about."

He reached the deck, wishing he'd had time to strap on his armor. He blinked for a moment in the full sunlight, his eyes slowly adjusting; with his large Elorian eyes, the sunlight always stung. Slowly the world came into focus. Fields swayed north of the Sern River, and forests sprawled to the south. The deck of the *Tai Lar* stretched before him, and five hundred other ships sailed behind the flagship, each lined with cannons and raising banners of the Red Flame, the Armada in all its glory.

"There he is! There's the pup who calls himself an emperor."

Jitomi blinked again. Several Ilari soldiers in lacquered armor moved aside, tugging back leashed panthers, forming a path of open deck. She stood there by the prow, hands on her hips.

"Naiko," Jitomi said, the word tasting foul.

She wore the armor of an Ilari noblewoman—heavy steel plates painted crimson, their edges tasseled. Two katanas hung from her belt, and a spear hung across her back. Her helmet was horned, the visor shaped as a sneering panther. When she raised that visor, she revealed a face no less vicious. Her lips smiled, baring sharp teeth, and her indigo eyes shone with cruelly.

"Little Jitomi," she said, her smile growing larger. She sauntered toward him. "When you were a child, you used to play with toy soldiers. Do you remember? Little things carved of metal and bone. You'd pretend to command them in great battles until I smashed the toys, making you cry." She snorted. "I told you then that you were no military ruler. Father had insisted mother bear him a boy. He kept pumping her full of babes, girl after girl, until finally he had the object of his desire." She stared at him in disgust. "You. A boy who's so frail, so weak, who cried when I slapped him instead of fighting back, who fled from the spiders I placed in his bed instead of crushing them. A sniveling weakling, and yet when you played with those toy soldiers, you thought yourself an emperor. And so I smashed those toys. And I smashed your face until you bled. And now, Jitomi . . . now I've come to end another one of your games."

Feeling queasy, Jitomi stared off the starboard bow. Her panther ship sailed alongside—a small black vessel shaped like the cat of Ilar. A dozen of her personal soldiers stood upon the smaller ship's deck, clad in black armor and armed with katanas. Here on the deck of the *Tai Lar*, seven female dojai stood behind Naiko, assassins in black silk and leather, daggers and throwing stars strapped to their belts.

Naiko was the deadliest killer Jitomi had ever known. Back in his youth, he had often seen her order prisoners and slaves into the arena, then fight and slay them for sport, laughing as their blood splashed her. Each of her soldiers, Jitomi knew, was a vicious killer, allowed to defend her only after defeating a hundred enemies in battle. Here facing him were perhaps the twenty most dangerous people in Moth.

And yet I command an army, he thought. *And no twenty, no matter how deadly, can defeat the might of Ilar's military.*

"Captain Han Gao," he said to a mustached warrior who stood to his left. "Disarm my sister, her dojai, and the soldiers in her ship. Escort them into the brig."

Naiko shook her head. "No, Jitomi. Your men will no longer obey you. You are the youngest child of Emperor Hashido, our father whom you murdered. Our eldest sister, Nitomi, is a prattle-mouthed fool who can't tell apart a soup bowl from a chamber pot. I am next in line, and these soldiers are mine to command." She turned toward the mustached captain. "Han Gao! Place my little brother in irons. Toss him into the brig. I'm taking command of this armada."

Before the soldiers could choose sides, Madori whipped around Jitomi and marched forward. Clad in only her robe and standing only five feet tall, she hardly made an intimidating figure, but she balled her hands into fists and gave Naiko her best glare.

"Listen to me very carefully, Naiko Hashido," Madori said. "I am Madori Greenmoat, daughter of Koyee, slayer of Lari Serin. You are nothing. Not here on this ship. Not here in Arden, my kingdom.

So get into your little kitty boat and sail away, and if you don't, I'm going downstairs to fetch my sword and slice off your damn head."

Naiko raised her eyebrows, examined Madori as one would a newborn pup, and laughed. "I like this one," the Ilari said. "I'll keep her around as a court jester." Then her face changed, scowling and rabid, and she raised her voice to a shout. "Now move, men! Imprison the boy or I'll flay your hides and weave sails from your skin!"

Soldiers rushed toward Jitomi.

He shouted. He drew his sword and swung it. He kicked as they grabbed him, barked out for order, cried out for Tianlong the dragon.

"Release me!" he roared. "Release me or—"

His sister approached, smiling crookedly, and swung her fist into his face.

Stars exploded and Jitomi went limp. Manacles clanked shut around his wrists, and his soldiers dragged him into the hull. The last thing he saw was Madori kicking in a soldier's grip, trying to reach him. Then a door slammed shut, sealing him in the belly of his ship, alone and chained in darkness.

CHAPTER SEVEN
IN BLUE

The ocean stretched on, an eternal dreamscape of blue and gray. Neekeya lay in her rowboat, the sun baking her skin and hair, her lips parched, her belly so tight she thought it could touch her back.

"Get up," she whispered. Her tongue felt like a strip of parchment in her mouth. "Get up, Neekeya. You have to row."

She blinked weakly. The sea stretched endlessly above her. Or was that the sky? All was blue here, heaven and water blending together. Timandra lay in endless sunlight, Eloria in endless night, but here was a new realm. Here was eternal blue, a different world, one she was trapped in, a single speck in eternity.

She forced herself onto her elbows. Blinking feebly in the light, she looked around her. The little rowboat swayed, and the water whispered all around her, rising and falling, spreading into all horizons. Judging by the position of the sun, she had not made much progress south.

She lifted a fish hook and scratched a rough map onto the boat floor.

"The desert of Eseer is to my left, far in the east." She sketched the Eseerian coast. "Daenor is in the northeast, and here in the south, many miles away, lies Sania."

She drew the island as she remembered it, a great land shaped as a horseshoe. As a child, she had read the book "Sari of Sania" many times; it told the stories of a young Sanian girl and her adventures, describing a world of sprawling savannahs, proud lions, lofty giraffes, and cities of gold and gems and wonder. Neekeya crawled toward the prow, leaned forward, and squinted at the southern horizon, trying to catch a glimpse of that distant land. She saw only blue. Sometimes she wondered if Sania were only a myth, a place from a storybook, no more.

"I should turn back," she whispered. "I can find a home in Eseer. I speak the language. Or I can even return to Daenor, live hidden in the swamps, feeding on frogs and crayfish, and—"

She shook her head wildly. No. Both Eseer and Daenor had fallen to the enemy, had been annexed to the Radian Empire.

"I will never live under Serin's banner," she swore. "I would sail to the end of the earth to escape him. I would rather drown than live under Serin's rule."

She grabbed the oars. She kept rowing.

The water stretched on.

The oars splashed.

The sun baked her.

Neekeya did not know how long she rowed. An hourglass was attached to boat's hull, but during her escape from the port, an enemy arrow had smashed it. Madori had once told her that in the darkness of Eloria, there were ways to calculate the passage of time by the movement of the stars, but here in the daylight, with the sun frozen in the same place, there was no way to tell. She could have been rowing for an hour, and she could have been rowing for a whole turn.

And still she saw no land.

Finally her arms felt too weak to continue. She gazed at them. Long ago, her arms had been strong and muscular, the arms of a warrior; she had often felt self-conscious about their width. Since leaving Teel University—by Cetela, it had been over a year ago—her body had grown slim and hard like the roots of mangroves. Her arms were now wiry, thin, still strong but growing weaker every turn. Without her armor—it still lay buried in the sand back in Daenor— her entire body seemed too fragile to her, withering away.

"I need to eat."

She placed down her oars and pulled her net up from the water; it had been dragging behind her. She sighed. The net had caught only a single panfish; it was no larger than her fist. She lifted the knife she had found on the boat, a gift from its previous owner, and gutted the fish. When she stabbed herself on its fins, she cursed and raised her bleeding finger to her lips. At least sucking the blood dampened her dry mouth.

She ate the paltry meal. The fish meat was raw and rubbery, and it barely subdued her hunger, but perhaps it would keep her alive for a few more strokes of the oars. What she really craved, more than a thousand panfish, was water—sweet, delicious water to heal her body. Yet until it rained, she had best push that thought out of her mind.

She placed the net back in the water, and she rowed on.

The boat rose and fell.

A distant fish breached the water, then vanished before she could catch it.

The sun baked her hair and limbs.

The endless blue stretched into the horizons.

Finally she could row no more; all the strength the panfish had given her was gone. She needed water. She craved water with every beat of her heart, every dry breath, every sway of the boat. She tugged the net back into the boat, and she found two panfish. She cut one open, drank its sweet blood, and chewed its meat. She saved the second in the tin bucket she had found in the boat.

She slept then, and in her sleep feverish dreams rose.

"Tam!" she cried, again and again.

And he kept falling, plunging into the lava, only to rise, burning and screaming and fall again into the molten rock. She kept trying to save him, but he died endlessly in her dreams, and Neekeya woke weeping.

"Why did you leave me, Tam?" she whispered. Her lips cracked and she sucked greedily at the blood. "Why?"

Her arms shook when she tried to grab the oars. When she touched her forehead, it felt so hot, and sweat beaded there. That was bad. She could not afford to lose any more moisture. She collected the sweat on her fingers and licked the droplets.

"Why did you let me fall?" Tam asked, sitting before her in the boat.

Neekeya shed tears, losing more moisture. Tam glared at her, his skin burned away, his bones showing through tatters in his muscles.

"Tam!"

"Why did you leave me in the lava?" he said. "I came back to you. I'm back. You let me burn." He pointed at her with a charred finger. "Why did you let me burn?"

"No!" she screamed. "You're not real."

She raised her sword, her only remnant from home, and swung the blade at him, weeping.

The sword cut through air.

He was gone.

Neekeya curled up on the boat floor, trembling.

"Visions," she whispered. "Visions of a feverish mind."

She was ill. Perhaps the raw fish had given her this fever, perhaps only her thirst and exhaustion. With shaky fingers, she reached for her waterskin, the old vessel she had carried with her through this past year of war. Empty again. Empty every time. Perhaps if she tried again later, she would find a forgotten drop. She checked the old tin bucket the fisherman had left in the boat, hoping for some rain water. Dry as a bone. Again.

The deep, mournful keen of her heart sounded across the sea.

It was the sound of a shattering soul. She was surprised she could emit a sound so sad.

Arms wobbling, she pushed herself onto her elbows and gazed off the starboard side. And there she saw him. A white creature, larger than her, a scar along his snout. His eye stared at her, large and round and wise, and water blasted from his spout, a fountain soaring, and he sang again. A beautiful dirge. A dolphin song.

"A spirit of the sea," she whispered. "A god of the blue." She smiled tremulously and reached out to it. "Thank you for blessing me."

She had heard of dolphins before; they were blessed, holy creatures in the lore of her land. And this one was special, pure white like an Elorian, an albino or perhaps a deity of the sea. Neekeya took her last remaining fish from her bucket. She did not know if she'd catch another, but this god of the water had blessed her with its presence. She would give him an offering.

She tossed the fish into his mouth. The albino dolphin accepted the meal, gave her a last look, then sank into the water.

And finally it began to rain.

Neekeya laughed. "Thank you, King Dolphin." She did not know why she thought him a king, but now he seemed a great king to her, wise and all powerful. "Thank you."

The rain fell, and she lay on her back, mouth open, drinking drop by drop.

The rain grew stronger.

The drops pattered against her, and the wind shrieked. The waves tossed the boat up and down. Lightning flashed and thunder boomed.

Neekeya clung to the boat. The rain drenched her and now sea water splashed into the boat too. The vessel rose and fell, and one oar spilled overboard. She managed to grab it just before it could sink, then stuffed both oars under the seat.

A great wave tossed the boat clear into the air. It crashed down with a clatter of fishing gear. Her bucket of rainwater overturned. The net tore free and sailed into the wind. The storm roared and the rain kept falling.

Neekeya clung to the boat. "Please, Cetela," she whispered. "Don't let me drown here. Let the rain stop."

The boat rose and fell again. Her knife and sword slid across the floor. The bucket rolled overboard and sank. Why had she ever come here? She had been a fool. The rain crashed down and lightning rent the sky, a demon of light.

Neekeya closed her eyes, trying to imagine she was back home in Daenor, snug in her bed, a storm raging harmlessly outside her window onto the marshlands.

The wind rose to a deafening shriek, and thunder boomed so loudly it shook the boat. A great wave tossed Neekeya into the air. The boat overturned beneath her. She crashed down into the water.

She sank. Salty water filled her mouth and stung through her nostrils. She floundered, feeling too weak to swim. The water tugged her down, yanked her sideways, and she kicked madly and thrashed and her face emerged over the surface. She gulped down air and swallowed water.

"Dolphin!" she shouted, knowing the animal was gone, knowing she would drown here.

The water tugged her back down.

She sank into the darkness.

All was shadows and mottles of fading light.

It seemed to her, as the darkness swirled and tugged at her feet, that was back in the dungeons under Eetek pyramid. She was fleeing the Magerians again through the mines, with Tam who had fallen. Again she saw him plunge into the pit, leaving her so soon after their wedding.

I cannot fall too.

She kicked.

She rose in the water.

Be like the dolphin.

She swam upwards, breached the surface, and gulped down air. She stayed afloat.

The boat was gone, and the waves tossed her up and down, and her head kept sinking, but she kept swimming. She laughed because the hosts of Serin could not kill her, and neither would this storm. She would stay alive for Tam. She would keep fighting. Even if all others fell, and the Radian fires burned all across the world, she would live.

I'm in the water and I'm safe from the fire.

When the storm died down, she floated on the salty water. She was alone in an ocean, the water stretching to the horizons. She had lost everything—her armor, her sword, her boat, her husband, her father. But she was still alive.

The rain had died to a drizzle when she saw the first shark fin.

Fresh fear filled her.

The shark swam closer, circling her. Two more emerged from the depths. Each was as large as her missing boat.

"Oh Cetela," she whispered.

Desperately, she scanned the sea for her boat and could not find it. The sharks circled nearer, and panic began to flood Neekeya. She panted and her limbs shook. A wave rose, Neekeya bobbed higher in the sea, and she saw it there. Her boat, overturned, still floated. It seemed about a mile away, a mere speck in the distance.

A shark drew so close it brushed against her.

Neekeya began to swim. *I'll never make it,* she thought. *Oh by the gods of sea and swamp, I'll never make it. Please, if there is any goodness to you, Idar, Cetela, and any other gods who might listen, save me this turn.*

She swam, grimacing, as the sharks drove in toward her.

With a song that brought tears to her eyes, a dolphin leaped from the water—an albino dolphin with a scarred snout—and slammed into one of the sharks.

An instant later, a dozen more dolphins emerged.

Their long noses slammed into the sharks. The dolphins were smaller, but they fought in a fury. The sharks swam away, turned back once toward Neekeya, seemed to decide her lanky frame more trouble than it was worth, and finally turned to flee.

The dolphin with the scarred nose, the one she had fed, swam up beneath her, gently lifting her from the water. She wrapped her arms around him.

"Thank you, friend." She kissed him. "Thank you."

The dolphins swam, returning her to her boat. When she struggled to turn it upright, the dolphins helped her push, and it seemed to her that they were as wise as men, perhaps wiser, surely kinder. When she had finally righted the boat and climbed back in, they swam alongside her, leaping from the water.

She had lost her oars and her sword. She leaned over the side and rowed with her hand. She could only move a few inches at a time this way, and she had to keep alternating sides. But she kept moving.

Her chin was raised, her lips tightened, when she saw land ahead.

CHAPTER EIGHT
REBORN

Tirus Serin, Sovereign of the Radian Empire, stood in his bedchamber, building a new daughter.

"Excellent," he said, strapping on her last piece of armor. He caressed the girl's cheek. "You are Lari Serin. You are returned to me."

She stood trembling before him, a young woman, perhaps twenty years old. Her hair was long and golden, her eyes blue, her face fair and soft. He had found her on the city streets, a milkmaid in the dregs of Markfir, a poor peasant girl with a little brother at her heels. A woman who looked like Lari. A woman who *was* Lari now.

Serin had torn off and burned her old clothes, a humble woolen skirt, apron, and kerchief. He had torn off her brother too and tossed the screaming urchin into the dungeon. Now she stood before him, clad in gilded armor, a sword at her waist. Now his daughter had returned from the dead.

You killed her, Serin thought. *You killed her, Madori. I will find you. I will break you. I will shatter every segment of your spine and keep you alive in a box, broken and screaming and begging for death.*

He found himself trembling with rage. The new Lari recoiled, and her lip wobbled.

"Please, my lord," the girl whispered. A tear streamed down her cheek. "Please let me see my brother."

Serin snarled and grabbed her shoulders. "You have no brother. I never had a son. You are Lari Serin, returned from the dead." He raised his fist. "Do you understand?"

She flinched. "Yes, my lord. But . . . the boy who was with me, is he—"

"Stop flinching! Lari is strong. Lari is a soldier, heir to an empire." He grabbed her arm, dragged her across the chamber, and stood her by the window. "Look! Look out the tower, Lari. Look at your domain."

They stood in the tallest tower of Solgrad Castle, pinnacle of Markfir. The chamber was lavish. Tapestries hung across the walls, depicting proud, golden-haired Radians slaying twisted nightcrawlers. Suits of filigreed armor stood at the room's corners, and many jeweled swords rose on stands, Radian eclipses upon their pommels. A great eclipse six feet in diameter, worked in gold and silver, hung above a plush bed. Serin's greatest treasure—his collection of Elorian skulls—stood upon shelves. Hundreds of the skulls stood here, all those he had personally slain. Upon each forehead he had engraved an eclipse, a symbol of his dominion. Countless more skulls—the victims of his soldiers—lay buried and burnt across the night; they too were his legacy.

When Serin had first moved into the capital, this chamber had been bare of any such trophies. Mageria's old, drunken king had lived here before Professor Atratus had slipped poison into his mug. Now this was a home to Serin, a great emperor, a slayer of nightcrawlers. From this tower, he could gaze over the city of Markfir and the landscape beyond.

Markfir, ancient capital of Mageria and now capital of the Radian Empire, was among the largest cities in the world, home to half a million souls. It rose across the foothills of Markshade Mountains—which in foreign lands men still called Teekat—sloping downward toward the plains. Solgrad Castle rose upon the city crest, perched like an eagle overlooking its territory. Avenues flared out from the palace grounds like rays from a sunburst, lined with buildings: homes of wood and clay with tiled roofs, stone barracks topped with Radian banners, Idarith temples whose domes sported the half-sun of their faith, and many inns, workshops, and silos of brick.

Three layers of walls spread out in three semi-circles from the mountains. The first contained the Old City, home to many historic buildings—some of them thousands of years old—the place where Mageria's very first people had lived. The city's oldest, richest families lived within this inner shell, some tracing their ancestry millennia back.

Since those ancient years, the city had expanded, and a second layer of wall contained newer buildings, these ones several hundred years old. Within this second layer lived wealthy merchants and tradesmen. Their family names were not as ancient, not as noble, but their coffers were deep, their manors large, their blood newer but still pure.

The third wall had been raised only recently to contain the city's expanding waistline. Within the past twenty years, many undesirables had clogged this third layer: peasants who thought they could live as city folk, travelers from Arden and Naya and other foreign kingdoms, and even Elorians who had moved to Mageria to seek a new life after the first great war. Those undesirables were gone now; Serin could still see the mounds of their mass graves outside the wall. Now his soldiers, many brought here all the way from Sunmotte Citadel in the north, occupied the third layer of Markfir: myriads of troops in steel, armed with swords, pikes, and bows. They stood on the walls. They mustered in the courtyards. They manned the turrets and gatehouses. They were waiting. Waiting for Madori to arrive.

"Look at the plains beyond the walls," Serin said, gripping Lari's arm. "The grasslands spread into the east, fabled for their herds of buffalo. The old banner of our kingdom displayed a buffalo, did you know? The buffaloes are nearly gone now, perhaps already extinct, hunted into nothingness . . . and this too will be the fate of the nightcrawlers. Beyond those plains, she's approaching. Madori. The woman who slew you before I resurrected you. She's coming here with a great army of nightcrawlers." Serin laughed. "I've allowed them to sail into the daylight; I left only a few hundred men at Fairwool-by-Night, knowing the nightcrawlers could make it through. Do you know why, Lari?"

The girl—his new daughter—shook her head silently. A fresh tear streamed down her cheek.

"I let Madori enter the daylight because I *want* her to come here. I want to watch it myself from this tower—the extinction of their race. And you will watch it with me. Thousands of nightcrawlers will have to crawl across the plains, weak in the sunlight, as my forces plague them along every mile. Madori will finally make it here with her ragtag army . . . and then, Lari, she will see our glory. Then her army will smash against our walls, and I will ride out to capture her myself." His breath quickened. "And it will be glorious."

"But . . . my lord, they say these Elorians are from Ilar, a cruel empire of bloodthirsty warriors." Lari shuddered. "They say they flay their enemies and drink blood from their skulls. They say . . ." Her voice dropped to a whisper. "They say that a dragon flies above them, the black beast Tianlong, that he can fly above walls and lay cities to waste."

Serin struck her.

He struck her so hard she fell to the floor.

"They are nightcrawlers," he said. "Before you died, you scorned them. You did not fear them." He stepped onto the joints of armor behind her knee, painfully bending her leg. "You will not speak of them in fear or awe. A dragon?" He scoffed. "I have creatures far greater growing in my dungeons. I created the beast Gehena and his monstrous steed; they are fighting in the north now, crushing Orewood and capturing its mines. And creatures even fouler now fester in the shadows. The nightcrawlers will see them soon. So will you. Come with me."

He tugged her across the chamber. They stepped through the doorway and walked down a staircase, coiling down the tower. Guards stood at attention along the steps, armed with swords and spears. Serin dragged his daughter through the halls and chambers of Solgrad Castle, this behemoth in the mountain's shadow: corridors lined with soldiers, porticoes overlooking lush gardens, a wall of battlements armed with catapults and ballistae, solariums full of summer flowers, and finally down stairs into the dungeons.

As large as its towers and halls were, most of Solgrad Castle lay underground. Stairways and tunnels burrowed deep like a hive of ants. They passed by smithies where burly men forged swords and spearheads, past chambers full of barrels of gunpowder, and by narrow hallways lined with prison cells where chained, beaten men screamed upon the walls.

Lari glanced around nervously, jumping whenever a prisoner screamed. Serin tightened his grip on her arm. The girl would have to learn some strength. He would temper her like a smith tempers steel.

A horrible shriek rose, echoing through the dungeons—not the cry of a prisoner but a louder, inhuman sound. A second cry answered, a sound like a dying horse. Lari gasped and whimpered.

"Do you hear them, Lari?" Serin whispered. "They call for blood. Come, we will visit them."

"But . . . please, my lord." Tears streamed down her cheeks. "My name is Ariana, not Lari. I think I saw my brother in one of these cells. Please, my lord, let me see him. Let—"

"Hush, Lari." He pulled her onward. "We're almost there."

Leaving the prison cells above, they plunged down a staircase and entered a massive chamber, a chasm large enough for armies to muster in. A ledge of stone thrust out, overlooking the pit.

The creatures waited there.

"Behold the avalerions," Serin said softly.

Lari screamed and tried to run back. Serin grabbed her and manhandled her onto the ledge of stone.

The creatures below snapped their beaks, beat their wings, and soared. Only feet away from reaching Serin and Lari, their massive chains tugged back their necks. The creatures crashed back down into the pit, clawing at one another, shrieking, begging to feed.

"Not yet, my children!" Serin cried down to them. He laughed. "You will hunger for a while longer. When the nightcrawlers come, you'll have all the flesh of the night."

The avalerions wailed—horrible, high-pitched sounds like cracking palaces of glass. The crumbling city of Pahmey, with its smashing towers and screaming nightcrawlers, had made this sound when Serin had destroyed it. The avalerions were ugly things, great vultures the size of whales. Black, oily feathers covered their wings, but their bodies were naked and covered with goose bumps like the skin of plucked chickens. Beaks of rusted iron grew from their bloated faces.

"They were humans once, do you know?" Serin said, holding Lari close. "Look at them. Look into their eyes. Do you see the bloodlust? The hatred? Only humans have such hatred in their hearts; no animal is as cruel as man. I found them in my army, hulking brutes, murderers. And I changed them. Grew them. Made them my children." He stroked Lari's hair. "And you too are my child. Who are you, daughter? Say your name."

She was trembling. "I am Aria—"

He gripped her and shoved her close to the edge, holding her just above the pit. The creatures inside went mad. They leaped upwards, snapping their teeth, reaching out their talons. Their chains pulled taut, keeping them only several feet away from the girl.

"Who are you?" Serin shouted, his voice so loud she started.

"I am Lari," she whispered, tears streaming down her cheeks. "I am Lari Serin. Your daughter."

He pulled her back from the edge. Good. The girl would learn. Serin would let none in his empire say that nightcrawlers slew his child. That would mean he was weak, that his family was weak. But he was strong. His daughter had survived the darkness. She stood here before him, noble and beautiful and proud.

"Very good," he said. "Very good, Lari. You're learning. You—ah! Look! It's lunch time."

The man emerged from behind them and stepped onto the ledge. He wore a leather apron, and he held a pole across his shoulders. A bucket hung on each edge of the pole, full of dank meat. When the man saw Serin, he knelt and bowed his head.

"My lord Serin! I've brought them their meal. As you said, my lord—just enough to keep 'em alive but still 'ungry."

"Rise, friend!" Serin said. "My daughter Lari would like to see the creatures feed."

The man rose and stepped closer, and when Lari got a closer look at the buckets, she gasped and covered her mouth. It was no ordinary meat inside those buckets; here were the severed hands of city thieves, bustling with flies.

"Your daughter?" said the man. "I . . . my lord! I thought that Princess Lari . . . I mean, begging your pardon, my lord, they're saying she died in the war. That the mongrel slew her. A horrible tragedy. I . . ." He glanced at Lari, his face twisting with confusion.

Serin sighed. He shook his head sadly. "Friend, I really did want them to eat only a snack to whet their appetite, a couple buckets of hands before they feast upon the nightcrawler army. Yet now they'll have to enjoy a larger meal."

The creatures in the pit squealed and tugged their chains. Their caretaker tilted his head, only seeming more confused. "My lord?"

Serin stepped forward. He grabbed the pole the man carried across his shoulders, knocking the buckets off its ends. The hands spilled onto the stone ledge. As the caretaker gasped, Serin dragged him toward the edge of the pit, then shoved him over.

Just as the man fell, Serin thrust out the pole, letting the caretaker grab one end.

The man screamed, dangling over the pit. His toes still touched the stone ledge. His sweaty hands gripped the wooden pole. Serin smiled, holding the other end of the staff. All he had to do was let go.

"My lord!" the caregiver cried. The avalerions below screeched and leaped up, snapping their beaks, rattling their chains. The dangling man hung only several inches above their reach.

"Step forward, Lari," Serin said calmly.

Shaking, she obeyed.

"Hold the pole," Serin said. "Hold it tightly so he doesn't fall."

Tears flowed down her cheeks, but she obeyed. Slowly, Serin released his grip of the pole, leaving Lari to hold it alone. The man tilted over the edge, feet scraping for purchase against the stone, holding his end of the stick.

"You hold his life in your hands, Lari," Serin said. "And now you have a choice. You can save him, proving yourself weak. Or you can let go, letting him fall . . . and you will prove yourself truly my daughter. And perhaps some turn, Lari . . . some turn I can have a son. Perhaps some turn your little brother will be freed from the dungeon, and he can join our family. Chose."

Lari wept.

She let go.

The caregiver tumbled into the pit. The avalerions cried out with joy and blood splattered as they fed. Serin stood over the ledge, watching, smiling, imagining the beasts flying over the fields and feeding upon Madori.

CHAPTER NINE
A SHADOW IN KINGSWALL

Thirteen turns since emerging into the sunlight, the Ilari Armada reached the occupied city of Kingswall, former capital of Arden and now a bastion of the enemy.

Madori stood upon the deck of the *Tai Lar*. She had doffed the heavy steel plates she had worn at Fairwool-by-Night, and she now wore the armor of a Qaelish warrior: a shirt of silvery scales and a simple, curving helm of bright steel. She held a shield in one arm, her katana in the other. Every other soldier around her wore Ilari armor—lacquered plates and faced visors that made them look like demonic isopods. Most of the Ilari fleet was comprised of heavy, iron-clad Ilari vessels, floating fortresses topped with pagodas. But among the fleet, Madori had found several ships seized from other forces: seven carracks of Arden taken only months ago upon the Inaro, a creaky old Leenish cog captured from smugglers, and a single Qaelish junk. She had scoured this ship, trying not to think of her kinsmen who had died here, and finally found the armor in its bowels.

I am a child of Qaelin, she thought as she stood here, back on the deck of the Armada's flagship. *And I will wear Qaelin's armor to battle.*

She turned to look at Koyee. Her mother stood at her side, also armored in Qaelish scales salvaged from the junk, and she too held a shield and katana.

"Mother," Madori said, "when you faced great battles when you were young, were you afraid?"

Koyee raised an eyebrow. "When I was young? Oh you little scoundrel. I'm not yet forty, you know." She frowned for a moment, seeming deep in thought, then nodded. "Yes, not yet forty."

"But were you afraid?" Madori insisted.

Koyee sighed. "I could speak some platitude about how courage is doing what's right even when you're afraid, how only the frightened can be brave, or some other such nugget of wisdom. But you'd still be terrified. And you'd still do what you need to do. Because you're my daughter. And you're like me."

Madori stuck out her tongue with a gagging sound. "I am nothing like you. You're so proper and prim." She growled. "I'm a rebel."

"When I fought my first battle, I was a filthy urchin off the streets, hardly proper and prim." Koyee narrowed her eyes. "Just stay near me, Madori, and fight well. We will slay Radians together."

Madori glanced toward the hatch leading under the deck.

"I wish he were here with us," she said softly. "Jitomi."

Her cheeks heated to remember that turn they had made love. She was not sure how she felt about Jitomi. Did she love him as he loved her? Or had she simply been afraid, lost, lonely, maybe simply curious, wanting to experience sex before she went to battle and perhaps died? She did not know, but now she missed him dearly. Since Naiko had taken command of the Armada, Madori had not seen her friend; Naiko kept Jitomi chained in the brig.

"He'll be safe down there," Koyee said softly and touched Madori's arm. "Perhaps the ship's prison is the safest place right now in Moth."

Madori nodded. "I know. But I wish Jitomi could be here with us, a sword in his hand, fighting with us to liberate Kingswall." She lowered her voice to a whisper. "I'd rather he led this host. I don't trust his sister."

Koyee sighed. "Nor do I."

Both turned to stare across the deck. Past hundreds of Ilari soldiers and panthers ready for war, Naiko stood at the prow. The wind streamed the empress's long white hair, and she raised her sword high. She was a figure in black and red, resplendent in the sun, all steel and might. She might as well have been the ship's figurehead. And yet Madori also saw cruelty in her, a passion for power rather than righteousness.

She seeks to conquer rather than liberate, Madori thought, *to crush rather than save. But I sailed into the daylight for freedom, not for conquest.*

Madori looked past the new empress toward the distant city. As the fleet sailed on, Kingswall grew larger. A pinch of nostalgia twisted her heart. She had spent her childhood summers in this city, the capital of Arden, sunlit land of her father. She still counted those summers among her most precious memories: long sunny turns running through the palace gardens with Tam, countless hours exploring bookshops and libraries along cobbled streets, the taste of sweet lemon cakes in the city bakeries, and the frosty ale Father had once bought her in a tavern here, her first taste of the wonderful drink.

The haven of her childhood had become a city of nightmares.

The raven banners of Arden no longer rose here, but real ravens flocked outside the walls, bustling over cages that hung from the battlements. Corpses rotted inside. New banners now rose from the towers, displaying a sun hiding the moon. Upon the city ramparts stood hundreds of Radian troops in black armor, armed with longbows. Madori knew that thousands more waited in the city. Kingswall had become a garrison to Serin's empire.

Madori took a deep, shuddering breath. She walked toward Grayhem, her dearest friend, and climbed onto his back. Around her the Ilari warriors, enclosed within black steel plates, sat astride panthers just as black. But she, Madori, was a warrior of silver scales, of a great gray wolf, of mixed blood, a woman of darkness fighting for her homeland of sunlight.

As the Armada sailed nearer, distant horns blared upon the city walls. Each blast of the horns made Madori shiver; they sounded like wailing men. More Radian troops raced into position on the walls, and a dozen warships left the piers and came sailing toward the invaders. Distant war drums boomed, and banners rose high, and the Radians cried out for war, for bloodshed.

"Drums!" Naiko howled upon the prow, and within an instant, a war drum beat upon each Ilari ship—five hundred drums all booming for war. Horns joined them from the decks, hundreds of deep, metallic cries. One of the hornblowers stood only a dozen feet away from Madori, and the sound nearly deafened her. All across the decks of Ilar, the soldiers brandished their katanas. Each of the ships held hundreds of warriors. They all now roared together.

The Radian warships sailed closer, great caravels and carracks and brigantines of wood and canvas, their hulls painted with eclipses. Cannons and archers lined their bulwarks.

"Cannons!" Naiko roared.

Across the Ilari ships, men lit fuses. The smell of gunpowder flared. Smoke blasted and fire lit the world. The deck shook beneath Madori. The guns of a dozen ships fired their cannonballs, and archers followed with arrows.

The hull of one enemy caravel shattered. The ship listed and another volley of cannon fire sent it sinking. The river was already won, Madori knew; the enemy had but a dozen ships to ward off hundreds.

Naiko placed her fingers in her mouth and whistled. "Tianlong! Tianlong, bear me on your back!" The great black dragon swooped, and Naiko climbed upon him and soared into the sky. "To the docks! Warriors of Ilar, to the walls! *Tai Lar*! *Daroma Min*! *Taroshi Dai*! With me!"

While most of Ilar's ships kept battling the Radian fleet, the three vessels Naiko had named—all towering *atakebune* ships, their hulls clad with iron and their decks bearing pagodas—turned toward the city, positioning themselves so their figureheads faced the heavy oak gates set into the walls.

Madori gripped her sword as the *Tai Lar*'s deck swayed beneath her. She stared at the city ahead, gritting her teeth. Her ship was only a few feet away from the boardwalk. Only a few feet beyond that, the city walls towered, topped with merlons and turrets. The gatehouse loomed ahead across the water. Its doors were carved of oak, banded with iron grills shaped as ravens.

"Burn them down!" shouted a Radian captain above the gatehouse.

A hundred Radian archers raised their bows. A hundred arrows sailed through the air, tipped with flame, to slam into the Elorian ships. Some arrows shattered against the iron-clad hulls. Others drove into the pagodas that rose upon the *atakebunes*' decks. A few arrows punched though Elorian armor; the men fell, gripping their wounds. Madori grunted as one arrow glanced off her side, cracking a scale in her armor.

"Fire!" cried another Radian upon the walls. A dozen cannons rose to appear between the merlons. Their fuses crackled.

Before the guns could fire, Naiko streamed above upon her dragon. "Ilar, cannons!" she roared.

Small bronze cannons, barely larger than men, lined the hulls of the three *atakebunes*—the *Tai Lar*, the *Daroma Min*, and the *Taroshi Dai*—guns for sinking enemy ships. But their greatest weapons hid within their iron figureheads. Men now rushed forth to light the fire.

The Radian cannonballs came flying down from the walls. One slammed into the *Daroma Min*—the *atakebune* sailed just east of Madori—and smashed its pagoda. Roof tiles rained. Another cannonball flew over Madori's head, missed her ship, and smashed into an Ilari *geobukseon* ship behind her. A third cannonball slammed into the *Tai Lar*'s hull, denting the iron. The ship swayed madly and Madori clung to her wolf.

An instant later, the Elorian guns fired.

The three *atakebunes*—each large as a fortress—hid massive cannons within their dragon figureheads, the muzzles so large Madori could have climbed into them. The great cannonballs, painted with demon faces, flew toward the city gates.

The ancient, oaken doors of Kingswall—doors sung of in legends and epic poems—shattered.

For a moment, the battle seemed to freeze.

As chips of wood and iron scattered, exposing the city beyond the walls, both Elorians and Timandrians stared in silence and awe.

Then Naiko swooped upon her dragon, sword raised high. "Ilar—into the city! For the glory of the Red Flame!"

The Elorian army roared for victory, thousands of voices rising in a storm.

"Be strong," Koyee said softly, climbing onto a panther.

Madori nodded upon her wolf. "Always."

As more cannons blasted and arrows flew, the three *atakebunes* sailed closer toward the boardwalk. They lowered their planks. With battle cries, the warriors of Ilar raced—some afoot, others astride panthers—onto the city boardwalk.

Madori and Koyee raised their swords, and their mounts burst into a run.

As soon as they leaped onto the boardwalk, a rain of arrows clattered down.

Madori raised her shield. Arrows slammed into the steel disk, so powerful they nearly knocked Madori off the saddle. One arrow punched right through the shield and scraped across her cheek. More arrows clattered against Grayhem; the nightwolf wore steel plates, the armor of panthers outfitted to his shape. Madori's nightwolf and Koyee's panther kept racing toward the shattered gates, hundreds of Elorian troops around them.

The walls towered above Madori, topped with parapets. The city's wooden doors had shattered, but its brick gatehouse still stood, a fortified archway within two towers. More archers fired from these battlements. The arrows rained down, tipped with flame. One arrow took down a panther to Madori's right. Another arrow slammed through an Ilari warrior's breastplate; he fell dead. The other Elorians kept racing forward, and more kept joining them, thousands of troops emerging from the ships.

Ahead of Madori, the first Elorians began to race through the shattered gates.

Upon the gatehouse battlements, Radians tilted barrels.

Bubbling oil spilled through murder holes in a sizzling rain.

Elorians screamed, the oil seeping through their armor, burning their skin. Radians cheered above and fired more arrows, taking down the invaders as they burned. As the lit arrows hit the oil, fire blasted out, rising like new gates, burning through men.

Grayhem bucked and yowled, freezing a dozen feet away from the flaming gatehouse. Raised in the wilderness and not trained for battle, he dared not run closer to the inferno. Upon his back, Madori stared in terror at the death, the blood. More oil spilled down. More Elorians screamed and fell, and more Timandrians cheered, and at that moment that was all they were to her—Madori no longer knew Ilar from Qaelin, Magerians from Ardishmen or Nayans, for all were simply children of darkness or children of light.

My two halves battling.

Her eyes stung, her heart hammered, and her breath quickened. The world seemed hazy. An arrow slammed into her armor, cracking a scale and cutting her skin. Her blood spilled. She looked up and

Koyee was shouting her name, calling to her, caught in a current of invaders. Madori could barely hear. All sounds faded, and more oil spilled, and an arrow slammed into her helmet. Her head rang. Her wolf reared beneath her, an arrow in his flank, daring not advance.

I'm going to die, Madori thought, her breath turning into a panicked pant. *I'm going to die here far from home. I won't even make it through the gates.* More Elorians were screaming ahead of her. Three men ran past her, burning, living torches, and leaped into the river. So much death. So much blood. So much—

A new voice spoke in her mind.

Breathe.

Madori sucked in air.

Breathe. Slowly. Feel the breath. Be aware. Be here.

It was Master Lan Tao speaking in her mind, she knew. As Grayhem whimpered, daring not enter the gauntlet of oil and flame, Madori forced herself to breathe, to feel the air entering her lungs, healing her, to exhale, to let all the fear flow away. She cleared her mind, becoming aware of all around her, no longer trapped within her terror. She was mindful of every arrow flying above. Every blast of a cannon. Every ship behind her. Every corpse ahead.

She stroked Grayhem's fur. "Go on, boy. Before they spill more oil." She pointed to the gates. "Run!"

Grayhem leaped forward, snarling as he raced. Flaming arrows flew down. One slammed into Grayhem's armor; the steel slowed the arrow enough that it only nicked his skin. Another arrow pierced Madori's shield.

A barrel of oil tilted above.

Grayhem leaped over Elorian corpses and through the gates.

The oil spilled down.

They landed inside the city.

The oil splashed against the ground behind them, spraying up to bite at Grayhem's heels. The nightwolf kept racing forward.

Burnt and bleeding, their armor bristly with arrows, they had entered the city of Kingswall.

* * * * *

A hundred other Elorians had made it into Kingswall; Madori breathed a sigh of relief to see Koyee among them. But hundreds of Timandrians stood here too—a mixture of Magerians in black armor and Ardishmen and Nayans who had joined their cause. Swords rang across the courtyard. Elorians swung katanas and fired arrows from atop panthers. Timandrian knights galloped forward on warhorses, thrusting lances.

Madori raised her blade. *The time for fear is ended. It's time to fight.*

She held the battle in her awareness, perfectly calm, moonlight upon a still pond. And she fought. And she killed.

Grayhem was perhaps a wild beast, not a trained nightwolf like those her uncle Okado and aunt Suntai had ridden in the last war, but he still fought in a fury, a wild beast of the moonlit plains slaying the sunlit enemies. Upon his back, Madori swung her katana. When a knight galloped toward her, Grayhem leaped into the air, dodging the lance, and Madori sliced into the knight's helm. They landed among a crowd of Radian swordsmen, and Madori swung her blade again and again, severing arms, cutting deep into men's chests and heads. Another knight galloped toward her, and Madori spun, summoned a crackling ball of magic, and lobbed the projectile at him. The knight fell, clutching his chest.

Behind Madori, more and more Elorians kept streaming into the city. They raced through the shattered gates. Their cannonballs sailed overhead, slamming into buildings in the city center. Their arrows flew everywhere.

Soon the Radian defenders lay dead, strewn across the courtyard and walls.

"To the palace!" Koyee shouted ahead upon her panther. She pointed her blade toward a boulevard. "With me!"

Madori rode after her mother. A thousand Elorians rode with her. The Palace of Kingswall rose a mile away upon a hill, overlooking the city—the place where Madori had spent her summers with Tam. Radian flags flew from its towers.

As Koyee shouted of liberating the city, and as Naiko flew above, roaring for conquest, Madori only thought: *This is my home.* She rode forth, lips tightened. This is where she had chased butterflies, where Tam and she had tried to fish in the koi pond using shoelaces for fishing lines, where she had once picked a bouquet of flowers for her mother, where she would spend hours under a tree, reading books of adventure. *And this is where I will bleed, where I will spill the blood of my enemies.*

More Radian forces rode down the boulevard to meet them, hundreds of horses and pikemen and swordsmen. The streets of Kingswall ran red with blood. Every heartbeat, another man fell dead. Cannonballs blazed overhead, smashing into buildings. Kindled arrows covered the sky, and houses burned. Madori kept driving forth, cutting men down. Her wolf fought beneath her, clawing at the enemies, ripping out throats.

It seemed a full turn of blood, death, and fire before they reached the palace grounds.

With battle cries, the Elorians raced through the gardens, the place of Madori's lazy childhood summers. Where she had once chased a dragonfly, she now chased a man and sliced his throat. Where she had once lain upon grass, imagining shapes in the clouds, she now sent soldiers crashing down, imagining shapes in their blood. Where she had once learned the names of flowers from her father, she now learned all the ways to kill a man. A place of childhood. A place of death. A liberation in fire, a libation of blood.

When the Elorians reached the gates of the palace and burst into its hall, they found the lord of the city kneeling.

General Velmore was a burly man, his yellow mustache thick, his shoulders wide. An eclipse shone upon his breastplate, formed of many gemstones. His captains emerged to kneel around him, similarly clad in black steel. In the hall of Kingswall, the Radian high command placed down their swords before the Elorian army.

Madori dismounted her nightwolf. At her side, Koyee dismounted her panther. With a hundred other Elorians, they stared at the Radian overlords.

"As Lord of Kingswall," said General Velmore, bowing his head, "I surrender this city. Spare our lives and we will fight you no longer."

Madori found herself trembling with rage. She took a step closer, sword raised. "Spare your lives?" Tears burned her eyes. "Spare your lives?" she repeated, voice rising to a shout. "Like you

Radians spared the lives of Pahmey's people? The lives of Elorians across Qaelin?" She took another step closer and placed the tip of her sword against the general's neck. "You slew millions! I watched them die." Her voice shook and tears streamed down her cheeks. "I watched as mountains of bodies burned. As wheelbarrows dumped thousands into pits. I watched as my land bled, as its people fell to the swarm of your master. Now you beg for mercy?"

The general stared up at her, and his eyes narrowed. "You are not fully Elorian."

Madori snarled. "No. I'm only half of the night. My father is a man of Arden, this kingdom you bled. This kingdom you conquered. This kingdom I will cleanse." She looked over the general's shoulder toward his throne. The skulls of Elorians lay at its feet, eye sockets wide and staring, trophies from this war or the last one. "You sat above those you slew, and now you beg for life!"

Madori raised her sword, prepared to strike, and felt a hand on her shoulder.

"Daughter, wait."

Panting, tears on her cheeks, Madori turned toward her mother. Koyee gazed her, eyes full of pity and fear.

"Madori, don't," Koyee whispered.

Madori trembled and still snarled. "Why not?"

"Because it hurts me to see you like this." Koyee gently pulled her back. "Because I cannot live in a world where my daughter is a killer, where she's consumed with vengeance. Don't let them turn you into monsters. An enemy can take your treasure, take your land, take the lives of those you love, but if he takes your soul, if he fills you with hatred, then he has truly won. So please, Madori. Do not let him turn you into a monster, though he himself is monstrous. Show him mercy."

Madori shook with rage. She thought back to the iron mine, to all those who had died there—the pit of bodies she had fallen into, the death all around her, disease, starvation. Suddenly she felt that pain again; the brand burned anew upon her shoulder, and the hunger clawed at her belly, and the whips of the overseers tore into her back. She raised her blade higher, throat burning, ready to slay the man . . . and let the sword drop.

She fell to her knees.

"No," she whispered. "No, I will not kill you. Because I saw cruelty. I saw too much death." She turned toward the Ilari soldiers who stood behind her, katanas raised. "Chain these men up. They will become our prisoners. They—"

A shard whistled through the air.

General Velmore clutched his chest. A crossbow bolt had driven through his armor and pierced his heart. He fell forward, dead before he hit the floor.

Madori gasped and looked toward the palace gates. Empress Naiko came walking into the hall, holding a crossbow. Her dojai assassins walked at her sides, women clad in black silk; they swung their arms, lobbing throwing stars, and the other Radian commanders clutched their throats, and they too fell down dead.

"Naiko, damn it!" Madori shouted. "They were surrendering."

The new empress snorted, already reloading her crossbow. "Watch your tongue, pup, lest my second bolt finds your heart. You've slain many sunlit demons in this battle; that's the only reason I now forgive your insolence." Naiko turned toward her soldiers in the hall. "Warriors of Ilar, we are victorious! Kingswall is ours! Go and claim your treasures."

The soldiers roared. With their visors shaped as snarling faces, the blood on their armor, and the blades in their hands, they seemed to Madori like demons. The troops moved across the throne room, tugging gems off statues, rummaging through dead men's pockets for coins, tearing rings off fingers and bracelets off arms. They banged down doors and marched through other corridors and chambers, crying out for loot.

"Naiko!" Madori shouted. "For pity's sake. We came to liberate this palace, not loot it. Call your men back!"

Yet Naiko only gave Madori a small, satisfied smile. With a groan, Madori raced out of the throne room into a corridor. Elorian troops were busy smashing statues and ripping off tapestries. They banged down doors, rushed into chambers, and overturned dressers and drawers, crying out in joy whenever they found coins. Palace servants screamed and fled from them. One old steward tried to hold the Elorians back from an Idarith charity box; the Elorians shoved him down, smashed the box open, and claimed the coins within. A few young women in livery tried to flee down a staircase; the Elorian troops grabbed them, slung them across their shoulders, and carried them off as if they too were spoils of war.

"Stop this!" Madori said and grabbed one of the Ilari soldiers. "We are liberators, not conquerors."

The man shoved her aside and returned to rummaging through an oak dresser. Madori raced down a corridor into another chamber. Two Elorians were inside, laughing as they tossed a weeping serving girl back and forth.

"Enough!" Madori roared and raced forward. She shoved the Elorians aside, allowing the girl to flee the chamber. "Back to your ships. Back!" She left the chamber and ran along the palace corridor. "Soldiers of Ilar—back to your ships! We've freed this city. Now . . ."

When she passed by a window, her breath died.

Below her, the city of Kingswall was crumbling.

Countless Ilari troops—a hundred thousand or more—were flowing through the city streets, kicking down doors, smashing windows, looting, laughing, killing. The blood of the city flowed. As Madori watched, Ilari troops dragged Idarith priests out of a columned temple and slit their throats on the street. Other Ilari were tugging young women out of homes, tossing them over their shoulders, and carrying them back to their ships. When their husbands and brothers tried to resist, the Ilari answered with swords. The corpses of the city's people—cobblers, tanners, monks, bakers, simple and humble people—piled up.

Madori stood at the window, frozen in terror.

"No," she whispered. "By the stars, no."

A soft voice answered at her side. "It is their reward, child. The spoils of their victory."

Madori turned to see Naiko standing at her side. The older woman stared out at the city, the wind streaming her long white hair, and a smile touched her lips.

"But . . . we came here as liberators," Madori whispered. "We are the heroes. We're on the good side! We are Elorians, warriors of justice. But I see monsters before me."

Naiko stroked Madori's cheek. "Heroes? Liberators? We are invaders, child. When your mother was your age, the sunlit demons invaded her lands. She stood upon the walls of Pahmey, fighting them off, slaying them as they marched through her gates. Her city fell then. And now you, her daughter, are the invader. Now you are the strong one, the conqueror." Naiko's eyes filled with cruel light. "Now the sunlit demons are those who are afraid, who perish. Look at them die, child."

Madori shook her head in horror. "My mother and I are Qaelish! Our empire is peaceful. We're not bloodthirsty like warriors of Ilar. Do you think the Timandrians know the difference between our nations? To them we're all Elorians, all the same, and now you stain my people with your bloodlust. You're no better than Serin."

Madori trembled. *What have we done? We've woken a panther to fight with us . . . and now that panther has gone rabid and cannot be tamed.*

Madori whistled and Grayhem approached her. She climbed onto his back, and she rode.

She rode out of the palace and into the bloody streets. All around her, the Ilari—no, she could not simply think of them as Ilari, as fighters of another land, for they were Elorians like her—the Elorians burned, plundered, murdered. Homes burned. Corpses covered the streets.

"Soldiers of darkness!" Madori cried. "Return to your ships!"

A flash of darkness streamed above. Madori raised her eyes and saw Koyee leaping from roof to roof upon her panther. She too cried out to the soldiers.

"Warriors of the Red Flame, to your ships!" Koyee was shouting.

Few seemed to listen. Madori rode her nightwolf up a temple's staircase, and they leaped onto the balcony, then across an alleyway and onto a home's roof. She stared south across the city toward the river, and new terror flooded her.

The *Tai Lar*, flagship of the Ilari Armada, was sinking.

Madori's heart seemed to freeze. The ship must have suffered cannonfire while she had charged toward the gates; its pagoda was smashed, and one of its masts had fallen. A crack split its deck, and each half of the ship was slowly submerging. The last of its soldiers and sailors were abandoning the wreckage in rowboats.

"Jitomi," Madori whispered.

Even her Yin Shi training could not calm her now.

"Jitomi!" she cried out.

Was he still chained in the brig? Had one of the sailors thought to free him? Madori kneed her nightwolf.

"To the boardwalk, Grayhem! To the ship!"

With a growl, the nightwolf leaped off the roof, vaulted across an alley, and landed atop a tavern. He kept running from roof to roof, traveling south through the city. All around them, Elorians were looting from shops and homes, and the ship kept sinking ahead.

* * * * *

Finally Madori rode out the smashed gates, leaving the city. Grayhem's paws pattered upon corpses. They raced across the boardwalk, and Grayhem leaped into the water. They swam toward the sinking ship, and Madori climbed onto the shattered deck.

"Jitomi!" she shouted.

The deck had split in half, and water gushed within the crack like river in a canyon. The ship's halves tilted inward, and Madori swayed. The battened sails blazed. The remains of the ship's pagoda rained roof tiles. A bronze dragon statue, once perched atop the pagoda, clanged down. Madori stumbled toward the staircase leading into the hull. She raced downstairs toward a torrent of gushing water.

"Jitomi!"

As Grayhem wailed upon the deck, Madori shrugged off her armor. Keeping only her sword, she held her breath and plunged underwater.

She swam down the rest of the staircase, along a corridor, and into the brig. A fish shot by before her eyes. Her lungs ached for air. She saw nothing, only murky water thick with blood and ash. Her chest felt ready to burst, and she swam upwards toward the ceiling. A pocket of air remained here, and when Madori emerged above the water, she gulped that air down. She looked around her. Most of the chamber was flooded; only these few inches of air remained, and—

"Madori!" The voice rose behind her. "Madori, over here!"

She spun around in the water, and she saw him there.

Thank Xen Qae.

Jitomi floated in the water, only his face above the surface. She swam toward him.

"My foot's still chained!" Jitomi said. "Chained to the damn wall."

"Where are the keys?" Madori shouted.

"I don't know! On Naiko."

Madori cursed. The empress was back in the city; if Madori raced to retrieve the keys, Jitomi would drown by the time she returned. Even as Madori swam here now, the water kept rising. Her head pressed against the ceiling; her chin touched the water.

She took a deep breath.

She sank under the water again.

She landed on the floor, her head underwater. Jitomi was standing on a chest, the chain running from his ankle to a metal pole. Her heart sank; the chain was thick, too thick for her sword to cut.

Madori had been chained before; once when led out of Teel, then in Serin's iron mine. She had tried to claim the chains then, to shatter them with her magic, and could not; the metal had been too thick, her power too weak. Yet this turn, she would have to do what she could not then.

She chose the metal links.

She claimed them.

She tried to shatter them . . . and could not.

Her lungs blazed with pain. She rose above the water and gulped air.

"Madori, hurry!" Jitomi said.

She plunged underwater again. She stared at the chains.

Use your Yin Shi! she thought. Yet how could she? Yin Shi relied on breathing, and she couldn't breathe underwater.

Yin Shi is not about breathing, Master Lan Tao seemed to speak in her mind. *It is about awareness. Be aware of the air in your lungs. Be aware of the water, the chains, the battle above, all sounds, all mottles of light.*

Exhaling slowly, Madori made her mind a clear pond, bringing the flooded brig into her awareness, bringing herself into a state of pure Yin Shi.

She chose the chains again.

She claimed then.

Full awareness. Full Yin Shi.

I can't do it! I've tried before!

You were weaker then, younger, afraid. Now you are Yin Shi.

She stared at the metal links.

They shattered.

She rose back up, gulped down air, and grabbed Jitomi's arm. "Swim!"

They swam up the stairs. Just as they emerged above the deck, the water overflowed it, and the ship finally sank beneath them.

The water swallowed the remains of the pagoda, then the masts. Bubbles rose as the last air trapped in the ship escaped, and the river churned. The froth tugged at Madori's feet, and she kicked and floundered, struggling to stay afloat. It felt like sea serpents were grabbing at her feet and tugging her down, and she had a sudden flashback of Pahmey vanishing into the sinkhole. Jitomi too struggled to stay afloat, and then the water gave such a tug that they both sank.

Under the surface, Madori kicked and beat her arms. Her sword tore free from her grasp, and she barely grabbed it before it could sink. Below her, she caught a glimpse of the ship shattering against the riverbed and sliding down into a murky grave of reeds.

She and Jitomi kicked and finally rose back above the water. They swam toward the bank and climbed onto the boardwalk.

Empress Naiko awaited them there, her hands on her hips, a crooked smile on her face. Her dojai stood around her, throwing stars in their hands.

"Growing up," Naiko   said, "my father often spoke of the Qaelish in scorn. He said that our northern neighbors were hardly Elorians at all; he called them weaker than pups who beg for a treat. Sometimes, when he was particularly disgusted with Jitomi's weakness, he would call the boy a Qaelish worm—the ultimate insult." Naiko nodded. "Now, seeing a Qaelish woman—even one mixed with the blood of sunlight—I truly see this weakness my father spoke of. You had the chance to raise your banners upon a conquered city, Madori. And yet you chose to save a drowning rat." Naiko raised her crossbow. "The weak deserve to perish. Ilar has grown strong by culling the cowards among us. Jitomi was meant to die in that river, but so be it; he will die at my crossbow instead."

Madori claimed the crossbow bolt.

It fired, whistling through the air.

Before it could hit Jitomi, Madori shattered the quarrel into a thousand shards. They slammed into Jitomi, drawing blood, but the wounds were skin deep.

As Naiko loaded another quarrel, Madori lunged forward with her sword.

Naiko fired.

Madori swung her blade, knocking the bolt aside. The dojai tossed their throwing stars; Madori claimed them all and froze them in midair. She kept charging. With a curse, Naiko dropped her crossbow and drew her sword.

The two blades slammed together.

Naiko laughed. "Do you think you can defeat me in swordplay? I've slain hundreds of men!" She swung her blade, forcing Madori back. "From childhood, my father would send me prisoners. I would fight them in our courtyard. I would slay them for sport." She swung again, and Madori parried. "No man or woman can defeat me."

The empress's dojai watched, thin smiles on their lips, not approaching; perhaps they knew their mistress enjoyed slaying her enemies herself.

Madori growled and swung her blade. "I am no prisoner. I am a warrior of Yin Shi. I bear Min Tey, Sheytusung renamed, a sword of legend."

With a laugh, Naiko parried and thrust, slicing Madori's arm. Blood spilled.

A growl rose, and Grayhem came racing toward the fray. The nightwolf leaped toward Naiko. With a thin smile, the empress tossed a throwing star. The shard of metal flew and slammed into Grayhem's neck.

The nightwolf yowled and crashed down.

Madori roared with rage. "Damn you!" She leaped toward Naiko, all her Yin Shi training forgotten, surrendering to her rage. She slammed her blade down again and again, as if she were swinging an ax at wooden logs. Naiko parried each attack, her smile growing.

"Good!" the empress said. "Good. Now I see strength. Now I see rage and hatred. Now I see the spirit you lacked in the city. If only you could show such hatred toward our enemies!"

Naiko swung her blade, slicing Madori's fingers.

Madori screamed, blood spurting, her fingers cut down to the bone. Her sword flew from her grasp and clattered against the cobblestones.

Naiko raised her blade above Madori.

"Sweet, innocent mongrel," Naiko whispered, head tilted. "I will gladly slay you first. I'd like my brother to see you die before I kill him too."

Naiko raised her katana further, prepared to swing it down.

Her blade melted.

Hot, molten metal dripped across Naiko's arm, and she screamed in pain.

Jitomi came walking forward. He lifted Min Tey and handed the katana back to Madori.

"Enough of this," Jitomi said. "Enough with violence, with bloodshed, with—"

Naiko dropped her molten sword and reached for a throwing star.

Madori lunged forward and drove Min Tey into the empress's face.

The blade crashed through Naiko's mouth and clattered against the back of her helmet.

"She should have worn her visor down," Madori said and tugged her sword back. The blade emerged, red and dripping. Naiko fell dead to the ground.

Madori knelt by Grayhem. The nightwolf lay on his belly, mewling, and licked her fingers. He yelped when Madori tugged the throwing star free from him; it had sunk deep. Madori sucked in breath, chose his wound, and healed it like she had learned in Magical

Healing class. She turned her attention to her fingers next; they were still bleeding heavily. She healed the cuts, leaving white scars.

As poor as I was at Offensive Magic, I was good at Healing, she thought with a small smile, flexing her fingers.

She turned around to see Jitomi kneeling by his fallen sister, his head lowered. The dojai stared down at their fallen mistress, faces blank. One among them muttered about Naiko's weakness; the others nodded.

Jitomi looked up at Madori. "It's strange," he said softly. "She tried to kill us, but still I grieve for her. Despite her cruelty, she was still my sister."

And the Serins are cousins to the Greenmoats, Madori thought. *And yet I slew Lari, and I will slay her father if I can.* She thought of Ferius, the cruel monk her mother had fought twenty years ago—Madori's uncle. Koyee had slain her own brother in battle. Perhaps in the seas of war, blood was not thicker than water.

Madori and Jitomi turned toward the city. Smoke rose from Kingswall, and the screams of the dying and the cheers of the invaders rose in a sickly symphony. A great black serpent shot through the smoke, and Tianlong came coiling down toward them.

"The city burns!" the dragon said.

Jitomi nodded and climbed onto his back. "My sister has fallen, Tianlong. I rule this army again, and we will withdraw it from the city." Sitting in the saddle, he reached down to Madori. "Fly with me."

She shook her head. "I stay with Grayhem. Bring them back, Jitomi. Bring them back under your rule. We leave this place."

He nodded. The dragon shot into the air and vanished back into the smoke.

Madori had sailed into this city a proud warrior, a liberator, a heroine, her chin raised and her chest puffed out with pride. As the Ilari Armada sailed away, they left behind a smoldering ruin, and Madori could only stand slumped upon their new flagship, head lowered.

"I thought we could save them," she whispered to her mother. "I thought that when Eloria invaded the daylight, we would come here as heroes."

Koyee embraced her and kissed her cheek. Mother and daughter stood together on the deck, staring westward. Past many leagues, deep in sunlight, rose Markfir, capital of the Radian Empire. Serin's home. The end of this war, an end of victory or ruin.

The Armada sailed on.

CHAPTER TEN
FALLEN GOD

Torin ran through the ruins with his ragtag band of fighters. Their
armor was dented and cracked. Mud and blood caked them. Their
beards had grown long, and their hair lay matted across their faces.
They scurried over piles of bricks, through holes in walls, under lone
archways and over fallen columns, mere rats in desolation, barely
men.

"Radians!" Torin shouted hoarsely, pointing.

The enemies came racing down a pile of rubble, firing arrows.
Torin ran toward them. The arrows whistled around him, but Torin
no longer cared. He had not slept or eaten for turns. He no longer
cared if he lived or died. Why should he? So many thousands died
around him every turn. Screaming, he swung his sword at the men.
Around him the others fought. Covered in grime, Cam swung down
his sword, cleaving a boy's skull; they were fighting mere boys now,
soldiers barely old enough to shave.

Within moments, the battle ended. Dozens of bodies covered
the debris.

Hogash, once a guardian of Orewood's gates, plunged his war
hammer down onto a wounded man. Blood splattered. Hogash spat.

"Good work, boys," he said. "Wish we had some ale to
celebrate."

Torin looked around him. He counted thirteen Magerian
corpses, seventeen Verilish ones. He saw no Ardish bodies. There
were no more Ardishmen left to fight, he supposed. Ten thousand
had marched here several months ago; most probably lay under the
rubble now. Torin doubted if any Ardishmen other than him and
Cam lived anywhere in Orewood; sometimes he doubted that any
lived anywhere in the world.

"I'd even go for rat's blood now," Torin said softly. "Ale? You
have lofty dreams."

Hogash laughed. He had once been a bluff man, proud and strong and wide of belly. He looked haggard now, eyes sunken, his laughter sounding more like a hoarse croak.

"More troops will come," Hogash said. He said the same every turn. "The great clans of the northern forests will muster. They'll march here. They'll bring aid."

Cam approached them. Torin had been seeking rats to eat all turn, and Cam looked much like a rat now himself, scrawny and ragged and hairy. "The northern clans did muster," the King of Arden said—or at least, the king of what had once been Arden. "They marched here, Hogash. You remember, don't you? Thousands of them, howling for war." Cam looked around him. "All dead. All under the rubble."

Cam climbed onto a piece of wall that still rose from ruins. It was rare to find walls that still stood in Orewood; most of the city had been leveled. Torin joined him, and they stood together, watching the landscape. Clouds covered the sky, allowing through only several beams of light. The rays fell upon nothing but devastation. The city's outer walls had fallen, taken down with magic and cannons. The city innards were in scarcely better shape. Of the palace only a single tower remained. Some turns the tower held the Radian banner, other turns the Verilish one. It seemed that every few hours, one force reclaimed the tower, only to lose it after another battle. Around that tower spread ruins: fallen temples, burnt homes, collapsed fortresses, and piles of corpses . . . everywhere corpses and the stench of death. Even the city's foundries stood in ruin, and the fabled iron mines lay buried. Without these prizes, Torin didn't even know why they kept fighting.

Orewood, capital of Verilon, had become a graveyard.

But no. Some still lived here. Hundreds, maybe thousands, still arrived every turn. Even now, as Torin looked south, he could see more Radian forces marching to Orewood, lines and lines of troops and wagons and chariots and riders. When he looked north, Torin could see more of Verilon's people traveling toward the ruins: men and women on bears, war hammers across their backs, and lines of children behind them. The children were barely older than twelve or thirteen, but they too held hammers, and they too would fight here.

They too would die. Torin had seen enough reinforcements arriving in Orewood to know: *They will not last more than a turn.*

"A Verilish soldier will only live for a turn on average," he said softly, looking at the line of bears and children. He turned back toward the southern Radian convoy. "A Radian with better armor, with more supplies—he'll last two or three turns, it seems. Idar, Cam. We've lived long, long past the average lifespan in this place."

Cam nodded. "This is the world now, my friend. A world of war. But I would not abandon this city, this pile of rubble. This is where we make our final stand." He gasped suddenly, raced off the wall, and leaped onto a pile of bricks. He grabbed something, laughed, and raised it over his head. "A beetle, Tor! A real beetle."

Torin frowned. "Cockroach. Those spread disease."

Cam shook his head. "Not a cockroach. Beetle. I'll split it with you. I—"

A dozen Verilish soldiers, Hogash among them, heard the young king. They began to advance, raising their hammers and licking their lips. Cam quickly stuffed the beetle into his mouth and swallowed. The Verilish soldiers cursed.

"Sorry, Tor, old boy," Cam said. "Had to eat it all myself. Couldn't let this greedy lot take a bite." He turned toward the north. "We should meet the new arrivals. They might have some food on them—real food."

Torin sighed. "The new arrivals will emerge into the northern quarters. That's a mile away. We'd never make it that way. Ruins are crawling with Radians. One under every brick."

"We've got to die some turn," Cam said with a wry smile. "I say we finally make our way north."

Torin turned to look at the Verilish soldiers. A few more were emerging from the ruins, little pockets of resistance. Every turn, the units fell apart and regrouped, gangs forming and disbanding and forming again. Every turn, most of them died, only for new groups to form. Fifty or more collected around Torin and Cam, weary souls, gaunt, haggard, clad in rags, bleeding, dying, starving.

Torin nodded. "North. We'll give the fresh meat a nice welcome." He grimaced to hear the Radian war drums in the south. "Will get us farther from that nasty lot of Radians too."

They scurried onward.

They raced through the shell of a building, perhaps once a temple, charred bones rising among the bricks. Arrows rained upon them from the walls. They fired back. They hacked with swords. A few of them died. They killed. They kept running.

They scuttled over a pile of collapsed, charred pieces of wood, the homes of the city's denizens. Charred skeletons of children lay around them. Smashed dolls tumbled beneath their feet. A cannon rolled toward them and fired, and the sound nearly deafened them, and three among them collapsed. The survivors kept running. Others joined them. More died. More emerged from the ruins to replace the fallen. They scurried onward.

It felt like they raced for hours, for turns. They found a cellar once; the home around it had fallen. Torin and Cam plunged down into the darkness. They found themselves around bodies, arrows in their chests. Maggots bustled, and the stench was like a living thing, but Torin and Cam slept here for a while. When they woke, they were tempted to eat the corpses, rotted as they were, but thankfully Cam found moldy bread under a fallen shelf. They feasted. They raced onward.

Finally—it could have been turns, it could have been years later—they reached the northern fringe of the city, and they greeted the new Verilish arrivals.

So did thousands of Radian troops.

The Radians raced forth to meet the northerners, to cut into the fresh meat. The Verilish screamed. They were humble foresters, loggers, fishermen, boys, girls. The Radians had been fighting this war for over a year now; they were hardened, survivors, and they slew with every breath, and they laughed as the blood sprayed them.

Torin and Cam watched as the new Verilish recruits fell.

"I thought you said they would last a turn on average," Cam said. Arrows sailed overhead, sinking into a group of charging Verilish bears; the riders upon them were already dead. "Has it been a turn already?"

Torin sighed. "A turn of life seems generous lately."

A group of Verilish boys, perhaps thirteen years old, charged into battle. They wore ragtag pieces of armor. They fought not with swords but with pointed sticks; all the swords of Verilon had been buried. A Radian cannon tore into them, scattering the boys apart. A couple of Radian troops, laughing and spitting, moved between the fallen and speared them, making sure none survived.

"Feel like killing a bit?" Torin asked.

Cam shook his head. "No. But there's nothing better to do here. Onward."

They raced forward. They slew the Radians before them. A few Verilish survivors joined them—a mixture of hardened old men, some of them veterans of the last war, and new recruits. Torin was surprised to see King Ashmog among them. The burly King of Verilon, the man who had once sentenced Torin to be mauled by a bear, was barely recognizable. He was thin now, cadaverous, and his beard had been ripped off, leaving raw cheeks. When he saw Torin, the ruin of a king limped toward him.

"My beard," he said, raising a tattered piece of hair like some old toupee. "I tore it off myself. With my old hands." His voice shook and tears filled his eyes. "They slew so many. My wives. My children. All dead. All dead, Torin." The king fell to his knees, chest heaving with sobs.

Torin patted the man on the shoulder. The clouds parted above, and a golden sunbeam fell upon the ruins. Torin looked and saw that in its light lay the corpse of a great bear, a creature large as a whale. He approached slowly, solemnly, and climbed onto a pile of rubble to stare down at the beast.

"Gashdov," Torin whispered. "The god of Verilon. He has fallen."

King Ashmog came to stand at his side. "You were supposed to save us, Kava Or," he said to Torin. His tears streamed. "You tamed Gashdov. You were prophesied to lead us to victory. And now my kingdom has fallen. Now my god lies dead while I, a man, linger on."

A deep, haunting pain filled Ashmog's eyes, and he tossed back his head and raised his arms, and he roared, a roar that shook the ruins, the roar of a bear.

"And I will die with him!" Ashmog cried. "I will die as he died."

The king tossed down his war hammer. With bare hands, he raced across the ruins toward a fragment of wall where Radians archers stood. Arrows flew, piercing King Ashmog, but still he ran. More arrows slammed into him. He ran onward, howling as if he himself were a bear, and reached the wall.

The Radians cursed and drew their swords. Ashmog scaled the crumbling wall, pierced with many arrows, bellowing with rage. He reached the top and crashed into the Radians, knocking them down, snapping their necks, biting into their throats, roaring as a wild beast until one man finally cut him down, cleaving his skull with a sword.

Ashmog fell from the wall and lay upon ruins, one more corpse, one among the countless.

Torin and Cam looked away. And they scurried on. Always. Live as rats. Hunt the rats. Survive another hour. Another turn. Until more troops arrived and maybe they had food, maybe they had more arrows, maybe they would die instead.

There was no more city to defend, only a nightmare, an afterlife of terror and endless pain.

Until they found hope.

Until they found a family.

It was snowing that turn. It was not yet winter, and yet it was snowing; perhaps the sky had collected so much ash it rained down, flakes of the dead. As the skies seemed to fall, it was under a burrow—a little hovel between two collapsed walls—that they found them.

It was Torin who entered first, seeking food, perhaps wafers from the pocket of a dead man, perhaps mice or beetles, perhaps—and some turn he knew it might come to that—a corpse not yet rotted. And there he saw them. Two figures huddled together, clad in robes, gaunt, eyes huge and haunted.

"Linee," Torin whispered. "Omry."

The Queen of Arden stared at him silently. Her face was pale. She tried to speak but nothing left her lips. Prince Omry reached out a frail hand as if begging for food.

"Linee?" rose Cam's voice behind. "Omry?"

They turned toward him and the king's eyes watered. Cam raced forward and embraced them.

"My wife!" Cam cried out, tears falling. "My son! My son!"

As they embraced, rage filled Torin, and jealousy, and hatred, and he trembled. Why was his wife not here? Why not his daughter? Where were Koyee and Madori?

But then they pulled him into their embrace, and he wept for them too, and he held them close.

"Come," Linee whispered. "We have a tunnel. We wait here sometimes for rain. Worms sometimes come out here in the rain, and they're good to eat. Come deeper."

They followed Linee down a crude crawlway and into a chamber. It was barely larger than a carriage. Two other souls huddled here: little Nitomi and towering Qato, the dojai of Ilar.

The Elorians stared at Torin with huge, glowing eyes.

"Torin," Nitomi whispered. The little woman sat wrapped in a cloak, shivering. For the first time since Torin had known her, the loquacious dojai had spoken only one word.

"Qato scared," whispered her giant companion.

Torin reached into his pockets and pulled out the loaf of bread. He had found it on the corpse of a new Verilish arrival. He had hoped to savor it, to save it for a special occasion; he supposed that occasion was now. They split the bread between them, and they ate silently. There was nothing to drink.

"What do we do?" Linee asked. "The men stay and fight for the smithies, for the smelters, for the mines. At least they did at first. I think now they stay for pride, for desperation, for fear . . . maybe simply because after so much bloodshed, they've forgotten another life. Do we stay and fight, Torin? Do we surrender? Do we flee?"

Torin look at her. He thought back to the first time he had met Linee—a beautiful young queen in Kingswall, silly and flighty, a girl who chased butterflies and loved talking of cupcakes and rainbows. Now her face was ashen, her eyes sunken, her hair scraggly, a ragged survivor. He could scarcely believe this was the same carefree girl he had known.

"The woods are swarming with Radians," Torin said. "Even if we made it south to Kingswall, that city is fallen. The Sern River must be rife with their ships. Perhaps there's nowhere left to go." Torin looked at a hole in the ceiling. A single ray of light fell through, and he saw a single patch of blue sky. A finch fluttered across it, a speck of gold, a symbol of life and hope. His eyes dampened. "There is still hope here. There is still life. We're still alive. I would have us stay and fight. And live. And see birds again, and smell flowers, and eat fresh bread, and live as we once did."

"Can there ever be such life again?" Linee asked.

"I didn't think so many times," Torin replied. "When I fought in Pahmey and saw that city fall to Ferius, I didn't think life could ever rise again. When I watched Yintao burn to the ground, and we fought along the Red Mile, I didn't think there could be more joy or light in the world. Yet we found new life, even after all that death, even after Bailey and Hem fell." His throat tightened. "We survived that war, and we found new life. And we planted new flowers and watched them bloom. And we brought new life into this world. Madori. Tam. Omry." He smiled at the young prince. "And we learned something: There is always hope."

"There is always hope," Linee whispered.

Clouds covered the sky outside. The ray of light vanished. Boots marched above and they heard the screams of a thousand more dying men.

CHAPTER ELEVEN
THE LOST HARP

North of Orida and all other lands of Moth, the *Orin's Blade* drove into ice and would sail no more. The longship had reached the top of the world.

Eris gazed at the wilderness before him. Sheets of ice stretched into the horizon, leading to distant mountains. White hills and boulders spread for miles, and gusts of wind raised swirls of snow. Behind him lay the ocean; before him the arctic.

"The land of giants," he said.

He was thankful for his thick fur cloak; through sheer willpower he stopped his teeth from chattering. His men looked just as cold; frost clung to their mustaches and beards, their faces were pale, and they tightened their furs around them.

Only Yiun Yee, a daughter of the endless night, seemed unaffected by the chill; her homeland was always frigid, and she still only wore her white silk gown. While her body was perhaps not cold, her demeanor was. Eris tried to meet her gaze, but she refused to look at him. For the past few turns, she had barely spoken to him, had shifted aside when he drew near.

She's still upset about the beast I slew, Eris thought. Why would Yiun Yee not understand that he had tried to save her? The serpent had nearly crushed their ship. It had tossed him into the waters and turned toward Yiun Yee. Yet when he had plunged his blade into the creature, saving her life, Yiun Yee had wept, had struck him, pitying the dead beast.

He sighed. He was a warrior. What did he know of pity? He believed in strength. In justice. In noble deeds. His father had cut Yiun Yee, so he had cut his father down. The sea serpent had risen to strike, so he had slain it. And it seemed Yiun Yee still begrudged him both acts.

Eris looked at his hands. They were calloused, blood-stained hands. The hands of a killer, yes, for he had killed with them many times. But they were also warm hands. Hands that longed to hold Yiun Yee, to caress her, to love her. They were hands that had claimed the Meadenhorn, that he would see cleanse Orida of evil.

Yet she only sees the bloodstains.

He strapped his shield across his back, climbed out of the longship, and landed on the ice. He looked back to his wife and his Oringard. "We walk from here. We're close."

They followed, taking with them their meager supplies: the last few skins of ale, a few fur blankets, what bundles of firewood remained, and what fish they had caught in the sea. Eris left two men to guard the longship—both had been wounded in the battle with Torumun, and the trek through the ice would only weaken them. The rest trudged northward into the endless white.

They walked for hours, their fur cloaks soon coated with frost and snow. A single banner rose above them, displaying an orca upon a white field. The arctic spread on. Drifts of snow. Great pillars and plains of ice. A bright white sun that would not warm them. The longship vanished behind them; the white would not end. Eris felt so small here; him and his men, such doughty men, were but specks here, lost in the wild.

But they were not the only life here. A turn into their march, they saw polar bears ahead, creatures that no longer lived in Orida; old pelts of their fur were all that remained of them back home. They shot one down with his arrows, and they camped for a short while, built a fire from their remaining logs, and ate the animal's meat. They walked on.

Ice.

Snow.

Shivering cold and endless white light.

As he trudged forward, covered in frost, the visions keep appearing before him; the arctic was a blank canvas for his memories. He kept seeing it again and again: returning home as a hero, only to see the Radian banner in his hall, to find his mother dead, to find Iselda, sister of a tyrant, in her place; his father swinging his sword and cutting Yiun Yee; Eris's own sword impaling the king, the blood that washed his hands, the terrible guilt, the sin of patricide he would never be cleansed of. It was a white land but his memories were red.

He looked toward Yiun Yee. Throughout his long years in shadow, seeking the lost horn of Orin, he had found comfort in her, a love and light that had guided him even in the darkness of endless night. And now, more than ever, he needed that comfort from her. He was tall and strong, among the mightiest fighters in his realm, but he needed her. And perhaps more than the blood on his hands, more even than the fall of his kingdom, he grieved for the coldness he now saw in her eyes.

"Yiun Yee," he said softly and drew nearer to her. "For long turns you've walked in silence, alone, no longer at my side. I cannot bring the wingless dragon back to life, but please do not let your love die too. Will you forgive a foolish warrior? I'm a man of the sword, not the heart; that you knew when we wed. Please, Yiun Yee, be my heart. Be the soul that I lack. Don't walk without me."

She lowered her head, and when she looked back up, tears filled her large indigo eyes. She stepped closer to him, and she held his hand. "You do not lack a soul, my husband," she whispered. "And you do not lack a heart. They call the cruel heartless. They call killers soulless. It is not so. Those whose hearts hurt, whose souls suffer— they shed more blood than heartless or soulless men."

"Will you then heal this heart, mend this soul?"

She nodded silently, a tear on her cheek, and squeezed his hand. They walked onward together, hands clasped.

They had walked for another turn, maybe two, before they reached the city of giants.

Had Eris not read about this place in countless epic tales, he might have thought it simply part of the wilderness. There were no buildings here, no roads, not even any tents or caves. But here was a city nonetheless, the place he had read about as a wide-eyed child, dreaming of adventure. Great henges of blue ice rose upon hills, each shard taller than the palace of Grenstad back home. Though the ocean was many miles away, the skeletons of whales rose from the ice, half-submerged, their ribs forming archways like the naves of temples. A great animal's skull, large as a mead hall, stared at the approaching Oridians, its fangs thrust into the ice like two columns.

Chunks of ice and stone lay strewn here in a field, and mountains rose all around like the walls of a great fort.

"Jotunheimr," Eris whispered in awe. "The land of giants."

Yiun Yee tightened her silk robe around her. "I see no one."

The Oringard glanced around with darting eyes and hefted their shields. Their hands strayed near their swords and axes. The old tales spoke of Orin taming the giants to his cause, leading them to cleanse Orida of spirits and ghosts, but in even older tales the jotnar—giants of the arctic—were vicious beasts who crushed the villages of men and fed upon the bones of children. Even under Orin's command, they were said to have gone into great rages, as likely to slay their allies as their enemies.

Eris took a step closer. He passed under the ribs of a whale, walking deeper into this land of bones and ice. The crystals of a henge rose to his left. Shards of shattered ice lay ahead like felled trees.

He raised the Meadenhorn above his head. "Jotnar! Hear me. I am Eris Grimgard, son of Bormund, defeater of Veniran the Half-Troll, slayer of the dragon Imoogi, descendant of Orin himself. I bear the Meadenhorn. Rise and meet me!"

Only a breeze and rustling snow replied.

No giants.

A dead city.

"This is a graveyard," said Halgyr. The beefy captain of the Oringard stared around with narrowed eyes. "Nothing but bones. The jotnar have left this place, if ever they lived here."

Eris shook his head. "They're here."

He took a step deeper into the jagged landscape, and before him he beheld a great pillar of ice, twice the height of a man, and within it shone a golden harp. Light gleamed through the crystal and gilded the harp strings like sunlight upon dewy cobwebs.

"The Harp of Lin Shai!" Yiun Yee whispered in awe. "It once was played in the halls of Leen, but it was lost to us many years ago. They say that only the royal family of Leen could play its music, and that any other musician, gifted as he or she may be, would produce only jarring notes." Her eyes watered. "It was a great heirloom of my family. And here it is, frozen in the northern sunlight."

She placed a hand upon the ice.

Trapped within the pillar, the harp glowed. The crystal emitted a single note, high and pure.

Yiun Yee gasped and withdrew her hand.

The landscape began to shake. Cracks appeared in the ice. Snow shifted. Rocks flowed down rising slopes. The henges of icy shards creaked and tilted. The landscape groaned like a creature awakening from slumber.

"What happened?" Yiun Yee whispered.

"I think you just rang the bell over their front door," Eris said.

The land trembled. Cracks raced across the ice, and the skeletons of whales shifted, their spines clattering and rising as if still alive. The icy shards forming the henges began to rise, growing taller, tilting and clinging together, taking new forms. Rocks rose into the air, flying toward the shards and snapping into place. Snow swirled and bones drove through ice like knives into flesh.

Eris gasped. The Oringard drew their swords. Before them, the ice, bones, and rocks clumped together, forming a score of giants.

The jotnar were craggy, weathered creatures. The bones of whales creaked within them, visible through their cracked, icy flesh. Frosted beards hung from their stony cheeks, and rocks shifted and grumbled within their bellies. Icicles formed their claws and teeth, and their faces were long, ugly things like ice grown over corpses. They drew nearer, hulking, staring down at Eris and his companions.

One among them wore a crown of icy crystals, and within each crystal rose the bones of a man's arm and hand. This jotun was taller than the others, and frosted hair fell across his rocky shoulders. A small heart, no larger than a man's fist, beat within his opaque chest, a pulsing red clump that spread out swirls of blood. Here stood Ymir, King of Frost, Lord of the Jotnar.

"Who has played the Harp of Shadow?" rumbled the giant, his voice like avalanches, like cracking boulders. "Who has woken us from our long sleep?"

Eris stepped closer to the frosted king. The jotun towered above him, thrice his height, the blood of his heart trickling down through his frozen limbs, red serpents trapped in ice. "Hear me,

Ymir, King of Frost! I am Eris, son of Bormund, descended of Orin who once led you to battle. I—"

"Who *led* us?" King Ymir's voice rose in a thunder, a sound so loud cracks raced along the ground, and Yiun Yee covered her ears with a grimace. "No mortal born of woman's womb has ever led the jotnar, for we are gods of the north, deities of ice. We answered Orin's plea for aid, for he was a noble man with god's blood."

"His blood flows within me," said Eris, remembering again how he had stabbed his father, how the blood of Grimgard, his royal house, had covered his hands.

"The blood of Orin has been diluted," said Ymir. "It is like a sculpture of ice, once grand, chipped away year after year, left to the mercy of the wind and winters, until it grows so small it becomes but a forgotten lump in an unforgiving hinterland. Thus has the House of Grimgarg fallen from glory, remaining but a band of islanders who'd sooner guzzle mead in thatch-roofed huts than ride to glorious battles or heed the council of their gods."

"I would heed your council were you to give it," said Eris, "were you to sit in our halls as you did of old, sharing your wisdom. If you would aid me now, as you aided Orin, I would see you returned to the Orinhall, honored guests, and would share our mead with you from the fabled horn which I bear." He raised the Meadenhorn again. "But the Orinhall has fallen to evil. Iselda, the Witch of Radian, has tempted my father, and then my brother after him. You spoke of Orin's blood diluted; she would pump that blood full of poison, forever vanquishing any hope of House Grimgarg's return to its old glory. If you still care for the blood of my house, for the descendants of Orin whom you've aided before, return with me now to my isle. Orin called upon you at his hour of greatest need, and you rid his land of the spirits that tormented men. Return with me now! Help me fight, jotun. Help me cleanse my hall of the sorceress, of the eclipse banner that hangs upon its walls."

"And rid it of your brother, of Prince Torumun?" said Ymir. "Yes, son of Orin, I know of your brother, your elder. With one hand, you would cleanse the hall of its foreign banners. With the other, you would strike your brother down, seeking to usurp him and claim his rightful throne."

Eris felt rage flare within him. He took a step closer to the giant. "My brother forfeited his throne when he aligned himself with the Magerian witch."

"And you forfeited all your bonds of family when you slew your father." Fresh, bright blood pumped through Ymir's icy body. "I know of your sin, and I will not aid you, lesser son of a house long fallen from glory. You may bear his horn, but you are not the hero Orin was."

Eris felt the old rage rise in him, the rage that had led him to slay so many enemies, to slay his own father, to slay the wingless dragon as it lay meekly upon his ship. He wanted to charge at the giant, to swing his sword, to cut through its heart. Yet he stilled his hand. Perhaps Yiun Yee had weakened him. Perhaps she had made him wiser.

A harp's note sounded again.

Eris turned his head.

Yiun Yee had placed her hands upon the icy crystal that contained the harp. Her hands did not touch the strings, for they were embedded deep within the ice, yet as she moved her fingers upon that ice, the harp sang. It sounded to Eris almost like a human voice, as if the harp were alive and crying out mournfully, a song beautiful yet sad.

"Harps are made to sing," she said softly as she played, moving her hands across the ice. "It's a saying in our land. I was never skillful at music, no matter how many times I wished to be a musician like the heroine Koyee. But here is the harp of my family. Here is the song of my home. Harps are made to sing, and mead is made for drinking, and homes cannot be lost." She looked at the giant. "This I know. Here is the song of my home, and that home awaits me in the darkness. Do not let my husband's home fall to ruin."

Her music continued, the harp strings trembling inside their icy prison, and the song was so beautiful, so mournful, that even the Oringard fell to their knees and wept to hear it. The giants gathered close, forming a ring around Yiun Yee and her music, and they too wept, their tears flowing down their icy cheeks.

"Harps are made to sing," whispered Ymir, King of the Jotnar. "For many years, we tried to play this harp, yet it sounded like a wounded animal, broken, afraid. We feared for it. We placed it in an altar of ice to protect its beauty." The giant fell to his knees, cracking the ice beneath him, and his tears flowed. "Yet the beauty of its song is one greater than I had ever imagined. Here is the song of a home, of a family."

Yiun Yee's fingers fluttered against the ice, playing her music. "And I have a new family now, Lord of Frost. For I am wed to Eris, and his hall is now my home too. Will you help us reclaim it? Not for glory. Not for the memory of old heroes long buried. But for the music of a home, for the light that can still fill frozen hearts."

The giants looked at one another, then down at Eris and Yiun Yee. She lowered her hands, and her song faded with a last quivering note.

For long moments, Ymir was silent. Then, slow as the beats of a frozen heart, the giant raised his hand, and he pointed southward. To the sea. To Orida beyond. He spoke in a voice deep as the oceans and unforgiving as the plains of ice upon which he lived.

"The jotnar will march."

CHAPTER TWELVE
THE ELEPHANTS OF SANIA

Neekeya no longer had the strength to row. She let the waves wash her boat ashore. When finally her boat rested in the sand, she stumbled out, took a few steps forward, and fell face down onto the beach. She kissed the sand, laughing weakly, her eyes too dry to shed tears. The shore was grainy, salty, filling her mouth. She lay prostrated, too weak to rise. A wave rushed over her, pushing her a few inches forward, then tugging her back toward the ocean.

Neekeya crawled. She dragged herself a foot forward. Then another. The water tugged at her feet, and she stared down at the beach, and she realized for the first time that universes existed within sand. These were not simply faceless grains but tiny rocks, each one a unique world, exoskeletons no larger than specks of dust, tiny seashells of all shapes, countless creatures and structures, an entire cosmos.

Do you too struggle and bleed? she thought, the sand on her lips. *Do you too fight and die and hope?*

Her eyes fluttered shut. Her cheek hit the shore, and the sun baked her, and she slept.

When she woke, she found seaweed tangled around her limbs. She chewed the long, rubbery leaves and the beads of fruit, finding some new vigor in the meal. A mollusk washed ashore, a little creature with a swirling shell. She cracked the shell open and drank the gooey saltiness within. This gave her enough strength to rise to her feet and look around.

Palm trees rose across the shore. The beach stretched out east and west. In the distance, she saw a hut built of wood and straw. Perhaps there would be aid there. Fresh water. Medicine for her feverish brow. She took a step across the sand. Her head spun. When she gazed down her body, she saw thin limbs caked with sand and salt, peeking through rents in her ragged cloak. She kept walking toward the hut, each step a battle.

The hut grew nearer, shaded under palms, and Neekeya saw a garden outside full of squash, beans, and bell peppers. Strings of fish hung outside to dry. An elderly man knelt in the garden, tending to the plants, and raised his head as Neekeya approached.

Neekeya took one more step closer, then fell again.

Once more she slept.

When finally she woke, she found herself lying in a hammock. She blinked feebly. Reed walls rose around her and a straw roof stretched overhead. Gourds stood on a windowsill, and outside she could see the ocean. An empty, dusty crib stood in the corner. Neekeya's eyes widened to see a ewer of water at her side. She drank greedily. The water was cold and infused with berries, sweet and wonderful. It dripped down her chin and neck and flowed down her throat, filling her with healing energy.

She climbed out of the hammock, opened a reed door, and stumbled out of the hut into the sunlight. The old man was back in his garden, watering a trellis of beans. He turned toward her and smiled.

"Are you ready for a meal?"

He had a brown, leathery face, and his eyes were kind, though Neekeya thought there was sadness in them too. Most of his teeth were missing, and his hair was white as snow. He wore a cotton tunic and a necklace of clay beads. He spoke Sanian, which Neekeya spoke well; the language was similar to the tongue of Daenor, for both people were from the same southern family of nations.

Neekeya nodded. "Thank you, elder."

He led her toward a table in the garden in the shade of palms. A little path, lined with flowers, led toward the beach, and the waves whispered. She sat in a wicker chair, and the elder brought out two plates. Upon each rested a fried fish, diced bell peppers, and spiced beans mixed with chilies. Neekeya wanted to be polite, to nibble her meal like a proper *latani*, but she was too famished. She bolted it down.

"Slow down!" the elder said, laughing. "You will choke on a fish bone."

"I thank you again," she said.

He bowed his head. "I am grateful for company. For many years I've lived here alone." That sadness returned to his eyes. "You are a child of Daenor. I hear it in your accent."

She nodded. "I sailed here alone from across the sea."

His eyes widened. "You are brave! That is a great journey even for large ships manned by many sailors."

"Brave or foolish," she said softly. She thought back to those turns before leaving into the sea—a widow consumed with grief, stumbling weak out of the marshes, desperate for any aid she could find, perhaps courting death. Perhaps yes, more foolish than brave, but at least she was a living fool.

She stayed with the kind old man for several turns, slowly recovering her strength. In payment for food, water, and shelter, she helped work in his gardens, patched his roof, and sang to him many old songs of Daenor which soothed him. Neekeya wished she could have stayed here forever, but she knew she must go on, to seek the city of Nhor in the Sanian savannah. As a child, Neekeya had met the royal family of Sania; they had visited her father in his pyramid. She remembered little of that visit, for she had been very young, but if they remembered her, and if they still held love for her family, perhaps they would aid her.

Finally, on her seventh turn with the old man, she felt strong enough to continue her journey.

"I'm sad to see you leave," said the old man. "Please take this with you, a parting gift." He handed her a tunic made from zebra fur, a garment finer than the tattered woolen tunic she wore. "It belonged to my wife . . . many years ago."

She accepted the gift, stepped into the hut, and donned the tunic. It fit her snugly, soft and warm and comforting.

"I will return here some turn," she said when she stepped back outside. "I will return with coins and gemstones to repay you."

"What use have I for coins or gemstones?" said the old man, laughing. "They are pretty things, perhaps, but with your company, you paid me a far greater treasure. Return not with gems and coins but with more songs, with more smiles. Return to warm an old man's heart in his final years alone upon the shore."

She nodded. "I will return." She kissed his leathery cheek.

She left the hut.

She walked south, heading between the trees, leaving the coast behind.

Across her back, she carried a leather pouch full of vegetables and fish. The palm trees gave way to pines, then to groves of acacia trees. She walked for what felt like a turn before she slept, then walked again. She navigated by the sun, keeping it at her back. Here in the deep southern hemisphere of Mythimna, the sun always hung a little lower in the sky, bright and hot but casting long shadows. On her second turn of walking, she reached the savannah.

The grasslands spread into the horizon, rustling in the wind. The grass was knee-high and golden, a second sea. Acacia trees rose in clumps like leafy islands, and distant yellow mountains rose from haze. In the maps Neekeya had seen, the fabled city of Nhon, capital of Sania, lay south from here by a great lake. Her books back home claimed that all Daenorians had come from Sania, immigrating north across the sea thousands of years ago, perhaps to escape famine or war, settling in the swamps and building great pyramids. Perhaps finding Nhon would feel like coming home.

As she kept walking, she saw tall, mottled animals ahead, stretching up their long necks to feed from the acacias.

Giraffes, she realized. She had heard of such animals, even had a wooden doll of one as a child. Her father had often called her a giraffe, for she had sprouted up tall at a young age. She smiled and approached them, hoping to see one close. Her father would never believe she actually saw one, he—

Her smile died.

She lowered her head.

My father is dead, she thought. *And so is my husband.* It was funny how the pain of losing them never left her, and yet she so easily still thought of them as alive.

She tightened her lips and kept walking. The priests of Cetela back home claimed that dead souls could reincarnate, returning to life as animals. Perhaps the giraffes ahead, these gentle giants, had once been men and women. Perhaps her father and husband would return, maybe even to this place, to roam the savannah. Neekeya did not know if those stories were true or simply tales to comfort the grieving, but perhaps now she needed comfort more than truth.

She kept walking, drawing closer to the mountains. The sun seemed to grow warmer with every step, and Neekeya soon ran out of water. A river flowed in the distance, and she saw animals approaching to drink—herds of wildebeests, antelopes, and hyenas. Pelicans and finches flocked above in great clouds. Mouth dry, Neekeya walked through the grasslands toward the water, seeking a clear spot on the bank.

She was only a few steps away when the growls rose behind her.

She spun around and hissed.

A lion crouched in the grass, staring at her, ready to pounce. The grass rustled around her, and Neekeya whipped her head from side to side. Several more lions padded closer, eyes golden and gleaming. They surrounded her, and they were hungry. They snarled, fangs bare.

Neekeya bared her own teeth right back at them.

I wrestled crocodiles in the swamps, she thought. *I faced down hordes of soldiers and dark mages. I will not cower from lions.*

Her sword was gone to the sea; instead, she lifted a branch and swung it in wide arcs. "Back! Back, beasts! Back or I'll hit you."

The lions growled and their fur bristled. Neekeya growled right back.

"Get back!" She stamped her feet, swinging her branch madly.

The lions hissed, then turned tail and fled.

Neekeya nodded in satisfaction and lowered her branch.

"Keep on running!" she called after them, pride welling inside her. "I beat crocodiles, and I can beat you. Get lost, cats! Get—"

Roars rose behind her, drowning her words.

Neekeya spun around, and her heart leaped into her throat.

Oh Cetela . . .

A dozen hippopotamuses, each quite a bit larger and angrier than a lion, were emerging from the river, rage in their eyes.

Neekeya did not bother swinging her branch this time. She ran after the lions. Behind her, the earth rumbled as the hippopotamuses chased. When she glanced over her shoulder, she felt the blood drain from her face. For such large, rounded beasts, they ran at a ferocious speed. Their mouths opened wide, revealing fangs like swords and gullets that Neekeya thought could swallow her whole. They were quickly gaining on her.

Had she survived battling Serin on the road, facing armies on the mountains and in the swamps, and crossing the sea to die here like this, a hunted beast, a death no nobler than that of a hunted antelope?

Her ankle twisted on a hidden rock and Neekeya fell. She flipped onto her back to see the hippopotamuses trundling toward her, and she raised her fists, prepared to fight before they trampled her and tore her apart.

Shards whistled above her.

Yipping battle cries rose.

Shadows fell upon her, and Neekeya leaped aside. A herd of elephants raced across the grasslands, beasts even larger than those chasing her. On their backs rode men and women clad in fur and feathers, and they fired bows with red fletching. The arrows sank into the hippopotamuses, drawing blood. The great river-beasts roared in pain, turned, and fled back into the water.

Neekeya leaped to her feet. The lions and hippopotamuses were gone. Now fifty elephants, each topped with an archer, surrounded her, and those arrows were pointed right at her chest.

"Sania just keeps getting better all the time," she muttered.

She had seen elephants before—Nayan warriors, bearing Serin's banners, had ridden them across Teekat Mountains into Daenor. These beasts were even larger, a breed with wider ears and longer tusks, creatures of the savannah rather than the jungle, symbols of Sania. Red and yellow rings were painted onto their tusks, and tasseled saddle bags hung across their wrinkly hides. Headdresses of gold and gemstones lay upon their lumpy brows. The riders on their backs sported just as much splendor. Red and white paint covered their bare chests, and many necklaces of beads, silver, gold, and gemstones hung around their necks. They wore skirts of colorful patches, and their hair hung in many braids, each braid tipped with a ring of precious metal. Arrows and spears hung across their backs, and they held bows engraved with holy runes.

One of the riders dismounted and landed in the grass before Neekeya. He walked toward her and frowned. Neekeya was a tall woman, but this man towered over her. His chest was bare and wide, and golden rings were painted around his arms. A golden amulet hung around his neck, engraved with an elephant's head, and he bore a feathered spear and wicker shield.

"Are you lost, wanderer?" the man said. "You are many leagues from Nhon, Atan Nor, or the plains where the wild tribes roam."

"I'm seeking Nhon," she replied. "I'm not lost but a traveler from across the sea. I am Neekeya, daughter of Kee'an, a *latani* of Daenor."

The man's eyes widened. "Neekeya?" he whispered.

She tilted her head and narrowed her eyes. "That's my name. Would you give me yours?"

He laughed and rubbed his eyes. "By the gods! It is you. I am Kota, son of King Odiga."

Now Neekeya's eyes were those to widen. "Kota! By Cetela, you've grown. You were a scrawny boy last time I saw you."

He laughed again. "And you were a little girl with scraped knees, speaking of magical artifacts, swamp monsters, and old spellbooks. It was many years ago, but I still have fond memories of my visit to Daenor." His smile faded, and he lowered his head. "I grieved to hear of the marshlands falling to the Radian enemy. We've just returned from the port of Atan Nor where Radian ships have been attacking. We repelled them but they muster still, flowing south from the marshlands that they claimed."

"Kota!" rose a voice from behind him. "She doesn't need to hear about our wars and the movements of troops. She's weary and thirsty and far from home, and you're regaling her with dull tales of your heroics."

A second rider leaped off an elephant and came walking toward them. She was slender and bore a spear bedecked with many feathers. Like Kota, she wore her hair braided. Her skin was dark and bared to the sun, aside from a beaded loincloth and many beaded necklaces that hid her chest. Arrows fletched with wide, red feathers peeked above her shoulder. She smiled at Neekeya, a smile of kindness and warmth.

"Adisa?" Neekeya whispered. "It *is* you."

The young Princess of Sania nodded. "I was only a little one when we last met. As were you." She approached Neekeya, hugged her, then handed her a water gourd. "Drink, Neekeya, then ride with me. We return to Nhon."

They refilled their gourds in the river, let their elephants drink, and then headed south through the savannah. Neekeya shared a saddle with Princess Adisa. She had never ridden on an animal before, not even a horse, and here upon the elephant she felt powerful as if she too were a princess of Sania.

They traveled for long hours through the grasslands until finally Neekeya saw the city ahead.

Forested hills rose in the distance, encircling a great shimmering lake. Mist hovered between the trees, and flocks of birds flew above in great clouds. From the forest rose many stone buildings, grand structures with many arches, thin towers, and steeples. The bricks were painted red and gold, the colors faded as if centuries old. Neekeya had never seen a grander city; this place would dwarf even Kingswall, the largest city she had seen in the mainland of Timandra.

Princess Adisa, who sat in front of Neekeya in the saddle, twisted around to face her. "Behold Nhon, capital of Sania. My home."

They rode on, leaving the grasslands and traveling across the forested hills. The trees grew so densely Neekeya didn't see the city walls until they were upon them. Those walls soared above them, craggy and mossy, weeds growing between their bricks. Two massive statues of elephants rose here, hundreds of feet high, robed in lichen and vines. Between these stone sentinels rose an archway that led into the city. The fifty elephants and their riders rode through the gates, entering Nhon.

They rode down a cobbled boulevard between palisades of baobab trees. Many buildings rose at their sides, constructed of heavy bricks, their arches lofty, their windows tall and thin. Monkeys leaped upon roofs and branches, and parrots flocked overhead, singing. As the procession made its way down the road, the city people came out to cheer for the heroes' return. They wore bright garments of stripes and checkers, and rings of many metals hung around their necks and arms.

Kota rode his elephant up beside Neekeya. The Prince of Sania—the boy she had known grown into a man—smiled at her. "What do you think of our home, Neekeya?"

She forced herself to smile back at him. "A place of wonder."

His smile widened, and pride in his city swelled his chest. But Neekeya's own smile was feigned. This was a city of wonder, it was true; its towers of painted bricks, palisades of trees, and wildlife were things of beauty. Yet as Neekeya rode the elephant through the city, she saw Kingswall fallen to the enemy, its gates smashed. She saw the pyramids of Eetek crumble. She saw the Radian rallies in Teel University, simmering cauldrons of hate that now spilled across Moth. As she looked around her, Neekeya could only imagine this place too crashing to the ground.

I must find aid here, she thought. *I must convince the king of this realm to sail north with me, to fight back . . . or even this distant island will burn.*

A cliff rose ahead, leafy with vines, and a waterfall crashed down the stone facade into the lake. Between stone and water rose the Palace of Sania, built of gray bricks and topped with three silver domes. Many guards stood here, clad in feathers, beads, and bronze-tipped spears. The elephant procession made its way toward the palace gates, and the riders dismounted. The waterfall crashed down at their side, spraying them with mist, and the palace archway loomed above, its keystone carved into the face of an elephant.

"You will speak with my father," Kota said to Neekeya, suddenly solemn. "We've been fighting the Radians along our coast ever since Eseer and Daenor fell. He would very much like to hear your tale, I believe."

"And I would very much like to tell it," Neekeya said.

Princess Adisa clasped Neekeya's hand. The princess gazed at her with soft eyes. "I'm with you, my friend. You're safe here."

The three entered the palace together—a tall prince, a young princess, and a *latani* of the northern marshlands. Neekeya found herself in a wide stone hall, its floor a great mosaic depicting many animals of the savannah; she saw lions, zebras, giraffes, and many elephants. Tall narrow windows broke the walls, letting in beams of sunlight. Trees grew inside the hall from stone pots, reaching toward the ceiling, and birds flitted between them. At the back of the hall, upon a stone throne, sat the king.

King Odiga was a large man, long of limbs and wide of belly, and he wore a lavish tunic of red cloth, a golden elephant upon the chest. Chains of gold hung around his neck and arms, and a crown inlaid with turquoise and sapphire topped his balding head.

He rose as his children entered the hall. "Kota! Adisa!"

The tall prince approached his father. He upended a sack, spilling out small metal eclipses—Radian pins.

"Ten of the enemy's ships assaulted the port of Atan Nor," Kota said. "A thousand men emerged from them, bearing the Radian banners. The commanders were Magerians, but most of the fighters were from Eseer and Naya. The city's defenses stood."

King Odiga's laughter rolled across the hall, and he clasped his son's shoulders. "We have repelled the enemy!"

Kota's eyes remained dark. "They struck with a thousand men. Perhaps they underestimated the strength of Sania. Perhaps they were testing that strength. But . . . father, many more gather in Eseer and Daenor. With me is Neekeya, daughter of Kee'an, who fled the devastation in Daenor. She speaks of great armies that muster there." He turned toward Neekeya. "Step forth, friend, and speak of what you saw."

Adisa squeezed Neekeya's hand. The princess whispered, "Be strong. I'm with you."

The two women stepped forward—a swamp warrior and a savannah princess. King Odiga approached Neekeya and examined her with narrowed eyes.

"Neekeya," he said. "I've not seen you in many years. Your father is a dear friend of mine. Hunting with him in the savannah and visiting his northern pyramids are among my dearest memories. I grieved to hear of Daenor's fall. Your father, is he . . ."

"Fallen as well," Neekeya said.

Odiga lowered his head. "I mourn him. Across the city, we will lower the banners of Sania in his memory, and I will host a vigil in his honor."

"I thank you, my king, and you deeply honor my father," Neekeya said, "but we have little time for ceremony, little time for grief. Sania is not safe, despite one assault repelled. Many thousands of Radians invaded my land, and I saw many of their ships mustering in our fallen port. I fear that more will sail here, a great armada, an army far larger than the one you've repelled. I've come here to bring you these tidings and to seek aid."

The corpulent king nodded. "You will find aid here, Neekeya, my friend. We will shelter you in this palace, and I will treat you as a daughter." He turned toward his son. "Kota, we must further defend the coast. I will send you back with a thousand men, and we will raise more among the southern tribes. I'll send masons and builders too; we will raise walls. Our island will not fall."

Neekeya took a deep breath and raised her head. "My king, when I warned my father about the Radian menace, I urged him to attack Markfir, capital of the Radian Empire. My father chose to stay in the marshlands, hoping Teeket Mountains defend us. Our land fell, and Teeket is greater than any wall. I would urge you to do what my father would not. Sail north! I will lead you through the swamps of Daenor and to the mountain pass. Fall upon Markfir and besiege its walls! Strike the snake's head rather than build walls and hope he does not slither over them."

The king's eyes darkened. "A sea guards a realm better than a mountain. Serin might have a mighty army on land, but his fleet is weak; men speak of the Elorians smashing many of his ships in the darkness of night. Neekeya, your father was a dear friend, and I mourn him, but I will not allow you to speak of war in my hall. War is a game for men, too harsh for women to play."

Princess Adisa snorted and spoke for the first time. "Yet you've sent me to war, Father, and I return to you a champion. I slew a dozen Radians upon the coast, and women fight among them too. Neekeya is wise. And you would be wise to listen to her."

King Odiga's face twisted, and a spark of rage filled his eyes. "What have I done to have my command questioned in my own hall! I offered Neekeya shelter. I could have easily sold her to Serin; he would pay greatly to possess the daughter of his marshland enemy. I could sell her still."

Neekeya gasped. She had thought to find shelter here, thought the king was wise and kind, yet now she saw a beast, a man who'd sell her for coin. She balled up her fists, prepared to fight, but Adisa placed a hand on her shoulder. The princess stared at Neekeya as if to say, *Leave him to me.*

"If you speak of such matters again, Father," Adisa said, turning back toward the king, "I would leave your hall and never more return. So would my brother." She turned toward Kota. "Wouldn't you?"

The tall warrior nodded, face stern. "I would. Neekeya is a friend of ours. Father, show her respect, I urge you. And I urge you to heed to her counsel."

Odiga roared, spraying saliva. "Heed her counsel? Sail north with an army, bog ourselves down in a swamp, die upon the mountains? For what, to save the mainland? When has Timandra's mainland ever cared about us?" He pointed a shaky finger at Neekeya. "Forever have the northern lands, the left wing of the world's moth, gazed down upon Sania in contempt. An island. A benighted wasteland, they think us. Why should I not let that mainland burn?"

Neekeya steeled herself. Perhaps this king was too brazen to fear a Radian invasion, but if she judged him right, she could tempt him with treasures.

"You wanted to sell me for coins," Neekeya said, meeting and holding his gaze. "Perhaps treasure is what you care for. So I will give you treasure." She looked toward Kota, and her eyes stung, and her belly twisted, but she knew she must do this. She looked back at the king. "Sail north with me, liberate my land . . . and I will give you that land. I will marry your son, so that your family rules the marshlands with me."

For a moment silence filled the hall. Prince Kota stared at her with wide eyes. Princess Adisa covered her mouth. King Odiga, meanwhile, narrowed his eyes shrewdly and tapped his chin.

Finally the king spoke, "You are not only a warrior and survivor, Neekeya. You are also a stateswoman."

She nodded. "Many suitors knocked on my father's door. I turned them all back. But I would wed now, and I would share the marshlands with your family, with your heir. But first you must reclaim those marshlands from the enemy. You spoke of the mainland scorning you." She smiled shakily. "So claim a piece of that mainland."

To her surprise, Kota knelt before her, and he held her hands. "*Latani*, you are wise, beautiful, and strong. But would you not ask me first how I feel about this marriage?"

"I don't have to," she whispered. "I saw how you gazed at me on our journey here."

Kota smiled, a smile blending embarrassment and mirth. "Then if my father approves, I vow to you: I will fight for you. I will reclaim your homeland from the enemy, and I will cross the mountains and attack that enemy at his doorstep."

They all looked at the king. Odiga stepped toward them and placed his hand on Neekeya's shoulder. "I told you that I would shelter you as a daughter, but now you will become a true daughter of Sania. We will form an alliance, Neekeya of Daenor, and we will celebrate the betrothal with a great feast. And then we will march to war."

Kota cried out in approval, and even Princess Adisa nodded and grinned. But Neekeya only closed her eyes, feeling the tears gather, and her chest shook.

Forgive me, Tam, she thought. *Forgive me. I love you and I'm sorry.*

CHAPTER THIRTEEN
THE MARCH OF GIANTS

In her dreams, even so many years later, Koyee still walked along the streets of Pahmey.

As she lay in her hammock in the belly of an Ilari ship, she found herself standing in Bluefeather Corner, covered in grime. She wore only a tattered old tunic of nightwolf fur, and she played a flute of bone. Ahead of her, the towering bluefeathers stood in their corral, clacking their beaks and beating their eyelids. The old soothsayer slumbered in the corner, while the delicious scents of mushroom soup wafted from the Fat Philosopher tavern. The city folk walked by as Koyee played her music: young women in silk dresses, their sashes embroidered, their jewels trapping the light of angler fish; urchin children in rags, racing along the cobblestones and laughing, clutching stolen fish and spiced bat wings from the city markets; weavers, glass-makers, chandlers, and other workers trudging toward their homes after long turns of labor; and even a wealthy merchant upon a palanquin, hands folded across his wide belly. Some people tossed coins her way. Others ignored her. She played on, and she slept in the alleyway, and she fought thieves with her katana, and she fought poverty with her flute.

In other dreams Koyee sat upon the sloping roof of a pagoda, gazing up at the sky as ten thousand lanterns floated toward the moon. The great wooden doll of Xen Qae moved down the street, taller than three men, its operators hidden within its robes, and fireworks rose to burst across the sky. Koyee watched and wept for the beauty, an invisible urchin who glimpsed the light of a nation, the hope of a people.

A people now gone.

Koyee grimaced, the pain clutching at her. She had fought in this city. She had stood upon its walls, firing arrows at the sunlit demons who invaded from the daylight. She had vaulted from roof to roof, firing down at the enemy, and she had lived in an occupied city, a yezyana in a mask, hiding in the Green Geode as the enemy forces drank wine and reached to grab at her.

And she had watched that city fall into darkness.

She had stood with Serin, his captive, chained and beaten, watching cracks and sinkholes greedily swallow her city, guzzling down its towers, shops, streets, homes, her memories, all those she loved and had fought for. Madori would perhaps never fully understand, nor would any of the Ilari she sailed with. But to Koyee this was not merely the loss of life, the loss of a great city; it was the loss of her youth, of her very soul.

"Pahmey," she whispered, unable to breathe, unable to stop those memories. Little Maniko, kind and gentle, teaching her to play "Sailing Alone" on the flute—fallen. Minlao Palace, the great Glow of the Moon, a crest of hope and light in a dark city—gone. Bluefeather Corner, her home in the shadows; the Green Geode, home to the yezyani who had become her sisters; the old graveyard, haven for the Dust Face Ghosts—all gone into shadows. The light of lanterns. The smells of the market. The laughter of children and the heat of the great public fireplaces. Forever silenced, forever darkened.

The pain was too great. Koyee thrashed in her hammock, feeling trapped in the web of some great spider. Finally she could bear it no longer. She stepped onto the floor. The ship's belly was a dark place, its windows curtained to keep out the searing, eternal light of Timandra. Several more hammocks hung in the shadows, their occupants deep in slumber.

Koyee padded toward the hammock at the back, the one where Madori lay sleeping.

She stood for a moment, looking down at her daughter, and some comfort filled Koyee but a new fear too.

Madori is the most precious thing in my life, she thought. *A beautiful child.* Madori had inherited Koyee's large eyes, delicate frame, and gentle features, but she had Torin's dark hair and tanned skin. A precious child. So fragile.

And I'm so scared, Koyee thought. She reached out and caressed Madori's short black hair. *I'm so scared for your father. I'm so scared that my sweet Torin is gone from us. And I'm so scared to lose you. I'm so scared for you to lose others, for you to feel pain like I feel, to never sleep without nightmares, to never know true peace because the pain can never fully heal.*

Madori mumbled in her sleep, roused by Koyee's touch, and opened her eyes to glowing, lavender slits. "Mother? Why are you crying?

Because you are pure and they hurt you, Koyee thought. *Because I cannot bear the thought of you suffering like I suffer.*

Madori was small, the hammock large, and Koyee climbed inside and lay beside her daughter. Madori's eyes closed again and she nestled close to Koyee, arms wrapped around her, as if she were again very young, a little girl scared of monsters in the closet and seeking the comfort of her mother.

Only now it's me, the mother, who is scared, who seeks comfort, Koyee thought.

She held her daughter close and kissed her forehead.

"You were so small when you were born," Koyee whispered. "You were born early, did you know? And I promised then to protect you. To make this world safe for you, a better world than the one I grew up in. I'm sorry, Billygoat. I'm sorry I failed you."

Madori mumbled in her half-sleep, wriggling and cuddling closer. "We'll win, Mother. We'll win."

Koyee closed her eyes, her daughter in her arms, and she knew something that Madori was too young to understand. There is no victory in war. Even should you slay your enemy, you have not won. The memories of war will forever scar you. The pain of loss and the lingering terror will forever fill your sleep.

But I can still fight, she thought. *For more times like this, holding my daughter close. For the hope of seeing Torin again. For the dream that some turn we all sit together in a garden, a family united, and find shapes in the clouds or the stars, seek brief moments of joy in a world of so much pain. For that I will fight on. Always.*

Finally sleep found her, and with her daughter held close, Koyee did not dream.

* * * * *

As in the years of old, the jotnar—giants of the arctic—walked onto the island of Orida.

They had swum through the sea like icebergs, and they emerged onto the shores like early winter sending up shards of frost. Beasts of stone and ice, of frosted beards and cold blue eyes, of beating hearts deep within crystallized rib cages, they lumbered across the rocky slopes, between the pines, and into the city of Grenstad. They moved between houses of clay and thatched roofs, long mead halls with beams carved as orcas, and between stone temples to the old gods. Lumbering beasts risen from myth, their jagged heads rose above roofs, and their feet sent fingers of frost across cobblestones.

Eris walked at their lead, clad in armor and fur, holding his horn high. Yiun Yee walked at his side, a princess in white silk, her skin pale, her eyes large and glowing. The people of the city gazed in awe, and many knelt, and many sang old songs. Soldiers raced toward them, sent from the palace to slay the outcast prince, but they too bowed and laid down their weapons, for here before them it seemed that Orin himself had returned from the ancient years, risen from legend to lead them again and restore their land to glory.

The Orinhall rose ahead in the shade of the mountains, a great mead hall with towering beams of giltwood. When Eris entered the hall, he found his brother upon the throne. Torumun held a drawn sword across his lap, and his father's crown topped his head. At his side stood Iselda, sister to Tirus Serin, clad in a burgundy gown.

"You are not welcome here, Eris the Kingslayer!" Iselda said. She pointed an accusing finger at him. "Last you entered this hall, you slew my husband—your own father. Now you come trying to usurp the throne. Your elder brother is true King of Orida, and he has taken me as a wife. As queen of this land, I charge you with regicide and patricide." The Radian queen turned toward the soldiers who lined the hall. "Men of Orida, place this man in chains. He will stand trial for his crime, and he will burn in a great pyre before our people."

Yet the first of the jotnar were now entering the hall behind Eris. Their joints of stone and ice creaked, their heads brushed the ceiling, and frost spread out from their feet. At the sight of the giants, the soldiers in the hall gasped. A few still held their swords; others placed down their weapons and knelt.

"Orin returns!" whispered one man.

"Orin returns with Ymir, king of the jotnar!" said another, voice awed, and tears streamed down his cheeks.

Eris took a step closer to the throne. Ignoring Iselda, he stared at his brother.

"Torumun," he said, "when you banished me from this hall, when you raised arms against me, I thought to return here and slay you, to claim the throne." He looked at Yiun Yee who stood at his side, seeking comfort from her soft gaze, then back toward Torumun. "But Yiun Yee taught me to be more than a warrior, more than a slayer of enemies. She taught me mercy. I should never have slain our father, even as he attacked my wife, and I don't wish to slay you. But I must cleanse this hall. Orida must remove the Radian banners and raise the orca flag again. Please, brother. Cast aside this woman who has bewitched you. Return to the ways of righteousness."

Torumun rose from his seat. He seemed to have aged since Eris had last seen him. White streaked his temples and yellow beard. His eyes were sunken and simmering with malice. Rather than the old armor of Orida, he wore a suit of black plates, and an eclipse sigil burned upon the breastplate, formed of rubies.

"Banish my wife?" Torumun said and laughed.

Eris narrowed his eyes. "Your wife? She is your stepmother!"

"No longer." Torumun's laughter was bitter. "You saw to that. You slew our father. You murdered him in this hall, all because he tried to rid us of your nightcrawler wife. Iselda is mine now. My wife. My prize." He pulled her close to him. "And she has shown me the true meaning of glory, and that glory lies under the Radian banners. Father was right to join Serin. Leave this place, brother! Your creatures of ancient stories cannot help you now. The jotnar perhaps are impressive for fools to look upon, but they are beasts of the old world. A new order rises. A new world begins. The hosts of Orida already muster, and our fleet gathers for assault. We will soon begin the invasion of darkness, and we will burn the isle of Leen and the northern coast of Qaelin." He sneered. "And your wife will be the first nightcrawler to die."

Eris shook his head. "You speak as father spoke. I slew him, it is true, but I will spare you." He looked at the soldiers who knelt before him—his brother's soldiers. "Sons of Orin, our old years of glory need not be mere legends. They can return. Remove the foreign banners that hang on these walls. Together we will cleanse the city. Escort Torumun and Iselda to the port, and give them a ship, and let them sail into exile. Let no more blood spill in this hall." He looked at Yiun Yee and held her hand. "May blood never spill here again."

Iselda stared at the kneeling soldiers in disgust, then back at Eris. Her face twisted, hatred blazed in her eyes, and she seemed more like a rabid beast than a woman.

"Exile? No, usurper. We will not go into exile." The sorceress spat toward the soldiers who knelt before Eris. "These men are weak. The blood of Orin is weak. But true soldiers muster to your south in Verilon. Very soon my brother's hosts will crush the resistance in Orewood, and then they will come here. Then true men will hold this hall, not the sons of farmers and shepherds who quake at the sight of some summoned goblins of ice. Torumun and I will return, Eris . . . return with an army of fire to melt your giants, burn your wife, and bring you back to Markfir so the emperor may see your bones shattered."

She wrapped her arms around Torumun and gave him a long, deep kiss, her body pressed against him. Then she turned toward Eris, glared, and spat toward him. Serpents of black smoke rose around her feet, coiling and hissing, wrapping around her and Torumun like a cocoon.

"Men, grab them!" Eris shouted.

His soldiers rushed forth and reached into the smoke, only to scream and pull back burnt hands. When finally the astral serpents dispersed, no sign of Iselda or Torumun remained, only a great eclipse charred into the floor.

CHAPTER FOURTEEN
THE HORNS OF ORIDA

Horns blared across the ruins of Orewood—loud, horrible, jarring banshee cries heralding death. Ravens took flight from the rubble, startled by the sound, leaving the corpses they had fed upon and vanishing into the clouds.

"Radian horns," Torin muttered. He crouched in the ruins, tending to a young soldier's wounded leg. The Verilish man groaned, face ashen. The leg would have to be amputated, Torin knew, though he wasn't sure he had the resolve to swing his sword and do the job.

"Lots of the bastards this time, by the sound of it," Cam said. The King of Arden himself had a wounded leg; a bandage wrapped around it, soaked red, and Cam winced when he shifted his weight. "Torin, old boy, my leg's in no shape for climbing. Be a good lad and go take a look."

Torin nodded and looked toward Linee. "Would you take over?"

Crouched among the ruins, the queen nodded and wiped her bloody forehead. More old blood stained her patches of dented armor, most of it not her own. She was better at healing than Torin anyway; she had already amputated and stitched up the limbs of several soldiers, including her own son's. Omry sat at her side, pale and shivering, his left leg ending below the knee.

"Go, Torin," Linee said. She approached the wounded soldier and winced at the sight of the man's wounded leg. She drew a long, curved knife.

The horns sounded again, metallic, cruel. Perhaps, at least, they would drown the screams of the wounded man. Grateful for his task, Torin rose with the creak of armor and joints; both had seen far too much wear. Pocked walls rose around them, a shell of crumbling stone, and thirty other soldiers hunkered here, all of them Verilish; Torin had not seen any other Ardishmen for many turns. He climbed the wall, walked along its jagged top, then made his way up the staircase of a tower. The tower's northern wall had fallen, affording a view of the Verilish camp: dozens of burrows between the ruins, each full of soldiers in bloody, dusty armor. Through the arrowslits on the tower's southern wall, Torin could see the sprawling, smoldering no man's land, a field of rubble and bones. To wander into that field, he knew, was death. The ravens had returned to the ruin, pecking at thousands of corpses.

Finally Torin made it to the top of the tower. Two tattered banners rose upon it: the bear of Verilon and the raven of Arden. Both banners seemed lurid to Torin now; the bear Gashdov had fallen, and the only true ravens here were feeding upon their dead. He stepped behind a merlon, crouched, and gazed south.

No man's land spread a mile long, nearly all its buildings fallen. Little more than a few arches, the stubs of columns, and chunks of wall rose here; the rest had fallen. Past this field of rubble rose the Radian side of the city, a great hive of crumbling forts, makeshift barracks, trenches, and the tattered standards of the enemy. The horns blared again, and the forest south of the city rustled. Fresh Radian forces began to emerge. Torin cursed.

"This might be the end," he muttered.

Throughout the past month or two, Radian reinforcements had arrived every few turns: a few wagons of food, a couple hundred frightened recruits pulled from southern villagers and towns, and sometimes even a knight or two with their footmen. But now, for the first time since the battle began, Torin saw a true new army arrive. Thousands of troops marched here, covered in black steel. Hundreds rode upon armored horses. Cannons rolled forth among them, shaped as buffaloes. On one banner Torin saw the sigil of a yellow citadel upon a crimson field.

These soldiers came from Sunmotte itself, Torin thought. *From Serin's own home.*

The Radians already in the city cheered as their comrades approached. The new arrivals did not even bother to set camp; at once they advanced toward no man's land, many swordsmen and horses and cannons, and began to travel across the rubble . . . toward Torin and his comrades.

"Oh Idar's beard," Torin whispered. He raced back down the tower and burst into the burrow he shared with Cam, Linee, and the others. "We're going to have company. Lots of company. Radians are arriving."

Cam cursed. "How many?"

"All of them, I think," Torin said. "They're entering the killing field and moving our way."

Cam grumbled and drew his sword. "This might be it, Tor."

Linee paled and moved toward her son. She hugged the prince close, her cheeks pale. Torin looked at them. His friends. His new family. They would die now, he knew. All of them would.

I'll never see Koyee and Madori again.

He drew his old chipped sword. "I don't have much to say." His voice was soft, weak with hunger and the long fight. "You all know what this means. Linee, I want you to take Omry and flee north of the city. Sneak into the forests. Try to survive, perhaps find a village, take a new name."

The queen shook her head, and tears filled her eyes. "I never ran from a fight. Not even when I was very young and afraid, when Camlin and I traveled Sage's Road through the night, when we fought in the deserts of Eseer, when we fixed the clock on the mountain. And I won't run now." She raised her knife. "This is my home now. And I'll die defending it if I must. Better to die here in battle, with my family around me, than in some forest in the cold of winter." She wiped her eyes and embraced Cam. "I love you, my Camlin. I love you so much."

Cam kissed her lips and held her close. "I love you too, Linee. Always. In this life and the next, my queen." He smiled tremulously. "I fell in love with you somewhere in the darkness of Eloria, and I've not stopped loving you since then, not for one instant." The horns blared again, and Linee started. Cam caressed her cheek. "We still fight together."

Torin moved toward the hole in the wall that served as their doorway. He waited. The horns wailed again. They would be here soon.

He frowned.

"The horns," he said. "They're . . . different."

He heard it again. He frowned. These horns were lighter, more melodious, and they sounded from the north, not the south where the enemy marched.

"Those aren't Radian horns," Cam said.

Distant voices rose in the north, chanting and deep. "Forward, Sons of Orin! For Orida! For King Eris! For glory and our northern isle!"

Torin gasped, raced back up the tower, and stared south. Hope and wonder blazed inside him like a great fire in the cold of winter. Thousands of horses came galloping from the northern forests into the city. Atop them sat thousands of men in bright armor and fur cloaks, their helmets horned, their wooden shields round. Their banners streamed, showing orcas. Behind the riders marched many soldiers on foot, rows and rows of them, a great army of metal and wood and fur.

"Orida brings aid," Torin whispered.

He turned back south. The Radians had already crossed half the city, moving closer. Their cannons crackled and fired. The great balls of iron flew through the air toward the Oridian host. The missiles tore through horses, but the rest of the cavalry kept charging, the riders calling out for battle. The city shook as the two forces crashed together.

Torin raced down the tower as the armies flowed across their hideouts.

And he fought.

And he laughed.

He was so weak, so thin, so weary and haunted, but he laughed as the hosts of Orida tore through the enemy, as the bright swords of the north cut down Serin's forces, as for the first time in many turns of death, hope kindled in Orewood. The warriors of the orca swept through the city like a wave cleaning debris off a beach.

When thousands of Radian troops had fallen dead, and the city defenders and the warriors of Orida charged against the enemy, Lord Gehena finally emerged to fight.

Three months ago, the towering mage had ridden toward the city walls, holding a severed head in each of his four hands. Gehena had tossed his grisly gifts toward the city, signaling the start of the assault, but since then the hooded creature had remained hidden in shadows. Now he emerged, the field commander of the Radians' northern front, a towering mage—he stood eight feet tall. He wore robes darker than the night, the hems burnt, and an iron helmet hid his face, revealing only blazing red eyes like forge fires. The creature walked afoot through the devastation, his four arms raised, and in each hand he held a weapon: a spear, an axe, a sword, and a hammer.

Watching from a ruined wall, Torin grimaced with sudden pain, blinded, nearly doubling over. Gehena had kept him imprisoned for eight months in a dungeon, then later a cart, and for most of those turns the mage had hurt him—sometimes by ordering his brutes to beat Torin, sometimes by casting magic himself, driving shards of pain through Torin's flesh. Now that pain flared in Torin's memory, so intense it felt real, and the scars of his imprisonment—they covered his body beneath his armor—blazed anew.

"Tor!" Cam said, clutching him. "Are you hurt? What's wrong?"

Torin could not reply, only stare in terror. If hope had kindled inside him with Orida's arrival, now, seeing Gehena, that hope seemed foolish, the hope of a starving prisoner as a guard taunts him with a meal he'd never serve.

"Archers, fire!" shouted an Oridian upon a tower, his long yellow hair billowing from under his horned helmet.

A hundred Oridian archers crouched among the ruins, tugged back bowstrings, and fired their arrows toward Gehena. The towering mage merely raised his eyes, and though Torin could not see Gehena's face—he never had, not even during his months of imprisonment—it seemed to Torin that the demonic mage sneered. Three feet away from Gehena, the arrows shriveled in midair and rained down as ash.

"Sons of Orin, charge!" cried an Oridian knight. The man thundered forth upon his horse, and twenty other riders rode with him, their horses armored, their banners fluttering in the smoky wind. Lances thrust. Torin crouched behind rubble, watching.

Gehena swung his four weapons. Lances shattered with fountains of wooden shards. The demonic mage's spear thrust, impaling a rider. His axe swung, cutting down a horse. His sword sliced through a knight, and his hammer sent another man crashing down. The horses kept charging, the riders aiming their lances, and the mage spun from side to side, blades spraying blood.

A lone horse, its rider dead, fled the carnage. The other riders lay dead around the demon-mage, torn apart.

Gehena tossed back his head and shrieked to the sky. It was a horrible sound, ear-splitting, its pitch higher than steam from a kettle, it volume louder than thunder. The ruins shook. A wall collapsed. The shriek coalesced into words that pounded Torin's ears.

"Will you hide as others fight for you, Torin the Gardener?" the towering mage cried. "Will you rely on saviors from afar, or will you face me yourself, man to man?"

Torin grimaced. The pain still blazed through him, the pain of his wounds, of his memories. Of Kingswall falling. Of his long months in the dungeon, worried for his family. Of the carnage in this city.

Slowly, clutching his sword, Torin emerged from behind the rubble and faced the mage.

"Torin, what are you doing?" Cam whispered, trying to tug Torin down. But it was too late. Gehena had seen him.

As thousands of men still fought across the ruins, Torin took a step across the debris toward the demon.

"I'm here, Gehena," he said. His heart thudded, sweat soaked him, but he kept walking. "I do not cower. I come to face you again, a sword in my hand."

He was being foolish, he knew. Feverish. Suicidal. But he kept walking. He kept thinking of the severed heads Gehena had tossed at him—the heads of his neighbors from Fairwool-by-Night. He kept thinking of the long months in Gehena's dungeon. And he thought of what else this demon might do if left free, of the pain Gehena could inflict upon Koyee, upon Madori, upon all other good souls in Moth.

And so I must stop him. I must do what I could not last time I fought him. I must kill him.

"I can see the fear in you, Torin Greenmoat," said the creature, "and you are right to be afraid. I see the doubt in you, and you are right to feel doubt." The demon raised his hand, and a ring of fire burst out around them, trapping them within walls of inferno. "You should have stayed hidden."

Torin shook his head. "No, Gehena. No magic. You want to face me? Face me in a fair fight. As you said, man to man, if indeed a man you are. No magical fires, serpents, bolts of lightning. Blade to blade. Doff your wizard's robes, let me see your form, and duel me."

The towering mage nodded . . . and removed his cloak. He let the garment drop to the ground.

Torin felt the blood drain from his face. Lord Gehena was not just thin; he was skeletal, his skin clinging to bones. That skin was red and raw as if burnt. Two of the mage's four arms were sewn on, the stitches dripping pus, and his legs seemed surgically extended, grafted onto goat hooves. But worst of all was Gehena's face. It was a withered face, the cheeks sunken, the mouth lip-less, the teeth sharp and yellow. It was a pained face. The face of a man who had felt too much agony, seen too much terror, heard too many screams, a face that hid a shattered mind.

Torin recognized that face. He had seen it upon every soldier after the fall of Yintao. Upon every survivor here in Orewood who fed on rats and waited for death. Many times, Torin had seen it when staring at his own reflection. It was the face of lost hope, of a cruelty born from lack of belief that any goodness could exist in this world. It was the face that, perhaps, Torin had always been fighting within himself.

Then Lord Gehena opened that shriveled mouth, shrieked again, and charged toward him.

The demon—for that was how Torin thought of Gehena now—swung his sword toward him. Torin parried, but the creature's spear thrust too. Torin raised his shield, blocking the blow, only for the axe and hammer to swing down. He leaped aside, and both weapons slammed into fallen bricks, shattering them.

A battle cry sounded, and Cam leaped through the ring of fire to fight.

"He has four hands," Cam said. "Figured I'd join to make the fight fair."

The shepherd-turned-king ran toward Gehena, sword swinging. The demon parried with his own sword. Torin swung his blade, only for Gehena to block the blow with his axe. The weapons swung in a fury, sparking together, clashing, chipping.

"Fools," hissed Gehena. "You cannot kill me. I was trained in the pits of Serin's forts. I was augmented with his magic, broken, rebuilt, formed to slay men." His blades swung again and again, slamming into Torin and Cam's weapons and armor. "You should have run."

A blow from Gehena's hammer slammed into Cam's breastplate, knocking the slender man down. Before Cam could rise, Gehena lashed all four weapons down toward Torin.

Screaming, Torin raised his shield and sword overhead. His sword snapped in half. The blows kept raining, pounding against his shield, and Torin fell to his knees, then onto his back.

Gehena loomed above him, laughing, his ribs rising and falling and stretching his desiccated skin. Sores burst upon his body. His hooves, surgically stitched onto his legs, slammed down at Torin's sides. The demon leered down at him, saliva dripping between his fangs. Torin lay on his back, moaning, clutching a hilt with only half a blade.

"And now, Torin, I will finally let you die."

Torin had shied away from amputating the wounded soldier's leg, but he had seen it done enough times. He swung the stub of his blade, aiming toward the stitches where Gehena's hoof met leg.

The blade cut through rotted flesh. The hoof tore off. Gehena screamed. As the demon fell down toward him, Torin raised the broken blade. Gehena fell onto the shard of steel, impaling himself, then burying Torin under his weight.

"Tor!" Cam limped forward, grabbed Gehena, and tugged him off. "By Idar's soggy britches, this thing weighs more than a horse."

Torin coughed and helped push. They rolled Gehena onto his back, and Torin struggled to his feet, staring down at the slain creature. A gust of wind blew, and Gehena dispersed into ash. The broken blade clattered down to the ground.

The ring of fire faded around them, revealing a field of dead. No more enemy troops fought. Verilish men, clad in fur cloaks and cast iron breastplates, cheered and raised their war hammers. Oridians chanted for victory, their helmets horned, their swords painted red.

Through the carnage, a figure in white came walking toward Torin. In his pain and delirium, he almost thought her a deity, a goddess in white.

An Elorian, he realized.

The woman reached him. She was young and fair, her eyes large and blue. Her white hair and flowing robes streamed in the wind. With her walked an Oridian lord, gold upon his armor, a filigreed mead horn hanging around his neck on a chain.

"The demon called you Torin," said the Elorian woman. "Are you . . . Sir Torin Greenmoat, the hero of the first war?"

Torin rubbed his aching neck. "Well, after this battle, I better be remembered as a hero of the second war too."

The Elorian woman clasped his hand. "I am Yiun Yee, Princess of Leen and Queen of Orida. With me is Eris, King of Orida."

Torin smiled at them wanly. "You're late. But if you join us on the road to Markfir, all will be forgiven."

Swaying weakly, he turned to look south. The ruins stretched ahead, and beyond them rose the pine forests of Verilon, but south from here, many leagues across forests and plains, lay the capital of the Radian Empire. That, Torin knew, was his destination. That, he knew, was where he'd meet Serin again.

CHAPTER FIFTEEN
LANTERNS IN THE DARK

Jin, Emperor of Qaelin, sat on his nightwolf, gazing at the port of
Eeshan.

Eeshan—the Gates to the North, the largest city along the
northern coast of Qaelin. Eeshan—the fair city that had fallen to
Verilon in the last war, that had risen from captivity into a great hub
of trade and industry. Eeshan—the last city still standing in his
empire, the last city not yet fallen to the sunlight.

Eeshan, Jin thought, the word like a prayer in his mind. *Maybe
our last hope in the darkness.*

All around Jin, thousands of his soldiers mustered for war. In
the port ahead, the lanterns of hundreds of ships swayed.

"For the first time," Jin whispered, "Qaelin will sail into the
sunlight."

His nightwolf growled beneath him, a beautiful silver animal
named Chon Bao. Born without arms and legs, Jin sat in a custom
harness that held his torso upright. Some of his empire's
philosophers had wanted to construct him limbs of gold, but why
should Jin pretend to have limbs? Shenlai the dragon had been
limbless, and he had been a great leader who had saved Qaelin in its
last war.

*Yet Shenlai, my dearest friend, has fallen. As a new fire burns, it is I who
must save my empire.*

Jin had been only a child in the last war, and great warriors had
helped him: Shenlai the dragon, Koyee the heroine, and Torin and
Bailey of the sunlight. Now, even as an adult, even with a great army,
Jin felt alone, and he was scared.

He looked around him at the port city. Tall, narrow houses
lined the streets, their tiled roofs curling up at the edges like scrolls.
Lanterns hung from the eaves, the tin shaped as the mocking faces of
spirits, candles within their eyes. Bats fluttered above, and a great

public fireplace roared in a cobbled square, its iron grill shaped as coiling dragons and dancing maidens.

And everywhere Jin looked, he saw his army. Qaelin's soldiers lined the streets, standing still and solemn as statues. Scale armor shone upon them. Their helmets were simple, polished steel. Each man held a spear and shield, and katanas hung across their backs. Most stood afoot, but like Jin many rode upon nightwolves, the beasts armored and as well trained as their riders.

Jin leaned forward, then sideways, guiding his wolf with the tilt of his limbless body. Chon Bao climbed onto a bronze dragon statue, letting the troops see their emperor.

"Soldiers of Qaelin!" he said. "Serin has destroyed the city of Pahmey, plunging it into darkness. Serin has burned Yintao and plundered its treasures. From here in Eeshan, upon our northern coast, we will strike back. We will show the Radian Empire that Qaelin still fights. We are the night!"

Thousands of soldiers raised their spears. "We are the night!"

Jin tilted in his harness. His nightwolf, understanding the signal, turned to face the port. When Jin leaned forward, the nightwolf jumped off the statue and began walking toward the boardwalk. The soldiers marched behind him, their boots thumping as one. In the water floated hundreds of ships: the junk ships of Qaelin, moonstars upon their sails and cannons lining their decks, and the long, elegant dragon-ships of Leen, diamonds painted upon their white hulls.

On the boardwalk, Jin saw a group of Leenish soldiers clad in flowing white robes over silvery breastplates. Between them stood the Emperor of Leen, an old man with a long snowy beard. He wore silk robes embroidered with white dragons—images of Pirilin, fallen dragon of Leen—and a great diamond, symbol of his empire, hung around his neck. The old man turned sad, indigo eyes toward Jin.

"Leen is a land of philosophers, harpists, poets, stargazers." The fleet's swaying lanterns reflected in his eyes. "I never imagined that Leen would invade the sunlight, would march to war. I never imagined that my own daughter, the gentle Yiun Yee, would marry a man of the sun."

Jin brought his nightwolf close to the old king's side. "The people of Leen are wise and peaceful, yet I've seen them fight. I rode upon Pirilin in the last war, and I fought alongside Leenish warriors." Jin shuddered to remember that war, to remember Pirilin sinking into the sea, forever lost from the night. "And your daughter's husband, they say, is himself a wise man who fights against the Radians. Yiun Yee too sails to fight Serin with the Oridian fleet. We will defeat Serin. We will save the darkness." He lowered his head. "Perhaps there's not much left to save. So much of our land has burned. Even as we speak, Radian troops assault the coasts of Leen and Ilar. But so long as we live, we will fight, even if we die upon the walls of Markfir."

He turned to look at the sea. *In Markfir, capital of Serin's empire, will I meet Koyee again?* Jin had not seen his friend in many years, and he missed her. Orida sailed to war, and they said that the Ilari Armada was already sailing in the sunlight. Perhaps at Markfir all free people would meet.

And perhaps you'll be there too, Koyee, at the great battle of our time.

Jin rode his nightwolf along a plank and onto a junk ship with silver, battened sails. All across the port, his soldiers boarded many other ships. Most would see the sunlight for the first time. Most perhaps would never see the night again. Each soldier carried a silver lantern, thousands of lights crawling onto the ships. In the daylight, Jin knew, thousands of these lights would go out.

They set sail, the ships of Eloria, hundreds of vessels, myriads of lanterns, and an emperor with the hopes of a nation upon his armless shoulders. The lights flowed over the black waters, across the shadows . . . and toward the light of day.

CHAPTER SIXTEEN
ELDMARK FIELDS

Torin had been riding across the plains for many turns when he finally saw Markfir in the distance.

After a summer of fire and blood, autumn had come to Moth, and cold wind ruffled Torin's hair and beard; both had grown long in the war, streaked with silver. His banner unfurled, revealing the black raven of Arden upon a golden field. He turned in the saddle, looking at the rest of his army. Only a dozen other raven banners rose here, a few last survivors of Arden come to join the assault.

But despite the scarcity of Ardishmen, the force—the Northern Alliance—sprawled across the grassy plains. Many of the soldiers were men and women of Verilon. They wore cast iron breastplates and pelts of bear fur, and their shaggy brown hair streamed in the wind. They carried massive war hammers—weapons too heavy for Torin to lift—and many among them rode bears instead of horses. The brown bear of Verilon appeared upon their green banners. Warriors of Orida comprised the rest of the Northern Alliance. They were large people, not as wide as the Verilish but just as tall, their hair golden, and the men sported long beards, and the women wore their hair in two braids; they reminded Torin of Bailey, and he missed his friend whenever he looked at these northern shieldmaidens. The Oridians too raised many banners, displaying a sea of orcas, and they rode many horses.

"Forty thousand warriors," Cam said, riding at Torin's side on a white courser. "There are more men than this defending Markfir, and they defend it from high walls." He looked at Torin. "Are we marching to an early death?"

Torin raised an eyebrow. "We've been doing that for years now. We're still alive."

"Some of us are," Cam said softly.

Torin looked back toward Markfir. The city lay across the flat wastelands men called Eldmark Fields, named after an ancient Riyonan emperor who had fallen here in some forgotten battle. No Radian force was marching forth to meet the invaders; the field was barren, flat, and empty, covered with only sparse grass. The city was still too far to see clearly, but even from this distance, Torin realized it was massive; hundreds of towers rose from it. This was a city even larger than Pahmey, its walls mighty and thick. Torin had seen Markfir embroidered onto a tapestry once—five or six cotton towers, maybe thirty soldiers upon its walls. The artist had been lazy; that tapestry would have to cover a city block just to depict the true might of Markfir.

Horse hoofs thundered, and Eris rode up to ride beside Torin. The King of Orida stared south, the wind in his golden hair, and his blue eyes narrowed. The autumn sun gleamed upon his bright armor and horned helmet.

"The bulk of Serin's forces linger in the darkness of Eloria," the northern king said. "He has spread himself too thin, launched too many fronts. His arrogance will be his downfall. We will slam through his gates, storm his palace, and hang him in the city square."

A shaggy bear padded forth, and upon the beast rose Hogash, burly and grumbling. Once Orewood's gatekeeper, the bearded man had risen to command Verilon's forces after his king had fallen. "Hang him?" Hogash spat across his saddle. "That death would be too kind for Serin. I will give him a better death. A slow one."

"We'll worry about Serin's fate later," said Cam, the third commander of the Northern Alliance. "High walls, tens of thousands of Radian soldiers, and probably hundreds of mages still separate us from the emperor. Let's cross those obstacles first."

Both Eris and Hogash nodded.

"The little king is wise," said Hogash.

And frightened, Torin thought, gazing at the three leaders. *And I'm frightened too.*

He looked back at the city; it was closer now, the sunlight gleaming upon the armor of its distant defenders. Torin had fought many battles, but here would be the greatest battle of his life, perhaps the greatest in Moth's history. Here the fate of this world torn between day and night would be decided. Here, upon Eldmark Fields, would all civilization burn in the Radian fire or rise to defeat it.

The Northern Alliance rode and marched onward, forty thousand soldiers and thousands of horses and bears, the free Timandrians of the north come south to strike at Serin's heart.

It must have taken hours, but it seemed to Torin that only moments passed before they reached Markfir.

The city lay in the shadow of the Teekat Mountains, which the Magerians called Markshade, the great range—once the western border of the fallen Riyonan Empire—that separated Mageria from Daenor in the west. To the north, east, and south of the city spread Eldmark Fields, the great grassy plains where buffaloes—sigil of the Magerian people—would roam in the turns of old, now hunted to extinction.

A moat surrounded Markfir, and beyond the water rose a ring of guard towers—well over a hundred of them—connected with walls of grayish-brown bricks. Each guard tower stared onto the fields with arrowslits like feline eyes, and red tiles covered their conical roofs. Beyond these fortifications rose a great hill, almost large enough to be called a mountain, covered with thousands of buildings. Most of the buildings rose several stories tall, all built of the same grayish-brown bricks, and their roofs too were tiled red. A hundred towers or more rose between homes and shops, all topped with battlements and archers. Even the Idarith temples, their steeples soaring hundreds of feet tall, had been converted into forts; archers stood in their belfries. At the city's crest, perched atop the hilltop, rose Solgrad Castle—Serin's imperial palace—a great complex with thick walls and four round towers overlooking the city below.

"By Idar," Torin whispered, sudden terror clutching him, so powerful that he winced and could barely look at the city.

Thousands of Radian troops manned the walls and towers, and they were all shouting for war. They beat drums. They blared horns. They waved swords and axes, and they chanted for victory.

"Radian rises!" boomed countless voices. "Radian rises!"

"A nice welcoming party they've set up," Cam muttered. The king's horse neighed and bucked.

Torin nodded. "We're honored guests. I say we ride up and make some trouble."

They advanced slowly toward the city gates, riders first. They had to move slowly, for the enemy had dug many hidden holes into the fields, each covered with a blanket of grass; several horses stepped into the traps to twist and even break their legs, and several men fell to crash down onto jagged spikes. Five hundred yards outside the city gates, the Northern Alliance halted.

"I'll go deliver our terms," Cam said.

Hogash snorted upon his bear. "Terms? The only term I have is to crush their skulls. Crush them. Like they did to Orewood."

"I thought we'd be gentlemanly about it," Cam said. "At least before we crush them."

The beefy Verilish commander sighed. "You Ardish are silly folk."

Cam rode forth, and Torin rode with him, until they stood just beyond the range of arrows. The gates and walls rose ahead, topped with thousands of troops.

Cam coned his palm around his mouth and cried out, "City of Markfir! Open your gates and send out your tyrant, the false emperor Tirus Serin. Send him forth and Markfir will be spared! Protect him and we will raze your city to the ground."

The soldiers upon the walls laughed. They banged their swords against their shields. They spat toward the field. They cried out obscenities, detailing various carnal acts Torin and Cam probably loved performing on nightcrawlers.

"Enough being gentlemanly for now?" Torin asked.

Cam nodded. "Quite enough."

The king looked over his shoulder at the rest of their troops, the forty thousand who waited in the field. He raised a silver horn and blew.

Torin raised his shield.

It begins.

Arrows flew. Catapults swung. The Battle of Eldmark Fields, the great battle for all of Moth, began.

* * * * *

Neekeya thrust her sword, slaying the last Radian defender of the pyramid. The corpse tumbled down the staircase that rose along the pyramid's southern slope, crashing down to the swamps below.

She looked around her, panting. Across the marshlands of Daenor, twelve other pyramids rose from the greenery, forming the shape of a great reptile. Across all thirteen peaks, soldiers climbed to tear down the Radian banners.

Kota, Prince of Sania, panted at Neekeya's side. He wiped his sweaty brow. "The air here in Daenor is so moist. I don't know how you can stand it."

The tall, dark-skinned man wore no armor as he fought; his bare chest gleamed with sweat, and he tugged off his helmet, letting his black braids spill down to his shoulders. The blood of his enemies coated his sword and arms.

My betrothed, Neekeya thought, staring at him, missing her fallen husband. *The man I had to marry to win this battle.*

Thousands of other Sanian soldiers were moving through the marshlands and climbing the pyramids, making sure all the Radian defenders were fallen. Elephants trudged through the marshlands, feeding upon the brush and drinking from the water; on their backs rode many Sanian archers.

"Thank you, Kota," Neekeya said softly. "Thank you for helping me reclaim my homeland."

She looked up the staircase. Only two steps above loomed the archway of Eetek Pyramid, leading into her old home. No more defenders emerged, and she heard no more enemy chants or taunts. Holding her sword before her, Neekeya climbed the last two steps, passed through the archway, and entered the hall.

She grimaced.

The Radian commander, governor of the occupied marshlands, lay dead on the floor, fallen onto his sword.

When Neekeya looked past the dead Radian, she gasped and covered her mouth. Tears leaped into her eyes.

Many smaller archways lined the hall, affording a view of the marshes. A skeleton was chained within one archway, arms and legs outstretched. The crows had picked the bones clean, but Neekeya recognized the skeleton's jeweled breastplate.

"Father," she whispered.

Kota entered the hall after her and winced. He pulled Neekeya into his arms and turned her head away.

"I'm sorry, Neekeya," the tall prince said, head lowered.

Princess Adisa, his sister, entered the hall next. The Sanian warrior-princess fought with a spear and a wicker shield, and her many braids chinked, strewn with beads of silver and gold. Behind her walked Sanian soldiers, armed with feathered spears. When Adisa gazed upon the scene, her eyes softened. The princess understood. She too approached Neekeya and joined the embrace.

As they walked down the staircase, back toward the swamps, the people of Daenor emerged from hiding—fishermen and farmers, a few thousand in all. At first they cheered; their land was liberated, the Radian forces slain. But when they saw Neekeya and Kota carrying the litter, the bones of their lord upon it, the people fell silent and lowered their heads.

Neekeya placed her father's bones into a *sheh'an*, the small reed boat of the marshlands, and covered them with a blanket of lichen. She waded alongside the *sheh'an*, the water rising to her waist, guiding the boat through the swamplands—her father's last journey. All around her, frogs trilled, herons hunted for fish, and the roots of mangroves rose in tangled webs. Dragonflies and fireflies flew above the water and between the branches. Mist floated.

She took her father to a stone platform that rose from the water, engraved with mossy birds and reptiles. Columns rose around the platform, supporting baskets of wilting flowers. Here was the place where Neekeya had married Tam, where her father had given her away to her sweet prince. Now here she would part from them.

She docked the boat with her father's bones, and she climbed out of the water onto the platform, lilies and moss clinging to her legs. Kota and Adisa rose to stand at her sides, and many others gathered upon fallen logs, boulders, and islets of grass—Daenorians and Sanian soldiers alike. All had come to pay their respects, to mourn with her.

Neekeya spoke softly. "The people of Daenor dig no graves, for our land is watery. We build no funeral pyres, for our wood is wet and will not easily burn. We do not entomb our dead in mausoleums of stone, for stones are things of life here, covered in moss and sheltering many small animals. To us in Daenor, life is precious, and our dead are given to the living, to the fish and birds and insects, so that our bodies may return into the land, become part of living things." She stared at the lichen blanket covering her father's bones. "The enemy chained my father in the air, letting birds feed upon him, and they meant it as a disgrace, but to a lord of Daenor to feed life, even in death, is an honor. And now I return my father's bones into the water, for from water all life has sprung, and to water all life must return." She tilted the boat over, letting the bones slide into the marshes. "From water to water. From life to life."

They all spoke around her, repeating the prayer. "From water to water. From life to life."

Tam's body was lost in the mines, and Neekeya's only memento from him was her wedding ring. Here upon this platform she had wed him, and so she lifted a stone that lay at her feet, and she placed it into the water.

Goodbye, Tam, she thought. *May your spirit find rest here in the marshes and in the plains of your distant home. I will always remember you. I will always love you.*

She did not wish to linger in the marshlands, not with her home desecrated, her family fallen. She turned and left.

Only a turn later, she was riding up Teekat Mountains upon the back of an elephant. Once more she wore armor of the marshes, the steel breastplate carved into the likeness of crocodile scales, the helmet shaped as a crocodile's mouth, and a necklace of crocodile teeth chinked around her neck. Before her in the saddle, Adisa sat armed with spear and bow. Behind them, all along the mountain pass, stretched a convoy of many elephants and warriors, both warriors of Sania and liberated Daenorians armed with whatever weapons they could spare.

Neekeya looked across this army and toward the distant pyramids rising from the haze. Again she was leaving her homeland, heading into danger. Perhaps this time she would never return.

She looked ahead. She kept riding. The army crested the mountains, and there in the distance she saw it—the plains of Mageria.

"Very soon, Serin, I'll knock on your door," Neekeya whispered, the cold wind fluttering her cloak. "Very soon we'll meet again."

CHAPTER SEVENTEEN
THE WALLS OF MARKFIR

Like lumbering giants of wood and metal, the siege towers advanced toward Markfir through a hail of arrows, cannon fire, and hurtling boulders.

Torin stood atop one of the siege engines, firing arrows toward the city walls. Five stories tall, the tower moved on wooden wheels. A dozen men stood behind it, pushing it forward, and dozens more filled the structure, waiting to attack the city walls. When Torin peered between the wooden battlements, he saw a dozen other wheeled towers rolling forth across Eldmark Fields, their front facades coated with metal plates.

"Remember, boys," Torin said to the soldiers who stood around him. All wore armor and held swords. All stared back solemnly. "We race onto the city rampart. We find the courtyard. We open the city gates and let everyone else in. No matter what happens, we must reach the gates."

They nodded silently.

The siege tower shook as arrows peppered it. One arrow even drove through the metal plates and wooden planks, its tip stopping only an inch away from Torin. Several archers within the siege engine stood at arrowslits, firing back toward the walls.

"Catapults, fire!" rose a shout from the city ramparts.

Across the walls of Markfir, catapults swung, hurtling boulders into the air.

"Answer fire!" rose a cry from far behind—Cam's voice back in the Alliance's formations.

Boulders sailed through the air. From here inside the siege tower, Torin couldn't see much through the arrowslits, but he glimpsed one boulder slam into a wooden tower to their right. Beams snapped, iron plates dented, and men fell screaming to the ground.

"Hold on!" cried an archer in front of Torin.

A shadow fell.

Through the arrowslits, Torin glimpsed a boulder flying their way. He grimaced.

An instant later, a blast of sound pounded in his ears. The siege tower shook madly. Wooden beams snapped. The boulder crashed through metal and wood, scraped along Torin's arm, then plunged down the middle of the tower, crashing through each of the five stories. Men screamed. Blood sprayed. Torin clung to a piece of wood, dangling over the pit the boulder had left.

"Keep shoving us forward!" Torin shouted at the men below. He clung to the siege tower, feet upon a wooden beam. A great hole gaped ahead, and many of the tower's beams had snapped, but the shell of the structure still stood. "Keep going, we're still standing!"

One soldier, a Verilish youth of perhaps fifteen years, grabbed Torin's arm. "Sir Greenmoat, we . . . so many dead." He pointed at a man beside him; the soldier lay across a beam, crushed, lifeless.

"We keep going," Torin said. "Now fire! Fire at the walls!"

The boy swallowed, and Torin noticed liquid dripping down his leg, but the soldier dutifully raised his bow and nocked an arrow. Torin joined him, firing his own arrows through the gaping hole the boulder had left. He could see the city walls clearly now. They were only a hundred yards away, rising beyond the moat. Hundreds of Magerian troops stood atop the ramparts, breastplates emblazoned with the Radian eclipse. They were firing arrows and chanting for victory.

Torin aimed. He fired an arrow. But the defenders kept rushing to hide behind merlons, and Torin could not hit them.

A boulder sailed toward the city, thrown from the Northern Alliance host. It flew over Torin's siege tower and slammed into Markfir's walls. Defenders rained down. A merlon cracked and crumbled, revealing more enemy archers. Torin fired and hit a man. To his left, men screamed as an enemy boulder slammed into another siege tower, smashing through it, sending attackers plunging down. Arrows filled the sky, tipped with fire. Another boulder slammed into Torin's siege tower, denting a metal plate and cracking more wooden beams. They kept moving forward, tilted and smashed but still rolling.

Through a hailstorm of arrows and boulders, they reached the moat.

"Drop the gangplank!" Torin shouted.

Typical siege engines had short planks, only a few yards long, a quick passageway from tower to rampart. To attack moated Markfir, the Alliance had built gangplanks as long as bridges. Around Torin, soldiers began sliding out their plank; it expanded section by section, unfurling like the wooden tongue of some great chameleon, spanning the moat below. Arrows flew toward them. One soldier screamed, an arrow in his chest, and fell.

"Remember, boys," Torin said. "Onto the rampart. To the courtyard. And open the gates. Once the others are inside the city, the hard part's over."

They stared back and nodded solemnly.

The gangplank slammed down onto the city wall, crossing the moat. With battle cries, soldiers raced onto the makeshift bridge and began running toward the wall's battlements. Torin raised his shield, gripped his sword, and ran with them.

The gangplank was wide enough for only two men to run abreast. The moat spread below, and Torin could see the boulders buried under the water. The height made his head spin. He looked back ahead, concentrating on the city rampart. A dozen men ran with him, shields and swords ready.

A storm of arrows flew toward them. Most shattered against the attackers' shields. One arrow glanced off Torin's helmet, and another scraped across his greave. The man who ran beside Torin lost his balance, screamed, and plunged down toward the moat below. He splashed into the water and slammed against a submerged boulder. He did not rise.

Torin kept running. More arrows flew. More attackers fell.

"Keep going!" Torin shouted. "To the rampart!"

An arrow slammed into his shield. Another man fell. More replaced him, rising from the remains of the siege engine. When Torin glanced left and right, he saw a dozen more wooden towers drop their gangplanks onto the walls.

Hope sprang in Torin. *We can do this. We can cross the wall. We can open the gates. And then forty thousand troops of the Northern Alliance will take this city.*

He was only a dozen yards away from the wall when the Radians tilted over the cauldron of oil.

The sizzling liquid spilled against the edge of the gangplank, forcing Torin to leap back. He tilted, nearly falling, and windmilled his arms. Before he could steady himself, the Radians on the walls dropped a torch onto the gangplank.

The oil caught fire, exploding with heat and sound and fury. Torin leaped another step back, slamming into a man behind him. The gangplank ahead blazed, a great wall of fire. Torin could not cross. More arrows flew from the inferno, slamming into his shield and armor. One punched through the metal, scraping his chest, and he cried out.

Through the flames, he glimpsed the Radians swinging axes against the blazing gangplank. Torin's heart sank.

He spun around, facing the siege engine and the men behind him. "Back!" he shouted. "Back into the siege tower, go—"

The gangplank creaked and began to crack.

Torin cursed, stared down at the boulders in the water, and took two steps forward, one to the right.

It was all he had time for. The plank collapsed. Wooden slats rained down. Torin fell with them.

In his last couple seconds on the bridge, he had managed to move over a spot of clear water. He splashed down between boulders and plunged underwater. At his sides, men crashed onto boulders, breaking apart, their blood splashing. Guilt exploded through Torin, as painful as the wounds, to see his comrades die as he lived. He kicked underwater and tugged madly at the straps of his breastplate, finally tearing it off. He kicked, swam, and his head rose over the surface.

Arrows hailed down. Torin cursed, dived underwater again, and swam to the edge of the moat. He climbed out by the ruins of the siege engine and ran behind its wheels for cover. Arrows peppered the land around him.

Bleeding and cursing, he quickly surveyed the battle. The other siege towers all burned. The other gangplanks too had crumbled. A few of the attacking troops—a group of Oridian fighters—were raising great ladders across the moat and climbing, but arrows plucked them down, and soon fire and axes sent the ladders crashing down.

Torin's heart sank as surely as the men in the moat. Not one man of the Northern Alliance had managed to reach the city's ramparts, let alone cross them.

He stared back toward the east where most of their forces—swordsmen, elephants, and horses still stood, waiting to enter the gates, those gates Torin and his men had failed to open. Upon his horse, Cam raised a horn and gave two short blasts. *Fall back.*

"Fall back!" Torin shouted to the survivors around him. Men were hunkering behind burning debris, and some survivors crawled out from the moat, limbs shattered. Most of the attackers lay dead, and arrows kept flying. "Fall back!"

Torin lifted a wounded man, slung him across his shoulders, and began to run. Around him, a handful of others rallied and ran with him. Arrows plunged down like fiery comets. One slammed into Torin's back, and he cried out, hoping his armor shielded him. He kept running. Arrows pattered down around his feet. An Oridian fell dead before him. A Verilish woman screamed, three arrows thumping into her back, and fell. Torin kept racing, the last few survivors of the assault around him.

Finally he was out of range, and he reached the rest of his army. Only twenty others had returned with him.

Cam dismounted and rushed toward them. Torin placed down the wounded man he carried, then stumbled toward his friend, nearly collapsing.

"I hate war," Torin said miserably. "I'm a gardener, not a soldier. I don't know why you keep dragging me into these messes, Cam."

Back at the city walls, the remains of the siege towers burned, and the enemy cheered.

CHAPTER EIGHTEEN
THE RED FLAME RISES

Serin stood upon the guard tower, gazing across the field toward the enemy forces.

"The raven flies back to its nest," he said. "The orca swims back into the depths. The bear retreats to his den. They were foolish to attack these walls."

Over a hundred towers surrounded the city of Markfir, walls stretching between them—the greatest fortification in the world. Serin stood on the tallest tower among them, the Sun's Eye. From these heights, hundreds of feet above the ground, he could see all of Eldmark Fields and the bleeding army from the north.

"Did you enjoy seeing that, Lari?" Serin asked, turning toward his daughter. "Did you enjoy seeing the bloodshed, the bodies burning, the arrows and boulders tearing into them? Look below, Lari. Do you see the corpses floating in the moat?"

His daughter trembled. She wore bright armor filigreed with gold, an eclipse upon the breastplate. A helmet topped her head, and she held both spear and sword. And yet her eyes still dampened, and her lips still shook.

"I enjoyed it, my lord," she whispered. "If you free my brother from the dungeon, I promise to enjoy every battle. I promise to be Lari, not Ariana anymore. My lord, please, I—"

He lifted his hand to strike, and she flinched and bit her lip. Instead of backhanding her, Serin caressed her cheek, his gauntlet scraping the skin like a razor.

"Call me 'Father,' my darling. I'm your father now."

She nodded, blinking tears away. "Yes, Father. But my brother, I saw him in the dungeon, I—"

"You have no brother, Lari!" He laughed. "But some turn you will bear me a grandson, a boy to become my heir."

A gagging, scraping sound rose behind Serin. He turned to see Headmaster Atratus clearing his throat; it sounded like a vulture regurgitating a mouse. The mage's bony fingers clutched the battlements like talons. The stooped, beak-nosed man stared off the tower, indeed seeming like some vulture gazing from an eyrie, waiting for a wounded animal to die before it swoops.

"Master," said the balding mage, "there are many powerful men who would marry the girl. The King of Eseer, a barbarian, perhaps would enjoy her. The Jungle King of Naya, barely more than an ape, would be glad to take her into his bed." He glanced toward Lari and licked his small, sharp teeth with a white tongue. "Yet it would be a shame to allow such a pure, beautiful daughter of Mageria be defiled by a lesser race. You've already sold your sister, the fair Iselda, to a foreign man from the Oridian backwater, and we saw how the Oridians repaid you. Your own daughter deserves a man of Mageria. Your grandson should be pure of blood."

Serin narrowed his eyes, staring at Atratus. "And I presume that you have such a man in mind."

Atratus bowed his head. "Master, you've named me your chief mage, and I've championed your cause for many years. I would gladly marry the girl Lari, even this . . . new Lari. I would give you a grandson of pure blood, strong of magic."

Serin stared at the headmaster, and a fire ignited inside him. How dared that twisted, bony creature crave his daughter, crave to steal Serin's precious prize? Serin had already lost his first Lari. He would keep his second Lari close. Precious. Safe. He glanced back toward his daughter, admiring her curved form, her large eyes, her pink lips.

She's not really my daughter, whispered a voice in his head. *I can claim her as my own. I can impregnate her myself. I can father my own grandson and heir.*

He turned back toward the battlements and gazed east. The alliance of rebels—those scum from the north—were setting camp across the field, raising tents and spreading out their forces.

"The enemy will not attempt to scale these walls again," Serin said, watching them. "They tested our strength. They failed. They will not be so foolish again. They will lay siege to our city, blocking the

649

roads, cutting off our supplies. Half a million souls live in this city, and the enemy will attempt to starve us." He looked back at Atratus. "I will allow no siege. The mages of Markfir must ride out and crush the enemy. And you will lead them, Atratus."

Atratus inhaled sharply. "Master, I am an educator. A man of learning, a teacher of youths." He glanced toward the hosts of thousands, then back at his emperor. "Master, I would remain at your side, your adviser, not rush into the field like a common soldier, like—"

"You taught Offensive Magic at the university, did you not?" said Serin. "You taught the art of war. Does the great teacher of war dare not ride to one?"

Atratus licked his dry lips. He glanced at the field, and a bead of sweat appeared on his brow. Yet he straightened as far as he could and nodded. "I will lead the assault, Master. Three hundred mages protect this city. I will lead them out." His voice trembled only the slightest. "Three hundred should be more than sufficient for our task. But . . ." He cleared his throat and twisted his fingers. "I would suggest bringing the avalerions. To strike fear into their hearts."

Serin sighed. "And to offer you some protection. But yes. The avalerions will rise and fly. And the enemy will fall."

* * * * *

Torin stood in a tent pavilion, his wounds bandaged. The commanders of the Northern Alliance stood with him: King Camlin of Arden, Lord Hogash of Verilon, and King Eris of Orida. With them stood a host of other lords, and Eris's Elorian wife stood here too—Princess Yiun Yee of Leen, clad in silk robes and no armor. As they gathered here in the field, the Radians still chanted upon the city walls.

"Our siege towers are gone, and there's not enough wood in these barren plains to construct more," Eris said, face grim. "It's unnatural for a land to be so barren of trees. It chills me."

"And even if we built more siege towers, the walls are too well defended," Torin said, wincing with the pain of his wounds. "Thousands of soldiers man those walls."

Cam pointed at the table that lay before them. A map of Mageria was unrolled across it. "So we set siege to the city. Serin will find little aid. Much of his Sunmotte garrison fell in Orewood, and most of his men are still deep in Eloria. If we cannot enter the city, then no one will—no farmer bearing produce, no merchant with supplies, no shepherd with sheep or goats. We'll starve him out."

"That can take a year or longer," Tanin said. "The city must be stocked well enough to last a long time."

Cam nodded. "We've been fighting this war for two years already. So long as we keep our supply lines open, we'll be well fed here. So we wait. Another year and Serin will be forced to open the gates, or he'll starve. He—"

Horns blared from the city.

Torin spun around to stare. He felt the blood drain from his face.

"Has it been a year already?" A chill ran through his bones. "The city gates are opening."

They stepped out from the pavilion and stared across Eldmark Fields. Indeed the enemy had opened the city's thick oaken doors, and a drawbridge slammed down, spanning the moat. Black horses began emerging from the city, two by two, and soon three hundred rode across the field. On them rode men in black robes, hooded, carrying no weapons and wearing no armor. The enemy's horns blared again and again from the walls, signaling doom.

"Mages," Cam said. He raised his own horn and trumpeted over the enemy's wails. A single, long blast. *Attack.*

Torin mounted his horse, a brown stallion named Geranfon, a gift from King Eris. He gritted his teeth and galloped forth to meet the mages.

Cam blared the horn again. *Attack! Attack!*

The Northern Alliance raced toward the enemy: thousands of riders upon horses, bearing swords, and thousands of Verilish warriors upon bears, swinging their war hammers. Only three hundred mages rode toward them, but Torin knew that one mage could slay many soldiers.

When only a hundred yards separated the forces, the mages stretched out their arms and blasted forth their magic.

"Shields up!" Torin shouted.

Streams of black smoke shot toward the charging riders. One blast slammed into Torin's shield, cracked the wood in half, and crawled up his arm, tearing at his vambrace. Torin grunted, tossed the halved shield aside, and kept riding. A mage galloped toward him, casting more magic. Torin rode by, rose in his stirrups, and swung his sword.

The blade sank into a protective shield of air, doing the mage no harm.

Torin spun his horse around to see the mages tearing through the Northern Alliance. Smoke tugged down horses and bears, ripped off armor, and tugged bones out from flesh. A smoky strand grabbed an Oridian rider several feet away and squeezed, crushing the armor like a tin cup. Blood leaked from inside.

Horror clutched Torin. *We were fools to ride here. We should have fled.*

He gritted his teeth.

No fear. Not now.

He charged back toward the mages and swung his sword at one of the robed, hooded men. The mage blocked the blade with a blast of magic. The man's black hood fell back, and Torin gasped.

He knew that face! He had seen it before! The man was balding, a ring of oily black hair surrounding his head. His nose was hooked, his eyes dark and glittering. He reminded Torin of a vulture, and then he remembered.

"Professor Atratus," Torin said, the name tasting like ash. He had seen the man only briefly when bringing Madori to Teel University, but he hadn't forgotten the malice in that face.

Atratus sneered and raised his hands. He blasted forth magic.

The black energy slammed into Torin's breastplate. His horse reared beneath him, and Torin fell from the saddle. He hit the ground.

"Warriors of Verilon, slay them!" rose a cry, and a herd of bears came charging forth. Hogash rode at their lead, swinging a war hammer, and behind him a hundred other warriors of Verilon brandished their own hammers and roared for victory. With a sneer,

Atratus turned away from Torin—perhaps thinking him dead already—and blasted his magic toward the Verilish assault.

Torin leaped to his feet. He tried to find Geranfon, but the horse had run off. All around him, mages, horsemen, and bears clashed in battle. Swords sliced at mages, struggling to tear through their shields of air. A Verilish man rode by and swung his hammer, knocking a mage off his horse. The young man—an albino mage with pink eyes—slammed down at Torin's feet. Torin growled and drove down his sword. The blade pierced through the mage's shield and into flesh, and the man gasped and reached out, struggling to summon more magic before Torin swung his sword again, finishing the job.

"I killed one!" Torin shouted. "They can be killed! Knock them off their horses, break their concentration, and slay them!"

All around him, the riders of the Northern Alliance—thousands of them—swung their weapons. King Eris thrust his lance forward, piercing a mage and knocking him off his horse. Another mage fell dead nearby, crushed by Verilon's hammers. Strands of magic shot out from the remaining mages, scattering corpses. Torin looked around for Atratus, but he could no longer see the mage. The dead covered the field; hundreds had already fallen.

But we're winning, Torin thought, panting as he moved through the battle, swinging his sword. *We're slaying the mages.*

He looked toward the city walls. "Is that all you've got, Serin? Only three hundred mages for us to crush?"

As if to answer him, shrieks louder than any horn rose from the city walls.

Torin looked up and froze. His hopes shattered and burned like the siege engines.

Great vultures were rising from the city, each as large as a dragon. Dank, oily feathers grew across their wings, though their bodies were naked as if plucked, their skin gray and bumpy. They opened their beaks and screeched again, revealing white tongues. Their claws were larger than swords, and their eyes shone red. Torin was instantly reminded of Gehena; these birds seemed molded from the same dark magic, stitched together, grown to monstrous size. An unholy cloud spread above them, shielding the sun, as if the sky offended them. Shadows fell across Eldmark Fields. The mages cheered at the sight of the beasts, crying out to them, "Avalerions! Avalerions!" Seven of the creatures flew toward the Northern Alliance . . . and swooped.

The oversized vultures plowed through the forces. Their talons slammed into bears, ripping them open. They scooped up horses and tossed them down. Their beaks tore through armor and bones.

"Shoot them down!" Cam was shouting somewhere in the distance. "Archers, fire!"

Archers rushed forth, knelt in the field, and fired their arrows skyward. The missiles slammed into the avalerions, seeming only to annoy them. The demonic vultures swooped again, driving through the hosts, tearing through the riders like wolves through a chicken coop.

Torin grabbed a horse, shoved off its dead rider, and climbed into the saddle. He raised his sword. "Men, rally here! Cut them when they swoop!"

The avalerions rose higher, circled beneath the clouds, and dived again. Claws drove through the army. Soldiers flew through the air, torn apart. Horses crumbled. Bears collapsed. The blood spilled everywhere. One of the avalerions flew toward Torin, screeching madly, rot dripping from its beak. Torin swung his sword. It clanged against the beast's talons, doing it no harm. The oversized vulture rose higher, dived again, and slammed into a host of charging horses—including Torin's. He flew through the air and crashed down hard. Men rained down around him.

The corpses of his comrades lay strewn around Torin, and the avalerions kept attacking, lifting men, tossing them down, and the remaining mages kept moving through the field, blasting out their magic. And Torin knew there was no hope.

Hope dies in Eldmark Fields, he thought, lying on his back, too weak to rise.

Horns.

More horns blared.

Not the shrieking horns of the enemy. Not the high, metallic calls of the Northern Alliance. Here were pure clarion calls, a sound like music.

Torin raised his head and stared to the east.

And there he saw it.

"Hope reborn," he whispered.

They marched across the plains, countless, covering the horizon. The dark clouds of magic parted as if driven back, and the sun emerged, its rays falling upon the new host. Their banners rose high, displaying a red flame upon a black field. A great serpent flew above them, a dragon of the night, his beard red, his scales black—the same dragon Torin had ridden as a young man.

"The army of Ilar," Torin whispered, tears in his eyes. "Elorians arrive. The night has fallen upon the lands of the day."

CHAPTER NINETEEN
LAST OF THE DRAGONS

Sitting upon Grayhem's back, Madori stared at the battle ahead and felt the blood drain from her face.

"*Shan dei*," she cursed.

The city of Markfir, a massive hive of towers and walls as large as fallen Pahmey, rose a mile away beneath a mountain range. Before the city spread a great killing field.

"Others attack Markfir," said Koyee, sitting at Madori's side upon a shadow panther. "Orca banners—Orida from North Timandra. Bear banners—that's Verilon of the pine forests. And . . . raven banners. Only a few but rising proud."

"Arden," Madori whispered, and tears leaped into her eyes. "Arden fights. Maybe Father is here."

Shrieks sounded on the wind, and Madori grimaced. Massive vultures, the size of dragons, were tearing into the assaulting free forces. Here flew avalerions; she had learned about such creatures at Teel University, foul things created from dead flesh and fire. Beneath the avalerions, mages rode black horses across the field, casting their magic, tearing apart the attackers. Thousands of Magerians still stood upon the city walls, mere specks from this distance, a massive force. Thousands of dead already covered Eldmark Fields.

Madori stared, barely able to breathe. Her fingers tingled. Her skull felt too fight. She had spent the journey here eager for battle, eager to strike at Serin. Now, seeing the death and bloodshed, she was afraid.

Tianlong streamed above, and upon the dragon's back, Emperor Jitomi blew his horn and cried out, "Ilar, hear me! Warriors of the Red Flame, fear no sunlight! We will crush the enemy. We will smash the city gates and slay the cruel tyrant. We are Eloria. We are the night!"

Upon thousands of panthers, Ilari warriors raised their katanas. Their eyes were weak in the daylight, but clouds hid the sun. They spread across the fields, some mounted, some afoot, some bearing swords, others bows and arrows, the might of Ilar—a hundred thousand strong. They all cried out together.

"We are the night!"

And Madori shouted with them, her katana raised above her head. She was not Ilari; she was a child of Qaelin, a different land of darkness. She was not even fully Elorian; her father was a man of sunlight. Yet now, chanting here, none of that mattered. She was a warrior—not fighting for one kingdom, not even fighting for one half of Moth. She would fight against evil, against the cruelty of the Radian Empire. With Ilar. With the free Timandrians fighting ahead. With Jitomi, the man she loved. With her mother. With all who fought against tyranny.

I am Madori Billy Greenmoat, she thought as the army roared for the night. *I was named after Bailey Berin, the great heroine of the first war. I will be brave like her.*

Koyee stood in her stirrups, clad in silvery scales. "Eloria! Ride! Ride for the night. Ride for fire and for shadow. Ride with me! To war! To victory! To shattering swords and singing arrows! Ride!"

And they rode, an emperor upon a dragon, thousands of Elorians upon panthers, and a single half-breed woman upon a nightwolf.

They rode across the fields, through light and shadow, toward the enemy.

The mages in the field turned toward the Elorians and reached out their arms. Bolts of magic blasted forth.

"Ride!" Koyee shouted.

"Ride!" Madori cried with her.

The Elorian army thundered across the field, the panthers growling, their eyes glowing. The blasts of magic hit them. A ball of smoke and metal shards crashed into a panther at Madori's side. The beast collapsed and rolled, spilling its rider. Another blast of magic plunged down like a comet, slamming into another Elorian. The man and his panther fell, crushed and burnt.

"Ride!" Madori shouted, sword raised. "We are the night!"

The projectiles kept slamming into them, tearing down rider after rider, but the survivors kept racing forward, thousands of them. The great avalerions swooped forth, and above her, Madori glimpsed Tianlong battling the beasts, snapping his jaws and whipping his tail. One avalerion plunged down, its throat torn out, and slammed into the ground ahead of Madori. Grayhem raced over the corpse as if bounding over a hill. Panthers growled and followed. Another avalerion crashed down dead, and Elorians fired from their panthers, slamming their arrows into the remaining beasts.

"For Eloria!" Madori cried, riding toward the mages ahead.

She raced between free Timandrians now—Verilish riders on bears, Oridians on horses—and reached the dark mages of the enemy.

The mages did not retreat. One, hidden in his black robes, blasted out magic and tore down three panthers. Another mage ascended in the air and shot out electricity, tearing Elorians off their mounts. Grayhem weaved between the enemies, leaping over blasts of magic, and bounded toward a mage ahead.

The mage turned his horse around to face Madori.

She lost her breath.

She trembled.

The mage stared at her, and his face twisted into a cruel smile.

"Atratus," she whispered.

His smile widened, revealing his small, sharp teeth, his hooked nose drooping to hide his top two incisors. He began walking toward her, stepping over corpses. "Hello, mongrel." He raised his hands, the fingers crackling with energy. "You have returned to me for your final lesson."

Madori screamed and hurtled forth her magic.

Her former professor sneered and blasted forth his own foul spells.

The projectiles crashed in midair, exploding and showering sparks. Instantly, Madori raised a shield of protective air. Not a second later, Atratus's magic flared again, slamming into the force field. Madori screamed, her shield shattering, the blast knocking her down.

She leaped up at once. She levitated shards of broken steel and tossed them forward. He waved the projectiles aside, cast out a ball of air and hardened smoke, and knocked her down again. She yowled, blood dripping down her chest.

Atratus stepped closer toward her, moving through the battle. All around the combatants fought—mages tearing down men and beasts, avalerions and dragon battling above. Fires blazed across the field and smoke unfurled. The stooped headmaster leaned over Madori and licked his chops.

"Your death will not be quick," he said, sending down tendrils of smoke. The strands wrapped around her. "I will toy with you first."

She tried to claim the strands, to rip them off, but his magic was too strong. She tried claiming his flesh, to tear it open, but a shield of air surrounded him; she could not break through. Tears budded in her eyes as he levitated her, as his strands squeezed, constricting her breath.

"Atratus . . ." she whispered hoarsely. "You . . . you will fail. You cannot win this battle."

Atratus sighed. "Your band of nightcrawlers will not enter the city. They will be crushed here upon the field. Already they fall. But I won't let you live long enough to see their defeat."

He tightened the strands further. Her scale armor cracked. Hovering a foot above the ground, she couldn't even scream in pain. Stars floated before her eyes. Darkness began to spread, closing in, darkness like the night, like the shadows of the Desolation where Master Lan Tao had taught her to fight.

Breathe, he spoke in her mind. *Breathe, Madori.*

I can't! Her tears streamed, and she saw nothing but Atratus's face, sneering, mocking her, the shadows all around it. *He won't let me breathe.*

Focus on the air already inside you. Like you did underwater. Become aware. Become a warrior of Yin Shi. Begin with your toes.

Her toes? By the stars, how could she focus on her toes now as the magic crushed her ribs? Yet she obeyed. She moved all her awareness toward her toes, shifting her attention away from the pain in her torso. She felt the tightness of her boots around them. The sharpness of her toenails which she had not properly trimmed. The air around her feet as she floated.

And she no longer felt the pain.

Expand it.

She expanded her awareness, taking in the battle around her, the smoke, the flames, the city beyond. She took all the world into her consciousness, became one with that world, living in the present, experiencing every instant. Time slowed to a crawl.

She was Yin Shi.

She chose and claimed the world.

She brought that world down upon Atratus.

Air slammed against him. A thousand shards of broken blades and armor and bone drove into him. The weight of the sky crushed him. Atratus screamed and fell, and his magic left her.

Madori crashed down to the ground, banging her knees. She did not waste an instant on the pain. She stretched out her arm, palm open, and shot out a blast of energy. The shard coalesced in midair, formed of smoke and debris, and drove into Atratus's chest.

He screamed and fell onto his back. Blood dampened his black robes.

Madori walked toward him, every step creaking with pain, the tip of her katana dragging across the ground. She stared down at the writhing, bleeding man. Suddenly he seemed pathetic to her, a frail, aging man in the mud.

"You call us worms," she whispered, "yet now you writhe in the dirt. Do you know where I learned my focus? In the night." She raised her sword. "Do you know where this blade was forged? In the darkness. You called Eloria weak, yet my Elorian half has always given me strength even in the sunlight. And now it spells your end."

She raised her sword high.

Lying on the ground, he screamed and summoned a shield of air.

Her katana drove through his magic and crashed into his chest.

He sputtered. Blood filled his mouth.

"I only wanted to be a healer," Madori whispered. "But you taught me to kill."

He gave a gasp, reaching toward her with his last breath, and then he breathed no more.

She tugged her sword free and looked around her at the battle. Her mother was fighting ahead upon a panther, leading a host of Elorian riders to slay another mage. Only two avalerions remained in the sky, and Tianlong flew between them, battling the pair. Bodies spread across Eldmark Field, fires burned, smoke rose in columns, and armies spread into the distance.

* * * * *

"Slay them and fly over the city walls, Tianlong!" Jitomi shouted, riding the dragon over the battlefield. "We must open the city gates!"

The armies fought below: mages on black horses, free Timandrians from the north, and a hundred thousand Elorians. Ahead, past smoke and flame and death, rose the walls of Markfir. The charred shells of siege towers lay before the moat, their shattered gangplanks sunken into the water. Upon the city walls, thousands of Radian defenders stood waiting for a new assault; they were armed with bows, catapults, ballistae, and cauldrons of sizzling oil, and the first assault had seemed to cause them no damage.

We must open the city gates and lower the drawbridge, Jitomi thought, *or even a hundred thousand men will be unable to cross the moat and walls.*

Tianlong roared and flew forth toward the walls, but two of the avalerions—rotting vultures the size of dragons—still lived, their bodies pierced with arrows. One was black and warty, the other gray and wrinkly. Both flew toward Tianlong, blood on their claws. They opened their beaks wide, revealing bits of human flesh.

Jitomi fired his crossbow, slamming a bolt into the wrinkly gray avalerion. The beast shrieked and dipped in the sky. The black avalerion soared, reached Tianlong, and lashed its talons.

Tianlong howled. The warty vulture's talons tore through him, and scales rained down toward the battlefield. The dragon's own claws were smaller, barely larger than human fingers, but his jaws were wide. He snapped his teeth, trying to grab the avalerion, to tear it open.

Jitomi loaded another quarrel and shot again. He hit the black avalerion's head, and the beast screeched. Tianlong plunged and closed his jaw around the warty creature's neck, biting deep.

The wrinkly gray avalerion, Jitomi's first quarrel still stuck in its chest, soared up and crashed against them.

Tianlong bellowed and spun through the sky. Jitomi gritted his teeth, clinging onto the saddle. The world turned upside down, and the crossbow fell, tumbling toward the ground.

"Fly, Tianlong!" Jitomi shouted and drew his katana. "Slay the avalerions! To the gates!"

Blood dripped from the dragon. Shreds of his skin hung loosely, revealing the cuts of talons. The black avalerion was still alive, its neck bleeding. It drew nearer, and Tianlong bellowed and shot toward it. The dragon rose higher, dodging the snapping beak, then plunged and drove his jaws into the avalerion's dark flesh. The dragon tugged back, ripping the beast open, and the rank vulture plunged down toward the battle.

Only the gray avalerion now remained, shrieking madly. Perhaps fearing to face Tianlong alone, it swooped toward a group of Elorian archers—easier prey.

"We must open the gates, Tianlong," Jitomi said, the wind nearly stealing his words. He stared at the city wall, fear driving through him. Catapults, archers, and cannons topped the ramparts. "We must fly high. We must open the gates and lower the bridge. Please, Tianlong."

The dragon nodded. He panted and his blood fell, and another one of his scales tore free and fell toward the battle. Yet still he flew onward.

Regaining some courage, the last avalerion soared, tossing aside dead Elorians. As Tianlong flew toward the city, the fetid bird rose to slam against the dragon's belly.

Talons lashed. The creature's beak closed around Tianlong's neck, cracking scales. The dragon tried to roar, to fight back, but only a whimper left his jaws.

Jitomi snarled, leaped from the saddle, and raced up Tianlong's neck. The dragon swayed, and Jitomi nearly fell but grabbed

Tianlong's horn. He drove down his katana, slamming the blade into the avalerion's wrinkly head.

The great vulture opened its beak, gave a last cry, then plunged down toward the battle. It slammed against the earth. Elorians rode toward it and drove swords into its hide.

Tianlong dipped in the sky, panting, his blood raining. "Jitomi, I . . . I must rest."

"You have to keep flying, Tianlong." Jitomi pointed his red sword at the city. "We have to fly over the walls. We must open the gates."

The black dragon nodded and kept flying across Eldmark Fields. He dipped again in the sky. "We will open the gates."

"Higher, Tianlong!" Jitomi shouted. "Higher, out of the range of arrows. Fly!"

The dragon tried to soar. He rose a few feet in the sky. He streamed toward the city walls.

A storm of arrows flew toward them.

"Tianlong, higher!"

But the dragon was too weak. Arrows slammed into him, tipped with fire. They drove into the wounds the avalerions had left. One arrow slammed into his mouth, tearing the palate. Another arrow slammed into Jitomi's armor, denting the steel and scratching his skin.

"Tianlong!" he cried hoarsely. "Fly!"

The dragon kept flying. He raised his head, and he let out a great roar, a roar that shook the battlefield and city. It was the roar of a lost dragon, the last of his kind. It was the roar of Ilar, an empire of fire and shadow. It was the roar of a people risen from darkness, striking back at the burning light, a people fighting against all hope. It was the roar of the night.

He kept flying.

Through arrows and smoke, bleeding, hurting, Tianlong flew forward, body snaking across the sky, red beard fluttering like a banner, a creature of pride and strength and magic. In the battlefield below, Elorians chanted for their champion, and even upon the city walls, Radians gazed with awe, for a few moments transfixed by the beauty of Eloria and her warriors.

Then, upon the wall, a ballista moved.

The great crossbow, large as a catapult, turned toward the dragon. Upon it lay a massive harpoon, larger than a man, a spike of jagged iron. Soldiers at its sides turned winces, and gears and ropes creaked, and Jitomi could barely breathe with horror.

The ballistae fired.

Jitomi cried out.

The harpoon sailed toward them, and Tianlong tried to bank, to dodge it, but he was too weak. Too hurt.

The iron shard drove into him, and Tianlong, last dragon of Eloria, fell from the sky.

They crashed into Eldmark Fields with a shower of dirt.

Jitomi fell from the saddle and rolled across the field. He struggled to rise. He crawled toward Tianlong and embraced his great scaly head.

"Don't die," he whispered. "Don't leave me alone."

The dragon stared at him, eyes narrowed and glowing, and it seemed to Jitomi that Tianlong smiled. Then his eyes closed and would open no more.

Thus the last dragon falls, Jitomi thought. *Thus an ancient wonder leaves Moth.*

He was near the city walls now, close to the moat. When he looked up, he saw arrows flying down toward him from the ramparts. Jitomi dived behind Tianlong. Arrows slammed into the dragon. One scraped against Jitomi. Another slammed into his shoulder, and he cried out in pain.

When he looked up, he saw the archers nocking new arrows.

"Jitomi!"

The cry rose across the field, and he looked east. His vision was blurred, but he made out a gray shape leaping forward, zigzagging across the field. Arrows fell, missing the target.

"Madori!" he cried.

She raced toward him upon her nightwolf. More arrows flew, hitting Tianlong. The nightwolf leaped forward and reached Jitomi.

"Come on!" Madori cried, reaching down from the saddle. She grabbed him and tugged him onto the nightwolf.

Grayhem spun back east and burst into a run. He raced from side to side, arrows falling around him. One scraped along his side, slicing fur. The nightwolf kept running, faster than a galloping horse, until they emerged from the range of arrows and rejoined the rest of their army.

In a crowd of Elorians, Grayhem halted and panted. An arrow in his shoulder, Jitomi stumbled off the wolf and lay on the ground, weary, bleeding, grieving.

"He's fallen, Madori," he whispered. "The last dragon."

She knelt beside him, grabbed the arrow in his shoulder, and tugged it loose. He grunted and his blood flowed.

"But you're still alive," Madori said, eyes flashing. "And you're still the commander of this force. Go get your wounds tended to. The battle continues." Her eyes were red and damp, and she knuckled them dry. "Go!"

He nodded. He squared his jaw. "The battle continues."

I will not die here, Tianlong, he swore. *I will win this war. For your memory. For all free people in both darkness and in light.*

CHAPTER TWENTY
MOONRISE AND SUNRISE

Serin stared down from the city walls at the corpses of his flying beasts and mages. The nightcrawlers were swarming across the field, cheering, staining his empire with their wretchedness.

And *they* were here. Serin saw them even from this distance. The mother and daughter. Koyee. Madori. The women he had vowed to break.

Rage.

Rage, white and blinding, flared in Serin.

"They slew my flying beasts," he whispered, voice trembling. "They slew my mages. They slew my servant Atratus." He clenched his fists, and a grin spread across his face. "They will feel so much pain."

"My lord," said Lari, "I'm frightened. Will the nightcrawlers hurt us? Will—"

He struck her.

He struck her with all his might, driving his gauntlet against her face. Blood showered. She yelped and would have fallen from the wall had Serin not grabbed her.

"I told you," he said. "Call me 'Father.'"

She is like an infant, he thought. *She will learn. She will grow into a true Lari.*

He dragged her off the wall and to a courtyard in the city. He mounted his horse and pulled her onto his saddle, seating her ahead of him. They rode through the city, many guards riding at their sides.

Markfir, one of the largest cities in Moth, was eerily silent this turn. Home to half a million souls, the city normally bustled with life: peddlers hawking every type of food from wheeled carts, urchins scuttling underfoot, buskers and fortune tellers standing at every street corner, and thousands of people walking the cobbled streets between shops and homes. This turn, with the enemy outside the walls, all those people were out of sight. The shops were closed. The people hid in their homes; many had boarded shut their windows. Soldiers stood everywhere, still and stern, their helmets hiding their faces.

Serin kept riding. They passed by many three-storied buildings of brown-gray bricks, their roofs tiled red. Barracks rose upon hills, their towers flying his banners. Temples rose above homes, their steeples scraping the clouds; archers now stood within their bell towers. The city had become a great fortress. Serin knew the nightcrawlers would never break through the walls, but even if they did, they would find only death.

He passed through the second layer of walls, then the third, finally entering the Old City. The buildings here were ancient; the very first people of Mageria had built them two thousand years ago. The bricks were *old* here, so old the mind could barely grasp their age, the craggy stone whispering of long-forgotten histories. Rather than having tiled roofs, these buildings were domed, their windows and doors arched. As the wind blew down alleyways, Serin imagined that he heard the ghosts of those lost generations.

They rode uphill toward Solgrad Castle, a massive structure whose foundations had been built thousands of years ago, expanded every generation. He dismounted, leaving the horse to his stable boy, and took Lari's hand. He pulled her past soldiers, through the gates, and into the palace hall.

His throne rose upon a dais beneath three draping banners; one showed the Radian eclipse, the second the buffalo of Old Mageria, and the third a tower beneath a mountain, sigil of the city. Guards stood between the columns, faces hidden in their helmets. Serin's sister stood by the throne, wearing a gown of the same crimson fabric, and a golden eclipse shone upon her throat. Iselda's hair cascaded across her shoulders, just as golden, and her blue eyes stared across the hall toward Serin and Lari.

The sorceress walked toward them across the dark tiles. When she reached them, she tilted her head, examining Lari's cut face. She caressed the trembling girl's cheek.

"Precious child," Iselda said. "You must learn not to disobey your father."

Serin ignored his sister and walked past her. Iselda had proven herself useless to him. He had sent her north to marry the King of Orida, to join their armies to his. And now the Oridians—those scum from the sea—lay siege to his city.

Past the throne, Serin saw him. He stood between two columns, clad in black steel, an eclipse upon his breast, as if he were a Magerian.

"Torumun," Serin said, not masking the disgust in his voice. "You stand here in my hall, dressed like us, my sigil upon your chest, husband to my sister . . . while your armies, the very armies I commanded you to lead into darkness, attack this great city of sunlight."

The Oridian prince was tall, almost as tall as Serin, his hair blond, his eyes blue. Clad in his black armor, he could almost pass for a true Magerian; both races were descended from the Old Riyonans, the people of northeastern Timandra. But rather than proving himself worthy of the Radian Order, this man had proven himself weak.

"It is my brother, the usurper named Eris Grimgarg, a craven and tyrant, who leads the hosts of Orida," said Torumun. The damn Oridians always spoke so formally.

"And who let him usurp Orida's throne?" Serin said.

Torumun stiffened. "He had giants with him, my lord. He—"

"I let you wed my sister!" Serin shouted. His voice was so loud Torumun started. "I let you wed her. I let you bed her. I took you into my hall as a brother. You vowed to align your army with mine. Now they attack my gates!"

Torumun had the grace to lower his head. "I am sorry, my lord. I am deeply ashamed." He looked up, and his eyes glittered. "I will find Eris and his wife, the nightcrawler he dragged back from the darkness. I will slay them both." He raised his chin. "I will prove myself worthy of the eclipse, my lord, I swear it. I will retake Orida and turn its armies against the nightcrawlers."

"And you will hand me your thumb," said Serin. "The left one."

Torumun frowned. "My lord?"

"You thumbed your nose at me, brother-in-law. So I think it only fair that you hand me that thumb."

The Oridian stiffened and glanced toward his wife. "Iselda, is—"

"Do as he says," said Iselda. She smiled thinly. "You don't want to cross him. If you don't give him your thumb, he'll ask for more."

Sweat beaded on Torumun's brow. "This is barbaric! I did not come here to play these games. I—"

"You came here seeking sanctuary," said Serin, "after you were banished from your own kingdom, a dog kicked away from his master's table. I took you in. I saved your life. I continue to save it every moment that I shelter you here. Your thumb! Draw your sword. Cut it off. Hand it to me now, here in this hall, or I will have your whole hand, then your arm, then your head."

The guards across the hall shifted, hands reaching toward their hilts. The blood drained from Torumun's face. Iselda approached him, placed a hand on his shoulder, and smiled.

When Serin left the hall, he smiled too. He returned to the city walls and gazed out at the enemy besieging him. He unfolded his handkerchief, grabbed the thumb within, and tossed it off the city walls as far as he could.

* * * * *

The last of the demonic vultures had fallen; so had Tianlong, last dragon of the night. The mages lay dead, and the surviving allies—a great coalition of free nations from both day and night—were searching for the wounded among the piles of dead. Upon the city walls, the Radian defenders shouted and jeered, awaiting another assault. For now, only death stretched between the forces, a no man's land of scattered flames and corpses. The battle lulled. As both sides nursed their wounds, crows descended to peck at the fallen.

Torin limped through the battlefield, aching, bleeding, cut and bruised a hundred times. But he did not care about his wounds, about the pain. He cared about only one thing now.

The Ilari might have news. His eyes stung. *If they traveled through Qaelin on their way . . . Oh, Idar, they might have seen Koyee and Madori.*

He walked between his comrades of the Northern Alliance, a collection of Timandrian warriors from three nations. He made his

way past horses and bears, across a field of dead, and toward the
Elorian army. The warriors of Ilar sat ahead upon great, black
panthers the size of horses, the beasts' eyes glowing yellow. The
riders seemed almost as beastly, clad in black steel plates, their
helmets shaped as snarling demons; their large Elorian eyes glowed
through holes in the visors, indigo and green and deep purple. Many
katanas hung across their backs, and tassels hung from their shields.

Torin tried to remember the Ilari dialect—it was similar to
Qaelish, a language he spoke well—to ask for news about his wife.
And then he saw her.

He froze and lost his breath.

Koyee sat upon an Ilari panther, but she wore Qaelish armor—
a suit of silvery scales and a simple, unadorned helmet of bright steel
which left her face bare. She turned toward him and met his eyes, and
Torin felt as if the pillars of creation tumbled around him.

He wanted to be strong. He wanted to be a soldier, a hero. But
his eyes watered, and his body shook, and he could barely stay
standing.

Koyee.

He had not seen his wife in over two years, not since that
summer he had taken Madori to Teel University. Over two years of
war, pain, fear. So many sleepless turns, worrying, not knowing if
Koyee lived or died. So many turns in darkness, afraid, missing her,
imagining her by his side.

Koyee.

The woman he had met over twenty years ago in the darkness
of Eloria, returning her father's bones into the night. The woman he
had fought in Pahmey, then loved, then protected, then married. His
lantern in the darkness. The very beat of his heart. His reason to live.
His love. His wife. His Koyee.

She dismounted and seemed almost hesitant, almost unsure.
Perhaps, with his beard and dented armor, she was uncertain it was
him. He reached out to her.

"Koyee."

Her eyes flooded with tears, and she ran toward him, and she
crashed into his arms, and she wept, and he wept with her. They

stood in blood, death all around them, embracing, kissing each other, trembling, laughing.

"Torin." She laughed through her tears, her body shaking with sobs. "Oh Torin. It's you. It's you."

He couldn't speak. He could only hold her. When words finally left his mouth, all he could say was, "I love you. Koyee, I love you."

She clung to him. "I love you too, Torin. I was so scared. Thank the stars, thank Idar, thank Xen Qae . . . oh Torin, I was so scared, and I love you so much."

He swept back strands of her hair. "Where's Madori? Is she . . . do you have news, is—"

"Father!"

He turned and saw her there. Madori ran toward him across the field, and she too wore Qaelish armor and bore a sword.

"Madori!"

His tears flowed anew, and Madori leaped into his arms and squeezed him, nearly crushing him, crying against him. "Father! I didn't know if you were dead. Oh, Father, thank Idar you're here." She frowned and tilted her head. "You look horrible."

He laughed weakly. "We all do. But we're together again."

Madori leaned her head against his chest, and the three of them held one another close, standing together in ruin, never wanting to break apart.

Horns.

Once more, horns blared across Eldmark Fields.

Torin turned toward the sound. From the north, great siege towers were rolling across the field. Torin narrowed his eyes. How could this be? All their siege towers had burned at the walls! Then Torin saw that here were greater structures, wider and taller, built of metal and leather. Many troops walked alongside the towers in neat rows, clad in scales and silvery cloaks, and they raised long standards bearing moonstars and diamonds. Thousands of the soldiers advanced toward the field. At their lead rode a man upon a nightwolf, armless and legless but proud and tall, a crown upon his head.

Torin had not thought he could shed more tears, but his eyes dampened again.

"The hosts of Qaelin and Leen," he whispered. "All of Eloria has risen."

* * * * *

The cannons fired for hours, blasting the walls of Markfir.

Torin stood in the field, covering his ears as the cannonballs kept flying. The projectiles shot across Eldmark Fields, slamming into the walls again and again, chipping off stones. Cracks spread across the ramparts. A turret crumbled and fell. Yet still the walls stood, for they were several feet thick, and even the guns of Eloria could not shatter them, no more than they could have shattered the mountains beyond.

"Keep firing at the gates!" Emperor Jin shouted, riding his nightwolf between the guns. "Smash them open!"

A cannon fired, rolling backwards in the field. Its cannonball flew across the field and moat and hit the city gates. The doors, carved of thick stone and reinforced with iron, withstood the attack.

Perhaps magic too reinforces them, Torin thought. *Perhaps we—*

Cannons fired from the city walls, great guns shaped as buffaloes, larger than the Elorian weapons. Cannonballs flew toward the Alliance. Torin cursed and raced for cover, diving into the ditch he had dug earlier that turn. More guns blasted. His head spun. Smoke covered the world. Men screamed. When Torin rose from the ditch, he found that an enemy cannonball had hit one Elorian fire team; the gunners lay dead, their corpses torn apart, little of them left to bury.

His ears ringing and his stomach churning, Torin turned away from the carnage. As healers rushed forth to scour the field for pieces of the dead, Torin walked toward Jin. The limbless emperor turned on his nightwolf. His face was sweaty, his eyes weary.

"How do you Timandrians stand this sunlight?" the Qaelish emperor said. "It's so bright and hot and burns the skin."

Torin looked up toward the veiled sky. "You're lucky it's overcast." He returned his eyes to the emperor. "Jin, the guns have done their work. We're already low on gunpowder. With your forces and siege towers, we have the might to assault the walls again." Torin sighed. "Our guns will be heard across Moth. Serin has more armies in this world, and they will be heading back home. We must slay him before he receives aid."

The young emperor nodded. "I'll summon the council."

As guns and catapults kept firing from both sides, the commanders of the Alliance met in the field. Several Elorians stood to one side: Emperor Jin, limbless, astride a nightwolf, leading the forces of Qaelin; Princess Yiun Yee and her father, the wise old Emperor of Leen; and Jitomi alongside several of his nobles, commanders of the Ilari host. With them gathered the commanders of the Timandrian forces opposing Serin: King Camlin and Queen Linee of Arden, and with them Torin; King Eris of Orida, tall and fair, his golden beard singed from enemy fire; and finally Lord Hogash, the bluff gatekeeper who now commanded Verilon's forces. After only a quick gathering, the guns blasting as they spoke, they parted.

The Alliance gathered for another assault. Nine Qaelish siege towers, constructed of metal sheets over iron beams, arranged themselves in a line. Men stood within them upon platforms, ready to turn levers and spin gears and wheels.

"Stay behind," Torin said to his daughter. He placed a helmet over his head. "Stay at the back of the battle where it's safe."

She glared and placed her hands on her hips. "Father, there's no way I'm staying behind. I fought for two years in this war, and I slew Professor Atratus myself, and I'm not staying behind now, and—"

"All right."

"—I refuse to just hide when the end is here, and I insist on killing Serin myself too, and—"

"All right, Madori." Torin scratched his chin.

"—and how dare you tell me to stay behind when . . ." She blinked. "Oh. All right." She grinned and leaped toward a siege engine. "I'll just climb in and—"

This time, it was not horns that rose across the field, interrupting her words. It was the sound of drums and the roar of countless men and beasts, a cry cruel and thirsty for blood.

Torin felt cold sweat trickle down his back.

Oh Idar . . . what fresh evil assaults us now?

The sound came from the south. He and Madori turned and stared, and both drew their swords.

With so many people already in Eldmark Fields, Torin could scarcely imagine more souls in one place. Yet now countless troops marched from the southern plains, swallowing the land. He dared not even estimate their numbers; he would not have been surprised if a hundred thousand marched here. Some rode camels and wore white robes, and they carried scimitars and spears. Others in this new host sported red, braided beards and wore tiger pelts, and they led living tigers upon leashes. All raised the Radian banners.

"The forces of Naya and Eseer," Torin said grimly. "Come to rescue Serin."

The new forces kept marching, no end to them. They beat their war drums, and they chanted for war.

"Radian rises! Radian rises!"

Horns blared across the Alliance camp. Men abandoned the siege towers and formed ranks, turning away from the city and toward the south. Torin mounted his horse, and Madori hopped onto her nightwolf. Koyee raced forward on her panther, her sword raised, charging toward the southern hosts.

"Alliance, attack! Fight!"

A heartbeat later, the alliance armies—a great gathering of free nations—charged after her, roaring and holding their weapons high. The hosts streamed across Eldmark Fields, banners high, horns blaring, countless troops covering the land, and slammed together in a great crash of metal and wood and screams.

Hope had begun to spring in Torin. He had thought that, with the Elorian hosts bolstering the Alliance, with the avalerions and the mages slain, they could scale the city walls, open the gates, storm the streets and slay Serin. Now he doubted they'd ever reach those walls again. The new enemies charged everywhere. Men and women rose upon camels, white robes flying in the wind, lashing scimitars. Tigers raced through the battle, tearing into soldiers. Jungle warriors fought in a wild horde, thrusting spears, laughing as they killed.

And everywhere, Alliance soldiers fell. The Elorians' eyes were weak in the sunlight, and when the clouds cleared, revealing the blazing sun, their eyesight grew even weaker. The enemy swarmed through their lines, cutting them down. The Timandrians of the Alliance were weary and wounded after long battles, and they too fell to the enemy swords and arrows.

We cannot defeat this new Radian army, Torin realized. *They are too many, too strong.*

A rainforest warrior raced toward him, swinging a sword. Torin parried from his horse and slew the man. At his side, more enemy soldiers swarmed toward Koyee, cutting into her panther. She fell off the beast, landed on her feet, and swung her katana in circles, holding them back. A crowd of men shoved forward, and Madori vanished into their ranks, crying out in fear and rage.

A tiger leaped toward Torin. His horse neighed and bucked, and the tiger lashed its claws, knocking the stallion down. Torin thumped down onto the ground. He swung his sword in mad arcs, struggling to hold back the enemy. He could no longer see his daughter and wife, no longer see any of his comrades. All he saw were the swords of the enemy and the dead around him.

CHAPTER TWENTY-ONE
THE GATES OF SUNLIGHT

As Neekeya rode the elephant down the mountain pass, she beheld a nightmare of such terror that she lost her breath.

"By Cetela," she whispered, feeling the blood drain from her face.

The city of Markfir still stood, its walls cracked but its gates still closed. Armies from every nation covered Eldmark Fields outside the city walls, spreading as far as Neekeya could see. To the north spread a great alliance of free nations from both day and night. To the south, charging against them, sprawled a force of Radians from the rainforest and desert. The enemy seemed more numerous than trees in the swamps, than grains of sand upon a beach, than the stars in the night sky which Madori had described so often. The chants rose from below, again and again. *Radian rises! Radian rises!*

Neekeya could barely breathe. The fear seized her.

She looked behind her. The combined forces of Daenor and Sania spread across the mountain pass. The Daenorians had come here from both the marshlands and their northern plains, uniting under her leadership. They wore crocodile armor and bore longswords and shields. The hosts of Sania bore wicker shields, spears, and many arrows, and many among them rode the fabled elephants of their island kingdom.

Prince Kota sat with her upon their elephant, holding a bow. War paints coiled across his chest, and strings of beads hung around his neck. The Sanian warriors fought bare-chested, fast and light, letting no armor slow them down. Kota turned in the saddle toward her, reached out, and squeezed her arm.

"We will fight together again, Neekeya, my swamp warrior."

She stared down at the enemy, then back up at her betrothed. Her breath shook, but she nodded. "We will fight well."

Neekeya had fought in battles before, but this one dwarfed them. All her other conflicts, combined, would have formed but a small corner of the battle of Eldmark Fields. Her fingers shook. Her chest constricted. She wanted to turn back, to flee, to hide behind the mountains. She could hardly bare to look at the bloodshed below, the carnage of Mythimna.

Then she saw a single raven banner rising from the crowd.

The banner of Arden. Tam's kingdom.

Her eyes stung. Tam had fallen saving her life. She would not abandon this fight, not abandon his memory.

She rose upon the elephant. She raised her crocodile standard in one hand, her sword in the other, and she cried for her troops.

"Warriors of Daenor! Warriors of Sania!" They stared at her, many thousands upon the mountains. "The enemy musters in the fields. We fight now. We fight for truth, for life, for freedom. I am Neekeya, a free woman. Fight now—with me!"

They roared and raised their swords and spears. Their cries seemed to shake the mountain.

They charged into battle, weapons rising as a forest.

Below upon the field, the Radian forces turned toward them, trapped between two foes. Commanders barked orders. Pikemen arranged themselves in lines, weapons thrust out. Archers tugged back bowstrings. Swordsmen stood in formations, blades drawn.

Neekeya's elephant kept charging down the mountains. Many more of the animals charged with her, and thousands of soldiers afoot raced behind. They reached the fields. Arrows tore into their ranks, but they kept charging. They flowed across the field. They slammed into the enemy with screams, blood, and a song of arrows and spears.

Neekeya fought in a haze, firing arrows down upon the enemy. When her elephant fell to their pikes, she fought afoot, swinging her blade. She was fighting in Teel again against Lari and her friends. She was fighting in the marshlands against the invading enemy. She was fighting to save her father, her husband, those fallen, those she knew were beyond saving.

She fought, shouting hoarsely, until her armor was dented, her arms sore, her sword chipped.

"Victory!" Kota was shouting.

"Victory!" cried Princess Adisa.

But there would be no victory to Neekeya, even as the enemy surrendered, as they turned to flee, as they lay dead. Too many had fallen, and she could find no joy in the death around her.

She stumbled through Eldmark Fields, over corpses, between cheering victors and kneeling prisoners, through smoke and scattered flames, a woman alone in a crowd of myriads.

Finally she saw them ahead, visions from her youth, two figures she had dreamed of so often, whom she had never thought she'd see again.

"Neekeya!" Jitomi cried and ran toward her.

"By Idar's soggy old britches, it's her!" shouted Madori, running forward.

They ran toward her across the charred, bloody field, leaping over shattered blades and shattered men. Until they had grabbed her, shaken her, called her name again and again, Neekeya did not believe they were real, did not believe that she still lived while so many had fallen.

"She's hurt," Jitomi said.

Madori examined her. "Covered in more bruises and scrapes than a cat in a doghouse. But they're only flesh wounds." She shook Neekeya. "Can you hear me?"

Neekeya blinked, looked around her, and finally her eyes dampened. It was real. They were here. She was alive.

"Madori," she whispered. "Jitomi."

She pulled them into her arms, held them close, and wept.

* * * * *

Eldmark Fields lay in desolation, a plain of ash and shattered spears, and Madori's heart felt just as broken.

The Alliance surrounded Markfir, half a league away from the walls. For an hourglass turn, they were besieging the city. For an hourglass turn, none would die. It was a time for burying the dead, a time for mourning, a time for shedding tears instead of blood. The banners of many nations were lowered across the Alliance camp, and the only horns that played were horns of mourning, not war.

Madori stood beside her nightwolf, her hand in his fur, feeling so empty, so . . . blank, unfeeling, shocked, a piece of parchment with no runes upon it.

He's dead. Tam is dead.

Neekeya had shared the news, her voice fragile, her eyes red. But Madori did not weep. She did not tremble. She barely felt a thing, only this hollowness, this disbelief.

Tam, my best friend . . . fallen.

She thought of all those childhood summers she had spent with Tam: sneaking into the kitchens of Kingswall Palace to steal blueberry pies, digging for worms and fishing in the river with makeshift rods, riding ponies and imagining they were dragons, wrestling in the grass and pretending to be knights, and a thousand other memories with him, perhaps the best memories Madori had.

And now he's gone.

It seemed surreal. Impossible. She wanted to weep for him, for all the countless souls who had died in this war, for her own haunting pain, for the nightmares of the Radian iron mine, for the scars that would forever cover her body and heart. Yet she could only feel numb.

She turned away from the fields. She looked back toward the other soldiers of the Alliance. King Camlin and Queen Linee sat nearby, tears in their eyes, their son fallen. Between them sat Prince Omry, Tam's twin brother; his face was pale, his foot amputated, and seeing his face—identical to Tam's—only shot more pain through Madori. A string of visitors kept approaching, speaking their condolences. Mostly the king and queen kept silent, staring ahead, as if they too were numb, but every few moments—like a wave in the sea—their tears fell, and they trembled, and everyone around them, even the gruffest soldiers, shed tears with them.

Madori looked back toward the city of Markfir. It lay over a mile away across the field. Thousands of ditches had been dug into that field. Countless bodies filled them. Countless more bodies lay buried or burnt across the rest of Moth. The city of Orewood in the north—reduced to rubble. The city of Yintao in the night—fallen and plundered. The city of Pahmey—gone into the abyss. Oshy. Fairwool-by-Night. Gone.

Madori had heard tales of the first war, the great War of Day and Night in which her parents had fought, the war from whose ashes she'd been born. But this war seemed worse, a tragedy from which the world might never recover. How could Moth survive after so much had fallen? And even if Madori should live, how could she ever find joy in a world of so much pain?

She stared at the soldiers on the walls of Markfir, at the hundreds of towers that rose within the city, at Solgrad Castle upon its crest. He waited there. Emperor Tirus Serin.

"You caused this war," she whispered. "You killed these people. We will meet again, Serin. I will fight you again. And this time I will kill you."

Yet her words tasted bitter, meaningless, empty cliches. Could Serin, one man, have truly caused all this death? How could any one man burn a world? As she stared at the city and the graves, it seemed to Madori that no one tyrant could be blamed.

Perhaps it's the nature of humanity to elevate tyrants to power. Perhaps more than any tyrant can be blamed for death and destruction, it's the shoulders he stands on that bear the shame. One despot falls. Another rises. Even should we sever the snake's head, a new head will grow. For we—sons, daughters, husbands, wives, the rich, the poor, humans afraid and angry—are the body of the snake. Perhaps our hearts are the true tyrants, not the figureheads we raise or the banners we sew.

She tightened her lips and gripped her sword's hilt. She could not change human nature. She could not remove fear, greed, and hatred from the hearts of men. But at least she could cut off one snake's head. She could not bring eternal peace, but perhaps she could end one war. That would have to be enough. That was all, perhaps, she could hope for.

Koyee and several Qaelish soldiers, their armor chipped and their hair stained with ash and blood, rode nightwolves toward Madori. Koyee dismounted and approached her daughter.

"We've spoken to the survivors of Naya and Eseer," Koyee said. "We've taken thousands of Nayan prisoners. With their commanders dead, they've lost the will to fight. We'll let them return to the rainforest, defeated."

Madori nodded, saying nothing.

Koyee continued speaking. "The Eseerian king, a friend to Serin, has fallen in the field, slain by a Daenorian arrow. A new lord has taken command of the surviving Eseerian forces, a kind and noble man; he will join us in attacking the city. Few Eseerians have ever held Serin much love; with their old Radian king fallen, they will now fight with us." She smiled thinly. "Our enemy has turned into a powerful ally."

Madori nodded again, silent.

"Madori . . ." Koyee's voice softened, and she touched her daughter's arm. "Do you hear? Are you all right?"

No, Mother. I'm not all right. How can you ask me that? After all that happened, how can you think I'm all right? I'm hurt. I'm grieving. I'm so scared.

But Madori only nodded again. She forced herself to raise her chin. "That's good. Serin's old allies turn against him." She tightened her grip on her sword's hilt. "It's time to assault the city. It's time to break in."

Koyee nodded. "It's time."

The hourglasses emptied. The turn of mourning was done. Under dark clouds, through rain and mud, the Alliance returned to the walls of Markfir.

The Elorian siege towers, built of metal, rolled across the landscape. The Timandrians from west of the mountains—Sanians and Daenorians—raised great ladders, hundreds of feet tall. Dojai assassins, clad in black silk, scaled the walls like scurrying insects. Thousands of soldiers converged upon the city. With siege towers, with ladders, and with grapples, they reached the ramparts of Markfir.

The city walls bled.

Madori leaped out of a siege engine. A gangplank stretched ahead across the moat, protected with walls and doors of metal; she was safe from fire until she emerged, screaming and swinging her sword, onto the wall. And here, between the merlons, hundreds of feet above the ground, she fought with steel. She fought with magic. She fought with Yin Shi. Her blade swung in arcs, sending Radians falling down into the eastern moat and the western courtyards. Her magic melted armor, blasted out cones of air, and sent men screaming down to their deaths. All around her across the walls, thousands battled, soldiers of every nation in Moth swinging their weapons, a great song of steel, the song of a torn world.

A staircase stretched down before her, leading to a courtyard by the city gates. Madori fought her way onto the stairs, sending Radians crashing down with every step. More soldiers ran up toward her; she knocked them down with blasts of magic. Arrows flew from towers deeper in the city; she blocked them with shields of air. At her sides, dojai were scaling down the walls with grapples and ropes, descending into the city.

"To the gates!" Torin was shouting somewhere in the distance. "Take the gatehouse! Open the gates!"

Madori leaped down four stairs at once, swinging her sword and knocking men back. She landed in the city courtyard, raised her head, and stared around her. Hundreds of Radians were charging her way.

The gates will open. She sneered. *They will open.*

She screamed and charged toward the army, katana raised. Behind her, dozens of Alliance soldiers ran with her.

The battle exploded across the courtyard, a sea of arrows, swords, axes. Men fell, crushed to death. Survivors fought atop corpses. Madori kept moving through the crowd, knocking men back with magic, until she reached the inner side of the gatehouse.

Madori breathed. In. Out.

Be aware. Hold the world in your awareness.

She chose the enemy soldiers around the gatehouse. She inhaled deeply. She claimed them. She shoved them backwards; the soldiers flew several feet in the air, knocked aside as from an explosion of gunpowder.

Madori ran toward the doors. A heavy bar lay in their brackets. She knelt, placed her shoulder under the bar, and struggled to rise, too weak to lift the heavy beam, too drained for more magic.

"Father, a little help!" she shouted. "By Idar!"

Torin ran toward her, as did other soldiers. They lifted the beam and let it fall to the ground. Two great Verilish warriors, seven feet tall with arms the size of Madori's entire body, swung their hammers at the door's padlock.

The padlock shattered.

Men roared and tugged chains, pulling the stone doors open. Madori swung her sword, slicing ropes. The drawbridge slammed down across the moat.

The floodgates broke.

Myriads of Alliance troops waited outside the gates. Roaring for battle, they began to stream into the city of Markfir.

CHAPTER TWENTY-TWO
THE QUEEN OF SUN AND STARS

As Eris charged into the city of Markfir, he kept glancing at his side. A short, slim soldier ran there, clad in the silvery breastplate, smooth helmet, and flowing white robes of Leen.

"Remember, Yiun Yee, stay near me!" he said as he ran into the courtyard. "Always."

She nodded, holding her katana high. "Always."

The battle raged ahead. Arrows flew from the rooftops. Radian and Alliance soldiers fought everywhere with swords and pikes. Eris had fought battles before; he knew of the blood, the terror, the noise, the weak knees, the thrashing heart. He had tried to convince Yiun Yee to stay behind, to await him outside the walls with the engineers, surgeons, and camp followers. She had refused. She had donned armor. She had drawn a sword. And now she fought at his side, charging into the city of the enemy.

Radians stormed toward him across the courtyard, and Eris fought.

He fought like he had never fought before. He had fought in battles, but none like this, the clash of nations, the world come to one city to shed the blood of Moth. And Eris Grimgard, son of Bormund, shed more blood this turn than in all his other battles combined. His sword sang. At his sides fought the Oringard, the legendary heroes who had traveled with him into the night, had helped him find the Meadenhorn which even now hung around his neck.

The Alliance moved through the city, street by street. And on every street the enemy awaited. From every building, archers sent down death. Eris had thought that all the enemy's mages had perished upon Eldmark Fields, but more now emerged, sending death from their fingertips. Men screamed as their hearts burst from the chests and thumped onto the ground, still beating. Others screamed as their bodies twisted, bones snapping. Eris charged toward the mages, swinging his sword, blocking their magic, cutting their flesh. Street by street. House by house. The streets ran red.

And always he stayed near Yiun Yee. Even as the battle flared, she remained in his shadow, shielded by his larger form. And she too killed. One Radian rushed toward her, axe swinging. She cut him down. Another man thrust a spear toward her; she parried, leaped forward, and drove her sword into his chest. Radian blood stained her white robes, and she would not flee even as her legs shook.

They were fighting their way up a narrow street, the brick walls of shops and homes at their sides, when Eris saw the sorceress ahead.

Iselda stood within a brick archway, clad in crimson, smiling. Several soldiers in black armor stood at her sides.

"Hello again, Eris," she said.

Eris froze from fighting. His armor was dented. His arms were bloody. He stared up at the woman—Serin's sister—the sorceress who had tempted his father, had corrupted his hall. The Oringard paused at his sides, panting. The sounds of battle rose from across the city, but for a moment this street was still.

Then Iselda pointed at Eris and his Oringard. "Slay them," she said to her soldiers.

Her Radians rushed forth.

Eris and the Oringard ran to meet them.

Here were no simple troops, Magerian boys drafted from city streets and farms. These Radians wore finer armor, and they fought like machines, every movement calculated; here were noble fighters trained from childhood. They did not simply swing swords wildly; they fenced with beautiful deadliness. Sweat beaded on Eris's forehead as he fought. He slew one man. At his side, one of the Oringard died. Another Radian fell.

Eris was so busy fighting he barely saw Iselda approach.

Her crimson robes fluttered as she walked toward Yiun Yee. A small smile played on her lips. Eris was forced to look away, to lock swords with a soldier. When he finally killed the man and looked back, he howled.

Iselda was smiling, magic flowing out from her fingers. The silvery, astral strands wrapped around Yiun Yee, pulling her close as if reeling in a fish. Magic muffled Yiun Yee; she couldn't even scream.

Eris raced forward and knocked into a Radian. He swung his sword, felling another man.

"Iselda!" he cried.

Before he could reach them, the witch pulled Yiun Yee close and wrapped her cloak around the two, a red cocoon. Eris leaped toward them. Smoke blasted out, and when he could see again, both Iselda and Yiun Yee were gone.

"Yiun Yee!" he shouted.

Around him, the Oringard slew the last of the enemies in the street. Eris ran. He ran through the city, calling for his wife. His men ran at his side. Radian troops ran toward them. The Oringard cut them down.

"Yiun Yee!" Eris cried.

His chest shook. His eyes stung. Iselda must have taken Yiun Yee to Solgrad Castle—to torture her, to kill her. He had to reach his wife. Why had he brought Yiun Yee here? Why had he placed her in danger? He ran, calling her name.

Yiun Yee. If he lost her, he would fall upon his sword. The woman who had met a beast, a mindless killer, and tamed him. The woman who had taught him mercy. The woman who had shown him he could be more than a warrior, that he could be a man of life as well as death.

And now, without her, all he brought was death, and the dead piled up before him as he fought.

He kept moving through the streets, calling for his wife. A burly soldier rushed toward him, all in black steel; Eris dueled the man and finally cut him down. Another man rushed toward him from behind a building, thrusting a spear. Eris knocked the spear down, leaped forward, and drove his sword into the soldier. Shadows swirled, and a mage came floating down the street toward him, black robes fluttering, a hood hiding his face. Eris roared in rage, leaped forward, and drove his sword through the mage's robes and into his chest.

The mage screamed.

It was a high scream, muffled.

Eris pulled back his sword. The magic holding the mage afloat shattered. The robed figure fell to the ground, reaching out to him. The hands, sticking out from the black sleeves, were pale and small.

Eris's breath froze.

Something cold and sharp broke inside him.

He knelt. His heart thrashed. His eyes stung. The fear would not let him breathe. He reached down, feeling numb, and pulled the mage's hood back.

Yiun Yee stared up at him, tears in her eyes, a cloth gagging her mouth. Blood spilled from her chest.

The world shattered.

More pain, more terror than Eris had ever known exploded inside him.

He tugged her gag free. She coughed, her lips shook, and she reached to him. "She . . . she put a robe on me, she . . ."

Tears flowed from Eris's eyes. His Oringard gathered around, staring silently. His chest shook. His fingers trembled as he pulled her robe back, revealing her wound, as he tried to bandage her, as he tried to save her life.

"Hold me," she whispered. She reached up a pale hand to touch his cheek. "Hold me as I leave."

He held her, shaking his head, tears flowing. "I'm sorry, Yiun Yee. I'm sorry. Don't leave me. I'm sorry." Sobs shook his body, and he held her close.

She kissed his cheek, and she smiled, and starlight filled her large indigo eyes.

"I forgive you," she whispered. "I love you, Eris. I love you always. I loved you on this earth, and I will love you from the stars. I travel to them now."

Her eyes closed.

He wept.

He held her lifeless body in his arms, and he tossed back his head, and Eris Grimgarg roared—a cry so loud that the entire city heard, a sound so discordant, so broken, a sound of something tearing inside him, something that could never heal.

"Yiun Yee! Yiun Yee! The stars have fallen. The moon has gone dark. Yiun Yee!" He rocked her in his arms, shaking, praying to see some spark of life, knowing it was gone. He kissed her forehead, and his voice dropped to a whisper. "You were brighter than moonlight. You were braver than dragons. I love you, my Yiun Yee."

Languid clapping sounded ahead.

"Lovely poetry, brother," rose a voice. "You should have become a bard, not a soldier."

He raised his eyes, still holding his dead wife, and saw Torumun ahead. Iselda stood at his side, smiling crookedly. A dozen Radian soldiers stood behind them.

Slowly, Eris placed his wife down and lifted his fallen sword.

"You did this," Eris whispered, voice hoarse. Blood dripped down his arms—his wife's blood.

Torumun tilted his head and frowned. "Dear brother, it does look like *you* are the one who slew her. I saw it. Your own hand drove your own sword into your nightcrawler's filthy heart."

Eris bellowed, a cry as much of rage as grief, and raced forward, sword swinging.

Torumun raised his own blade, smiling thinly, and parried.

The two fought. They fought like fire and ice. They fought like day and night. Their blades clanged, sparking, banging against the walls of homes. Their boots thudded against the cobblestones.

Torumun laughed as he fought. "You've never been able to best me in swordplay, little brother! You won't best me now." He laughed. "I will slay you, and I will dump your body in the moat, and I will hang your wife's body in the halls of Orida."

Eris screamed, lunged forward, and thrust his sword madly. Torumun smiled, sidestepped, and lashed his sword along Eris's hip below the breastplate.

Eris gasped, pain exploding through him. Blood spilled down his thigh. He glanced at the wound. It was deep. He stared back up at his brother, snarled, and lunged forward again. He found an opening, thrust his sword, but the blade clanged against Torumun's armor, unable to pierce it.

Torumun swung again, cutting deep into Eris's shoulder.

Eris faltered. He wanted to cry for his Oringard for aid, but they were busy fighting their own duels.

He fell to his knees. He rose again. Torumun struck, and the blow rang against Eris's helmet, and Eris fell. His sword clattered across the cobblestones.

Torumun stood over him and shook his head sadly.

"And thus your life ends, brother. You could have served me. Now you die like a worm. Farewell."

Torumun raised his sword high and swung it down. With his last whisper of strength, Eris raised the Meadenhorn. Torumun's blade hit the artifact and shattered into many shards.

For an instant, Torumun stood frozen in shock, holding a blade-less hilt.

Eris grabbed one of the fallen steel shards, rose to his feet, and drove the metal deep into Torumun's throat.

His brother gasped. He tried to speak. He tried to pull the shard out. He fell, sprawled out, and would not rise.

Eris stood panting, bleeding, shaking. Around him, the Oringard defeated the last Radians in the street.

My father, Eris thought in a haze. *My wife. My brother. I slew them all. What remains of me?*

Iselda walked toward him through the carnage. Her eyes were sad, as if some spell had lifted from them. She seemed very fair, tall and pale, her golden hair shining, her eyes the deepest blue. The sorceress placed a hand on Eris's wounded shoulder.

"You fought bravely, Eris," she said. "You proved yourself stronger than your father. Stronger than your brother." Iselda caressed his cheek. "I will let you take me. I will be your wife. Return with me to Orida, and we will rule together, and the world will bow before—"

Eris lifted his fallen sword and drove it into Iselda's chest.

As she died, he wept.

He looked around him at all those he had killed, the death he brought wherever he went.

"All I wanted was to retrieve the Meadenhorn," he whispered, holding it up, gazing upon its beauty, the filigree and jewels that shone. "An heirloom. A blessed thing, the horn Orin drank from. It saved my life . . ." He lowered his head. "It saved me as I killed all others around me. It is a cursed thing."

He unslung the horn off his neck. He tossed it aside. His Oringard stared at him, silent.

"My lord," said Halgyr, the squat, bearded lord of the Oringard. "You are wounded and need healing."

Eris gazed at him with clouded eyes. "Halgyr, you are strong and wise. Lead them. Lead the Sons of Orin. Become more than a soldier. Become a king."

Halgyr raised his chin. "You lead us, Eris Grimgarg. You are our only king. You are Orin Reborn."

Eris shook his head. "I am Orin fallen."

He raised his brother's sword. And he fell upon it. He closed his eyes and he thought of his wife, of the stars in the night that he would gaze at so often, wondering at their distance and beauty. He oared toward them in a great longship, the waves black, sailing toward halls of mead and song, toward Yiun Yee.

The Oringard stood around him, staring down at their king, heads lowered.

Halgyr knelt and held the fallen king's hand. Head bowed, he spoke softly. "He fell with honor, though his heart was filled with shame. He died nobly, though he lived believing himself ignoble. He fought the enemy bravely, saving many lives, though he thought himself a murderer. We will carry on his name and the name of his fair wife, the wise daughter of the night. Forever will Orida remember Eris and Yiun Yee, the sun and moon of our island." He placed a hand upon his king's head, and his gruff face softened. "Farewell, my king of sunlight." He turned toward Yiun Yee and gazed at her calm, pale face, a countenance fair even in death, and at her eyes that stared toward the sky. "Farewell, my queen of shadow. May the sun and moon forever shine upon you."

With that, Halgyr rose, walked down the street, and lifted the Meadenhorn upon its chain. He hung it around his neck, and his fellow Sons of Orin gathered behind them. They lifted the bodies of their king and queen and bore them out of the battle and into legend.

CHAPTER TWENTY-THREE
TORN

"To the castle!" Madori shouted, riding Grayhem through the city. "Friends, with me!"

Many soldiers of the Alliance ran with her, fighting for every step. His dragon fallen, Jitomi now rode a shadow panther, the beast clad in armor as black as its fur. Neekeya had lost her elephant in the battle; she now shared Grayhem's saddle, clinging to Madori with one hand, swinging her sword with the other. Thousands of other humans and animals battled around them, a great swarm covering the city.

"Onto the roofs, Grayhem!" Madori cried, pointing upwards. "The streets are too crowded."

The nightwolf seemed to understand. He leaped onto a building, jumping from window to spout, until he was racing across the tiled roof. Jitomi's panther followed, racing close behind. They vaulted off the roof, sailed over a street, and landed on the next house. They sailed across another street, then kept leaping from roof to roof. All around them, countless soldiers clogged the streets, battling over every cobblestone. Madori spotted her parents fighting a few blocks away, leading a host of Qaelish warriors through the city's third and final layer of walls.

She returned her eyes to the city crest. Solgrad Castle rose there upon the hill, the mountains rising behind it. That was where he lurked. She felt him, felt his eyes staring from the castle tower. She felt his sword cut her again, like it had cut her on the road outside of Teel. The scars of that battle remained. That battle would now resume.

"To the castle, Grayhem," Madori said, pointing ahead. "Take us there."

They vaulted across a wide street swarming with troops. Arrows flew from below, hitting their armor. They kept riding.

Jitomi's panther leaped at Madori's side, a shadow darting forth. Soon they were only a few hundred yards away from Solgrad Castle. It loomed above, the greatest building Madori had ever seen. She could make out the gates ahead, several guards outside them.

Sitting behind her in the saddle, Neekeya tightened her grip around Madori's waist. "Only several men guard the doors, but he'll have many soldiers around him."

Madori nodded. "And we bring many with us. With magic. With wolf and panther. With swords and arrows. We end this now."

She looked behind her. The Alliance troops were storming forth. Many of their nightwolves and panthers had also taken to traveling the roofs; hundreds now rode behind Madori. Thousands more raced up the streets.

"With thousands of swords," she whispered. "We end this."

Leading the pack, Grayhem sailed across another street when the explosions rocked the city.

Sound slammed into Madori. She screamed, not even hearing herself, and grimaced, unable to cover her ears while holding shield and sword. Smoke blasted across her an instant later, and debris peppered her. The smell of gunpowder flared. Bricks flew through the air. Grayhem leaped through the explosion, landed upon a roof instants before it crumbled, then vaulted again and landed in a courtyard. Jitomi and his panther landed beside the nightwolf, coated with dust.

Grayhem turned around, and Madori felt the blood drain from her face.

Several city blocks were gone. The devastation spread in a ring. Ancient buildings, thousands of years old, had collapsed into rubble. Dust and smoke rose in clouds, and the smell of gunpowder joined the stench of death. A hundred Alliance troops lay upon the ruins, torn apart. Thousands more were buried.

"He surrounded the castle with barrels of gunpowder," Neekeya whispered. She dismounted and stared at the ruins, dust painting her gray. Her eyes reddened. "He . . . he must have killed thousands of his own people to stop us."

Madori stared past the rubble. A mile away, the rest of their forces were still battling Radians in the streets, advancing only foot by foot. She sneered and spun back toward the castle.

"And so I face him alone."

She began riding uphill toward the castle, eyes narrowed, her katana raised, leaving her friends behind.

Jitomi raced up toward her upon his panther. "Madori! We cannot storm the imperial palace without an army."

Neekeya ran alongside. "Madori, we must turn back."

She kept riding, ignoring them, staring ahead at the castle gates. *You're in there, Serin,* she thought. *You're watching me now, awaiting me.* Her fingers tingled around the hilt of her sword. *I'm coming to you.*

"We won't need to storm the castle," she said softly. "He knows we're coming. He's waiting for us. And I will face him alone." She looked at her friends. "Go back. Go rejoin the others. I must do this now."

They kept advancing with her, moving away from the ruins toward the castle.

"We parted from you once," Jitomi said. "It took a long time to reunite."

Neekeya nodded. "We stick together from now on. Always."

Moans, screams, and clanging steel rose behind them in a chorus. Silence lurked ahead. They rode across a courtyard strewn with rubble and approached the castle gates. Only a dozen guards stood here, armed with pikes; they charged forward. The three young mages, summoning their training from Teel, cast forth blasts of dust and air. The magic slammed into the guards with the force of a typhoon, knocking them back against the castle walls. They slumped down, unconscious. Another blast of magic shoved the doors open.

Shadows loomed inside. Madori could see nothing but darkness, and cold air flowed from within. She felt as if she stood outside a tomb; she hoped it was not her own.

Madori halted her nightwolf and dismounted. She kissed Grayhem. "You've brought me this far, noble hunter of the moonlit plains. Return now to your comrades who fight beyond the rubble. Do not follow me into the shadows."

He stared into her eyes and bared his fangs. He growled as if to say, "I am a creature of shadows. I come with you."

Madori shook her head. "I will not bring you into danger. We fought in great battles, but here lies my greatest fight, the greatest danger. I cannot bear to see you face it, to lose you." Her eyes stung to remember how Naiko had wounded the nightwolf, and her voice dropped to a whisper. "I've lost too many friends already." She pointed east, away from the castle. "Go, Grayhem! Go!"

The nightwolf wouldn't budge. Eyes damp, Madori summoned her magic. Her tears fell as she thickened the air, as she magically shoved the wolf away, kept him shielded from the castle. His howl tore at her. He clawed at the wall of air, trying to reach her, wailing as she turned away.

I'm sorry, she thought. *I cannot place you in more danger.*

Katana raised, Madori stepped through the castle doorway and into shadows.

* * * * *

As Madori walked through the shadows, she imagined herself back in Eloria, traveling across the great lifeless plains of Qaelin toward the Desolation. She had felt so alone then, so afraid, seeking guidance, seeking a teacher of war. Now again she walked in darkness, seeking not training but the battle itself. And now again she felt afraid.

But I'm not alone.

She looked at her companions. Jitomi walked to her right, clad in dark armor, the dragon tattoo nearly invisible upon his pale face in the shadows. The Elorian boy who had approached her at Teel University two years ago. The Elorian man she had kissed, made love to, perhaps even loved.

Neekeya walked at her left side. Her dark skin and midnight hair nearly vanished into the shadows, but Madori knew that the marshland warrior held a great light inside her. The tall, awkward girl who had attracted so many snickers at Teel, speaking of magical artifacts, offering friends lint-covered toffees from her pockets, and smiling obliviously even as others tormented her. The warrior who had fought for the proud marshes of Daenor, who had returned home with the armies of Sania, who had led men in battle and fought against the horde of an empire.

And one among us is missing, Madori thought. *Tam is not here. Our quartet is forever broken.*

Torchlight blazed ahead, casting back the shadows. They found themselves in a grand hall, windowless, lined with columns. The tiles were black, the walls red. A throne rose ahead, and upon the wall behind it draped three great banners, long as dragons, of the Radian Order.

Serin sat upon the throne, legs splayed out, while Lari stood at his side.

Madori gasped and narrowed her eyes. She had killed Lari! She had stabbed her in the grave of skeletons, had—

This's not Lari, she realized. *It's a lookalike. A trick.*

"Welcome, friends!" Serin said, rising to his feet. He clapped languidly. "You've done well to come this far. I've been anxiously awaiting your arrival. Welcome!"

Madori wasted no time. She summoned particles of smoke and fire from the torches, tugged them down to form a hovering ball, and lobbed her projectile. The magic blasted forward, crackling and shrieking.

The flames and smoke shattered against Serin's shield of air.

Neekeya gave a wordless cry and raised her palms, and Serin's armor began to redden, to heat and creak. Jitomi snarled and blasted forth strands of smoke; they coiled around Serin and tightened, cracking the emperor's invisible shield, beginning to constrict him.

Serin only grinned and raised both palms.

Neekeya and Jitomi screamed, levitating a dozen feet in the air. Serin thrust his hands forward. The young Ilari emperor and the marshland warrior flew through the hall, slammed against columns, and slumped to the floor. Serin laughed, curled his right hand's fingers like a puppeteer, and a stone statue of himself tilted over and slammed down onto Jitomi, crushing the young man. When Neekeya tried to rise, Serin yanked down his left hand as if tugging a rope. A chunk of ceiling came loose and slammed onto Neekeya, burying her under rubble.

Madori screamed and ran toward the emperor, sword swinging.

Serin raised his palm, and Madori slammed into an invisible wall of air. She kicked, trying to break through, to cut her way forward with magic and steel, but she remained frozen.

"Poor little mongrel . . ." Serin said. "Struggling like a mouse between the cat's paws." He raised his hand, levitating her into the air. Madori thrashed, unable to free herself. "I want you to see something, mongrel. I have a little show for you. Do you enjoy theater? Behold, then, the theater of your life."

Holding her aloft with one hand, Serin swept his other hand to the left and right. The Radian banners behind the throne parted like curtains.

Madori stared between the banners . . . and screamed.

Behind the curtains lay a great chamber, its brick walls painted with sunbursts. The floor sloped inward like a bowl, and many writhing, squirming creatures filled the declivity. Their skin was pale gray and wrinkly, their eyes huge and red. Fangs stretched out from their mouths, and claws grew from their fingers. Naked and warty, they climbed above one another, snapping their teeth, mewling, whimpering. Their bones pushed against their skin; she could see the ribs clearly, even hints of red where the hearts beat.

They were Elorians.

Not Elorians like the ones Madori had always known, proud and noble people of the night. Here were Elorians like those the Radians drew in their books, sculpted as their gargoyles, and burned as effigies in their rallies—the twisted, evil creatures who hungered for the flesh of Timandrians, sub-humans with minds of shadow. True nightcrawlers. The creatures saw Madori and reached toward her. Some tried to climb out of the pit, only to slide back down onto their brethren.

"I made them myself," Serin said. "From the Elorians I captured in the night. I had to . . . modify them a bit, to coax out their true forms. Soon the world will see the evil of the nightcrawlers."

But it was not the creatures—these nightcrawlers in the pit—that made Madori shed tears, that made her heart ache, her belly twist, her soul crack. It was what she saw above the pit.

Her parents.

Torin and Koyee were wrapped in strands of magic, held afloat in the chamber like marionettes on strings. Gags of tar filled their mouths. The astral ropes bound their arms and legs, nearly tearing through the limbs. The creatures below kept leaping, reaching up their claws, snapping their teeth, trying to grab Torin and Koyee, to feed upon them.

Her parents stared at Madori, tears in their eyes, entreating her to flee.

Madori wept and tried to reach toward them, unable to break through Serin's magic.

"If they fall into the pit," Serin said, "they will not die. No. The nightcrawlers will infect them, turn them into fellow beasts. Only my magic now keeps Torin and Koyee afloat. I found them in the battle easily enough; they were not hard to recognize even in the crowd. But, sweet Madori . . . if I let them drop, they will become very, very hard to recognize."

Finally Madori found her voice. "Mother! Father!" Held in Serin's magic, she could not move forward, only stretch out her arm, trying to reach them.

Serin tsked. "You might consider calming yourself, sweetest mongrel. Only a slight lapse in my concentration, and my magic will falter. I will not be able to keep Torin and Koyee floating above the pit." He looked at her and tilted his head. "Fight me, and I'll have to dedicate more magic toward you, away from holding your parents above their fate. Kill me and they will certainly fall." He lowered Madori to the floor. "Now place down your sword . . . and we will talk."

Finally freed of his magic, Madori wanted to leap forward, to stab Serin, to end this war, to kill this tyrant. She took only half a step forward, and Serin smiled. Her parents dipped a few inches in the cavern. The creatures in the pit squealed with hunger, leaping up with more vigor. One scraped Koyee's foot, drawing blood. Serin only smiled wider, never removing his eyes from Madori.

Trembling, Madori took a step back.

"Now drop your sword," said Serin.

Never removing her eyes from her parents, Madori obeyed. Min Tey clattered onto the floor.

"Good!" said Serin. "Such an obedient cur. Now we shall negotiate your terms of surrender. It's quite simple. You will speak to the commanders of this so-called Alliance. Your parents being who they are, you're the closest this horde has to a figurehead. You will order the treacherous Timandrians who oppose me to return to their lands; they will have another chance to join my empire. You will then order the nightcrawler mobs to retreat back into the darkness; let them lurk again in shadows, far from my walls. Once their retreat is completed, and this city is safe from their aggression, I will release your parents."

"Only to kill us," Madori said, voice stiff. She stared at Torin and Koyee, and she wanted so badly to speak to them, to rush to them. She wanted so badly to rush toward her friends too, to Neekeya and Jitomi who lay hurt, buried under stone, perhaps dying. But she forced herself to stare into Serin's eyes.

The emperor sighed. "I do confess, mongrel, that for two years now, that has been one of my goals. Yes, to kill you. To kill your parents. I often delighted in the daydream of slaying you. But I think I will delight more in letting you live. Letting you escape. Withdraw your armies, and you will reunite with your parents. I will arrange to transport the three of you to a distant island of my choosing; I know of several beyond the coasts of Daenor. You'll be allowed to live out your lives there—under guard, of course, but otherwise free to enjoy the warm weather, blue waves, and the delights of coconut cuisine. From time to time, you may be tormented with memories, with guilt, with pain for all those I slew, for your cowardly escape from war while so many died. And I, while I sit here in my a palace, a great emperor, will in turn enjoy thinking of you living under my rule, knowing that you lost, that you will grow older and linger under my dominion."

Madori growled. "So that's your deal? I withdraw the Alliance assault, let you keep your throne, and my family and I get to live out our lives in exile?"

Serin raised his eyebrows. "You may also choose the alternative, of course. Attack me with your sword or magic. Maybe you will even slay me. Maybe you will die assaulting me, but in a few moments, your fellow Alliance troops will barge into this hall and finish the job. I doubt I could withstand all those nightcrawlers you brought here, even with my magic. I do confess, mongrel, that you have brought an army to my doors that I cannot defeat. But . . ." He sighed and looked back toward the pit. "Choose my death, and you know your parents' fate. It will be too late to save them." He looked back at her. "Choose, Madori Billy Greenmoat. Your life and the life of your parents . . . or my death. You may only choose one."

Madori stood, swordless, powerless. She looked behind her at her friends. Neekeya and Jitomi moaned, trapped under the fallen stones. She could save them, see them retreat back to their lands. She looked back toward her parents. Torin and Koyee hung above the creatures, eyes pleading with her to keep fighting, even if she let them die. She knew that was the choice they wanted her to make.

I have to save them, Madori thought. *I can use my magic. I can hold them up myself! I can . . .*

She knew she could not. She had never excelled at levitation; even when rested and healthy, she still struggled to hold afloat even small figurines. Weary and wounded, she could not hope to keep her parents levitated. She could not save them. If she slew Serin, she would watch them fall.

"Yet how can I let you die?" she whispered. "I love you."

They stared at her, eyes damp. Her father, Torin, the man she had once thought so foolish, so embarrassing—the man Madori loved more than anything, the man she knew was a great hero, a noble soul, the wisest and strongest man in the world. Her mother, Koyee, the woman Madori would clash with so often, the woman she had fled to Teel—the woman Madori wanted to be like, the woman she admired more than any storybook heroine, the greatest woman she knew.

"Father," she whispered. "Mother. I cannot let you fall."

The creatures in the pit screeched, leaping up, trying to reach the floating pair.

How can I watch you fall? How can I watch you become the creatures in the pit? Her body shook. *How can I lose you?*

"Choose, sweetling," Serin said, voice soft. "You must choose now."

Madori lowered her head. She closed her eyes. She thought back to the iron mine in the darkness, her most forbidden, dark memory. She thought of how the overseers had reduced her people to skeletal, dying things, consumed with disease and starvation, their bodies broken. And she thought of summer childhoods before the pain of youth, of working in the spring gardens with her father, of reading picture books with her mother while snow fell outside, of joyous years, of home, of family, of love.

And Madori knew what she had to do.

She knew the only choice she could make.

"I cannot see you fall, Father and Mother," she whispered, looking back up at them, and she saw the tears in their eyes. Her own tears fell. "I love you both so much. And I'm so sorry." She inhaled slowly, filling her lungs with calming air, with the awareness she had learned under the stars. "I am torn between day and night. I am a daughter of both worlds. The people of sunlight and the children of darkness must hear me, must learn to live in peace, must learn to end our endless wars. I love you, Mother, more than the stars love the night. I love you, Father, more than gardens love the sun. And I must bring stars and sun together. I must become who I was meant to be."

She lifted her sword.

She raced forward, perfectly calm, perfectly aware, one with light and shadow, one with Moth.

Serin gasped, eyes wide, as Madori shoved her blade through his chest and into his heart.

As the emperor collapsed, as his breath died and his body slumped to the floor, Madori wept and reached out to her parents, trying to race forward, to still save them, to hold them aloft, knowing she could not, knowing they would fall, knowing she had decided their fate.

Above the pit of screeching creatures, Torin and Koyee remained suspended.

Madori gasped and blinked tears from her eyes. Serin was dead! Her sword had pierced his heart! And yet her parents still floated above the writhing creatures, held up with magic. Madori laughed and her breath shook. Was this all only an illusion, a bluff?

"Mother! Father!"

No. They were real. Oh, by the stars, they were real. The gags left their mouths, and they cried out to her, calling her name again and again.

"How can this be?" Madori whispered.

Soft footsteps padded up toward her. Madori spun around and her eyes widened. The young woman in Lari's armor stood staring at her, smiling tremulously.

"I was never very good at Offensive Magic or Healing," the young woman whispered. "But I was always one of Teel's best students of levitation. My grandmother, Headmistress Egeria, always said so. I'll bring them to you."

The Lari lookalike curled her fingers inwards, gently pulling Torin and Koyee away from the pit. When they hovered above the solid floor again, the young woman released the magic. The smoky tendrils left Madori's parents, and they rushed toward her.

Madori wanted to hug them, to cry, to tell them she loved them, but she turned away. She raced toward her friends.

"Help me!" Madori said. "Help me free them! Lari—or whoever you are—help me lift the rocks off them!"

The young mage nodded and levitated the bricks off Neekeya and the fallen statue off Jitomi. The two lay on the floor, moaning. Blood covered them.

Madori knelt by Neekeya, examining her injuries. The Daenorian's leg was broken, but she seemed otherwise unharmed, and she even managed to smile weakly. Madori forced herself to breathe, to focus, to bring the shattered bone into her awareness. She had always been a good healer. She claimed the broken bone, guided it back into place, and molded it back together. Neekeya gasped, and her eyes closed, and she slept.

"She's all right," Madori said, relief flooding her, and raced toward Jitomi.

When she reached him, her heart sank.

"Oh . . . Jitomi." Her eyes dampened anew. "My Jitomi."

His injuries were worse. She saw that at once. She brought his body into her awareness, exploring his wounds in her mind, and the terror flooded her. His ribs had snapped, piercing his organs. Blood filled his insides. These were injuries beyond what she could heal.

"Jitomi," she whispered, her voice so high, so soft, fragile as a bird.

He blinked at her. He smiled softly. He reached out a trembling hand, and she clutched it.

"We'll find a better healer than me," she whispered. Her tears splashed his face, trailing down his dragon tattoo. "Just stay with me a little longer. Just a little longer."

He reached out his second hand and caressed her cheek. "You're beautiful, Madori, and strong and wise and good. You brought new light into my life. I loved you in the darkness and in the light, and I'll love you from whatever lands I travel."

She shook her head. "Don't you travel anywhere. Not without me. Don't you dare." She gently embraced him. "Please, Jitomi. Don't leave me." Through trembling lips, she spoke the secret inside her, the secret she had dared not reveal even to herself until now, the secret she knew was true, had known was true for moons now. "I carry your child with me. You must live. You must live to be a father."

His eyes widened. His lips curled into a smile, a smile of surprise, of awe, of joy. He breathed out shakily, and he did not breathe again.

Madori shook with sobs. She lowered her head, touched her forehead to his, and cradled him close and would not let go.

CHAPTER TWENTY-FOUR
THE SOLDIERS OF AUTUMN

Upon Eldmark Fields the cyclamens grew, a carpet of lavender and blue. Upon Eldmark Fields, the gravestones rose, row by row, the soldiers of autumn, soldiers of stone.

Koyee stood on the hill, overlooking the field. She had come here to a field of death, of screams; a field of boys dying in the mud, crying to their mothers as they tried, in vain, to hold their wounds from spilling; a field of daughters, torn from their homes, spears in their hands, weeping for a womanhood that would never come, for a new spring they would never see. Here in Eldmark Fields, under a carpet of stones and cyclamens, lay the soldiers of autumn. Here in Eldmark Fields lay sleeping a generation.

We betrayed them, Koyee thought, gazing upon the rows and rows of gravestones. *We promised our children a better world. We promised them winters of snowmen and hot chocolate by fireplaces, not winters shivering in hovels, afraid and alone. We promised them summers of sun, not fire. We promised them autumns of warm quilts, of jumping in dry leaves, of roasting chestnuts and pumpkin pies; not an autumn of dying.*

"Here, in Eldmark Fields, we buried a generation," she whispered. "Here, in Eldmark Fields, the youth of Moth shattered and wept. Goodbye, soldiers of autumn. Goodbye, children of Moth."

A cold breeze blew, and the field of cyclamens rustled, spreading for miles, a blanket for those sleeping beneath it.

Koyee had never been a composer, only the player of other people's songs—the songs she had learned in the night. Yet this turn, standing outside of Markfir before the field, she pulled out her flute, and she played a new song, a song she had composed. Her notes flowed down the hill, and all the survivors of the war—the children of every nation—turned to listen. It was a song of cyclamens in the breeze. A song of pale stones between the flowers, rows on rows. It was a song for lost children. A song for the cold autumn of her betrayal. A song for hope, for a new spring, for a dream of peace. It was the song of Moth.

Later that turn, Koyee stood with her daughter on the walls of Markfir. Before them spread the fields. Behind them sprawled the city streets where Idarith priests walked, swinging bowls of incense and chanting out prayers; their temple had taken charge of the city until an heir to Mageria would rise.

"Mother," Madori said softly, the wind ruffling her short black hair. "Before I was born, you fought in another war."

Koyee nodded. "I did."

"And you . . . you fixed a clock." Madori turned to look at her, her eyes soft and damp. "On Cabera Mountain. You made the world turn again, made day and night cycle. But then you decided to break the clock. To freeze the world again between day and night. Do you think . . . do you think we should fix the clock again?"

Koyee sighed and placed her arm around her daughter. "Often I had thought this. For long years, I wore a gear around my neck, taken from Cabera. Many times, I was tempted to return to the mountain, to fix the clock like I did during the last war. When the Radians invaded the dusk, I almost wanted to flee south, to return the gear to the clock."

"So why didn't you?" Madori whispered.

"Serin's forces overwhelmed us at Oshy. He stole the locket from my neck. But I would not let him steal the gear; it's too precious." She smiled thinly. "The Cabera gear lies somewhere in the Inaro River. Perhaps by now, it has reached the southern sea and is lost forever."

Madori bit her lip and nodded. "So Mythimna will forever remain Moth, split in two." Suddenly tears filled her eyes, and she trembled. "Mother, I'm sorry."

"For what, sweetness?" Koyee whispered, embracing her daughter.

"I was going to let you fall. You and Father." She clung to Koyee. "In the castle, I . . . Serin said I could save you. That I could flee with you and Father to an island. But . . . I had to kill him. I had to save Moth. I had to let you fall."

Koyee kissed her daughter's forehead. "We didn't fall."

"I didn't know you wouldn't. I made a choice. A choice to sacrifice you. Can you forgive me?" Madori stared at her with huge, damp eyes. "I love you."

Something seemed to break inside Koyee, and her own tears fell, and she held her daughter so tightly she nearly crushed her. "I love you too, Madori. There is nothing to forgive. You make me proud."

They looked back toward the fields. The gravestones spread in rows, and the carpet of cyclamens rustled in the wind.

CHAPTER TWENTY-FIVE
CHILDREN OF DUSK

Two and a half years after leaving Fairwool-by-Night to become a mage, Madori Greenmoat returned home.

She had left her home a young woman, only sixteen, wearing purple clothes she had sewn herself, sporting two black strands of hair that framed her face, the rest of her hair cropped short. She had left in a creaky old cart, heading into the unknown. She had left confused, angry, not knowing who she was. A youth, troubled and yet innocent.

She returned home a woman, a healer and a warrior. Instead of sitting in an old wooden cart, she rode upon Grayhem, a proud nightwolf. Instead of wearing old homemade clothes, she wore the polished scale armor of a Qaelish warrior, and a katana of legend hung across her back. Only one thing she kept from those old years; she was growing her two strands of hair again. After all, some things were not meant to change.

She looked to her right side. Ariana—Headmistress Egeria's granddaughter—rode there upon a black gelding. She no longer looked like Lari; she had removed her Radian armor, and instead she wore a gray tunic and dark leggings. Her little brother rode on the saddle before her, freed from the Radian dungeon.

"My grandmother often spoke of you, Madori," the young woman said with a smile. "The girl from the dusk, she called you. And here we are. At the dusk."

Ariana pointed ahead and smiled. A mile away, the sunlight of Timandra faded into shadow, and beyond lay the endless night.

A gasp sounded to her left, and Madori turned toward Neekeya. Her friend rode a white mare, her eyes wide, and a smile spread across her face.

"The night lies ahead," the Daenorian whispered. "A land of magic. I always dreamed of seeing the darkness. Well, at least since I met you, Madori. Do they have magical artifacts in the night?"

Madori smiled. "Maybe, Neekeya. If they do, I trust you to find them."

Madori gave Grayhem a soft tug on the reigns, and he slowed his pace, letting her two friends ride ahead. Two other travelers caught up with her, and soon Madori rode between her parents. The three stared together at the dusk, and sadness filled Madori.

"I miss Fairwool-by-Night," she said. "And I miss Oshy."

Torin leaned sideways in his saddle, reached out, and patted her arm. "We'll always miss all that we lost. We'll always mourn. And we'll build. A new home. A better home."

Madori looked behind her at the others. A hundred survivors of the war rode along the riverbank. Elorians. Timandrians. One people.

The river sang to their south, its surface glinting with sun beads, and grasslands rustled to their north, lush with wildflowers. They rode across where Fairwool-by-Night had once stood, a field of flowers and memories, only the old Watchtower still standing. The pain suddenly seemed too great to Madori, and she kept staring forward, lips tight, as they crossed the wilderness that had been her old home.

A hundred souls, they rode into the dusk and traveled through the soft light. Duskmoths rose to fly around them, and Madori felt some of her pain ease. The little creatures seemed to favor her, perhaps acknowledging the duskmoth tattooed onto her wrist. When she reached out her palm, one moth landed on her fingertips, its one wing black, the other white. A moth shaped like the world. A moth shaped like her heart. The little animal seemed to look at her, seemed to comfort her, to tell her that her pain had ended, that her new journey began. It tilted its antennae, then flew off into the sky.

"This is the place," Madori said softly. She halted her nightwolf. "Here."

A hundred horses halted in the soft light. The sun glowed behind them, half-hidden behind the horizon, a semicircle of gold casting out white rays between the trees. To the east the moon glowed in a deep blue sky. The river flowed to the south, and hills rose in the north, covered with soft grass. A place of shadows and light. Of day and night. Of peace after fire.

They all dismounted, and Madori stood at the place where the duskmoth had landed upon her fingertips. The center of her life, a mixed child, had always lain in the dusk. Here was her anchor. From the dusk she had come; to here she returned.

The others gathered around her, and Madori spoke to them. "Thousands of years ago, our world fell still. For thousands of years, our world has been as a duskmoth, one wing in darkness, the other in light. For too long, we fought—children of sunlight and children of darkness. For too long, we hated, feared, burned, killed. But I'm a child of both daylight and darkness. For most of my life, my two halves fought their own war, and I didn't know who I am. But I know now." She looked west toward the sunlight, then east toward the moon. "I'm a child of Moth. We are all children of Moth. Here in the dusk, there are no sunlit demons, no nightcrawlers. No Timandrians or Elorians. We're all the same here. People in a torn world, a people united." She turned toward Torin, cleared her throat, and whispered, "Father, the seed!"

He blinked at her, then seemed to remember his task. He nodded hurriedly, reached into his pocket, and pulled out an acorn. He spoke to the crowd as if reciting. "Here do I, Torin Greenmoat, a man born in sunlight, plant a seed from my land." He knelt, dug a little hold, and planted the acorn.

Madori turned toward her mother and frowned, urging her to speak.

Koyee smiled softly. She stepped forward, holding a silken lantern, and lit the candle inside. "And here do I, Koyee of the night, release a lantern from my land." She let go, allowing the lantern to float into the twilit sky.

Madori spoke again to the crowd. "Our village is founded. In Qaelish, my mother's language, the word for healing is: *Lentai.* I name this village Lentai-in-Dusk. And may it forever be a place of healing and peace."

For a few hours they rested, ate, and played soft songs on flutes and harps. Until they built houses they would live under the sky.

Until they built beds they would sleep on the grass. It would be a while before this was a proper village, Madori knew. But it already felt like a home.

Soon after her speech, two of the war's survivors approached Madori. One was the short, slim Nitomi, clad as always in her black dojai silks. The second was the towering Qato, her cousin.

"It's time," whispered Nitomi.

Madori lowered her head. "So soon?"

Nitomi nodded. Once she had been a happy little thing, excitedly spouting out loud, bubbly words. Now the dojai spoke softly. "I've spent too long away. I lost my father in this war. And I lost my older sister. And I lost my brother." She looked around her, eyes damp. "This is a good place, but it's not my home. Hashido Castle awaits me back in Ilar, its hall empty. My inheritance. It's time to go home . . . and it's time to take my brother home."

Madori knew this was coming, but those last words still stabbed her with cold grief. She nodded, approached Grayhem, and pulled the urn from his saddlebag. She stared at the round granite box for a moment, passing her fingers again and again over its cold surface.

"Here, Nitomi," she finally whispered. "Take him home. Jitomi's ashes belong in the night."

Nitomi reached out, hesitant. Then her eyes flicked down to Madori's rounded belly. The dojai paused, then pulled her hands back. She shook her head.

"No," Nitomi whispered. "He belongs here. With you."

The diminutive dojai wiped her eyes, then turned away and mounted her panther. The towering Qato looked down at Madori, then nodded once.

"Goodbye, Madori," he said. "Qato will miss you."

Madori blinked. *Well, I'll be.*

"Goodbye, Qato," she managed to whisper.

He nodded again, then turned and mounted his own panther. The two dojai began riding east toward the shadows of night. Before vanishing from view, they turned back toward the camp, and Nitomi called out, "Come on, Neekeya! It's dark in the night, and you'll get lost without us, so you better hurry, because if you get lost we'd never find you, so come on!"

The tall Daenorian nodded and walked toward them, leading her horse. For once, Neekeya did not wear her crocodile armor; instead, a silk *qipao* dress hugged her body in the style of the night. When she passed by Madori, she paused and smiled.

"Are you sure you don't want to visit Ilar with us?" Neekeya asked.

Madori nodded. "I've been to the night before. Eloria is beautiful. Enjoy your journey, Neekeya. Gaze upon the face of the moon, the glowing fish of the dark rivers, the countless lights of the stars. And then return to us here. I'm not letting you be away from me for too long again!"

The two women embraced, and Neekeya plated a kiss on Madori's cheek. "The prince of Sania still expects me back on his island, you know. I did vow to wed Kota in return for his aid. But maybe if I linger a little longer in the darkness and shadows, he won't mind. It's a large world, and there's still so much to see."

"Neekeya, come on!" Nitomi cried, bouncing in her saddle. "I'm bored and I want to go!"

Neekeya laughed, smiled at Madori, then turned and walked into the shadows with the dojai.

For a few moments, Madori stood in silence, holding the urn to her chest. Then she sighed and turned back toward the others.

"Well," she said, "let's build some houses."

And they built.

And the turns went by, and Lintai-in-Dusk grew, the shells of houses rising in the soft light, a village shared between Timandrians and Elorians, a village for all of Moth.

Many more villages will rise in the dusk, Madori thought. *Towns and cities, a great civilization of people like me . . . people not Timandrian or Elorian but simply children of Moth.* She placed her hand on her belly. *Like my child.*

In early spring, when the first leaves budded from the trees, that child was born.

Madori lay in her bed, exhausted but smiling, and cradled her newborn son to her breast. The babe was beautiful, she thought—a little wrinkly, a little red, but beautiful nonetheless. She cuddled him close, and he nursed at her breast. His hair was black like hers, but his eyes were large and blue—his father's eyes.

"I name you Tom," she whispered and kissed his forehead. "Tom Greenmoat."

When she showed the boy to her parents, they looked happier than she'd ever seen them. Torin kept gazing at the baby in wonder, speaking of how he looked just like his own father. Koyee spoke less and smiled more.

"Can you believe it?" Madori said to her. "You're a grandmother."

Koyee, who was not yet forty and looked barely older than Madori, nodded. "It's strange. I often still feel like a child myself."

As Madori held her son, she wished Jitomi could have been here with her, could have raised Tom with her. But she knew that she had the help of her parents, of all her village. And she knew that Jitomi was with her, if not his spirit than his memory. Whenever she looked into her son's eyes, she would remember Jitomi.

And I will remember myself, she thought. *Myself in Iron Mine Number One, hurt, afraid, dying. And I will remember the fall of Pahmey, the genocide of Qaelin. And I will remember the killing fields of Eldmark, the multitudes dying together, their blood feeding the plains.* She winced and closed her eyes, even as she held her son close. The brand on her shoulder, given to her in the mine, still hurt some turns, and she knew that these memories would never leave her. She knew that the nightmares would forever fill her sleep. She knew that she'd never forget the wagons of dead, the pits of skeletons, the screams, the stench of the dying. She knew that even many years from now, happy in her new home, her joy would be a fragile thing, a delicate shell around a broken core. She knew that the nightmares—waking in cold sweat, unable to breathe, crying and begging for life—would forever fill her sleep.

She stroked her child's hair.

"My parents fought a war," she whispered to him, "and when I was born, they swore to protect me. They swore that I would know peace. And yet a new war blazed, a fire more destructive than any before it. And I don't know if I can protect you, Tom. I don't know if

I can give you a better life, a life safe from such pain. But I promise that I'll try. I promise that I'll never let you go, that I'll always love you."

Her son gurgled and reached out a tiny hand to grab her hair. She smiled and kissed his fingertips.

* * * * *

On a chilly autumn turn, Madori and her son walked through the village of Lintai-in-Dusk. Many homes rose around them, built of white stone, their roofs tiled blue. Statues stood in twilit gardens, and lanterns hung from poles, glowing gold and silver. Many villagers walked around Madori down the cobbled road, heading toward the hill.

"Mama, why do we need a university?" Tom bit his lip, thinking for a moment. "What's a university?"

"A place of learning," Madori said.

"Like learning numbers and letters?"

She nodded and mussed the boy's hair. "Yes. A place for adults to learn things they don't know."

They kept walking through the village, dressed in white silk. All around, their fellow villagers wore their finest garments, and many held floating lanterns on strings. Madori and Tom walked around a copse of trees, and they saw the university ahead upon the hill. It was the largest building in the village, larger even than the old library in Fairwool-by-Night, and indeed many of its bricks had been taken from that fallen library.

Tom paused and stared at the building in wonder. The lanterns reflected in his large indigo eyes. "It's as big as a dragon!"

Feet shuffled, and Madori turned to see Professor Yovan approaching them. The elderly man stepped on his long white beard and wobbled for a moment, then grumbled, tossed the beard across his shoulder, and smiled at Tom.

"Indeed, my boy!" said the old professor. "I was quite surprised when your mother invited me to teach within its walls. Lovely building, indeed. Bit smaller than Teel, but the air here is cooler too, and I do quite enjoy the soft light of the dusk."

Madori smiled at her old teacher of Magical Healing. "Go, professor. Headmistress Ariana waits."

Yovan cleared his throat and nodded at her. "Yes, quite. Did you know, little boy, that Ariana is the granddaughter of Egeria, the former headmistress of Teel University?"

Madori smiled. "Yes, professor, I know. And I'm not a little boy, though my son is."

He blinked. "Yes, yes, of course. Well then. Carry on." With that he shuffled on, nearly tripping over his beard again.

The villagers gathered in a courtyard outside the university portico. Ariana spoke to the crowd, and Madori could scarcely believe that here stood the same woman kidnapped by Serin, forced to become his new daughter. Headmistress of Lintai University, Ariana now seemed as confident and wise as Egeria had been. She spoke of learning ways of peace, not war. Of learning wisdom, not hatred. She spoke of a great university for all people of Moth, a place of healing, a place not only of knowledge but of wisdom.

"What are you going to learn here, Mother?" Tom asked when the ceremony ended. They stood outside between the trees as villagers released their lanterns, letting the soft lights rise into the sky.

"Healing," Madori said.

"But you already know how to heal."

Madori thought of Jitomi, how she had held him as he lay dying.

I could not heal your father, my child, she thought, a lump in her throat.

"I will learn more," she said softly.

Tom thought for a moment, brow furrowed. "When you become a healer, will you be able to heal my father? To bring him back?"

The words stunned Madori into silence. For a moment she only stared at her son, and then she knelt and held his arms. "Sweetness, your father can never return. You know that, right? I won't be able to bring him back, even after studying here."

Tom lowered his head and nodded. "I thought so. I wanted to be sure."

She hugged him, then mussed his hair. "Now go to Grandpapa and Grandmama. Sing to them the new songs I taught you."

His face brightened and he ran off, already singing even before he reached Torin and Koyee in the crowd.

Madori smiled softly and looked back at the university. Perhaps, like the village she had founded, this university would become her legacy, the legacy of Moth. A place of healing. Of wisdom. Of peace.

"May the world know only healing," she said softly, gazing at the university, the village, the light in the west and the darkness in the east. "May we build a world not of warriors, not of conquerors, not of victors or emperors. May we build a world of musicians, of painters, of healers." She gazed at the duskmoth tattooed onto her wrist and her voice dropped to a whisper. "And may I be healed. May all souls torn in two find some healing."

She smiled, tasting tears on her lips, and raised her eyes. A single duskmoth flew above her, rising into the sky like one of the floating lanterns. Between the shadows and light, it seemed to Madori that the moth no longer had one black wing, the other white, but that it was painted all in gold, beautiful and whole.

THE END

NOVELS BY DANIEL ARENSON

Dawn of Dragons
Requiem's Song
Requiem's Hope
Requiem's Prayer

Song of Dragons
Blood of Requiem
Tears of Requiem
Light of Requiem

Dragonlore
A Dawn of Dragonfire
A Day of Dragon Blood
A Night of Dragon Wings

The Dragon War
A Legacy of Light
A Birthright of Blood
A Memory of Fire

The Moth Saga
Moth
Empires of Moth
Secrets of Moth
Daughter of Moth
Shadows of Moth
Legacy of Moth

Made in the USA
San Bernardino, CA
11 September 2018